Earth Trek
Volume 1

WHAT IS ALL THE FUSS
ABOUT RELIGION?

EarthTrek
Volume 1

What Is All The Fuss About Religion?

ISBN: 1- 4392 -3930-4

Published by WCM Press

Cover Design: W Bahtiar & Devid S
English Editor : Stephen Till

CHAPTERS

Dedicated to:

My beloved husband Marcel Alexander Moormann
My beloved daughter Heraldine Ardana Moormann
And to my entire family

To my sources of inspiration:
Dr. Rashad Khalifa
Erich Von Daeniken
Dr. Maurice Boucaille
Karen Amstrong
Harun Yahya
Prof. Arsyo Santos
Prof. Frank Joseph Hoff
Acharya S
Dan Browne
Muhammed A. Asadi
Arifin Muftie
Dr. Richard Carrier
Fahmi Basya
Eckhart Tolle
Dr. Wayne Dyer
Agus Mustofa
Oprah Winfrey
Sir Scott Ridley

And to
All Truth Seekers

Introduction
(Please don't skip these pages...)

First of all, I can not believe this book is finally published! Thank you so much to WCM Press and Amazon.com, and especially thanks to you for reading this book, hopefully until the end. You have no idea how long I have been overloaded with all the thoughts that I am about to share with you on the next pages.

These EarthTrek Trilogy books are the resume of my personal study in search of Truth which has taken on and off around 30 years of my life and are a compilation of many, many authors' works. Some of the information might also come from TV programs as well as the Internet.

Kindly accept my apology for not writing long acknowledgment to the books authors, TV producers and website owners that I should be thanking to. Presently I don't even have all the books that I have read over the years, so sometimes I might refer to information from a particular book, TV program or website without naming the source,   since honestly, I do not remember some of them any longer.

I also hope for your understanding for the way how I write in such a casual manner in simple English. This is because what you are about to read is my own personal mental journey and also because I am not an English native-speaker. I am neither a scientist, nor a historian nor am I a religious scholar. I am just an average person who happens to read a lot of books; travels a great deal and likes to contemplate about life. I am just an average 'Joe' or 'Jane' - to be more precise - looking for the meaning of life. A Truth Seeker, just like you. I hope that qualifies me to write these books and share the information. I just cannot contain these observations within myself any longer, I have to share it with anyone who is open minded enough to hear what I have gathered.

This first book of EarthTrek Trilogy is mainly about religious comparison study. The main message is that all the major religions in the world, be it monotheist or polytheist religion, *originally* came from One Source. In fact, I believe that there is only One Religion for all of mankind. Although sadly this One True Religion has been corrupted by human's hands throughout the ages, hence there appear to be many different religions contradicting and fighting against one another.

On the way to prove the above conclusion, I can not avoid looking as if I am criticizing *people* of all religions. Yes, *all*... mostly people of the three main monotheist religions: Judaism, Christianity and Islam. However, I am not criticizing the religion itself – this is definitely not my intention - but the *people* (including myself) who sometimes interpret and practice religion incorrectly.

I am writing this book in search of Truth and one cannot define truth without recognizing the false. Hopefully this book can make us all ponder and *stop disagreeing*.

Allow me to suggest you to read the whole book from front to back and not skipping any chapter, because you might misunderstand the main message that I am trying to share with you. Bear in mind that I am not a scientist, so please don't get bogged down by the inexact scientific data.

I am merely sharing my spiritual/mental journey and hoping that this information might be a food for thought. Once again, I have no intention to offend any particular race or religion, because I believe in the advice of an ancient Wise Book that says:

"Call to the way of your Lord with wisdom and goodly exhortation.."

May peace be with us
Anita Herawati Moormann

CHAPTER ONE

IN SEARCH OF GOD

*T*he purpose of this book is to share the evidence that all the religions in the world, be it monotheist or polytheist religions, even pagan religions that have vanished from today's world *originally* come from One Source. In fact, I believe that there is only one religion for all of mankind. Although sadly this One True Religion has been corrupted by human's hands throughout the ages, hence there appear to be many different religions contradicting and fighting against one another.

But before I start sharing with you my deepest thoughts - my personal spiritual/mental journey in search of Truth, allow me to introduce myself and tell you about my background. This is so you can follow my 'train-of-thoughts' and understand why I 'dare' to write these trilogy books and come to the above conclusion. I hope you won't get bored... ☺

⟨⟩⟨⟩

I am an Indonesian woman, who was born in 1968 in a big family of 8 children. I am married to a Dutch man and together we have a daughter. I spent around 20 years of my life abroad, starting from Malaysia, ex-Yugoslavia, Switzerland, Germany, Check Republic and Holland. Having to live so long outside of Indonesia, I have come to notice that until about 8 years ago, most people in America and Europe (except for some Dutch) do not know

1

much about Indonesia. I remember clearly the time when most people didn't even know where Indonesia is or had even heard of it.

Since 1998, Indonesia has very often appeared in the news, mostly because of the bombings and other bad things that are happening lately. Today almost everybody in the world who owns a TV set and watches CNN has heard about Indonesia. However, I would like to show you the view from an insider's angle. Even though most of you have heard about Indonesia, I am sure the age old question that I used to hear so often: "Where on earth is Indonesia?" is still out there.

WHERE ON EARTH IS INDONESIA?

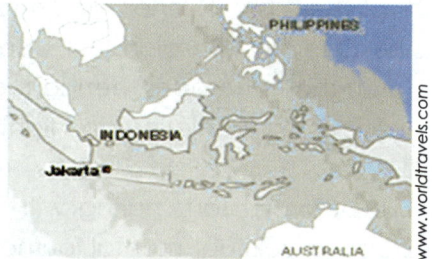

Location of Indonesia

Indonesia is the biggest archipelago in the world - it consists of more than 17,000 large and small islands. Yes, you read correctly: over 17,000 islands. And yet many people don't know where it is. If you look at the globe, and turn it on the side where Australia is, then look at the area where the Asian main continent is, you will see a chain of many islands in between, you can't miss it. That's Indonesia - a big stretch of island groups, continuing to the Melanesian smaller islands group then to the Polynesian islands.

Today, Indonesian people are a mixture of Malays, Chinese descendants, some Indian descendants, a few Arab descendants, some Aborigines (the people from the island of Papua New

Guinea - half of that big island belongs to Indonesia) and a few Eurasians (mainly mixture between Indonesians and ex Dutch colonials). At present there are more than 100 languages in Indonesia, not dialects but distinct languages.

Sometimes I think most people don't know where Indonesia is, being the biggest archipelago in the world, and the 4th or 5th largest populated country in the world, because the names of each individual islands are more well-known than the name of the country itself. I believe most people have heard of Java, Sumatra, Borneo or Irian Jaya (i.e half of Papua).

By now, you are probably wondering why I am writing at length about Indonesia when the title of this book concerns religion. This is because I have noticed that most of the time religion is (mistakenly) intertwined with racial and cultural issues.

ISLANDS OF THE GODS
My first 'taste' of religion/culture experience was when I lived in Penang Island, Malaysia. I lived there since I was 5 years old. My father was posted as a Consul, so we lived in the diplomatic area of the island. At the age of 8, I studied in an English Christian Primary School, where most of the students were Chinese and Eurasians. I was the only Indonesian in that school. At that school, I didn't receive any different treatment because of religious difference, but I did feel some kind of racial discrimination.

You see, in the 1970's there was some kind of unspoken hierarchy among the races in Malaysia. Although, I am note sure whether this is a general issue in all parts of Malaysia, or only in my school. The Eurasians (mostly Chinese or Malays mix with Europeans mainly English) were on top of the rank, then comes the Chinese, then the Malays and after that the Indians (Tamils). In that school every grade was divided into 3 different classes: the Red class, the Blue class and the Green class. The division was done according to the intelligence level. Somehow being Indonesian (which was

3

still considered as Malay), as soon as I entered the school, I was placed in the Green class. I was just a child, but I understood what was going on and I felt it was unfair. However, I didn't make a fuss about that, I just decided to prove that I deserve to be in the Red class, even though my English was very, very poor back then. Thus, about 6 months later I managed to be transferred to the Red class.

Another significant experience was at home. Since we lived in the diplomatic area, there were many foreigners around our house. The neighbors next to us were a rich Chinese family. They were not a diplomatic family but they were rich, their servants however were a whole Tamil Indian family. Behind our house lived a German family. All of my neighbors had children around my age.

My youngest sister and I were closely befriended with the children of the German family but sometimes we also played with the other children. One day, all the children from these four families played together and we had to make two groups from the eight of us. You know how children pick side by showing the outside of the palm or the inside of the palm? It is a short of 'scissor, rock, paper' kind of game. We would call the outside of the palm 'black' and the inside of the palm 'white', then whoever shows the same side of the palm stays in the same group.

We were all very young, probably between 5 until 10 years of age. So we put our hands behind our backs then on the count of '3' we showed our palms. My little Indian friend showed her inner palm - which should be 'white' of course - my German friend shouted innocently and said "But her palm is also so dark, that doesn't count as white!"

I remember looking (and feeling) how hurt and embarrassed my Indian friend was. I just said to my German friend: "Well, she is Indian, and Indian's skin color is that way. So that counts as 'white' because she was showing her inner palm."

I felt what my Indian friend felt, but I was too young to describe or identify what kind of feeling it was. I just knew it was an unpleasant feeling. I guess that was my first encounter with 'innocent' racism.

Another incident happened when I was having dinner in a local restaurant, where people eat outside on long benches, a typical Asian fast food stall. At this kind of restaurant people eat very closely to one another, sometimes when it's full, people have to share a table.

One day, we (I must have been with my parents or elder sisters) had to share the table with some Chinese and some Malays. The Chinese ordered some pork meat, then all of the sudden the Malays just stood up from the table and walked away because the Malays who are Moslems are not supposed to eat pork. I could feel the Chinese were offended. Again, I felt something unpleasant. But I still didn't know quite exactly yet what it was.

I used to go to my Chinese neighbors and saw their praying altar, with statues of Chinese gods. Then I used to stand and look at the pictures of their Indian servants' gods, they are totally different. But all of them are images of humans. Strange humans, I thought, one of the Indian gods is even blue skinned, and another has elephant head. To me, they are all so fascinating and enigmatic.

One night, I saw a Hindu festival of Taipussam parade in front of my house. I ran and stared in horror at those people being pierced by some short of arrows on their tongues, back of their bodies, arms, everywhere practically. I felt so sick to the stomach. Even though there was no blood, it was such a scary scene to watch, especially for a child. As a child, I was also terrified whenever I saw a statue of crucified Jesus on a cross. But then again, I also felt the same way when I saw the Moslems sacrificing cows and goats during the Iedl Adha (the remembrance of when Abraham was about to sacrifice his son). Although, I already understood back then, that since we eat meat, those animals had to be slaughtered somehow.

However, my general feeling of my own family's religion was a sense of peaceful family gathering. I loved it when it's Iedl Fitr time, the end of the fasting period for the Moslems. I was still too young to fast, but I was always so happy whenever my four older sisters and oldest brother who lived in Kuala Lumpur and Jakarta came to visit us in Penang Island during that celebration, and my mother would cook special festive food.

And then, I also remember the Christmas time where my older brother, my youngest sister and I would have Christmas dinner together with the European children in some fancy hotel with my parents. I loved that too; the colorful Christmas trees, the gifts, the snowy decorations and the funny Santa Claus.

All of those religious impressions were stuck in my head, but I was still too young to digest all of it.

⟳⋆⟲

At the age of 11, I came back to Jakarta, Indonesia. And all of the 'cosmopolitan' feeling seemed to be forgotten. Being a daughter of a diplomat I was already so much used to international crowds. In the 1970's Jakarta was far less cosmopolitan in comparison to Kuala Lumpur or even Penang Island, one could hardly see a white person walking down the street.

Therefore, at first I felt a little bit depressed seeing everyone looking the same and speaking the same language. I missed the cosmopolitan flair. But on the other side, I also didn't (consciously) feel the mild racial issues that I sometimes felt in Malaysia. You see, Malaysia is just a smaller neighbor archipelago country, and it has more or less the same cultural mix as Indonesia, but to me it felt so different. In Indonesia, back then one could hardly feel the cultural difference, because almost all the Chinese, Indians and the few Arabs in Indonesia speak fluent Indonesian, but that was not the case in Malaysia. Only when I was older did I understand that the Chinese in Indonesia were obliged to speak Indonesian, as well as having Indonesian names beside their Chinese names!

So anyway, in Jakarta I went to a local school and that's where I started to learn more about religion. After a short adjustment, I found that period living in Jakarta between the age of 11 and 18 was actually one of the happiest times of my life. I loved the peacefulness in Indonesia back then. In all my life living and traveling to many countries, I have never seen beggars as cheerful as in Indonesia. They are poor and yet we can see them laughing and joking around the streets of Jakarta.

Another thing I used to be very glad about Indonesia was its harmonious religious life. Historically, Indonesia has been a religious country since millennia. I try to be as cautious as possible whenever referring to history because I know that any historical data that I use may be disagreed by some one else. After reading so many books, I realize that almost *every* single data concerning our world history differs from one historian to another, from one nation to another. I will analyze world religious history in depth later in my next books: EarthTrek Vol. 2 and 3. I have to warn you that some of the information that I have gathered will not be easy to swallow. There are so many 'hidden facts' in our world religious histories that will truly shock most readers.

So for now, I am taking the historical data of Indonesia from what I have learned in Indonesian public school. Throughout this book I will be using BCE or Before Common Era (equivalent to BC or

Before Christ) and CE or Common Era (equivalent to AD or Anno Domini) whenever indicating a specific year.

During the pre-historical times, Indonesians had been practicing all kinds of polytheism, animism and shamanism religions. By the time of the Sriwijaya Empire, the old Indonesian kingdom's name – which stretched from the middle islands of modern Indonesia (Kalimantan and Sulawesi) to some parts of Thailand at ca. 400 CE – 1300 CE (some historians say between 600 CE – 1300 CE), almost the whole kingdom was practicing Buddhism.

At around 800 CE the biggest Buddhist temple in the world at the time – Borobudur - was built in the Mataram Kingdom of Java. The Borobudur Temple was one of the centers of pilgrimage for Buddhists around the ancient world. After the fall of Sriwijaya and Mataram, another giant kingdom appeared under the name of Majapahit, which stretched out from Malay Peninsula to some islands in the Philippines at around 1300 CE. This kingdom practiced Hinduism, which was introduced by Indian gurus and traders.

Indonesia has a very long historical link with India. In fact the Latin name of Indonesia is Indos Nesos which means: Islands of the Indians. Apparently, during the exploration era, Europe (the Old World) was obsessed with India, among others because of its spices. The Europeans ended up 'finding' the New World (America) and called the natives Red Indians, probably thinking they have found India at first. Then they 'found' Jamaica and after realizing that it was not India, called it West Indies and finally ended up in Indonesia, which in many ways has many similarities to India and called it Dutch East Indies. Funny, how our history was shaped, isn't it?

Islam came gradually between the 13th and 14th century CE (some historians say it was earlier) to Indonesia, brought by Indian and Arab traders as well as scholars. Just as the previous religions that came to Indonesia, Islam was accepted by most Indonesians. Then Christianity came to the archipelago around the 16th century CE. Christianity was brought to Indonesia by European colonials. This is probably the reason why not many Indonesians were attracted to convert into Christianity. Although most of the people in the eastern part of Indonesia, i.e. the Moluccan Islands and North Sulawesi, are mostly Christians, these are the parts where the European colonials first set foot in Indonesia.

Today around 90% of the population of Indonesia are Moslems, the rest are a mixture of Protestants, Catholics, Buddhists and Hindus. With one of the biggest populated countries in the world, this makes Indonesia the largest Moslem population in the world. Yes, the biggest Moslem population is in Indonesia and not some Middle Eastern country.

With that diverse religious background it is important to note that many of the Moslems in Indonesia are not real practitioners. Many of them are just registered as Moslems on their identity cards. Many Indonesian Moslems are still practicing Islam in combination with other religions or believes such as the Kejawen (old Javanese belief which is allegedly rooted from Hinduism mixed with Buddhism) and in most remote islands are still combined with the old belief of animism (belief in the force of different animals, plants, rocks or other natural forces).

That religious diversity was the one thing that fascinated me most growing up in Indonesia. It's a common thing for most Indonesians to believe in one religion and have other family members with different religions and we all lived in peace. In fact the biggest mosque in Jakarta is located right on the same street as the biggest cathedral.

I have always been fascinated by people and culture... including religion. I loved the fact that we didn't have to go to school for every single holy day of those five major religions... ☺

I loved the tradition that everyone congratulated and visited everyone else during their religious holidays. I loved when it was Ramadhan time (the Islamic fasting month), where all the kids came back from the mosque and played happily because that's the only month where they are allowed to play and stay up late after the night prayers; I loved it when the streets in Jakarta was so brightly colored with lamps and decorations during Christmas; I loved to watch the monks chanting in Borobudur temple (via television) during the Waisak celebration or when I could watch the *wayang* stories (Hindu heroic epics told in a form of puppets) of Mahabharata or Ramayana the whole night on TV during the Hindu holidays.

I loved the fact that I have family members who are Christians, and Kejawen practitioners as well as Moslems. I loved to learn about all the religions even though I was a little confused about them when I was very young.

Most Indonesians had to learn about all the five religions in school. About the different holy days, basic teachings and oh, what I loved the most were the stories of the prophets. They were all so different yet similar and all are so enchanting.

But as a Moslem, I had to pray and fast. Of course, being a child, it was not easy, especially when I saw my Christian friends receiving gifts during Christmas. While during my religious holy day (Iedl Fitr), where yes, I got new clothes and shoes too but only after fasting for a whole month.

～٥٭٥～

FAITH ON TRIAL

When I was 17 years old, I read a book from Erich Von Daeniken, 'Chariots of the Gods'. You see, in Indonesia back then, every book was screened by the government. Indonesia as a Republic is still a very young country. Indonesia gained independence from the Dutch in 1945 (and even acknowledged later by the UN). There was a time when the communist party was getting quite powerful in Indonesia, therefore today every Indonesian is obliged to choose a religion out of the five official religions. Well, of course this is only a simplified version of the history, the full history itself is much more complicated and I am not going into further detail since this is not the main topic of this book. I just intend to describe how Indonesians are familiar with many different religions.

Anyway, there was a time when, all books which had any political issues or 'radical' religious and philosophical issues were heavily screened. Provocative books such as Erich Von Daeniken's were of course forbidden in Indonesia. But somehow, by accident I got my hands on it. That book almost shook me to the core. Even though some would say that Von Daeniken's theories are over-stretched and apparently some of the numerical data that he put in his book are exaggerated, the main idea is so convincing and totally plausable!

According to Von Daeniken we are not the only intelligent beings in the universe. His theory being that a long time ago from a galaxy far, far away - and I just love, love Starwars.... ☺ came a colony of space ships which landed on earth, at the time a place filled with half human - half savage cave drawing hominids.

Those intelligent beings coming with their spaceships were perceived as gods by the savages. The savages worshiped them. The aliens taught them how to read and write, how to cultivate and finally how to build cities. Alledgedly, it seems like there is a missing link between our savage pre-historical period and the time of city buildings of our ancient civilizations. According to Von Daeniken, those aliens were the reason why there are so many ruined cities from ancient civilizations popping up out of nowhere around the globe: such as the Aztec and Egyptian.

That is because those alien 'gods' went back to their own galaxy, after intermingling with the primitive people of the earth in order to create a better species (i.e. Homo Sapiens). That's why there are so many mummy traditions on this planet, waiting to be awakened by the gods who had promised to return and award them with eternal life. And that's how religions were created.

I am not saying that I agree or disagree with this theory; although I have also always thought, that there is no way in this mega vast universe, there is only one insignificant blue speck of a planet called the earth which is populated by intelligent creatures! Why did God create the rest of the vast universe if the only intelligent creatures He created wouldn't even be able to witness it all? So I agree with Von Daeniken, that human being is just being arrogant thinking that we are the 'paramount' of God's creation.

Another thing that has always fascinated me is mythology. I love myths, I love stories. I think we all love stories. I think that's why most of us are addicted to watching TV or films or even reading books. Why else?

One of the oldest memories I could remember was sitting on the floor of my parents' house, digging thirstily into any story or myth from ancient civilizations in the old fashioned Encyclopedia Britannica (there was no Internet yet). Even before I could read, I was fascinated just looking at the pictures. My imaginations ran wild whenever I saw pictures of some gods or goddesses from the ancient Greek, Roman, Indian, Aztec, Persian or Egyptian civilizations. I loved looking at the pictures of the mythical creatures like Pegasus, Gorgon or looking at the pictures of the magical weapons and chariots of the Hindu gods. I knew most of the stories about the prophets and messengers of God, from the creation of the world, from Adam and Eve, to Noah, Abraham, Moses, Jesus and finally Muhammad. But somehow those stories never seemed to add up in my mind, whilst I would love to believe that all of them were true. However, that's not possible; most of those stories were contradictive to logic and science. Thus, finally I gave up like most of us do, I came to the conclusion that: myth is myth, religion is religion and science is science... and there is no connection between all of them. Point.

I was so disappointed about that 'fact' until I read Erich Von Daeniken's book which connected beautifully all the myths, religions and well, not really science but at least logic. I felt tortured by Von Daeniken's theory, torn between two poles, because deep in my heart I still believed there is a God, a Supernatural Power that is good, that is guiding me somehow and whispers in my heart and conscience. I don't believe an alien creature is doing that to me.

Bear in mind this was in the 1980's where science fiction movies were not as many as today. Star Wars was not even finished being filmed! So were other movies, such as Stargate or the latest Indiana Jones which I believe are also inspired by Von Daeniken's theory (or Zecharia Sitchin – another popular book writer of alien origin of human, his books are the main source of the hot topic concerning the End of Days in 2012). On the other hand, I couldn't find any proof of God; whilst Von Daeniken's theory seemed like a possibility. (More detail in EarthTrek Vol. 2 - From Myth to the Ultimate Reality)

Children today, who watch so many science fiction movies, might not be as shocked as anyone from my generation or older generations who read a theory like that. This is good in a way, but on the other hand, many science fiction movies are so far-fetched, the historical data and mythical names so jumbled up and inaccurate that children today might even be more confused and misinformed then children from my generation ever were.

Anyway, I couldn't get this alien origin of human theory out of my mind. Hmm.... that's sounds like a possibility!

Thus... all this time I have been praying to an alien creature?
No way!
Why would I do that?
So... there is no heaven and hell?
Why should I pray then?
What a waste of time!

TO WHITE MEN'S LANDS

www.europeancities.com

Prague, Athens, Bluche, Duesseldorf and Amsterdam

I had just graduated from high school and went for university study in Jakarta for a few months, when my father was posted as Ambassador to ex-Yugoslavia and Greece. I joined him there for a while.

That was the first time I met European Moslems (from ex-Yugoslavia and Albania), and that was also the first time I really saw with my own eyes how much hate could be caused in the name of religion. I was there in late 1980's, right before the civil war started. It was horrible. There were many local Yugoslavian staff who had been working for the Indonesian Embassy for many years. They were befriended before the war, then all of the sudden after the situation heated up they became grouped according to their religions. I felt so sad witnessing all that.

I couldn't understand why it was happening? It never happened in Indonesia before. I remember saying gladly to any foreigner who would discuss about religion with me, how peaceful the religious life in Indonesia was. When they said that "Religion is the cause of war" I would say (gladly again): "Not in Indonesia." Oh boy, was I wrong! If only I knew, that the religious atmosphere in Indonesia would change too, like today.

After Beograd, I left to Switzerland for my study. Here I ended up in one of the most expensive dormitory schools in the world. There were about 400 students in my batch coming from 60 different countries; multiple different races of rich, spoiled brats! ☺ That was such an experience.

At the beginning of the school year, we hang out in different groups according to our races. So there were the African group, the Latin American group, the European/American/Australian group, the Asian group and the Middle Eastern group.

There were quite a few racial incidents in that school, especially at the beginning of the first year. I couldn't help wondering how on earth young people could be so ignorant and racist if that didn't begin with our families and/or local upbringing.

Misunderstandings between races were such a common thing as well as many other ridiculous incidents. At that school, we would dine together in the *salle-a-manger* (dinning room). One day during lunch, a white student from South Africa asked a black student from Kenya to pass her some bread. The black student from Kenya passed the bread with her bare hands. What a scene the white South African student made! She started yelling and saying how dare a black person passed her bread with bare hands. It was so terrible to see that.

Then there was another incident, where a student from Saudi Arabia called another student from the Philippines by clapping his hands. Oh boy! You should see how the Philippina girl yelled back at him. That was kind of funny though. You see, there are many Philippinos working as domestic helps in the Middle East that the Arab boy thought all Philippinos must be identical with servants and therefore he clapped his hands to call her just like he usually did in his own country. Not realizing that the Philippina girl is a daughter of a very rich general from President Marcos's regime! Oops.. ☺

There were quite a few incidents like that in my school. It was sad and sometimes hilarious to see how ignorant we were, having been programmed by our families, culture, religions and societies. Fortunately, by the end of the third year (almost) all of us had become good friends, ignoring the racial issues entirely. There were still groups, not based on races anymore but because of similarity in characters or interests.

I believe that was one of the best international experience and education for all of us. We all sat together watching CNN during the first Gulf War, and just worrying about our (pro)Iraqi and (pro)American friends' families; or during the US Panama Invasion without taking political side at all. I am sure the whole world in general could learn something from these youngsters open minded and true cosmopolitan outlook.

Before I came to Europe, I did not know that many Europeans dislike Middle Eastern people. And since for most people, Islam is identical to Middle East, the anti-Islamic feeling is also very tangible. Meanwhile in Indonesia, most people, especially in the villages look up to Arabs. Many (non-traveling) Indonesians (ignorantly) think that everyone from the Middle East must be 'enlightened' spiritually. Therefore, I was really surprised and I couldn't understand this anti-Islamic sentiment.

In Europe, many people don't believe in religion anymore but it seems like everyone has all kinds of opinion about it and unfortunately in a slightly negative way. Many people also do not really believe in Christianity anymore apart from seeing it as some kind of family tradition. I also found out that not many Westerners really know what Christianity is all about; the same way they don't know much about Islam. But they seem to have all kind of negative opinions about Islam. In Indonesia we are taught to respect all the religions. It's a common thing if people ask you: "What is your religion?", just in order to make sure that we don't ask or say the wrong things to each other and to make sure when to congratulate others on their holy days. But in Indonesia people among different religions do not really talk or discuss about religion to each other.

Therefore, I could not understand that notion back then, to me it seemed quite absurd to have such strong opposition about something that one doesn't really know what it's all about. It's like hating your enemy without knowing why. Only after sometime, living in this very cosmopolitan society, did I finally start understanding the reasons behind the negative emotions towards the Moslems. (This was in early 1990's - before the bombing attacks became 'popular').

I don't like to generalize people into stereotypes; unfortunately sometimes we have to do that to explain certain phenomena. Anyway, I started learning and observing more about the characteristic of the different nations. I learned that there are many different types of Middle Eastern people.

I learned that most of the Middle Easterners living in Geneva are among the richest people in the world. While in Germany most of the Middle Eastern people come from Turkey. The Turks were 'imported' to Germany after the Second World War, when there were not many working native males left to build the country. Meanwhile in the Netherlands most are from Morocco and in France from Algeria.

In Germany, in most big cities at least, the Turks are quite welcomed by the Germans because most of them speak German and they can more or less adapt to the culture. So do the Algerians in France, because of the long connection since the time of the French colonization of Algeria. Most of the Algerians are quite apt in picking up the French language. Algerian food is also very popular in France.

But not in the Netherlands, surprisingly enough for a country which is among the most tolerant to foreigners, the Dutch have quite a strong antipathy towards the Moroccans. I must add that the Moroccans also made the least effort to adjust to the Dutch culture in comparison to the Algerians or the Turks in other parts of Europe.

Through my observations, it looks like the Moroccans are also more hot tempered and more nationalistic in comparison. Of course, there are a few exceptions. And of course, my observations might be wrong. But from what I saw, frictions between the Moroccans and the native Dutch are very common. Or maybe I think this way, because when I lived in Amsterdam, my apartment was located in the vicinity of the so-called Moslem area. There are several mosques around the apartment complex. (Almost) every single month, the glass door of my apartment would be pelted with stones by the Moroccan youngsters who had gotten into a fight with some Dutch youngsters.

Remember when I said, that religion is (mistakenly) intertwined with racial issue? This is what I mean. That kind of behavior created such a strong dislike among the Europeans. But then again, maybe it was the Dutch youngsters who provoked them first. I wouldn't know...

Thus, most Westerners misunderstand Islam since they assume that Islam is identical with Middle Eastern people. Strangely enough, although most Westerners don't know much about Islam, almost all of them know about the rule of 'haram' (forbidden) for Moslems to drink alcohol and eat pork.

Back to my school in Switzerland... almost everyone who was considered as 'cool' drank alcohol. Almost all the Westerners did.

So did the Middle Eastern kids. But of course, they were judged heavily, before all the students could get along well interracially. The Westerners called them hypocrites, being Moslems but still drinking alcohol. However, in fairness, these Middle Eastern kids were no different than any other kids in the world, right..

They couldn't escape from the 'cool trend' which was going on, such as drinking alcohol. These Middle Eastern kids were just as rebellious, confused and looking for identity like any other teenagers in the world. Moreover since they came from strict Islamic countries, the temptation was probably even bigger for them.

I could understand both sides. I could understand why the Europeans thought the Middle Eastern kids were being hypocritical. On the other side, I could understand the Middle Eastern kids too, they were just being kids. After all, they didn't invent the rule of alcohol prohibition, right?

Unfortunately, with the additional of cultural history (which has been brained washed for centuries) in the mind of these kids from different races and the love for drama and teenage egos – several clashes inevitably happened under the influence of alcohol. Somehow most of the Middle Eastern kids tend to be hotter tempered in comparison to other races. So at the end it was always Islam that got the blame.

❧

I said already before that most of religious issues are intertwined with racial issues. I would like to adjust it now. Most religious wars are just a mask for racial issues and in most cases it goes even deeper than that - it is just a cover for economical issues.

At the end it's about money, about having the most power to have more provisions and to control others. In the olden days, it was a fight to gain more land; today it's about oil or natural resources, which is just the same thing actually.

Before I went to Europe, I read a book which was written by a Frenchman who studied Islam. He mentioned that Christians in Europe see Moslems as some kind of primitive, devil worshippers. I couldn't believe that at first. In Indonesia, the Christians don't think that way about the Moslems. Nor do the Moslems think that way about the Christians. Only after living in Europe I could see what he meant.

It then got worse all over the world.. with the so-called terrorist attacks. When it just started, I still thought that it is because many people are not well informed about other religions. I still thought: "In Indonesia where most people are familiar with all of the religions, nothing like this would happen".

But suddenly in 1998 chaos struck in Indonesia too. I was still living in Europe, it was such a blow for me who put a high price on the religious peace in Indonesia when I saw the news on TV. All of the sudden, the five religions that had been living for so long in harmony just clashed with one another. Especially Islam and Christianity. How did that happen?

I have always been interested in myth, religion, culture and history since as long as I could remember. But all this mess in the world has made my passion for these topics even deeper. So I read any book I can get my hands on concerning the above topics. Finally, I found enough evidence to the conclusion that I have mentioned at the beginning of this chapter. At first I wanted to keep this to myself, but then I thought I should share my journey with anyone who is just as confused as I was and looking for answers. I was taught that religion is meant to teach people how to be good. So what are these wars in the name of God is all about? This is how my search for God began. When I was a child it started with these questions:

Would one believe in God if one was never told to do so?
Would anyone convert to another religion other than the religion of their parents, if they knew that the inherited religion is not the 'right' one? Would I?
Would I still be a Moslem if I wasn't born in a Moslem family?
Why are there so many religions?
Is it good to be good because one is scared to be punished in hell? Is that really good or just plain scared?
I was taught that Islam is the only right religion.
But I couldn't help thinking, aren't the other children taught the same thing about their religions too?
So… which one is the right one?

But after living in Europe, meeting and discussing with many agnostics and atheists, the list of questions became longer:

What is religion?
Is religion really necessary in life?
Is there prove that God exist?
What is all the fuss about religion?

CHAPTER TWO

WHAT IS RELIGION?

Pagan, Hindu, Buddhist, Jewish, Christian and Islamic Houses of Prayer

*T*o find the answers, I think the first logical step is to see what the definition of religion is. There are many definitions concerning what it is. The following is according to the Oxford English Dictionary: 'A strong belief in a supernatural power or powers that control human destiny'.

I know that many 'modern' people think that religion is not important and primitive. However, if we look at the world today everyone is forced to admit that religion still has a strong grip in our lives if not stronger than before. The clash of many religions has such a big impact on everyone's life. Just switch on CNN and you will know what I am talking about.

Apparently, religion has always had this impact in human's history. Some historians have agreed that the first societies established in human history are most likely of a religious origin.

Studying religion can be very complex, many of the historical facts are intertwined (not to mention purposely or not, hidden from the public) and many are contradictive. This book is my personal spiritual/mental journey, so this is just the conclusion of my own autodidact study for almost 30 years.

I am trying to simplify the historical facts and the scientific theories that are used to write this book – the purpose of this book is to become food for thought and not to make you even more confused. Therefore, if you want to have further detail, please search personally.

There are many religions in this world, many ancient ones have perished. There are literally religions from A – Z: Aladura, Asatru, Atheism, Baha'i, Bon, Buddhism, Cao Dai, Chinese Religion, Chopra Center, Christianity (Catholic, Protestant, Orthodox), Christian Science, Confucianism, Deism, Druze, Echankar, Epicureanism, Falun Gong, Gnosticism, Greek Religion, Hare Krishna, Hinduism, Islam, Jainism, Jehova Witness, Judaism, Mahikari, Mayan Religion, Mithraism, Mormonism, New Age, New Thought, Rastafari, Sabian, Scientology, Seventh-Day Adventists, Shinto, Shikism, Stoicism, Taoism, Unification Church, Unitarian Universalism, Urantia, Wicca, Zen and Zoroastrianism. I am sure there still many more, and we are not even counting the hundreds or even thousands of sects.

It is not easy to put religion in certain categories, since many of the concepts are intertwined. But for the sake of simple explanation all religions can be categorized in the following 2 types:

1. **Polytheism** is a belief that there are plural gods and/or deities and/or spirits. The examples are (most) Hinduism sects and almost all ancient civilizations religions: Egyptian, Aztec, Sumerian, Greek, Roman, etc. Polytheism also includes :
   - **Animism**, a belief that souls inhabit all objects from inanimate objects to plants, animal and even natural phenomena.

- **Pantheism**, a belief that everything, the universe or nature and God are equivalent.
- **Shamanism**, a traditional belief and practices concerned with the communication with the spirit world.
- **Paganism**, basically any other religious beliefs other than those of the main world religions - all kinds of spiritual, cultic or beliefs of any folk religions fall into this category.

2. **Monotheism** is a belief in one Creator God. There are 3 major monotheisms in the world at present: Judaism, Christianity and Islam.

Today there are 5 major religions that have the most influence in the world. There are (in order of the most followers): Christianity, Islam, Hinduism, Buddhism and Judaism.

Although, Buddhism doesn't really teach about God or gods, it teaches more about enlightenment without discussing about God – therefore, some scholars categorize Buddhism as philosophy and not a religion.

According to some historians today religions are divided into stages of progression from simple to more complex societies, especially from polytheism to monotheism and from gradual philosophical evolution to organize.

Thus, the starting point is tribal societies whose religion is animistic that involves shamans and totems. Since the group is tribal, there is no permanent sanctuary. Cultic rites centre on identification with wild animals and taming the spirits, often of the hunted.

As society developed into chiefdoms and small kingdoms, religious rites began to serve different functions. Agriculture became important and so fertility gods were introduced (often female, as it is women who have the power to produce life). The status of the 'big man' (or chief) was supported with mythic tales of heroes and demigods, whom he may be descended from.

When these small kingdoms merged into larger groups (often through conquest), different cults merged. The conquest of one group by another is therefore recorded in an epic tale of the conquest of the conquered group's god by the victor's (e.g. some Hinduism gods and the Babylonian Marduk). Another solution was to merge different religious traditions, for example, the Romans' identification of their gods with the Greeks' and the Greeks' adoption of Anatolian (today Turkish) myths and characters.

Finally, the growth of the city state brought about progression to the most 'civilized' level of religion, i.e. ethical monotheism. Generally, it is believed that Judaism is the first monotheist religion in the world, although some historians say that monotheism began in Egypt with Akhenaton (a Pharaoh from ca. 1375 BCE) who has established monotheism religion in Egypt. However, his successor Tutankhamen brought polytheism back to Egypt and some say its remnants grew into Judaism, Persian Zoroastrianism and Greek Philosophy to endow Western society with the most progressive form of religion.

Nevertheless, it is still widely held that ethical monotheism (e.g. Judaism, Christianity, Islam, some forms of Hinduism and some form of Buddhism) was encouraged by the growth of city states. This was partly due to the role of a hierarchical society with a god-like absolute ruler. A more powerful force is needed to regulate social issues as society moved from the smaller clan to a more cosmopolitan lifestyle. Questions of justice and value that had been previously answered by the family and small tribe were now to be pursued independently. Ethical monotheism answered society's need for a moral guide and motivation, whilst a unique personal God who was sovereign over all areas of life answered people's feelings of isolation and powerlessness. (Ref: Wikipedia)

The above theory is now doubted because archeological findings have shown that some ancient cultures were already more cosmopolitan and more advanced than the early period of Judaism. As the matter of fact, the Great Pyramid of Giza remained the tallest man-made structure in the world for thousands of years, unsurpassed until the 160 meter tall spire of Lincoln Cathedral was completed at around 1300 CE. And according to historians, the Egyptians who build the Great Pyramid were believers of polytheism. The more sophisticated and cosmopolitan Roman Empire also had remained to believe in polytheistic religion long after the birth of Judaism.

Many people in the West today concluded that religion is just man-made invention. But is it true? So let's analyze this together. Analyzing religion is incomplete without analyzing the source of it: God. So who is God? Is there a Supernatural Power in the universe? If yes, can we prove it by science? Is there only one or more?

PROVING GOD'S EXISTENCE THROUGH SCIENCE
Before we analyze about God's existence let's see the different view of people's belief concerning God. Basically this can be simplified and categorized in the following groups:

1. **Atheist** – a person who does not believe in neither God nor gods.

2. **Agnostic** – a person who is skeptical in the existence of God, because he or she believes that it is not possible to have absolute knowledge of the existence of God or gods. There are many types of agnostic, from the one who says: "I don't

know and neither do you." or "I don't know, but maybe you do." until: "I don't know and who cares anyway?"

3. **Polytheist / Animist / Pantheist / Pagan** – it is not easy to differentiate the beliefs of these groups of people, because the concepts are similar and sometimes intertwined. For the sake of simple explanation we can categorize them as Polytheists – because all of these people do not believe in One Creator God.

4. **Monotheist** – a person who believes in One God.

Most so-called modern and intelligent people in the world especially in the West belong to the atheist and agnostic groups. Most of them believe that science is the only thing that can answer all of the questions and problems in the world. They believe only in what they can see or proof by science.

Appropriately, it is a common saying that religion and science cannot go together harmoniously. If this was true, I think it is totally understandable that many intelligent people become atheists or agnostics. I have to admit that this is a rational approach because I also believe that if God exists, His guidance (i.e. religion) must be in accordance with science. The other way around is just absurd.

So let's examine what our scientific study concludes about the existence of a Super Natural Power or powers.

Is there a God? To some people, the affirmative answer is the only one there can be, while to others believing in it is no more than a calculated bet. The French philosopher Pascal concluded that belief was the wisest bet because the believer will either have bliss if he/she is right or oblivion if he/she is wrong, whereas the atheist has the less attractive alternatives of oblivion or damnation.

To some people the word 'nature' is some kind of force responsible for shaping life, but can there be justification in saying that 'nature' is a concrete intelligent force responsible for creating as well as shaping life? Or, is 'nature' merely an abstract man-made label that acts as an easy answer to the more urgent questions in our attempt to explain the cause of things? According to the Concise Oxford Dictionary the definition of 'nature' is the phenomena of the physical world collectively, including plants, animals, and the landscape, as opposed to humans or human creations.

According to science today, if we were to trace the age of the earth we would have to go back in time 4.5 billion years. The age of our galaxy, the Milky Way, would take us even further back 12 billion years, while as the estimated age of the entire universe is around 18 billion years.

If the 'terrestrial nature' represents the earth and everything on it, there would still remain a very long period of time prior to the formation of the earth when there would have been no meaning to the word 'nature'. Still, some force had to account for what occurred before.

If we were to chart the age of mankind against the age of the universe we would find it very insignificant in universal terms. According to evolution theory today – the alleged first Homo Sapiens, whom evolutionist believe to be our direct ancestors, walked on earth a mere 200,000 years ago. Clearly then the school of thought that claims that God is not an External Being but is to be found inside each of us is naive and pretentious. It is naive because if we were to claim that God exists *only* inside us then we would have to believe that before 200,000 years ago there was no God. Even if one employs Darwin's theory of evolution to suggest some kind of link between man and ape, and as a result associate an older age for mankind, one would still have to say that God did not exist before 4 - 2 million years ago, that is when the first alleged human-apes (Australopithecus) walked on earth. It is also pretentious because no matter how clever we think we are, we are only one species of creatures on one planet that revolves around one star. The star, being the sun, is merely one star among billions other similar stars that belong to our galaxy, the Milky Way. In the universe there are billions of other galaxies!

The failure of science to provide adequate answers to these questions, and in the quest for the Truth, lead many people seek the answers in religion.

Through adopted faith, whether it is researched or most commonly inherited, we seek to find God. However, it may make better sense to reverse the procedure. It may be wiser to seek God first and then search for His true word. After all God, has always existed while as the establishment of any faith or religion is a time related event.

There are those who will completely do without an intellectual approach to belief insisting that for them belief is in the heart and not the mind. Whilst we must understand and respect this point of view so far as the first part of the search goes, and that is the initial belief in God, it is of prime importance that the process of selecting a faith to believe in should not be left to the heart alone, but is a matter that should be researched thoroughly by taking time to consider and debate all points of view. This is necessary because of the unfortunate yet intentional misguidance and misrepresentation conducted by various religious organizations. Sadly, all major religions in the world today can be accused of corruption in one way or another.

Furthermore, we tend to be more inclined to the view that even though a spiritual or emotional belief may appear to be of great strength, yet if it is not supported intellectually; it may often be vulnerable to crack. We often come across people who have suddenly acquired a very intense faith only to completely lose it after a period of time. For as the saying goes 'easy come easy go'. On the other hand, a slow contemplated intellectual approach has a better chance of endurance because it is built on reason.

Today we live in an age of reason and not of blind faith. It is thus necessary for any intelligent person to debate all matters and not succumb to the influence of our native environment alone. We should not rely on the religious background passed on through parents or the society alone. We have no choice as to which faith we were born into but we all have the free will to seek the Truth. We should adopt a faith only when we are totally convinced that it is the Truth, don't you think?

THE BIG BANG

Today the Big Bang Theory is the dominant and reliable scientific theory about the origin of the universe, with the most evidence to support it. According to the Big Bang theory, the universe was created sometime around 18 billion years ago from a cosmic explosion that hurled matter in all directions.

In 1842 Christian Doppler – an Austrian mathematician and physicist, confirmed that the sound's pitch gets higher as the sound source approached him, and lower as the sound source moved away from him.

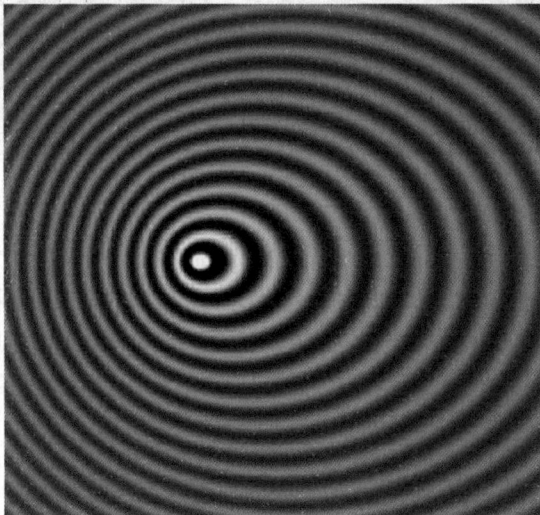

www.wikipedia.org/wiki/Doppler-effect

Doppler Effect

The universe consists of billions of galaxies and each galaxy has a vast number of stars. To study a galaxy, scientists record light from it on a strip film. If the galaxy is moving away from our galaxy, the lines on the spectrum will be towards the red end of the film; this is called the Red Shift.

In 1912 Vesto Slipher – an American astronomer, measured the first Doppler shift of a 'spiral galaxy' and soon discovered that almost all such galaxies were moving away from earth. A spiral galaxy is a type of galaxy that has a rounded swelling shaped with a flat surface, surrounded by a disk and encase by a spherical halo (circle of light).

A Spiral Galaxy

In 1927, George Lemaitre, a Belgian Roman Catholic priest, professor of physics and astronomy, predicted that the moving away movement of the galaxies was due to the expansion of the universe. In 1931 Lemaitre went further and suggested that the universe began as a simple 'primeval atom'.

In 1948, a contrasting theory called the Steady State Theory was proposed by Fred Hoyle, Thomas Gold, Hermann Bondi and some other scientists. This theory which also sometimes called as the

Infinite Universe Theory or Continuous Creation basically proposes that the universe has no beginning and no end.

Although this theory had a large number of supporters amongst cosmologists in the 1950's and 1960's, the number of supporters decreased markedly in the late 1960's after the discovery of the Cosmic Microwave Background Radiation (the left over of the radiation caused by the Big Bang explosion). So, today only a very small number of supporters of this theory remain.

Huge strides in Big Bang cosmology have been made since the late 1990s as a result of major advances in telescope technology as well as the analysis of copious data from satellites such as COBE (Cosmic Background Explorer), the Hubble Space Telescope and WMAP (Wilkinson Microwave Anisotropy Probe). Cosmologists now have fairly precise measurement of many parameters of the Big Bang model, and have made the unexpected discovery that the expansion of the universe appears to be accelerating.

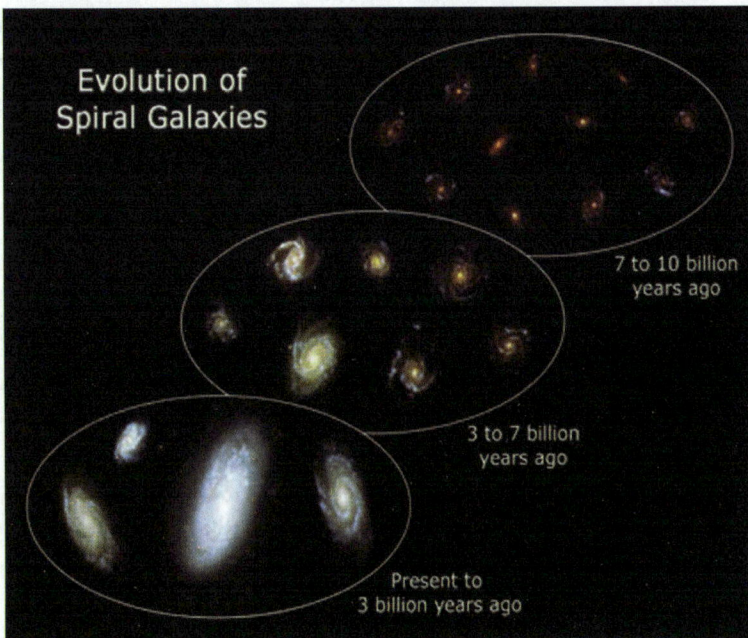

Evolution of the Spiral Galaxies

Most scientists today agree that the universe was 'born' out of the Big Bang and had a beginning. The universe is not 'beginning-less' it must have started from nothing. Although, scientists still do not know what have caused it. <u>The energy needed to split the primordial atom is so immense that nothing in this natural world may be the cause of it</u>. Thus, most scientists today have to accept the theory of the 'born' finite universe, which is expanding.

∂⋆σ

There are 2 theories that can be used to prove that the universe is finite and has a beginning: the Olbers' Paradox and/or the Laws of Thermal Dynamic.

THE OLBERS' PARADOX

The visible night sky is dark. If the universe is infinite, eternal and static, then the sky should be as bright as the surface of the sun all the time! This problem is called the Olbers' Paradox.

If the universe is uniformly filled with stars, then no matter which direction we look, our line of sight will eventually intersect a star (or other bright thing). Now it is known that the stars are grouped into galaxies, but the paradox remains: our line of sight will eventually intersect a galaxy.

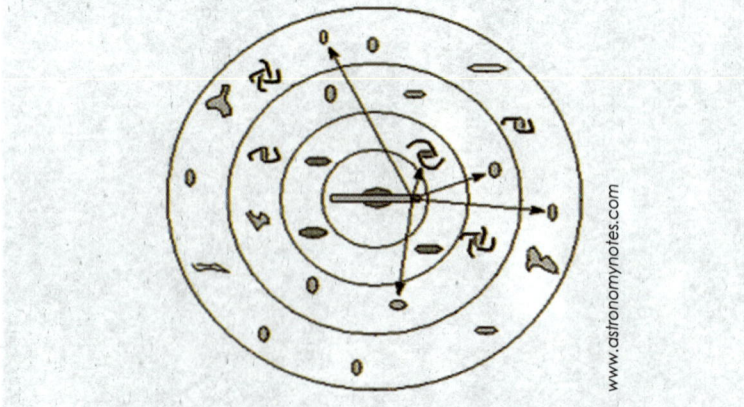

www.astronomynotes.com

Sky That Never Gets Dark According to Olbers

The brightness of the star does decrease with greater distance but more stars are further out. The number of stars within a spherical shell around us will increase by the same amount their brightness decreases. Therefore, each shell of stars will have the same overall luminosity and because there are a lot of ever bigger shells in an infinite universe, there is going a lot of light!

Any intervening material absorbing the starlight would eventually heat up and radiate as much energy as it absorbed, so the problem remains even if we try these 'shields'.

Looking at trees within a big flat wood in direction of the horizon shows the same effect: the mass of dark trees will hide the horizon (imagine the trees now as lights).

THE THERMAL DYNAMICS
Now let's argue that the universe is finite (very large but finite) but still has no beginning. Here we refer to the Laws of Thermal Dynamics which govern the movement of heat between different bodies.

The second Law of Thermal Dynamics states that heat travels from hot bodies to cooler bodies and not the opposite. If for example a hot oven is placed in a cold room the oven will warm the room, this is because heat will be transferred from the hot oven to the cold room. Never will the amount of heat originally in the room cause the oven to get hotter. This transfer of heat between the oven and the room will continue until the oven has used up its entire fuel source (e.g. a gas cylinder). When that point is reached the oven will start to cool until such a point when the temperatures of both the oven and the room become equal. To calculate the amount of time during which the oven will continue to warm the room we need to know two things:

1-   The amount of gas left in the cylinder.
2-   The rate at which gas is consumed.

If for example there is 500 c.c. (cubic centimeters) of gas left in the cylinder and the oven uses up 10 c.c. every hour, with a simple division we find that the oven will continue to warm the room for 50 hours (call this stage A). After 50 hours the oven will start to cool until the point is reached where the temperatures of the oven and the room are equal (call this stage B).

Now let us apply this to the universe as a whole. We know that the total amount of energy in the universe is equal to the sum of energy in all the stars, galaxies, ...etc. This is a finite amount no matter how large it is. These stars will continue to radiate heat, light and other types of radiation into the vast space of the universe, in the same way in which the oven would warm the space inside the room. So if we think of all the stars and all other active bodies in the universe as the oven and the vast empty space as the empty room we can deduce the following:

From what is known about the life and death of stars in modern theories of cosmology, it is known that they would continue to radiate energy until they consume all their resources. To be precise, when all the Hydrogen, that constitutes the vast majority of the mass of stars, has been converted into Helium and other heavier elements in a process of continuous nuclear reactions. After that stage the stars start to collapse and end up as cold dead bodies.

Since the amount of matter in the universe (in the form of stars, nebula, quasars.....etc.) is finite, then these energy sources will radiate energy into the universe for a finite length of time. In our example of the oven and the room we calculated that time to be 50 hours. Theoretically, and if we can calculate the total amount of energy in the universe, and also the rate of consumption of energy, we can also calculate the length of time (although obviously not as accurately as in the case of the oven) in which the stars will continue to radiate energy. For argument's sake, let us assume that the universe will continue to radiate energy for another 50 billion years. Since there is still plenty of energy available in the universe we are still in stage A.

Now if we go back to our original debate, and try to decide whether the universe had a beginning or has it always been there, we can quickly reach the conclusion that if it had always been there, or in mathematical terms if the age of the universe goes back to infinity, it should have been a cold and dead place by now simply because: infinity is older than 50 billion years. If the age of the universe is infinity, we should have been at stage B a long time ago,. The accuracy of the figure 50 billion is of no importance to the result, for whatever figure we choose to make it, it will always be less than infinity.

What that means is that the universe had a definite beginning. That beginning, for arguments sake, being less than 50 billion years ago. The birth of new stars in the universe does not affect our analysis, they are not born out of the void, and they are merely a conversion of hot gases into hot new stars. Their birth is not an addition to the total amount of matter that already exists in the universe. The total amount of matter remains constant. After a time all the hot gases in the universe will be used up and no new stars will be born. As for the newly born stars, they too will eventually consume all their energy and die.

⟨σ✲σ⟩

The truth is the sky is neither always bright nor it is totally dark. Now, if we accept that the universe is finite and had a definite beginning, the next step would be to debate whether that beginning was caused by an Intelligent Power or by mere chance.

IS THE UNIVERSE CREATED BY A CREATOR OR MERE CHANCE?
Here we refer to the well-known Law of Conservation of Matter. This law states that 'matter cannot be created nor destroyed'. What that means is that all that we are able to do is convert one

form of substance to another. We can never create matter from nothing, and similarly we cannot turn matter into nothing. Trees are brought down to make wood and paper, sand is used in the making of glass, etc., but we can never create wood or glass out of vacuum. Similarly we cannot completely destroy wood or glass, for even if we burn wood, we are only converting it to ashes and gases that are given off in the process.

We have also shown that all matter had a definite beginning or a moment in time when it came to exist, the moment when the universe was created (the Big Bang). By joining these seemingly contradicting statements together:

1- Laws of physics states that matter cannot be created.

2- Since the universe had a definite beginning, we can say that it was created.

The universe appears miraculously, so to speak. Therefore, it is only rational to say that the universe was created by a Power that is above and independent of the Laws of Physics as we know them. That Power is clearly not restricted or confined to the basic Laws of Physics but far more superior. Neither can this Power be of a physical essence. It is also justifiable to expect this Power not to have had a beginning because the concept of a beginning and for that matter Time in general, has been shown to be a dimension of the physical universe only.

In his Theory of Relativity, Einstein stated that time, space and matter were all created when the universe was born, and that before that moment Time did not exist. It is not easy for the human mind to envisage the concept of No Time, but if one accepts that Time is only a dimension of the physical world the idea becomes more acceptable. Further still, since the universe had a definite beginning before which nothing existed, then such an awesome event (the creation of the universe) cannot be attributed to chance, since before that initial moment of creation nothing existed, not even Chance!

This law makes it impossible to attribute a 'natural' cause to the start of the universe. The energy had to come from somewhere, the energy whose radiation we still receive. A superior non-physical Power and Creator is the only possible explanation to this argument.

THE LAWS OF PROBABILITIES

The Laws of Probabilities offer another interesting argument: If we throw a dice, the chance of obtaining double 6 is 2.7% or 1 out of 36. What this means is that on average if we throw the dice 1000 times, the chances are that we should get double 6 around 27 times. Now if we throw the dice 1000 times and we obtain double 6 every single throw then there is a design, a system or a controlling force behind the throws. We can hardly call it chance.

The science of genetics offers vivid evidence that chance could not be a factor in the process of creation due to the very precise combinations necessary in the building of cells. These requisite combinations defy all Laws of Probabilities.

On a larger scale, we only need to look at the universe to be able to marvel at the endless examples of precision and beautiful design. Every field of scientific knowledge seems to testify to the existence of a Master Creator. It does not seem difficult to dismiss the possibility of Chance. The universe cannot be created by Chance or accident. A fitting quote here is that of an American Biologist and Zoologist, Professor Edwin Conklin, he stated:

"The probability of life originating from accident is comparable to the probability of the Unabridged Dictionary resulting from an explosion in a printing company."

THE CONSTANTS

Many thinkers: Pythagoras, Plato, Cusanus, Keppler, Leibniz, Fibonacci, Newton, Planck and Einstein are convinced that the existence of numbers and geometrical shapes are the concept of the universe. Galileo said that "Mathematics is the language of God when He created the universe".

The universe is filled with numbers that repeat themselves (periodic) which are structured and systematic. For example: the orbit of the moon, earth and other planets, the number of DNA and chromosomes, the characteristics of the atoms, all the chemical elements, and so forth.

As a layman, the simplest example that I can understand is the constant of water (binary compound) which is: H_2O. When 2 atoms of Hydrogen are joined with 1 atom of Oxygen it becomes water. Always! Now, this is one of the Laws of the Universe.

Scientists calculate that during the first few minutes after the expansion began, roughly 25% of the Hydrogen in the universe was converted into Helium. Scientists also say that if the Strong Force had been slightly more intense all the Hydrogen in the universe would be converted into Helium. In such case life would never exist for 3 reasons:

1. There would be no water without Hydrogen.
2. Hydrogen is necessary for proteins and nucleic acids that are needed for life.
3. Stars that have only Helium is extremely short lived and could never reach the 3 billion years figure that our system took for life to appear.

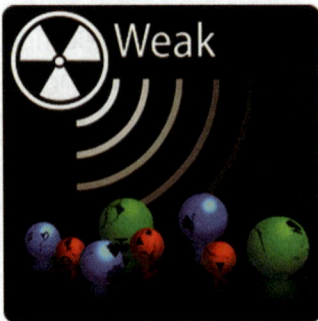

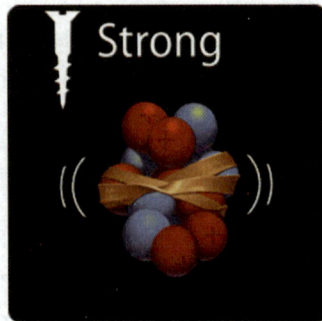

www.particlephysics.ac.uk.gif

Illustration of Weak and Strong Forces effect to Matter Particles

But if the Strong Force were a little weaker, things would not exist as the protons could not stay together in the cores of atoms. So the constant figure of the Strong Force of Attraction is exactly what is needed to create life in the universe. Had nature opted for a slightly different set of numbers, the world would have been a very different place and we would not be here to see it. Thus, to believe that life originated without an Intelligent Designer becomes really absurd.

Even (many) intelligent scientists have to admit that without external cause (i.e.: the Supernatural Power or what we call God) the Big Bang and the creation of life in the universe is impossible. The only logical hypothesis by studying the nature is that an Intelligent Being created the heavens and the earth. And this Being cannot be human or like anything in the natural world.

THE MECHANICAL ARGUMENT
The mechanical argument is also in support of the concept of a Creator. "For every action there is a reaction, equal to it and opposite in direction.'

Everything that has moved was moved by something else. If we go back in time, tracing everything to its original mover, we would ultimately arrive at that which was not moved by anything else. This analysis will also lead us to the unavoidable conclusion of an Initial Creator.

THE DEVELOPMENT VS DESTRUCTION ARGUMENT
Everything left unattended gradually disintegrates. If one builds a house and leaves it unattended, in a few weeks it will become full of dust. In ten years or so the paint will start falling off. After a hundred years or so some of the walls will start to weaken and fall, and maybe in a thousand years or so the whole house will be flat to the ground. In other words, if left unattended, any organized structure or system will eventually become one of chaos. Never

will chaos suddenly spring into a system. A house will never spring into being of its own doing.

If we try to analyze what has actually happened on earth we realize that it was quite remarkable. When the earth was first formed it was a very hostile hot planet with no form of life whatsoever. Somehow, simple forms of life, more complex forms of living creatures and human appeared.

The trend has been reversed; instead of things crumbling they have in fact developed all the time to higher forms of being. Chaos has developed into a system. Has the earth been attended all the time?

It is amusing, to put it mildly, to observe humans so full of vanity thinking we are the masters of everything merely because we are given some intelligence to discover some of the Laws of the Universe. In reality, we have no authority in setting or altering such laws. With the aid of the physical senses, we are given a view over a Divine masterpiece, but considering we are mere spectators within the huge universe, we can indeed be very pompous.

THE MACRO/MICRO PATTERN

There is so much symmetry in the universe to be able to go through all of it, but one particular design has special appeal. And that is the Macro/Micro pattern.

If we look at the universe at large we find that it is composed of vast areas of empty space and also other areas containing shapeless matter in the form of hot gases, dark matter and formed stars. These stars group together to form galaxies. Our galaxy Milky Way has within it no less than 100 billion individual stars. Our star, the sun, has nine planets (or eight planets since Pluto is no longer considered as a planet) in orbit around it. Most of these planets have a number of moons again in orbit. The basic force that governs the movement of all these bodies is gravity. The moons rotate around their planets, which all rotate around the mother star, which in our case is the sun. Similarly, all these stars revolve round the center of gravity of the galaxy. Galaxies group together to form clusters of galaxies and once again individual galaxies revolve round the center of gravity of the cluster. Clusters group together to form super-clusters, and these obey the same laws. These are the largest units in the universe as we know it today.

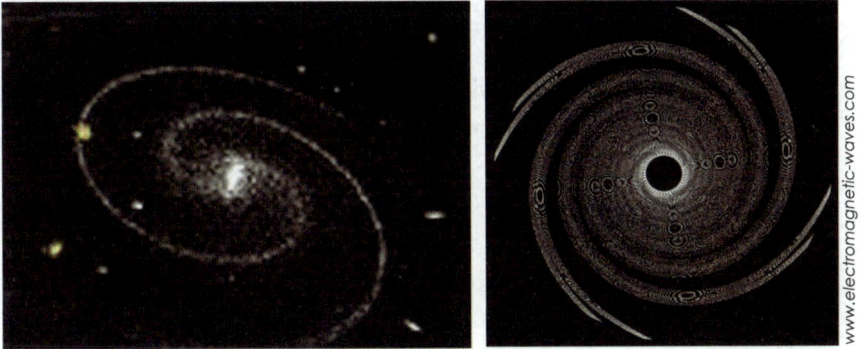

Illustration of a Spiral Galaxy and a Rotation of A String of Coupled Photons

When we proceed in the opposite direction, we notice that the similarity is truly remarkable. If we examine the atom which is the smallest form of substance able to exist in a chemical reaction, we find that it is composed of electrons revolving round a nucleus, in the same way as stars revolve round the center of gravity of their galaxies. Are we but seeing the finger prints of the Creator? If one searches one can surely find God. God's marvels are all around us.

The more we advance on the path of science in all directions, micro and macro, the arguments that there is an Intelligent Designer becomes increasingly eloquent. The origin of the 'laws' of nature and the precise values of the 'constants', without life could never have originated, necessitate intelligent design.

When analyzed logically, the 'God hypotheses' emerges as a factual reality. <u>This in essence is pure science</u>.

Thus, looking at the facts that nature provides us, leaves us with only two options:

1.   See it or acknowledge the prove based on science, or
2.   Ignore or reject it, which will be the same as   abandoning science itself.

Just as Annie Dillard – the winner of Pulitzer award for non-fiction book in 1975 – wrote it beautifully:

> "The universe was not made in jest but in solemn incomprehensible earnest. By a power that is unfathomable secret, and holy and fleet. There is nothing to be done about it, but ignore it or see it."

If we accept that the creation of the universe must have been the work of Supreme Intelligent Power, we are faced with another puzzle and that is: how many Gods are there? Is God one, or could there be more than one God?

ONE GOD OR MANY GODS?

Here the reference is made to some basic word definitions. The words 'absolute' and 'relative' is straight forward in what they mean. Anything relative is that which can be compared to or related to other things. Whenever we describe an object we are always describing it in relation to other things. On the other hand an absolute is that which is self-existent and conceivable without relation to other things.

If we return to our example of the room and the oven we can say that the oven is hotter than the room but that does not mean that the oven is hot in an absolute sense, for if we were to place this oven inside an active volcano it would seem very cool in comparison. An athlete is a very fast runner compared to road pedestrians but is indeed very slow compared to a motor car, and so on until it becomes clear that anything we see in life is relative because there will always be something that is cooler, bigger, older ....etc.

If we go back to our Big Bang theory we realize that what brought it about must have been a Power that is above all the Laws of Physics that governs the universe. When scientists study the evolution of the universe they trace it back to the moment of creation or the Big Bang, but when they reach that point they find that all the Laws of Physics cease to be. Had they considered the same situation in a forward direction they would have realized that the Big Bang was the moment when all the laws of physics have actually began to be. We have also noted that the force that brought about the Big Bang, and in effect the creation of the universe, could not have been related to this universe in any physical sense, for it is clearly the cause and not the effect of the universe. Since this Supreme Power is the cause then it must have been existent prior to and independent of the universe. Thus we can say that nothing in this universe can be related to that Supreme Power, and if nothing can be compared or related to that power, then by definition that power is absolute.

The absolute God means that nothing is like or akin to Him, for if we were to consider the possibility of the existence of more than one God, immediately the question will arise as to: which god came first, which god is more powerful and so on, and that would ultimately reduce these gods to being relative because comparisons will arise.

If God is absolute, by definition, God must be One.

Furthermore, if the universe would be controlled by more than One God, then each god will fight for dominancy, as confirmed in the Hindu and Greek epics. Indeed, in all polytheist teachings there are stories about the gods fighting amongst each other for dominion. No matter how fascinating and enchanting those stories are, they are not in accordance with science.

If truly all the gods are fighting for dominancy, the whole universe would have been in total chaos. Yes, there is chaos on the earth, but that is caused by human, not by nature. Nature always follows the basic Laws of Physics. We know that whenever a ruler of a country changed, there is always some alterations in the country's policy.

That must be the case if the universe is ruled by many gods... imagine what would happen if each of the ruling god decides to change the force of earth's gravity or the rotation of the sun or the neutral pH of water...

I hope nobody will take this following statement as an offence. I find it very difficult to accept that sometimes the actions of the gods in all the polytheist religions that we know; are not of good example. For instance, the supreme ruler of the Greek gods, Zeus, killed Cronus (his father) to gain power. Zeus was married to his own sister, Hera, and he still had many other wives who were willingly married to him, or even raped by him! I am sorry, but I just can not believe that this kind of stories is truly the true story of our universe. These kind of similar stories exist in all polytheist religions.

Science has proven that there is only one Original Source, one Original Force, One God. This means I can rule out the choice of being an atheist, agnostic and polytheist, since these groups are not in accordance with the above scientific proof. For me, after studying the information above, this far my choice to find the Truth is only left with monotheism.

Although, I know that some teachings of polytheism are in accordance with science. For example, scholars have found amazing scientific information 'hidden' in between the fascinating epics of the Rig Veda - the religious book of the Hindus. I have also read books about the Buddhist teachings concerning the power of the focused mind and the importance to stay in the Now (Zen Buddhism teaching) that may also be proven scientifically, mostly likely by using the Laws of Quantum Mechanics.

But I am looking for the whole Truth. To me, partial truth is not the Truth. Especially when dealing with Truth concerning God and religion. We will discuss some of the teachings of Hinduism and Buddhism towards the end of this book and will go into further analysis concerning the correlation between polytheist and monotheist religions, which is surprisingly even more intertwined than most people are aware of, in my next two books (EarthTrek Vol. 2: From Myth To The Ultimate Reality and Vol. 3: The Chronicle). But, at the moment, let's stick to the monotheism religions first, shall we?

So how can we search for the Truth? We know that the history of religions (all religions), *especially* the monotheist religions, is full of bloody fights and wars. Although this doesn't necessary mean that the teachings are wrong; it just proves that the followers of these religions can be violent, right? Can we really analyze the teaching of a religion by the action of its followers? I believe not. I believe the way to analyze the teaching of a religion is by reading its religious scripture.

CHAPTER THREE

THE MONOTHEISTIC RELIGIOUS BOOKS

The Tanakh, the Christian Bible and the Quran

*T*his far, my journey in search for the Truth is heading towards monotheist religions. Let's analyze the brief known history of the monotheist religions (that I know of):

1. **Aten**

    Aten is a monotheistic religion that was 'founded' by Akhenaton - an Egyptian pharaoh who is believed to have lived around 1375 BCE. He believed in the One God but then his successor - Tutankhamen brought his people back to the old polytheist religion. Unfortunately, no intact scripture of the teaching of Aten can be found to be studied today.

2. Zoroastrianism

Zoroaster or Zuruzhustra was a prophet from Persia (today Iran), who taught monotheism. The time when Zoroaster lived is still not really defined yet, most probably he lived between 1400 BCE and 1000 BCE. The religious book is called the Avesta. Although Zoroastrianism is still considered as monotheism, it also believes in the concept of dualism: it teaches the followers to believe in One God (Ahura Mazda), who is always in constant battle with the evil spirit (Angra Mainyu) who is just almost as powerful. Today there are only around 200,000 followers of this religion in the world.

For the moment, I choose to analyze deeper the study of the three major monotheist religions in the world today, which are: Judaism, Christianity and Islam. Although, there are a few other monotheistic religions (such as Sikhism and some sects in Hinduism), but they do not have many followers; unlike the three Abrahamic religion (i.e. Judaism, Christianity and Islam).

3. Judaism

Jewish tradition believed that the Jewish Patriarch started with Prophet Abraham. Although, the nationality of Abraham is still a matter of dispute today. The name 'Israel' (another name for Jacob – Abraham's grandson) and the term 'Judaism' came from the name of one of the sons Jacob. According to most historians Abraham came from Mesopotamia – a region corresponding to modern Iraq, north eastern Syria, southeastern Turkey and south western Iran. The main religious book of Judaism is called the Tanakh in Hebrew or also called the Old Testament in the Christian Bible. The time when Abraham lived is also still a matter of argumentation it ranges between 2000 BCE - 1700 BCE.

4. Christianity

According to most historians, Christianity began in the 1st century CE in Jerusalem as a Jewish sect, but quickly spread throughout the Roman Empire and today it is the world's largest religion. Though the life of Jesus is a matter of academic debate, most biblical scholars say that Jesus was born ca. 4 BCE, grew up in Nazareth in Galilee (today Palestine) and was crucified in Jerusalem ca. 33 CE with the consent of the Roman Governor of Judea Province, Pontius Pilate. The main sources of information regarding Jesus' life and teachings are the four canonical (Church Law) Gospels and which are compiled in the New Testament. Apart from the New Testament, Christians also read the Old Testament of Judaism as their religious book. Thus, the Christian Holy Bible consists of both the Old and New Testaments.

5. **Islam**

    Islam means 'submission to the will of God and peace'. Moslems use the phrase 'God willing' very often in daily conversation, since Moslems believe that everything happens only if God wills it. The same phrase is also used frequently by the other two previous monotheist religions: Judaism and Christianity. The prophet of Islam who delivered the Quran – Muhammad was born in 570 CE in Mecca, Saudi Arabia. The teaching of Islam is contained in the Quran which means the 'Recitation'. The Quran mentions many times that God also revealed the Torah (the first 5 books in the Old Testament) and the Christian Gospels (or the Injeel in Arabic) before God revealed the Quran. So Moslems believe that the other previous two books were also divinely revealed.

Thus, the Christian Bible contains teachings from the Old Testament (Jewish Tanakh). And the Quran contains teachings from both the Christian Bible and the Jewish Tanakh – so, theoretically all the three religious books should actually contain the same message. In reality today, only the main message is the same: the Oneness of God (to a certain degree), but the rest of the details of these three books are not the same and some contradict the other. So which one is the Right one?

If there is no contradiction, they might all be right. But if there are contradictions, they cannot all be right. Yes, they might all be wrong too..

Let us analyze the origin of these three books first. This is not an easy study for this is a history of thousand of years altogether (from Abraham to Muhammad). It doesn't matter from which source I take there is always objection from other parties. If you are looking for more detailed information, please conduct a comparison study yourself (from non-prejudice sources). I have read many shocking religious historical facts which I will share in my next two books of the EarthTrek Trilogy.

For the moment, I am only sharing with you the most common accepted history today. The main source of the following text is from Dr. Maurice Boucaille – author of 'The Bible, The Quran and Science'.

ORIGIN OF THE OLD TESTAMENT

www.sahallquist.files.wordpress.com

Moses and the Ten Commandments

The essential data for the following historical survey were taken from the entry of 'The Bible in the Encyclopedia Universalis' by J.P. Sandroz, a professor at the Dominican Faculties, Saulchoir.

To understand what the Old Testament represent, it is important to retain this information, correctly established today by highly qualified specialists.

The Hebrew Bible is called the Tanakh – which is an acronym based on the initial Hebrew letters of each of the text's three parts: **T**orah (Law), **N**evi'im (Prophets) and **Kh**etuvim (Writings). The Torah is the most important document in Judaism, revered as the inspired words of God and traditionally said to have been revealed to Moses.

The Tanakh consists of 24 books – which are the same books found in the Christian's Bible. However, the order of the book is different, and also Christians count these books as 39 instead of 24. For a matter of consistency, through out this book, if possible, I will refer to the Hebrew Bible as the Old Testament and the Christian Bible concerning only the teaching of Jesus as the New Testament.

Following is the list of the 39 books of the Christian version of the Old Testament:

1. Genesis
2. Exodus
3. Leviticus ⎫ The Torah / Pentateuch / 5 Books of Moses
4. Numbers
5. Deuteronomy ⎭

The rest are:

6.Joshua	15.Ezra	24.Jeremiah	33.Micah
7.Judges	16.Nehemiah	25.Lamentations	34.Nahum
8.Ruth	17.Esther	26.Ezekiel	35.Habakkuk
9.Samuel I	18.Job	27.Daniel	36.Zephaniah
10. Samuel II	19.Psalm	28.Hosea	37.Haggai
11.Kings I	20.Proverbs	29.Joel	38.Zechariah
12.Kings II	21.Ecclesiastes	30.Amos	39.Malachi
13.Chronicles I	22.Song of Songs	31.Obadiah	
14.Chronicles II	23.Isaiah	32.Jonah	

The Old Testament is a collection of works of greatly differing length and many different genres. The first incomplete writings were done, probably between the 10th and 11th century BCE, at the beginning of the Israelite Monarchy. It was at this period that a body of scribes appeared among the members of the royal household. The texts that were written down were: a certain number of songs, the prophetic oracles of Jacob and Moses, the Ten Commandments and the legislative texts which established a religious tradition before the formation of the law. All these texts constitute fragments throughout the various collections of the Old Testament.

It was not until a little later, possibly during the 10th century BCE, that the so called 'Yahvist' text of the Pentateuch was written. It is called 'Yahvist' because God is named Yahweh in this text. This text was to form the backbone of the first 5 books ascribed to Moses. This text which comes from the southern kingdom (Judah) deals with the origin of the world up to the death of Jacob.

Later, the so called 'Elohist' text was added. It is called 'Elohist' because God is named Elohim in this text. Then only the so called 'Sacerdotal' version – from the preachers in the Temple at Jerusalem was written.

www.essential-architecture.com

Destruction of the Temple of Jerusalem

At the end of the 9th century BCE and the middle of 8th century BCE, the prophetic influence of Elias and Elisha took shape and spread. We have their books today. This is also the time of the Elohist text of the Pentateuch which covers a much smaller period than the Yahvist text because it limits itself to facts relating to Abraham, Jacob and Joseph was written. The books of Joshua and Judges date from this time.

The 8th century BCE, saw the appearance of the writer-prophets: Amos and Hosea in Israel, and Micah in Judah.

In 721 BCE, the fall of Samaria (the capital city) put an end to the Kingdom of Israel. The Kingdom of Judah took over its religious heritage. The collection of Proverbs dates from this period, distinguished in particular by the fusion into a single book of the Yahvist and Elohist texts of the Pentateuch; in this way the Torah was constituted. Deuteronomy was written at this time.

In the second half of the 7th century BCE, the reign of Josiah coincided with the appearance of the prophet Jeremiah, but his work did not take definitive shape until a century later.

Before the first deportation to Babylon in 598 BCE, there appeared the Books of Zephaniah, Nahum and Habakkuk. Ezekiel was already prophesying during this first deportation. The fall of Jerusalem in 587 BCE marked the beginning of the second deportation which lasted until 538 BCE.

The Book of Ezekiel, the last great prophet and the Prophet of Exile, was not arranged into its present form until after his death by the scribes that were to become his spiritual inheritors. These same scribes were to resume Genesis in a third version, the so-called 'Sacerdotal' version, for the section going from the Creation to the death of Jacob. In this way a third text was to be inserted into the central fabric of the Yahvist and Elohist texts of the Torah. It was at this time that the Lamentations appeared.

On the order of King Cyrus the Great of Persia, the deportation to Babylon came to an end in 538 BCE. The Jews returned to Palestine and the Temple at Jerusalem was rebuilt. The prophets' activities began again, resulting in the books of Haggai, Zechariah, the third book of Isaiah, Malachi and Daniel.

The period following the deportation is also the period of the Books of Wisdom: Proverbs was written definitely around 480 BCE, Job dates from the 3rd century BCE, Ecclesiastes dates from the fourth century BCE, as do the Song of Songs, Chronicles I & II were written one century before Christ. The books of Ruth, Esther and Jonah are not easily datable.

All these dates are given on the understanding that there may have been subsequent adaptations, since it was only around one century before Christ that a shape was first given to the writings of the Old Testament. Thus, the Old Testament appears as a complete document from its origin to the generally believed to be the birth of Christianity - between the 11th century or the 10th century BCE and the 1st century BCE.

ORIGIN OF THE NEW TESTAMENT

www.catholic-resources.org

The Four Evangelists

The majority of Christians believes that the Gospels were written by direct witnesses of the life of Jesus and therefore constitute unquestionable evidence concerning the events highlighting his life and preaching. The value of the authors of the Gospels has as witnesses are always presented to the faithful as axiomatic (self evidently true). In the middle of the 2nd century CE, Saint Justin the Martyr did, after all, call the Gospel as the 'Memoirs of the Apostles'.

There are four authors or evangelists of the New Testament: Matthew, Mark, Luke and John.

Matthew was believed as a well - known character, he was 'a custom officer employed at the tollgate or customs house at Carphanaum', it is also said that he spoke Aramaic and Greek.
Mark is identifiable as Peter's colleague. Peter was one of Jesus' first disciples.
Luke was the 'dear physician' of whom Paul talks about.
John was the Apostle who was always near to Jesus, son of Zebedee, fisherman on the Sea of Galilee.

However if we read the following text, which is mainly based on an article of Cardinal Danielou – we will find quite different information:

Modern studies on the beginning of Christianity show that this way of presenting the identities of the evangelists hardly corresponds to reality. Their identities are still a matter of dispute until today.

As far as the decades following Jesus' mission are concerned, it must be understood that events did not at all happen in the way they have been said to have taken place and that Peter's (one of Jesus' 12 Apostles) arrival in Rome in no way laid the foundation for the Church. On the contrary, there was a struggle between the second half of the 2nd century CE between two groups.

One was what one might call Pauline Christianity (followers of Paul) and the other Judeo-Christianity. It was only very slowly that the Pauline Christians triumphed over Judeo-Christians.

Cardinal Danielou quotes Judeo-Christian writings, which express the views of Jesus of this community (initially formed around the apostles), the Gospel of the Hebrew (coming from a Judeo-Christian community in Egypt). This might be the oldest writings of Christian literature. This writing was later to be classed as Apocrypha – to be concealed by the victorious Church, which was to be born of Paul's success.

Saint Paul in Athens

Judeo-Christianity predominated not only in Jerusalem and Palestine during the first hundred years of the Church, but it was until Rome, Corinth (in modern Greece) Galatia, Colossae and Antioch (all three are in modern Turkey). The Judeo-Christians have now disappeared as a community with any influence, but one still hears people talking about them under the general term of 'Judaistic'. They petered out quickly in the West. In the East however it is possible to trace them in the 3rd and 4th century CE in Palestine, Arabia, Transjordania, Syria and Mesopotamia (modern Iraq, northeastern Syria, southeastern Turkey and southwestern

Iran). Others joined in the orthodoxy of the Great Church at the same time preserving traces of Semitic culture; some still persist in the Churches of Ethiopia and Chaldea (a Hellenistic part of Babylonia – today modern southern Iraq).

Who was Paul? Paul was the most controversial figure in Christianity. Saint Paul the Apostle was also called as the 'Apostle to the Gentiles'. (Gentile is a term for non-Jewish people). According to the Book of Acts, Paul was born in Tarsus, Cecilia in Asia Minor, or modern-day Turkey, under the name Saul, "an Israelite of the tribe of Benjamin, circumcised on the eighth day" (Philippians 3:5).

However, Paul's own letters never mention this as his birthplace, nor is the name 'Saul' alluded to. Acts records that Paul was a Roman citizen — a privilege he used a number of times in his defense, appealing against convictions in Judea to Rome (Acts 22:25 and Acts 27:29). According to Acts 22:3, he studied in Jerusalem under the Rabbi Gamaliel, well known in Paul's time. According to Acts 18:3 he worked as a tentmaker.

Paul wrote several letters (epistles) to various churches. These epistles were circulated within the Christian community, they were prominent in the first New Testament canon ever proposed and they were eventually included in the orthodox Christian canon. They are the earliest written books of the New Testament. Paul's influence on Christian thinking has, arguably, been more significant than any other single New Testament author.

Paul had not known Jesus during his lifetime and he proved the legitimacy of his mission by declaring that Jesus, raised from the dead, had appeared to him on the road to Damascus.

After Jesus' departure, the 'little group of Apostles' formed a 'Jewish sect that remained faithful to the form of worship practiced in the Temple'. However, when the observances of converts from paganism were added to them, a 'special system' was offered to them as it were. The Council of Jerusalem in 49 CE exempted them from circumcision and Jewish observances; although many Judeo-Christians rejected this concession. Paul separated himself from the Judeo-Christian group.

Paul and the Judeo-Christians were in conflict over the questions of pagans who had turned to Christianity. For Paul, himself a circumcised Jew - circumcision, Sabbath and form of worship practiced in the Temple were henceforth old fashioned, even for the Jews. Christianity was to free itself from its political-cum-religious adherence to Judaism and open itself to the Gentiles.

For the Judeo-Christians who remained 'loyal Jews' Paul was a traitor: Judeo-Christian documents call him an 'enemy', accusing him of 'tactical double-dealing'. Until 70 CE, Judeo-Christianity represents the majority of the Church and Paul remains isolated. The head of the community at that time was James, a relation of Jesus. James's successor was Simeon, son of Cleopas, a cousin of Jesus.

After the Jews had been discredited in the Empire, the Christians tended to detach themselves from them. The Hellenistic peoples of Christian persuasion then gained the upper hand; Paul won and Christianity separated itself politically and sociologically from Judaism.

From 70 CE until around 110 CE the four Gospels from Mark, Matthew, Luke and John were produced. But the letters of Paul still predate them.

Evangelist Matthew

Matthew is the first of the four Gospels as they appear in the New Testament. This position is perfectly justified by the fact that it is a prolongation, as it were, of the Old Testament. It was written to show that 'Jesus fulfilled the history of Israel'. To do so, Matthew constantly refers to quotation from the Old Testament which show how Jesus acted as he were the Messiah the Jews were awaiting. Matthew constantly brings the leading position of Jesus' attitude towards Jewish law. The main principles which are: praying, fasting and dispensing charity are resumed here.

According to O. Culmann author of 'The New Testament' - Matthew's community was trying to break away from Judaism while at the same time preserving the continuity of the Old Testament.

There are also political factors to be found in the text. The Roman occupation of Palestine naturally heightened the desire of this country to see itself liberated. They hoped for God to intervene in favor of the people He had chosen among all others, as He had already done many times.

Who was Matthew? The opinion that he was a tollgate officer at the house of Carphanaum when Jesus called him as his disciple was no longer held today.

Matthew was no longer acknowledged as one of Jesus' companions. His true identity is still a matter of dispute today, however one undisputable opinion about who he was: is that he was writing 'for people who speak Greek, but nevertheless know Jewish customs and the Aramaic language'.

Evangelist Mark

This is the shortest of the four Gospels. It is also the oldest, but in spite of this it is not a book written by an apostle. At best it was written by an apostle's disciple. O. Culmann considers that many turns of phrase corroborate the hypothesis that the author was of Jewish origin, but the presence of Latin expressions might suggest that he had written his Gospel in Rome. He addresses himself moreover to Christians not living in Palestine and is careful to explain the Aramaic expressions he uses.

Tradition has indeed tended to see Mark as Peter's companion in Rome. This was because in the final section of Peter's first letter – assuming that he really wrote the letter, was a sentence as follow: "The community which is at Babylon (what is probably meant Rome), which is likewise chosen, sends you greetings, and so does my son Mark."

Papias, Bishop of Hierapolis in ca. 150 CE ascribe this Gospel to Mark as Peter's interpreter and the possible collaborator of Paul, which could place Mark's Gospel to be placed after Peter's death between 65 CE – 70 CE.

Evangelist Luke

Luke is a cultivated Gentile convert to Christianity. His attitude towards the Jew is immediately apparent. Luke leaves out Marks' most Judaic verses and highlights the Jews unwillingness at Jesus' words, throwing into relief his good relations with the Samaritans, whom the Jews detested. Matthew, on the other hand, has Jesus ask the apostles to flee from them.

Who was Luke? An attempt has been made to identify him with the physician of the same name referred to by Paul in several of his letters. There was a Luke who was Paul's traveling companion, but was he the same person? O.Culmann thinks he was.

Evangelist John

John's Gospel is radically different from the other three. It is so different that Father Roguet who wrote the 'Initiation to the Gospel' - calls it 'a different world'. It is different in the arrangement, choice of subject, description, speech, style, geography, chronology and even differences in theological outlook. Father Roguet wrote that Jesus' word was recorded in a style that is striking, much neared to the oral style. In John all is meditation, to such extent indeed that one sometimes wonder if Jesus is still speaking or whether his ideas have not been extended by the evangelist's own thoughts.

Who was John? This is a highly debated question and extremely varying opinions have been expressed on this subject. Some believe that John is the son of Zebedee and brother of James. Many details are known about this apostle and are set out in works for mass publication. Popular iconography puts him near Jesus, as in the Last Supper prior to the Passion.

The fact that this Gospel was written so late is not a serious argument against this opinion, for most likely the first version was written around the end of the 1st century CE - which is around 60 years after Jesus' departure, so it is still possible for John who was very young at the time of Jesus. It is unthinkable however, that an episode so basic to Christianity, one indeed that was to be the mainstay of its liturgy, i.e. the Mass, should not be mentioned by John. In contrast, there are stories which are unique to John and not present in the other three.

ORIGIN OF THE QURAN

The religious book of the Moslems is called the Quran (Recitation). Moslems believe that the Quran was revealed by the Archangel Gabriel to Muhammad in a period of 23 years. It started in the year of 610 CE when Muhammad was 40 years old. The Quran was revealed little by little in accordance to the circumstances that needed guidance from God throughout the life of Muhammad.

The content of the Quran is not presented the same way like the Old and New Testaments. The Old Testament tells about the prophets lives in a complete story style. The New Testament tells about the biography of Jesus also in a complete story style. However, in the Quran the story of the prophets are scattered throughout the 114 surahs (chapters). Almost all of the prophets' names in the Quran are also mentioned in the Old Testament. Usually the Quran uses parts of the stories of the prophets and Jesus to set example for the readers of how to behave in certain life situations.

Professor Hamidullah wrote in the preface to his French translation of the Quran (1971): "The sources all agree in stating that whenever a fragment of the Quran was revealed, the Prophet (Muhammad) called one of his literate companions and dictated to him, indicating at the same time the exact position of the new fragment in the fabric of what had already been received. Description note that Muhammad asked the scribe to reread to him what had been dictated so that he could correct any deficiencies.. "

Diverse materials were used for this first record; parchment, leather, wooden tablets, camel's scapula, soft stone for inscriptions, etc. At the same time however, Muhammad recommended the Moslems to learn the Quran by heart. Thus, there were Hafizun – Moslems who knew the whole of the Quran by heart and spread it abroad.

Since Muhammad's time up to today, Moslems acquired the habit of keeping vigil during Ramadhan, and of reciting the whole of the Quran in addition to the usual prayers expected of them. Several sources add that Muhammad's scribe Zaid Ibn Thabit was present at the final bringing - together of the texts. Elsewhere, numerous other personalities are mentioned as well.

Not long after Muhammad's death (632 CE), his best companion Abu Bakr, the first Caliph (ruler) of Islam, asked Muhammad's former scribe, Zaid, to make a copy; this he did. On Omar's initiative (the future second Caliph), Zaid consulted all the information he could assemble at Medina – the Hafizun, copies of the book written on various materials belonging to private individuals, all with the object of avoiding possible errors in transcription. Thus the first copy of the Quran was obtained.

The sources say that the second Caliph – Omar in 634 CE, subsequently made a single volume that he preserved and gave on his death to his daughter Hafsa – a widow of Muhammad.

The third Caliph of Islam, Uthman, who held the caliphate from 644 CE – 655 CE, entrusted a commission of experts with the preparation of the great recession that bears his name. It checked the authenticity of the document produced under Abu Bakr, which had remained in Hafsa's possession until that time.

The commission consulted Moslems who knew the text by heart. The agreement of the witnesses was deemed necessary before the slightest verse containing debatable material was retained. It is indeed known how some verses of the Quran correct others in the case of prescriptions (law): this may be readily explained when one remembers that Muhammad's period of apostolic activity stretched over 23 years. The result is a text containing an order of surahs (chapters) that reflects the order followed by Muhammad in his complete recital of the Quran prior to his departure.

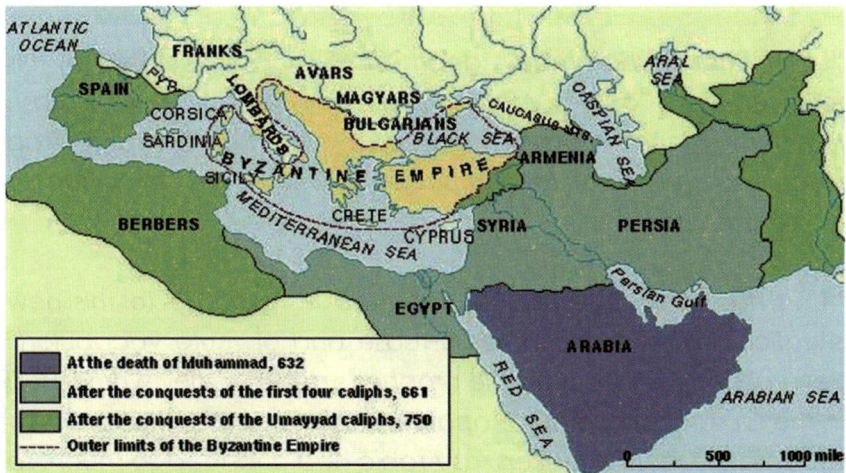

The Moslem Territory at the End of the 8th Century CE

According to Islamic scholars the reason why the first three Caliphs, especially Uthman, to commission collections and recessions of the text is because Islam's expansion in the very first decades following Muhammad's death was very rapid and it happened among people whose native languages were not Arabic. The Moslem territory had become the second largest empire during the medieval time - after the Mongolian Empire under Kubilai Khan. Absolutely essential steps had to be taken to ensure the spread of a text that retained its original purity: Uthman's recession had this as its objective.

World's Oldest Quran in the Library of Uzbekistan, Tashkent

The following statement is from The Foreign Vocabulary Of The Quran, Arthur Jeffery 1938:

"Soon after Muhammad's death in 632 CE, armies led by his followers burst out of Arabia and conquered the Near East, Northern Africa, Central Asia, and parts of Europe. Arab rulers had millions of foreign subjects, with whom they had to communicate."

"Thus, the language rapidly changed in response to this new situation, losing complexities of case and obscure vocabulary. Several generations after the prophet's death, many words used in the Quran had become opaque (not transparent) to ordinary sedentary Arabic-speakers, as Arabic had changed so much, so rapidly. The Bedouin speech changed at a considerably slower rate, however, and early Arabic lexicographers sought out Bedouin speech as well as pre-Islamic poetry to explain difficult words or elucidate points of grammar. Partly in response to the religious need to explain the Quran to Moslems who were not familiar with Quranic Arabic. Arabic grammar and lexicography soon became important sciences. The model for the Arabic

literary language remains to this day the speech used in Quranic times, rather than the current spoken dialects."

Uthman sent copies of the text of the recession to the centers of the Islamic Empire. The copies attributed to Utman still exist in Tashkent, Uzbekistan and Istanbul, Turkey today. The older documents known to the present day, that are to be found throughout the Islamic world are identical; the same is true for documents preserved in Europe. There are also fragments in the Bibliotheque Nationale in Paris which, according to the experts, date from the 8th and 9th century CE.

The Quran is thought to be one of the first texts written in Arabic. Some critics have also commented on the arrangement of the Quranic text with accusations of lack of continuity, absence of any chronological or thematic order, and presence of repetition. It is known amongst the Moslems that there are some spelling differences in the Quran – therefore some non-Moslems scholars argue that the Quran is not authentic. Others have praised the Quran's style as a book of divine guidance, and its eloquence has been described as near perfect by Dr. Francis Steingass due to the Quran's '*ability to transform savage tribes into civilized nations*'.

The above are only simplified descriptions concerning the origin of the three books. We can get further into the detail, but for the moment I think it is already enough to give a brief information about the authenticity of all the three books. We will go into further detail in the next two books of the EarthTrek Trilogy.

One thing is for sure: 900 years is a very long time. So, how authentic the historical data and teaching of the Jewish prophets in today's Old Testament, is of course a matter of dispute.

And which evangelist's version of the New Testament are we suppose to believe? Matthew, Mark, Luke or John? They can not all be right – because they are all writing about Jesus' biography but some of the data are missing in the other and some are contradictive.

And although some non-Moslem scholars accept the history of the Quran as the above; they do not accept its divine origin; some say that Muhammad put forth verses and laws that he claimed to be of divine origin; and that numerous version of these revelations circulated after his death in 632 CE.

To me, the historical background of how a religious book was written down is less important than how morally correct is the content of the book. Because I believe a book revealed by God must be flawless. So how do we prove whether the teaching of a religion is truly revealed by God or not? I think the most logical approach is by analyzing its religious and moral teachings; accuracy of historical data (among others: concerning the lives of the prophets) and its compatibility with our modern scientific data.

CHAPTER FOUR

GOD OF THE MONOTHEIST RELIGIONS

*A*lthough Judaism, Christianity and Islam claim to be monotheist religions, the presentations of God in all the three Holy Scriptures are so different to one another. The difference seems so striking that many Christians generally think that God of the Old Testament is not the same as the Christian God. Most Jewish and Christians also think that Allah of the Quran is a different God then their God. Is it so?

The word God in English, comes from the Gothic root 'Gheu' which means either 'the one invoked' or 'the one sacrificed to'. This word becomes: God in Anglo-Saxon; Gott in German; Khoda in Persian; Khooda in Hindu; Deva in Indo-Iranian; Dyaus in Sanskrit; Deus in Latin; Theos in Greek; Dia in Gaelic; Dieu in French; Dios in Greek (than becomes Zeus); and Tiu in Old Teutonic, these words can be defined as the proper name of the One Supreme Being as well as the generic name of the divinely worshipped entity in polytheistic religions (i.e. pagan gods).

NAMES OF GOD IN JUDAISM

God is called by numerous different names in Judaism. These names of God have been a source of debate amongst biblical scholars. Most scholars agree that in the Hebrew Bible, the personal name of the God of Israel is YHVH, whereas the other names are titles which are ascribed to Him. This is similar to how a man may be called by his name, or by 'Father', 'Husband', 'Boss', 'Sir', 'Son', 'Brother', 'the Nice Man', etc.

In medieval times, God was sometimes called THE SEVEN:

1. YHVH

יהוה

The Tetragrammaton of YHVH in Hebrew

English translation :   YHVH, YHWH or JHVH or Yahweh or LORD, Lord.

The name of God in Judaism is YHVH. YHVH is a tetragrammaton (a four - letter) that consists of the Hebrew letters: Yod – Heh – Vav – Heh. The meaning is 'to be', so as third person singular it means 'He is' and when God is represented as speaking, the meaning is 'I am'.

Because Judaism forbids pronouncing this name outside of the Temple in Jerusalem, the correct pronunciation of the tetragrammaton may have been lost, as the original Hebrew texts only included consonants. Pronouncing this name is considered as a blasphemy, for which capital punishment is prescribed in Jewish law.

According to Rabbi Haim Levi, YHVH is the symbol of all universal existence translated from Hebrew as follows:

HVH (Hayah) means: was
HVH (Hoveh) means: is
YHY (Yehiye) means: will be

The combinations of these words convey the meaning of past, present, and future which make up the four - letter name of God. God is then YHVH because all three tenses are part of His own existence or spiritual Oneness. He is the Creator of time and unaffected by it. As is Einstein's Theory of Relativity, the name YVHV may be understood as God is He who fills all time at the same time simultaneously, even as He fills all space. He is still today and will be unto eternity. He is above all limitation found in the word 'before' as well as the word 'after'.

The letters of YHVH is also a number or series of numbers as follows: Yod = 10 ; He = 5 ; Vav = 6 ; He = 5.

The total of these numbers are 26 (10+5+6+5), which for one thing represent also the number of twists used by the Sefardim (Jews of Spain) when tying their Tzitzit (tassels worn by Jews on the corner of four-cornered garments) for their talits (Jewish prayer shawl).

www.media.washingtonpost.com

A Jewish Tzitizt

There are also 10 generations from Adam to Noah; another 10 from Noah to Abraham, from Abraham to Sinai there are 6 generations. So the total is 26 generations.

2. Adonai

English translation   : Lord or my Lord.

Since pronouncing YHVH is avoided out of reverence for the holiness of the name, Jews use the term 'Adonai' instead in prayers. Adonai maybe translated also as 'Lord'. Formally, this is plural (my Lords), but the plural does not refer to plural gods, but is used here as an expression of majesty (*pluralis majestatis* in Latin). The singular form is Adoni, or 'my Lord'. This calling was also used by the Phoenicians for the god Tammuz and is the origin of a Greek god named Adonis.

The translation **Yehovah** or **Jehovah** was created by adding the vowel points of **Adonai** to the tetragrammaton YHVH done by the early Christian translators of the Hebrew Bible who did not know that these vowel points only served to remind the reader not to pronounce the divine name.

Hashem is the term used by the Jews to address God in conversation, while Adonai is strictly used for prayers. Hashem means 'the Name'.

3. El

English translation :   God (only when referring to the One God) otherwise it can also mean god or gods (as in polytheistic concept).

'El' appears in other Semitic languages such as Phoenician and Aramaic. The literal meaning of this word is 'power' or 'divine', the common translation in English is God or god. In Hebrew 'El' is used both in the singular and plural, both for other gods and for the God of Israel. As a name of God of Israel, however, it is usually attached with an epithet such as: El Elyon (Most High God), El Shaddai (God Almighty), El Elohe Israel (God, the God of Israel), El Elim (God of gods), etc.

4. Elohim

English translation :   God (only when referring to the One God)
otherwise it can also mean god or gods
(as in polytheistic concept).

Grammatically Elohim is the plural form of El. **Eloah** Is also considered as the singular form of Elohim, this word is rarely used. This word is an equivalent of the word 'Ilah' which means 'a god' in Arabic, or 'Elaha' in Aramaic. The meaning is 'He who is the object of fear or reverence'. This word also describes gods of other religions. However, when referring to God it always takes a singular form in the Hebrew Bible. Other scholars interpret the -im ending commonly used to define a plural form, is used here as an expression of majesty (pluralis majestatis) or excellence (pluralis excellentiae) expressing high dignity or greatness. Some Christian scholars use the plural form of Elohim as evidence for the basic Trinitarian doctrine in Christianity.

5. Eheyeh-Asher-Ehyeh

English translation :   'I am that I am' or 'I shall be as I shall be'.

According to Rabbi Haim Levi, the reason why God used the name Eheyeh-Asher-Ehyeh (when Moses asked Who was speaking to him via the burning bush) may be understood as an indication that there are numerous names to describe God. Each of which is a different way in which He reveals himself through the ages.

6. Shaddai

English translation :   Almighty.

Shaddai was an ancient Amorite city on the bank of Euphrates river (today Syria). It has been conjectured that El Shaddai was therefore the 'god of Shaddai' and associated in tradition with Abraham. According to Exodus 6:2,3 Shaddai is the name by which God was known to Abraham, Isaac and Jacob.

7. Zebaot

English translation   : Hosts.

This word frequently attached to the name YHVH and Elohim. For instance, YHVH Elohe Zebaot (YHVH God of Hosts) or Elohe Zebaot (God of Hosts).

Other names of God in Judaism

Shalom (Peace), Shekhinah (Dwell), Hamakom (The Place), Adir (Strong One), Adon Olam (Master of the World), Aibishter (The Most High), Avinu Malkienu (Our Father, Our King), Boreh (The Creator), Emet (Truth), Kadosh Israel (Holy One of Israel), Ribbono shel 'Olam (Master of the World), Ro'eh Yisra'el (Shepherd of Israel), Tzur Israel (Rock of Israel), and a few more.

The 72 Lettered Name

In the Kabbalah (the ancient Jewish tradition of mystical interpretation of the Tanakh) there is the 72 Lettered Name which based from 3 verses in Exodus (14:19-21), where each of the verses contains 72 letters and when combined they form 72 names, known collectively as the Shemhamphorasch. The Kabbalah explains that the creation of the world was achieved by the manipulation of the sacred letters that form the names of God.

THE NAMES OF GOD IN CHRISTIANITY

Christianity uses the Old Testament as a part of its religious scripture; therefore in general the names of God are the same as in Judaism. Additionally, most Christian denominations also believe in the Trinity, which consists of God the Father, Jesus the Son and the Holy Spirit. These are the English names of the Christian Godhead or Holy Trinity:

1. God - the Father

Yahweh or **Jehova** is the common vocalization of God's personal name based on YHVH. Because of Jewish concerns for avoiding blasphemy, the name in English Bible is often avoided and replaced with **LORD**, **Lord**, the **Lord God** or simply **God**.

Some other names for God the Father are: Heavenly Father, The Light, King of Kings, Lord of Lords, Lord of the Hosts, Ancient of Days, The Principle, The Mind, The Soul, The Life, The Truth, Love, Spirit, Alpha and Omega. These names are considered synonymous and indicative of God's wholeness.

2. God - the Son

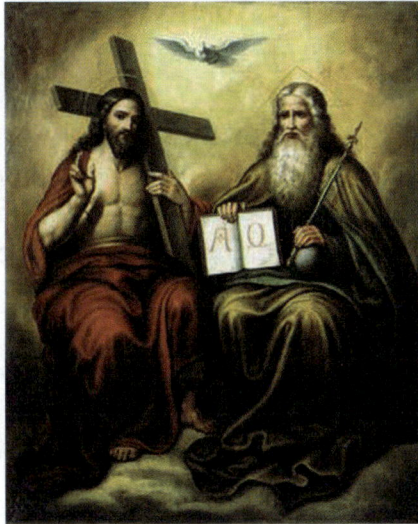

The Holy Trinity

Jesus / Iesus / Yeshua / Joshua / Yehoshua is a Hebraic personal name meaning 'Yahweh saves/helps/is salvation'.

Christ means 'the anointed' in Greek.

Khristos is the Greek equivalent of the Hebrew word **Messiah**. The Messiah is the leader/saviour promised deliverer of the Jewish nation prophesied in the Old Testament. It also means 'the anointed'.

Other titles referring to Jesus are: God, Prophet, Lord, Son of Man, Son of God, Apostle, Lamb of God, King of the Jews, King of Kings, Rabbi (literally means 'my teacher'), Redeemer, Christ - the New Adam, Liberator, Saviour of the World, Paraclete, Mediator of the New Covenant, The Bridegroom, High Priest, Logos in the Flesh, The Living Word, Head of the Church and Emmanuel.

3. God - the Holy Spirit

In Hebrew the name for the Holy Spirit is Ruach haQodesh (very similar with its Arabic term which is Roohul Qoodus).

THE NAMES OF GOD IN ISLAM

ALLAH

Allah is the 'name' of God in Islam. Actually Allah is the Arabic word of God in English. So it is not so much a name as a title, unlike YHVH in Hebrew which can truly be defined as the name of the God of Israel or Jesus which is the name of one of the Triune Godhead in Christianity.

The word Allah has the same Semitic root referring to 'the Divine' of El in Canaanite, Ilu in Mesopotamian, El/Elohim/Eloah in Hebrew and Elaha/Alaha in Aramaic (a language that some biblical scholars assume as the mother tongue of Jesus). Although in Hebrew both El and Elohim might mean 'god', 'gods' or 'the One God'; the word Allah only means 'the One God'. The Arabic word for a 'god' is Ilah.

Allah for God has always been used before (and after) Islam by the Arabic-speaking Jews, Christians and others when they speak about God. Allah is not only the One God of the Moslems nor is Allah the One God of Arabs. In the Indonesian Christian Bible the word for God is 'Tuhan Allah'. In Maltese the word for God that is worshipped since 52 CE (before the advance of Islam) to the present is 'Alla'.

Below are two examples of a verse from Arabic Quran and another one from Arabic Bible. The underlined pictograms are the word Allah in the Arabic Quran and the Arabic Bible:

بِسْمِ اللهِ الرَّحْمٰنِ الرَّحِيْمِ

*In the Name of **God**, the Compassionate, the Merciful.*
*Bismi-**Allah**i al-Rahmani, al-Raheem.*
***(Quran** 1:1)*

فِي الْبَدْءِ خَلَقَ اللهُ السَّمَاوَاتِ وَالأَرْضَ

*In the beginning **God** created the Heaven and the Earth . . .*
*Fee al-badi' khalaqa **Allah**u as-Samaawaat wa al-Ard . . .*
***(Bible**: Genesis 1:1)*

Although most modern English translation of the Quran keeps the word Allah untranslated, this was not the case in the 1940's and 1950's. Today there are still some Quran translators who translate the word Allah into 'God'. For example: Rashad Khalifa, Muhammad Asad, Arberry, George Sale and JM Rodwell.

In English the word god is for male form; the female form is goddess. The plural form for god/goddess is gods/goddesses. The word Allah does not have plural or gender form. In the English translation of the Quran, the pronoun used for Allah is 'He' because there is no other option. Using the term 'She' would imply God's gender, and 'It' is of course degrading.

In the Quran, sometimes God (Allah) refers to Himself as 'We'. This 'We' in the Quran is also an expression of majesty (*pluralis majestatis*) and excellence (*pluralis excellentiae*) and not referring to plural gods, the same principal that is also used in the word 'Elohim' of the Hebrew Bible.

The Beautiful Names of God

The Quran refers to the attributes of God as God's 'most beautiful names'. Traditionally there are 99 beautiful names of God. Here are some of the names:

Ar-Rahmaan (The Compassionate)	Ar-Raheem (The Merciful)
Al-Malik (The King)	Al-Qudoos (The Holy)
As-Salaam (The Source of Peace)	Al-Muhaimin (The Protector)
Al-Mutakabbir (The Majestic)	Al-Azeez (The Mighty)
Al-Khaaliq (The Creator)	Al-Ghaffar (The Forgiver)
Al-'Aleem (The All Knowing)	Al-Hakam (The Judge)
Al-Kabeer (The Most Great)	Al-Hakeem (The Wise)
Al-Kareem (The Generous One)	Al-Haqq (The Truth)
Al Wasi (The Vast, The All-Embracing)	Al-Wadood (The Loving)
Al-Majeed (The Most Glorious One)	Al-Hayy (The Alive)
Al-Mu'eed (The Reproducer)	Al-Mubdi' (The Originator)
Al Muhyi (The Giver of Life)	Al-Ahad (The One)
Al-Mumeet (The Creator of Death)	As-Samad (The Eternal)
Az-Baatin (The Hidden)	Az-Zaahir (The Manifest)
Al-Barr (The Source of All Goodness)	Al-Haadi (The Guide)
Al-Alameen (The Lord of the Worlds)	An-Noor (The Light) ...

May We Use the Word God Instead of Allah When Quoting Quranic Verses?

Before I begin with further analysis about the concept God in the three monotheist religions by quoting the three Holy Scriptures, it is necessary that I respond to the above question which has become a common topic of debate amongst Moslems.

Clearly it is a misunderstanding to think that Allah is only the God of Moslems. The Quran itself never mentions Allah as only the God of Moslems or the God of Arabs for that matter; unlike the Old Testament which mentions several times that YHVH is the God of Israel.

Strangely enough, although every Moslem believes that the Quran is universal and that Allah is the only One God of all mankind, some Moslems *do* feel offended whenever one uses the English word 'God' when referring to Allah.

Although it is clear that Allah is 'just' the Arabic word for the One God, the Divine, and the Supreme Being in English. Talking to English speaking people about God using the word Allah is very much the same like speaking to Arabic speaking people about Allah using the word God. Many Moslems do not realize, that when they insist on the use of the word Allah which is the Arabic word for God they immediately creates the illusion that Allah is a whole different deity than God of the whole world. It creates a God that belongs only to the Moslems. In the Internet I found a comment written by a Moslem convert that I believe can enlighten our point of view concerning this matter (http://www.submission.org/allah-god.html):

The word "ALLAH"
A Comment by : Abu Iman Robert Squires

Assalamu Alaikum (may peace be with you),
I would like to strongly concur with your observations about the use of the word "Allah" in English and any other language. Both from my conversion experience in America and my experience doing da'wah (missionary endeavor) *here in Kuwait, it is definitely 100% - without a shadow of a doubt - better to use the word "God" when making da'wah* (missionary endeavor) *to English speaking people.*

79

This alone is enough to open many hearts and minds since many people think that Muslims worship a different God. I've come across some Arab brothers who insist in using only the word "Allah". They somehow think that it implies Tawhid (*the Oneness of God*) while the word "God" implies the Trinity, etc., etc.

You know, the problem with such people is not their knowledge of Arabic, but their ignorance of English. The mushriks (*disbelievers*) at the time of the Prophet (saws) used the word Allah, and so do Arabic-speaking Christians. The word itself in no way implies tawhid (*the Oneness of God*). The reason it implies tawhid to Muslims is that they're Muslims. Others use this word in ways that are nothing but shirk (*polytheistic manner*).

The word God implies tawhid (*the Oneness of God*) to me because I have the Islamic concept of Him. It's all in the concept, but has nothing to do with the word itself. Also, there are statements in some da'wah (*missionary endeavor*) pamphlets that say "all prophets since Adam used the word Allah" and that "the word Allah is exactly the same as the Aramaic word Jesus used for God".

The first statement is baseless and can be proved to be logically incorrect from the Quran. The second statement is incorrect, but the words are only similar, but NOT exactly alike. This whole trend of using "Allah" in English seems to come about rather recently. Most of the translations and writings done back in the 1940's and 1950's used the word "God", which is a perfectly good translation of the word Allah in Arabic. M.M. Pickthall being the main exception, since he seemed to have used "Allah" in all of the translations that I've seen.

The change came, I believe, as a result of Nasserite Arab Nationalism. Many Arabs I know over here still don't know the difference between Islam and Arab Nationalism! They seem more interesting in defending their pride heritage than really spreading the message. But this is in no way limited to Arabs, I've dealt with Pakistanis, Malaysians, Turks and Afghanis that have the same hang-up.

The mentality of some of these brothers almost approaches that of the Bani Isra'il - the "our God vs. your God" mentality! By the way, I've never met an English-speaking convert to Islam (or Spanish-speaking, or French-speaking) who disagreed with me on this point. Most them went through a stage wondering why (some) Muslims insist on using Allah.

I should also add that I know a lot of Muslims that use "God" when speaking English. I find this rather common among most Egyptians that I know. In Morocco, where I visit quite frequently, the also use Dieu when they parlez francais.

Insh'allah (God willing), more Muslims will realize this and our da'wah (missionary endeavor) will become more effective. This is a BIG barrier, but many Muslims don't realize it. Many come up with baseless reasons to justify it (for whatever reason). What do we converts know anyway!!! Ha! Another point before I go...some people like to try to draw exact parallels between English and Arabic words which just don't fit.

The word "ilah" in Arabic can be used for a false god or for Allah. (Like when God says (paraphrased) the "ilah" of Ibrahim", and numerous other example.) Anyone who can read the Quran should know this. However, unlike the word "god" in English, which ALWAYS implies a false god. Non-native English speakers sometimes mistakenly believe that "god" and "God" are the same English word, but they are not. They carry completely different meanings. If they doubt this, then they simply don't know how to speak the English language. And to say that the word "Allah" can only be used for the Supreme Almighty Creator is refuted by the Quran itself.

It clearly says (and I paraphrase here rather liberally) that Christians say that "Allah is Jesus". There you have it, applying "Allah" to something that isn't "Allah" right there in the Quran. You see, what people really mean to say is that you SHOULDN'T use "Allah" for anything except the Almighty Creator, but you still CAN. The same thing goes for the word God.

People can use it in the wrong way, but that doesn't make it right. The truth is that this word too should only be used for the Almighty Creator. Remember...God has sent prophets to everyone in their OWN LANGUAGE, i.e. a language that they can understand. How many more people around the world wouldn't be dying on SHIRK (polytheistic manner) if many Muslims woke up and started making da'wah (missionary endeavor) in a way people can understand? Well, I've spoken my peace.

Abu Iman Robert Squires

After the above explanation, I truly hope now Moslem readers are not offended that I choose to use the English word God when quoting verses from the Quran.

RESEMBLANCES & DIFFERENCE IN THE CONCEPT OF GOD IN JUDAISM, CHRISTIANITY & ISLAM
Now, let's analyze the concept of God in the Old Testament, New Testament and the Quran. Language is a big barrier in order to examine these ancient books. I wish I could speak and read Hebrew, Aramaic, Greek and Arabic. Unfortunately, I can't. I am able to read and write in Arabic, but I have just beginning to learn the grammar and vocabulary of this extremely detailed language. So like most non-Semitic people in the world, I have to rely on the translation of these scriptures.

I have to inform you that since this book quotes and refers to many sources, the translation of the scriptures into English might be taken from a number of different translators. In this book, most of the Old and New Testament English translations are quoted from the New International Version (NIV) Bible, New American Standard Bible or the King James Version.

Whenever I quote a verse from the Bible, I write the book name, chapter and verse number. In addition I also noted NT = New Testament, which means that the verse refers purely to Christian teaching; and OT = Old Testament, which means that the verse refers to both Judaism and Christian teachings.

For a quick Biblical verses search I recommend you to go to: http://www.biblegateway.com/keyword/.

As for the Quran translations that I am using here are mostly from the Minister of Religion of the Kingdom of Saudi Arabia, Yusuf Ali or from Rashad Khalifa. For a quick Quranic verses search I recommend the: www.islamawakened.com/Quran/default. htm. It is an excellent website for the transliteration of the Arabic Quran to English, and comparison of 16 English translators.

PS: one is not allowed to claim that verses quoted from the Quran as the Quran itself without being accompanied by its original Arabic text. This is in order to maintain the authenticity of the text. Therefore whenever I quote verses from the Quran, I write 'Quran translation' below or above it.

~ఠ★ర~

From the above information concerning the names of God, we can clearly see that in principal there are some resemblance and difference in the concept of God in all these three Semitic monotheist religions.

RESEMBLANCE:

1.   Most of the Semitic names of God clearly originated from the same root.

2.   All three religions have the same concept of using the attributes of God as different appellations for God.

3.   The use of *plural majestatis* and *plural excellentiae* for God in Judaism and Islam, which according to some scholars has been used as Trinity defense in Christianity.

DIFFERENCE:

God's Oneness

JUDAISM & CHRISTIANITY

Dear Jews, correct me if I am wrong, but the concept of monotheism in the Old Testament is not really clear. Because, in the Old Testament, God states that none is like Him, but God also states that He has begotten a son (David). If David is God's son, doesn't that make David a sort of god too?

Some verses mention that 'there is only one God, and there is no other but Him'. But another verse mentions that 'God is greater than all other gods'. This verse might lead us to the understanding that there is only one God for Israelites, but other gods of the Gentiles exist besides Him, right?

I was really surprised after reading the stories of the prophets in the Old Testament. There are so many stories concerning YHVH defending the Israelites against the influence of other gods! There are also many stories about God punishing the Israelites for whoring after other gods! (Yes, the word 'whoring' is used in the King James Version).

Hence, it is really difficult not to come to the conclusion that the Old Testament actually teaches monotheism in the sense to believe in YHVH which is one God amongst many other gods. I am not sure that this fits with the definition of monotheism according to the Concise Oxford Dictionary which is 'a belief that there is only one God'. How can there be only one God, when other gods exist too?

> You shall not have no other gods before Me.
> (OT: Exodus 20:3)

> Remember the former things, those of long ago; I am God, and there is no other; I am God, and there is none like Me.
> (OT: Isaiah 46:9)

> I am the Lord, and there is no other; apart from me there is no God.
> (OT: Isaiah 45:5)

> Now I know that the LORD is greater than all other gods, for He did this to those who had treated Israel arrogantly.
> (OT: Exodus 18:11)

> And the LORD said unto Moses, Behold, thou shalt sleep with thy fathers; and this people will rise up, and go a whoring after the gods of the strangers of the land, whither they go to be among them, and will forsake me, and break my covenant which I have made with them.
> (OT: Deuteronomy 31:16) KJV

> God said to David:
> "You are my son today I have begotten you".
> (OT: Psalm 2:7)

CHRISTIANITY

And please don't be angry, dear Chirstians, but the concept of monotheism in Christianity is even less definable, because of the following verses that are used by most Christian scholars as the base of the Trinity doctrin:

God said to Jesus:
"You are my son today I have begotten you".
(NT: Hebrew 5:5)

Therefore go and make disciples of all nations, baptizing them in the name of the Father and of the Son and of the Holy Spirit.
(NT: Matthew 28:19)

ISLAM

The Quran's concept of monotheism is clear and absolute.

Say: He is God, the One and Only;
God, the Eternal, Absolute;
He begetteth not, nor is He begotten;
And there is none like unto Him.
(Quran translation 112:1-4)

It is not consonant with the majesty of the Most Gracious that He should beget a son.
(Quran translation 19:92)

.. our God and your God is One, and to Him do we submit.
(Quran translation 29:46)

Physical Description of God

JUDAISM & CHRISTIANITY

Although the Old Testament mentions that none is like God, it also mentions that God made man after His image. God also walks in the garden; sometimes He sleeps and He also appeared physically in front of Abraham. These description makes God human-like.

Therefore, although Judaism forbids the drawing of God, in Christianity God (the Father) is pictured like a human being.

www.museumrome.com

Illustration of God and Adam in the Sistine Chapel

And God said, let us make a man in our image, after our likeness.
(OT: Genesis 1:26)

The LORD appeared to Abraham near the great trees of Mamre ...
(OT: Genesis 18:1)

Then the man (Adam) and his wife heard the sound of the LORD God as He was walking in the garden in the cool of the day ...
(OT: Genesis 3:8)

... For in six days the Lord made heaven and earth, and on the seventh day He rested, and was refreshed.
(OT: Exodus 31:17)

<u>ISLAM</u>
Since none is like God, the Quran only describes the physical matter of God in a form of a parable... which is Light upon Light. It explains further that God is great and encompasses everything but He is also very close to us; and no vision can grasp God. Thus, clearly He is not human-like.

God is the Light of the heavens and the earth. The parable of His light is …. Light upon Light!...
(Quran translation 24:35)

No vision can grasp Him. But His grasp is over all vision: He is above all comprehension, yet is acquainted with all things.
(Quran translation 6:103)

And whatever is in the heavens and whatever is in the earth is God's; and God encompasses all things.
(Quran translation 4:126)

… We are nearer to him than (his) jugular vein.
(Quran translation 50:16)

… and know that God cometh in between a man and his heart..
(Quran translation 8:24)

God's Omnipotence and Unerringness

<u>JUDAISM & CHRISTIANITY</u>

Although the Old Testament mentions that God is Almighty, it also indicates that God is not free of error. God in the Old Testament sometimes feel grief, regrets His actions, jealous (of other gods!), sometimes unfair, not All-Knowing, breaks His promise and even forgets.

He determines the number of the stars and calls them each by name. Great is our Lord and mighty in power his understanding has no limit.
(OT: Psalm 147:4-5)

And GOD saw that the wickedness of man (was) great in the earth, and (that) every imagination of the thoughts of his heart (was) only evil continually. And the LORD

repented that he had made man on the earth, and it grieved him at his heart.
(OT: Genesis 6:5-6)

But God remembered Noah and all the wild animals and the livestock that were with him in the ark, and he sent a wind over the earth, and the waters receded.
(OT: Genesis 8:1)

... they hid from the LORD God among the trees of the garden. But the LORD God called to the man, "Where are you?"
(OT: Genesis 3:8-9)

You shall not bow down to them or worship them; for I, the LORD your God, am a jealous God, punishing the children for the sin of the fathers to the third and fourth generation of those who hate Me.
(OT Exodus 20:5)

The Lord said: "I will break my covenant with them".
(OT: Leviticus 26:44)

With the pure you show yourself pure and with the crooked you show yourself perverse.
(OT: 2 Samuel 22:27)

ISLAM
In the Quran, God is Omnipotent, Self-Subsisting, All-Knowing, fair, never errs, never forgets, never breaks His promise and never advocates injustice.

... till God accomplisheth His purpose: for God hath power over all things.
(Quran translation 2:109)

He said, "The knowledge thereof is with my Lord in a record. My Lord never errs, nor does He forget. "
(Quran translation 20:52)

Most surely your Lord is watching.
(Quran translation 89:14)

God! There is no god but He, the Living, the Self-subsisting, Eternal. No slumber can seize Him nor sleep...
(Quran translation 2:255)

And God's is the East and the West, therefore, whither you turn, thither is God's purpose; surely God is Amplegiving, Knowing.
(Quran translation 2:115)

Such is God's promise - and God never breaks His promise - but most people do not know.
(Quran translation 30:6)

O you who believe stand out firmly for justice as witnesses to God even as against yourselves or your parents or your kin.
(Quran translation 4:135)

God's Dominion and His People

JUDAISM & CHRISTIANITY
The Old Testament states that God's dominion covers the world, but God's salvation is only for the Israelites.

The earth is the LORD's, and everything in it, the world, and all who live in it.
(OT: Psalm 24:1)

For the Israelites belong to me as servants. They are my servants, whom I brought out of Egypt. I am the LORD

your God.
(OT: Leviticus 25:55)

… and say to him, 'The LORD, the God of the Hebrews, has met with us. Let us take a three-day journey into the desert to offer sacrifices to the LORD our God.'
(OT: Exodus 3:18)

… "This is what the LORD, the God of Israel, says: 'Let my people go, so that they may hold a festival to Me in the desert.'
(OT: Exodus 5:1)

CHRISTIANITY

In the New Testament God's salvation is extended for the Gentiles, but the Jews still have the first place.

I am not ashamed of the gospel, because it is the power of God for the salvation of everyone who believes: first for the Jew, then for the Gentile.
(NT: Romans 1:16)

ISLAM

In the Quran, God is Lord of the worlds. The plural worlds, is understood today as an indication concerning the existence of multiple universes. His salvation is universal.

All praise is due to God, the Lord of the worlds.
(Quran translation 1:2)

Surely those who believe, and those who are Jews, and the Christians, and the Sabians, whoever believes in Allah and the Last day and does good, they shall have their reward from their Lord, and there is no fear for them, nor shall they grieve.
(Quran translation 2:62)

WERE ALLAH (and YHVH) PAGAN MOON GODS?

Clearly, according to the Quran, Allah or God is not only the One God of the Moslems, let alone only God for the Arabs... God in the Quran is Lord of the Worlds. Now, I am neither a Jew, nor Arab. Can you understand my point of view if this far, I am more incline to the One God that is described by the Quran?

It really surprises me however, that there is a growing argumentation outside the Moslem circle, especially in the Internet that Allah was a pagan Arab moon god from pre-Islamic times. This argumentation has been made popular since 1991 by a Christian apologist pastor, Robert Morey, who based his claim upon an archeological site in Hazor, Palestine and Hureidha, Hadhramaut, Yemen.

Morey says: "In the 1950's a major temple to the moon god was excavated at Hazor in Palestine. Two idols of the moon god were found. Each was a statue of a man sitting upon a throne with a crescent moon carved on his chest. The accompanying inscriptions make it clear that these were idols of the moon god. Several smaller statues were also found which were identified by their inscriptions as the "daughters" of the moon god."

Archaeological Site In Hazor

The evidence from Hazor suggests that the interpretation of the statue of a man with an inverted crescent suspended from his necklace and holding a cup-like object in his right hand, which Morey labeled as moon god, is disputed among the scholars. This statue (only one statue, by the way, not two as Morey claims) could be of a deity, king or priest. None of the scholars, however, say that the statue represents a moon god, let alone the statue representing Allah.

Below is the principal object of interest that is the statue which Morey has labeled as a moon god. The statue, about 40 cm in height, depicts a man with an inverted crescent suspended from his necklace and holding a cup-like object in his right hand, while the other hand rests on his knees.

A Statue of a Man with an Inverted Crescent on His Chest

There is a difference of opinion among the scholars concerning this statue. It is not too hard to understand why this is the case. It seems illogical that a god should hold offering vessels in his hand; the god is usually the one who receives offerings.

Therefore, the statue should, in all probability, depict a priest or a worshipper of a god, who himself is in a way considered present, either invisibly or in the upright stelae of the sanctuary. Furthermore, the statue of a man holding an offering was seated at the left hand side of the shrine. This can hardly be a proper position for a revered god, whose position is usually arranged in the centre of the sanctuary.

Regardless of the difference of opinions concerning the nature of statue found at Hazor no scholar has ever identified this statue with a moon god, nor do they say that 'accompanying inscriptions' suggest that the statue was that of a moon god.

Apart from this, Morey also claims that several smaller statues were also found 'which were identified by their inscriptions' as the 'daughters of the moon god'. However, no such statues or inscriptions accompanying them were found in Hazor.

Actually, Morey made the claim based on a hypothesis made earlier in 1920's by a Danish scholar Ditlef Nielsen. Ditlef Nielsen theorized that all ancient Arabian religion was a primitive religion of nomads, whose objects of worship were exclusively a triad of the Father Moon, Mother Sun and the Son Venus star envisaged as their child. The logic of the proponents of Nielsen's hypothesis is that since Shams (sun) is feminine in epigraphic South Arabian, the other principal deity must be masculine and this was equated with the moon. The relationship between Father Moon and Mother Sun produced Son-Venus star, their child.

Nielsen's triadic hypothesis met much refutation by many scholars. W. Montgomery Watt a Professor in Arabic and Islamic Studies at the University of Edinburgh pointed out: "The divergent theories of Dietlef Nielsen are not generally accepted. These recount what is known about a large number of gods and goddesses and about the ceremonies connected with their worship. As our knowledge is fragmentary and, apart from inscriptions, comes from Islamic sources, there is ample scope for conjecture. These matters are not dealt with here in any detail as it is generally agreed that the archaic pagan religion was comparatively non-influential in Muhammad's time."

William F. Albright - an American archaeologist, biblical scholar, linguist and expert on ceramics - issued a general warning regarding Nielsen's study of the South Arabian pantheon. Although Albright noted Nielsen's contribution to the study of South Arabian pantheons, he concluded that he had "gone much too far in trying to carry it through Near-Eastern polytheism in general." Albright also pointed out Nielsen's strong tendency to over-schematize the material and hence the latter's work should be used with great caution.

Other modern scholars such Ryckmans, Breton and Beeston have also rejected the lunar association of the ancient South Arabian deities. However, the thesis of Dr. Dietlef Nielsen still has many followers amongst people who are still insisting to prove that Allah was a pagan moon god. As previously mentioned, one of the most ardent supporters is Robert Morey. Robert Morey is a strong critic of Wicca, non-Evangelical Christian beliefs and Islam.

Arguably, the names of moon god in ancient Arabia were Wadd, 'Amm, Sin, Ilmuqah and Hubal. None of them was called Allah. Morey explained that Allah derived from a combination of Ilmuqah and the word Ilah (which means god or gods in Arabic). He came to that conclusion by pointing the similarities between the words Ilah to Allah. However, as we have seen previously, the word for God (i.e. El, Elohim, Eloah, Ilu, Alla, Elaha, Alaha and Allah) in many ancient Semitic languages do sound almost the same. This does not mean that his theory is correct. In fact, in English the word God and god (for pagan gods) have the exact same spelling; the only difference is the capitalization. But no one claims that God was originally a pagan god, right? Because we understand that the concepts of the two words are totally different.

If Morey wants to prove that Allah was (or is) a moon god, he should use verses from the Quran. But there is not a single verse in the Quran that points to that direction.

> And He it is Who created the night and the day and the sun and the moon; all (orbs) travel along swiftly in their celestial spheres.
> (Quran translation 21:33)

The above is definitely not a statement from a moon god. The most intriguing twist is that although Morey supports (or elaborates) the theory of Allah moon god by Dr. Nielsen Dietlef, ironically he chooses to dismiss another theory from the very same Dietlef who also claims that YHVH of the Old Testaments was actually also a moon god and a part of the triad of YHVH/Ba'al/Astart! This means if Ditlef's theory was confirmed, Morey would have had to agree that the God that he believes in, i.e. the God of the Old Testament was also a moon god. This is utter non-sense, of course.

> If there be found among you, within any of thy gates which the LORD thy God giveth thee, man or woman, that hath wrought wickedness in the sight of the LORD thy God, in transgressing his covenant, and hath gone and served other gods, and worshipped them, either the sun, or moon, or any of the host of heaven, which I have not commanded; and it be told thee, and thou hast heard of it, and enquired diligently, and, behold, it be true, and the thing certain, that such abomination is wrought in Israel.
> (OT: Deuteronomy 17:2-4)

Another reason why some people still insists that Allah was a pagan moon god is because the crescent moon is an internationally recognized symbol of Islam. The symbol is featured on the flags of several Moslem countries, and it has also become the official emblem for the International Federation of the Islamic Red

Crescent Societies (the equivalent of the Red Cross). The truth is that, the crescent moon symbol actually predates Islam by several thousand years. All kinds of celestial symbols have been used by many different ancient races around the globe as deities. The crescent moon a symbol of the goddess Diana was adopted as the symbol of the city of Byzantium (today modern Istanbul). When the Moslem Turks conquered this city in 1453, they adopted the city's existing flag and symbol. The Turks of the Ottoman Empire ruled over the Moslem world for hundreds of years. This was the beginning of the affiliation of the crescent moon with the Moslem world. After centuries of battle with Christian Europe, it is understandable how the symbol of this empire became linked in people's minds with Islam as a whole.

But even if, the moon were a symbol of Islam, Morey's argumentation is still unfounded. The symbol of Judaism is the star (of David); the symbol of Christianity is the cross. Does that mean that Jews worship stars and Christians worship the cross? Of course not.

Furthermore, the early Moslem community did not really have any symbol. During the time of Muhammad, Islamic armies and caravans flew simple solid-colored flags (generally black, green or white) for identification purposes. In later generations, the Moslem leaders continued to use a simple black, white or green flag with no markings, writing, or symbolism on it. Historically, Islam has no symbol.

～۵٭۵～

Now, that we have studied the most important theological aspect of the three monotheist religions, let's compare their religious teachings with modern scientific data.

Let's start with the origin of the universe..

CHAPTER FIVE

THE MONOTHEIST RELIGIOUS BOOKS VERSUS SCIENCE

*T*he New Testament does not explain about the origin of the universe. Christians use both the Old and New Testaments as their religious book. So in this particular topic we can only do a comparison study between the Old Testament and the Quran.

The commentaries below are mostly quoted from the book of Dr. Maurice Boucaille author of The Bible, Quran and Science.

THE CREATION OF THE WORLD ACCORDING TO THE OLD TESTAMENT

> *In the beginning God created the heaven and the earth. And the earth was without form, and void; and darkness was upon the face of the deep. And the Spirit of God moved upon the face of the waters.*
> *(OT: Genesis 1: 1 - 2)*

It is quite possible to admit that before the Creation of the earth, what was to become the universe as we know it was covered in darkness. To mention the existence of water at this period is however quite simply pure allegory. Science has indicated that at the initial stage of the formation of the universe a gaseous mass existed. Thus, it is an error to place water in it.

> And God said, Let there be light: and there was light. And God saw the light, that it was good: and God divided the light from the darkness. And God called the light Day, and the darkness he called Night. And the evening and the morning were the first day.
> (OT: Genesis 1: 3 - 5)

The light circulating in the universe is the result of complex reactions in the stars. At this stage of the Creation however, according to the Bible, the stars were not yet formed. The 'lights' of the firmament are not mentioned in Genesis until verse 14, when they were 'to give light upon the earth'. It is illogical to mention light on the first day, when the cause of this light was created three days later. The fact that the existence of evening and morning is placed on the first day is moreover, purely allegorical; the existence of evening and morning as elements of a single day is only conceivable after the creation of the earth and its rotation under the light of its own star: the sun.

> And God said, Let there be a firmament in the midst of the waters, and let it divide the waters from the waters. And God made the firmament, and divided the waters which were under the firmament from the waters which were above the firmament: and it was so. And God called the firmament Heaven. And the evening and the morning were the second day.
> (OT: Genesis 1: 6 - 8)

The topic of the waters is continued here with their separation into two layers by a firmament that in the description of the (Noah's) Flood allows the waters above to pass through and flow onto the earth. This image of the division of the waters into two masses is scientifically unacceptable.

And God said, Let the waters under the heaven be gathered together unto one place, and let the dry land appear: and it was so. And God called the dry land earth; and the gathering together of the waters called he Seas: and God saw that it was good. And God said, Let the earth bring forth grass, the herb yielding seed, and the fruit tree yielding fruit after his kind, whose seed is in itself, upon the earth: and it was so. And the earth brought forth grass, and herb yielding seed after his kind, and the tree yielding fruit, whose seed was in itself, after his kind: and God saw that it was good. And the evening and the morning were the third day.

(OT: Genesis 1: 9 - 13)

The fact that the continents emerged at the period in the earth's history, when it was still covered with water, is quite acceptable scientifically. What is totally untenable is that a highly organized vegetables kingdom with reproduction by seed could have appeared before the existence of the sun (in Genesis it does not appear until the fourth day) and likewise the establishment of alternating nights and days.

And God said, Let there be lights in the firmament of the heaven to divide the day from the night; and let them be for signs, and for seasons, and for days, and years: And let them be for lights in the firmament of the heaven to give light upon the earth: and it was so. And God made two great lights; the greater light to rule the day, and the lesser light to rule the night: he made the stars also. And God set them in the firmament of the heaven to give light upon the earth, And to rule over the day and over the night, and to divide the light from the darkness: and God saw that it was good. And the evening and the morning were the fourth day.

(OT: Genesis 1: 14 - 19)

Here the Biblical author's description is acceptable. The only criticism one could level at this passage is the position in the description as a whole. Earth and moon emanated, as we know, from their original star, the sun. To place the creation of the sun and moon after the creation of the earth is contrary to the most firmly established ideas on the formation of the elements of the solar system.

—⟳⋆⟲—

The Old Testament also gives a misinformation concerning the time of the Creation. This can be done by calculating the total life spans (i.e. the genealogy) of the prophets from Adam until Abraham which is only ca. 2,123 years – which puts the time of the creation of the universe at around 4000 BCE. This is unacceptable by our scientific fact today that gives the approximate time of the Big Bang at around 18 billion years ago!

Additionally, science has proven that the universe is expanding, but the Old Testament also states that the world cannot be moved.

> The LORD reigneth, he is clothed with majesty; the LORD is clothed with strength, wherewith he hath girded himself: the world also is stablished, that it cannot be moved.
> (OT: Psalm 93:1)

—⟳⋆⟲—

I was taught to believe that the Old Testament was of divine origin. So, how come its description of the creation of the world is not in accordance with science? Who made that mistake? What happened to the original revelation of God that was written in the Old Testament? God wouldn't have made that mistake. There are only 2 possible explanations for this: either the Old Testament was not revealed by God or it has been altered by men.

Ironically, some (non-Moslem) scholars say that the Quran is a copy of the Old Testament – but when we analyze the verses of the Quran concerning natural phenomena in the world, we will see that it cannot be true, since not only the verses in the Quran are in accordance with modern science, the details and style are totally different then the verses of the Old Testament.

QURANIC VERSES CONCERNING NATURAL PHENOMENON

Now, look at what is written in the Quran concerning our world and we have to bear in mind that it is revealed around 1400 years ago. Meanwhile the Western world only 'found out' that the earth is rotating around the sun around 600 years ago:

Illustration of the Big Bang

THE BIG BANG

Do not the rejecters see that the skies and earth were bound together then We disunited (or separated) them...
(Quran translation 21:30)

In the above statement, the Quran gives an accurate description of the Big Bang, a theory of the origin of the universe widely accepted by scientists today. The Quran, many centuries before the Big Bang theory was presented, confirmed the 'common origin' or source of everything in the universe. It is stating that the earth and the skies had one common origin.

In the words of Martin Rees, who is one of the leading cosmologists in the world states in his book, Our Cosmic Habitat:

> "Our universe may once have been squeezed to a single point, but EVERYONE whether on earth or Andromeda, or even on the galaxies remotest from us can EQUALLY claim to have started from that point..."

THE GASEOUS UNIVERSE

... Then He (God) rose over towards the heaven when it was smoke..
(Quran translation 41:11)

The Quran uses the Arabic word 'dukhan' which stands for smoke to describe the early stage of the universe, which is a perfect analogy for gas and particles in suspension and the gasses being hot. Scientists have only very recently confirmed that the universe was indeed, at an early stage, a gaseous mass composed of Hydrogen and some Helium, a big mass of hot gasses. The Quran is more accurate in describing the gasses as 'smoke' rather than the word 'mist' or 'fog' used frequently by scientists as the gasses were hot. The Quran used these analogy centuries before anyone in the world had any idea about Helium and Hydrogen, yet even today scientist use a crude form of the same analogy.

The Belgian cosmologist George Lemaitre, lecturing in 1930, around 1300 years after the Quran, described this stage of cosmic evolution as: " ... the filling of the heavens with smoke."

THE EXPANDING UNIVERSE

> *And the sky We built it with might and We cause the expansion of it.*
> *(Quran translation 51:47)*

The Quran talks about a universe that is continually 'expanding'. The fact that the universe is not static but in a state of expansion was discovered by the American astronomer Edwin Hubble in the late 1920s.

THE DEATH STARS

> *... when the stars lose their lights.*
> *(Quran translation 77: 8)*

That one day all the stars will loose their lights or die is a known scientific fact today. Our own sun is a dying star.

THE BLACK HOLES

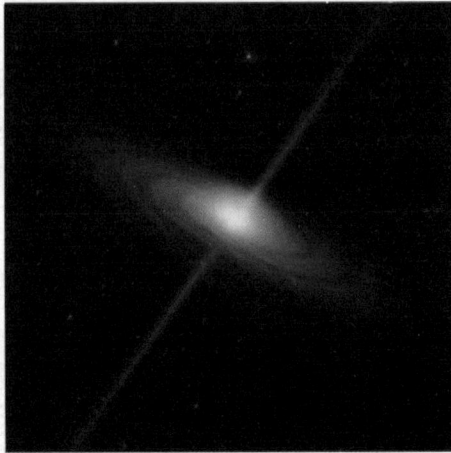

physics.technion.ac.il

The Black Hole

> *I swear by the sky and the (phenomena of) Tariq.*
> *And what will explain to you what Tariq is?*
> *It is a star that pierces (or makes a hole).*
> *(Quran translation 86 : 1– 3)*

The Quran is aware of the phenomenon of 'black holes', stars that have collapsed under their intense gravitational field, so that even light cannot escape. This concept was first stated by John Michell in 1767 and given the term the 'black hole' by John Wheeler in 1968.

The Quran uses the word 'Tariq' in Arabic, this word is left untranslated by some translators, actually it literally signifies a puncture or a minute hole. Martin Rees states in his book: "Space is already being punctured by the formation of black holes."

Black holes are objects literally 'cut off' from the rest of the universe. It is wrapped in a zone called 'event horizon'. Once the event horizon is crossed, nothing can return. A camel falling into the event horizon would literally be stretched to the dimension of a yarn and can pass through the 'eye of the needle' is the analogy used in the Quran. Inside the event horizon time itself comes to a standstill.

THE MOVEMENT OF THE SUN

He (God) created the skies and the earth in truth.
He coils the night upon the day and He coils the day upon the night.
He it is who has created the night and day, and the sun and the moon.
They all, in their orbit, swim.
(Quran translation 39:5)

At a time when a geocentric cosmology was in vogue, the Quran not only corrected the erroneous notions associated with that world-view, but made clear that night and day were caused by a coiling motion. The Quran uses the Arabic verb 'kawarra' which in its original usage signifies the 'coiling' of a turban around the head. A perfect analogy to the movement that causes night and day, i.e. the earth's rotation.

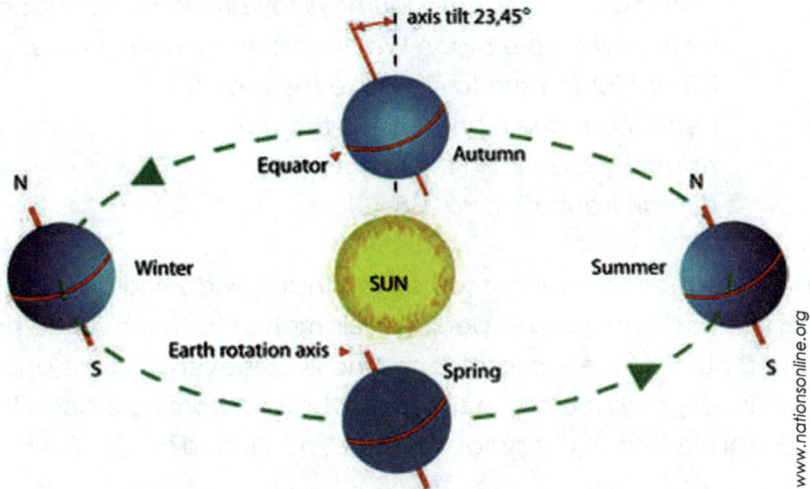

axis tilt 23,45°

N

Equator

Autumn

N

Winter

SUN

Summer

Earth rotation axis

S

Spring

S

www.nationsonline.org

Earth Rotation Around the Sun

The above verse stated that day and night is brought about by orbital motion similar in principal <u>but</u> distinct from the orbital motion of the sun and the moon. They <u>all</u> says the Quran (all signifies night, day, the sun and the moon) swim – which signifies movement with one's own motion.

To make this notion of a rotating earth causing the night and day even clearer, the Quran mentions that the night 'merges' into the day and the day 'merges' into the night.

> *Thou (God) causest the Night to merge into the Day, and Thou causest the Day to merge into the Night..*
> *(Quran translation 3:27)*

And that night 'interchange' into each other.

> *It is God Who interchanges the Night and the Day; verily in these things is an instructive example for those who have vision!*
> *(Quran translation 24:44)*

And the sun constantly journeys towards a homing place
for it, And for the moon We have determined phases.
It is not for the sun to overtake the moon,
Neither can the night outstrip the day.
And they all swim in their own orbits.
(Quran translation 36 : 38-40)

The sun's movement is not something that is evident to our eyes or experience but requires special equipment. Modern science has found out that the sun rotates around its axis every 26 days and is continually on a journey in space towards its 'homing place', the central nucleus of our galaxy, just like mentioned in the Quran.

www.carpecrustulum.wordpress.com

The Moon

Also the Quran is known to be the first book known today to use the modern term 'phase' associated with the moon's appearances. By stating that the sun is not permitted to 'overtake' the moon, the Quran is making clear for astronomers, in their own terminology, that the sun and the moon are revolving around the same object. It also makes clear that the movement of the sun and the moon are not the cause of night and day. Since on the first part it says that the sun cannot overtake the moon, and that night cannot outstrip day.

Not only this, the Quran also completely debunks the geocentric hypothesis when it states:

> By the Sun and its brightness, and by the moon when it imitates it. (i.e. the moon reflecting the sun's brightness)
> And by the day which reveals it.
> By the night that conceals it.
> (Quran translation 91 : 1 – 4)

The above statement of the Quran not only reveal the reflected nature of the moon's light but also debunks the erroneous claim of the geocentric that the sun's movement causes the day and night. It is the morning that 'reveals' the sun and the night that 'conceals' the sun, not the other way around. In other words, the sun is stationary relative to night and day. The movement that causes night and day is not the movement of the sun!

THE ORIGIN OF LIFE

> ... We made from water every living thing. Will they not then believe?
> (Quran translation 21:30)

> And it is He Who has created man from water.
> (Quran translation 25:54)

> God has created every moving (living) creature from water. Of them there are some that creep on their bellies, and some that walk on two legs, and some that walk on four. God creates what He wills. Verily God is Able to do all things.
> (Quran translation 24:45)

The Quran mentions that all life 'originated' from water. Man is 'created' of water and so are all the animals of earth. These statements to an Arab would have sounded ridiculous in that day and age.

Even today such statements in the Quran might cause most of us to wonder. The fact that all life originated from water is well established by the scientific community. We have found evidence that support the fact that the first living beings were cyan bacteria also called blue-green algae, and they existed in water. It is a fact that human beings and animals were created of water is also well established since cytoplasm the basic components of 'life' in any animal cell is over 80% water!

THE EMBRYO

> And that He (God) creates the pairs, male and female,
> From Nutfah (ejaculated drop of semen - male and female discharges) when it is emitted.
> (Quran translation 53:45-46)

The Quran says that the 'ejaculated drop of semen' determines the sex of the human baby. It is common knowledge that semen is the fluid that is ejaculated by males during sexual acts. Females do not possess such 'ejaculated semen'.

The sex of the baby, whether it will be male or female, will indeed be determined by the 'ejaculated drop', i.e. the father's sperm, as mentioned in the Quran. It has been scientifically established only recently that the female ovum contains only X-chromosomes. If the ejaculated drop, of the father's sperm bears the Y-chromosomes, the offspring will be male; otherwise the offspring will be female. No one living at the time of Muhammad or even Darwin for that matter had any knowledge of such genetics, foretold centuries earlier in the Quran.

THE SEQUENCE OF OUR SENSES

> ... And He (God) gave you hearing and sight and feeling and understanding..
> (Quran translation 32:9)

The above verse has as its context the creation of mankind. The special senses of hearing, seeing and feeling, develop on a baby inside its mother's womb in the exact same order as mentioned in the above verse. The primordial of the internal ears appear before the beginning of the eyes, and the brain (the site of feeling and understanding) differentiates last.

THE CIRCULATION OF BLOOD

> And surely in the cattle, there is a lesson for you. We give you to drink what is inside their bodies, from between digested food and blood, pure milk, pleasant to those who drink it.
> (Quran translation 16:66)

The above verse of the Quran calls our attention to the food distribution functions of blood. It should be kept in mind that a Moslem scientist formally discovered the circulation of blood 600 years after Muhammad's death and it was made known to the West by William Harvey 400 years later. It is a fact that digested food is transported via blood and then becomes the constituent of milk secreted by the mammary glands.

THE ATOM

> ... (God is) the Knower of the unapparent. Not an atom's weight in the skies or the earth, nor anything smaller than that, or larger, escapes Him, but is in a clear record.
> (Quran translation 34:3)

It was not until 1897 that the concept of the 'indivisible atom' was challenged when the English physicist J.J. Thomson, working at the Cavendish Laboratory in Cambridge found ways to study bits that had been broken off atoms. And yet the Quran clearly states that there are things 'smaller' than an atom 1400 years ago.

THE FEMALE BEE

The Quran mentions the bee, which leaves its home in search for food, in the verse that discusses honey (Quran 16 : 68 – 69). It uses the female verb in describing the bee, in Arabic 'faslukee'. Does anyone except the expert know how to differentiate between the male and female bee? Even today, let alone at Muhammad's time, we need a specialist to differentiate between a male and female bee. The Quran is accurate when it mentions that the female bee leaves their homes in search for food; the males never leave their homes for food, it is the females who have to feed them.

LIGHTING THE DARK AGES – ANCIENT ARAB AND PERSIAN SCHOLARS

By Deane Morrison

Published on March 18, 2005

The period between the fall of the Roman Empire and the beginning of the Renaissance has been called the Dark Ages because, during that time, the light of learning lay dormant in Europe. But elsewhere, and perhaps nowhere more than in the Arab-Muslim world, it not only shone but brightened.

The eve of a visit to campus by Ismail Serageldin is a good time to look at the contributions of Arabs and Persians to modern science and mathematics. Director of Egypt's Library of Alexandria (Bibliotheca Alexandria), Serageldin, a proponent of agricultural and scientific progress in developing countries, heads an institute whose namesake, the original library at Alexandria, was a Mecca for scholars in the ancient world.

To get an idea how pervasive the influence of Arab mathematicians was during the Middle Ages, visit the MacTutor History of Mathematics Archive and look for biographies of mathematicians born between 500 AD and 999 AD. You'll find the vast majority of names are Arabic.

One of those names is Muhammad ibn Musa Al-Khwarizmi, born in what is now Uzbekistan around 780 AD. Never heard of him? He's well known in mathematical circles for a work in which he preserved and expanded on the work of Diophantus, a Greek. The work was titled 'Ilm Al-Jabr Wal Muqabalah', 'the science of transposition and cancellation'. The Arabic 'Al-Jabr' became the Latin 'Algebra', the name given to the branch of mathematics Diophantus had founded. Al-Khwarizmi's own name got twisted into 'Algorism', meaning 'the art of calculating', what we now call Arithmetic.

Even more important, Al-Khwarizmi drew on the work of Hindu as well as Greek mathematicians, picking up the Hindu numerals, including the zero, which was unknown to users of Roman numerals. His work was translated into Latin, and the numerals - called Arabic numerals, despite their Hindu origin - went with it.

The numerals were passed to Europe through the Italian mathematician Leonardo Fibonacci. It took a while, but the Arabic numerals turned mathematical calculations upside down. Today, no one can envision doing long division or any number of other manipulations without them.

The Persian scientist Rhazes, also called by the Arabic name Abu-Bakr Muhammad ibn Zakariyya Ar-Razi, was born near what is Tehran around 845 AD. He studied medicine and became the chief physician of Baghdad's biggest hospital. He is credited with being the first to distinguish clearly between smallpox and measles describing his experiments so well that modern scientists can reproduce them. Rhazes also concocted (combined ingredients) what is now called plaster of Paris and described how it could be made into casts to keep broken bones in place.

The most prominent physicist of the Middle Ages was Alhazen (Arabic name: Abu-'Ali Al-Hasan ibn Al-Haytham), born in Basra (Iraq) about 965 AD. Fascinated by optics, he corrected an old notion that people see by rays of light emanating from the eyes and reflecting from objects. Alhazen realized that the Sun or some other source emits light before it's reflected off objects and into the eye. He also explained that lenses magnify objects because of the curvature of their surface, not because of any intrinsic property of the material the lens is made from.

He did much work on reflection and refraction of light, including studies of the rainbow and the focusing of light through lenses. He made a pinhole camera and parabolic mirrors, the type now used in telescopes. The world had to wait nearly six centuries - until the days of German astronomer Johannes Kepler, who was heavily influenced by a Latin translation of Alhazen's work - to see further progress in optics.

The dry air and clear skies of the Middle East led Arabian science to make its most famous marks. Pick up a star chart, and you'll see all kinds of Arabic names for stars.

There's Algol, 'the winking eye of the demon' in the constellation Perseus; Aldebaran, 'the eye of Taurus', the bull (from Al Dabaran, 'follower' - of the Pleiades star cluster); and Betelgeuse, the brightest star in Orion. The name Betelgeuse is from the Arabic Ibt al Jauzah, or 'Armpit of the Central One', via a long line of intermediate names.

"Arab and other Muslim astronomers made numerous observations of star positions," says U of M astronomy professor Terry Jones. "Much of the ancient Arabs' contribution to astronomy consisted of preserving and refining the knowledge of others, especially Greeks and Egyptians."

For example, Arabian astronomer Albategnius (Arabic name: Abu-'Abdullah Muhammad ibn Jabir al-Battani), born in what is now southeastern Turkey around 858 AD, made a mark by improving on the work of the ancient astronomer Ptolemy, who had drawn up a model of the universe with the Earth at the center.

Albategnius noted, among other things, the position of the Sun among the constellations at the moment the Sun appears smallest - that is, when Earth is farthest from the Sun. Observing the Sun's position for himself at that moment, he realized the Sun was no longer in the position where Ptolemy had said. He concluded that this position changed slowly and calculated a rather accurate value for the motion. Today, we know this phenomenon happens because the Earth's elliptical orbit itself rotates. Albategnius became the most respected of Arabian astronomers in the eyes of Medieval Europeans.

To read more on the development of science during ancient and Medieval times, see Isaac Asimov's Biographical Encyclopedia of Science and Technology, the source for much of this article.

There are still many more extraordinary scientific findings made by ancient Moslem scientists, but the following are the famous ones: some are known in the West by their Latinized names, because their works were translated into Latin. The translation of Arabic scientific texts, and the introduction of Indian-Arabic numerals into Europe, are some of the most important factors sparkling the European Renaissance.

Al-Farghani (Alfraganus), 850 CE, wrote the Elements, a summary of Ptolemaic Astronomy studied in Europe until 1600 CE.

Ibn al-Haytham (Alhazen), 1038 CE, astronomer and physicist. He wrote the Optical Thesaurus, the first important work on dioptrics (the optics of the eyes), which influenced the work of Roger Bacon, the 13th century CE English scholar.

Umar Khayyam, 1123 CE known mostly as a Persian poet, he became famous in the West when his book of poems; the Rubaiyat were translated into English. However, he was also a famous philosopher, mathematician and astronomer. He made important developments in geometry and corrected the calendar which was being used at that time.

Ibn Sina (Avicenna), 1037 CE probably the most famous Arab scientist of them all. He wrote on astronomy, physics, and medicine, which he also practiced, and his great medical textbook was taught in Europe for 700 years.

Al-Biruni, 1048 CE, was one of the greatest Arab encyclopeadist of science. He wrote books on mathematics, astronomy, astrology, geography, history and botany.

Ibn Rushd (Averroes) 1198 CE, famous Arab scientist and philosopher, whose writings were very influential for hundreds of years. Among other things, he wrote important commentaries on Aristotle that was studied in Europe.

Here are some English astronomy and mathematic terms coming from Arabic language: Algebra, Algorithm, Almanac, Azimuth, Cipher, Nadir, Sine, Zenith and Zero.

⊸⋆⊸

I know for most people who are not familiar with the history of Islam the above information might come as a surprise, you might even think that I am biased. So before I go further I think it is necessary that I quote few words from highly educated Westerners who knows about the Quran, to give you more information from a neutral perspective.

Dr. Maurice Boucaille - French surgeon
"The Quranic Revelation appeared 6 centuries after Jesus. It resumes data found in the Hebraic Bible and the Gospels since it quotes frequently from the Torah or the Pentateuch of Moses (i.e: Genesis, Exodus, Leviticus, Numbers and Deuteronomy) and the Gospel. The Quran directs all Moslems to believe in the Scriptures that precedes it (4:136). It stresses the important position occupied in the Revelation by God's emissaries, such as Noah, Abraham, Moses, the Prophets and Jesus - to whom they allocate a special

position. His birth is described in the Quran, and likewise in the Gospels, as a supernatural event. Mary is also given a special place, as may be seen by the fact that chapter 19 bears her name."

"We must note here that the above facts concerning Islam are not generally known in the West. It is hardly surprising, when we consider the way so many generations in the West were instructed in the religious problems facing humanity and in what ignorance they were kept about anything related to Islam."

"The use of such terms as 'Mohammedan religion' and 'Mohammedans' has been instrumental – even to the present day – in maintaining the false notion that beliefs were involved that were spread of a man among which God (in the Christian sense) had no place. Many cultivated people today are interested in the philosophical, social and political aspects of Islam, but they do not pause to inquire about the Islamic Revelations itself, as indeed they should."

"In what contempt the Moslems are held by certain Christian circle! I experienced this when I tried to start an exchange of ideas arising from a comparative analysis of Biblical and Quranic stories on the same theme. I noted a systematic refusal, even for the purposes of simple reflection, to take any account of what the Quran had to say on the subject in hand. It is as if a quote from the Quran were a reference to the Devil!"

And further he said:

"It makes us deem it quite unthinkable for a man of Muhammad's time to have been the author of such statements on account of the state of knowledge in his day. Such considerations are what give the Quranic revelation its unique place and forces the impartial scientist to admit his inability to provide an explanation which calls solely on materialistic reasoning."

Arthur J Arberry – Quran translator
"The Quran is a book apart."

Keith L. Moore - Head of the Department of Anatomy at the University of Toronto
"It is clear to me that these statements (from the Quran) must have come to Muhammad from God. This proves to me that Muhammad must have been the messenger of God."

Professor Alfred Kroner - Chairman of the Department of Geology at the Institute of Geosciences, Johannes Gutenburg University, Mainz, Germany
"Somebody who did not know something about nuclear physics 1400 years ago could not, I think, be in position to find out from his own mind for instance that the earth and the heavens had the same origin, or many other of the questions that we have discussed here."

E. Marshall Johnson - Professor and Chairman, Department of Anatomy, Daniel Bough Institute, Thomas Jefferson University, Philadelphia, Pennsylvania
" The Quran describes not only the development of external form but emphasizes also the internal stages – the stages inside the embryo of its creation and development, emphasizing major events recognized by contemporary science. If I was to transpose myself into that era, knowing what I do today and describing things, I could not describe the things that were described. I see no evidence to refute the concept that this individual Muhammad had to be developing this information from some place. So I see nothing in conflict with the concept that divine intervention was involved. There is nothing here (the Quran) in conflict with the concept that divine intervention was involved in what Muhammad was able to say."

Professor Palmer – American marine biologist
"Scientists today are only confirming what was already written in the Quran years ago."

CHAPTER SIX

THE INTELLIGENT LANGUAGE
OF THE UNIVERSE

Mathematics is the language of God, when He created the universe

Galileo Galilei (1564 CE– 1642 CE)

*I*f you are surprised finding out about how accurate the Quran is concerning the facts in natural phenomena, you will be even more surprised reading what I am about to share with you in this chapter.

I know many people especially in the West today are skeptical about religion, even more so about Islam, to put it mildly. Of course, I am aware of the negative predicate that is attached to Islam today. However, as I have mentioned at the beginning of this book, this is not necessarily because of the teaching of religion itself.

Although many 'modern' people still believe that God exists, most are not convinced that religion truly comes from God or that God is actually involved in our lives.

If God, who has created us and the whole world, exists, don't you think He would be sending us guidance? Is it possible that

He created all these without any purpose? Is it possible that He created us and then left us living our lives without any guidance? Will we truly vanish after we die? Yes, our body will dissolve, but what about the soul? Soul is somekind of energy, right? Energy can not be destroyed. Where does it go after the dead body rots? What happen after this life on earth? Do we really think our actions on earth do not have any consequence to our souls in the after life at all?

Although there are many contradictive teachings in the three monotheistic religions as we have analyzed so far, all three agree that God actually cares about us. That our actions in life is monitored by God. If this is true, then it makes sense that God must have given guidance for us about how to live our lives the way He intended us to do. And if there is only One God of all mankind, than His guidance must be one also. His guidance must be the same for all us, because all of us are His creatures.

I can not believe that God would only give guidance to a particular race, at a particular time. Because it wouldn't be fair for the other races and also for the people who were not born yet before the guidance was revealed, right?

His guidance, or His words must be flawless. I cannot believe in any religion notwithstanding how many generations of my family have believed in that religion nor how many millions followers it has, if this religion is not making sense to me. If God would give guidance it would never be in contradiction to science. It is just simply impossible. How could it be? He is the Creator of our universe. Science might not be able to understand the whole of His law. But science that has been proven correct today cannot contradict His law. In fact, this is exactly what the Quran says: that God has been giving us guidance since the beginning of time. This guidance has been given to every race of mankind via His prophets. But mankind has always altered His guidance. This sounds like the Truth, don't you think?

The fact is, 'modern' men are not the only ones who are skeptical about God and His guidance. Human has always been skeptical, since the dawn of time. Ancient nations too have always demanded a guidance, clear proves, a sign, a miracle of God's existence. But even when God showed them a miracle, people before us too had denied it.

> *(All) people are a single nation; so God raised prophets as bearers of good news and as warners, and He revealed with them the Book with truth, that it might judge between people in that in which they differed; and none but the very people who were given it differed about it after clear arguments had come to them, revolting among themselves...*
> *(Quran translation 2:213)*

> *And every nation had an apostle; so when their apostle came, the matter was decided between them with justice and they shall not be dealt with unjustly.*
> *(Quran translation 10:47)*

> *And if you reject (the truth), nations before you did indeed reject (the truth); and nothing is incumbent on the apostle but a plain delivering (of the message).*
> *(Quran translation 29:18)*

> *And one of His signs is the creation of the heavens and the earth and the diversity of your tongues and colors; most surely there are signs in this for the learned.*
> *(Quran translation 30:22)*

> *And those who have no knowledge say: Why does not God speak to us or a sign come to us? Even thus said those before them, the like of what they say; their hearts are all alike. Indeed We have made the communications clear for a people who are sure.*
> *(Quran translation 2:118)*

(One of) the communications meant in the above verses comes in the form of Book of guidance from God. The Quran says that Books of guidance have been given to mankind, but human have always altered them. The Books that are mentioned by name in the Quran are: the Torah (the first 5 books in the Old Testament), the Injeel (the Gospel) and the Quran.

> He has revealed to you the Book with truth, verifying that which is before it, and He revealed the Torah and the Injeel (the Gospel) aforetime, guidance for the people, and He sent the Quran.
> (Quran translation 3:3)

> Woe, then, to those who write the book with their hands and then say: This is from God, so that they may take for it a small price; therefore woe to them for what their hands have written and woe to them for what they earn.
> (Quran translation 2:79)

What the Quran means with 'the signs' (ayah in Arabic) may also be translated as miracles. In the past, prophets had been performing miracles, by God's will, but people who disbelieve remained in their disbelief.

> And nothing could have hindered Us that We should send signs except that the ancients rejected them…
> (Quran translation 17:59)

> And if they see a miracle they turn aside and say: Transient magic.
> (Quran translation 54:2)

Most of us have heard about the miracles performed by the prophets as told in the Bible, for instance the parting of the sea during Moses' time; Jesus' raising the dead, etc..

For us today all those miracles are only (his)stories; either we believe they really happened or we don't. Those miracles happened in the past and we didn't witness them.

Actually, there is a miracle which was hidden in the Old Testament that we could have witnessed today. Unfortunately, since the Old Testament has been altered by human hands, this miracle is not complete anymore. Fortunately, this eternal miracle still exists in the Quran in its complete form and still can be witnessed today. What is it?

God says in the Quran that there will be no more books (i.e. written guidance) revealed for us after the Quran. And, although the previous scriptures revealed by God have been altered by human's hands, the Quran will be protected by God Himself from any manipulation.

How? Apparently, mathematics may be used as a language which is exact and cannot be manipulated. This language can be understood objectively by every intelligent being in the whole universe (including intelligent extraterrestrial beings).

The Quran is guarded by strict mathematical code. Many Moslems are also not aware of this. It is characterized by a unique phenomenon never found in any human authored book. What does this mean? Allow me to explain: let's say someone tells you to write a ten page essay about yourself.

Each line should rhyme at the end. In this essay you are only allowed to use exactly 50 A's, 25 B's and 15 C's. Do you think you can do that? Maybe. But you wont be able to convey the original message that you wanted to say and probably your sentences would be strange, don't you think? Now, just imagine writing a whole book which is scientifically accurate that way.

The Quran is written that way and even more complicated. Thousands of people are able to memorize the Quran by heart down to the alphabets! I am sure you know how difficult, close to impossible it is to memorize a book. Ask any author on which page he or she wrote a certain sentence in his or her book. I am sure he or she won't remember – all of them. Well, I sure don't.

The Quran also tells us that it is written in Arabic for a reason. Today most of the Middle Eastern countries may be considered as Islamic countries, but it was not so in past. Before the advance of Islam, the Middle Eastern countries were followers of many different religions. The Middle East has been agreed by most scholars as the cradle of civilizations, i.e.: Sumer, Babylon, Assyria and Egypt (at the border of Africa and Middle East). Arabia was not included as one of the advanced ancient civilizations. In the past Arabs were pagan nomads, scattered all over the Middle East. Apparently, they are considered as the most hot-headed but also brave, superstitious, ignorant and disbelief (in God) tribes in the Middle East, if not in the world.

So God must have purposely revealed the Quran, the last divine guidance to this tribe. The reason behind it is most likely because if such a difficult tribe can be made into God fearing tribe; that means other races should be able to do so. Unfortunately, some Arabs remain the same way – as you can witness yourself. They are still fighting amongst each other even after embracing Islam. But this has nothing to do with the Quran at all.

> The Arabs of the desert are the worst in unbelief and hypocrisy, and most fitted to be in ignorance of the command which God hath sent down to His Messenger but God is All-Knowing, All-Wise.
> (Quran translation 9:97)

But then:

> *But some of the desert Arabs believe in God and the Last Day, and look on their payments as pious gifts bringing them nearer to God and obtaining the prayers of the Messenger. Aye, indeed they bring them nearer (to Him): soon will God admit them to His Mercy: for God is Oft-Forgiving, Most Merciful.*
> *(Quran translation 9:99)*

Of course, God knows that the Arabs would behave in extreme different ways, even after the Quran was revealed. This becomes a sort of trial from God for other nations, so only a true Truth Seeker will be willing to learn about the Quran.

Why, you say, does God make it so difficult? Of course, God could have made it easy for us. But the truth is, nothing in life comes easy. Aren't we all constantly challenged and tested in all aspects of life? God purposely make it that way, just like every aspect in this world, so only true people of understanding – people who truly learn, ponder and willing to understand the universe can really see through and find out the truth. As the Quran confirms:

> *... only the men of understanding that pay heed.*
> *(Quran translation 13:19)*

So why is the Quran written in Arabic? The answer is, it doesn't matter in what language a guidance is revealed, be it in Finnish or Italian or Chinese or even English, most human will always disbelieve in it.

> *And if We had made it a Quran in a foreign tongue, they would certainly have said: Why have not its communications been made clear? What! a foreign (tongue) and an Arabian! Say: It is to those who believe a guidance and a healing; and (as for) those who do not*

believe, there is a heaviness in their ears and it is obscure to them; these shall be called to from a far-off place. (Quran translation 41:44)

In fact, the Quran says that God had also sent other apostles to other nations in their own languages. Well, many amongst us still don't believe, right?

And We did not send any apostle but with the language of his people, so that he might explain to them clearly.. (Quran translation 14:4)

The Quran is not only for Arabs, it is the last Book of guidance amongst a succession of divine Books from the same One God:

And before it the Book of Musa was a guide and a mercy: and this is a Book verifying (it) in the Arabic language that it may warn those who are unjust and as good news for the doers of good.
(Quran translation 46:12)

The Bible is the most printed book in the world. But the Quran – which means 'the Recitation' is probably the most recited book in the world. Its perfection in language is unarguable amongst the linguists. Its combination of perfection in language, meaning, intonation, melody, rhythm when done correctly may have a strong hypnotic power – just like the Gothic chanting or the Buddhist mantra. I know, I know, not when the Quran is recited forcefully and intrudingly through loudspeakers competing with other just as forceful recitals – like in many places in Indonesia.

For laymen, the meaning of the Quran might be difficult to understand, because its topics and historical stories are not chronologically ordered like the Bible. It is also not basing its theological teaching upon dramatic epics like the Hindu books or Greek myths. The Quran speaks directly concerning education, charity and so on.

Most of the stories in the Old and New Testaments and the Quran are similar, but none are exactly the same. The stories in the Quran are not written in the form of story telling. For example, the story of the Creation is not written in one chapter like the Genesis. A chapter in the Quran might consist of many different stories and teachings. I.e.: verses 1 – 5 might tell the story of Adam, then 6 – 8 talk about Josef, 8 – 10 talk about charity and so on. Why is this? This may be explained by the mathematical codes, which I am about to share with you.

So how could thousands of people are able to memorize the Arabic Quran by heart to the alphabets? It is almost impossible to memorize a book, although some Hindu priests are also able to memorize the Vedas. However, I don't think anyone can memorize the Old Testament because there are so many names in it and sometimes the names are repeated but the sequel are not the same. The New Testament (Gospel) has 4 versions, and I believe it is almost impossible to memorize one version of the Gospel by heart to the alphabet.

Please don't take my statement above as an attack. I am not an Arab. In fact, my big family – like any other Indonesian families – consists of many different religions. Some of my aunts are Christians and my grandparents still used to believe in Kejawen (a mix of Hindu/Buddhist religion with Javanese beliefs). My husband is Dutch of Roman Catholic background.

Going back to the Quran, how could thousands of people are able to memorize it? It is because the Arabic Quran is written like a poem and the end of (almost) every sentence in one chapter rhymes. Let me give you an example:

Bismillahi rrahmaani rrahiym
Qul huallahu hu ahad,
Allahu samad,
Lam yalid,
Walam yulad,
Walam yakulahu kufuwan ahad.

In the name of God, Most Gracious, Most Compassionate
Proclaim, " He is the One and only God."
The absolute God.
Never did He beget.
Nor was He begotten.
None equals Him.
(Quran transliteration and translation 112: 1 – 4)

I put an asterisk in front of the *Bismillahi rrahmaani rrahiym (*In the name of God, Most Gracious, Most Compassionate) because every single chapter of the Quran begins with this sentence. Except for one chapter, I will get back to this later. This sentence is called the Basmallah.

I have to go through this explanation first, because it is necessary to decode the mathematical phenomena that I am going to share with you. This Basmallah sentence is necessary to understand and to unlock the secret.

I am trying to explain this matter as simply as I can, but just like studying a Chinese book, we have to know a little about the style of the writing, right..

In Arabic the writing of Basmallah looks like this:

بِسْمِ اللهِ الرَّحْمٰنِ الرَّحِيْمِ

Arabic writing starts from right to the left. Some of the consonants can be joined together (B, M, L, etc) some cannot . There is no independent alphabets for the vocals (A, E, I, O, U) instead they use the following signs to determine vocal sounds of: A, I and U.

There is an exception of one vocal which may be counted as an alphabet which is called the Alif (A). This alphabet has the same word root like Alfa in Roman alphabet.

Ok, enough with the linguist lesson. Now let's proceed with the decoding of the Quran. So let's talk about mathematics, from the simple ones first.

A few years ago Dr. Tariq Al Swaidan discovered that the total number of words that are mentioned in the Quran as equal or opposite to another are mathematically equal. For example the word 'life' and 'death' in the following verse:

> Nay! do those who have wrought evil deeds think that We will make them like those who believe and do good-- that their **life** and their **death** shall be **equal**? Evil it is that they judge. (Quran translation 45:21)

Although this makes sense grammatically, the astonishing fact is that the number of times of the word 'life' mentions in the Quran is 145 and the number of times the word 'death' is also 145, therefore not only is this phrase correct in the grammatical sense but also true mathematically, i.e: 145 = 145.

Upon further analysis of various verses, he discovered that this is consistent throughout the whole Quran, where it says one thing is like another or opposite of one another. See below for the astonishing result of the number of times certain words appear in the *Arabic* Quran (the result might be different in other language Quran translations due to grammatic difference). Read carefully and see if you can also understand the wisdom behind it:

* Life	145	* Death	145
* Earthy life	115	* Afterlife	115
* Angel	88	* Satan	88
* People	50	* Messenger	50
* Calamity	75	* Thanks	75
* Charity	32	* Blessing	32
* Mind	49	* Light	49
* Tongue	25	* Sermon	25
* Hardship	114	* Patience	114
* Man	24	* Woman	24

Now, look at how many times the following words appear in the Arabic Quran:

* Month	12
* Day	365

And look at this one:
Sea is mentioned 32 times, and land is mentioned 13 times.

Sea + land	= 45
Sea	= 32/45*100 = 71.1111111%
Land	= 13/45*100 = 28.888889%
Sea + land	= 100.00%

Modern science has only recently proven that water covers 71.111% of earth, while land covers 28.889%. Is this a coincidence?Maybe yes...

Now, let's check the more complicated mathematical phenomena that are found in the Quran. If you are one of those people who dislike complicated calculations or just simply to lazy to do calculation, don't worry.. the calculations here are very basic and yet the revelations are truly, truly miraculous... They appear like simple calculations and yet these calculations are impossible to imitate. Don't just take my word, you have to check it yourself. So, I strongly suggest that you get your calculator and read this chapter carefully and check the numbers yourself. I guarantee you: they will blow your mind away..!

THE PRIME NUMBERS

The following is the explanation of 'prime numbers' by Arifin Muftie, author of Matematika Alam Semesta (Mathematics of the Universe). Prime number is the base of mathematics, it is included as one of the mystery of the universe. For most laymen, it is hard to understand how prime number can be the base of the universe. But most thinkers like: Pythagoras, Plato, Cusanus, Kepler, Leibniz, Newton, Planck and Einstein were convinced that the existence of numbers (constants) and geometrical shapes are the concept of the universe. That's what Galileo Galilei meant when he said that "Mathematics is the language of God when He created the universe."

Prime number is one of the oldest mysteries in mathematics that has never been solved. Prime numbers are numbers that can only be divided into round numbers by number 1 and itself. For example: 12 is not a prime number. Because it can be divided by 2, 3, 4 and 6. While 23 is a prime number because it can only be divided by 1 and 23. If 23 is divided by 2 for example it becomes 11.5 (not a round number).

There are indefinite prime numbers, even though it becomes lesser and lesser the further we count. It is puzzling scientists why these numbers cannot be divided by any other number.

Apparently, these numbers are used in this modern era for codification of important matters and secret matters at the banks, insurances and calculations of nuclear weapons as security systems with millions of numbers that cannot be divided by any other number. This is needed because with any other numbers the codes would be easy to crack down. This phenomenon was founded by Dr. Peter Pflichta from Düsseldorf – a German (now a Moslem or a Submitter in English term) expert in mathematics and chemistry.

Scientists – like Dr. Carl Sagan and Dr. Frank Drake who found the Cryptogram as intergalactic communication, communication code breaker - believe that prime numbers are the universal numbers that can be understood by all intelligent species as their communication language. This language is mysterious because it is connected to the planning of universal cosmos.

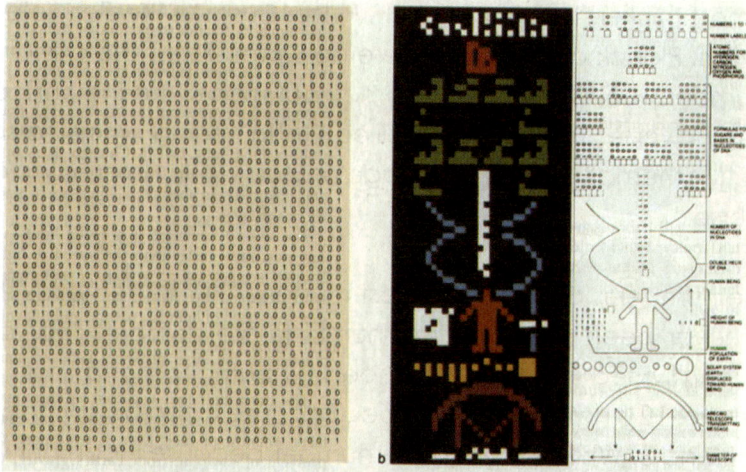

An Example of Interstellar Message in Mathematical Code

The majority of astrophysics also believe that there is a 'cosmic code' in the universe, which is also known as the Theory of Everything, which means that there are constant numbers in the universe that are interconnected to one another based on the command (programming) of the Designer.

And if that command can be deciphered, then this will give more scientific knowledge of other related matters.

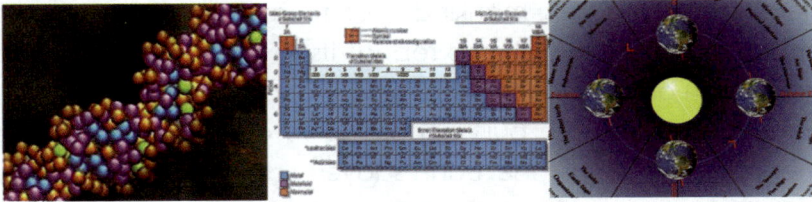

DNA Chain, Periodic Table of Elements and the 12 Stars Constellations

Below is the table of the 1st until the 19th prime numbers for a reference to our further analysis of the mathematical phenomena in the Quran:

Order	Prime Numbers
1st	2
2nd	3
3rd	5
4th	7
5th	11
6th	13
7th	17
8th	19
9th	23
10th	29
11th	31
12th	37
13th	41
14th	43
15th	47
16th	53
17th	59
18th	61
19th	67

THE MYSTERIUS NUMBER 19

It is a common knowledge amongst scientists today that the Super Intelligence created the universe using certain codes of numbers.

The universe teaches mankind that there is work in periodic terms. Certain period always repeat itself in certain systematic order. Such as the moon, earth, planet and star orbits. The DNA, the chromosomes are built according to certain numbers, the characters of atoms, the earth's layers, atmospheres and the certain characters of chemical elements.

The following mathematical secret in the Quran was not known for centuries, until finally an Egyptian-American biochemist named Dr. Rashad Khalifa was able to reveal it. In 1976 he did a research, (most likely based) on this particular verse in the Quran:

> Over it are **nineteen.**
> And We have set none but angels as guardians of the Fire. And We have fixed their number only as a trial for the disbelievers, in order that the people of the Scripture (Jews, Christians and Moslems) may arrive at a certainty and that the believers may increase in Faith, and that no doubt may be left for the people of the Scripture and the believers, and that those in whose hearts is a disease (of hypocrisy) and the disbelievers may say: "What does God intend by this example ?" Thus God leads astray whom He wills and guides whom He wills. And none can know the hosts of your Lord but He. And this is nothing else than a reminder to mankind.
> (Quran translation 74 : 30 – 31)

Some verses in the Quran are difficult to understand, sometimes it speaks in a riddle. Or maybe they sound like a riddle because our knowledge is not high enough to understand what they mean (yet). Such as the above verses.

As mentioned before, Moslems believe that the verses of the Quran were revealed by the Archangel Jibril (Gabriel) gradually in a time span of 23 years. Some of the verses came down unannounced, some came down whenever Muhammad proposed a question from his followers. Apparently the above verses came down as the 'answer' to the questions of how many angels are guarding the Fire (Hell).

So Dr. Rashad Khalifa tried to find out why that verse mentions such an 'odd' number like **19**. Using a modern computer he started the research. And these are the results of his research:

1. (Almost) every chapter in the Quran begins with the Basmallah (In the name of God, Most Gracious, Most Compassionate). In Latin the Basmallah is written this way: Bismillahi rrahmaani rrahiym - 26 alphabets are needed to write this sentence. But in Arabic, since the vocals do not count as alphabet (except for some 'A' which is needed to create an affix), it is counted differently:

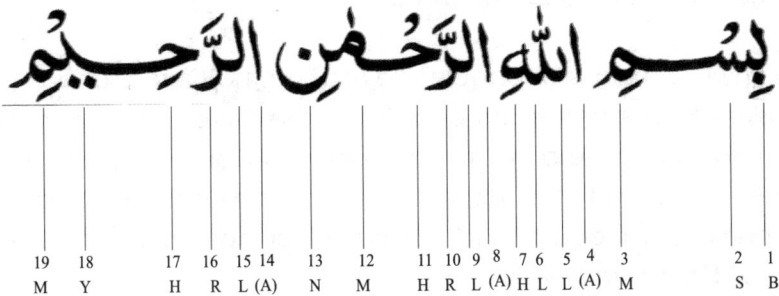

$$بِسْمِ اللهِ الرَّحْمٰنِ الرَّحِيْمِ$$

19	18		17	16	15	14		13		12		11	10	9	8	7	6	5	4		3		2	1
M	Y		H	R	L	(A)		N		M		H	R	L	(A)	H	L	L	(A)		M		S	B

From the left to the right:
B S M (A) L L H (A) L R H M N (A) L R H Y M
So there are **19** alphabets that are needed to write this sentence.

2. The sentence Basmallah consists of 4 words, which means:
Ismi (In the name of)
Allah (God)
Arrahmaan (Most Gracious)
Arrahiym (Most Compassionate)

God (Allah) in the Quran is mentioned 2,698 times.

And 2,698 is equal to **142** x 19

Is this a coincidence? Maybe yes..

But when we add the numbers of all the verses where the word 'Allah' (God) occurs, we obtain a total of 118,123.

Now 118,123 is also divisable by 19:

118,123 = 6,217 x **19**.. Is this still a coincidence?

3. There are 114 surahs (chapters) in the Quran. This means that number can be divided by 19 into a round number, which is 6. 114 = 6 x **19**.

4. If all the chapters in the Quran begin with Basmallah, it would mean that the total number of Basmallah can also be divided by 19 – because there are 114 chapters. But there is 1 (one) chapter which doesn't begin with Basmallah.

Meanwhile millions of people are reciting the Quran, and every Moslem knows that each chapter of the Quran 'should' begin with Basmallah. And yet there is one, only one chapter which doesn't begin with the Basmallah. Why? And isn't it amazing that no one dares to add it (or to 'correct' it) for more than a thousand years? Now here is why.

Since one chapter is missing the Basmallah. That would mean that the sentence of Basmallah in the Quran only remains 113 instead of 114, right? 113 divided by 19 is 5.947368... If this is the case, then the previous calculation can be called a coincidence. But this is not the case.

The Basmallah is missing in chapter 9 but in chapter **27** there is another Basmallah sentence to be found apart from the beginning of the chapter, it can be found on verse **30**. That means there is one Basmallah missing, but there 2 Basmallahs in another chapter. So the total remains 114, which is dividable by 19. So: 114 (-1+1) = 6 x **19**.

And also chapter 9 consists of war verses, it tells about the breach of peace treaties between the Quraisy (Muhammad's own clan who at first rejected his prophethood) and the Moslems. Therefore, the Basmallah sentence of God Most Compassionate is not 'appropriate' to begin this chapter. Meanwhile chapter 27 consists of the story concerning Queen Sheba who submitted with Solomon to the One God. Therefore, the Basmallah is written twice here for it is 'appropriate' to show God's compassion. So there is antagonist between the content of these two chapters.

5. And not only that, if we add the chapter and the verse number of 27:30 it becomes, 27 + 30 = 57 = 3 x **19**! And there is still more: if you count the chapters from chapter 9 until 27: it is **19** also! (9,10,11,12,13,14,15,16,17,18,19,20,21,22,23,24,25, 26,27)

6. And there is still more! If you add the chapter's numbers from chapter 9 until 27: 9+10+11+12+13+14+15+16+17+18+19+20+21 +22+23+24+25+26+27 = 342 = 18 x **19**!! Do we still think this is a coincidence? Then what a coincidence that is!

The result of the research doesn't just stop there. The Quran was revealed gradually. Remember that the Quran is not ordered by the sequence of the time of revelation. When checked by the sequence of the revelation, these are the numbers:

7. The **first** revelation (96 : 1-4) consists of 19 words   = **1** x19

8. The **second** revelation (part of 68) consists of 38 words = **2** x 19

9. The **third** revelation (part of 73) consists of 57 words   = **3** x 19

10. And the **last** revelation (110) consists of 19 words again   = **1** x 19

11. The first revelation is placed on chapter 96 which the **19**th chapter if counted from the end of the Quran (114 until 96).

12. If we add the chapters number from behind (114) to the first revelation (96): 114+113+112+111+......+96 = 1995 = 105 x **19**!

13. I have mentioned previously that the Quran mentions the word 'day' 365 times and 'month' 12 times. But the word 'year' in the Quran is mentioned 19 times! Has the Quran make a mistake then? Well, look at this explanation: the Arabs use moon calendar. Now, according to the Metonic cycle in astronomy the earth and moon meet again in the same position periodically every **19** years! Or every 235 months of moon calendar = **19** years of sun calendar. The above shows that the Quran is ordered with a mathematical interlocking system – from the front and behind. Just as the Quran itself confirms:

> *But God doth encompass them from behind!*
> *(Quran translation 85: 20)*

And also this shows that the Quran has very deep meaning in each of its word and can only be fully understood by readers who have wisdom and quite high knowledge in science. It also means that both the sun and moon calendars are God's.

There some chapters in the Quran which begin with initials or code alphabets. Arabic alphabets have names, which are similar to Roman alphabet, i.e. Alif = Alfa = A; Ba = Beta = B; Ta = Teta = T, Lam = Lamda = L, etc. This is difficult to envision for people who are not familiar with the Quran. So let me give you and example:

> **Alif Lam Mim**.
> *This is the book; in it is guidance, sure, without doubt, to those who fear God. Who believe in the Unseen, are steadfast in prayer, and spend out of what We have provided for them (for charity).*
> *(Quran translation 2: 1 – 3)*

You see, on the first verse, there is a set of alphabets: Alif Lam Mim. Which are: A, L, M. This has been puzzling the readers for more than a thousand years. What does it mean?

Finally, Dr. Rashad Khalifa counted the number of Alif (A), Lam (L) and Mim (M) in that particular chapter, where it begins with those alphabets. And this is the result:

14. The total of the mentioned alphabets are as follows:

Alif (A)   = 4,502
Lam (L)   = 3,202
Mim (M)   = 2,195
                 ———— +
                   = 9,899 = 521 x **19**!!

15. There are 14 alphabets that are used for this series of alphabet, there are 14 combinations (i.e. ALM, ALMR, ALMS, ALR, YS, TSM, etc) and are spread in 29 chapters. So : 14 +14+29 = 57 = 3 x **19**!

16. Chapter 36 starts with double alphabets which are: Ya, Sin or Y, S. The total of Y's and S's in this chapter is as follows:

Ya (Y)   = 237
Sin (S)   = 48
                 ———— +
                   = 285 = 15 x **19**!

The list goes on. I am not going to write them all here. Remember when I asked you whether you could write an essay of 10 pages with certain amount of alphabets? Just imagine, who could have written the Quran? Definitely not Muhammad. So the next question is, why **19**?

A. The number **19** is considered a unique number in mathematics which belongs to the group of prime numbers. Prime numbers can be considered as one of God's characters which is unique and can not be divided by anything else, except by Himself.

Never did He beget. Nor was He begotten.
(Quran translation 112: 3)

B. Number **19** consists of number 1 and 9, where 1 is the first number and 9 is the last number in our decimal system. This also symbolizes another of God's character which is the First and the Last, or Alpha Omega.

He is the First and the Last, the Evident and the Hidden: and
He has full knowledge of all things.
(Quran translation 57:3)

C. Number **1** symbolizes God's Oneness. And **9** is the biggest independent number which symbolizes one of God's characters which is the Most Great.

Proclaim, " He is the One and only God."
(Quran translation 112:1)

..God is the Greatest..
(Quran translation 29:45)

D. Number 19 is connected to God's Oneness. One in Arabic is WAHD. Just like the Romans, the Arabs also put value to their numbers, it is called the gematrical value. For example: the Romans value of X = 10, C = 100, M = 1000; the Arabs alphabets value of Alif (A) = 1, Ba (B) = 2, and so forth. The gematrical value of WAHD is W = 6, A = 1, H = 8, D = 4. The total is = 6+1+8+4 = **19**!

E. The numbers **1** and **9** are also two numbers that look similar in Arabic and Latin numerals. In Arabic 19 looks like this ١٩.

**THE SPECIAL CHAPTER 19 IN CONNECTION TO
ADAM, MARIA AND JESUS**

The title of the **19**th chapter in the Quran is called Maria or Maryam in Arabic. This chapter was revealed right before Muhammad told his followers to seek refuge in Habash (today Ethiopia) for being constantly attacked by the Quraisy. Back then, Habash was a Christian land ruled by a wise king called Negus. The disbelieving Quraisy dissuaded King Negus to reject the Moslems. But the king decided to let the Moslems take refuge in his country after he was told concerning what had just been revealed by Gabriel concerning Maria and Jesus. This chapter is considered as special for it has multilevel of mathematic codification as follows:

1. The exact timing of the revelation – if this chapter had been revealed a little later, Muhammad's followers would probably have not been welcomed in that Christian land.

2. The name Adam and Jesus are both mentioned for the **19**th time in this chapter .

3. The **19**th time the name Adam is mentioned in (**19** : 34) The **19**th time the name Jesus is mentioned in (**19** : 58) If you count from 34 to 58 you will come to a number: **25**. Both Adam and Jesus are mentioned **25** times in total in the Quran!

> Verily, the **likeness** of Jesus before God is the likeness of Adam. He created him from dust, then God said to him: "Be!" - and he was.
> (Quran translation 3 : 59)

4. Chapter 19 consists of 98 verses, whereas **25** of the verses are of prime numbers:
2, 3, 5, 7, 11, 13, 17, 19, 23, 29, 31, 37, 41, 43, 47, 53, 59, 61, 67, 71, 73, 79, 83, 91 and 97.

5. In (19 : **34**) where Jesus' name is mentioned for the 19th times, is the verse where Maria's name is mentioned for the **34**th time!

> Such (was) Jesus the son of Maria: (it is) a statement of truth, about which they (vainly) dispute.
> (Quran translation 19:34)

Now, seriously.. what intelligence being can make something like this?

19 and 81

One of the most intriguing prime number is 19. Even though Pythagoras, Euler and Gauss have tried to solve the mystery, they still could not solve this complex structure. Dr. Peter Plichta argued that it seems all mathematical formulae and numbers are connected to the two math poles of the universe. For example:

The polar number of 13 is 87. I.e.: 13 + 87 = 100
The polar number of 25 is 75. I.e.: 25 + 75 = 100

Number **81** is special because it completes number 19 (19 + 81 = 100). And the total of those two numbers are= 1 + 9 + 8 + 1 = **19** (If you do this with all the numbers below 100, the total is always **19**!)

If we analyze the connection of the two numbers further as follows: 1:19 = 0,**05263157894736842**1052631578947368...

The numbers repeat periodically, exactly on the **19**th digit after the coma. And interestingly enough if we add those numbers:

0 + 5 + 2 + 6 + 3 + 1 + 5 + 7 + 8 + 9 + 4 + 7 + 3 + 6 + 8 + 4 + 2 + 1 the total is **81**!

Now:
1:81 = 0,012345 6**79** ...

Oops! The number **8** is missing even though the rest of the numbers appears periodically. Why is the number 8 missing? Why not other numbers? It has been guessed that it has something to do with the number **19**.

Well... **19** is the **8**th prime number ! (2, 3, 5, 7, 11, 13, 17, 19!)

For the Chinese the number 8 symbolizes the Pat Kwa, the 8 wind directions, it is a powerful number, the number of richness, power, harmony and balance. The Quran says that 8 is the number of angels who will bear the throne of our Lord on the Judgement Day!

> *And the angels will be on its sides, and **eight** angels will, that Day, bear the Throne of your Lord above them.*
> *(Quran translation 69 : 17)*

THIRTY (30)

There are **30** numbers mentioned in the Quran: 1; 2; 3; 4; 5; 6; 7; 8; 9; 10; 11; 12; 19; 20; 30; 40; 50; 60; 70; 80; 99; 100; 200; 300; 1,000; 2,000; 3,000; 5,000; 50,000 and 100,000. Their total is 162,146 = 8,534 x **19**!

It is interesting that the Quran mentions number **30** only twice in (7 : 142) and (46 : 15). The total of the chapters and verses digit numbers are = 7 + 1 + 4 + 2 + 4 + 6 + 1 + 5 = **30**.
Amazing, isn't it?

FIFTY SEVEN (57)

It is indeed strange that one of the chapters in the Quran being a religious book is entitled as one element from the Chemical Periodic Table: **Chapter 57 : Iron**. But that is the Quran.

The question is: why iron? What is so special about iron? Why not other metal which is more valuable? Like gold, for example.

*We sent aforetime Our Messengers with Clear Signs and sent down with them the Book and the Balance (of Right and Wrong), that men may stand forth in justice; and We **sent down Iron**, which is **mighty**, as many benefits for mankind, that God may test who it is that will help, unseen, Him and His Messengers: for God is Full of Strength, Exalted in Might (and able to enforce His Will).*
(Quran translation 57:25)

1. The first thing that interest many of the Quran translators is the sentence ' .. sent down Iron..'. What does the Quran means by the Iron being sent down? Is it sent down from the sky? Only after our scientific knowledge advanced, do we understand what that means. According to Professor Amstrong from the NASA: Iron belongs to the category of heavy metal – metal that can not be made on the earth. This is because the energy in our solar system is not sufficient to produce the element of iron. The energy that is needed to produce iron is estimated around 4 times the energy of our solar system, which means iron has got to be produced by a star which is much bigger than our sun! Whereby this star must have exploded as a nova or supernova and the residues of the explosion scattered in space as meteorites which contain Iron until it is then absorbed by the earth's atmosphere at the beginning of the earth's creation billion of years ago. Which means the Quran is right literally by using the word: sending down the iron to the earth!

2. The second thing that is quite striking is the word 'mighty' to describe iron. On the first instance, most people would think of the usage of iron for weapon's purpose. But the Quran means beyond that. One of the great benefits from God for mankind is the 'design' of the earth. The earth and its content are protected by the Van Allen Belt which is surrounding the earth like a shield of highly charge electro magnetic field. This 'mighty' belt is not to be found on other planets in our solar system.

Van Allen Belt

The radiation from this belt creates a high energy which consists of proton and electron, which surround the earth up to thousands of kilometers. This belt is protecting the earth from the mega explosion of the sun which happens every 11 years, which is called the Solar Flares. Without the Van Allen Belt the earth would be shattered by these Solar Flares which has power equivalent to 100 million atom bomb of Hiroshima!

How was this belt formed? It is formed by the biggest core of the earth which is **Iron** and Nickel. Both of these elements have big magnetic fields which can not be found on other planets on our solar system. Except for Mercury, with very low radiation.

3. The third thing is the number of this chapter: 57. The Arabic word for Iron is Al Hdyd. The gematrical value of AL HDYD is (A = 1, L = 30), H = 8, D = 4, Y = 10, D = 4. The total is = (1 + 30) + (8 + 4 + 10 + 4) = **31 + 26** = **57**! So it is the same as the number of the chapter! And 57 = 3 x **19**!

4. According to Peter Van Krogt, an expert in elementimology – iron has been used as long as human can remember. The Latin name for it is Ferrum which means 'the holy element' a derivation of and Anglo Saxon word: Iren. During the Roman Caesar of Marcus Aurelius and Commodus, Iron has been associated with the myth of the planet Mars.

Modern chemistry states that Ferrum or Fe in short has 8 isotopes (atoms which has the same amount of protons but different amount of neutron). Whereby only 4 of the isotopes of Ferrum are stabile. These are the chemical symbols of the stabile ones: Fe-54, Fe-56, **Fe-57** and Fe-58. Ferrum has atomic number of **26**. (**26** is the total gematrical value of HDYD!)

5. One of the stabile isotopes of iron is the Fe-**57** (again the same number like the number of the chapter!). This isotope has **31** neutrons (the same gematrical value of AL). The rest of the isotopes have different number of neutrons.

6. The mass atom of Fe-57 is **56,9354**. (569,354 = 29,966 x **19**!)

7. It is not a coincidence that the above verse from the Quran is positioned on chapter 57, verse 25. Again: 5 + 7 + 2 + 5 = **19**!

8. The word '**iron**' is mentioned **9** times in **6** different verses. One of them is in (18:**96**). This verse is telling about an '**iron** door or wall' located 'in between two mountains' which was built by Zulkarnain. One day this iron door or wall will be leveled to the ground – which will be one of the signs of the End of the World. It is still argued today who is Zulkarnain, some propose that he is Iskandar Zulkarnain (Alexander the Great) or Cyrus the Persian Emperor or Akhnaten of Egypt or even Buddha.

9. Some scholars argue that they have found the 'iron door' which is meant by the Quran to be located in Derbent – ex Uni Soviet as is mentioned in the Encyclopedia Columbia.

It mentions that the Iron Door was built by the Persian as a protection wall against the attack from invaders from the North. This door still exists today and is called the Caucasian Wall but also sometimes called the Alexander Wall. There is another theory that says that it was actually talking about the most ancient part of the Great Wall of China, which was architect by Zulkarnain/Akhenaton! I will discuss about this in more detail in the next books of the EarthTrek Trilogy.

～ᴓ✦ᴓ～

Wow! Isn't that amazing? My head already spin just trying to understand it when the first time I read about this. How on earth a human being could have written something with such complicated mathematics/physics/chemistry calculation, in poetic form, tells a prophecy and still makes sense?

Have you seen how intertwined everything is? But then again isn't our world is just as intertwined as this? For the Creator of the universe this is all nothing. I am not even including all of the mathematical phenomena that have been decoded in the Quran, there are many more. And I am convinced many more to come. Apparently every single number in the Quran is coded and has meaning behind it!

However, I would like to share another phenomenon that spins my head even more. Let's go back to the mysterious number 19. For this one you really need a calculator to see the 'miracle' yourself.

THE MYSTERIOUS GRAPHIC OF NUMBER 19
Elaborating the research of number 19 in the Quran, Fahmi Basya an Indonesian mathematician did further test. He combined the principal of the prime number 19 and another principal in the Quran that mentions that God creates everything in pairs and then multiplies them.

And of everything We have created pairs that you may be mindful.
(Quran translation 51:49)

The Originator of the heavens and the earth; He made mates for you from among yourselves, and mates of the cattle too, multiplying you thereby..
(Quran translation 42:11)

The above verses maybe understood as the base of the multiplication of all creatures by cell division, which starts from nothing (0) into 1 cell, into 2 cells, into 4 cells, into 8 cells, etc.

So let's see what happen if both these principles are combined into one frame:

1. Let's draw a vertical line based on the 19 system. In the decimal system we start with number 0 and end with number 9. So in the 19 system we start with number 0 and end with number 18.

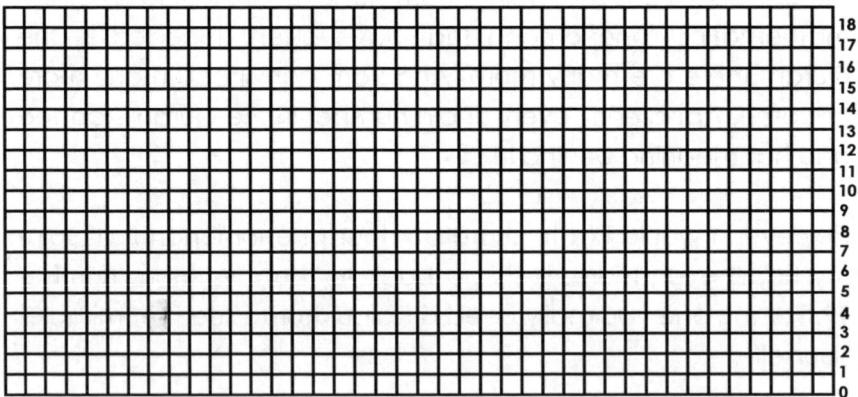

2. Then let's draw a horizontal line also starting with number 0, then number 1 followed by its double multiplication (like cell multiplication). We have to put the numbers starting from the right to the left since we are now using the Arabic system. But first, we have to convert the numbers into the 19 system.

In the decimal system (based on 10) the number is as follows: 0,1,2,3,4,5,6,7,8,9, right... and then after that the numbers repeat like this: 10, 11, 12, 13, 14, 15, 16, 17, 18, 19... and so forth. Using the 19 system the calculation becomes like this:

Sequence	Multiply by 2	Based on 19	Last Digit
1	1	1	1
2	2	2	2
3	4	4	4
4	8	8	8
5	16	16	6
6	32	13	3
7	64	7	7
8	128	14	4
9	256	9	9
10	512	18	8
11	1024	17	7
12	2048	15	5
13	4096	11	1
14	8192	3	3
15	16384	6	6
16	32768	12	2
17	65536	5	5
18	131072	10	0
19	262144	1	1
20	524288	2	2

The first column is the sequence of the numbers.

The second column is the previous number in the same column multiply by 2 (like cell multiplication). I.e.: 1x2=2 ; 2x2=4 ; 4x2= 8, and so forth.

The third column is the conversion of the numbers in the second column based on the 19 system. No number can exceed 18.

Think of a clock. A clock is based on the 12 system. 13 o'clock is the same as 1 o'clock in the afternoon, right? How do you count it? 13 – 12 = 1. Let's say there is 26 o'clock, so that would be 26 – 12 – 12 = 2 o'clock. Now use the same principle based on the 19 system.

1	=	1			
2	=	2			
4	=	4			
8	=	8			
16	=	16			
32	=	32	- 19	= 13	
64	=	64	- (3x19)	= 7	
28	= 128	- (6x19)	= 14 And so forth.		

The fourth column is the last digit number of column 3. E.g: if the number on the third column is 1, the fourth column is also 1. If the number on the third column is 16, the fourth column is 6 (the last digit).

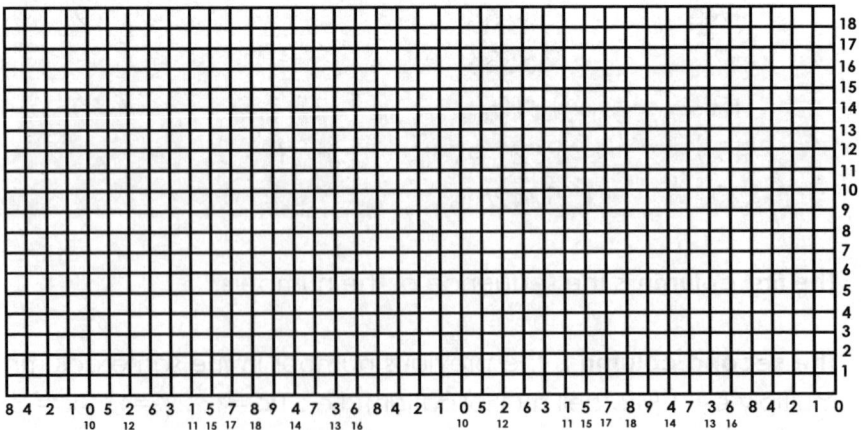

8 4 2 1 0 5 2 6 3 1 5 7 8 9 4 7 3 6 8 4 2 1 0 5 2 6 3 1 5 7 8 9 4 7 3 6 8 4 2 1 0
  10   12   11 15 17 18   14   13 16   10   12   11 15 17 18   14   13 16

Then let's put only the numbers in the last column on the horizontal axis. So now the graphic looks like the previous graphic: the vertical axis is from 0 until 18 and the blue numbers on column 4 are placed on the horizontal axis.

Then let's place dots, according to the third column. If the number on the horizontal column is 4, we put the dot on number 4 on the vertical axis. If it is 18 then we put the dot on number 18 on the vertical axis, even though on the horizontal axis only the last digit appeared (8). So the graphic becomes like this:

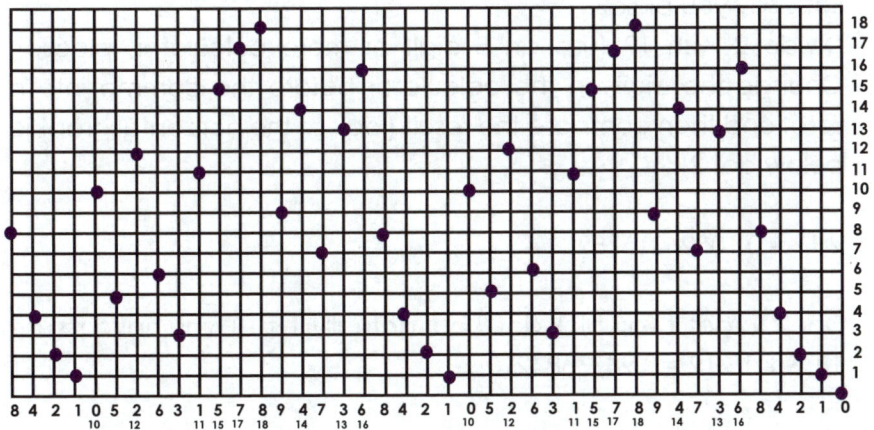

And this is what happens if we connect the dots:

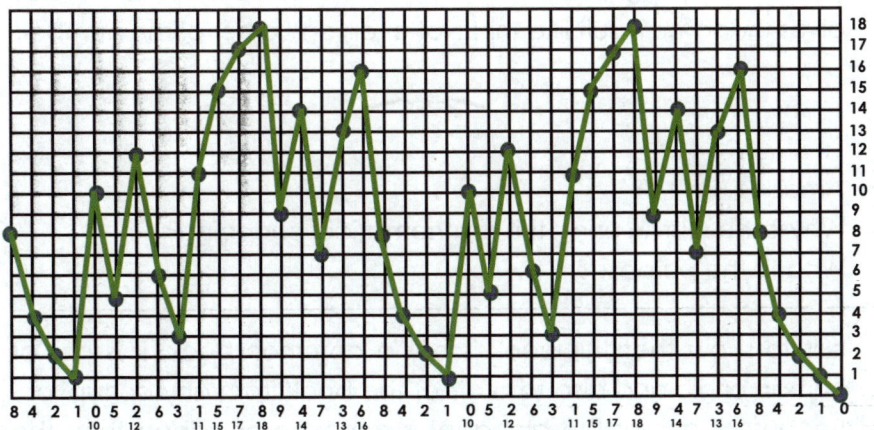

151

Remember how Allah (God) is written in Arabic? If we connect the dots, they do look like a repetition of God, God, God in Arabic… don't they? (Even when we turn it up-side-down!)

w٦

Do you think this is too far-fetched?
Pick a dot then, any dot.
Let's say you pick 2.
Divide 2 with 19 (use an 8 digit or more calculator, please). Change the digit on the calculator before the comma into a zero, and then compare the result (look at the horizontal graphic below dot 2).

2:19 = 0,10526315789…

Don't forget if you pick dot 8 but actually it is 18, you have to use 18. So: 18:19 = 0,9473684210…

Go ahead pick another number.. The result will always be the same like the graphic… Try with any calculator that can show you as many digits as possible. No other number in this universe gives the same result like this! Not even any other prime number.

—∘∗∘—

Amazing, isn't it?
Why is the Quran using this mathematical encoding?
What is the purpose?

It is to show that this book is not a common book, it is not of human origin and also to protect the book from any corruption. Because if any of the alphabet is removed or added then the whole calculation will tumble down. There is not a single ancient book in this world which has not changed or altered by its own author on the printing, or quoted, changed and mistranslated by other authors, etc. There is always some adjustment done, some changes done and before we know it the original message is already missing.

Just like our words, you know that game... where ten people line up and tell a story to another person, at the end of the line the message are usually not the same anymore. Imagine that this happens over a period of thousands of years.

This is mentioned in the Quran itself:

> *We have, without doubt, sent down the Message; and We will assuredly guard it (from corruption).*
> *(Quran translation 15:9)*

> *No falsehood can approach it from before or behind it: it is sent down by One Full of Wisdom, Worthy of all Praise.*
> *(Quran translation 41:42)*

Actually, this numerical phenomena of the Quran also existed in the Old Testament. Apparently, this 'numerical structure' is also used in the Jewish prayer. Here is an article that I found in the Internet (www.19.org):

Joseph Dan writes that Rabbi Judah was critical of the French and British Jews when they altered the Morning Prayer by adding a few words (Studies In Jewish Mysticism, Association for Jewish Studies, 1982). Rabbi Judah argued that such an addition destroys the numerical structure of the prayer. Here is an excerpt from Rabbi Judah: The people (Jews) in France made it a custom to add (in the morning prayer) the words: 'Ashrei temimei derekh' (blessed are those who walk the righteous way) and our Rabbi, the Pious, of blessed memory, wrote that they were completely and utterly wrong. It is all gross falsehood, because there are only **19** times that the Holy Name is mentioned (in that portion of the morning prayer) and similarly you find the word 'Elohim' **19** times in the periscope of Ve-'elleh shemot. Similarly, you find that Israel is called 'sons' **19** times, and there are many other examples. All these sets of **19** are intricately intertwined, and they contain many secrets and esoteric meanings, which are contained in more than eight large volumes.

Therefore, anyone who has the fear of God will not listen to the words of the Frenchmen who add the verse 'Ashrei temimei derekh', and blessed are the righteous who walk in the paths of God's Torah, for according to their additions the Holy Name is mentioned twenty times and this is a great mistake. Furthermore, in this section there should be 152 words (152 = **19** x 8) but if you add 'Ashrei temimei derekh' there are 158 words. This is nonsense, for it is a great and hidden secret why there should be 152 words, but it cannot be explained in a short treatise. In order to understand this religious phenomenon, we have to take the basic contention of this treatise exactly as it is stated: every addition or omission of a word, or even of a single letter, from the sacred text of the prayers destroys the religious meaning of the prayer as a whole and is to be regarded as a grave sin, a sin which could result in eternal exile for those who commit it.
(Studies In Jewish Mysticism)

And now, even more fascinating, the Quran - which was revealed approximately 600 years before Rabbi Judah made the above critic (at around 12th century CE) - already prophecied about it:

> Say, 'What if it (the Quran) is from God and you disbelieved in it? <u>A witness from the Children of Israel</u>

has borne witness to a similar phenomenon, and he has believed, while you have turned arrogant. Surely, God does not guide the wicked people.
(Quran translation 46:10)

Unfortunately, in the Old Testament the coding is not complete anymore as in the Quran due to the age long alterations. This must be true, because otherwise the Quran would have not come to existence then. But of course, this is already planned by God. And today we do not have the Gospel that was written during the time when Jesus was still alive. Furthermore, most of the Bibles that are circulating publicly around the world today are only translations in many languages and are not represented together with the original language. Of course, any translation from one language to another is never exactly the same.

Yes, the Quran is also translated into many languages. However, to be called the Quran, the translation has to be accompanied by the original Arabic language. This is to guard the authenticity. Translations might be wrong and not exact. In fact, the newer translation of the Quran has become more accurate year by year, especially concerning the natural phenomena of the world. Because the exact meaning of some verses can only be interpreted after recent scientific findings.

What is the purpose of this mathematical coding? It is explained in the following verses concerning the number 19:

> *Over it are **nineteen**.*
> *And We have set none but angels as guardians of the Fire; and We have fixed their number only as a trial for Unbelievers, in order that:*
> 1. *the People of the Scripture (Jews, Christians as well as Moslems) may arrive at certainty, and the Believers may increase in Faith,*
> 2. *and that no doubts may be left for the People of the*

Scripture and the Believers,

3. *and that those in whose hearts is a disease and the Unbelievers may say, "What symbol doth God intend by this? Thus doth God leave to stray whom He pleaseth; and guide whom He pleaseth; and none can know the forces of thy Lord, except He.*

4. *And this is no other than a warning to mankind.*
(Quran translation 74: 30-31)

Strangely enough, despite the amazing numerous phenomena that we have just witnessed, some Moslems actually accused Dr. Rashad Khalifa of making this up. Probably it is because they have not seen or checked the actual proof themselves. If the explanations above are still not enough to proof that these phenomena truly come from God, allow me to quote another verse from the Quran to confirm it. The following verse should be enough to show that it is not a coincidence that number 19, is somekind of base of God's calculation when He revealed the Quran:

... He (God) keeps count of all things (i.e. He knows the exact number of everything).
*(Quran translation **72 : 28**)*

Look at the number of the surah (chapter) and the number of the above verse. Chapter 72: verse 28. The total is: 7 + 2 + 2 + 8 = **19**! Again... "He keeps count of all thing."

CHAPTER SEVEN

WHY ARE WE FIGHTING ?

*N*ow let's go into the laws concerning war – an aspect which caused most debate, critics and friction amongst the three religions.

When I was younger I used to be scared listening to my religious teacher in school talking about the law of war and punishment system in religion, especially from the one religion that I am most familiar with – Islam. I thought that the rules are too harsh. And I wished that there were no such law system.

But the older I get, the more I understand the nature of men, the more I see how chaotic and unjust the world can be without law system (even with law system our world is still chaotic) – finally I understand that law and punishment system is desperately needed. I decided to learn from all the three monotheistic religions' scriptures concerning law and punishment. I must say, I was surprised many times to find out what I am about to share with you.

There are many issues concerning human's interaction that need to be put in order (i.e. law). Humans do not always know how to deal with these justly. Who else can lay down a better law and inform us how to deal with these issues if not our Creator? In fact, in college I was taught that the basic laws in many Western countries today come from the Roman law, which is originally from the Bible.

Religion is not only about praying and giving charity; there are other uncomfortable issues that have to be regulated including war. Apparently Buddhism was a sect of Hinduism that is against any sort of violence; more or less in the same relation as Christianity to Judaism.

I wish all the problems in the world can be solved without physical force at all. But that is not the case. Even on the personal level, it is almost impossible to settle everything without being harsh or firm at all. Sometimes it is just needed. Let's face it there are bad and even evil people in this world. The question is: how to deal with evil without becoming a part of evil itself. What to do when our right is violated by others?

War is amongst one of the most terrifying things in this world. I used to be totally against war in any form. I used to think that we should be able to solve all our conflicts by using diplomacy. Unfortunately, this is not the case. Just look at the history of our earth; it is full of bloody battles and wars.

Some historians explain that in the absence of war, progress and civilization would have been hindered in some nations. They say that war is a social necessity which nations practice in order to solve their social problems which defy peaceful solution. Human communities have plunged into fights not only for the mere accomplishment of material aims but for the achievement of moral needs as well.

Hegel, a pioneer of the study of historical development, for instance, says that change can take place only when there are opposing forces which struggle against one another so that a new product, stronger than the rest, issues from the clash. This view was later adopted by Marx and Engels. Some people also argue that war is a way of nature to keep the balance to encounter over population in the world. Well, I don't know about this argument, I personally think that there must be other ways to deal with over population.

But despite what I personally think, it is a fact that our earth's history is full of wars. Although, after having attained a certain level of scientific and cultural progress, even the most 'civilized' countries in the West still tend to solve their problems by way of war. So the more sensible question is: how to set rules during a war? Let us see what the three monotheistic religions say about this issue.

Many so-called religious people in the world do not read their scriptures entirely and yet most of us judge each others action. This can be very dangerous and misleading.

A fair judge learns everything about the law or at least knows where to look for a particular law reference to decide a case. It is impossible to become a fair judge if he or she knows the law only partially. Just imagine what would happen if a judge only knows the law partially. Not only that he or she would make an unfair judgment, but also most likely the rest of us would probably lose our faith in the law system all together.

Unfortunately, this is what is happening with religion today. Very few people really read the religious scripture wholly. So some people who claim to follow the teaching of a certain religion only follow a part of its teaching and ignore the rest. And some other people, who are leading these religious people, take advantage of that. And the rest of the world condemns the religion – unfortunately, also without knowing the full teaching of religion, i.e. the law of God.

I think we all owe to ourselves to learn about it, don't you think? I was surprised when comparing what the three monotheistic religions have to say about war.

WAR VERSES

According to the Old Testament

And Moses spake unto the people, saying, arm some of yourselves unto the war, and let them go against the Midianites, and avenge the Lord of Midian. Of every tribe a thousand, throughout all the tribes of Israel, shall ye send to the war.

So there were delivered out of the thousands of Israel, a thousand of every tribe, twelve thousand armed for war. And Moses sent them to the war, a thousand of every tribe, them and Phinehas the son of Eleazar the priest, to the war, with the holy instruments, and the trumpets to blow in his hand.

And they warred against the Midianites, as the Lord commanded Moses; and they slew all the males. And they slew the kings of Midian, beside the rest of them that were slain; namely, Evi, and Rekem, and Zur, and Hur, and Reba, five kings of Midian: Balaam also the son of Beor they slew with the sword.

And the children of Israel took all the women of Midian captives, and their little ones, and took the spoil of all their cattle, and all their flocks, and all their goods. And they burnt all their cities wherein they dwelt, and all their goodly castles, with fire. And they took all the spoil, and all the prey, both of men and of beasts. And they brought the captives, and the prey, and the spoil, unto Moses, and Eleazar the priest, and unto the congregation of the children of Israel, unto the camp at the plains of Moab, which are by Jordan near Jericho.

And Moses, and Eleazar the priest, and all the princes of the congregation, went forth to meet them without the camp. And Moses was wroth with the officers of the host, with the captains over thousands, and captains over hundreds, which came from the battle. And Moses said unto them, Have ye saved all the women alive?

Behold, these caused the children of Israel, through the counsel of Balaam, to commit trespass against the Lord in the matter of Peor, and there was a plague among the congregation of the Lord. <u>Now therefore kill all the boys, and kill every woman that hath known man by lying with him. But all the girls, that have not known a man by lying with him, keep alive for yourselves.</u>
(OT: Numbers 31: 3 – 17)

When thou goest out to battle against thine enemies, and seest horses, and chariots, and a people more than thou, be not afraid of them: for the Lord thy God is with thee, which brought thee up out of the land of Egypt.
And it shall be, when ye are come nigh unto the battle, that the priest shall approach and speak unto the people, and shall say unto them, Hear, O Israel, ye approach this day unto battle against your enemies: let not your hearts faint, fear not, and do not tremble, neither be ye terrified because of them; for the Lord your God is he that goeth with you, to fight for you against your enemies, to save you.
And the officers shall speak unto the people, saying, What man is there that hath built a new house, and hath not dedicated it? Let him go and return to his house, lest he die in the battle, and another man dedicate it.
And what man is he that hath planted a vineyard, and hath not yet eaten of it? Let him also go and return unto his house, lest he die in the battle, and another man eat of it.
And what man is there that hath betrothed a wife, and hath not taken her? Let him go and return unto his house, lest he die in the battle, and another man take her.
And the officers shall speak further unto the people, and they shall say, What man is there that is fearful and fainthearted? let him go and return unto his house, lest his brethren's heart faint as well as his heart.
And it shall be, when the officers have made an end of speaking unto the people that they shall make captains

of the armies to lead the people. When thou comest nigh unto a city to fight against it, then proclaim peace unto it. And it shall be, _if it make thee answer of peace, and open unto thee, then it shall be, that all the people that is found therein shall be tributaries unto thee, and they shall serve thee._

And if it will make no peace with thee, but will make war against thee, then thou shalt besiege it: And when the Lord thy God hath delivered it into thine hands, _thou shalt smite every male thereof with the edge of the sword: But the women, and the little ones, and the cattle, and all that is in the city, even all the spoil thereof, shalt thou take unto thyself; and thou shalt eat the spoil of thine enemies, which the Lord thy God hath given thee._

Thus shalt thou do unto all the cities which are very far off from thee, which are not of the cities of these nations. But of the cities of these people, which the Lord thy God doth give thee for an inheritance, thou shalt save alive nothing that breatheth: But thou shalt utterly destroy them; namely, the Hittites, and the Amorites, the Canaanites, and the Perizzites, the Hivites, and the Jebusites; as the Lord thy God hath commanded thee: That they teach you not to do after all their abominations, which they have done unto their gods; so should ye sin against the Lord your God.

When thou shalt besiege a city a long time, in making war against it to take it, thou shalt not destroy the trees thereof by forcing an axe against them: for thou mayest eat of them, and thou shalt not cut them down (for the tree of the field is man's life) to employ them in the siege: _Only the trees which thou knowest that they be not trees for meat, thou shalt destroy and cut them down;_ and thou shalt build bulwarks against the city that maketh war with thee, until it be subdued.

(OT: Deuteronomy 20:1 – 20)

According to the New Testament

Then Jesus said to him, "Put your sword back into its place; for all those who take up the sword shall perish by the sword".
(NT: Matthew 26:52)

According to the Quran

You may fight in the cause of God against those who attack you, but do not aggress. God does not love the aggressors.
You may kill those who wage war against you, and you may evict them whence they evicted you. Oppression is worse than murder. Do not fight them at the Sacred Mosque, unless they attack you therein. If they attack you, you may kill them. This is the just retribution for those disbelievers.
If they refrain, then God is Forgiver, Most Merciful. You may also fight them to eliminate oppression, and to worship God freely. If they refrain, you shall not aggress; aggression is permitted only against the aggressors.
(Quran translation 2: 190 – 193)

Thus, Moses in the Old Testament gave us two different commands of what to do during a war; the first command is that we have to kill all the enemies including non-virgin women and boys. But another command is not to cut the trees, kill all the men only (not the boys) but to keep the rest to serve us. I hope no one would be offended, when I say I don't believe that this kind of teaching comes from God. These verses must have been altered by men. I can not find any other explanation for this.

It is probably interesting to note, that while many non-Moslems are aware that there are verses concerning the conduct of war in the Quran, most are not aware that the Old Testament contains a lot more verses of war. Joshua (the successor of Moses) alone was noted in the Old Testament to have defeated 31 kings during his leadership (Joshua 12:24). Almost all these kingdoms were destroyed, the entire people slew and the cities burned.

Meanwhile, the New Testament is saying something completely the opposite. Christianity came and made a complete prohibition of violence altogether. Although, personally I would love to embrace this teaching, I know this teaching is practically impossible to apply in the real world.

The more I study the Old and New Testaments the more extreme differences I learn. This is like having two parents, who contradict one another. Not only is this confusing, at the end of the day, it becomes unwise. A parent should not be too strict to their children, but also not too lenient. This is for the children's own interest. In a larger scale, without a clear law, the people of a country will be confused, feeling insecure and finally, the country might end up in the hands of anarchists.

Now, because of the above teachings many Christians sacrificed their lives in the cause of prohibiting war, which also means the prohibition of the military profession itself. Meanwhile, some other Christians made tremendous efforts to reconcile the New Testament teachings and the necessities of the State, and their efforts resulted in a differentiation between permissible war and prohibited war. A war is fair and just, according to them, when it is declared by the prince or ruler, provided his motive is truthful without greed or cruelty.

Although this ruling does make sense, it is not stated anywhere in the New Testament – and ironically this statement can be found in the Quran.

So in accordance to the 'adjusted' rule, in the fourth century, after the establishment of a State under the leadership of Constantine the Roman Emperor, Christianity used force in order to uproot paganism from the Roman Empire.

I think when comparing the above three teachings, the verses in the Quran concerning war make the most sense. Unfortunately, today some fanatic Moslems have taken parts of the Quran verses in order to justify their violent actions. And already with the long history of antipathy towards the Middle Eastern countries, many non-Moslems end up condemning Islam.

In order to gain a proper understanding of many verses in the Quran, it is important to understand and know the historic context of the revelations. Many revelations in the Quran came down to provide guidance to Muhammad and the fellow Moslems based on what they were confronting at that time. The following verse is one such verse which is very often misinterpreted.

> Recall that your Lord inspired the angels: "I am with you; so support those who believed. I will throw terror into the hearts of those who disbelieved…
> (Quran translation 8:12)

The above verse concerning war in the Quran was revealed during the Battle of Badr, which occurred in Arabia in the early 7th century CE. A battle where the pagans of Mecca traveled more than 200 miles to Medina with an army of about 1,000 men to destroy the Moslems of only around 300 men. Previous to that Muhammad and the Moslems had suffered severe persecutions and were tortured for 13 years in the city of Mecca. And during those 13 years the Moslems did not fight back. Then they fled Mecca and found a sanctuary in the city of Medina, but they were once again threatened.

Here, the above verse was revealed and gave the order for the Moslems to fight to defend their lives and faith. So, it was a war to defend themselves and their faith. But of course many of the Moslems were surprised by the revelation that allowed them to fight back, since they have been passive previously. The above revelation is to assure them that God was on their side.

However, the Quran only allowed us to fight, strive and kill the enemy *during* the fight. Even during a war, the Quran teaches the highest moral law of war. One is not allowed to kill civilians, i.e. children, women (except for women soldiers, these are not civilians) or any one who is not fighting in the war. This is clear because the Quran also says:

> ... *Whosoever kills a human being without (any reason like) man slaughter, or corruption on earth, it is as though he had killed all mankind ...*
> *(Quran translation 5:32)*

We are also ordered not to fight, if the enemy wants a peace treaty:

> *But if the enemy inclines towards peace, do thou (also) incline towards peace, and trust in God: for He is One that hears and knows (all things).*
> *(Quran translation 8:61)*

Compare the above with these verses of the Old Testament says:

> *And the Lord said, Go ye after him through the city, and smite: let not your eye spare, neither have ye pity: Slay utterly old (and) young, both maids, and little children, and women: but come not near any man upon whom (is) the mark; and begin at my sanctuary. Then they began at the elderly men who (were) before the house. And he said to them, Defile the house, and fill the courts with the slain: go ye forth. And they went forth, and slew in the city.*
> *(OT: Ezekiel 9:5-7)*

Unfortunately, many people innocently or deliberately misquote religious teachings without full knowledge, whilst others seek to change God's revelations. Mankind has been doing this throughout the ages. It can be both dangerous and misleading. A little knowledge is a dangerous thing.

I contend that the above verses concerning Moses' words from the Old Testament have also been altered, whether intentionally is debatable.

It is very easy to misquote any religious teaching. Previously, I have quoted a verse from the New Testament which clearly says that Jesus came with a message of peace to earth. But imagine what manner of misquotation one could have done with the following verses:

> *Do not suppose that I (Jesus) have come to bring peace to the earth. I did not come to bring peace, but a sword. For I have come to turn a man against his father, a daughter against her mother, a daughter-in-law against her mother-in-law.*
> *(NT: Matthew 10: 34-35)*

In international law, there is a set of well-established rules concerning the obligations of nations toward each other in times of war and peace. The first of these is that a country should base its relations with other countries on terms of peace so that it may exchange benefit and cooperate with others in order to promote humanity to utmost perfection. Peaceful ties like these, they say, should not be broken except in extreme urgencies that necessitate war, provided that all peaceful steps have failed in terminating the cause of dispute.

This is what the Quran has always been teaching, and the relations of Moslems with others are primarily based on peace and confidence. The Quran forbids the killing of people merely because they embrace a different faith, nor does it allow us to fight against those who disagree with them on religious questions. It urges its followers to treat such people kindly, even during religious discussion or argument the Quran teaches us to do that in the best manner:

> And do not dispute with the followers of the Books (Jewish and Christians) except by what is best (of manners), except those of them who act unjustly, and say: We believe in that which has been revealed to us and revealed to you, and our God and your God is One, and to Him do we submit.
> (Quran translation 29:46)

> God does not forbid you from befriending those who do not fight you because of religion, and do not evict you from your homes. You may befriend them and be equitable towards them. God loves the equitable.
> God forbids you only from befriending those who fight you because of religion, evict you from your homes, and band together with others to banish you. You shall not befriend them. Those who befriend them are the transgressors.
> (Quran translation 60: 8-9)

In another place, the Quran says:

> .... Therefore, if they leave you alone, refrain from fighting you, and offer you peace, then God gives you no excuse to fight them.
> (Quran translation 4:90)

And there is also:

> If they resort to peace, so shall you, and put your trust in God. He is the Hearer, the Omniscient.
> (Quran translation 8:61)

Instructions like these pave the way for the establishment of peace, and go in harmony with the present tendency to set down principles that call for the abolishment of war. Islam, in fact, makes of peace a special greeting which Moslems exchange whenever they meet by saying, "Peace be unto you" (Assalamualaykum). Moslems also utter this statement at the end of every prayer.

So, the Quran only allows war as a means to solve some social problems at a time when tyranny was the sole obstacle in the face of the call for justice.

Cases in Which the Quran Permits Fighting

A. Fighting in Self-Defense:

Upon examining closely the Quranic passages in which God requests Moslems to fight, we find them clarify that war should be a means to drive away aggression and tyranny.

The Quran says:

> Permission is granted to those who are being persecuted, since injustice has befallen them, and God is certainly able to support them. They were evicted from their homes unjustly, for no reason other than saying, "Our Lord is God." If it were not for God's supporting of some people against others, monasteries, churches, synagogues, and mosques - where the name of God is commemorated frequently - would have been destroyed. Absolutely, God supports those who support Him. God is Powerful, Almighty.
> (Quran translation 22: 39 - 40)

As for victorious believers, God says:

> They (the believers) are those who, if We appointed them as rulers on earth, they would establish the regular prayers and the obligatory charity, and would advocate

righteousness and forbid evil. God is the ultimate ruler.
(Quran translation 22:41)

This means, military victory should not lead to expansion or dominance as is the case with colonial regimes, nor should it lead to control over sources of wealth, or to behave arrogantly in the land to raise a race above another. Victorious believers had better 'establish regular prayers' to attain spiritual exaltation by worshipping God, and to purify their spirits. They 'establish the obligatory charity' and thus establish social justice by supporting the right of the needy to live a decent life. They 'advocate righteousness' by spreading benevolence and right among people, and 'forbid evil' by fighting against evil and corruption and uprooting them from society.

B. Fighting in the Cause of God

The Quran commands us to establish justice on earth, and this requires us to stand in the face of injustice and oppression, wherever they may be, and eliminate the source so that they can not take hold of the earth, or enslave people or dominate their welfare, but establish the Word of God on earth, without doubtful intentions. In the Quran, this is called the 'strife in the cause of God' and the 'fight in the cause of God'. The Quran commands:

> *You shall strive for the cause of God as you should strive for His cause....*
> *(Quran translation 22:78)*

> *You shall fight in the cause of God, and know that God is Hearer, Knower.*
> *(Quran translation 2:244)*

The cause of God is the cause of justice. Every fight in the cause and support of freedom is a fight in the cause of God; and every fight to drive away oppression and support the oppressed against the oppressor, or to support right and justice is a fight in the cause of God. Every effort done to attain or protect justice is also done in the cause of God. The Quran demands believers to fight in the cause of God, without any worldly intentions. The following verses, sent down to Muhammad in Medina, clarify the aims of war:

> Those who readily fight in the cause of God are those who forsake this world in favor of the Hereafter. Whoever fights in the cause of God, then gets killed, or attains victory, we will surely grant him a great recompense. Why should you not fight in the cause of God when weak men, women, and children are imploring: "Our Lord, deliver us from this community whose people are oppressive, and be You our Lord and Master."
> (Quran translation 4:74 – 75)

A hint is made here that, in the Quran, war is not for oppressing or enslaving people; it is waged for the cause of God and weak people, like those in Mecca who were persecuted and oppressed by the pagan Meccan. It is the duty of every believer to support people like these and relieve them from oppression, people who no longer have any supporter and thus turn to God for refuge. Then the Quran says:

> Those who believe are fighting for the cause of God, while those who disbelieve are fighting for the cause of tyranny. Therefore, you shall fight the devil's allies; the devil's power is nil.
> (Quran translation 4:76)

Evil means amongst others transgression of limits. Thus when one transgresses limits, behaves arrogantly, enslaves others and deprives them of their rights or of having a share in the riches of the earth, he is said to be fighting 'in the cause of evil' which God criticizes severely. The aim of fighting in the cause of God is to

171

spread Divine Law (which calls for justice and freedom of religion) in the world without there being any selfish intent or arrogance, as God wants the case to be:

> We reserve the abode of the Hereafter for those who do not seek exaltation on earth, nor corruption. The ultimate victory belongs to the righteous.
> (Quran translation 28:83)

Comparison Between the Quran and the International Law Concerning War

The Quran permits war but keeps it within the limits of mercy. The Quran has set down certain rules, the most merciful and considerate to people, and required people to observe them.

Such rules go in line with the principles of international law in many ways, but differ in that they are divine rules legalized through religion and executed through faith.

A. International law determines that the citizens who are not regular members of an army are not considered as fighters, and hence should not be inflicted with harm; only regular soldiers (or armed men/women engaged in a war) are considered as fighters. The Quran agrees on this point, for it says:

> You may fight in the cause of God _against those who attack you_, but do not aggress. God does not love the aggressors.
> (Quran translation 2:190)

It is an act of transgression when believers fight those who do not fight them, people like their enemy's children and wives, as well as their sick, old and clergy – or in other word: civilians.

B. International law forbids killing the wounded, torturing the enemy, destroying them by treachery or deception, or using bombs, missiles or weapons which add to their torture. It also prohibits the poisoning of wells, rivers and foods; it recommends that the corpses of the dead be respected, and prohibits any severity or mayhem be inflicted on them, regardless of the nationality of the dead.

The Quran applies the same principles, for when Muhammad appointed an army or troop leaders, he instructed him to follow the Quranic laws closely, not to be the aggressor or transgress the limits nor make any corruption on the earth.

> ... Do not make corruption in the land...
> (Quran translation 2:11)

C. International law prescribes a number of principles regarding the proper treatment of captives. They should not be killed, injured, ill-treated or humiliated if they surrender or if they are deprived of their freedom. The Quran also urges the kind treatment of captives in general, and God commends the righteous that they treat such people hospitably, saying:

> They (the believers) donate their favorite food to the poor, the orphan, and the captive. "We feed you for the sake of God; we expect no reward from you, nor thanks".
> (Quran 76: 8-9)

The above verse instructs believers to donate their favorite food (not just any food, but their favorite) amongst other to the captives. So clearly torturing captives is out of question.

Those who Seek Protection

Among the principles in the Quran which reveal tolerance toward the enemy in the time of war, is one which allows individuals and groups of the enemy who actively fight against Moslems, to get in touch with Moslems and to reside in Moslem lands under the protection of the Quranic law which is known as the 'Law of Protection'. The Quran ensures the protection of such people and requires Moslems to protect them with all they can afford as long as they are in Moslem territories. It even offers them certain privileges and releases them from certain obligations, which Moslems have to observe.

The purpose of this Law of Protection is to give these people a chance to learn the truth about Islam. In this way, Moslems could effectively spread the message of their faith. The origin of this lies in God's words:

> If one of the idol worshipers sought safe passage with you, you shall grant him safe passage, so that he can hear the word of God, then send him back to his place of security. That is because they are people who do not know. (Quran translation 9:6)

Thus, when they accept the Word, they become Moslems and brethren, and no further question arises. If they do not see their way to accept Islam, they will require double protection: (1) from the Islamic forces openly fighting against their people, and (2) from their own people, as they detached themselves from them. Both kinds of protection should be ensured for them, and they should be safely escorted to a place where they can be safe.

The Quran deals with this point at length and permits the Moslem individuals to protect and settle a covenant with one or a group of non-Moslems. This measure of protection and guarantee on his part is to be respected.

The Quran does not make specific demands regarding such measures, except that which ensures safety to Moslems, like making certain that those under protection have no force or resistance of their own, and that there is no likelihood of a tendency on their part to spread intrigue or spy on Moslems. To this effect, the Quran confirms the right of the leader to annul an individual's right for protection if this annulment be for the general good of Moslems.

Covenants in the Quran

Treaties have always been an important means to strengthen relations and settle disputes peacefully. They are based on mutual confidence between parties, without which peace collapses.

The Quran reserves special respect to treaties and allots to them all possible guarantees, so that we may rise with such treaties above personal desires and passions. Many Quranic verses require believers to abide by their covenants:

> ...You shall fulfill your covenants, for a covenant is a great responsibility.
> (Quran translation 17:34)

In describing the qualities of truthful believers, God says that:

> When it comes to deposits entrusted to them, as well as any agreements (covenant) they make, they are trustworthy.
> (Quran translation 23:8)

In the view of the Quran, refusal to keep up trust is like rejecting the virtues of humanity:

> The worst creatures in the sight of God are those who disbelieved; they cannot believe. You reach agreements with them, but they violate their agreements every time; they are not righteous.
> (Quran translation 8 : 55 – 56)

By honoring covenants with others, the Quran does not mean to gain colonial authority or make stratagems to cheat people so as to attain strength over other nations - but to establish peace:

You shall fulfill your covenant with God when you make such a covenant. You shall not violate the oaths after swearing (by God) to carry them out, for you have made God a guarantor for you. God knows everything you do. Do not be like the knitter who unravels her strong knitting into piles of flimsy yarn. This is your example if you abuse the oaths to take advantage of one another. Whether one group is larger than the other, God thus puts you to the test. He will surely show you on the Day of Resurrection everything you had disputed.
(Quran translation 16: 91 – 92)

The Quran charges Moslems to keep up their covenants, even if it might prevent them from rushing to the support of their brethren who live in a non-Moslem State with whom they have a treaty of mutual alliance. The Quran considers that Moslems, in spite of their different races and nationalities, constitute one Nation, and that every aggression inflicted on one Moslem community is an aggression against the Islamic Nation as a whole. The Quran says:

...However, if they need your help, as brethren in faith, you shall help them, except against people with whom you have signed a peace treaty. God is Seer of everything you do.
(Quran translation 8 : 72)

However, if the opponents violate the terms of the treaty, the Moslems are allowed to fight them:

If they violate their oaths after pledging to keep their covenants, and attack your religion, you may fight the leaders of paganism - you are no longer bound by your covenant with them - which they may refrain.
(Quran translation 9:12)

Now, I know many of you still wonder: what about those suicide bombers, who blow themselves up in public places? Well, these bombers blow themselves without making any investigation about who are going to be killed by their actions. So the answer is plain and simple: they are not true believers, what they are doing is against everything which is taught in the Quran.

> *O you who believe! When you go to war in God's way, make investigation, and do not say to any one who offers you peace: You are not a believer. Do you seek goods of this world's life! But with God there are abundant gains; you too were such before, then God conferred a benefit on you; therefore make investigation; surely God is aware of what you do...*
> *(Quran translation 4:94)*

The next question would probably be what about the rest of Muhammad's wars? To write the history of Islam will make this book too long, beside the fact that I am not a historian. My purpose of writing this book is to find the true guidance of God.

However, it is important to explain about the wars during Muhammad's time in order to explain the rule of war in Islam. On the next few pages I am quoting some words from authors who write about the history of Islam. I also suggest watching an old Hollywood movie called 'The Message' which shows the history of Muhammad, played by Anthony Quinn and Irene Papas.

The following is a short version of Muhammad's history. Coming from a simple family background, Muhammad (re)established and spread the teaching of Islam. At the same time he proved himself as a strong, true and effective leader. Today, more than 13 centuries later, his influence is still strong and deeply rooted.

The Arab Bedouins were tough and brave soldiers. But they were not many and they were always fighting amongst themselves.

Muhammad was the first person in history, due to his strong believes in the One God, who managed to lead this small Arab troop to make extraordinary conquests.

In 622 CE Moslems were only a very small oppressed group in Mecca, and by 740 CE the Moslems territories already cover Persia, Egypt, Syria, Palestine, Turkey and Spain.

Most of us, do not realize that the countries mentioned above were non-Moslems at Muhammad's era and they did not speak Arabic either. Before the advance of Islam, the main religion of the Persians was Zoroastrianism, most Egyptians were Christians (due to the influence of the Greek/Roman rulers), most Syrians were Christians, most Palestinians were Jews or Christians, most Turkish and Spanish were Christians. Today, most of these people are Moslems (except for the Spanish).

So why are many Moslems being oppressed or oppressing others today? It is because many so-called 'Moslems' are not following the true teaching from the Quran any longer.

Moslems did indeed wage many wars, just as the Jews and Christians did both before and after that. After the revelation of the verses with commandment to fight (back), several wars occurred between the Moslems and the pagan Arabs. In none of these wars, however, were the Moslems the inciting party.

Furthermore, the Prophet Muhammad established a secure and peaceful social environment for Moslems and pagans alike by signing the peace agreement of Hudaybiya which conceded to the pagans most of their requests. The parties who violated the terms of the agreement and restarted hostilities were the pagans.

With rapid conversions to Islam, the Islamic armies mustered a great force against the pagan Arabs. However, Muhammad conquered Mecca without bloodshed and in a spirit of tolerance. If he wished, Muhammad could have taken revenge on pagan leaders in the city.

Yet, he did not do harm to any one of them, forgave them and treated them with the utmost tolerance. When they were victorious, the Moslems were commanded not to destroy the churches nor the synagogues, nor to force the people to convert to Islam.

The people were allowed to continue to practice their religion without persecution or being forced to convert. (Compare for example with Numbers 31, and Deuteronomy 20. Also compare with the great Spanish inquisitions).

Muhammad sent eight letters to the neighboring rulers who already had history of oppression and tyranny. While this might seem arrogant, we must understand that as a prophet like any other prophets, Muhammad too had a message to be delivered from God.

If we read the Old Testament we will see that many Jewish prophets also went to war to deliver the same message. Even today, the United States of America and the United Nations become involved to help oppressed nations. Moslems during Muhammad's leadership also did not go to war and force people to embrace Islam nor colonize the countries. All the conquered countries were left to rule their territories under the Islamic law, not Muhammad's law.

TESTIMONY OF SOME WESTERN SCHOLARS ON THE MOSLEM CONQUEST

According Hamilton Gibb author of: Whither Islam

I have always held the religion of Muhammad in high estimation because of its wonderful vitality. It is the only religion which appears to me to possess that assimilating capacity to the changing phase of existence which can make itself appeal to every age. I have studied him - the wonderful man and in my opinion far from being an anti-Christ, he must be called the Savior of Humanity. I believe that if a man like him were to assume the dictatorship of the modern world, he would succeed in solving its problems in a way that would bring it the much needed peace and happiness: I have prophesied about the faith of Muhammad that it would be acceptable to the Europe of tomorrow as it is beginning to be acceptable to the Europe of today.

**According to George Bernard Shaw author of:
The Genuine Islam**

The extinction of race consciousness as between Moslems is one of the outstanding achievements of Islam and in the contemporary world. There is, as it happens, a crying need for the propagation of this Islamic virtue.

According to Sir Thomas W. Arnold the author of: The Preaching of Islam, A History of the Propagation of the Moslem Faith

...of any organized attempt to force the acceptance of Islam on the non-Moslem population, or of any systematic persecution intended to stamp out the Christian religion, we hear nothing. Had the Caliphs (the first 4 Islamic rulers after Muhammad's death) chosen to adopt either course of action, they might have swept away Christianity as easily as Ferdinand and Isabella drove Islam out of Spain, or Louis XIV made Protestantism penal in France, or the Jews were kept out of England for 350 years. The Eastern Churches in Asia were entirely cut off from communion with the rest of Christendom throughout which no one would have been found to lift a finger on their behalf, as heretical communions. So that the very survival of these Churches to the present day is a strong proof of the generally tolerant attitude of Mohammedan governments towards them.

According to The History of Christianity in the Light of Modern Knowledge, A Collective Work, Harcourt Brace and co.
Against unbelievers he (Muhammad) enjoined his followers to undertake a holy warfare, but only when attacked. The earlier Moslem leaders did not try to impose their faith upon other nations.

According to John L. Esposito author of Islam: The Straight Path
Eschewing vengeance and the plunder of conquest, the Prophet instead accepted a settlement, granting amnesty rather than wielding the sword toward his former enemies.

According to from Karen Amstrong author of Muhammad: Prophet of Our Time
Islam has a far better record than either Christianity or Judaism of appreciating other faiths. In Moslem Spain, relations between the three religions of Abraham were uniquely harmonious in medieval Europe. The Christian Byzantines had forbidden Jews from residing in Jerusalem, but when Caliph Umar conquered the city in 638 AD, he invited them to return and was hailed as the precursor of the Messiah.

According to Barnaby Rogerson author of: The Heirs of the Prophet Muhammad
The wars of conquest and the establishment of the Islamic empire after Muhammad's death were not inspired by religious ideology but by pragmatic politics. The idea that Islam should conquer the world was alien to the Quran and there was no attempt to convert Jews or Christians.

According to Dr. Gustav LeBon author of: Civilization of the Arabs
The reader will find, in my treatment of the Arabs' conquests and the reason of their victories, that force was never a factor in the spread of the Quranic teachings, and that the Arabs left

those they had subdued free to exercise their religious beliefs. If it happened that some Christian peoples embraced Islam and adopted Arabic as their language, it was mainly due to the various kinds of justice on the part of the Arab victors, with the like of which the non-Moslems were not acquainted. It was also due to the tolerance and leniency of Islam, which was unknown to the other religions.

The mercy and tolerance of the conquerors were among the reasons for the spread of their conquests and for the nations' adoptions of their Faith and regulations and language, which because deeply rooted, resisted all sorts of attack and remained even after the disappearance of the Arabs' control on the world stage, though historians deny the fact. Egypt is the most evident proof of this. It adopted what the Arabs had brought over, and reserved it. Conquerors before the Arabs - the Persians, Greeks and Byzantines - could not overthrow the ancient Pharaoh civilization and impose what they had brought instead.

A few impartial European scholars, who are well-versed in the history of the Arabs, do confirm this tolerance. Robertson, in his book 'Biography of Charlequin', says that the Moslems alone were the ones who joined between Jihad and tolerance toward the followers of other faiths whom they had subdued, leaving to them the freedom to perform their religious rites.

According to Michel Michaud author of: History of the Crusades Islam, besides calling for Jihad, reveals tolerance toward the followers of other religions. It released the patriarchs, priests and their servants from the obligations of taxes. It prohibited, in special, the killing of priests for their performance of worship, and Omar Ibn Al-Khattab did not inflict harm on the Christians when he entered Jerusalem as a conqueror. The Crusades, however, did slay Moslems and burn the Jews when they entered the city.

According to Count de Castri author of:
Islam - Impressions and Studies

After the Arabs yielded to, and believed in the Quran, and people received enlightenment through the True Religion, the Moslems appeared with a new show to the peoples of the earth, with conciliation and treatment on basis of free thinking and belief. The Quranic verses then succeeded one another, calling on kind treatment, after those verses in which warnings had been addressed to the heretic tribes.

Such were the instructions of the Apostle after the Arabs had embraced Islam, and the Caliphs who succeeded Muhammad followed his example. This makes me say with Robertson that the people of Muhammad were the only ones who combined kindness to others and the pleasure of seeing their Faith spread. It was this affection that pushed the Arabs on the way of conquest. The Quranic spread its wings behind its victorious troops that invaded Syria and moved on like a thunderbolt to North Africa, from the Red Sea to the Atlantic, without leaving a trace of tyranny on the way, except what is inescapable in every war, and never did they massacre a nation who rejected Islam.

The spread of Islam and the submission to its authority seem to have another reason in the continents of Asia and North Africa. It was the despotism of Constantinople which exercised extreme tyranny, and the injustice of rulers was too much for people to bear. Islam was never imposed by sword or by force, but it got into the hearts of people out of longing and free will, due to the talents of stimulation and captivation of people's hearts, lodged in the Quran.

Many historians admit that the spread of Islam among the Christians of the Eastern Churches was mainly due to a feeling of dissatisfaction that arose from the doctrinal sophistry which the Hellenistic spirit brought over to Christian theology. It was also due to the abundance of good that such Eastern Christians

183

found in Islam, and due to its ability to rescue them from the disorder they were struggling in. In Caetani, for instance, one reads, "*Known for its preference of simple and plain views, the East suffered, religiously, a great deal from the evil consequences of the Hellenistic culture which turned the refined teachings of Christ into an ideology rampant with complicated doctrines and doubts. This led to the rise of a feeling of despair, and even shook the very foundations of religious belief. When, at last, news suddenly came from the desert of the New Revelation, such Eastern Christianity, being torn by inner splits, was shattered.*"

"*Its foundations were shaken, and, due to such doubts, the clergy of the church were taken by despair. Christianity was incapable, after this, of resisting the appeals of the New Faith which eliminated, with a mighty blow, all the trivial doubts and offered graceful, positive qualities in addition to its doubtless, simple and plain principles. It was then that the East forsakes Christ and threw itself into the lap of the Prophet of Arabs*".

According to Napoleon Bonaparte – founder of the French Empire (1769 – 1821)

Author Cherfil in his book 'Bonaparte et L'Islam' page 105 quoted Napoleon's words as follows: "*Moses explained the existent of God to his people, Jesus to the Romans and Muhammad to the whole world 6 centuries after Jesus. The Arabs were pagans when Muhammad introduced the worship to the God that is worshipped by Abraham, Ismaeel, Moses and Jesus. However, the sect of Arius and other Christian sects disturbed the harmony of the East with teachings of the characteristic of God the Father, God the Son and the Holy Spirit, meanwhile Muhammad said: " There is no other God than God who has no father, no child and that Trinity is a mislead teaching." Muhammad was a royalty who unite all the warriors. In just a few years the Moslems were able to conquer half of the earth globe. They have saved more souls and destroyed the pagan gods and altars in 15 years more than what Moses and Jesus followers ever could in 15 centuries. Muhammad was a great man. Should the revolution that he started was not prepared by circumstances; he would surely be seen as a god."*

According to Goethe – German philosopher (1794 – 1832)
Muhammad rose and called the Arabs to monotheism. With that religion he intended to awaken a race in Asia and Africa. Beside that he also intended to break the primitive paganism that has imprisoned mankind. Muhammad awakens the Persian Empire who was fallen asleep, repented the Eastern Roman Empire so that they will stop having arguments that divided because of hypothesis of Greek philosophy.

It is undeniable that all the Prophets of the world have powers to bring goodness for mankind, like sunshine, rain and wind that revive the dry earth into green earth. We should acknowledge their prophet hood. The prove of their goodness can be seen by the fact that they all lived in faith, peaceful and harmonious soul, with passion and strong will, devoted and patience through all kind of diversity, strong against the mental corruption and the decreased moral of the people.

They believe that these will disappear when we fight against the corruption and do daily prayers. If all that is taught in Islam, then by definition we are all Moslems.

Michael H. Hart author of: The 100, a Ranking of the Most Influential Persons in History
In his book Michael Hart ranks Muhammad as the number 1 most influential person in history. He wrote that: *"Muhammad was the only person in history who has managed to reach extraordinary success in the sense of religion and humanity."*

JIHAD IN ISLAM
A word which is often heard and associated with the acts of certain individuals, claiming to act in the name of Islam, is the Arabic word: Jihad. Its significance plays an extremely crucial

role in the image of Islam. But what does this so widely known word mean?

Jihad has a great significance in the lives of Moslems. Like any language, Arabic has unique words which have a particular meaning which cannot be translated precisely. The best translation known for such a word is the following: a sincere and noticeable effort (for good); an all true and unselfish striving for spiritual good.

Jihad as presented in the Quran implies the striving of spiritual good. This Jihad particularly involves change in one's self and mentality. It may concern the sacrifice of material property, social class and even emotional comfort solely for the salvation and worship of God alone.

Examples of this Jihad would be to exceed in the sincere act of good deeds, to worship God alone, to study the scripture in detail, to help the poor and the orphans, to stand for people's right for freedom, to work honestly and support the family, to be equitable, never bear witness to false testimony, frequent and stay in good terms with friends and neighbors, and the restraining of the doing of sins (stealing, lying, cheating, adultery, insulting people and gossiping, etc). Jihad emphasizes on the individual. Jihad also includes the striving and establishing of justice. Before one can strive for justice in his/her community, justice must be one of his/her main religious and moral principles. Apart from that, Jihad may also reflect the war aspects in Islam. The fighting of a war in the name of justice, to deter an aggressor, for self defense, and/or to establish justice and freedom to practice religion , would also be considered a Jihad .

> You shall strive (jihad) for the cause of God as you should
> strive for His cause...
> (Quran translation 22:78)

The previous Quranic verse incites man to strive, in the cause of God. The cause of God is justice for all.

> O you who believe, you shall be absolutely equitable, and observe God when you serve as witnesses, even against yourselves, or your parents, or your relatives. Whether the accused is rich or poor, God takes care of both. Therefore, do not be biased by your personal wishes. If you deviate or disregard (this commandment), then God is fully Cognizant of everything you do."
> (Quran translation 4:135)

Since this verse shows that God accepts only justice, fighting in the name of God is fighting in the name of justice. But, contrary to many people's interpretation, Jihad is anything but a holy war, the media and public misunderstand this.

Professor Tariq Ramadan who studied Islam at the University of Geneva and al-Azhar University in Cairo and is currently senior research fellow at St Antony's College, Oxford – makes clear that Muhammad did not shun non-Moslems as 'unbelievers' but from the beginning co-operated with them in the pursuit of the common good. Islam was not a closed system at variance with other traditions. Muhammad insisted that relations between the different groups must be egalitarian. Even warfare must not obviate the primary duty of justice and respect.

When the Moslems were forced to leave Mecca due to persecution by the Meccan establishment, Ramadan shows, they had to adapt to the alien customs of their new home in Medina, where, for example, women enjoyed more freedom than in Mecca. The Hijrah (the Moslems migration from Mecca to Medina) was a test of intelligence, the emigrants had to recognize that some of their customs were cultural rather than religious, and had to learn foreign practices.

Ramadan also makes it clear that, in the Quran, Jihad was not synonymous with 'holy war'. The verb Jihad should rather be translated: 'making an effort'. The first time the word is used in the Quran, it signified a 'resistance to oppression' (25:26) that was intellectual and spiritual rather than militant. Moslems were required to oppose the lies and terror of those who were motivated solely by self-interest, they had to be patient and enduring.

Only after the migration, when they encountered the enmity of Mecca, did the word Jihad take connotations of self-defense and armed resistance in the face of military aggression. Even so, in mainstream Moslem tradition, the greatest Jihad is not warfare but reform of one's own society and heart, as Muhammad explained to one of his companions, the true Jihad was an inner struggle against egotism. In the light and essence of Islam and the Quran, there is no war which is holy, under any circumstances whatsoever. In fact the whole text of the Quran and the religion of Islam revolve around the concept of peace, not war. Islam is also a word that shares the same root of the Arabic word Salaam meaning peace. The term 'holy war' has never been mentioned in the Quran. War is unholy, thus, Jihad must mean anything but holy war. And the way of Jihad has various ends..

> Your striving (jihad) is most surely (directed to) various (ends).
> (Quran translation 92:4)

CHAPTER EIGHT

EYE FOR EYE, TOOTH FOR TOOTH

*L*et us now analyze the punishment system in the three religions. According to the Old Testament the crimes that would be punished by death in the **Old Testament** are the following:

> *He that smiteth a man, so that he die, shall be surely put to death. And if a man lie not in wait, but God deliver him into his hand; then I will appoint thee a place whither he shall flee. But if a man come presumptuously upon his neighbour, to slay him with guile; thou shalt take him from mine altar ,that he may die. And he that smiteth his father, or his mother, shall be surely put to death. And he that stealeth a man, and selleth him, or if he be found in his hand, he shall surely be put to death. And he that curseth his father, or his mother, shall surely be put to death.*
> *(OT: Exodus 21: 12 –1 7)*

> *If a man be found lying with a woman married to an husband, then they shall both of them die, both the man that lay with the woman, and the woman: so shalt thou put away evil from Israel.*
> *(OT: Deuteronomy 22:22)*

Thus, according to the Old Testament the crimes that are punishable by death are: killing, striking and cursing the parents, slavery and adultery. In the following verses are some more crimes that are punishable by stoning to death:

If a bull gores a man or a woman to death, the bull must be stoned to death, and its meat must not be eaten. But the owner of the bull will not be held responsible. If, however, the bull has had the habit of goring and the owner has been warned but has not kept it penned up and it kills a man or woman, the bull must be stoned and the owner also must be put to death.
(OT: Exodus 21: 28 – 29)

Say to the Israelites: 'Any Israelite or any alien living in Israel who gives any of his children to Molech must be put to death. The people of the community are to stone him.
(OT: Leviticus 20:2)

A man or woman who is a medium or spiritist among you must be put to death. You are to stone them; their blood will be on their own heads.
(OT: Leviticus 20:27)

Anyone who blasphemes the name of the LORD must be put to death. The entire assembly must stone him. Whether an alien or native-born, when he blasphemes the Name, he must be put to death.
(OT: Leviticus 24:16)

So the assembly took him (a man who gathered sticks on Sabbath day) outside the camp and stoned him to death, as the Lord commanded Moses.
(OT: Numbers 15:36)
Stone him to death, because he (fake prophet) tried to

turn you away from the Lord your God, who brought you
out of Egypt, out of the land of slavery.
(OT: Deuteronomy 13:10)

Take the man or woman who has done this evil deed to
your city gate (i.e. idolatrous) and stone that person to
death.
(OT: Deuteronomy 17:5)

Then all the men of his town shall stone him (for gluttony
and drunkard) to death. You must purge the evil from
among you. All Israel will hear of it and be afraid.
(OT: Deuteronomy 21:21)

There are a few more crimes that are punishable by stoning to death mention in the Old Testament. When the first time I read the above verses I was shocked. Please try to understand that I am not writing this to judge people of certain races. I just want to find the truth and share it with you. I believe in One God and I want to know His true guidance for us. I think: people are just the same every where in the world. There are ignorant people in every race as there are rational people in every race. Apparently stoning to death is an ancient punishment which is done by many races – especially amongst the Semitic race. Although, there is also evidence this was done in ancient Greece.

Stoning to death is a very cruel way of punishment. I always feel sick to the stomach whenever I hear about it. So I was really surprised to find out how many verses concerning stoning to death are in the Old Testament.

I have read in the Internet that this punishment is still executed in the Jewish community, but I hear and read more frequently in the media concerning this method of execution amongst the so-called Moslem society. Islam has been accused by non-Moslems (especially in the West) amongst other because of this kind of harsh punishment. So I am even more surprised to found out that: stoning to death is not mentioned anywhere in the Quran!

So how come? Well, as I have just stated above, it is because it is an ancient Semitic tradition. And apparently, tradition is hard to die – even though it is not taught by the Quran.

So now let's see what the **New Testament** say how to deal with evil person – since the New Testament does not talk about any death punishment at all:

> But I (Jesus) tell you, do not resist an evil person. If someone strikes you on the right cheek, turn to him the other also.
> (NT: Matthew 5:39)

> If someone strikes you on one cheek, turn to him the other also. If someone takes your cloak, do not stop him from taking your tunic.
> (NT: Luke 6: 29)

Now, I wish we could all live the way it is taught in the New Testament. Although realistically speaking this is almost impossible to do. And besides that, is it truly wise to be so passive against injustice this way? Crime needs to be punished (or reformed, to be more precise) in order to prevent its re-occurrence. Even the most 'civilized' country in the world would never use this law of 'kindness' which is taught by the New Testament. Not even in countries where the majority of the populations are Christians.

Here, again the teachings of the Old and New Testament are extremely different. So once again, I think the following punishment from the **Quran** makes more sense and just:

O you who believe! Retaliation is prescribed for you in the matter of the slain, the free for the free, and the slave for the slave, and the female for the female, but if any remission is made to any one by his (aggrieved) brother, then prosecution (for the blood wit) should be made according to usage, and payment should be made to him in a good manner; this is an alieviation from your Lord and a mercy; so whoever exceeds the limit after this he shall have a painful chastisement.
(Quran translation 2:178)

Thus, retaliation is permitted, but we have the choice to forgive as well (remission). Isn't this the law that is applied by the 'civilized countries' today? Let us analyze this rule on a more personal level.

Just imagine (God forbid) someone in our family got killed. Would we stone the killer to death? Maybe we might feel like doing that, but most likely we would rather the killer receive death penalty in a different way, right? I don't think we would feel treated fairly if we are not allowed to retaliate though. Would we offer another family member to be killed or harmed? That's just insane!

OK, let's say we decide to forgive the killer. Would we feel good if we just let the killer go unpunished? Don't you think it is dangerous for the society if we leave such behavior unsanctioned? What if the one who is killed was the bread winner of the family? Surely receiving an amount of money for the pain and injustice that have been inflicted to our family member is the least what we may expect.

And notice that the Quranic law mandates the same rule for free man, woman as well as for slaves. Before we discuss further concerning slavery in general, let's first compare the above verse of the Quran to the unfair treatment for a slave in the Old Testament:

If a man beats his male or female slave with a rod and the slave dies as a direct result, he must be punished, but he is not to be punished if the slave gets up after a day or two, since the slave is his property.
(OT: Exodus 21:20-21)

Now let's see what the punishment for adultery is:

In the Old Testament

If any man take a wife, and go in unto her, and hate her, and give occasions of speech against her, and bring up an evil name upon her, and say, I took this woman, and when I came to her, I found her not a maid: then shall the father of the damsel, and her mother, take and bring forth the tokens of the damsel's virginity unto the elders of the city in the gate: and the damsel's father shall say unto the elders, I gave my daughter unto this man to wife, and he hateth her; and, lo, he hath given occasions of speech against her, saying, I found not thy daughter a maid; and yet these are the tokens of my daughter's virginity.

And they shall spread the cloth before the elders of the city. And the elders of that city shall take that man and chastise him; and they shall amerce him in an hundred shekels of silver, and give them unto the father of the damsel, because he hath brought up an evil name upon a virgin of Israel: and she shall be his wife; he may not put her away all his days.

But if this thing be true, and the tokens of virginity be not found for the damsel: then they shall bring out the damsel to the door of her father's house, and the men of her city shall stone her with stones that she die: because she hath wrought folly in Israel, to play the whore in her father's house: so shalt thou put evil away from among you.

If a man be found lying with a woman married to an husband, then they shall both of them die, both the man that lay with the woman, and the woman: so shalt thou put away evil from Israel.

If a damsel that is a virgin be betrothed unto an husband, and a man find her in the city, and lie with her; then ye shall bring them both out unto the gate of that city, and ye shall stone them with stones that they die; the damsel, because she cried not, being in the city; and the man, because he hath humbled his neighbour's wife: so thou shalt put away evil from among you.

But if a man find a betrothed damsel in the field, and the man force her, and lie with her: then the man only that lay with her shall die. But unto the damsel thou shalt do nothing; there is in the damsel no sin worthy of death: for as when a man riseth against his neighbour, and slayeth him, even so is this matter: for he found her in the field, and the betrothed damsel cried, and there was none to save her.

If a man find a damsel that is a virgin, which is not betrothed, and lay hold on her, and lie with her, and they be found; then the man that lay with her shall give unto the damsel's father fifty shekels of silver, and she shall be his wife; because he hath humbled her, he may not put her away all his days.

(OT: Deuteronomy 22:13 – 29)

In the New Testament

You have heard that it was said, 'Do not commit adultery.' But I tell you that anyone who looks at a woman lustfully has already committed adultery with her in his heart.

(NT: Matthew 5:27 - 28)

If your right eye causes you to sin, gouge it out and throw it away. It is better for you to lose one part of your body than for your whole body to be thrown into hell.

(NT: Matthew 5 : 29)

But, the New Testament also says:

> And the scribes and Pharisees brought unto him a woman taken in adultery; And when they had set her in the midst, they say unto him, Master, this woman was taken in adultery, in the very act. Now Moses in the law commanded us, that such should be stoned: but what sayest thou? This they said, tempting him, that they might have to accuse him. But Jesus stooped down, and with his finger wrote on the ground, as though he heard them not. So when they continued asking him, he lifted up himself, and said unto them, He that is without sin among you, let him first cast a stone at her. And again he stooped down, and wrote on the ground. And they which heard it, being convicted by their own conscience, went out one by one, beginning at the eldest, even unto the last: and Jesus was left alone, and the woman standing in the midst.
> When Jesus had lifted up himself, and saw none but the woman, he said unto her, Woman, where are those thine accusers? Hath no man condemned thee? She said, No man, Lord. And Jesus said unto her, Neither do I condemn thee: go, and sin no more.
> (NT: John 8: 3 – 11)

In the Quran

> (As for) the fornicators and the fornicator, flog each of them, (giving) a hundred stripes, and let not pity for them detain you in the matter of obedience to God, if you believe in God and the last day, and let a party of believers witness their chastisement.
> The fornicator shall not marry any but a fornicators or idolatress, and (as for) the fornicators, none shall marry her but a fornicator or an idolater; and it is forbidden to the believers.
> And those who accuse free women then do not bring four witnesses, flog them, (giving) eighty stripes, and do

not admit any evidence from them ever; and these it is
that are the transgressors, except those who repent after
this and act aright, for surely God is Forgiving, Merciful.
And (as for) those who accuse their wives and have no
witnesses except themselves, the evidence of one of
these (should be taken) four times, bearing God to witness
that he is most surely of the truthful ones.
(Quran translation 24: 2 – 6)

Now let's analyze which of the above theological law is most sensible and just. Again I am not talking about what is being practiced today. I am aware that there is a great deal of cruelty and injustice happening out there. But right now we are analyzing the scriptures, not the current practice.

Most of the time, when we hear someone being punished, especially if it is 'too' cruel in our eyes and also in the name of religion, we tend to judge the religion instead of looking at why that religion imposes such punishment.

Let's position ourselves as the cheated party. If you are a man, imagine that your wife sleeps with another man, vice versa if you are a woman. Being cheated by our spouses must be one of the most painful experiences in life. It doesn't only destroy the trust, but also our self-esteem not to mention the disgust, jealousy, humiliation and the damage that maybe caused by such action to the whole family (i.e. children if there are any). So now... how would we want justice to be done in such a case?

The Old Testament's jurisdiction for adultery is stoning to death. Well, once again.. too cruel. Some of us would probably want our partner who cheats on us to die, but in fact we don't really want that to happen, right... especially not by stoning to death.

The New Testament presents mixed messages. According to John the adulterer is to be left unpunished, repenting is enough. But according to Matthew ... well, I think this is a little bit too strict, because looking lustfully is already considered as committing adultery. Especially since the punishment of the eyes that cause us to sin is to pluck them out. And that has to be done by the crime doer himself/herself. I think the chance that it would happen is practically none.

The Quran way... well, at least it is not death sentence. I don't like this idea either... but then again justice has nothing to do with liking or not. Flogging is painful, but so is being cheated. Then again, the pain of being flogged will go away; meanwhile the pain of being cheated might not go away forever. Why does the punishment have to be witnessed? The reason is most likely due to a psychological reason.

Since the Quran does not mention how hard the flogging has to be done, some Moslem scholars argue that the flogging is only to be done symbolically (not too hard), because the main purpose of such punishment is to stop the person from doing it again – therefore the witness is mentioned here.

Psychologically, the most efficient way to stop a compulsive cheater is by applying social pressure and scandalizing the crime. The Quran is more elaborate on this rule. A crime of adultery can be very damaging for many parties, therefore the accusation of such action is also explained in detail in the Quran. Many families are broken because of adultery. Since family is the core of society then the accusation of adultery should not be taken lightly either. The Quran gives redemption for the punishment – if the crime doer repents, then God will forgive him/her.

Personally, I still think that flogging sounds harsh, but I am kind of forced to admit that it is probably the most just way. Even in the West today, where corporeal punishment is not enforced any longer, I am not surprised if 'crime of passion' is still tolerated by many people. A crime of passion, refers to a crime in which the perpetrator commits a crime, especially assault or murder, against a spouse or other loved one because of sudden strong impulse such as a jealous rage or heartbreak rather than as a premeditated crime. In the United States civil courts, a crime of passion is referred to as temporary insanity. In some countries, notably France, *crime passionel* (or crime of passion) was a valid defense during murder cases; during the 19th century.

So which of the three religious punishments for adultery is most fair? Punishment by death, pluck the eyes out (or something even more private) or being flogged? I dislike them all equally... but justice is justice. And...

> *.. it may be that you dislike something in which God has placed a great deal of good.*
> *(Quran translation 4:19)*

STEALING

Stealing is another crime that is condemned by all the monotheist religions – actually by all laws of the world. Now let's analyze this one:

In the Old Testament

> *If the theft be certainly found in his hand alive, whether it be ox, or ass, or sheep; he shall restore double. If a man shall cause a field or vineyard to be eaten, and shall put in his beast, and shall feed in another man's field; of the best of his own field, and of the best of his own vineyard, shall he make restitution.*
> *(OT: Exodus 22:3-4)*

In the New Testament

> *Jesus replied, " 'Do not murder, do not commit adultery, do not steal, do not give false testimony, honor your father and mother,' and 'love your neighbor as yourself."*
> *(NT: Matthew 19:19)*

And if your right hand causes you to sin, cut it off and throw it away. It is better for you to lose one part of your body than for your whole body to go into hell.
(NT: Matthew 5:30)

In the Quran

And (as for) the man who steals and the woman who steals, cut their hands as a punishment for what they have earned, an exemplary punishment from God; and God is Mighty, Wise. But whoever repents after his iniquity and reforms (himself), then surely God will turn to him (mercifully); surely God is Forgiving, Merciful.
(Quran translation 5: 38 – 39)

The punishment for stealing according to the Old Testament is quite elaborate, I hope that the above verses that I quote is enough to represent the basic rule.

So far, the Old Testament has been the harshest during our comparison study concerning the punishment systems between the three monotheistic books. But it is not so concerning the punishment system for stealing. According to the Old Testament the punishment (basically) is to pay back the same value of the stolen good or double of it.

Surprisingly enough the punishments for stealing according to the New Testament and the Quran sounds very similar, which is to cut the hand. This sounds very cruel, doesn't it? I was really surprised when I first read this punishment in the New Testament. Although most non-Moslem do not know much about Islam, most of them know about this punishment in Islam and strongly condemn it. Ironically, actually this punishment is also mentioned in the New Testament.

There is a 'slight' difference, however, between the punishment of stealing in the New Testament and the Quran. According to the

New Testament it is cutting of the hand (and throwing it away). According to the Quran is also cutting the hand, unless the thief repents. Now how do we know when someone repents and really reforms after a crime? I think that means this punishment should be applied when the person commits the same crime again.

Once again, personally I think this is too harsh. Until one day I watched an English talk show program 'Kilroy'... he invited many victims of robbery to attend one of his shows. These are all 'civilized' English people. I could not believe my ears when a few of them actually suggested that the punishment of stealing (robbery) should be cutting off the hands, so that way the thief (robber) can not do the crime again. They explained how devastating it is to be robbed in their own houses. For some, the fear and violation of privacy cannot be restored even after the crime doer is convicted to jail. Some of the victims cannot get back their sense of security for many years.

Well, I guess we don't know how we would react or feel until something like this happens to ourselves. But then again, what if the thief is only stealing a piece of bread? Or even stealing a hundred dollars from us? Is it justified to cut his or her hands off for that?

Now, the Old Testament, the New Testament and the Quran also mentioned the Law of Equivalence.

According to the Old Testament

> Eye for eye, tooth for tooth, hand for hand, foot for foot. Burning for burning, wound for wound, stripe for stripe. And if a man smite the eye of his servant, or the eye of his maid, that it perish; he shall let him go free for his eye's sake. And if he smite out his manservant's tooth, or his maidservant's tooth; he shall let him go free for his tooth's sake.
> (OT: Exodus 21: 24 – 27)

201

According to the New Testament

Ye have heard that it hath been said, An eye for an eye, and a tooth for a tooth: But I say unto you, That ye resist not evil: but whosoever shall smite thee on thy right cheek, turn to him the other also.
(Matthew 5: 38 – 39)

According to the Quran

And we decreed for them in it that: the life for the life, the eye for the eye, the nose for the nose, the ear for the ear, the tooth for the tooth, and an equivalent injury for any injury. If one forfeits what is due to him as a charity, it will atone for his sins. Those who do not rule in accordance with God's revelations are the unjust.
(Quran translation 5:45)

This is probably the best example to see how the three scriptures could teach exactly the same teaching, down to the words... and yet, the details are different.

The Old Testament teaches the Law of Equivalence for everyone, except for slaves. The New Testament teaches us to ignore the Law of Equivalence, just give in and more. The Quran teaches us that the Law of Equivalence is valid, unless the victim decides to forgive.

Now, let's combine the above rule with the punishment system of stealing. There are some scholars who explain that the Quran does not mean the cutting of the hand by chopping it off. I agree with this argumentation, because I don't think that it is fair if the thief is only stealing a piece of bread out of hunger. Meanwhile, the Law of Equivalence in the Quran is clear about being fair.

So what could cut the hand means besides chopping it off? There is another verse in the Quran that talks about cutting the hand (this story is not told in the Old Testament) – the following verse is the story of Josef when he was sold as a slave to an Egyptian man and then the Egyptian man's wife tried to seduce him. After failing, she tried to defend herself by showing to her friends how irresistible was Josef, that she could not restrain herself. So she prepared a meal and gave each of her friends a knife and asked Josef to appear in front of them. And when the women saw Josef, they cut their hands out of amazement because of his good look.

> So when she (the Egyptian master's wife) heard of their sly talk she sent for them and prepared for them a repast, and gave each of them a knife, and said (to Josef): Come forth to them. So when they saw him, they deemed him great, and <u>cut their hands</u> (in amazement), and said: Remote is God (from imperfection); this is not a mortal; this is but a noble angel.
> (Quran translation 12:31)

From the above verse we can clearly see that cutting the hand doesn't mean to chop it off. No one who is sane would do something like that to themselves. So what they did was cutting but not deep, more like leaving a scar on their hands.

This theory is supported by the use of the mathematical coding of the Quran. In chapter 6: The Intelligent Language of the Universe - we have learned that the Quran uses same numbers whenever referring to two verses which are related to one another. Now, the verse that talks about the punishment of cutting (as in marking, not severing) the hand of a thief is stated in 5:38. The surah (chapter) and the verse numbers add up to 5+38 = **43**. The other place in the Quran where 'the hand is cut' is found in 12:31. This is where we read how the women who admired Joseph 'cut' their hands. Obviously, they did not sever their hands; no one would do that. The surah and verse numbers add up to 12+31=**43**, the same total as in 5:38.

This gives mathematical confirmation that the Quranic law calls for marking the hand of the thief, not severing it. According to the Law of Equivalence in the Quranic criminal justice, the thief who is convicted of stealing a hundred dollars from you must work for you until you are fully paid for the hundred dollars you lost plus any other damage and inconvenience that theft may have caused you. And the thief's hand will be cut (marked) if the thief does not repent. So again; the main punishment is not to torture but rather to put social pressure on the criminal.

The above reasoning, however, may not be applied when we follow the rule in the New Testament. The punishment for theft can not be 'adjusted' accordingly. Since the New Testament says 'cut it (the hand) off and throw it away'. There is no space for argument here. We would have to choose between cutting the hand (and throw it away) or ignore the crime all together.

⎯ᴏ✶ᴏ⎯

Once again, the Quran has proven that it is wise in its teaching on every level of human's aspect. So how come the punishment in the so-called Islamic countries today is so cruel? It's because mankind tends to transgress.

Sometimes we judge things rashly without understanding the reasoning behind it. Let me give another example: the Old Testament and the Quran teach us the 'halal' or 'kosher' way to slaughter animal for eating purpose, which is by slicing the jugular vein with a sharp knife.

Let's see the explanation of Wikipedia Encyclopedia concerning jugular vein.

The jugular veins are veins in the neck, carrying blood from the head. There are external and internal jugular veins. The internal jugular vein provides venous drainage for the contents of the skull.

204

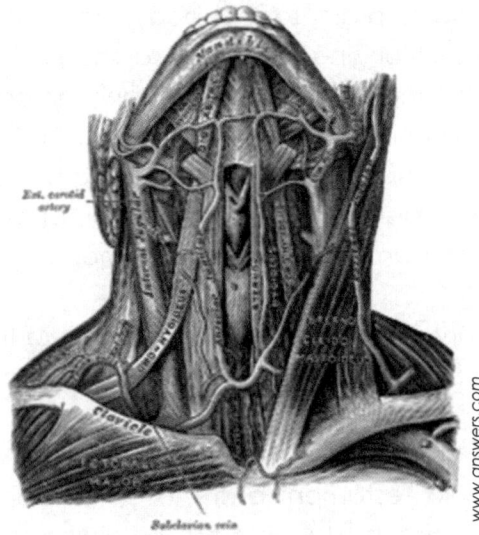

Vena Jugularis

The jugular vein is the major point of damage when performing Jigai, a traditional way for Japanese women to commit suicide. This method was most commonly used because of its quick, painless, and certain outcome. The jugular is stereotypically what dogs and other animals are thought to go after with the intent of killing another animal, it will incapacitate the opponent with little effort.

It is also the Islamic method of slaughtering animals. Moslems traditionally pronounce "God is Great" before pulling a sharpened blade from a concealed place, and then slicing through both veins in the neck, as this numbs creatures and brings about instant death. The resulting halal (allowed) meat is made from the animal to consume after all the blood is drained from the openings. Jews also slaughter animals through the jugular vein; the result is called 'kosher' meat.

In regular Western slaughter houses the animal is given an electrical shock (stunned) on the head to make it unconscious. It is then slaughtered. The animal is then temporarily left alone to allow the blood to drain from its body. From there, the meat is then processed. Stunning (by electrical shot) affects the central nervous system and as a result many animals can die from the effect of the stunning. In this process, most of the blood will still remain in the animal's body. The remaining blood in the animal is a source of fermentation and destruction of meat quality. This means bacteria can grow easily on the meat.

On the contrary, if an animal is slaughtered via the jugular vein, the central nervous system works properly and the entire animal's blood will be allowed to drain.

Why do the Old Testament and the Quran command us only to eat meat which is slaughtered by slitting the jugular vein? Because, although slaughtering animals by slicing the throat (jugular vein) seems cruel, actually it is more compassionate towards the animal and healthier for human consumption.

And of course, God is the only one who knows what is best for His creatures although sometimes we might think that we know better.

While we are at the topic of jugular vein, I would like to get back to a verse that I have quoted on the chapter concerning war. The following verse is one of the verses that had been quoted in the recent controversial film 'Fitna' made by the Dutch parliamentarian Geert Wilders. 'Fitna' is an Arabic term used to describe 'disagreement and division among people' or a 'test of faith in times of trial'. In the chapter concerning war, I did not quote the full verse, therefore I put (...) 3 dots at the end of it. I purposely did that because it will lead us to a great misunderstanding before we discuss about the jugular vein. So here is the full verse:

> Recall that your Lord inspired the angels: "I am with you;
> so support those who believed. I will throw terror into the

hearts of those who disbelieved. <u>You may strike them above the necks, and you may strike even every finger.</u>"
(Quran translation 8:12)

Wow! What a scary verse, huh.. Well, we need to look deeper to understand the humanitarian reasoning behind this verse. First of all, this is a promise from God to the believers that during a war against evil one should never be discouraged because God is on our side. Even when we are outnumbered (remember, this verse came down during the Badr battle where the Moslems where outnumbered by far against the Quraisy). Actually, this message goes for every aspect in our lives. It tells us not to be discouraged when facing obstacles in life, when we know that we are doing the right thing.

Secondly, we have to remember that the purpose of a war is to eliminate evil. So there are two ways of doing it: kill the enemy, but kill compassionately... therefore the commandment of striking above the neck. As cruel as it sounds, killing through the neck (i.e. jugular vein) is the least painful and quick way of death. This means in modern terms, during a war we should only use weapons that ensure quick death instead of prolong torture. Unfortunately, today we also use weapons that do not kill people instantly, this is a torture.

The other option, if we intent not to kill, but only to paralyze the enemy to disable them to fight against us any longer... then choose a way which is less cruel. Nobody can use any weapon when the fingers are struck. It does sound scary, but this is after all a law during war.

———❂———

Now, back to the punishment system.. in most countries today the above mentioned punishments for adultery and stealing are not practiced. Although, we know through the media in some Islamic

Middle Eastern countries, strangely the punishment from the Old and the New Testaments are executed (i.e.: stoning to death for adultery and chopping off the hands for theft). I don't know how it is in other so-called Islamic countries, but in Indonesia adultery is left unpunished and stealing is punished by jail sentence, like in most Western countries.

Physical punishments seem harsh, but physical punishment last shorter in duration than a spell in prison. Physical punishment and social pressure will most likely also have more constructive impact on the criminal rather then imprisonment. Apart from that, physical punishments do not take the freedom of a person.

Is the prison system really the wisest way to deal with crime? Look at any Hollywood movies concerning prisoners. Most of the prisoners are not reformed; in fact they just make better links in the prison and become even more criminal minded in order to survive in jail and in the outside world after they are released.

And where does the money come from to provide for prisoners? Tax money from you and me. Is it fair that we have to pay and support their needs, since they cannot earn money themselves? Why do we have to pay for the crimes that they committed? And also, if the thief that steals a hundred dollars from us is put in prison, what do we get? And if the thief has a wife and children, why should they also be punished? By putting the thief in prison, the whole family would be deprived of their father and most likely the financial support from the father who is in jail. This is not a wise way to reform a criminal, instead it is just putting a burden on the society.

Today almost every country in the world applies the prison system. So let's see, is prison system truly the wisest way to punish/rehabilitate crime? The following text is from an American Harvard student:

THE PRISON DILEMMA
America's Penal System Makes a Mockery of Democracy

By Roopal Patel and Peter McMurray

How ignorant are we at Harvard? If we were to ask the host of recommendation-writing teachers, employers, and community leaders who helped get us here, we would hear a flattering chorus of affirmation: we are the best (except CalTech), the brightest, the richest, blah, blah, blah. We've heard it all before. But what if we asked our neighbors right here in Cambridge? A conversation with the average Harvard Square denizen-a random Pit kid, homeless person, or cab driver-would quickly reveal some of the deficiencies in our education. Most of us (myself most certainly included) probably don't have a clue about the 'real world' of poverty, crime, and homelessness that surrounds our secluded lives. Maybe our so-called 'liberal education' isn't quite liberal enough. Among the many deficiencies of our education, one of the most grievous is that of America's current situation regarding prison systems.

Despite all of our moral reasoning, political campaigning, and service-oriented extracurricular, it seems that we've consistently missed the bus with prisons. It's not that the penalties don't affect us. Prisons are draining our tax dollars, ruining families, and destroying lives.

But sadly enough, we find more time to worry about the MCAT, acappella groups, and crew races than about prisons. And in the mean time, the problems plaguing our prison systems including overcrowding, lack of adequate health care, exploitative prison labor, and systematic brutality are getting worse.

A War On Prisoners
Since 1980, America's prison population has more than tripled, creeping up to the two million mark. The number of females in prison has quadrupled. The strangle-hold our prisons have on the black population is particularly staggering: although blacks only make up 12% of the

total population, they represent nearly half of the prison population. We've outgrown even our most ambitious prison-building programs, resulting in overcrowding, disease, and a general failure to help and reform prisoners. And fueled by America's cry for a "war on crime" - including tougher sentencing, fewer parole opportunities, and more police-the prison epidemic looks like it will continue to spread.

Granted, many Harvard students are well aware of such statistics. Some would agree with the graffiti on JFK Street that the time has come for "No More Prisons;" others would argue that these people are in prison because they committed a crime. But while such debates rage on across the country, we have failed to notice more fundamental problems with our prison system, particularly those of human rights abuses. International human rights groups, from the UN to Amnesty International, have condemned our treatment of prisoners, but their cries have fallen on deaf-and painfully ignorant-ears.

Among the many offenses that America has committed against its prisoners, three have received particular attention: brutally-enforced labor programs, lack of health care, and felony disenfranchisement.

Stolen Labor, Stolen Lives
Since the first American penitentiary was built in 1817, prisoners have been set to work in hopes of decreasing idleness and helping prisoners learn to make a positive contribution to society. Within two years, however, this fine ideal of productive rehabilitation was turned into a cheap-labor-for-hire system for local factories and a precedent was set for exploiting prison labor for financial gain.

Nearly 200 years later, this privatized work force produces over $1.3 billion in goods. Not surprisingly, this flourishing market has attracted the attention of private corporations and stockholders nationwide, who have now invested almost $3 billion in prison construction alone. In advertising for a conference on private prisons, one New York-based investment firm advertised the following: "While arrests and convictions are steadily on the rise, profits are to be made-profits from crime. Get in on the ground floor of this booming industry now!" As any Ec10 student could easily explain, the increased opportunity for profit has led to a desire to cut costs, leaving prisoners with an average wage between $0.23 and $1.23, hardly the 'prevailing wage' called for by the free labor market. Any prisoner who opts not to work is then deprived of family visits, phone calls, and many recreational privileges. And if a prisoner causes any disturbances, guards stand ready to maintain order and security violently.

Corporate America is quick to defend such actions on the grounds that prisoners are learning useful job skills and a work ethic. Unfortunately, prisoners are forced into labor-intensive, menial trades such as clothes and textile manufacturing. Not only do these jobs exploit cheap labor, their practical application after release seems unlikely, as most US and transnational corporations have moved their operations to Third World countries. Upon release, prisoners find themselves with few job skills and a prison record that will further discourage any potential employer.

Cruel and Usual
Beyond these sweatshop-like conditions, however, American prisons are violating international standards of prison maintenance. The recent reinstatement of prison chain gangs-labor used as punishment-violates United Nations standards as found in the UN Standard Minimum Rules (1955). These rules explicitly state: "No prisoner shall be employed, in the service of the institution, in any disciplinary capacity." As with most UN standards, prison regulations are largely ignored by the United States. International condemnation is mounting, led by none other than the Chinese, whom we have criticized for years for their institutional prison labor. While Chinese prison exports are decreasing, our own sales are beginning to boom.

Another major issue for prisons is health care. The UN also called for adequate health care sufficient to "meet all requirements of health" and provide necessary treatments for sick, pregnant, or mentally ill patients. Furthermore, with the presidential campaign in full swing, it seems that health care discussions have become the order of the day. Even so, prisoners are largely left outside the issue. At the most basic level, many prisoners are suffering and dying prematurely from a variety of treatable diseases. One of the most threatening in recent years has been hepatitis C. Most states don't routinely screen inmates for hepatitis, and the few states that do screen generally find that roughly 1/3 of all prisoners test positive. Six months ago, Georgia Dept. of Corrections began to test inmates, only to conclude that they expected a six fold increase in cases reported by this June. Not only is the disease expensive to treat, but it does irreparable damage to the body, inflicting serious damage to the livers and kidneys and often leading to cancer.

As with most epidemics, the costs-both in terms of lives lost and money for treatment and research-are climbing higher with every day of inaction.

Mental illness also plagues prisons. A 1997 Justice Dept. study found that about 16% of the prison population suffers from mental illness. And although all jails and prisons are required by law to have personnel trained to treat such problems, adequate care for the mentally ill seems to be almost non-existent. Many critics also accuse prison psychiatrists of failing to recognize mental illness, especially in minorities. Statistics seem to confirm such accusations, as 23% of white state prisoners are deemed mentally ill as compared to 14% of blacks. Regardless of racial disparity, however, it seems that most mentally ill prisoners fail to receive the professional treatment they require.

Another fundamental health problem with prison facilities is the lack of drug and alcohol rehabilitation efforts. Recent studies indicate that 80% of all jailing are related to alcohol or illegal drugs as a result of violating drug or alcohol laws, being intoxicated or high when committing crimes, or committing crimes to support addictions. Despite such evidence, an estimated 75% of all state prisoners fail to receive needed drug treatment. Countless studies have shown the impact of drug rehabilitation programs: drug treatment significantly reduces the rate of future offenses, prison maintenance expenses, and the size of the overall prison population. But few voters and lawmakers seem to feel that America's 'war on drugs' should be followed through with drug rehabilitation, as though pure punishment, not reform, were the aim of our prisons.

Punishment Without Representation

Finally, prisoners are losing yet another right that we Americans hold so dear to our hearts: the right to vote. For all the political flair at Harvard-from campaigning to debating to voting-it seems that many students are unaware of the fact that 46 states and the District of Columbia prohibit inmates from voting while serving a felony sentence. Massachusetts, one of the four states that does allow felons to vote, is currently moving to join the 'tough on crime' bandwagon and take the vote away from felons. 32 states prohibit felons on parole to vote. And 14 states disenfranchise felons even after their sentence is complete.

Felony disenfranchisement is a form of retributive punishment: incarcerated criminals have broken the social contract; which guarantees their rights as long as they live in accordance to the laws determined by that society. By breaking that contract, they have taken benefits from society that they have not earned, and this action justifies taking their rights away. A retributive system of government, however, does not alleviate crime within a society. In order to correct the fundamental problems that cause crime, we should implement a penal system based on reform. A system of reform recognizes the rights of incarcerated felons.

Felony disenfranchisement means that almost 4 million Americans will not be voting in the upcoming elections, 1.4 million of whom are ex-offenders who have completed their sentence. Even more disturbing than the sheer number of voters who have lost the vote is the mounting racial inequality; 13% of all black males are currently disenfranchised. At our current pace, three in ten of the next generation of black males can expect to be disenfranchised at some point in their lifetime. Slowly but surely, the American legal system is taking away the vote from the 'untouchables' of society-the poor, the homeless, racial minorities-and consequently corroding the very essence of a democratic state: the voice of the people.

Apathy or Activism?

America's prison system is failing. Inhumane labor practices, pathetic health care, and discriminatory disenfranchisement are taking their toll on our prisons and, perhaps more importantly, our society as a whole. Our 'war on crime' is slowly becoming a corporate takeover of the lower classes of American society, and we're all sharing the costs. America has once again emerged as a world leader, but this time, it's for our outrageous human rights violations under the pretense of "law and order." As many critics have pointed out, a new kind of slavery has sprung up in America.

But we Harvard students have more important things to worry about. And after all, we aren't the ones committing the crimes, so why should we care? It doesn't really matter so long as it doesn't hurt us, right?

Once again, Harvard is outdoing itself, as we set ourselves up in an ignorant state of self-approval. We have failed to recognize the community that we live in, a community that extends from our brilliant professors to the kids in the Pit, from Neil Rudenstine to all our favorite Spare Change vendors. It's time that we look beyond our own existence and reach out to those who weren't born in the lap of luxury, to those who had to drop out of high school to help support their family, to those who never got the chances we have.

It's time to wake up, shake off our ignorance, and take action before it's too late.

CHAPTER NINE

IN VINO VERITAS

Wine Making in Ancient Egypt

ALCOHOL

Alcohol, especially wine has been consumed by many civilizations around the world for millennia. The earliest evidence suggesting wine production comes from archaeological sites in Georgia and Iran, dating from 6000 BCE to 5000 BCE. The archaeological evidence becomes clearer, and points to domestication of grapevine, in early 'Bronze Age' sites of the Near East, Sumer and Egypt from around 3000 BCE.

The oldest known evidence suggesting wine production in Europe and second oldest in the world comes from archaeological sites in Greece and is dated to 4500 BCE. The same archaeological sites in Greece also contain remnants of the world's earliest evidence of crushed grapes. In Egypt, wine became a part of recorded history, playing an important role in ancient ceremonial life. Wine was possibly introduced into Egypt by the

215

ancient Greeks. Traces of wine were also found in China, dating from 2000 BCE and 1000 BCE.

Wine was common in classical Greece and Rome. Dionysus was the Greek god of wine and wine was frequently referred to in the works of ancient authors Homer and Aesop. Since Roman times, wine (potentially mixed with herbs and minerals) was assumed to serve medicinal purposes as well. During Roman times it was not uncommon to dissolve pearls in wine for better health.

In medieval Europe, the Christian Church was a staunch supporter of wine which was necessary for the celebration of the Catholic Mass. In some places in Europe, beer was banned and considered pagan and barbaric while wine consumption was viewed as civilized and a sign of conversion.

Wine (and all other intoxicant) is forbidden in the Islamic religion. Although, after Geber and other Moslem chemists pioneered the distillation of wine, it was used for other purposes, including cosmetic and medical uses. In fact the 10th century CE Persian philosopher and scientist Al Biruni described a number of recipes where herbs, minerals and even gemstones are mixed with wine for medicinal purposes.

─ ⌒☆⌒ ─

Do you remember the story about the Middle Eastern teenagers and the Western teenagers in my school in Switzerland? How the Middle Eastern students were being judged for drinking alcohol? Well, I guess looking at origin of wine which is most probably invented by their forefathers, the taste of wine or alcohol is still genetically inherited in their blood. (Just kidding... ☺)

Alcohol does make one joyful (or less tense to be more precise) when it is drank in a small portion. In fact, when I was still studying in Switzerland one of my teachers who was crazy about wines repeatedly said: "In Vino Veritas" – in wine is the truth. He was truly convinced about that. Tragically, he died after being gunned down by his boyfriend; most likely when he was under the influence of alcohol.

I don't need to write in length about the pros and cons of alcohol. Everyone knows that alcohol is useful for medicinal purpose, but nothing good comes out of drunkenness. Although many people who consume alcohol claim that they have it under control.

Almost everyone knows that alcohol is forbidden by the Quran. But how it is mentioned in the Quran – most people do not know. What about in the Old and the New Testaments?

In the Old Testament

He who loves pleasure will become poor; whoever loves wine and oil will never be rich.
(OT: Proverbs 21:17)

Do not join those who drink too much wine or gorge themselves on meat. For the drunkard and the glutton shall come to poverty: and drowsiness shall clothe a man with rags.
(OT: Proverbs 23:20 – 21)

In the New Testament

For the kingdom of God is not meat and drink; but righteousness, and peace, and joy in the Holy Ghost. For he that in these things serveth Christ is acceptable to God, and approved of men. Let us therefore follow after the things which make for peace, and things wherewith one may edify another. For meat destroy not the work of God. All things indeed are pure; but it is evil for that man who eateth with offence. It is good neither to eat flesh, nor to drink wine, nor any thing whereby thy brother stumbleth, or is offended, or is made weak. Hast thou faith? Have

it to thyself before God. Happy is he that condemneth not himself in that thing which he alloweth. And he that doubteth is damned if he eat, because he eateth not of faith: for whatsoever is not of faith is sin.
(NT: Romans 14: 17 – 23)

Do not get drunk on wine, which leads to debauchery. Instead, be filled with the Spirit.
(NT: Ephesians 5:18)

In the Quran

They ask you about intoxicants and gambling. Say: In both of them there is a great harm and only some benefit for humankind, and their harm is greater than their usefulness..
(Quran translation 2:219)

What? So do the Old Testament and the New Testament forbid wine or not? I can not believe my eyes when I first saw that actually there are more verses that indicate abstinence of wine in the Old and New Testament than in the Quran!

We all know that there is benefit to intoxicants (by definition of Oxford: alcoholic drink or drugs that cause someone to lose control of their faculties) but the harm is greater than the benefit. Although the harm is not because we will never get rich if we consumed it. Unless if we become an alcoholic and finally unable to work anymore. Look at the choice of words used by the Food and Drug Administration in the United States concerning the innovative medical drugs whose *'benefits are less than their harmful side effects'* are banned from the market. This is exactly what is written in the Quran around 1400 years ago.

SWINE FLESH

What about meat then? As mentioned above the New Testament forbids meat without any explanation what kind of meat.

While according to the **Old Testament**:

> It shall be a perpetual statute for your generations throughout all your dwellings, that ye eat neither fat nor blood.
> (OT: Leviticus 3:17)

> Ye shall therefore put difference between clean beasts and unclean, and between unclean fowls and clean: and ye shall not make your souls abominable by beast, or by fowl, or by any manner of living thing that creepeth on the ground, which I have separated from you as unclean. And ye shall be holy unto me: for I the LORD am holy, and have severed you from other people, that ye should be mine.
> (OT: Leviticus 20:25 – 26)

> Nevertheless these ye shall not eat of them that chew the cud, or of them that divide the cloven hoof; as the camel, and the hare, and the coney: for they chew the cud, but divide not the hoof; therefore they are unclean unto you.
> And the swine, because it divideth the hoof, yet cheweth not the cud, it is unclean unto you: ye shall not eat of their flesh, nor touch their dead carcase.
> These ye shall eat of all that are in the waters: all that have fins and scales shall ye eat. And whatsoever hath not fins and scales ye may not eat; it is unclean unto you. Of all clean birds ye shall eat.
> But these are they of which ye shall not eat: the eagle, and the ossifrage, and the ospray. And the glede, and the kite, and the vulture after his kind. And every raven after his kind.
> And the owl, and the night hawk, and the cuckow, and the hawk after his kind. The little owl, and the great owl, and the swan. And the pelican, and the gier eagle, and the cormorant. And the stork, and the heron after her kind,

and the lapwing, and the bat. And every creeping thing
that flieth is unclean unto you: they shall not be eaten. But
of all clean fowls ye may eat.

Ye shall not eat of anything that dieth of itself: thou shalt
give it unto the stranger that is in thy gates, that he may
eat it; or thou mayest sell it unto an alien: for thou art an
holy people unto the LORD thy God. Thou shalt not seethe
a kid in his mother's milk.
(OT: Deuteronomy 14: 7 – 22)

Meanwhile in the **Quran**:

Forbidden to you is that which dies of itself, and blood, and
flesh of swine, and that on which any other name than
that of God has been invoked, and the strangled (animal)
and that beaten to death, and that killed by a fall and
that killed by being smitten with the horn, and that which
wild beasts have eaten, except what you slaughter, and
what is sacrificed on stones set up (for idols) and that you
divide by the arrows; that is a transgression. This day have
those who disbelieve despaired of your religion, so fear
them not, and fear Me. This day have I perfected for you
your religion and completed My favor on you and chosen
for you Islam as a religion; but whoever is compelled by
hunger, not inclining willfully to sin, then surely God is
Forgiving, Merciful.

They ask you as to what is allowed to them. Say: The good
things are allowed to you, and what you have taught the
dogs and birds of prey, training them to hunt-- you teach
them of what God has taught you- so eat of that which
they catch for you and mention the name of God over it.
(Quran translation 5 : 3 – 4)

Once again the Quran is much more lenient than the other
two Testaments. And even in the case of compelled hunger
this prohibition may be overruled. There are a lot more ruling
concerning what is clean and unclean animals in the Old

Testament than is mentioned above. But what is the definition of clean or unclean? And why are the Children of Israel not allowed to eat unclean animal, but strangers are allowed?

The Quran doesn't classify animal because they are clean or not. Animals are also God's creatures - just like us:

> And there is no animal that walks upon the earth nor a bird that flies with its two wings but (they are) genera (species) like yourselves; We have not neglected anything in the Book..
> (Quran translation 6:38)

I believe all the three religious books are saying the same thing originally. The Old Testament is clear about saying that swine flesh is forbidden. The New Testament is not that clear; in fact it says that we should avoid all meat. However, Jesus likened dog and pig to those people who after receiving divine teaching failed to profit from them and abuses them for self-serving purposes:

> Do not give holy to dogs - they will only turn and attack you. Do not throw our pearls in front of pigs-they will only trample them underfoot.
> (NT: Matthew 7:6)

Now let's analyze this topic by common sense, do you believe the saying "We are what we eat"? The Ayurvedic priests understand about the effect of healthy or clean eating to our body. I am sure you have also heard the phrase "Mens sana in corpore sano" – a sound mind in a sound body – which was first quoted by the Roman poet Juvenal.

Many Far Eastern traditions also discourage the eating of pork. The 3,000 year old Confucian Book of Rites says, "A gentleman does not eat the flesh of pigs and dogs." Although many Chinese are keen eaters of pork today, physicians of ancient China recognized pork-eating as the root of many human ailments. Buddhists, Jains and Hindus usually also avoid eating any kind of meat.

Clean eating (tayyab in Arabic), meaning eating food that do not pollute the body, is not a new phenomenon. In fact on August 23, 2004 – BBC News Online in UK spoke to the experts concerning the connection between our emotional behaviors towards the food that we eat.

God's command to abstain from pork eating is based on the same reason as above, hygiene and of the cultivation of purity of character. Pork is not so poisonous as to kill people right on the spot but latently. It will destroy slowly. It is certainly not as nourishing as any other meat and it causes prolonged suffering.

Abstention from eating pork is a measure to safeguard health. Of all the domestic animals, pig is the greediest, eating anything including human excreta and its own babies! It is the cradle of harmful germs and parasites. Its meat is carrier of diseases to man, thus making it unfit for human consumption. I saw a Hollywood movie once (I can't remember the title – it was a mafia movie) where someone kills a person and to get rid of the body he threw the dead body in a pigsty!

Yes, other cattles can also be a medium for diseases too (in fact, we can catch diseases from anything) – but a pig causes by far many more diseases, amongst others because of its lack of sweat gland.

All the three religions also prohibit blood of any type. This is because of chemical analysis of blood shows that it contains an abundance of uric acid, a chemical substance which can be dangerous to human health. Uric acid in humans is excreted as a waste product, 98 % of the body's uric acid is extracted from the blood by the kidneys and removed through urination.

Do you remember the way of slaughtering an animal to produce 'halal' or 'kosher' meat? That is by making incision through the jugular veins, leaving all other veins and organs intact, in order to kill the animal by total loss of blood from the body, rather than an injury to any vital organ.

If the organs, for example the heart, the liver or the brain are crippled or damaged, the animal could die immediately and its blood would congeal in its veins and would eventually permeate the flesh. This implies that the animal flesh would be permeated and contaminated with uric acid and therefore very poisonous. Only today do our dieticians realize such a thing.

Now, a pig cannot be slaughtered at the neck for it does not have a neck! And because its lack of sweat gland, pig's biochemistry excretes only 2% of its total uric acid content, the remaining 98% remains as an integral part of the body.

However, every creature was created by God for a purpose. Muhammad always encouraged his followers to be kind to animals. Although we should not eat the meat of the pig, it doesn't mean that we should hate pigs. We should show them the same kindness as any other animal, and not abuse or torture them.

Pigs score high on tests devised to determine animal intelligence; in other words, they are very smart. Many believe that pork would taste better if the pigs were kept in a state of filth, but this is not the natural inclination of the pig. When left to their own devices, it is said that pigs do not like to soil their sleeping quarters. As for their tendency to wallow in mud, that is done mainly to keep cool – for the lack of sweat gland. But this doesn't mean that when kept clean it becomes healthy to eat pigs.

ILLNESS CAUSED BY PORK MEAT

Influenza (flu) is one of the most famous illnesses which pigs share with humans. This illness is harbored in the lungs of pigs during the summer months and tends to affect pigs and human in the cooler months. Sausage contains bits of pigs' lungs, so those who eat pork sausage tend to suffer more during epidemics of influenza. Pig meat contains excessive quantities of histamine and imidazole compounds, which can lead to itching and inflammation; growth hormone, which promotes inflammation and growth; sulphur - containing mesenchymal mucus, which leads to swelling and deposits of mucus in tendons and cartilage, resulting in arthritis, rheumatism, etc.

Sulfur helps cause firm human tendons and ligaments to be replaced by the pig's soft mesenchymal tissues (embryonic tissue which develops into connective and skeletal tissues), and degeneration of human cartilage. Eating pork can also lead to gallstones and obesity, probably due to its high cholesterol and saturated fat content. The pig is the main carrier of the taenia solium worm, which is found in its flesh. These tapeworms are found in human intestines with greater frequency in nations where pigs are eaten. This type of tapeworm can pass through the intestines and affect many other organs, and is incurable once it reaches beyond a certain stage.

1 in 6 people in the US and Canada has trichinosis from eating trichina worms which are found in pork. Many people have no symptoms to warn them of this, and when they do, they resemble symptoms of many other illnesses. These worms are not noticed during meat inspections, nor are they killed by salting or smoking. Few people cook the meat long enough to kill the trichinae. The rat (another scavenger) also harbors this disease. There are dozens of other worms, germs, diseases and bacteria which are commonly found in pigs, many of which are specific to the pig, or found in greater frequency in pigs.

And the cholesterol, which results from pork's analysis in the body appear in the blood in the form of semi-cholesterol pleomorphic which led to a rise in the blood pressure and arteriosclerosis and they from the dangerous factors that introduced filling of the heart muscle. Professor Roff found that cholesterol that is found in the cancer rover cell is like the cholesterol which is found when eating the pork.

The pork is rich with the compounds that contains a high rate of sulfur and all affect the tissues absorption ability to the water as sponge that take the shape of vast bag and this led to the deposition of the mucous substance in sinews, ligaments, cartilages between vertebrae and to degeneration in the bones.

And the tissues that contains sulfur are damaged by rotten producing a spread bad odor and caused hydrogen sulphate gas and it was noticed that the containers that contains the pork although it is perfectly closed it's odor spreads from the room after few days as a result of it's bad rotten odor and it's unsustainable odor. Contrastly, other types of meat was passed by the same experiment and it was found that the rotten of beef is slower than the pork and this rotten odor doesn't spread from it. The pork contains a high ratio of growth hormone which has a great effect on the infection (material's ends), also it has an effect on the stomach growth (the potbelly) and increase the growth rate especially the designed for growth and cancer development. According to professor Roff studies these fatty meals that contain pork consider essential in cell's cancer turning as it contains the growth hormone and it has a great effect in rising blood cholesterol.

It's amazing that pig is rich pasture for more than 450 epidemic diseases and it is playing the role of intermediary to transform 57 diseases to man, in addition to these diseases that are caused from eating pork as dyspepsia, the atherosclerosis and many others. The pig itself is responsible to transform 27 epidemic diseases to human and some other animals. (Ref: Dr. Mohamed Nezar Al-Dakr)

So.. what are the Jews, Christians and Moslems fighting about? A true One God believer is supposed to follow a doctrine of peace. And yet, Jews and Christians say that Moslems are too strict. While Jews and Christians are supposed to be practicing and avoiding the same things that are taught by the Quran. Moslems say that Jews and Christians are misguided, and yet some Moslems actually practice what is written in the Old Testament that is not commanded in the Quran. While most Jews and Christians do not practice what is written in the Old nor the New Testament. Jews say that Christians are not practicing their rituals, and Christians say that the Jewish rituals are old fashioned - yet they both read the same scripture. Oh, people are just the same everywhere...

Who is to blame? I blame it on our own racial prejudice, our tendency to exaggerate, our social programming, historical manipulation and most of all our own unwillingness to learn and find out about the Truth.

I blame it on our own ignorance...

CHAPTER TEN

DAUGHTERS OF EVE

www.stefaniespeaks.files.wordpress.com

Adam and Eve

N ow let's discuss about what the three scriptures say about another hot debated religious topic: women.

ADAM AND EVE

The three monotheistic religions agree on one basic fact: both women and men are created by God. However if we really examine, the stories are 'slightly' different in fundamental ways.

According to the Old Testament

And God said, Let us make man in our image, after our likeness: and let them have dominion over the fish of the sea, and over the fowl of the air, and over the cattle, and over all the earth, and over every creeping thing that creepeth upon the earth. So God created man in his own

image, in the image of God created he him; male and female created he them. And God blessed them, and God said unto them, Be fruitful, and multiply, and replenish the earth, and subdue it: and have dominion over the fish of the sea, and over the fowl of the air, and over every living thing that moveth upon the earth.
(OT: Genesis 1: 26 – 28)

And the LORD God formed man of the dust of the ground, and breathed into his nostrils the breath of life; and man became a living soul.
(OT: Genesis 2:7)

And the LORD God commanded the man, saying, Of every tree of the garden thou mayest freely eat: but of the tree of the knowledge of good and evil, thou shalt not eat of it: for in the day that thou eatest thereof thou shalt surely die. And the LORD God said, It is not good that the man should be alone; I will make him an help meet for him. And out of the ground the LORD God formed every beast of the field, and every fowl of the air; and brought them unto Adam to see what he would call them: and whatsoever Adam called every living creature, that was the name thereof. And Adam gave names to all cattle, and to the fowl of the air, and to every beast of the field; but for Adam there was not found an help meet for him. And the LORD God caused a deep sleep to fall upon Adam, and he slept: and he took one of his ribs, and closed up the flesh instead thereof; and the rib, which the LORD God had taken from man, made he a woman, and brought her unto the man. And Adam said, This is now bone of my bones, and flesh of my flesh: she shall be called Woman, because she was taken out of Man. Therefore shall a man leave his father and his mother, and shall cleave unto his wife: and they shall be one flesh.
(OT: Genesis 2: 16 – 24)

According to the Quran

And when your Lord said to the angels, I am going to place in the earthly representative, they said: What! Wilt Thou place in it such as shall make mischief in it and shed blood, and we celebrate Thy praise and extol Thy holiness? He said: Surely I know what you do not know. And He taught Adam all the names, then presented them to the angels; then He said: Tell me the names of those if you are right.They said: Glory be to Thee! we have no knowledge but that which Thou hast taught us; surely Thou art the Knowing, the Wise. He said: O Adam! inform them of their names. Then when he had informed them of their names, He said: Did I not say to you that I surely know what is unseen in the heavens and the earth and (that) I know what you manifest and what you hide?

And when We said to the angels: Make obeisance to Adam they did obeisance, but Satan (did it not). He refused and he was proud, and he was one of the unbelievers. And We said: O Adam! Dwell you and your wife in the garden and eat from it a plenteous (food) wherever you wish and do not approach this tree, for then you will be of the unjust. But the Satan made them both fall from it, and caused them to depart from that (state) in which they were; and We said: Get forth, some of you being the enemies of others, and there is for you in the earth an abode and a provision for a time. Then Adam received (some) words from his Lord, so He turned to him mercifully; surely He is Oft-returning (to mercy), the Merciful.
(Quran translation 2: 30 – 35)

Although the above verses sound similar if we read carefully we can see that the Quran does not mention that Eve was created from Adam's rib. Furthermore, the Quran does not mention that human is created in the image of God. All these facts might seem minor, but the impact it has on humanity is unbelievably immense.

IS IT EVE'S FAULT?

In the Judeo-Christian version God prohibited both of them from eating the fruits of the forbidden tree. The serpent seduced Eve to eat from it and Eve, in turn, seduced Adam to eat with her. When God rebuked Adam for what he did, he put all the blame on Eve, *"The woman You put here with me - she gave me some fruit from the tree and I ate it."* Consequently, God said to Eve:

> I will greatly increase your pains in childbearing; with pain you will give birth to children. Your desire will be for your husband and he will rule over you.
> (OT: Genesis 3:16)

To Adam He said:

> Because you listened to your wife and ate from the tree .... Cursed is the ground because of you; through painful toil you will eat of it all the days of your life...
> (OT: Genesis 3:17)

While the following is according to the Quran:

> And We said: O Adam! Dwell you and your wife in the garden and eat from it a plenteous (food) wherever you wish and do not approach this tree, for then you will be of the unjust. But the Satan made them both fall from it, and caused them to depart from that (state) in which they were; and We said: Get forth, some of you being the enemies of others, and there is for you in the earth an abode and a provision for a time. Then Adam received (some) words from his Lord, so He turned to him mercifully; surely He is Oft-returning (to mercy), the Merciful.
> (Quran translation 2: 35 – 37)

Again, a careful look into the two accounts of the story of the creation reveals some essential differences. The Quran, contrary to the Bible, places equal blame on both Adam and Eve for their mistake. Nowhere in the Quran can one find even the slightest hint that Eve tempted Adam to eat from the tree or even that she had eaten before him. Eve in the Quran is no temptress, no seducer and no deceiver. Moreover, Eve is not to be blamed for the pains of childbearing. God, according to the Quran, punishes no one for another's faults. Both Adam and Eve committed a sin and He forgave them.

EVE'S LEGACY

The image of Eve as temptress in the Bible has resulted in an extremely negative impact on women. All women were believed to have inherited from their mother, the Biblical Eve, both her guilt and her guile. Consequently, women are all untrustworthy, morally inferior, and wicked. Menstruation, pregnancy, and childbearing are considered the just punishment for the eternal guilt of the cursed female sex. In order to appreciate how negative the impact of the Biblical Eve was on all her female descendants we have to look at some more verses concerning women in the Old Testament:

> I find more bitter than death, the woman who is a snare, whose heart is a trap and whose hands are chains. The man who pleases God will escape her, but the sinner she will ensnare....while I was still searching but not finding, I found one upright man among a thousand but not one upright woman among them all.
> (OT: Ecclesiastes 7:26-28)

Further in the Jewish literature that can be found in the Catholic book of Eccletiasticus (not to be confused with Ecclesiastes):

> No wickedness comes anywhere near the wickedness of a woman.....Sin began with a woman and thanks to her we all must die.
> (Catholic Ecclesiasticus 25:19,24)

The Biblical Eve has played a far bigger role in Christianity than in Judaism. Her sin has been pivotal to the whole Christian faith because the Christian conception of the reason for the mission of Jesus Christ on earth stems from Eve's disobedience to God. She had sinned and then seduced Adam to follow her suit. Consequently, God expelled both of them from Heaven to earth, which had been cursed because of them.

They passed on their sin, which had not been forgiven by God, to all their descendants and, thus, all humans are born in sin. In order to purify human beings from their 'original sin', God had to sacrifice Jesus, who is considered to be the Son of God, on the cross. Therefore, Eve is responsible for her own mistake, her husband's sin, the original sin of all humanity, and the death of the Son of God. In other words, one woman acting on her own caused the fall of humanity. What about her daughters? They are sinners like her and have to be treated as such. Listen to the severe tone of St. Paul in the New Testament:

> A woman should learn in quietness and full submission. I don't permit a woman to teach or to have authority over a man; she must be silent. For Adam was formed first, then Eve. And Adam was not the one deceived; it was the woman who was deceived and became a sinner."
> (NT: I Timothy 2:11-14)

All women are denigrated because of the image of Eve the temptress. If we now turn our attention to what the Quran has to say about women, we will soon realize that the Islamic conception of women is radically different from the Judaeo-Christian one.

> For Moslem men and women, for believing men and women, for devout men and women, for true men and women, for men and women who are patient, for men and women who humble themselves, for men and women who give in charity, for men and women who fast, for men

and women who guard their chastity, and for men and women who engage much in God's praise - For them all has God prepared forgiveness and great reward.
(Quran translation 33:35)

The believers, men and women, are protectors, one of another: they enjoin what is just, and forbid what is evil, they observe regular prayers, practice regular charity, and obey God and His Messenger. On them will God pour His Mercy: for God is Exalted in power, Wise.
(Quran translation 9:71)

And their Lord answered them: Truly I will never cause to be lost the work of any of you. Be you a male or female, you are members one of another.
(Quran translation 3:195)

Whoever works evil will not be requited but by the like thereof, and whoever works a righteous deed - whether man or woman - and is a believer- such will enter the Garden of bliss.
(Quran translation 40:40)

Whoever works righteousness, man or woman, and has faith, verily to him/her we will give a new life that is good and pure, and we will bestow on such their reward according to the best of their actions.
(Quran translation 16:97)

It is clear that the Quranic view of women is no different than that of men. They, both, are God's creatures whose sublime goal on earth is to worship their Lord, do righteous deeds, and avoid evil and they, both, will be assessed accordingly. The Quran never mentions that the woman is the devil's gateway or that she is a deceiver by nature. All men and all women are His creatures; that is all.

According to the Quran, a woman's role on earth is not limited to childbirth. She is required to do as many good deeds as any other man is required to do. The Quran never says that no upright women have ever existed. To the contrary, the Quran has instructed all the believers, women as well as men, to follow the example of those ideal women such as the Mary (Jesus' mother) and the Pharaoh's wife (the Pharaoh during Moses's time):

> And God sets forth, As an example to those who believe, the wife of Pharaoh: Behold she said: 'O my lord build for me, in nearness to you, a mansion in the Garden, and save me from Pharaoh and his doings and save me from those who do wrong.' And Mary the daughter of Imran who guarded her chastity and We breathed into her body of Our spirit; and she testified to the truth of the words of her Lord and of His revelations and was one of the devout. (Quran translation 66:11-13)

SHAMEFUL DAUGHTERS?

In fact, the difference between the Old Testament and the Quranic attitude towards the female sex starts as soon as a female is born. For example, the Old Testament states that the period of the mother's ritual impurity is twice as long if a girl is born than if a boy is (Leviticus 12:2-5). Another verse states explicitly that:

> The birth of a daughter is a loss.
> (Catholic Ecclesiasticus 22:3)

In contrast to this shocking statement, boys receive special praise:
> A man who educates his son will be the envy of his enemy.
> (Catholic Ecclesiasticus 30:3)

The Old Testament made it an obligation on Jewish men to produce offspring in order to propagate the race. At the same time, it did not hide their clear preference for male children:

Your daughter is headstrong? Keep a sharp look-out that she does not make you the laughing stock of your enemies, the talk of the town, the object of common gossip, and put you to public shame.
(Catholic Ecclesiasticus 42:11)

Keep a headstrong daughter under firm control, or she will abuse any indulgence she receives. Keep a strict watch on her shameless eye, do not be surprised if she disgraces you.
(Catholic Ecclesiasticus 26:10-11)

Before the advent of Islam, pagan Arabs also treated their daughters in a similar manner. Pagan Arabs used to practice female infanticide. The Quran severely condemned this heinous practice:

When news is brought to one of them of the birth of a female child, his face darkens and he is filled with inward grief. With shame does he hide himself from his people because of the bad news he has had! Shall he retain her on contempt or bury her in the dust? Ah! What an evil they decide on?
(Quran translation 16:59)

It has to be mentioned that this sinister crime would have never stopped in Arabia were it not for verses in the Quran that condemn this practice (16:59, 43:17, 81:8-9). The Quran, moreover, makes no distinction between boys and girls. The Quran considers the birth of a female as a gift and a blessing from God, the same as the birth of a male. The Quran even mentions the gift of the female birth first:

To God belongs the dominion of the heavens and the earth. He creates what He wills. He bestows female children to whomever He wills and bestows male children to whomever He wills.
(Quran translation 42:49)

FEMALE EDUCATION

The difference between the New Testament and the Quranic conceptions of women is not limited to the newly born female, it extends far beyond that. Let us compare their attitudes towards a female trying to learn her religion.

> *As in all the congregations of the saints, women should remain silent in the churches. They are not allowed to speak, but must be in submission as the law says. If they want to inquire about something, they should ask their own husbands at home; for it is disgraceful for a woman to speak in the church.*
> *(OT: I Corinthians 14:34-35)*

How can a woman learn if she is not allowed to speak? How can a woman grow intellectually if she is obliged to be in a state of full submission? How can she broaden her horizons if her one and only source of information is her husband at home? Now, to be fair, we should ask: is the Quranic position any different? One short story narrated in the Quran sums its position up concisely.

Khawlah was a Moslem woman whose husband Aws pronounced this statement at a moment of anger: "You are to me as the back of my mother." This was held by pagan Arabs to be a statement of divorce which freed the husband from any conjugal responsibility but did not leave the wife free to leave the husband's home or to marry another man. Having heard these words from her husband, Khawlah was in a miserable situation. She went straight to Muhammad to plead her case. Muhammad was of the opinion that she should be patient since there seemed to be no way out. Khawla kept arguing with Muhammad in an attempt to save her suspended marriage. Shortly, the Quran intervened; Khawla's plea was accepted. The divine verdict abolished this iniquitous custom. One full surah (Chapter 58) of the Quran whose title is 'Almujadilah' or 'The Woman Who Is Arguing' was named after this incident:

> *God has heard and accepted the statement of the*
> *woman who pleads with you (Muhammad) concerning*
> *her husband and carries her complaint to God, and God*
> *hears the arguments between both of you for God hears*
> *and sees all things...."*
> *(Quran translation 58:1)*

A woman in the Quranic conception has the right to argue even with Prophet Muhammad himself. No one has the right to instruct her to be silent. She is under no obligation to consider her husband the one and only reference in matters of law and religion.

UNCLEAN IMPURE WOMAN?

The laws and regulations concerning menstruating women are extremely restrictive in the Old Testament. It considers any menstruating woman as unclean and impure. Moreover, her impurity 'infects' others as well. Anyone or anything she touches becomes unclean for a day:

> *When a woman has her regular flow of blood, the impurity*
> *of her monthly period will last seven days, and anyone*
> *who touches her will be unclean till evening. Anything she*
> *lies on during her period will be unclean, and anything*
> *she sits on will be unclean. Whoever touches her bed*
> *must wash his clothes and bathe with water, and he will*
> *be unclean till evening. Whoever touches anything she*
> *sits on must wash his clothes and bathe with water, and*
> *he will be unclean till evening. Whether it is the bed or*
> *anything she was sitting on, when anyone touches it, he*
> *will be unclean till evening.*
> *(OT: Leviticus 15:19-23)*

The Quran does not consider a menstruating woman to possess any kind of 'contagious uncleanness' nor curse. She practices her normal life with only one restriction: married couples are not allowed to have sexual intercourse during the period of menstruation. Any other physical contact between them is permissible:

> *They ask you about menstruation: say, "It is harmful; you shall avoid sexual intercourse with the women during menstruation; do not approach them until they are rid of it. Once they are rid of it, you may have intercourse with them in the manner designed by God. God loves the repenters, and He loves those who are clean."*
> *(Quran translation 2:222)*

It has to be understood that whom God means with clean here are both women and men, not only the women. Some Quran translators use the word 'sickness' or 'illness' for menstruation, but this is not precise. We know today that menstruation is not a sickness. The exact translation is harmful. It is harmful when a couple have sexual intercourse while the woman is having menstruation. Although, most doctors will tell you that it is fine to do so, the following report says differently:

> In a health letter on September 25, 1995, the U.S. Centers for Disease Control and Prevention reported that avoiding sex that causes bleeding, or takes place while a woman is menstruating, cuts the risk of HIV infection.

> This CDC report was presented at the 11th meeting of the International Society for Sexually Transmitted Disease Research, which was held in New Orleans, Louisiana from August 27-30 in 1995. The CDC's letter focused on a case controlled analysis conducted by W.J. Kassler, in which 95 HIV transmission were closely studied. Kassler and his colleagues found that bleeding during sex accounted for 11% of the cases, and concluded that this type of transmission was a risk for both men, with a ratio of 8:1, and women, with a ratio of 4:1.

Kassler also found that for women, having sex during menses, which accounted for 20% of the cases studied, was associated with a six-fold risk of transmission.

BEARING WITNESS

Another issue in which the Quran and the Bible disagree is the issue of women bearing witness. It is true that the Quran has instructed the believers dealing in financial transactions to get two male witnesses or one male and two females:

> O you who believe, when you transact a loan for any period, you shall write it down. An impartial scribe shall do the writing. .... Two men shall serve as witnesses; if not two men, then a man and two women whose testimony is acceptable to all. Thus, if one woman errs, the other will remind her. It is the obligation of the witnesses to testify when called upon to do so...
> (Quran translation 2:282)

A woman testimony is equal to the man's testimony except in one case only, the financial transactions. Financial transactions are the only situations where two women may substitute for one man as witness. To be honest, I have not found a satisfactory explanation to this rule. The best explanation that I could find so far is that it is to guard against the possibility that one of the women is the wife of the man, and thus cause her to be biased. Generally, it is a agreed that women are more emotional than men. Especially when it comes to financial issues, women (especially women with children) tend to be more emotional, because they have more financial issues to worry about.

Another probable reason is because in general men are better in mathematics and women are better in language skills. However, this is a hot debate which is still ongoing. Apparently, many experiments have been done, and there is still no unanimous result. Because when we look around, during mathematics tests in school actually many girls score better then boys, however it is undeniable that engineering, physics and mathematics findings and (top level) banking managerial positions are still occupied by men.

The reason however, is not because men are more intelligent than women. Many recent studies have concluded that IQ performances of men and women vary little. A research in England has shown a greater variance in the IQ performance of men compared to that of women, i.e. men are more represented at the extremes of performance, and less represented at the median.

Female brains are more compact than male brains in that, though smaller, they are more densely packed with neurons, particularly in the region responsible for language. Also, females have language functions evenly distributed in both cerebral hemispheres, while in males they are more concentrated in the left hemisphere. This puts males more at risk for language disorders like dyslexia.

One thing is for sure, men and women are NOT the same, but we are EQUAL. The perfect symbol to describe this dynamics is probably the yin-yang symbol of the Chinese.

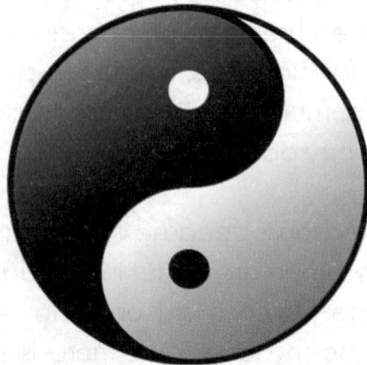

So back to the financial transaction: if a woman's witness in general was worth half that of a man, the verse would have stated so clearly. But obviously that is not the case. Women's testimony in all other matters is equal to that of a man or even supersedes his testimony as in the case of a wife testifying against her accusation of adultery.

If a man accuses his wife of unchaste behavior, he is required by the Quran to solemnly swear five times as evidence of the wife's guilt. If the wife denies and swears similarly five times, she is not considered guilty and in either case the marriage is dissolved. Why is this? Again the answer is probably psychological, and only God knows what the reason is. Probably, because in general men have higher sex drive than women, meanwhile women (usually) only cheat when they are extremely unhappy. Maybe this recent article that I found in the Internet can be the answer:

"New research shows men are better at detecting a cheating partner than females, and they're more likely to suspect infidelities that don't exist. A US study of heterosexual couples has found that men are the more suspicious of the sexes when it comes to straying, but a leading Australian sex researcher says they are only more suspecting because they are more likely to cheat."

> And (as for) those who accuse their wives and have no witnesses except themselves, the evidence of one of these (should be taken) four times, bearing God to witness that he is most surely of the truthful ones. And the fifth (time) that the curse of God be on him if he is one of the liars. And it shall avert the chastisement from her if she testifies four times, bearing God to witness that he is most surely one of the liars; And the fifth (time) that the wrath of God be on her if he is one of the truthful.
> (Quran translation 24:6 – 9)

On the other hand, in the Jewish society women cannot bear witness because of the verses in Genesis 18:9-16, where it is stated that Sara, Abraham's wife had lied. It should be noted here that this story narrated in Genesis 18:9-16 has been mentioned more than once in the Quran without any hint of any lies by Sara (11:69-74, 51:24-30). In the Christian West, both ecclesiastical and civil law debarred women from giving testimony until late last century. If a man accuses his wife of being unchaste her testimony will not be considered at all according to the Bible. The accused wife has to be subjected to a trial by ordeal. In this trial, the wife faces a complex and humiliating ritual which was supposed to prove her guilt or innocence (Numbers 5:11-31). If she is found guilty after this ordeal, she will be sentenced to death. If she is found not guilty, her husband will be innocent of any wrongdoing!

Besides, if a man takes a woman as a wife and then accuses her of not being a virgin, her own testimony will not count. Her parents had to bring evidence of her virginity before the elders of the town. If the parents could not prove the innocence of their daughter, she would be stoned to death on her father's doorsteps! If the parents were able to prove her innocence, the husband would have to pay a fine of one hundred shekels of silver and he could not divorce his wife as long as he lived:

> If a man takes a wife and, after lying with her, dislikes her and slanders her and gives her a bad name, saying, 'I married this woman, but when I approached her, I did not find proof of her virginity,' then the girl's father and mother shall bring proof that she was a virgin to the town elders at the gate. The girl's father will say to the elders, 'I gave my daughter in marriage to this man, but he dislikes her. Now he has slandered her and said I did not find your daughter to be a virgin. But here is the proof of my daughter's virginity.' Then her parents shall display the cloth before the elders of the town, and the elders shall take the man and punish him. They shall fine him a hundred shekels of

silver and give them to the girl's father, because this man has given an Israelite virgin a bad name. She shall continue to be his wife; he must not divorce her as long as he lives. If, however, the charge is true and no proof of the girl's virginity can be found, she shall be brought to the door of her father's house and there the men of the town shall stone her to death. She has done a disgraceful thing in Israel by being promiscuous while still in her father's house. You must purge the evil from among you.
(OT: Deuteronomy 22:13-21)

VOWS

According to the Old Testament, a man must fulfill any vows he might make to God. He must not break his word. On the other hand, a woman's vow is not necessarily binding on her. It has to be approved by her father, if she is living in his house, or by her husband, if she is married. If a father/husband does not endorse his daughter's/wife's vows, all pledges made by her become null and void:

> *But if her father forbids her when he hears about it, none of her vows or the pledges by which she obligated herself will stand ....Her husband may confirm or nullify any vow she makes or any sworn pledge to deny herself.*
> *(OT: Numbers 30:2-15)*

In the Quran, the vow of every Moslem, male or female, is binding on him/her. No one has the power to repudiate the pledges of anyone else. Failure to keep a solemn oath, made by a man or a woman, has to be expiated as indicated in the Quran:

> *He [God] will call you to account for your deliberate oaths: for expiation, feed ten indigent persons, on a scale of the average for the food of your families; Or clothe them; or give a slave his freedom. If that is beyond your means, fast for three days. That is the expiation for the oaths you*

have sworn. But keep your oaths.
(Quran translation 5:89)

Companions of Muhammad, men and women, used to present their oath of allegiance to him personally. Women, as well as men, would independently come to him and pledge their oaths:

> *O Prophet, when believing women come to you to make a covenant with you that they will not associate in worship anything with God, nor steal, nor fornicate, nor kill their own children, nor slander anyone, nor disobey you in any just matter, then make a covenant with them and pray to God for the forgiveness of their sins. Indeed God is Forgiving and most Merciful.*
> *(Quran translation 60:12)*

A man could not swear the oath on behalf of his daughter or his wife. Nor could a man repudiate the oath made by any of his female relatives.

WIFE'S PROPERTY

The three religions share an unshakeable belief in the importance of marriage and family life. Nevertheless, blatant differences do exist among the three religions with respect to the limits of this union. In the Judeo-Christian tradition, unlike Islam, a husband is considered as the master of his wife. The Jewish tradition regarding the husband's role towards his wife stems from the conception that he owns her. This conception has been the reason behind the double standard in the laws of adultery and behind the husband's ability to annul his wife's vows. This conception has also been responsible for denying the wife any control over her property or her earnings.

As soon as a Jewish woman got married, she completely lost any control over her property and earnings to her husband. Thus, marriage may cause the richest woman to become practically penniless. The Talmud describes the financial situation of a wife as follows:

> How can a woman have anything; whatever is hers belongs to her husband? What is his is his and what is hers is also his...... Her earnings and what she may find in the streets are also his. The household articles, even the crumbs of bread on the table, are his. Should she invite a guest to her house and feed him, she would be stealing from her husband.
> (Jewish San. 71a, Git. 62a)

The fact of the matter is that the property of a Jewish female was meant to attract suitors. A Jewish family would assign their daughter a share of her father's estate to be used as a dowry in case of marriage. It was this dowry that made Jewish daughters an unwelcome burden to their fathers. The father had to raise his daughter for years and then prepare for her marriage by providing a large dowry. Thus, a girl in a Jewish family was a liability and no asset. This liability explains why the birth of a daughter was not celebrated with joy in the old Jewish society (see the 'Shameful Daughters?' section).

The dowry was the wedding gift presented to the groom under terms of tenancy. The husband would act as the practical owner of the dowry but he could not sell it. The bride would lose any control over the dowry at the moment of marriage. When she works after marriage and all her earnings had to go to her husband in return for her maintenance, which was his obligation. She could regain her property only in two cases: divorce or her husband's death. Should she die first, he would inherit her property.

In the case of the husband's death, the wife could regain her pre-marital property but she was not entitled to inherit any share in her deceased husband's own property. It has to be added that the groom also had to present a marriage gift to his bride;

yet again he was the practical owner of this gift as long as they were married.

Christianity, until recently, has followed the same Jewish tradition. Both religious and civil authorities in the Christian Roman Empire (after Constantine) required a property agreement as a condition for recognizing the marriage. Families offered their daughters increasing dowries and, as a result, men tended to marry earlier while families postponed their daughters marriages until later than had been customary. Under Canon law (church law), a wife was entitled to restitution of her dowry if the marriage was annulled unless she was guilty of adultery. In this case, she forfeited her right to the dowry which remained in her husband's hands. Under Canon and civil law a married woman in Christian Europe and America had lost her property rights until late 19th and early 20th centuries CE.

For example, women's rights under English law were compiled and published in 1632. These 'rights' included: "That which the husband hath is his own. That which the wife hath is the husband's." The wife not only lost her property upon marriage, she lost her personality as well. No act of her was of legal value. Her husband could repudiate any sale or gift made by her as being of no binding legal value. The person with whom she had any contract was held as a criminal for participating in a fraud. Moreover, she could not sue or be sued in her own name, nor could she sue her own husband. A married woman was practically treated as an infant in the eyes of the law. The wife simply belonged to her husband and therefore she lost her property, her legal personality, and her family name.

Islam, since the 7th century CE, has granted married women the independent personality which the Judaeo-Christian West had deprived them until very recently. In Islam, the bride and her family are under no obligation whatsoever to present a gift to the groom. A girl in a Moslem family is no liability. A woman is so dignified by Islam that she does not need to present gifts in order to attract potential husbands. It is the groom who must present the bride with a marriage gift. This gift is considered her property and neither the groom nor the bride's family have any share in or control over it. In some Moslem societies today, a marriage gift of a hundred thousand dollars in diamonds is not unusual. The bride retains her marriage gifts even if she is later divorced. The husband is not allowed any share in his wife's property except what she offers him with her free consent. The Quran has stated its position on this issue quite clearly:

> *And give the women (on marriage) their dower as a free gift; but if they, of their own good pleasure, remit any part of it to you, take it and enjoy it with right good cheer. (Quran translation 4:4)*

The wife's property and earnings are under her full control and for her use alone since her, and the children's, maintenance is her husband's responsibility. No matter how rich the wife might be she is not obliged to act as a co-provider for the family, unless she herself voluntarily chooses to do so. Spouses do inherit from one another. Moreover, a married woman in Islam retains her independent legal personality and may keep her family name.

DIVORCE

The concept of gender equality in Islam is stressed by the non-superiority of either sex over the other. It came at a time when it was necessary to elevate the degraded status of women and grant them rights equal to those of men. The equality of women in Islam is evident by the unprecedented legal rights given to them under a monotheistic religion as defined in the Quran.

As one of many examples, consider the rights of women in marriage and divorce. Both men and women have equal rights to contract a marriage as well as to dissolve it. The precondition of marriage is merely the mutual agreement by both parties. A woman in Islam can divorce her husband at any time if she feels that she has been dealt with unjustly or when the marriage is not based upon mutual responsibilities toward each other.

The three religions have remarkable differences in their attitudes towards divorce. Christianity abhors divorce altogether. The New Testament unequivocally advocates the indissolubility of marriage:

> But I tell you that anyone who divorces his wife, except for marital unfaithfulness, causes her to become adulteress, and anyone who marries the divorced woman commits adultery.
> (NT: Matthew 5:32)

This uncompromising ideal is, without a doubt, unrealistic. It assumes a state of moral perfection that human societies have never achieved. When a couple realizes that their married life is beyond repair, a ban on divorce will not do them any good. Forcing ill- matched couples to remain together against their wills is neither effective nor reasonable.

Judaism, on the other hand, allows divorce even without any cause. The Old Testament gives the husband the right to divorce his wife even if he just dislikes her:

> If a man marries a woman who becomes displeasing to him because he finds something indecent about her, and he writes her a certificate of divorce, gives it to her and sends her from his house, and if after she leaves his house she becomes the wife of another man, and her second husband dislikes her and writes her a certificate of divorce, gives it to her and sends her from his house, or if he dies, then her first husband, who divorced her, is not allowed to

marry her again after she has been defiled.
(OT: Deuteronomy 24:1-4)

Even worse according to the Catholic teaching:

> *A bad wife brings humiliation, downcast looks, and a wounded heart. Slack of hand and weak of knee is the man whose wife fails to make him happy. Woman is the origin of sin, and it is through her that we all die. Do not leave a leaky cistern to drip or allow a bad wife to say what she likes. If she does not accept your control, divorce her and send her away.*
> *(Catholic Ecclesiasticus 25:25)*

Islam occupies the middle ground between Christianity and Judaism with respect to divorce. Marriage in Islam is a sanctified bond that should not be broken except for compelling reasons. Couples are instructed to pursue all possible remedies whenever their marriages are in danger. Divorce is not to be resorted to except when there is no other way out.

In a nutshell, Islam recognizes divorce, yet it discourages it by all means. Let us focus on the recognition side first. Islam does recognize the right of both partners to end their matrimonial relationship. Islam gives the husband the right for Talaq (divorce). Moreover, Islam, unlike Judaism, grants the wife the right to dissolve the marriage through what is known as Khula'(also divorce). Khula' is the right of women in Islam to give divorce or get separation from her husband. After divorce the husband is responsible to finance the education, food and residence of their children. The young children preferably live with the mother. Older children have the right to live with father or mother, as they decide.

If the husband dissolves the marriage by divorcing his wife, he cannot retrieve any of the marriage gifts he has given her. The

Quran explicitly prohibits the divorcing husbands from taking back their marriage gifts no matter how expensive or valuable these gifts might be:

> But if you decide to take one wife in place of another, even if you had given the latter a whole treasure for dower, take not the least bit of it back. Would you take it by slander and a manifest wrong?
> (Quran translation 4:20)

In the case of the wife choosing to end the marriage, she may return the marriage gifts to her husband. Returning the marriage gifts in this case is a fair compensation for the husband who is keen to keep his wife while she chooses to leave him. The Quran has instructed Moslem men not to take back any of the gifts they have given to their wives except in the case of the wife choosing to dissolve the marriage:

> ... It is not lawful for you (men) to take back any of your gifts except when both parties fear that they would be unable to keep the limits ordained by God. There is no blame on either of them if she give something for her freedom. These are the limits ordained by God so do not transgress them.
> (Quran translation 2:229)

In some cases, a Moslem wife might be willing to keep her marriage but find herself obliged to claim for a divorce because of some compelling reasons such as, cruelty of the husband, desertion without a reason, a husband not fulfilling his conjugal responsibilities, infidelity, etc. In these cases the Moslem court dissolves the marriage.

In short, Islam has offered the Moslem woman some unequalled rights. She can end the marriage through Khula' - sue for a divorce. A Moslem wife can never become chained by a stubborn uncooperative husband. It was these rights that enticed Jewish women who lived in the early Islamic societies of the 7th century CE seek to obtain bills of divorce from their Jewish husbands in Moslem courts. The Rabbis declared these bills null and void. In order to end this practice, the Rabbis gave new rights and privileges to Jewish women in an attempt to weaken the appeal of the Moslem courts. Jewish women living in Christian countries were not offered any similar privileges since the Roman law of divorce practiced there was no more attractive than the Jewish law.

Let us now focus our attention on how Islam discourages divorce. A Moslem man should not divorce his wife just because he dislikes her. The Quran instructs Moslem men to be kind to their wives even in cases of lukewarm emotions or feelings of dislike:

> ... *Live with them (your wives) on a footing of kindness and equity. If you dislike them it may be that you dislike something in which God has placed a great deal of good.*
> *(Quran translation 4:19)*

However, Islam is a practical religion and recognizes that there are circumstances in which a marriage comes to the verge of collapse . In such cases, a mere advice of kindness or self restraint is no viable solution. So, what should be done in order to save a marriage in these cases? The Quran offers some practical advice for a spouse (husband or wife) whose partner (wife or husband) is the wrongdoer.

For the husband whose wife's ill-conduct (i.e. indecent, rebellious or wicked) is threatening the marriage, the Quran gives four types of advice as detailed in the following verses:

> *The men are made responsible for the women, and God has endowed them with certain qualities, and made them the bread earners. The righteous women will cheerfully*

accept this arrangement, since it is God's commandment and honor their husbands during their absence. As to those women on whose part you fear disloyalty and ill-conduct:

(1) Admonish them,

(2) refuse to share their beds,

(3) beat them; but if they return to obedience seek not against them means of annoyance: For God is Most High, Great.

(4) If you fear a break between them, appoint two arbiters, one from his family and the other from hers; If they wish for peace, God will cause their reconciliation.

(Quran translation 4:34-35)

On the first glance, the above verses sound harsh towards women, right? But if we analyze further, actually there is deep psychological wisdom embedded beneath it. Remember, the above verses are concerning the case of marriages where the wives are heading towards disloyalty and ill-conducts.

The first three are to be tried first. If they fail, then the help of the families concerned should be sought. It has to be noted, in the light of the above verses, that beating the indecent wife is a temporary measure that is resorted to as third in line in cases of extreme necessity in hopes that it might remedy the wrongdoing of the wife. If it does, the husband is not allowed by any means to continue any annoyance to the wife as explicitly mentioned in the verse. If it does not, the husband is still not allowed to use this measure any longer and the final avenue of the family-assisted reconciliation has to be explored.

Although men and women are equal we are forced to admit that there are certain things that the other gender cannot do. Men and women complete one another. A man would never be able to give birth to a child. And on average man are just stronger physically than women - not in men's ability to endure pain, but in strength. Although there are some reports of domestic violence caused by women, statistic shows that cases of domestic violence caused by men are far more frequent. The following is the data on domestic violence in America:

Domestic violence represented by wife beating or abuse is rampant in this country and around the world. While the exact numbers on domestic violence incidents differ, because this is such an under-reported crime there are statistics on which most experts agree.

1. In 1984 the US Surgeon General declared domestic violence as this nation's number one health problem. (US Surgeon General)

2. A woman is beaten every 15 seconds by her partner; it happens at some time in 25-35 % of American homes; 4,000 women die from such abuse each year. (FBI)

3. Physical abuse by male social partners is the single most common source of injury among women ages 15 to 44, more common than auto accidents, muggings and rape by a stranger combined. (U.S. Surgeon General, 1989)

4. In USA, medical costs from domestic violence total at least $3-5 billion annually. At least another $100 million can be added to the cost to businesses in lost wages, sick leave and absenteeism. (Sylvia Porter, For Your Money's Worth)

5. Women of all cultures, races, occupations, income levels, and ages are battered - by husbands, boyfriends, lovers and partners. (Surgeon General Antonia Novello, as quoted in Domestic Violence: Battered Women, publication of the Reference Department of the Cambridge Public Library, Cambridge, MA)

6. Approximately one-third of the men counseled (for battering) at Emerge are professional men who are well respected in their jobs and their communities. These have included doctors, psychologists, lawyers, ministers, and business executives. (For Shelter and Beyond, Massachusetts Coalition of Battered Women Service Groups, Boston, MA 1990)

Statistics as these should awaken all those in denial of the fact that wife beating and abuse is an endemic disease in all different cultures, religions and communities. It is as common in Western as it is in Eastern societies.

Men in Eastern (and Western) societies do not abuse their wives because of scriptural teachings, but because of a natural instinct of domination and aggression. God, knowing this, has therefore decreed a perfect law to help men control their temper and to solve any problems before resorting to physical aggression. These statistics reflect the failure of modern societies in treating this perilous condition in men. Despite advances in modern psychology and improved understanding of behavioral patterns of men, civilized and uncivilized, a successful solution to this aggressive behavior has not been found by man.

So at first glance the Quran may appear as if promoting physical abuse of women. But when reading the verse carefully one realizes that it actually prohibits abuse and beating of women by using the best psychological approach.

The advise to first talk and then avoid sexual contact, provides the necessary time and space for both parties to cool off, reason, examine the problem and reach a favorable agreement for both of them. Abuse of a wife will not happen if the man learns to follow the clear commandments of God in this verse and in the order decreed. Abuse will only happen when a man does not follow these commandments, and thus fails to cool off and reason with himself or with his wife.

Chapter (surah) 4, where the above verse can be found, entitled 'The Women', is one of the longest chapters in the Quran. It deals with many of the rights and responsibilities of women, rights that were first available to Western women only a few decades ago, and some that still aren't. The theme of this chapter is to defend women's rights, and countering injustice and oppression of women. Thus, any interpretation this verse must be in favor of the women, not the other way around.

Unfortunately the above verse is extremely abused by many Moslem men in the world. While disregarding their own obligations and their own righteousness, these men only focus on the third step of handling this difficult condition as described in the verse, skip the first two necessary steps and give them the excuse to beat their wives. Once again, we have to remember that the right given to the man in that verse can only be claimed when you have a situation with a righteous man on one hand dealing with a situation in which his wife commits 'Neshooz' which is an unrighteous, disloyal, wicked and rebellious act.

Abusing this law, and the attempt to apply it to regular daily marital disagreements, is not warranted by the strong and selective wording of the verse. Furthermore, for a man to take this action, he must first give that woman all the rights God has given her and follow all aspects of the commandment without skipping any part of it. God clearly says in the Quran that He has decreed for the men and the women rights and obligations equitably.

In reality, a believing husband would most probably never come to the stage where he would actually lay a hand on his wife. He would be much too careful to examine his own motives first, as a God fearing man, before exercising this right. As we see in the verse immediately following, when the marriage reaches this stage it is already on it's way to end, as the very next words in the Quran reads; "If a couple fears separation..."

Most women in the world today do not enjoy the protection the above verse grants them. Instead they are unjustly abused, verbally and physically, by unrighteous men in unrighteous ways, and get beaten up for the most trivial of reasons, or for no reason at all. According to this verse even if the husband has a good reason, he is not allowed to lay a hand on his wife until he has passed all the previous steps. We also learn that one of the traits of a believer is that he/she is able to suppress anger:

> They (believers) are suppressors of anger, and pardoners of the people. God loves the charitable.
> (Quran translation 3:134)

And now, for the wife whose husband's ill-conduct (i.e.: violent, irresponsible or indecency) is threatening the marriage, the Quran gives the following advice:

> If a wife fears cruelty or desertion on her husband's part, there is no blame on them if they arrange an amicable settlement between themselves; and such settlement is best.
> (Quran translation 4:128)

In this case, the wife is advised to seek reconciliation with her husband (with or without family assistance) or to separate in an amicable terms. It is notable that the Quran is not advising the wife to resort to the two measures of abstention from sex and beating. The reason for this disparity is to protect the wife from a violent physical reaction by her already misbehaving husband. Such a violent physical reaction will do both the wife and the marriage more harm than good – just as the above statistic has proven to us. The above verse doesn't mean that a man is allowed to beat a woman, and not the other way around.

Let's face it, what would happen in reality if a wife beats her already violent husband? The most probable chance is that she will end up being beaten worst. So it is better for her to leave him if the situation is already beyond repair.

The nature and essence of a healthy relationship between a husband and wife is beautifully expressed in the following verse from the Quran:

Among His proofs is that He created for you spouses from among yourselves, in order to have tranquility and contentment with each other, and He placed in your hearts love and care towards your spouses. In this, there are sufficient proofs for people who think.
(Quran translation 30:21)

Their Lord responded to them: "I never fail to reward any worker among you for any work you do, be you male or female, you are members of one another (i.e. equal)...
(Quran translation 3:195)

To sum up, the Quran offers married couples much viable advice to save their marriages in cases of trouble and tension. If one of the partners is jeopardizing the matrimonial relationship, the other partner is advised by the Quran to do whatever possible and effective in order to save this sacred bond. If all the measures fail, the Quran allows the partners to separate peacefully and amicably.

FEMALE INHERITANCE

Another important differences between the Quran and the Bible is their attitude towards female inheritance of the property of a deceased relative.

The **Old Testament**'s rules of inheritance are outlined as the following verses:

And thou (Moses) shalt speak unto the children of Israel, saying, If a man dies, and has no son, then ye shall cause his inheritance to pass unto his daughter. And if he has no daughter, then ye shall give his inheritance unto his brethren. And if he has no brethren, then ye shall give his inheritance unto his father's brethren. And if his father have no brethren, then ye shall give his inheritance unto his kinsman that is next to him of his family, and he shall

> *possess it: and it shall be unto the children of Israel a statute of judgment, as the Lord commanded Moses.*
> *(OT: Numbers 27:8 – 11)*

A wife is given no share in her husband's estate, while he is her first heir, even before her sons. A daughter can inherit only if no male heirs exist. A mother is not an heir at all while the father is. Widows and daughters, in case male children remained, were at the mercy of the male heirs for provision.

Christianity has followed suit for long time. Both the ecclesiastical (religious law) and civil laws of Christendom barred daughters from sharing with their brothers in the father's patrimony. Besides, wives were deprived of any inheritance rights. These iniquitous laws survived till late in the last century.

Among the pagan Arabs before Islam, inheritance rights were confined exclusively to the male relatives. The Quran abolished all these unjust customs and gave all the female relatives inheritance shares:

> *From what is left by parents and those nearest related there is a share for men and a share for women, whether the property be small or large - a determinate share.*
> *(Quran translation 4:7)*

Moslem mothers, wives, daughters, and sisters had received inheritance rights thirteen hundred years before Europe recognized that these rights even existed. The division of inheritance is a vast subject with an enormous amount of details (4:7,11,12,176). Why are there so many details? Just look around, and we will see how many problems and broken family caused by unfair inheritance settlements. The general rule is that the female share is half the males except the cases in which the mother receives equal share to that of the father.

This general rule if taken in isolation from other legislations concerning men and women may seem unfair. In order to understand the rationale behind this rule, one must take into account the fact that the financial obligations of men in the Quran far exceed those of women (see the 'Wife's property?' section). A bridegroom must provide his bride with a marriage gift. This gift becomes her exclusive property and remains so even if she is later divorced. The bride is under no obligation to present any gifts to her groom. Moreover, the Moslem husband is charged with the maintenance of his wife and children.

The wife, on the other hand, is not obliged to help him in this regard. Her property and earnings are for her use alone except what she may voluntarily offer her husband. Besides, one has to realize that Islam vehemently advocates family life. It strongly encourages youth to get married, discourages divorce, and does not regard celibacy as a virtue. Therefore, in a truly Islamic society, family life is the norm and single life is the rare exception. That is, almost all marriage-aged women and men are married in an Islamic society. In light of these facts, one would appreciate that Moslem men, in general, have greater financial burdens than Moslem women and thus inheritance rules are meant to offset this imbalance so that the society lives free of all gender or class wars.

PLIGHT OF WIDOWS

Because of the fact that the Old Testament recognized no inheritance rights to them, widows were among the most vulnerable of the Jewish population. The male relatives who inherited all of a woman's deceased husband's estate were to provide for her from that estate. However, widows had no way to ensure this provision was carried out, and lived on the mercy of others. Therefore, widows were among the lowest classes in (ancient) Israel and widowhood was considered a symbol of great degradation:

Fear not; for thou shalt not be ashamed: neither be thou confounded; for thou shalt not be put to shame: for thou shalt forget the shame of thy youth, and shalt not remember the reproach of thy widowhood any more.
(OT: Isaiah 54:4)

But the plight of a widow in the Biblical tradition extended even beyond her exclusion from her husband's property. According to Genesis 38, a childless widow must marry her husband's brother, even if he is already married, so that he can produce offspring for his dead brother, thus ensuring his brother's name will not die out.

Then Judah said to Onan, "Lie with your brother's wife and fulfill your duty to her as a brother-in-law to produce offspring for your brother".
(OT: Genesis 38:8)

The widow's consent to this marriage is not required. The widow is treated as part of her deceased husband's property whose main function is to ensure her husband's posterity. This Biblical law is still practiced in today's Israel. A childless widow in Israel is bequeathed to her husband's brother. If the brother is too young to marry, she has to wait until he comes of age. Should the deceased husband's brother refuse to marry her, she is set free and can then marry any man of her choice.

The pagan Arabs before Islam had similar practices. A widow was considered a part of her husband's property to be inherited by his male heirs and she was, usually, given in marriage to the deceased man's eldest son from another wife. The Quran abolished this degrading custom:

And marry not women whom your fathers married - except what is past - it was shameful, odious, and abominable custom indeed.
(Quran translation 4:22)

Widows and divorced women were so looked down upon in the Biblical tradition that the high priest could not marry a widow, a divorced woman, or a prostitute:

> The woman he (the high priest) marries must be a virgin. He must not marry a widow, a divorced woman, or a woman defiled by prostitution, but only a virgin from his own people, so he will not defile his offspring among his people.
> (OT: Leviticus 21:13-15)

The Quran, on the other hand, recognizes neither castes nor fatal persons. Widows and divorcees have the freedom to marry whomever they choose. There is no stigma attached to divorce or widowhood in the Quran:

> When you divorce women and they fulfill their terms (three menstruation periods) either take them back on equitable terms or set them free on equitable terms; But do not take them back to injure them or to take undue advantage, If anyone does that, he wrongs his own soul. Do not treat God's signs as a jest.
> (Quran translation 2:231)

> Those of you who die and leave widows should bequeath for their widows a year's maintenance and residence. But if they (the widows) leave (the residence) there is no blame on you for what they justly do with themselves.
> (Quran translation 2:240)

POLYGAMY

Let us now tackle another one of the most frequently asked questions in Islam: polygamy. Polygamy is a very ancient practice found in many human societies. The Old Testament does not forbid polygamy. On the contrary, the Old Testament and Rabbinic writings frequently attest to the legality of polygamy. King Solomon is said to have had 700 wives and 300 concubines:

> But king Solomon loved many strange women, together with the daughter of Pharaoh, women of the Moabites, Ammonites, Edomites, Zidonians, and Hittites: of the nations concerning which the LORD said unto the children of Israel, Ye shall not go in to them, neither shall they come in unto you: for surely they will turn away your heart after their gods: Solomon clave unto these in love. And he had seven hundred wives, princesses, and three hundred concubines: and his wives turned away his heart.
> (OT: 1 Kings 11: 1 – 3)

Also, David is said to have had many wives and concubines (2 Samuel 5:13). The Old Testament does have some injunctions on how to distribute the property of a man among his sons from different wives (Deuteronomy 21:15-16). The only restriction on polygamy is a ban on taking a wife's sister as a rival wife (Leviticus 18:18). Although ironically, according to the Old Testament, Jacob married two sisters: Rachel and Leah. The Talmud advises a maximum of four wives. European Jews continued to practice polygamy until the 16th century CE. Oriental Jews regularly practiced polygamy until they arrived in Israel where it is forbidden under civil law. However, under religious law which overrides civil law in such cases, it is permissible.

What about the New Testament? According to Father Eugene Hillman in his insightful book, Polygamy Reconsidered, "Nowhere in the New Testament is there any explicit commandment that marriage should be monogamous or any explicit commandment forbidding polygamy." Moreover, Jesus has not spoken against polygamy though it was practiced by the Jews of his society.

Father Hillman stresses the fact that the Church in Rome banned polygamy in order to conform to the Greco-Roman culture (which prescribed only one legal wife while tolerating concubinage and prostitution). He cited St. Augustine, "Now indeed in our time, and in keeping with Roman custom, it is no longer allowed to take another wife." African churches and African Christians often remind their European brothers that the Church's ban on polygamy is a cultural tradition and not an authentic Christian injunction.

Polygamy was a way of life in the Middle Eastern countries (as well as most African and Asian countries, and even a sect of Christian Mormon) until the Quran was revealed. When the earth was young and under-populated, polygamy was probably one way of populating it and bringing in the human beings needed to carry out God's plan.

So why not polyandry? Polyandry is the term for practice of a woman who has plural husbands. The purpose of polygamy in the ancient days is most likely to populate the earth, and a man can produce multiple offspring by mating with many wives. However, a woman can only get pregnant once every nine months even with many husbands. Apart from that, in general, by nature men have tendencies towards polygamy while women tend to prefer monogamy.

By the time the Quran was revealed, the world had been sufficiently populated. Actually, it is a total misconception to say that Islam invented polygamy or commanded polygamy. It is more precise to say that the Quran put down the first limitations against polygamy, because previous to the Quran revelations, it seems men were allowed to have unlimited number of wives (or maybe the verse concerning unlimited wives has also been altered by men).

Thus, polygamy is permitted in the Quran, but under strictly observed circumstances. Any abuse of this divine permission incurs severe retribution. Thus, although polygamy is permitted by God, we should examine the circumstances carefully before saying that a particular polygamous relationship is permissible.

An example here, which widely misunderstood is of the Prophet Muhammad. He was married to one wife, Khadijah, until she died. Thus, Khadijah and her children had Muhammad's full attention for as long as she was married to him, 25 years. So, Muhammad had one wife - from the age of 25 to 50. During the remaining 13 years of his life, he married the aged widows of his friends who left many children of his deceased friends, needing a complete home with a fatherly figure, and Muhammad provided that.

Other than marrying widowed mothers of orphans, there were three political marriages in Muhammad's life. His close friends Abu Bakr and Omar insisted that he marry their daughters, Aisya and Hafsah, to establish traditional family ties among them. The third political marriage was to Maria the Christian Egyptian, she was given to him as a political gesture of friendship from the ruler of Egypt. It is important to know that apart from Aisya, the rest of Muhammad's wives were widows and some were older then him.

Apart from that, Muhammad had more than one wife, during the peak of his mission; he was almost always on a war. So the accusation of him being a 'playboy' is far from the truth. If he was, he would not have gone to war while having many wives and also he would have chosen young, non-married women.

Muhammad's example tells us that a man must give his full attention and loyalty in marriage to his wife and children in order to raise a happy and wholesome family. Providing a fatherly figure for orphans is the only specific circumstance in support of polygamy mentioned in the Quran. The Quran repeatedly says that Moslems have to treat orphans (and widows) justly. So the rule of polygamy in the Quran is connected to taking care of orphans and/or widows.

The Quran emphasizes the limitations against polygamy in very strong words:

> O people! be careful of (your duty to) your Lord, Who created you from a single being and created its mate of the same (kind) and spread from these two, many men and women; and be careful of (your duty to) God, by Whom you demand one of another (your rights), and (to) the ties of relationship; surely God ever watches over you.
> And give to the orphans their property, and do not substitute worthless (things) for (their) good (ones), and do not devour their property (as an addition) to your own property; this is surely a great crime.
> And *if* you fear that you cannot act equitably towards orphans, then marry such women (the mothers of the orphans) as seem good to you, two and three and four; but if you fear that you may not be equitable in treating more than one wife, then you shall be content with one, this is more proper, that you may not deviate from the right course.
> (Quran translation 4:1 – 3)

And what most polygamist 'Moslem' men conveniently 'forget' to read is the following verse:

> You cannot be equitable in a polygamous relationship, no matter how hard you try, but be not reluctant (from one) with total reluctance, so that you leave her in suspense..
> (Quran translation 4:129)

Any married man knows how difficult it is to deal with just one wife, let alone four wives, right? The Quranic limitations against polygamy point out the possibilities of abusing God's law. Therefore, unless we are absolutely sure that God's law will not be abused, we had better resist our lust and stay away from polygamy.

If the circumstances do not dictate polygamy, we had better give our full attention to one wife and one set of children. The children's psychological and social well-being, especially in countries where polygamy is prohibited, almost invariably dictates monogamy. A few basic criteria must be observed in contemplating polygamy: it must alleviate pain and suffering and not cause any pain or suffering and if we have a young family, it is almost certain that polygamy is not suggested.

Thus, the Quran does not command polygamy. It does allowed polygamy as a solution in certain cases (it start with the word 'If' instead of 'do' or 'don't'). The rule concerning polygamy also has its restrictions. The Quran, contrary to the Bible, limited the maximum number of wives to four under the strict condition of treating the wives equally and justly. It should be understood that the Quran is not exhorting the believers to practice polygamy, or that polygamy is considered as an ideal. In other words, the Quran has 'tolerated' or 'allowed' polygamy.

Why is polygamy permissible? The answer is simple: there are places and times in which there are compelling social and moral reasons for polygamy. As the above Quranic verse indicates, the issue of polygamy in Islam cannot be understood apart from community obligations towards orphans and widows. Islam as a universal religion suitable for all places and all times could not ignore these compelling obligations.

In most human societies, females outnumber males. In the U.S. there are at least 8,000,000 more women than men. In a country like Guinea there are 122 females for every 100 males. In Tanzania, there are 95.1 males per 100 females. What should a society do towards such unbalanced sex ratios?

There are various solutions, some might suggest celibacy, others would prefer female infanticide (which still happens in some societies today!). Others may think the only outlet is that the society should tolerate all manners of sexual permissiveness: prostitution, sex out of wedlock, homosexuality, etc.

For other societies, like most African societies today, the most honorable outlet is to allow polygamous marriage as a culturally accepted and socially respected institution. The problem of the unbalanced sex ratios becomes truly problematic at times of war. Native American Indian tribes used to suffer highly unbalanced sex ratios after wartime losses. Women in these tribes, who in fact enjoyed a fairly high status, accepted polygamy as the best protection against indulgence in indecent activities. European settlers, without offering any other alternative, condemned this Indian polygamy as 'uncivilized'.

However, after the Second World War, there were 7,300,000 more women than men in Germany (3.3 million of them were widows). There were 100 men aged 20 to 30 for every 167 women in that age group. Many of these women needed a man not only as a companion but also as a provider for the household in a time of unprecedented misery and hardship. The soldiers of the victorious Allied Armies exploited these women's vulnerability. Many young girls and widows had liaisons with members of the occupying forces. Many American and British soldiers paid for their pleasures in cigarettes, chocolate, and bread.

We have to ask our own conscience at this point: What is more dignifying to a woman? An accepted and respected second wife as in the native Indians' approach, or a virtual prostitute as in the 'civilized' Allies approach? In other words, what is more dignifying to a woman, the Quranic prescription or the theology based on the culture of the Roman Empire?

It is interesting to note that at an international youth conference held in Munich in 1948 the problem of the highly unbalanced sex ratio in Germany was discussed. When it became clear that no solution could be agreed upon, some participants suggested polygamy. The initial reaction of the gathering was a mixture of shock and disgust. However, after a careful study of the proposal, the participants agreed that it was the only possible solution. Consequently, polygamy was included among the conferences final recommendations.

The world today possesses more weapons of mass destruction than ever before and the European churches might, sooner or later, be obliged to accept polygamy as the only way out. Father Hillman has thoughtfully recognized this fact, *"It is quite conceivable that these genocidal techniques (nuclear, biological, chemical..) could produce so drastic an imbalance among the sexes that plural marriage would become a necessary means of survival.... Then contrary to previous customs and law, an overriding natural and moral inclination might arise in favor of polygamy. In such a situation, theologians and church leaders would quickly produce weighty reasons and biblical texts to justify a new conception of marriage."*

To the present day, polygamy continues to be a viable solution to some of the social ills of modern societies. The communal obligations that the Quran mentions in association with the permission of polygamy are more visibly present in some Western societies than in Africa. For example, In the United States today, there is a severe gender crisis in the black community. One out of every twenty young black males may die before reaching the age of 21. For those between 20 and 35 years of age, homicide is the leading cause of death. Besides, many young black males are unemployed, in jail, or on dope. As a result, one in four black women, at age 40, has never married, as compared with one in ten white women. Moreover, many young black females become single mothers before the age of 20 and find themselves in need of providers. The end result of these tragic circumstances is that an increasing number of black women are engaged in what is called 'man-sharing'. That is, many of these hapless single black women are involved in affairs with married men. The wives are often unaware of the fact that other women are 'sharing' their husbands with them. Some observers of the crisis of man-sharing in the African American community strongly recommend consensual polygamy as a temporary answer to the shortage of black males until more comprehensive reforms in the American society at large are undertaken. By consensual polygamy they mean a polygamy that is sanctioned by the community and to which all the parties involved have agreed, as opposed to the usually secret man-sharing which is detrimental both to the wife and to the community in general.

The problem of man-sharing in the African American community was the topic of a panel discussion held at Temple University in Philadelphia on January 27, 1993. Some seventy of the speakers recommended polygamy as one potential remedy for the crisis. They also suggested that polygamy should not be prohibited by law, particularly in a society that tolerates prostitution and mistresses. The comment of one woman from the audience that African Americans needed to learn from Africa where polygamy was responsibly practiced elicited enthusiastic applause.

Philip Kilbride, an American anthropologist of Roman Catholic heritage, in his provocative book Plural Marriage For Our Time, proposes polygamy as a solution to some of the ills of the American society at large. He argues that plural marriage may serve as a potential alternative for divorce in many cases in order to obviate the damaging impact of divorce on many children. He maintains that many divorces are caused by the rampant extramarital affairs in the American society. According to Kilbride, ending an extramarital affair in a polygamous marriage - rather than in a divorce, is better for the children. *"Children would be better served if family augmentation rather than only separation and dissolution were seen as options"*. Moreover, he suggests that other groups will also benefit from plural marriage including elderly women who face a chronic shortage of men and the African Americans who are involved in man-sharing.

Billy Graham, the eminent Christian evangelist also recognized this fact: "*Christianity cannot compromise on the question of polygamy. If present-day Christianity cannot do so, it is to its own detriment. Islam has permitted polygamy as a solution to social ills and has allowed a certain degree of latitude to human nature but only within the strictly defined framework of the law. Christian countries make a great show of monogamy, but actually they practice polygamy. No one is unaware of the part mistress's play in Western society. In this respect Islam is a fundamentally honest religion, and permits a Muslim to marry a second wife if he must, but strictly forbids all clandestine amatory associations in order to safeguard the moral probity of the community.*"

It has to be added that polygamy in Islam is a matter of mutual consent. No one can force a woman to marry a married man. Besides, the wife has the right to stipulate that her husband must not marry any other woman as a second wife. The Old Testament, on the other hand, sometimes resorts to forcible polygamy. A childless widow must marry her husband's brother, even if he is already married (see the "Plight of Widows" section), regardless of her consent (Genesis 38:8-10).

It should be noted that in many Moslem societies (outside of the Middle Eastern countries) today the practice of polygamy is rare since the gap between the numbers of both sexes is not vast. In Indonesia, just recently, there was a case of a well-known religious preacher who decided to practice polygamy and surely enough his popularity rate went down soon afterwards. This means although polygamy is permitted, *most* Moslems (in Indonesia anyway) understand that it should be done out of necessity not out of lust. Because, if the intention of the man is purely to support the orphans and widows financially, he doesn't necessarily have to marry the mother, right?

CHAPTER ELEVEN

LIBERTE, EGALITE ET FRATERNITE

Balance of Justice

'L iberty, equality and brotherhood' was the rallying cry of the French Revolutionaries who brought an end to the oppression, inequalities and privileges of the absolute monarchy of France.

This revolution (1789–1799) was a period of political and social upheaval in the history of France and Europe as a whole, during which the French governmental structure, previously an absolute monarchy with feudal privileges for the aristocracy and

Catholic clergy, underwent radical change to forms based on Enlightenment principles of republic, citizenship, and inalienable rights.

The French Revolution was caused by the huge national debt created by the many wars of the 18th century CE, and the burden of a grossly inequitable system of taxation. The Roman Catholic Church - the largest landowner in the country levied a harsh tax on crops known as the 'dime'. While the dime lessened the severity of the monarchy's tax, it nonetheless served to worsen the plight of the poorest that faced a daily struggle with malnutrition. Meanwhile the noble class continued to life decadently despite the financial burden on the populace.

Maximilien Robespierre came to power in France shortly after the French Revolution began. As a philosopher of the Enlightenment, he supported the separation of Church and State in France. His policy of 'de-Christianization' promoted humanism and made France a secular nation. In July 1790, the National Constituent Assembly published the Civil Constitution of the Clergy. This document declared that the Pope was no longer the head of the Catholic Church in France. The Civil Constitution of the Clergy also declared that the French government had the right to confiscate all church land, which stretched across most of the French territory. Clearly, both the de-Christianization of France and the Civil Constitution of the Clergy represented Enlightenment ideas regarding religion and the separation of Church and State.

The Enlightenment not only changed the way people viewed religion, but it also changed the way people viewed the government, and it's political and social policies. Citizenship, democracy, and human rights were all important aspects of the Enlightenment.

As a result, the phrase 'liberty, equality, brotherhood', became a popular slogan of the French Revolution. Revolutionaries fought for a government by the people and for the people. They wanted a government where all men had the right to vote, and all citizens were equal before the law. The Revolution offered a chance to make these ideas a reality.

The most influential effect of the French Revolution was the shift from Absolute Monarchy to Republicanism. This not only reduced the power of a single ruler but transferred the power to the citizens. France was the largest European nation to convert to Republicanism at the time.

The effects of the French Revolution are not only felt by France but by almost every nation in the modern world. One of the most important effects is the spread of democracy and the Declaration of the Rights of Man (1789). (Main source of the above text: A Documentary Survey of the French Revolution by John Hall Stewart)

—❦—

So far we have analyzed the background, law and theological aspects of the three religions. Now, let's see what these religious books say about human rights in general. To keep it simple let's just analyze the topic of human rights in the three monotheistic books according to the above basic three categories: Freedom, Equality and Brotherhood.

FREEDOM
There are basically 3 types of freedom that is affirmed by democracy:
1. Religious
2. Political
3. Economical

Religious freedom
To analyze about religious freedom according to its history would

probably take another book, because throughout history religious freedom hardly ever existed. Sadly, this still persists today. Here is a very short list of religious persecution throughout our history:

- Much of the Jews population of the Kingdom of Judah was deported from Jerusalem and dispersed throughout the Babylonian Empire after King Nebuchadnezzar II seized Jerusalem in 586 BCE.
- Christians were persecuted by the Romans that began during the sadistic Emperor Nero's regime (1st century CE).
- 20.000 Yemeni Christians were massacred in a fire-pit by the Jew Dzu Nuwas (6th century CE).
- The Hindu King Sudhanvan from Ujjain (an Indian territory) ordered that all Buddhist from Ramesvaram until Himalaya to be killed (14th century CE).
- During the Spanish Inquisition around 60 millions Native Americans were killed (15th century CE).
- All Jews and Moslems were either persecuted or expelled from Spain in 1492.
- Tortures and even mass murders between Christian sects in Europe are uncountable especially between the 16th and the 17th century CE. The most notably in the Massacre of Saint Bartholomew's Day in 1572 where around 100,000 of the Huegenot Sect (Calvin Protestants) were killed by the Catholic mass in France.
- Many witches (pagans) were tortured and killed in Salem, America (1692).
- The number of witches killed in Europe is estimated between 200,000 – 500,000 (between the 16th – 18th century CE).
- Mormons were massacred in Missouri, America (1838).
- The most infamous case of anti-Semitism in the 20th century was the Holocaust, a systematic mass murder of European Jews by the Nazis.
- In mainland China members of the spiritual group Falun Gong were tortured in camps.
- In Iran, the constitution recognizes four religions whose status

is formally protected: Zoroastrianism, Judaism, Christianity and Islam. The constitution, however, also set the groundwork for the institutionalized persecution of the Bahais.

- Between 1950's and 1970's Buddhist nuns in Tibet suffered from persecution since within Tibetan society and Buddhist institutions their status was not equal to that of monks.
- Around 1.5 million Christians have been killed by the Janjaweed, the Arab Muslim militia, and even suspected Islamists in northern Sudan since 1984.
- In New Delhi, India more than 100 acts of violence have occurred in the past year against Christians. This included the stoning of Christian schools, the digging up of graves and desecrated icons.
- Thousands of Bosnian Moslems were slaughtered and expelled during the ethnic cleansing in the Srebrenica Massacre in 1995.
- And of course, the recent (and still on going) bombing attacks done by fanatic Moslems in the name of Jihad.

The list goes on…

⎯⎯ᴏ⋆ᴏ⎯⎯

The first constitution of human right in most (civilized) country is the freedom of religion. This right was written in the 18th century, but as we can see on the above list, religious persecution is still going on. Men from all religions have had their share in persecuting other men and women from other religions.

All religions teach peace, and yet we kill each other continuously just because of different beliefs. So, to find out the true teaching of religion, I am not going to refer to history, but let's analyze what the religious books say about this.

According to the Old Testament
If there arise among you a prophet, or a dreamer of

dreams, and giveth thee a sign or a wonder, And the sign or the wonder come to pass, whereof he spake unto thee, saying, Let us go after other gods, which thou hast not known, and let us serve them; Thou shalt not hearken unto the words of that prophet, or that dreamer of dreams: for the LORD your God proveth you, to know whether ye love the LORD your God with all your heart and with all your soul.

Ye shall walk after the LORD your God, and fear him, and keep his commandments, and obey his voice, and ye shall serve him, and cleave unto him.

And that prophet, or that dreamer of dreams, shall be put to death; because he hath spoken to turn you away from the LORD your God, which brought you out of the land of Egypt, and redeemed you out of the house of bondage, to thrust thee out of the way which the LORD thy God commanded thee to walk in. So shalt thou put the evil away from the midst of thee.

If thy brother, the son of thy mother, or thy son, or thy daughter, or the wife of thy bosom, or thy friend, which is as thine own soul, entice thee secretly, saying, Let us go and serve other gods, which thou hast not known, thou, nor thy fathers; Namely, of the gods of the people which are round about you, nigh unto thee, or far off from thee, from the one end of the earth even unto the other end of the earth; Thou shalt not consent unto him, nor hearken unto him; neither shall thine eye pity him, neither shalt thou spare, neither shalt thou conceal him: But thou shalt surely kill him; thine hand shall be first upon him to put him to death, and afterwards the hand of all the people.

And thou shalt stone him with stones, that he die; because he hath sought to thrust thee away from the LORD thy God, which brought thee out of the land of Egypt, from the house of bondage.

(OT: Deuteronomy 13: 1 – 10)

Thus, the Old Testament not only allows religious persecution, in fact, it clearly says that Jews are commanded by God to stone to death anyone who is teaching any other religion than Judaism.

According to the New Testament

Jesus answered, "I am the way and the truth and the life. No one comes to the Father except through me.
(NT: John 14 : 6)

The New Testament does not mention how to deal with others who are non-Christians; however it clearly mentions that anyone who does not follow the way of Jesus may not come to the Father (i.e. God).

According to the Quran

Surely, those who believe, those who are Jewish, the Christians, the converts; <u>anyone</u> who:
(1) believes in God, and
(2) believes in the Hereafter, and
(3) leads a righteous life,
will receive their recompense from their Lord; they have nothing to fear, nor will they grieve.
*(Quran translation 2:62 **and** 5:69)*

There is no compulsion in religion…
(Quran translation 2 : 256)

You shall have your religion and I shall have my religion.
(Quran translation 109 : 6)

The Quran clearly states that we should not force our religion to anyone, it is a personal choice and thus, persecution because of different belief or religion is not allowed.

Freedom is one of God's great gifts to men. I know for most non-Moslems the above verse might come as a surprise. Islam today is falsely accused as against freedom and tolerance. This notion comes from the ignorance of the non-Moslems and the misbehaviour of the so-called 'Moslems' themselves. How could Moslems persecute non-Moslems for not embracing Islam , when even saying bad words against pagan gods is forbidden by the Quran? Why? Because we could never convey the message of the True Religion by insulting others.

> Believers, do not say bad words against the idols lest they (pagans) in their hostility and ignorance say such words against God...
> (Quran translation 6:108)

The Quran clearly spells out that freedom should be the foundation of the ideal society that God has in mind for humanity. The Quran clearly let us choose to believe in Him or not, it is up to us to be able to see the Truth or not. The Quran does not only forbid religious persecution, it also teaches that any attempt or even just a discussion between different religions should be done in the best manner.

> Call to the way of your Lord with wisdom and goodly exhortation, and have disputations with them in the best manner...
> (Quran translation 16: 125)

Instead of fighting concerning religion, the Quran teaches us to remind each other, that there our God is the same, for there is only One God, the True God of (all) human.

> And do not dispute with the followers of the Book except by what is best, except those of them who act unjustly, and say: We believe in that which has been revealed to us and revealed to you, and our God and your God is One, and to Him do we submit.
> (Quran translation 29:46)

Political Freedom

I am really sorry to say that I failed to unearth any verse in the Old and New Testament concerning political freedom. Maybe, I just have not read careful enough. But from the many verses that have been quoted in the previous chapters, I think it is already clear enough that women have neither political freedom nor equality in the Old and New Testament. So even if I could find verses that support political freedom and equality in the Old and New Testament, they will contradict some of the verses that have been quoted in this book alone.

By contrast, the Quran does support political freedom and suggests that Moslems should decide affairs in a democratic way. Women also have freedom of speech, as discussed in the previous chapter about women.

> .. Their (Moslems) affairs are decided after due consultation among themselves, and from Our provisions to them they give (to charity).
> (Quran translation 42:38)

However, the Quran reminds us again that on top of our decision there is still God's law that has to be put into practice. And what is that? Not to forget that our decision has to be unselfish. Most of human's affair is concerning provision or money, so no matter what it is that we have agreed among us, we should never forget to spare some to charity for the poor people.

Economical Freedom

The New Testament is against the accumulation of wealth:

> Again I tell you, it is easier for a camel to go through the eye of a needle than for a rich man to enter the kingdom of God.
> (NT: Matthew 19:24)

In matters of economic gain, the Old Testament is the same as the Quran: it is permissible to gain wealth and trading is allowed as long as it is fair, although excessive interest or usury is prohibited. There is a difference, however, between the Old Testament and the Quran rules concerning usury. The Quran forbids usury. Point. The Old Testament forbid usury only amongst children of Israel, but allows them to practice it unto strangers!

> *Unto a stranger thou mayest lend upon usury; but unto thy brother thou shalt not lend upon usury: that the LORD thy God may bless thee in all that thou settest thine hand to in the land whither thou goest to possess it.*
> *(OT: Deuteronomy 23:20)*

> *You may say to yourself, "My power and the strength of my hands have produced this wealth for me." But remember the LORD your God, for it is he who gives you the ability to produce wealth, and so confirms his covenant, which he swore to your forefathers, as it is today.*
> *(OT: Deuteronomy 8: 17 – 18)*

> *He does not lend at usury or take excessive interest. He withholds his hand from doing wrong and judges fairly between man and man.*
> *(OT: Ezekiel 18:8)*

The Quran says:

> *O you who believe! Do not devour your property among yourselves falsely, except that it be trading by your mutual consent..*
> *(Quran translation 4:29)*

> *...God has allowed trading and forbidden usury..*
> *(Quran translation 2:275)*

EQUALITY

It is sad to see that in today's world, we can still see all kind of unequal treatment among mankind. Be it due to racial, gender and/or material possession. Worst of all is mankind's long history of slavery. We say that slavery is banished in the today's world. And yet we still see poor, uneducated children who are forced to work below minimum wages. Isn't this still some kind of slavery?

Captured Slaves in Africa

Here is a short history of slavery:

The history of slavery covers many different forms of human exploitation across many cultures and throughout human history. Slavery, generally defined, refers to the systematic exploitation of labor for work and services without consent and/or the possession of other persons as property. There is no clear timeline for the formation of slavery in any formalized sense. Slavery in the ancient cultures was known to occur in civilizations as old as Sumer, and found in every ancient civilization, including ancient Egypt, the Akkadian Empire, Assyria, ancient Greece, Rome and parts of its empire, and Saudi Arabia. Such institutions were a mixture of debt-slavery, punishment for crime, the enslavement of prisoners of war, child abandonment, and the birth of slave children to slaves. In the Roman Empire, probably over 25% of the population

281

was enslaved. In ancient Athens about 30% of the population consisted of slaves.

During the Roman Empire, the people subjected to slavery came from all over Europe and the Mediterranean. Greeks, Africans, Germans, Thracians, Gauls (or Celts), Jews, Arabs, and many more were slaves used not only for labor, but also for amusement (i.e. gladiators and sex slaves). If a slave ran away, he was liable to be crucified! By the late Republican era, slavery had become a vital economic pillar in the wealth of Rome. Slavery was so common, and citizenship restricted so firmly (only to native-born adult males), that the slaves in Rome far outnumbered the citizens.

In the Viking era starting ca. 793 CE, the Norse raiders often captured and enslaved weaker peoples they encountered. In the Nordic countries the slaves were called thralls. The thralls were mostly from Western Europe, among them were many Franks, Anglo-Saxons, and Celts. There is evidence of German, Baltic, Slavic and south European slaves as well. The slave trade was one of the pillars of Norse commerce during the 6th through 11th centuries CE.

Chaos and invasion made the taking of slaves habitual throughout Europe in the early Middle Ages. In Carolingian Europe (ca. 780 – 920 CE) approximately 20% of the entire population consisted of slaves. So many Slavs were enslaved for many centuries that the very name 'slave' derived from their name, not only in English, but in other European languages.

The Arab world traded in slaves for over a millennium. The Arab or Middle Eastern slave trade is thought to have originated with trans-Saharan slavery. The slave trade from East Africa to Arabia was dominated by Arabs and Africans traders in the coastal cities of Zanzibar, Dar Es Salaam and Mombassa. Male slaves were employed as servants, soldiers, or laborers, while female slaves were traded to Middle Eastern countries and kingdoms by Arab, Indian, or Oriental traders, some as domestic servants and others as sex slaves. Some sources estimate that between 11 and 17 million slaves crossed the Red Sea, Indian Ocean, and Sahara Desert from 650 CE to 1900 CE.

The Mongol invasions and conquests in the 13th century CE made the situation worse. The Mongols enslaved skilled individuals, women and children and marched them to Karakorum or Sarai, whence they were sold throughout Eurasia. Karakorum is a large mountain range spanning the borders between Pakistan, China, and India, located in the regions of Gilgit, Ladakh, and Baltistan. It is one of the Greater Ranges of Asia, often considered together with the Himalaya, but not technically part of that range.

http://en.wikipedia.org/wiki/Karakoram

Baltoro Glacier in Central Karakorum

The 15th century CE Portuguese exploration of the African coast, commonly regarded as the harbinger of European colonialism, also marked the beginnings of the slave trade which was to become a major element of this colonialism until the end of the 18th century CE.

The Atlantic slave trade peaked in the late 18th century CE, when the largest numbers of slaves were captured on raiding expeditions into the interior of West Africa. These expeditions were typically carried out by coastal African kingdoms, such as the Oyo Empire (Yoruba) and the kingdom of Dahomey, through more formal trade agreements with European traders or by slave raiding parties through more informal bounty agreements. The people captured on these expeditions were shipped by European traders to the colonies of the New World (America).

Human Sacrifice in an Aztec Temple

In Pre-Columbian Mesoamerica the most common forms of slavery were those of prisoners-of-war and debtors. People unable to pay back a debt could be sentenced to work as a slave to the person owed until the debt was worked off. Most victims of human sacrifice were prisoners of war or slaves. According to Aztec writings, as many as 84,000 people were sacrificed at a temple inauguration in 1487!

Slavery was commonly used in the parts of the Caribbean controlled by France and the British Empire. The Lesser Antilles islands of Barbados, St. Kitts, Antigua, Martinique and Guadeloupe, which were the first important slave societies of the Caribbean, began the widespread use of African slaves by the end of the 17th century CE, as their economies converted from tobacco to sugar production. The slaves were treated terribly, often beaten and raped. They had such miserable lives that death was considered a welcome release.

In 1619 twenty Africans were brought by a Dutch soldier and sold to the English colony of Jamestown, Virginia. Approximately one Southern family in four held slaves prior to war. According to the 1860, US census, about 385,000 individuals owned one or more slaves.

Between 1933 and 1945, the Nazi regime created many Arbeitslager (labour camps) in Germany and Eastern Europe. Prisoners in Nazi labour camps were worked to death on short rations and in bad conditions, or killed if they became unable to work. Millions died as a direct result of forced labour under the Nazis.

Between 1930 and 1960, the Soviet regime created many Lageria (labour camps) in Siberia. Prisoners in Soviet labor camps were worked to death on extreme production quotas, brutality, hunger and harsh elements.

Slavery in China has repeatedly come in and out of favor. Due to the enormous population of the region throughout most of its history, China has had an almost unlimited workforce of cheap labor. Thus, the economy would naturally rely on a system of serfdom, slavery, or a combination of both. Approximately 5% of China's population was enslaved in ancient Han China (206 BCE - 220 CE) and slavery continued in China until the early 20th century CE.

As the Japanese Empire annexed Asian countries, from the late 19th century CE onwards, archaic institutions including slavery were abolished in those countries. However, during the Pacific War of 1937-1945, the Japanese military used hundreds of thousands of civilians and prisoners of war as forced labour, on projects such as the Burma Railway. As many as 200,000 women mostly from Korea and China, and some other countries such as the Philippines, Taiwan, Burma, the Dutch East Indies (Indonesia), Netherlands, and Australia were forced into sexual slavery during World War II.

Modern day

According to Human Rights Watch, there are currently more than 40 million bonded laborers in India, who work as slaves to pay off debts; a majority of them are Dalits. There are also an estimated 5 million bonded workers in Pakistan. As many as 200,000 Nepali girls, many under 14, have been sold into the sex slavery in India. Nepalese women and girls, especially virgins, are favored in India because of their light skin.

The Arab or Middle Eastern slave trade continued into the early 1900s, and by some accounts continues to this day. As recently as the 1950s, Saudi Arabia had an estimated 450,000 slaves, 20% of the population. There are currently an estimated 300,000 women and children involved in the sex trade throughout Southeast Asia. It is common that Thai women are lured to Japan and sold to Yakuza -controlled brothels where they are forced to work off their price. Just as recently as in 2004 the government acknowledged to the United Nations that at least 25,000 Brazilians work under conditions 'analogous to slavery'. The top anti-slavery official puts the number of modern slaves at 50,000. More than 1,000 slave laborers were freed from a sugar cane plantation in 2007 by the Brazilian government, making it the largest anti-slavery raid in modern times in Brazil.

There is practically not a single race in this world who can truly claim that it is clean from history's dark shadow of slavery. Actually, all of us are still to blame. We can pretend that we are not supporting slavery at all, when in fact most of us still buy products using cheap child labor somewhere in India, China or Africa. Now, let's get back to our religious scriptural study.

According to the Old Testament

When Noah awoke from his wine and found out what his youngest son had done to him, he said, "Cursed be Canaan! The lowest of slaves will he be to his brothers." He also said, "Blessed be the LORD, the God of Shem! May Canaan be the slave of Shem.
(OT: Genesis 9:24-26)

Because the Israelites are my servants, whom I brought out of Egypt, they must not be sold as slaves.
(OT: Leviticus 25:42)

Your male and female slaves are to come from the nations around you; from them you may buy slaves. You may also buy some of the temporary residents living among you and members of their clans born in your country, and they will become your property.
(OT: Leviticus 25:44-45)

"If a man sells his daughter as a servant, she is not to go free as menservants do. If she does not please the master who has selected her for himself, he must let her be redeemed. He has no right to sell her to foreigners, because he has broken faith with her. If he selects her for his son, he must grant her the rights of a daughter. If he marries another woman, he must not deprive the first one of her food, clothing and marital rights. If he does not provide her with these three things, she is to go free, without any payment of money."
(OT: Exodus 21: 7 - 11)

According to the New Testament

There is neither Jew nor Greek, slave nor free, male nor female, for you are all one in Christ Jesus.
(NT: Galatians 3:28)

Servants, be obedient to them that are your masters according to the flesh, with fear and trembling, in singleness of your heart, as unto Christ; Not with eye service, as men pleasers; but as the servants of Christ, doing the will of God from the heart; With good will doing service, as to the Lord, and not to men: Knowing that whatsoever good thing any man doeth, the same shall he receive of the Lord, whether he be bond or free. And, ye masters, do the same things unto them, forbearing threatening: knowing that your Master also is in heaven; neither is there respect of persons with him.
(NT: Ephesians 6:5 – 9)

According to the Quran

And marry those among you who are single and those who are fit among your male slaves and your female slaves; if they are needy, God will make them free from want out of His grace; and God is Ample-giving, Knowing.
(Quran translation 24 : 32)

… do not compel your slave girls to prostitution, when they desire to keep chaste, in order to seek the frail good of this world's life; and whoever compels them, then surely after their compulsion God is Forgiving, Merciful.
(Quran translation 24 : 33)

And what will make you comprehend what the uphill road is? (It is) the setting free of a slave.
(Quran translation 90: 12 – 13)

Shockingly, according to the Old Testament slavery begins after the Deluge (Flood), by the curse of Noah to one of his own sons! Noah in the Quran is described as a righteous man, who would never advocate such heinous practice like slavery. Although, the Old Testament forbids the enslavement between the Israelites, it actually commands the Israelites to take slaves from amongst other nation! Furthermore, it contradicts the prohibition by saying that "if a man sells his daughter...." as if it is permissible to sell one's own daughters to slavery, right? Wow!

The New Testament considers slaves as equal to free men. However, the New Testament does not renounce the institution of slavery; it also says that slaves ought to serve their masters wholeheartedly. Eventhough, at the same time, slave owners must also treat their slaves fairly. The Quran does not only treats slaves as equal to free men but it also encourages us to free them and forbid slavery for sex. Why does the Quran still mention concerning slavery then? Because it is unrealistic not to mention it at all, since slavery was such a common practice during the Quranic revelation, and it still continues today!

Probably it is interesting to know, that two of the first converts from pagan to Islam were a woman (Khadijah – Muhammad's wife), and a slave Zaid Ibn Haritha (Muhammad's freed slave). The first Islamic muezzin - a person at the mosque who leads the call (adhan) to Friday service and the five times daily prayer – chosen by Muhammad because of his beautiful voice was a freed black Ethiopian slave called Bilal. His respected stature during the birth of Islam is an evidence of the importance of pluralism and racial equality in the foundations of the religion.

BROTHERHOOD
The Quran calls every believers as brothers-in-faith one to another despite their racial differences. Although this brotherhood still should not be above our sense of justice.

... However, if they need your help, as brethren in faith, you shall help them, except against people with whom you have signed a peace treaty. God is Seer of everything you do.
(Quran translation 8 : 72)

━━✦━━

Most people today tremble when watching news on CNN concerning some Islamic countries who intend to execute Islamic Law in their country. I am not surprised if this fear does not only arise amongst non-Moslem, but also amongst some Moslems as well. Myself included.

Why? Because, although the Quran commands freedom and equality, many so-called Moslem countries are not democratic in nature, instead, most of them are monarchy countries. Most 'Catholic' countries that hold high the value of democracy are also monarchy in the essence of religion, i.e. rank of Popes, Bishops - just like the 'Islamic' countries today with the religious scholars and Imams. Not a single Islamic country today has succeeded to apply the law entirely from the Quran. I have met several Indonesian women who worked in Saudi Arabia as house maids. They told me the most horrific stories about how their Arabian bosses treated them during their employment in that country. They practically treated and punished them as slaves during medieval time!

Thus, it is truly ironic, after the above analysis it is quite obvious that the USA and Western European countries (the so-called 'enemies of Islam' according to the fanatic Moslems) actually both as societies and nations practice 'God's Law of Freedom of Choice' as laid out in the Quran, in fact more so than any other nation in the world! The basic law of freedom and democracy in the USA and Western European countries, when applied, is parallel to the requirements advocated in the Quran.

There is a big difference, however, the Quran repeats again and again that above human's law, God's Law must still prevail. The practice of democracy must still be aligned with God's Command. Every decision must be based on moral ethic, logic and fairness, not only based upon the majority vote. And who can be more just and true but God? So why are we so scared if a country decides to apply the law according to God's Law? Doesn't the Western countries law originally came from the Bible?

Most 'modern' people believe that the voting system in democracy is the best way to find solution or settle a dispute. I agree, but there must be another guidance to put into consideration: if the majority of the people are correct in their choice/decision, then we should proceed. If not, we should find another guidance to solve the problem.

We always tell our children not to follow just about anything other children do. And when they say: "But everyone else is doing it, Dad, Mom!" What do we say then? "If everyone jumps over the bridge, would you follow as well?" Right? We should not simply agree with the majority of people without any justified background, or else unfairness will surely prevail.

CHAPTER TWELVE

PROPHETS OF GOD

commons.wikimedia.org

A Prophet

*T*here is One Supernatural Power. There is One God. There must be only One Message from this One God. So, why are there so many prophets and religions – teaching different messages?

According to Judaism

There are different opinions concerning how many prophets are there. A Jewish tradition says that there were 600,000 male and 600,000 female prophets. But only 48 male prophets left permanent messages to mankind. The prophet names that are mentioned in the Old Testament begin with Adam and end with Noahbiah. Although some Jewish works, like the Talmud states that Gentiles (non-Jews) may have prophets too, generally, Judaism does not accept that any of the prophets that are acknowledged in other religions are genuine prophets. Judaism holds that no true prophet may deliver other faith or religion as successor to Judaism.

According to Christianity

The New Testament states that Christians should judge the authenticity of a prophet by their fruits, by checking whether their prophecies come true or not. The New Testament also contains several warnings about false prophets. Some Christians believe prophecy ended with the coming of Jesus. Although the majority believe that John the Baptist was also a prophet at the time of Jesus. Whether Christians believe that Jesus was a prophet, Son of God or one of the gods in the Trinity – is still a matter of dispute today. We will go in detail concerning this matter later.

According to Islam

In general, it is agreed that there are 25 prophet names that are mentioned in the Quran – starting from Adam until Muhammad. This doesn't mean that there are only 25 prophets, since the Quran says that God has chosen prophets amongst every nation. Each of the prophets is believed to have been assigned a special mission by God to guide the whole or a group of mankind, depending on the mission assigned to each. The message that they brought are all the same – which is to believe and worship the One God, believe in the Judgment Day and to do good on earth.

—⊙⋆⊙—

So, Moslems believe in all the prophets mentioned in the first 5 books of the Old Testament (the Torah) and the original Gospel.

And Christians believe in all the prophets mentioned in the Old Testament. On the contrary, Jews believe that the last prophet was Noahbiah – not Jesus. And neither Jews nor Christians believe that Muhammad was the last prophet. Hmm…

Still, many Christian scholars believe that the coming of Jesus was already mentioned in the Old Testament, here are two examples thereof:

> But you, Bethlehem Ephrathah, though you are small among the clans of Judah, out of you will come for me one who will be ruler over Israel, whose origins are from ancient times.
> (OT: Micah 5:2)

Christians believe that Jesus was born in Bethlehem in Judea during the time of King Herod.

> Therefore the Lord himself will give you a sign: The virgin will be with child and will give birth to a son, and will call him Immanuel.
> (OT: Isaiah 7:14)

Jesus was born of Maria, who was a virgin. Immanuel is a name which may be translated as 'existing within God'. Therefore, many Christian scholars believe that the above verse is prophesizing the coming of Jesus.

—⊙✲⊙—

Many Moslem scholars also believe that the coming of Muhammad was also mentioned in the Old Testament, as the following examples:

> The burden upon Arabia. In the forest in Arabia shall ye lodge, O ye traveling companies of Dedanim. The

inhabitants of the land of Tema brought water to him that was thirsty, they prevented with their bread him that fled. For they fled from the swords, from the drawn sword, and from the bent bow, and from the grievousness of war.
For thus hath the Lord said unto me, Within a year, according to the years of an hireling, and all the glory of Kedar shall fail: And the residue of the number of archers, the mighty men of the children of Kedar, shall be diminished: for the Lord God of Israel hath spoken it.
(OT: Isaiah 21: 13 -17)

Arabia, and all the princes of Kedar, they occupied with thee in lambs, and rams, and goats: in these were they thy merchants.
(OT: Ezekiel 27:21)

The prophet that came from Arabia is Muhammad. Tema is an oasis in the north of Medina in Saudi Arabia (according to J. Hasting's Dictionary of the Bible) - where Muhammad and his persecuted followers migrated to flee from the swords of the 'mighty' men of Kedar.

Who is Kedar? According to Genesis 25:13, Kedar was the second son of Ishmael, the ancestor of Muhammad. See also Ezekiel 27:21 that clearly explains 'all the princes of Kedar' are Arabs merchants. Therefore, Moslems believe that the above verses foretold about the battle of Badr in which the few ill-armed faithful Moslems miraculously defeated the 'mighty' men of Kedar, who sought to destroy Islam and intimidate their own folks who turned to Islam.

*And I will shake all nations, and the **Himdah** (desire) all the nations will come; and I will fill this house with glory, says the Lord of hosts. Mine is the silver, mine is the gold, says the Lord of hosts, the glory of my last house shall be greater than that of the first one, says the Lord of hosts;*

*and in this place I will give **Shalom** (peace), says the Lord*
of hosts.
(OT: Haggai 2:7-9)

Some English Bibles translated the word 'Himdah' as desire.
Actually, the word Himdah in Hebrew has the same root of Hmd
- consonants pronounced Hemed -- in Arabic means 'to praise'
which is the root and the meaning of Muhammad's name. The
name 'Muhammad' is the transliteration of an Arabic name from
the passive participle of Hmd, i.e. 'the praised one'. Other Arabic
names from the same root include Mahmud, Ahmed, Hamid
and Al-Hamid, one of the beautiful names of God meaning 'The
Blesser'.

The word Shalom has the same root and meaning of the Arabic
'Salam' which means also 'peace and submission' which is also
the root of the word Islam itself. Therefore, Moslems believe that
the above verses are prophesizing the coming of Muhammad
and Islam.

Here is another one from the vision of Isaiah:

> *And the vision of all is become unto you as the words of*
> *a book that is sealed, which [men] deliver to one that*
> *is learned, saying, <u>Read this, [I pray thee]: and he saith,</u>*
> *<u>I cannot; for it [is] sealed: And the book is delivered</u>*
> *<u>to him that is not learned, saying, Read this, [I pray</u>*
> *<u>thee]: and he saith, I am not learned.</u> Wherefore the*
> *Lord said, Forasmuch as this people draw near [me]*
> *with their mouth, and with their lips do honor me, but*
> *have removed their heart far from me, and their fear*
> *toward me is taught by the precept of men: Therefore,*
> *behold, I will proceed to do a marvelous work among*
> *this people, [even] a marvelous work and a wonder:*
> *for the wisdom of their wise [men] shall perish, and the*
> *understanding of their prudent men shall be hid. Woe*

*unto them that seek deep to hide their counsel from
the LORD, and their works are in the dark, and they
say, Who seeth us? and who knoweth us? Surely your
turning of things upside down shall be esteemed as the
potter's clay: for shall the work say of him that made it,
He made me not? or shall the thing framed say of him
that framed it, He had no understanding? [Is] it not yet
a very little while, and Lebanon shall be turned into a
fruitful field, and the fruitful field shall be esteemed as
a forest? And in that day shall the deaf hear the words
of the book, and the eyes of the blind shall see out of
obscurity, and out of darkness."*
(OT: Isaiah 29:11-18)

According to Islamic tradition, Prophet Muhammad was
illiterate. His entire life he never learned to read nor write. The
exact circumstances of this first revelation were as follows: it was
the habit of Muhammad to frequently remove himself from the
midst of his fellow Arabs and their heathenistic actions and spend
many days secluded in the cave of Hiraa in the mountains of
Mecca where he would pray to God according to the religion
of Abraham. When Muhammad was 40 years old (610 CE), the
angel Gabriel suddenly appeared before him. Gabriel ordered
him to "Iqra!" (read, recite, repeat, proclaim). Muhammad, in
his terror thought he was being asked to read, so he stammered:
"I am unlettered." The angel Gabriel again ordered him to
"Iqra!" Muhammad again replied: "I am unlettered." The angel
Gabriel now took a firm hold of him and commanded him "Iqra
in the name of God who created!" Now Muhammad began to
understand that he was not being asked to read, but to recite,
to repeat. He began to repeat after him, and Gabriel revealed
to him the first verses of the Quran, those at the beginning of the
chapter:

*Read(Iqra): In the name of your Lord who created,
Created man from a clot. Read(Iqra): And your Lord is*

the Most Bounteous, Who teaches by the pen, Teaches
man that which he knew not.
(Quran translation 96:1 – 5)

The word Gabriel used to command Muhammad was the Arabic word 'iqra'. It is derived from the Arabic root word 'qara'. If we were to go back to the original Hebrew form of the verses of Isaiah 29:11, we would find that the actual word which is translated into English as "Read this (I pray thee)" is the Hebrew word qara' {kaw-raw'}.

Isn't it an amazing 'coincidence' that the Hebrew text used not only a word with the same meaning, but the exact same word? This very same prophecy was mentioned quite clearly in the Quran:

> *Those who follow the Messenger, the unlettered Prophet*
> *whom they find written in the Torah and the Gospel with*
> *them. He enjoins upon them that which is right and forbids*
> *for them that which is evil. He makes lawful for them all*
> *things that are good and prohibits for them all that is foul*
> *and he relieves them from their burden and the fetters*
> *that they used to wear. Then those who believe in him,*
> *honor him, assist him, and follow the light which is sent*
> *down with him: they are the successful.*
> *(Quran translation 7 : 157)*

And here is a very clear one from the Gospel of Barnabas. The Gospel of Barnabas was accepted as a Canonical Gospel in the Churches of Alexandria, Egypt until 325 CE. In 325 CE, the Nicene Council was held, where it was ordered that all original Gospels in Hebrew script should be destroyed. An Edict was issued that anyone in possession of these Gospels will be put to death. Although, today the Gospel of Barnabas is not presented in the New Testament, this Gospel still survived, we can still read it in the following website: www.barnabas.net/barnabasP39.html. And here is what is written in chapter 39:

299

Adam besought God, saying: "Lord, grant me this writing upon the nails of the fingers of my hands." Then God gave to the first man upon his thumbs that writing; upon the thumb-nail of the right hand it said: "There is only one God" and upon the thumb-nail of the left it said: "<u>Muhammad is Messenger of God</u>." Then with fatherly affection the first man kissed those words, and rubbed his eyes, and said: "Blessed be that day when you shall come to the world." (Gospel Barnabas : chapter 39)

The name Muhammad appeared in many chapters in the Gospel of Barnabas (chapter 39, 41, 44, 54, 55, 97, 112, 136, 163 and 220). Christians believe that these verses were inserted by Moslems.

I don't know what to think of this particular issue. Chronologically, it is not possible. Since this Gospel was 'rediscovered' by archbishop Anthemios of Cyprus in 478 CE. Meanwhile, Muhammad was born only in 570 CE, and he only started his mission 40 years later.

On the other hand, after reading many, many religious historical books, and realizing how many religious books had been altered by men of different races, I won't be surprised if indeed it is true that the Moslems inserted verses concerning Muhammad in the Gospel of Barnabas (of course on later date then 478 CE). Whether this is true or not, I found the context of the above verses seem strange. The fact that it mentions Muhammad's name being written on Adam's thumb-nail does not correspond to any Quranic verse and it simply sounds like a fairy tale.

⚬✶⚬

It is not very difficult to guess what the reason is for certain race to reject other prophets from another race. Again and again, this is another example of religion being intertwined with racial issue. The main reason is to prove the supremacy of one nation above another.

I personally cannot believe that only certain races are guided by true prophets of God. I think the explanation of God giving guidance to all nations is the only one that makes sense. We are all God's creatures, so why would God only give guidance to one nation and neglects the rest. That won't be fair.

So what really happened? As we have analyzed in the previous chapters; the topics that are discussed in these three religions are the same, although almost all the details are different. This far, my logic tells me that the Quran makes the most sense in comparison to the other two scriptures. Yes, I was born in a Moslem family, but I did not come to this conclusion because of my upbringing. I really studied all the three scriptures in search of the Truth. Actually, I do not only study these three scriptures, I am studying some Hindu and Buddhist books too. I believe you too can see why I come to this conclusion, right? And talking about racial supremacy... well, I am neither Arab nor Jew. And yes, I am aware that many Moslems practice religion radically and I will share with you in detail concerning the cause of this extremity in chapter 17.

Obviously (originally) the scriptures are telling the stories of the prophets in order to give us examples of how to lead a righteous life no matter in what circumstances we are born into. No matter how different and difficult our life situation is, we are commanded by God to act correctly. According to the scriptures, all the three religions have been rejected at one time or another. The Jews were enslaved by the Egyptians – they fled Egypt. The Christians were persecuted by the Romans – they hid and forgave the Romans. The Moslems were persecuted by their own people (the Quraisy) – at first they hid, then they fled, afterwards they fought back and finally they forgave the Quraisy.

In almost all the cases, it seems like Judaism has the simplest but harshest rules (i.e.: eye for eye). Christianity is more complicated, because it demands an almost inhuman perfection to be compassionate (i.e. no eye for eye – turn your other cheek). While Islam, is the middle ground of the two teachings; the rules in the Quran have more layers, more 'if' clauses (i.e. eye for eye, and if... but forgive is better...).

If we are open minded enough, we can clearly see how the newer rules in religion actually gets more sophisticated; just as human's society gets more complex since the time of Jacob to the time of Muhammad. Or probably, to be more precise, the 'newer' religion actually brings the teaching back to the original teaching which has been altered through the passage of time.

Either way, I believe all the Scriptures are telling stories about the prophets in order to give examples of good moral behaviour for us, right? But I am sorry to say, after reading the Old and New Testaments further, not only do I got confused by some of the stories but sometimes I even feel disappointed. So, I dare to say that I am convinced some of the stories are not originally from God. I believe that these Testaments originated from God, but clearly they have been altered by men.

There are many stories of the prophets in these Testaments that are not giving good examples. I am sure many people, even Jews and Christians do not read the Old and New Testaments *entirely*. Why?

The Bible (both Old and New Testaments) is an enchanting book with many amazing stories, but it is not easy to read. Apparently the total words in the Bible are around 788,000 words, while there are 'only' around 77,000 in the Quran. That means the Bible is more than 10 times the Quran word-wise. There are many stories in the Bible that are not told in the Quran. I think one of the reasons why many people do not read the entire Bible is because of the thickness, and also there are soo many names in it, that makes it very difficult to follow the stories.

Well, at least that was the case with me. When the first time I read the Bible, I was confused after only reading the first few pages of Genesis (the first book in the Old Testament). I loose track of who is who because only in Genesis chapter 10, for example, there are more than 100 names of people and cities listed in it! In the King James' Version this chapter is only written in half a page. No wonder, many people do not realize that there are many 'strange' stories to be found in the Bible. If you are interested to read the stories, I have compiled almost all of them in EarthTrek Volume 3: The Chronicle.

Here is one story that I just fail to understand its moral teaching. Or why this kind of story is even told in a religious book?

> *And Lot went up out of Zoar, and dwelt in the mountain, and his two daughters with him; for he feared to dwell in Zoar: and he dwelt in a cave, he and his two daughters. And the firstborn said unto the younger, Our father is old, and there is not a man in the earth to come in unto us after the manner of all the earth: Come, let us make our father drink wine, and we will lie with him, that we may preserve seed of our father. And they made their father drink wine that night: and the firstborn went in, and lay with her father; and he perceived not when she lay down, nor when she arose.*
>
> *And it came to pass on the morrow, that the firstborn said unto the younger, Behold, I lay yesternight with my father: let us make him drink wine this night also; and go thou in, and lie with him, that we may preserve seed of our father.*
>
> *And they made their father drink wine that night also: and the younger arose, and lay with him; and he perceived not when she lay down, nor when she arose. Thus were both the daughters of Lot with child by their father.*
> *(OT: Genesis 19: 30 – 36)*

What ethical example is the Old Testament trying to teach us? That it is fine to perform incest to repopulate the world? Although in the above case, it is only Soddom and Gomorrah that were destroyed. Ok, I can still buy that... but is it really necessary to go in such detail? Yes, when we read further... a lot, further.. like in other books already, we will learn that the above action finally took its toll... the descendants of Lot and his two daughters missed out in some inheritance. But even this explanation still leave unanswered questions. Such as: why did the descendants have to pay for the mistake committed by their ancestors? Why Lot, a prophet, let himself got so drunk like that?

Here is another one from the New Testament:

> Jesus left that place and went to the vicinity of Tyre. He entered a house and did not want anyone to know it; yet he could not keep his presence secret. In fact, as soon as she heard about him, a woman whose little daughter was possessed by an evil spirit came and fell at his feet. The woman was a Greek, born in Syrian Phoenicia. She begged Jesus to drive the demon out of her daughter.
> "First let the children eat all they want," he told her, "for it is not right to take the children's bread and toss it to their dogs." "Yes, Lord," she replied, "but even the dogs under the table eat the children's crumbs."
> Then he told her, "For such a reply, you may go; the demon has left your daughter." She went home and found her child lying on the bed, and the demon gone.
> (NT: Mark 7:24 - 30)

In the above story, Jesus symbolized the Jews as the children, and the Gentiles as the dogs. Now, although finally Jesus did help the Greek woman's child, at first he was reluctant. The usual explanation for this strange and racist behaviour is because Jesus wanted to test the woman's faith first. But come on, seriously... I don't believe that Jesus would have used such a degrading comparison. Just imagine how we would have reacted today if someone we look up to would say such a thing. I believe that this story too has been altered to proof the supremacy of one race above other races. I don't believe that both of the above stories truly are religious teaching coming from the One God, God of all men, our One God. Do you?

⁓ᴏ⋆ᴏ⁓

So why are there so many prophets? Why are there so many religions? Why are the teachings of the monotheistic religions who worship the same One God so diverse? Why are there so many nations with different languages in this planet? Why doesn't God just make one nation? Why doesn't God put a stop to all these (religious) wars?

According to the Old Testament

Now the whole world had one language and a common speech. As men moved eastward, they found a plain in Shinar and settled there.

They said to each other, "Come, let's make bricks and bake them thoroughly." They used brick instead of stone, and tar for mortar. Then they said, "Come, let us build ourselves a city, with a tower that reaches to the heavens, so that we may make a name for ourselves and not be scattered over the face of the whole earth."

But the LORD came down to see the city and the tower that the men were building. The LORD said, "If as one people speaking the same language they have begun to do this, then nothing they plan to do will be impossible for them. Come, let us go down and confuse their language so they will not understand each other."

So the LORD scattered them from there over all the earth, and they stopped building the city. That is why it was called Babel - because there the LORD confused the language of the whole world. From there the LORD

305

scattered them over the face of the whole earth.
(OT: Genesis 11: 1 - 9)

So according to the Old Testament, God scattered us to become many nations with different languages in order for us not to challenge Him, in order to confuse us so we do not understand each other. Is this so? Isn't God omnipotent? Why is He so threatened by humans?

The New Testament does not explain concerning this issue. But obviously, as we have seen in the story concerning the Greek woman, Jesus considered the Jews to be on higher ranks than the Gentiles.

According to the Quran

On the contrary to the Old Testament that says God made us into different nations to confuse us, the Quran actually says that He did so in order for us to know, to learn from each other and to test which ones of us act in the best of conducts.

> *O people, we created you from the same male and female, and rendered you distinct peoples and tribes, that you may recognize one another. The best among you in the sight of God is the most righteous. God is Omniscient, Cognizant.*
> *(Quran translation 49:13)*

> *(All) people were a single nation; then God raised prophets as bearers of good news and as warners, and He revealed with them the Book with truth, that it might judge between people in that in which they differed; and none but the very people who were given it differed about it after clear arguments had come to them, revolting among themselves...*
> *(Quran translation 2:213)*

And We did not send any apostle but with the language of his people, so that he might explain to them clearly..
(Quran translation 14:4)

..if God please He would certainly make you a single nation..
(Quran translation 16 : 93)

Do men think that they will be left alone on saying, we believe, and not be tried?
(Quran translation 29 : 2)

O Children of Israel, remember My favor which I bestowed upon you, and that I blessed you more than any other people.
(Quran translation 2:47)

And when We made a covenant with the children of Israel: You shall not serve any but God and (you shall do) good to (your) parents, and to the near of kin and to the orphans and the needy, and you shall speak to men good words and keep up prayer and pay the poor-rate. Then you turned back except a few of you and (now too) you turn aside.
[Quran translation 2:83]

And most certainly We gave Moses the Book and We sent apostles after him one after another; and We gave Jesus, the son of Maria, clear arguments and strengthened him with the holy spirit. What! Whenever then an apostle came to you with that which your souls did not desire, you were insolent so you called some liars and some you slew.
(Quran translation 2: 87)

Woe, then, to those who write the book with their hands and then say: This is from God, so that they may take for it a small price; therefore woe to them for what their hands have written and woe to them for what they earn.
(Quran translation 2 : 79)

And the Jews say: The Christians do not follow anything (good) and the Christians say: The Jews do not follow anything (good) while they recite the (same) Book. Even thus say those who have no knowledge, like to what they say; so God shall judge between them on the day of resurrection in what they differ.
(Quran translation 2: 113)

He has revealed to you the Book with truth, verifying that which is before it, and He revealed the Torah and the Gospel aforetime, a guidance for the people, and He sent the Quran.
(Quran translation 3: 3)

So according to the Quran, the teachings of all the prophets were originally the same. The Quran tells stories of almost all the prophets of the Old Testament; the difference is in the Quran every story about the prophets gave good examples for us. And if they made mistakes (and they all did, since they were all humans too), they received the consequences and repented.

The Quran confirms that God had blessed the Jews above other nations at one time (by raising many prophets from among them), until they started to reject some prophets and altered the Old Testament. The Quran also says that Jesus was a prophet; and not the Son of God. So, let's discuss about the controversial status of Jesus in the next chapter.

CHAPTER THIRTEEN

SON OF GOD?

*H*ere comes one of the most difficult topics that I am sharing with you in this book. Please open your heart while reading this chapter which is concerning one of the most sensitive topics in Christianity. Once again, I have no intention to criticise any religion, I am merely sharing information and my thoughts in search of Truth.

Some historians have agreed that the first society that has been established in mankind's history was most likely of religious origin – which confirms what the Quran says that God has given guidance (i.e. religion) to every nation of man. But mankind has always altered the teaching, one of the strongest tendency is to alter the monotheist teaching into polytheist (or atheist), by describing God in a human-like form, by picturing God and making God into many lesser gods. Just look at the ancient temple, tombs and palace ruins – eventhough the Quran says that mankind has always been informed about the One God, in almost all ancient ruins archeologists found some depiction of multiple gods.

I think our ancestors kept on falling into polytheism because the concept of this Invisible One God, who is Most Great, who encompasses everything and yet is nearer to man than his jugular vein is very difficult to understand, difficult to imagine. This reason makes us fail to understand the nature of God.

Human beings are visual beings, therefore we can not stop imagining and trying to picture God in a physical form. Hence, mankind keep on falling into polytheism again and again.

How can we picture God, when none is like Him? When vision cannot comprehend Him? When God is Most Greatest! How big is the greatest? Bigger than the sun? Bigger than the universe? How can we see the universe? It is already impossible for us to see with naked eyes how the earth rotating around the sun. Now, this Great God is closer to us than our jugular vein! Our jugular vein is located inside our necks, around our throats!

The only analogy I could think of is this: imagine a single cell in a human body. How could a cell ever be able to 'see' and understand the human body? When the human body encompasses that cell and is inside (or merge with) it?

Even if this cell manages to get out of the human body, how could it be able to see the human body which is so big in comparison to itself? It has to 'stand' so far apart in order to see the whole body, and with such great distance, its vision will be impaired, of course. It's a loose – loose situation!

Unfortunately, many of us only 'believe what we can see'. But in reality we cannot see most of the things in this universe! And I am not talking about ghost or anything here... We can not see electricity current. Without the help of technology, we also cannot see atoms.

If we can only believe what we see, we would still believe that the sun rotates around the earth. No matter what science has confirmed, we still 'see' the sun rotates around the earth, right? If we can only believe what we see, we would still believe that solid matter does not vibrate. Sometimes, we forget how small and insignificant we are. Just because dogs cannot see color, it doesn't mean that colors do not exist, right?

310

So, why is it so important that we do not picture God? Because, beside the fact that we cannot (vision cannot comprehend Him), when we do picture God it is always wrong.

Now, we have read the description of God according to the Quran. If all the other religious books describe God this way, I believe we won't come up with so many guesses about how God looks like - which is of course, always misleading. The picturing of God has also misled some Truth Seekers, who use religious books other than the Quran, to conclude that God is an alien. Surely aliens are also just other creatures of God. However, since religion is very important to us, we never stop trying to picture God. History has proven that mankind has always been doing this, even people who are so-called monotheist believers.

Just look at the paintings of God in Christendom. Doesn't God in those pictures look like Zeus - the Greek patron god?

The Lord God of the Bible and Zeus

This is not God. I know, those pictures look nice, don't they? I can fully understand the fascination of looking at pictures or statues of some 'divine' beings… especially when they are big. I cannot stop looking at the pictures of the sphinx, or the Indian gods for example. We are just built this way – to be tested. Yes, I know visualization can help us to materialize things… but we should never attempt to visualize God.

Look at the picture of God and Adam in the Sistine Chapel. I wonder why so many pictures of humans and angels during the early Roman Christendom epoch are almost naked? That doesn't look very religious, or decent... it is even totally the opposite of the first teaching of the Bible where Adam and Even feel shame due to their nakedness, right?

How did something like this happen in a monotheist religion? I have already listed the verses from the Bible that mention God who created man in His own image, who sleeps, gets jealous, walks in the garden, etc.

Verses like these indirectly make God human-like. Especially the verse that mentions that men are created in the image of God. Another point that has always bothered me is the verse that says God rested on the seventh day. On which part of the world did He rest on the seventh day? We know that daytime can only happen at one half of the earth, while the other half will be night. And why did God rest? What happened to the other part of the world, which was still day time when He rested?

Another tendency of human is to exaggerate, especially if it is concerning someone or something that we adore. Buddha started as a prophet, a spiritual teacher from India/Nepal, but then centuries later, many worship him as the 'Enlightened One'.

Here is another one, according to the New Testament around 2,000 years ago the Romans persecuted the Christian-Jews and even crucified Jesus. Then ca. 300 years later the same person they hunted and killed becomes their God! And the capital of Christianity today is in Vatican City – the religious capital city of the persecutor. What happened?

Simcha Jacobovici and Charles Pellegrino in their book 'The Jesus' Family Tomb' also express this odd phenomenon by using the following analogy:

According to most scholars, Jesus was crucified around 30 AD. Christianity became the official religion of the Roman Empire under Constantine the Great's regime in 312 AD. There is around three hundred years that separates the time of Jesus' crucifixion – as a guilty Jew that was accused of rebellion against the Roman Emperor and the time of Jesus' elevation as the highest God – if not the only God – for the exact same Empire. In a short period of time, Jesus' disciples who were a persecuted Jewish sect became the most dominant religion in the civilized world. Meanwhile, this was happening when other Jewish messiahs, such as Bar Kochba were still fighting against the Roman ruler.

Think about it. For Jesus to be accepted by the Romans, would be like convincing the Americans today that the leader of the Vietcong (*of the Vietnamese rebel*) was actually a peace lover and a son of God. (*I would use Osama ben Laden as an example - author*). That must have been difficult to accept.

So, one method used by the early Jesus followers who weren't Jews, to achieve the transformation of Jesus' movement from a persecuted Jew sect into a non-Jew world religion, is by separating themselves from the Jew Christian. Before the destruction of Jerusalem in 70 AD, that method was not possible, because no matter what, Jesus, his family, the prophets and their influential followers were all Jews. The people, who had touched Jesus, talked to him, shared bread with him and believed in his message were all Jews. However, after Jesus' crucifixion, a Jew named Saul who later became St. Paul, lead the non-Jew followers and threatened to defeat the original Jewish followers.

—∘⋆∘—

From a prophet of monotheistic religion, suddenly Jesus becomes a God of the Trinity. What is Trinity? Trinity is one of the oldest pagan traditions in the world, and <u>this Trinity doctrine is not mentioned anywhere explicitly in the Old nor the New Testaments.</u>

TRINITY

So when did the ideology of Trinity begun? There are many Trinity doctrines in the ancient world. But most probably ancient Babylonia (today Iraq) is the original place of this doctrine. According to most scholars this civilization flourished around 5,000 years ago. Below is the list of Trinity gods in many ancient traditions:

Babylon	: King, Prince and Queen
	Nimrod, Tammuz and Semiramis
	Shamash, Sin and Ishtar
Egypt	: Osiris, Horus and Isis
India	: Brahma, Wisnu and Shiva
Phoenician	: Ba'al, Tammuz and Ashtoreth
Greek	: Zeus, Apollo and Hera
Roman	: Jupiter, Mars and Venus
Christianity	: Father God, Jesus and the Holy Spirit

Ancient Pagan Trinity Symbols

The above are Trinity symbols from India, Babylon, Celts, and the one in the middle is the symbol of the All-Seeing Eye of the Egyptian Sun God - Ra which can be found in 1 US Dollar bill.

Ancient Pagan Worship Artifacts of the Trinity

Egypt

India

Babylonia

Norwegian

Germany

France

www.sabbatarian.com

The above artifacts were found in archeological excavations and historical museums. If we look at history, it is obvious that the worship of a Triune Godhead had been done by many ancient religions before Christianity.

The word Trinity comes from Trinitas, a Latin abstract noun that means 'three-ness', 'the property of occurring three at once' or 'three are one'. Thus, Trinity means three gods incarnation from one another. The basic concept of Trinity comes from the reflection of the three-in-one nature of the universe. For example: matter has three states: solid, liquid and gas. Any color of light can be formed from the three primary colors: red, yellow and blue. Time in our universe has three dimensions: past, present and future. There are three domains habitable on earth: land, sea and air. The nature of man is expressed as: mind, body and spirit. And yet, they are all one.

Now, although the above explanation makes sense, other numbers might apply also. Such as: two-in-one. Nature reflects itself in a dual system. For example: male and female. Yin and yang. Macroscopic and microscopic. Good and bad. Dark and light. True and false. Nothing and being.

In fact, there are also religions which base their doctrine on this dual reality, such as Zoroastrian - although some say that it is a monotheistic religion, it believes also in dualism, in short: two-in-one.

So why one then? Because this is the only explanation that is consistent with the scientific prove that we have today. As we have examined in Chapter 2.

There is only One Supernatural Power that originated the universe; He is the source of everything. Thus, obviously there are 'traces' or 'blue print' from Him all over the universe. His energy is everywhere. The best analogy that I can come up with is this: a drop of water contents the same essence of the sea. But a drop of water is still not the sea. A drop of water will never have the same power like the sea. Of course, this comparison is ultra miniscule in comparison of God and His creatures – for the sea does not create the drops of water. We have to be very careful not to turn around Reality.

The above Trinity method of thinking is the basic ideology that becomes the teaching of paganism. In pantheism we even elevate the whole humanity's importance in the universe. Again and again we try to elevate human's importance in the universe. Yes, we are all a part of God. So are the animals, the plants and the stars. Everything. But that doesn't mean that we are all gods. The Creator and His creatures are just not the same. We are not creators. Whatever we create is in fact only reassembling, restructuring things that we find in nature. Historically, human has never created a single atom out of nothing, and never will. Point.

Yes, there is Oneness in all the three aspects of life; this is also true for every number in the universe. But God is beyond all that. God is the Source of it. We are all beings and beings are things. And the opposite of thing is nothing. No-thing.

In fact, both the Bible and the Quran agree with science that the universe starts from nothing. This No-thing is One. This No-thing is the Creator of the universe, the Supranatural energy that caused it. This Supranatural energy is not the universe – although His energy permeates all which is in the universe. If monotheist keeps on juggling and arguing about this One-ness we will surely end up believing in the existence of plural gods. It doesn't matter whether we say two–in-one or three–in-one, it is still not one… even mathematically it is still plural. And this believe is condemn by all the three monotheistic religions.

> I am the Lord, and there is no other; apart from Me there is no god.
> (OT: Isaiah 45:5)

> I, the Lord, am your God who brought you out of the land of Egypt, that place of slavery. You shall not have any other gods beside me. <u>You shall not carve idols for yourselves in the shape of anything in the sky above or on the earth below or in the waters beneath the earth; you shall not bow down before them or worship them.</u> For I, the Lord, your God, am a jealous God....
> [OT: Deuteronomy 5:6-9]

> "The most important one," answered Jesus, "is this: 'Hear, O Israel, the Lord our God, the Lord is one.
> (NT: Mark 12:29)

> Pagans indeed are those who say that God is a third of a trinity. There is no god except the one God.
> (Quran translation 5:90)

It is totally illogical to claim ourselves as monotheists and still believe in the Trinity. Every Trinity teaching always has depiction or statues of the three gods – including Christianity, although this is strictly forbidden in the Bible itself. There are pictures or statues of Jesus or Maria or the saints in almost every church. And Christians do worship to the direction of the altar where usually the statue of crucified Jesus or Maria is placed. I know, this doesn't mean that Christians are worshipping the statues, it is just symbolic.

But with all due respect, dear Christians: isn't this the exact same reasoning the pagan use? They also know that the statues are just symbols to some other 'divine' beings they believe to be gods. They are not really worshipping the statues, but the 'spirits' which are symbolized by the statues. So what is the difference?

More food for thought, why is Jesus pictured as having light hair (sometimes blond) and blue eyes with European features? Jesus was a Jew. Please, don't bite my head off, but please search inside your heart, would any Westerner worship Jesus if he was pictured as a Jewish man (i.e. Semitic looking)? In a TV program made by BBC there is a picture of how Jesus would have looked like, made by an American artist, an expert in creating 3D computerized feature out of a skull. The picture has been aired on a program made by BBC about the history of Jesus. The picture is made out of the assumption of what Jesus would look like from a skull of an average Jew man of the 1st century CE. You can see the picture in the Internet (Google), just type: Jesus BBC.

Would any Westerner worship the Semitic looking Jesus as passionately as the Westernized version of Jesus? Probably not. Do you think this is absurd? Well, have you seen a picture of a black Jesus? I have. Do you think this is absurd? Well, actually this is not more absurd than the depiction of a blond, blue eyed Jesus. No one really knows how Jesus looked like, but most likely he was not blond and blue eyed.

Why are we doing this? Isn't it obvious that some races in the world just want to claim Jesus to come from their own cultural heritage? This is all unjustified, of course.

In truth is, we have been doing this since the dawn of time. Have you ever seen a picture of Buddha? I am talking about the depiction of the Chinese, overweight looking Buddha. Now, there is no way Buddha would look like that. Buddha was an Indian prince (born in today's Nepal) who was a vegetarian and almost always on a fast. He could not have been overweight. Dear Christians and Buddhists, please don't get me wrong, I have no intention to criticize Jesus or Buddha. Actually, quite on the contrary, **I believe Jesus and Buddha were true great spiritual masters, and we could never do them justice by trying to depict them** – especially the way we do by fitting their looks according to our nationalistic point of views. This is misleading.

Back to Trinity in Christianity, if Jesus would have taught that he is one of the Gods in Trinity, why didn't he say so? Why did he have to say it in such riddles? Why did he say God is one? Why did the Trinity doctrine appeared only around 300 years after his departure, when Christianity has already become the major religion of the Roman Empire – once a pagan nation who believed in Trinity?

My conclusion to all the above religious doctrines is this: all those teachings are just made by men. Many men from many nations who want to claim God only for their nation or race. But aren't we smarter than that? So, is Jesus really the son of God? The Old Testament mentions about sons of God. A theory suggests that it applies for all children of Adam. In fact, this same context can also be found in the Gospel of John:

> *To all who believed him and accepted him (Jesus), he gave the right to become children of God, children born not of natural descent, nor of human decision or a*

husband's will, but born of God.
(NT: John 1:12)

But many Christians believe that Jesus literally is the son of God. The concept of son of God is not a new concept in human history. There are few traditions of sons of gods: the Sumerians believe that Gilgamesh was half human, half god.

Probably, the most well-known myths concerning sons of gods; are the ones of the ancient Greeks and Romans. For example: Virgil Aenas was Son of the goddess Venus; Dionysus, Apollo and Hercules were sons of Zeus – the father god.

Now, is it a coincidence that Jesus the Jewish Prophet suddenly transformed into Jesus the Son of God after the Romans converted into Christianity? Weren't the ancient Romans pagan people? Isn't this exactly what the Quran says about Trinity? Here is another food for thought; Jesus taught of humbleness, he even said this:

> *Again I tell you, it is easier for a camel to go through the eye of a needle than for a rich man to enter the kingdom of God.*
> *(NT: Matthew 19:24)*

Jesus also told his disciples to sell all their possessions to give to the poor. Jesus was clearly against the accumulation of material possessions, so how come the capital city of Christianity today, i.e. the Vatican City is so decadent. Yes, it is beautiful but it does not relate to the teaching of Jesus. Do you ever wonder what Jesus would say if he sees this?

Why are there many churches filled with golden plated statues of Maria and the saints? And why do the Pope and all his Cardinals dressed in such a pompous way? They almost look like royalty from the olden days.

The Dome of St. Peter's Basilica, Vatican City

It might come as a surprise for many Christians, that one of the longest chapters in the Quran is called Maryam (Maria) – named after Jesus' mother. In fact, Maria is the only woman mentioned by name in the Quran! Jesus name is mentioned 25 times in the whole Quran; far more often the name of Muhammad – which is only mentioned 4 times (excluding names that are written in brackets). The Quran is clear about who Jesus is. Jesus was one of God's prophets. His miraculous birth was explained very simply in Quran: he was born miraculously of a virgin. But this should not be taken as a sign of divinity. The Quran clearly explains that to do something like that is very easy for God, just as the way God had created Adam without a father or a mother. It is also interesting to note that Adam's name, like Jesus, is also mentioned 25 times in the Quran:

> *Surely the likeness of Jesus is with God as the likeness of Adam; He created him from dust, then said to him, Be, and he was.*
> *(Quran translation 3:59)*

Some Christians explain that Jesus is one of the Gods in Trinity incarnated in human form by using the following metaphor: a human being can not talk to ants. So how can a person talk to ants? That human being has to somehow transform himself into an ant. Since in a human form, this person would be far too great for the ants to see and also in an ant form, the human can communicate in the ant's language.

Yes, that makes sense. But God is so much powerful than that, He can do whatever He wants. For thousands of years He had sent prophets and messengers, so why the sudden need for sending His son to earth? Out of desperation? Not to mention sacrificing His only son on the cross to save mankind. This doesn't even make sense. I think the Quran version makes more sense. If God would have wanted to, He could have make us all believe in Him. No sweat.

> ... so if He (God) please, He would certainly guide you all.
> (Quran translation: 6:149)

Please, don't get me wrong. I believe that Jesus was upright, loving and kind. I believe that his teaching is good. But I don't believe that he is God or son of God. How can I believe in that when many verses in the New Testament concerning this matter are contradictive?

So how did this Trinity teaching begun in Christian's history? The first recorded use of the word Trinity in Christianity begun in about 180 CE by Theophilus of Antioch, who implicitly point to the context of Trinity by using the term: "God, His Word, and His Wisdom". Actually, the term 'Trinity' or 'Triunity' never appeared in the Old or New Testaments. Various verses from both Testaments have been cited as supporting this doctrine, while other passages are cited as opposing it.

Who is Theophilus of Antioch? Theophilus was a Patriarch of Antioch (today Turkey), his death probably occurred at 183 – 185 CE. We gather from his remaining writings that he was born a pagan, not far from the Tigris and Euphrates, and was led to embrace Christianity by studying the Jewish and Christian Scriptures, especially the prophetical books.

He wrote Apologia ad Autolycum to convince a pagan friend, Autolycus about the divine authority of Christianity. His arguments were drawn almost entirely from the Old Testament, with very few references to the New Testament. He made the truth of Christianity by demonstrating that the books of the Old Testament were older than the writings of the Greeks and that they were divinely inspired. However, some of the theories that he proposed were absurd, i.e.: he asserts that Satan is called the dragon (Greek: drakon) who revolted from God; he also ridicules those who maintain the spherical form of the Earth.

Theophilus transcribes a considerable portion of Genesis chapters 1- 3 with his own allegorizing comments upon the successive work of the Creation week. The sun is the image of God, the moon of man, whose death and resurrection are prefigured by the monthly changes of that luminary. The first three days before the Creation of the heavenly bodies are types of the Trinity - the first place in Christian writings where that terminology is known to occur: i.e. "God, His Word and His Wisdom".

Then, in about 200 CE Tertullian, an early Christian author who was raised in Carthage (modern Tunisia) gave the first exposition of the formula of Trinity which is the 'three Persons, one Substance', i.e. the 'Father, Son and Holy Spirit'. Finally in 325 CE, Trinity was established in the Council of Nicea. So, what exactly happened at this famous council? What did the Roman Emperor decide in front of some 250 quarreling Christian bishops?

"The Council of Nicea was of great importance in Christianity and even in world history," wrote historian W.H.C. Frend. It was during this council that the doctrine of Christ's divinity was formally affirmed for the first time. Never before in world's history had the entire church gathered to determine policy and doctrine (let alone at the bidding of the Roman emperor).

The following article, written by the late writer and biographer Robert Payne (d. 1983), is excerpted and adapted from his book 'The Holy Fire: The Story of the Early Centuries of the Christian Churches in the Near East' (1957). Today some biblical scholars may debate about the historical details, but no other narrative conveys as well the human dimension of this critical event.

THE COUNCIL OF NICEA

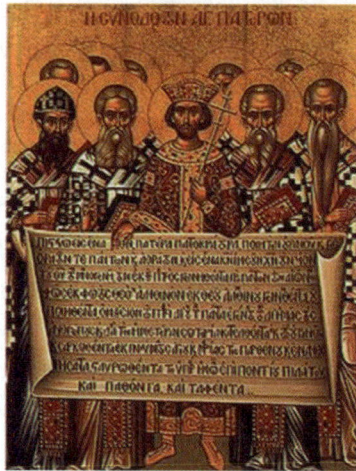

www.pcontent.answers.com

Council of Nicea

Pope Alexander of Alexandria *(in modern Egypt)* had called a meeting of the presbyters *(priests)*. According to the historian Socrates, the aging 'pope' (some early senior bishops were called 'papa' - that is, 'father') with perhaps too philosophical minuteness began to lecture on the theological mystery of the Holy Trinity. Alexander had been discussing the Father, the Son, and the Holy Ghost for some time when he was interrupted by one of the presbyters called Arius, a native of Libya. In combating Alexander, Arius fell into a new heresy, for he announced, "If the Father begat the Son, then he who was begotten had a beginning in existence, and from this it follows there was a time when the Son was not".

Here, at some time in 319 AD, the cry of the Arians - "There was a time when the Son was not" - was first heard. The words were to have an extraordinary influence on the shaping of the church. They were dynamite and split the church in two, and these words, which read in Greek like a line of a song, still echo down the centuries.

THE ISSUE
Alexander was appalled by the new heresy and knew that desperate measures would be necessary to combat it. Once it is admitted that "there was a time when the Son was not," then a bewildering series of further heresies follows. High as he is, the Son is now infinitely lower than the Father. The words are like a wedge, splitting the monotheism of the church. Athanasius (Alexander's chief deacon assistant) saw the danger clearly, and he seems to have taken over from Alexander the task of refuting Arius.

It was a very simple heresy. All Arius said was that if the Father begat the Son, then the Son must have had a birth, and therefore there was a time when the Son of God did not exist. He had come into existence according to the will of the Heavenly Father, and therefore he was less than the heavenly Father, though greater than man. Christ was no more than a mediator between man and God. No, answered Alexander and Athanasius; Christ is absolute God. In our own heretical age, the dispute between Athanasius and Arius may appear to be a splitting of hairs, but it was not so at the time. But the difference between Christ the mediator and Christ the God is a very real one, and whether Christ is of the same substance (homo-ousios) or a like substance (homoiousios) to God the Father is a matter of importance to all Christians, not only theologians. Arianism brought Christ down to earth, making him at once inferior to the Father, and more popular. His heresy had the power to destroy the Church.

ROUND ONE
The clergy of Alexandria were assembled to discuss the matter, and most of them signed an urgent letter to Arius, begging him to acknowledge his heresy.

Arius refused. Alexander had no alternative but to summon a synod of the bishops of Egypt and Libya and depose Arius and his followers. But the people wanted something they could sing, and this Arius provided in abundance. "There was a time when the Son was not" became a catch phrase. There were many other catch phrases, hymns and songs, "to be sung at table and by sailors, millers, and travelers."

The people took up the cause of Arius, who withdrew to Palestine and later to Nicomedia (*in modern Turkey*), where he was protected by the bishop. Here in a corner of Asia Minor not far from Byzantium (*modern Istanbul*), Arius continued to taunt the pope of Alexandria. Already the evil that had begun in the church of Alexandria was running through all Egypt, Libya, Upper Thebes, Palestine, and Asia Minor.

THE EMPEROR STEPS IN

Inevitably it came to the ears of the emperor; he decided to send Hosius to Nicomedia and Alexandria with a letter written in his own hand, ordering by imperial prescript an end to the quarrel. But he had acted too late, the quarrel was blazing furiously. "In every city," wrote a historian, "bishop was contending against bishop, and the people were contending against one another, like swarms of gnats fighting in the air". There had been bloodshed in the streets. Constantine decided to call a general council to resolve the conflict, in a small city of Nicea in Bithynia (*modern day Turkey*), a few miles from Nicomedia. By Constantine's orders, 1,800 bishops were invited to attend the council. These bishops came from Syria and Sicilia, Arabia, Palestine, Egypt, Libya, Mesopotamia, Persia, Scythia, and Europe.

VICIOUS DEBATES IN SONG

The conference was now open. Everyone was suddenly arguing. There was a wild waving of arms. Arius burst out into a long, sustained chant, having set his beliefs to music. These chants and songs were sung by the people, and Arius may have thought the emperor would listen more keenly to chanting than to a disquisition on the faith. The anti-Arian bishops were appalled, closed their eyes, and put their hands over their ears. Finally, Eusebius of Caesarea (*today Israel*) suggested a creed that he had first heard as a child, an astonishingly beautiful creed that was to form the basis of the creed finally adopted. This creed read:

> We believe in one God, the Father Almighty, maker of all things visible and invisible, and in one Lord Jesus Christ, the Word of God, God from God, Light from Light, Life from Life, the only begotten Son, the Firstborn of every Creature, begotten of the Father before all worlds, through whom also all things were made. Who for our salvation was made flesh and lived among men, and suffered and rose again on the third day, and ascended to the Father, and shall come again in glory to judge the quick and the dead; And in the one Holy Ghost. Believing each of them to be and to have existed, the Father, only the Father, and the Son, only the Son, and the Holy Ghost, only the Holy Ghost...

This creed the emperor accepted, and the Arians, seeing in it nothing that specifically destroyed their position, would have accepted it if their opponents had not seen that this creed failed in any way to resolve the conflict. It was necessary to state the creed in such a way that the Arians would be forced to deny their essential tenets. Pope Alexander discussed the matter with Hosius. Constantine, turning against the Arians he had previously favored, suggested that Christ should be defined as *homoousios* - one in essence with the Father - and this definition should be included in the creed.

The orthodox bishops were gaining strength. A new creed, formed by patching together the old creed and a new, more vigorous statement of the anti-Arian position, was finally announced by on June 19. It read:

> We believe in one God, the Father Almighty, maker of all things visible and invisible. And in one Lord Jesus Christ, the Son of God, begotten of the Father, only begotten, that is, from the substance of the Father, God from God, Light from Light, very God from very God, begotten not made, of the same substance as the Father, through whom all things were made, both things in Heaven and things in earth; who for us men, and for our salvation, came down and was made flesh, was made man, suffered and

rose again the third day, ascended into Heaven, and shall come to judge the quick and the dead. And in the Holy Ghost. And those who say "There was a time when he was not" and "He did not exist before he was made" and "He was made out of nothing" or those who pretend that the Son of God is "of another hypostasis or substance" or "created" or "alterable" or "mutable," the Catholic Church anathematizes.

In this form, the Nicene Creed left much to be desired. It was tortured, blunt-edged, without poetry or rhythm, and without the nobility of the creed of the church of Palestine. But many words that gave a living significance to the original creed - "the Word of God," "the Firstborn of every creature," "begotten of the Father before all worlds" - were in fact deliberately omitted to show that the triumphant Alexandrians would allow no compromise, no loophole for the Arians and were bent on avoiding all misunderstanding.

POETRY FROM CHAOS
In its original form, the Nicene Creed was a weapon: it was to become a more sublime article of faith in time, when poetry and ornament and a less abrupt rhythm were fashioned for it by the simple process of adding words. These words, which gave depth and resonance to the Creed, were added at the Council of Constantinople in 381 AD, and finally approved at the Council of Chalcedon (a district in modern Istanbul) in 451 AD. Then the second clause came to read:

> And in one Lord Jesus Christ, the only-begotten Son of God, begotten of the Father before all worlds, Light from Light, very God from very God, begotten not made, being of one substance with the Father, through whom all things were made; who for us men and for our salvation came down from the heavens and was made flesh of the Holy Ghost and the Virgin Mary, and was made man, and was crucified for us under Pontius Pilate, and suffered and was buried, and rose again on the third day according to the Scriptures, and went up into the heavens, and sits on the right hand of the Father, and is to come again with glory to judge the quick and the dead, and of his kingdom there shall be no end.

Arius was publicly anathematized (*cursed*). According to the historian Socrates, Constantine issued an imperial prescript ordering that all the books of Arius should be burned "so that his depraved doctrine shall be entirely suppressed and so that there shall be no memorial of him left in the world." The punishment for concealing any book compiled by Arius was death!

⟋ᴑ✶ᴑ⟍

When the Roman Emperor Constantine saw the great religious division among the different geographical parts of his empire he became concerned that this might affect the stable condition of the current rule that Rome had on these areas. So out of concern for the Roman Empire he put into motion what is historically called the (First) Council of Nicea at 325 CE.

The emperor saw these divisions as threatening to the civil harmony of the empire and he knew he had to do something to stabilize the situation and return the control to Rome as it once had on its entire civilization. Constantine was not concerned with the truth, he was concerned with peace and control. So, in his imperial wisdom, he implemented a meeting of the religious leaders of these divided areas which were under the Roman law. The resulting declaration of that meeting would set into motion what is called the Trinitarian Doctrine. However, the church leaders had great difficulty coming to an agreed declaration which could be unanimously decreed. Many declarations were submitted and turned down for lack of total agreement on the part of the religious leaders. The final declaration was settled and the religious leaders returned to their lands with a new decree to base their religious yet still divided.

WHO IS JESUS?
Isn't it hard to believe that the concept of Trinity in the most influential religion in the world was decided in such a way, around 300 years after the generally accepted time of Jesus' departure?

Obviously, Trinity was not the original teaching of Jesus himself. In fact, the New Testament itself has prophecied that this would happen!

> *For the time will come when they will not endure sound doctrine; but after their own lusts shall they heap to themselves teachers, having itching ears.*
> *(2 Timothy 4:3)*

So: who is Jesus? I am not going to answer this question myself, but below is a condensed version of an article by Lisa Spray, author of 'Jesus; Myth and Message'.

Most people growing up in the West have a pretty definite idea of who Jesus Christ was and what he taught. Jesus of Nazareth was born of a virgin, grew up in Palestine and spent the later years of his rather short life teaching of the coming of the Kingdom of God. He began a new religion, which was to become one of the driving forces in Western civilization. For those who worship him, he is the son of God, part of the Godhead, or God Himself. To millions of people, this is the truth. But is it? Well, partially. Many of the major tenets of Christianity developed centuries after the death of Christ. Some of them are contrary to his actual teachings. We will examine some of these using the Bible itself as our main reference.

At the core of those doctrines is the identity of Jesus Christ. For most Protestant denominations, Jesus is part of the Trinity and might be defined as God's manifestation or revelation of Himself in human form. Catholics also accept the Trinity and bestow upon Mary the title of the 'Mother of God,' thus asserting that Jesus is, for the Catholics, truly man and truly God.

Some of the more recently formed denominations have quite a different view. For instance, Jehovah's Witnesses do not accept the Trinity and see Jesus as the ransom sacrifice to redeem humanity, not God Himself. And Unitarians generally see Jesus as a great teacher and example, but fully human and God's son only in the same sense that all humans are His children.

On the scholarly front, there has long been a wide range of understandings of Jesus. He has been seen as an Essene (*an ancient Jewish sect*) scholar, a member of a radical Jewish political movement, a witty rabbi, and many other things. For years a number of scholars have worked to discern the historical figure of Jesus Christ from the background of the scriptural narrations and whatever other sources they could find. That interest continues today, as is witnessed by the recent paper back reprinting of Albert Schweitzer's book The Quest of the Historical Jesus, and the new release of John Crossan (The Historical Jesus, Harper Collins, 1991).

For some scholars, like John Bowden, the search has ended in serious questioning and skepticism. For others the skepticism goes farther. As an example, G. A. Wells poses the following question about Jesus, "Can we really be sure that a person described in these terms ever had any earthly existence?" His answer is summed up by the last thought in his book, "is it not time to look elsewhere than in the Scriptures for guidance in our living, and to stop basing our decisions and choices on ancient fantasies?" (Who Was Jesus? G. A. Wells, Open Court Publishing, La Salle, IL, 1989.)

John Hick, H. G. Wood Professor of Theology at Birmingham University, compares the exaltation of Jesus to the status of God with the deification of Buddha in Buddhism. He blames the innovation of the incarnation doctrine on a human tendency to elevate the founder of any given religion. He states (Ibid. p.170):

Buddhology and Christology developed in comparable ways. The human Gautama came to be thought of as the incarnation of a transcendent, pre-existent Buddha as the human Jesus came to be thought of as the incarnation of the pre-existent Logos or divine Son. In the Mahayana the transcendent Buddha is one with the Absolute as in Christianity the eternal Son is one with God the Father.... We are seeing at work a tendency of the religious mind, which is also to be seen within the history of Christianity. The exaltation of the founder has of course taken characteristically different forms in the two religions. But in each case it led the developing traditions to speak of him in terms which he himself did not use, and to understand him by means of a complex of beliefs which was only gradually formed by later generations of his followers. Each essay in The Myth of God Incarnate is a careful piece of honest scholarship and soul searching commentary. Such work requires the moral courage to step out of one's upbringing, indeed, out of one's culture, and allow the objective examination of one's own faith. The unanimous conclusion of these courageous theologians is that the concept of God incarnate is indeed innovation and not part of the teachings of Jesus Christ.

If in Jesus the fullness of God himself is permanently incarnate, Jesus can be directly worshipped as God without risk of error or blasphemy. A cult of Christ as distinct from a cult of God then becomes defensible, and did in fact develop. The practice of praying direct to Christ in the Liturgy, as distinct from praying to God through Christ...slowly spread, against a good deal of opposition, eventually to produce Christocentric piety and theology. An example of the consequent paganization of Christianity was the agreement to constitute the World Council of Churches upon the doctrinal basis of 'acknowledgement of our Lord Jesus Christ as God and Savior'- and nothing else.

Perhaps it was only when Christocentric religion finally toppled over into the absurdity of 'Christian Atheism' that some Christians began to realize that Feuerbach might have been right after all; a Chalcedonian Christology could be a remote ancestor of modern unbelief, by beginning the process of shifting the focus of devotion from God to man....

Similarly, it could not resist the giving of the title Theotokos, Mother of God, to Mary. The phrase 'Mother of God' is prima facie blasphemous, but it has had a very long run, and the orthodox have actively promoted its use, fatally attracted by its very provocativeness.

The doctrine of Christ as God's divine son has here humanized deity to an intolerable degree. The strangeness of it is seldom noticed even to this day. A sensitive theologian like Austin Farrer can dwell eloquently upon a medieval icon of the Trinity, and a philosopher as gifted as Wittgenstein can discuss Michelangelo's painting of God in the Sistine Chapel, and in neither case is it noticed that there could be people to whom such pagan anthropomorphism is abhorrent, because it signifies a 'decline of religion' in the only sense that really matters, namely, a serious corruption of faith in God.

At one time or another we have all asked ourselves: Who is God? Who was Jesus?

In trying to answer this question we will be drawing on many sources of information, a few of which most Christians have not explored. Back to our question. Was Jesus God? The answer may come as a shock to many Christians, as it did to me. Jesus never said he was God. Actually, he said over and over, and in many ways, that he was not God. Jesus was a practicing Jew, and such a concept is now, and would have been then, totally against the Law of Moses (Mosaic law). The next few quotes from the Bible show us that Jesus was a devout and learned Jew, a rabbi:

> Jesus returned in the power of the Spirit to Galilee, and his reputation spread throughout the region. He was teaching in their synagogues, and all were loud in his praise. He came to Nazareth where he had been reared, and entering the synagogue on the Sabbath as he was in the habit of doing, he stood up to do the reading.
> (Luke 4:14-16)

As a rabbi, what did Jesus teach? Throughout the New Testament, Jesus exhorted us to worship God alone and keep the Mosaic commandments. The first and best known commandment in both the Old Testament and the New Testament advocates total and absolute devotion to God alone:

The Lord our God is Lord alone! Therefore, you shall adore the Lord your God with all your heart, with all your soul, with all your mind, and with all your strength.
(Deuteronomy 6:4-5) (Mark 12:29-30)

Jesus especially stressed this First Commandment:

The scribe said to him: "Excellent, Teacher! You are right in saying, 'He is the One, there is no other than He.' Yes, 'to love him with all our heart, with all our thoughts and with all our strength, and to love our neighbor as ourselves' is worth more than any burnt offering or sacrifice." Jesus approved the insight of his answer and told him, "You are not far from the reign of God."
(Mark 12:32-34)

Again, Jesus' straightforward injunctions to follow the commandments in general, and the First Commandment in particular, are throughout the New Testament. Significantly, he described the First Commandment as 'The Great Commandment' (Mark 12:29). The statement of this injunction is very strong:

I, the Lord, am your God who brought you out of the land of Egypt, that place of slavery. You shall not have any other gods beside me. You shall not carve idols for yourselves in the shape of anything in the sky above or on the earth below or in the waters beneath the earth; you shall not bow down before them or worship them. For I, the Lord, your God, am a jealous God....
(Deuteronomy 5:6-9)

For Jesus, this commandment meant more than just an injunction against physically worshiping idols. Often people use phrases like 'he worships the ground she walks on', or 'he's my idol'. These phrases show the subtle idol worship that pervades our daily lives. Jesus taught the absolute devotion to God alone. On one occasion a lawyer stood up to pose him this problem:

"Teacher, what must I do to inherit everlasting life?" Jesus answered him: "What is written in the law? How do you read it?" He replied: "You shall love the Lord your God with all your heart, with all your soul, with all your strength, and with all your mind; and your neighbor as yourself." Jesus said: "You have answered correctly. Do this and you shall live."
(Luke 10:25-28)

We see that Jesus stressed pure worship of the Father, in spirit and truth. It is not possible that Jesus could have so strongly taught total devotion to God, and then advocated his own worship.

EARLY CHRISTIAN JEWS
It is also very clear that the early Christians still considered themselves to be Jews, and thus subject to the Mosaic laws revealed in the Torah. Dr. George M. Lamsa, in his book New Testament Origin makes a point of the Jewish origins of Christianity, and his quote from Matthew stresses Jesus's adherence to Mosaic law: Christians for some time continued to worship in the Jewish temple and in the synagogues, to observe Jewish customs and traditions, and to keep the Mosaic Law and the Sabbath. For nearly two centuries the bishops of Jerusalem were Semites. In other words, the followers of Jesus were loyal to the teachings of the prophets as expounded by their Master, who had told them that he had not come to destroy the law and the prophets but to fulfill them. Jesus said:

> Think not that I am come to destroy the law, or the prophets: I am not come to destroy, but to fulfill. For verily I say unto you, till heaven and earth pass, one jot or one title shall in no wise pass from the law, till all be fulfilled. Whosoever therefore shall break one of these least commandments, and shall teach men so, he shall be called the least in the kingdom of heaven: but whoso shall do and teach them, the same shall be called great in the kingdom of heaven.
> (Matthew 5:17-19)

Evidently Jesus left no doubt in the mind of his disciples in regard to his loyalty to the commandments and the teachings of the prophets. On his own identity Jesus's statements throughout the Bible suggest that any idea of exalting him to divinity was unthinkable. In Matthew's gospel, Jesus denounces in the strongest terms those who exalt him by calling him `Lord':

> "None of those who cry out, `Lord, Lord,' will enter the kingdom of God but only the one who does the will of my Father in heaven. When the day comes, many will plead with me, `Lord, Lord, have we not prophesied in your name? Have we not exorcised demons by its power? Did we not do many miracles in your name as well?' Then I will declare to them solemnly, `I never knew you. Out of my sight, you evil doers!"
> (Matthew 7:21-23)

Jesus would not even accept the praise of a man who called him good:

> "Good teacher, what must I do to share in everlasting life?" Jesus answered: "Why do you call me good? No one is good but God alone."
> (Mark 10:17-18)

If Jesus would not even allow himself to be called good, he certainly would not claim divine qualities. Perhaps some of the difficulty that humans have is that we do not really recognize the qualities of God. When we say that He is omnipotent and omniscient, we do not fully realize what that means - that God can do anything and that He knows everything, including our innermost secrets, and those we are not even aware of yet. Unless we do realize the full meaning of these qualities, it is possible to think of Jesus as having had them. But the next section shows clearly that he did not.

ONLY GOD HAS DIVINE QUALITIES
Surely, when Jesus prayed in the Garden of Gethsemane he demonstrated that he was neither omnipotent nor omniscient:

"Father, if it is your will, take this cup from me; yet not my will but yours be done."
(Luke 22:42)

Jesus made it clear in many, many ways that he was not God, that God is greater. Nowhere is this more definitely stated than when he spoke to his disciples about his imminent departure:

If you truly loved me you would rejoice to have me go to the Father, for the Father is greater than I.
(John 14:28)

JESUS'S PRAYER

As demonstrated above, and throughout the Gospels, Jesus prayed to God. This certainly argues against his being God. God would not pray to Himself. There were times when Jesus felt the need to pray with special urgency. Luke reports that, on one occasion, Jesus prayed very hard:

In his anguish, Jesus prayed with all the greater intensity, and his sweat became like drops of blood falling to the ground.
(Luke 22:44)

Jesus also prayed to God that the people might believe in him as God's messenger. This specifically defines the role of Jesus as deliverer of God's message:

...Jesus looked upward and said, "Father, I thank you for having heard me. I know that you always hear me but I have said this for the sake of the crowd, that they may believe that you sent me."
(John 11:41-42)

One of the most compelling pieces of evidence that Jesus was not God is in the way that he taught the disciples to pray.

One day he was praying in a certain place. When he had finished, one of his disciples asked him: "Lord, teach us to pray, as John

taught his disciples." He said to them, "When you pray, say: 'Our Father in heaven, hallowed be your name, your kingdom come, your will be done on earth as it is in heaven. Give us today our daily bread, and forgive us the wrong we have done as we forgive those who wrong us. Subject us not to the trial but deliver us from the evil one.' "
(Luke 11:1-4) (Matthew 6:9-13)

Note that Jesus taught us to pray to the Father, our Creator, not to himself. In fact, he did not mention himself in any way, nor did he indicate that we should pray in his name. His instructions were very specific - we are to pray to God alone. This would not be the case if Jesus himself were God.

REPORTED DYING WORDS
Even in the narration of his death, in the Gospels of Matthew and Mark, there is an incident that contradicts the concept of Jesus' divinity. According to these two references, Jesus was put on the cross and left to die, then:

> At that time Jesus cried in a loud voice, "Eloi, Eloi, Lama Sabachtani?" which means, "My God, my God, why have you forsaken me?"
> (Matthew 27:46) & (Mark 15:34)

It is not logical that God would ever say: "My God, my God, why have you forsaken me?" This utterance was recorded in both Gospels in Jesus' mother tongue, Hebrew/Aramaic, to emphasize the accuracy of transmission. Thus, according to this Christian narration, Jesus could not have been God.

EXAMINATION OF VERSES
We have seen that there is significant scriptural evidence that Jesus was not God. On the other hand, there are numerous other verses understood by many Christians to mean that he was divine. The rest of this chapter examines those verses.

It is appropriate at this time to quote from Michael Goulder, Staff Tutor in Theology, Birmingham University. Goulder states in The Myth Of God Incarnate: *...In my early ministry I was still a trembling believer in Chalcedonian orthodoxy - Jesus was God the Son, of one substance with the Father, who came down from heaven. Trembling beliefs do not alter themselves: they are reinforced daily by the repetition of the liturgy. When I look back, I think that the firmest plank on which my creed rested was the familiar passage in John 1, "The Word became flesh and dwelt among us...." This was not alone, for there were similar statements in Col. 1 and Phil. 2, and hints of the same in many of the Pauline letters, and in Hebrews. Where had St. John got the doctrine from? Not from Jesus.*

In these lines we see some of the Biblical references understood by many people to mean that Jesus is God. We also see in the same lines that Goulder found those roundabout statements do not bestow divinity upon Jesus.

> I cannot do anything of myself. I judge as I hear, and my judgment is honest because I am not seeking my own will but the will of Him who sent me.
> (John 5:30)

> My doctrine is not my own; it comes from Him who sent me. Any man who chooses to do his will know about this doctrine- namely, whether it comes from God or is simply spoken on my own. Whoever speaks on his own is bent on self-glorification. The man who seeks glory for him who sent Him is truthful; there is no dishonesty in his heart.
> (John 7:16-18)

In John 8:40, Jesus describes himself as 'a man who has told you the truth which I have heard from God'. Thus again we see that Jesus delivered the Word of God. Much of what we recognize today as the basic teachings of Christianity came to us through Paul. Remember that though Paul was the major missionary to the Gentiles in the years immediately following the crucifixion, he never met Jesus. All of his understanding of Jesus and what he taught came secondhand and through the visions which he had. Most of Paul's own teachings come to us through letters which he wrote to various Christian communities. His Epistle to the Colossians is an example. It was partly from this letter that Michael Goulder originally derived the idea of Jesus's divinity:

> He is the image of the invisible God, the first-born of all creatures. In him everything in heaven and on earth was created, things visible and invisible, whether thrones or dominations, principalities or powers; all were created through him, and for him. He is before all else that is. In him everything continues in being.
> (Colossians 1:15-17)

This obviously is Paul's teaching, not that of the man who said:

> Why do you call me good? No one is good but God alone.
> (Mark 10:18)

How can people be saved only by believing in Jesus if the New Testament itself teaches: Each man should look to his conduct; if he has reason to boast of anything, it will be because the achievement is his and not another's. Everyone should bear his own responsibility.... A man will reap only what he sows.

Clearly Jesus was not just any man. Though fully human, he was special. He was born miraculously of a virgin. He spoke with great wisdom as a newborn infant, and indeed, was a prophet from birth:

> She came with him to her family, carrying him. They said, "O Mary, you have committed something gross. O descendant of Aaron, your father was not a bad man, nor was your mother unchaste." She pointed to him. They said, "How can we talk with an infant in the crib?" (The infant spoke and) said, "I am a

servant of God. He has given me the scripture, and made me a prophet. He made me blessed wherever I go, and enjoined me to observe the contact prayers and the obligatory charity for as long as I live. I am to obey my mother; He did not make me a disobedient rebel. And peace be upon me the day I was born, the day I die, and the day I get resurrected."
(Quran 19:27-33)

Jesus worked great miracles even imparting life to clay birds and resurrecting the dead by God's leave. The teachings he brought are among the most beautiful ever given to mankind. If we all followed what he preached, the world would be a very wonderful place - heaven on earth - and the Kingdom of God, which he announced, would have indeed come to our planet. Jesus was the Messiah for whom the Jews waited. Though some Bible scholars have questioned whether Jesus ever claimed to be the Messiah, it is quite clear in the Gospel of John when Jesus was speaking to the Samaritan woman at the well:

> The woman said to him: "I know there is a Messiah coming." (This term means Anointed.) "When he comes, he will tell us everything." Jesus replied, "I who speak to you am he."
> (John 4:25-26)

The Quran confirms this:

> The angels said, "O Mary, God gives you good news of a Word from Him whose name shall be 'The Messiah, Jesus, son of Mary. He will be prominent in this world and in the Hereafter, and one of those closest to Me.' "
> (Quran 3:45)

All of the signs and miracles that Jesus manifested is 'God worked through him'. Jesus always recognized that he had no real power of his own. What he did was the will of his Omnipotent Lord:

I cannot do anything of myself. I judge as I hear, and my judgment is honest because I am not seeking my own will but the will of Him who sent me.
(John 5:30)

The Quran tells us that as a messenger to the Children of Israel he was to proclaim:

I am here to confirm the previous scripture, the Torah and to revoke certain prohibitions imposed upon you. I come to you with proof from your Lord. Therefore, you shall observe God, and obey me. God is my Lord and your Lord; you shall worship Him alone. This is a straight path.
(Quran 3:50-51)

And he said unto them, What things? And they said unto him, Concerning Jesus of Nazareth, which was a prophet mighty in deed and word before God and all the people.
(Luke 24:19)

For a complete reading of the above article you can read Lisa Spray's book or read on the Internet at www.submission. org/jesus.html.

CHAPTER FOURTEEN

ASTROLOGICAL SONS OF GOD

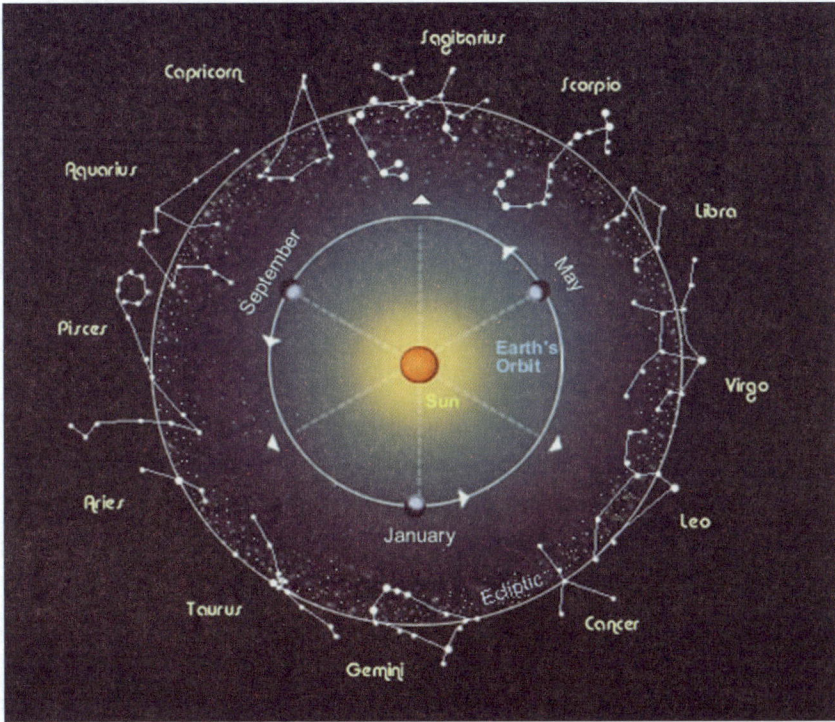

Zodiac Belt

*I*n this chapter I will share with you a really shocking information concerning the origin of the sons of gods myths in ancient religions. Since this book is getting too thick as it is, for the moment I am only sharing the brief explanation without going into the historical background. The historical background will be analyzed in the next two volumes of EarthTrek.

Almost all the ancient pagan religions originated from the worship of the sun. The reason is obvious, since the sun is deemed to be the source of life. Beside the sun, other heavenly bodies were also considered as divine by the ancients. The study of the influence of these heavenly bodies is known as astrology.

Although, it is true that astrology can be a fascinating and even helpful study to learn about the characteristic of people and nature, it can be dangerously misleading when it is taken to the degree of religious belief. However, this is exactly what happened in ancient times , and unfortunately still persists today, albeit in a subtler form.

According to astrology there are 12 constellations of stars encircling our solar system. This is called the Zodiac Belt. These 12 constellations were personified in myths sometimes as magical creatures or humans. We are still familiar with these 12 constellations of stars today which are used for horoscope prediction and are called the 12 star signs (i.e: Aries, Taurus, Cancer, etc.)

The sun is perceived as passing the 12 constellations in a year which reflects the 12 months of the year, the 4 seasons and the equinoxes (the time when the day and night are of equal lengths). The sun was perceived as the high god, because of its life giving and saving qualities. There are numerous sun gods in the ancient world, such as: Apollo, Surya, Amon-Re, etc.

The following are some myths concerning those sun gods or sons of gods which are surprisingly very similar to one another. The main source of this chapter is from a movie called Zeitgeist, a movie that conveys information that was originally written in a book called Suns of God by Acharya S (D. Murdock) – a Bachelor of Liberal Arts with degree in Greek Civilization and classically educated in archaelogy, history, mythology and languages.

HORUS of Egypt
ca. 3000 BCE

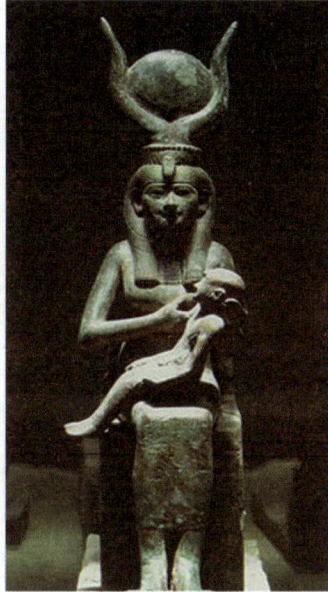

www.touregypt.net

Horus and Isis

Horus was born of the virgin Isis-Meri on December 25 and his birth was announced by a star in the east and attended by three wise men. Horus taught in the temple when he was a child. He was baptized when he was 30 years old by 'Anup the Baptizer'. Horus performed miracles and raised a man named El-Azar-us, from the dead. Not only did Horus walk on water, he was also crucified, buried in a tomb, and then resurrected. Horus was known as 'the Way', 'the Fisher', 'the Truth', 'the Light', 'God's Anointed Son', 'the Son of Man', 'the Good Shepherd', 'the Lamb of God', and 'the Word'. He was also was called 'the KRST', or 'Anointed One'. There was a trinity with Horus: Atum the Father and Ra the Holy Spirit. In the later years Horus had 12 disciples known as Har-Khuttie. Horus had an enemy (originally this was also the dark side of Horus, or his other face). This evil enemy was 'Set' or 'Sata'. Horus struggles with Sata for 40 days in the wilderness. Some claim that this myth represents the triumph of light over dark. This triumph is most noted on December 25.

KRISHNA of India
900 BCE (some say 3000 BCE or even much older)

Khrisna Sharing Little Food With Many People

Khrisna was a Hindu god who was born of a virgin called Devaki. Mother Devaki after being visited by spirits to announce the impending birth of an immaculately conceived a child who is a sun god and the 'Son of God'. A bright star in the east signaled his coming and his birth was attended by wise men, as well as shepherds. Krishna was presented at birth with frankincense, myrrh, and gold. Krishna worked miracles, restored sight, cast out devils, and raised the dead. Krishna was baptized in the River Ganges, a version of Khrisna myths told that he was crucified between two thieves, died, buried, and resurrected in 3 days and worshipped as the 'Savior of men'. The name Krishna is derived from the word 'KRST' which means 'the anointed one'. He proclaimed himself the 'Resurrection' and the 'Way to the Father'. He was said to be without sin, of royal descent, and raised by a human father that was . . . a carpenter.

He preached of a great and final day of judgment and used parables to teach the people about charity and love. In death he stood transfigured in front of his disciples. Krishna was called the 'Shepherd god', 'Lord of lords', 'the Redeemer', and the 'Universal Word'. He was considered, 'Alpha and Omega' as well as being omniscient, omnipresent and omnipotent.

MITHRA of Persia
ca. 1200 BCE

Mithra

Mithra was born on the December 25. He was also born of a virgin, with a few shepherds present. Mithra, a traveling teacher and master, had 12 disciples as he performed miracles. Mithra was buried in a tomb, died, and after 3 days was resurrected and rose again! Known as 'the Way', 'the Truth', 'the Light', 'the Redeemer', 'the Messiah', 'the Savior', 'the Word', 'the Son of God' and 'the Good Shepherd', Mithra was sometimes pictured carrying a lamb on his shoulders. Sunday was sacred to the followers of Mithra and called it 'the Lord's Day'. Mithraism hit Rome in the 1st century BCE as the Mithraic cult fled Persia. Here it flourished as the sun god Natalis Solis Invicti.

The leader of this religion ruled from what is now Vatican hill, which is a place previously sacred to Mithra. The male religious leader was called Papa (which is how we get the word 'Pope'). Books in honor of Mithra were called 'Helio Biblia', which translates to us as either 'Sun Book' or 'Holy Bible'. He was prophesized to return to battle evil forces in a second coming. His disciples bestowed on him a word that means 'pure essence'. That word is 'Jezeus'.

ATTIS of Phrygia
ca. 204 BCE

Attis and Nana

There are some rather confusing variations on the myths of Attis. One traditions says that Attis was a son of goddess Cybele earthly incarnation, the virgin Nana, who miraculously conceived him by eating an almond or a pomegranate. Thus, Attis was a typical 'god without a father', the virgin's son. The virgin mother Nana who was actually goddess Cybele herself, was also known as Inanna by the Sumerians, Mari-Anna by the Canannites, Anna Perennea by the Sabines (an ancient Italian tribe), and Nanna, mother of the dying god Balder, in northern Europe (Walker, The Woman's Encyclopedia of Myths and Secrets, p. 77).

Attis the handsome Phrygian (today Turkish) shepherd was also sometimes called the 'Good Shepherd'. His goddess mother, Cybele loved him intensely but Attis fell in love with a nymph and jealousy overcame the mother. In a rage she cast a spell of madness on Attis and he castrated himself at the foot of a pine tree. As his life blood dripped to the earth violets sprang up. He became a sacrificial victim and savior, slain to bring salvation to mankind. His body was eaten by his worshippers in the form of bread (the Eucharist of Attis).

In another version, like his priests he was castrated, then crucified on a pine tree, where his blood poured down to redeem the earth. Thus, it was then death and sadness entered the world. Cybele, full of remorse took the body to a cave and wept. She first buried Attis but then used her power to restore him to life and they were reunited, thus bringing nature back to life and hope and salvation into the world. After the resurrection Attis was given the title as 'the most high god, who holds the universe together'. Cybele founded the cult where the pine tree is considered as sacred. Attis' passion was celebrated on March 25, exactly nine months before the solstice festival of his birth, December 25.

Another tradition says that Attis was killed by a boar sent by Zeus, possibly an identification of Attis with the Syrian god known as the Lord Adonis. The day of Attis' death was Black Friday, or the Day of Blood. Attis died and was buried. He descended into the underworld (hell). On the third day he rose again from the dead. His worshippers were told: "The god is saved; and for you also will come salvation from your trials." This day was the Carnival or Hilaria, also known as the Day of Joy. People danced in the streets and went about in disguise, indulging in horseplay and casual love affairs. This was the Sunday; the god arose in glory as the solar deity of a new season.

In prehistoric Phrygian Empire, Cybele was worshipped for over 500 years. The cult was duly moved to Rome and established in 191 BCE on the Palatine Hill in the heart of the city. Later the cult incorporated that of Attis who probably never had any following independent of her. The high priest or Archigallus of Cybele was identified with Attis.

DYONISUS/BACCHUS, IXION
and other Greek/Roman gods
ca. 200 BCE

Bacchus Crucified on a Cross Tree

www.lost-history.com/mysteries5.php

Ixion Crucified on a Wheel

www.askwhy.co.uk

The Greek god Dyonisus or Bacchus, born on December 25, was crucified in 200 BCE. He also performed miracle such as turning water into wine. He was referred to as 'King of Kings', 'Alpha and Omega' and after his death was resurrected.

Prometheus, was a grandson of Uranus the Father Sky, had his liver eaten by an eagle only to be resurrected everyday. Adonis born on December 25 was son of the virgin Myrha. Hermes born on December 25 was the son of the virgin Maia, as well as a member of a holy trinity Hermes Trismegistus. Ixion of Rome, a son of Ares the War god was crucified on a wheel.

NIMROD of Babylonia
ca. 2000 BCE

Ninus a.k.a Tammudz a.k.a. Nimrod

Nimrod was represented in a dual role of God the Father and Ninus, the son of Semiramis, and her olive branch was symbolic of this offspring produced through a 'virgin birth'. Ninus was also known as Tammuz, who was said to have been crucified with a lamb at his feet and placed in a cave. When a rock was rolled away from tile cave's entrance 3 days later, his body had disappeared. Nimrod was symbolized by a fish.

Nimrod married his own mother, Semiramis. Legend has it, after his untimely death, she claimed that a full-grown evergreen tree sprang overnight from a dead tree stump, which symbolized the springing forth unto new life of the dead Nimrod. On each anniversary of his birth, she claimed, Nimrod would visit the evergreen tree and leave gifts upon it. December 25 was the birthday of Nimrod.

There are many more gods or sons of god with similar characteristics to the above. In fact they can be found all over the ancient world. I.e.: Buddha, Salivahana of Bermuda, Crite of

Chaldea, Baal of Phoenicia, Indra of Tibet, Bali of Afghanistan, Jao of Nepal, Wittoba of Balingonese, Odin of Scandinavia, Xamolxis of Greece, Zoar of Bonzes, Adad of Assyria, Deva Tat of Siam, Alcides of Thebes, Eros of the Druids, Thor of Gaul, Cadmus of Greece, Quaxalcoatl of Mexico and Ischy of Formosa. All the above attributes clearly remind us of the most famous son of God in today's biggest religion in the world: Christianity.

JESUS of Nazareth
ca. 4 BCE – 33 CE

www.fest-cornerstone.org

Jesus – With The Sun Disc Symbol

Jesus was born on December 25. He was born of the Virgin Mary. The eastern star signaled his birth and three wise kings came to adorn him, bringing myrrh, frankincense and gold. At the age of 12 he was a child teacher. At the age of 30 he was baptized by John the Baptist. Jesus had 12 disciples and he performed many miracles, such as healing the sick, walking on water and turning water into wine. After being betrayed by Judas, his disciple, Jesus was crucified and buried. After 3 days he was resurrected. He was called by many names, such as: 'King of kings', 'Son of God', 'Light of light', 'Lamb of God', 'the Saviour', 'the Way', 'Alpha and Omega' and many more.

Yes, not all the myths are exactly the same, but very similar. So now the questions are:

Why these attributes?

Why December 25?

Why many of them were born of virgins?

Why were many of their births signified by the eastern star?

Why were there 3 kings adorning some of their birth?

Why were many of them dead for 3 days before resurrected?

Why the 12 disciples?

The birth sequel of these gods or sons of god is actually astrological. The star in the east is Sirius, the brightest star on the night sky which on December 24 aligned with the 3 stars on the Orion constellation. These 3 stars are called today as in the ancient times the 'Three Kings'. The 'Three Kings' and the 'Star in the East' point to the birth of the 'sun god' (the point of the sunrise) at the winter solstice at December 25!

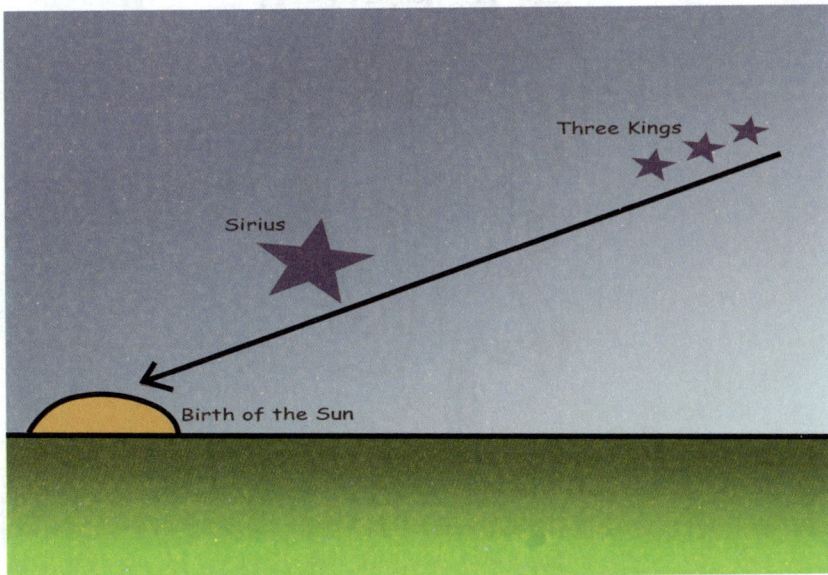

Northern Sky On December 25

This is why the 'Three Kings' follow the 'Star in the East' in order to locate the sun rise (the birth of the sun).

353

The Virgin Mary is the constellation Virgo, also known as 'Virgo the virgin'. Virgo in Latin means virgin. The glyph symbol of Virgo is the altered shape of M.

Virgo Glyph

This is why many of the virgin mothers of the above gods start with the initial M, such as: Mary of Jesus, Isis-Mare of Horus, Maya of Buddha, Myrha of Adonis and Maia of Hermes.

hsci.cas.ou.edu

Constellation Virgo

The constellation Virgo rules during the month of September and October or the autumn season, the season before winter. Therefore it is said to give 'birth' to the sun god after its resurrection. This constellation is also called the 'House of Harvest'. The symbol of Virgo is a virgin holding a sheaf of corn or wheat.

From autumn to winter, the days become shorter from the northern hemisphere's point of view, the sun seems to move further and smaller. The shorter the day, the longer the night and this symbolizes the process of death to the ancient; it was seen as the death of the sun.

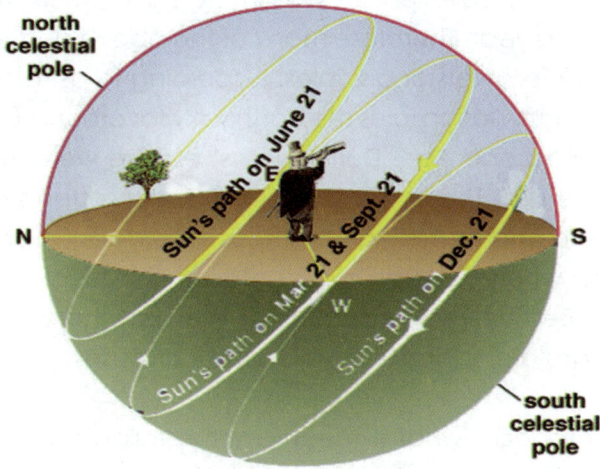

Sun Movement Seen from the Northern Sky

By December 21, the sun seems to disappear totally, for it moves south continually and makes its lowest position in the sky. On this day the sun stops moving to the south (at least perceivably) for 3 days (December 22, 23 and 24). During these 3 days the sun is at the vicinity of the Southern Cross constellation or the Crux.

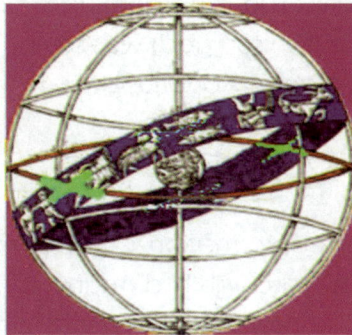

Earth in the 'Middle' of the Crux Constellation

And after this day, the sun moves one degree north on December 25, foreshadowing longer days, warmth and spring. Thus, it was said that the sun died on the cross for 3 days and then it was resurrected.

There are 12 constellations of stars in the Zodiac Belt, where the sun travels in a year. Therefore many of the above gods or sons of gods had 12 followers or disciples. According to astrology, each of the star constellation rules the earthly sky for around 2,160 years which is called one Age. During Jesus' era we were in the Age of Pisces the Fish. This is why Christianity is also often symbolized by a fish. The end of the Age of Pisces should be around the 2nd millennium, where we are now entering the Age of Aquarius the Water Bearer. The 12 sectors of the sky where the 12 star constellations are 'placed' is called the 12 Houses.

So, this is probably what it meant by the following verse in the New Testament, where one of Jesus' disciples asked when the next Passover will be and Jesus answered:

> And he (Jesus) said unto them, Behold, when ye are entered into the city, there shall a man meet you, bearing a pitcher of water; follow him into the house where he entereth in.
> (NT: Luke 22:10)

The symbol of Aquarius is a man bearing a pitcher of water. So could it be that Jesus (the sun god) was saying that after the Age of Pisces comes the Age of Aquarius?

Of course, the above information is not complete. And if you do further research you will find many different versions of each myth. That is the problem with myths, since they are orally transmitted for a long period of time, usually there have many different versions. Therefore, we can not really argue concerning the details. Because even if the details are not exactly the same, we can still see the striking similarities in the storyline, theme and ideology.

What happened to the original monotheistic teaching of Jesus? The name 'Jesus' in Hebrew is either Yeshua, Joshua or Ioshua. Christ or 'Krst' is just a Greek/Roman title, which was given to him much later, meaning the 'anointed one'. So, how come Jesus' teachings become similar to the teachings of ancient pagan religions then?

It is really not that difficult to see that the original teaching of Yeshua, the Hebrew Messiah, has been mixed up with ancient pagan religions - both ancient Eastern and Western religions/tradition. Just look at Christmas. Why do we associate Christmas today with snow, reindeer, and elves? There is no such thing in Jesus' life. Jesus lived in today Israel – a country in the Middle East. So: why the pine tree? What is the connection between Jesus the Jewish prophet and Santa Claus – a mythological man who is believed to come from the Northpole?

I was really surprised when I read in Wikipedia that the celebration of Christmas was and still is a topic of hot debate amongst Christian scholars. The debate started since the 4th century CE, when this feast disappeared after Gregory of Nazianzus resigned as Archbishop of Constantinople (today Istanbul) in 381 CE, although it was reintroduced by Saint John Chrysostom who became the Archbishop of Constantinople at around 400 CE.

The importance of Christmas increased gradually after Charlemagne was crowned on Christmas Day in 800 CE. Christmas during the Middle Ages remained a public festival, incorporating ivy, holly, and other evergreens, as well as gift-giving. Caroling also became popular, and was originally a group of dancers who sang. The group was composed of a lead singer and a ring of dancers that provided the chorus. Various writers of the time condemned caroling as lewd, indicating that the unruly traditions of pagan Saturnalia may have continued in this form. Saturnalia was a feast with which the Romans commemorated the dedication of the temple of god Saturn. Originally celebrated for a day, on December 17, popularity grew it to week long extravaganza, ending on December 25.

During the Protestant Reformation (1517 - 1648) in Europe, Puritans condemned Christmas celebration as 'trappings of popery' and the 'rags of the Beast' and they banned Christmas in 1647. The Roman Catholic Church responded by promoting the festival in an even more religiously oriented form. The Restoration of Charles II in1660 ended the ban, but many clergymen still disapproved of Christmas celebrations.

Debates about Christmas in America still continue to this day! Not only concerning the theological aspect but also concerning the environmental issue of cutting trees for Christmas decoration.

∽∘⋆∘∼

I know the above information must be really shocking for most Christians. I was truly surprised too when the first time I read about it. I know you must have thousands of questions and objections. If you are interested to know further about the historical facts, I will elaborate in the next two volumes of the EarthTrek Trilogy. Believe it or not, I have gathered even more shocking information from reliable sources... not only concerning Christianity, but also Judaism, Islam, Hinduism and Buddhism! In chapter 17, I will share with you how similar ideology also creeps into the teaching of Islam.. but before that let's finalize our analysis concerning the true religious teachings first, ok..

CHAPTER FIFTEEN

GATE OF HEAVEN

So let's talk about the religious practices then... If truly all religions originally have the same message then all their religious practices should be same too, right? What religious practices are actually commanded by God? The Quran says: charity, fasting, praying and (at least once in a lifetime, if possible) pilgrimage.

Actually, Judaism, Christianity and even Hinduism as well as Buddhism also command the same practices. Here, I am not going to analyze the different practices, but just the same ones.

CHARITY
It is obvious why we are commanded to do this good practice. What is the purpose of charity or alms? It is to help equalize the economical level, to teach compassion, tolerance, gratefulness and to protect the weak and unfortunate.

According to the Old Testament
In this way you also will present an offering to the LORD from all the tithes you receive from the Israelites. From these tithes you must give the LORD's portion to Aaron the priest.
(OT: Number 18:28)

When you have finished setting aside a tenth of all your produce in the third year, the year of the tithe, you shall

give it to the Levite, the alien, the fatherless and the widow,
so that they may eat in your towns and be satisfied.
(OT: Deuteronomy 26:12)

According to the New Testament

All the believers were one in heart and mind. No one
claimed that any of his possessions was his own, but
they shared everything they had. With great power the
apostles continued to testify to the resurrection of the Lord
Jesus, and much grace was upon them all. There were
no needy persons among them. For from time to time
those who owned lands or houses sold them, brought the
money from the sales and put it at the apostles' feet, and
it was distributed to anyone as he had need.
(NT: Acts 4:32-35)

Woe to you Pharisees, because you give God a tenth
of your mint, rue and all other kinds of garden herbs, but
you neglect justice and the love of God. You should have
practiced the latter without leaving the former undone.
(NT: Luke 11:42)

According to the Quran

Alms are only for the poor and the needy, and the officials
(appointed) over them, and those whose hearts are made
to incline (to truth) (the 'reverts') and the (ransoming
of) captives and those in debts and in the way of God
and the wayfarer; an ordinance from God; and God is
knowing, Wise.
(Quran translation 9:60)

They ask you as to what they should spend. Say: Whatever
wealth you spend, it is for the parents and the near of kin
and the orphans and the needy and the wayfarer, and
whatever good you do, God surely knows it.
(Quran translation 2:215)

The rules of charity are somewhat different in each religion. I believe main principle should be the same, which is to donate money for the less fortunate. Although some religions command the followers to donate to their religious constitution, religious leaders and/or priests.

The Quran teaches us 2 types of charity:
1. Sadaqa - this is a voluntary charity. The amount and time is not prescribed.
2. Zakat or alms - this is an obligatory charity. According to the Quran all adult believers of sound mind and body with a set level of income and assets are expected to pay Zakat. Zakat is to be distributed to eight categories of individuals: 1.orphans, 2.the poor, 3.travelers, 4.beggars, 5.debtors, 6.slaves, 7.the officials whose jobs are to collect the zakat and 8.the reverts.

Usually we call people who change one religion to another is called 'converts'. But according to the Quran, since there is only one Religion, i.e. one Truth, the proper term for such people should be 'reverts' ... which means people whose hearts are inclined to the Truth.

Zakat is essentially a personal exercise with no intermediary control, and could be given directly to its recipients, although a central treasury often collects it. Apart from the group of people mentioned above, everyone else has to work for their provision. According to the Quran, there are neither monks nor priests entitled to receive money from the believers. The Quran teaches us that there is no human intermediary between God and human, in matters of good deeds. I agree with this point. Why should adults with sound mind and body who decide to study more about religion be entitled not to work and earn their own living? In fact, throughout history the practice of giving tithe to a religious institution has been corrupted beyond imagination (I will share more information on this matter in my next books).

FASTING

According to the Old Testament

Then all the children of Israel, and all the people, went up, and came unto the house of God, and wept, and sat there before the LORD, and <u>fasted that day until even</u>, and offered burnt offerings and peace offerings before the LORD.
(OT: Judges 20:26)

According to the New Testament

And when he (Jesus) had <u>fasted forty days and forty nights</u>, he was afterward an hungered.
(NT: Matthew 4:2)

Defraud ye not one the other, except it be with consent for a time, that ye may give yourselves to <u>fasting</u> and prayer; and come together again, that Satan tempt you not for your incontinency.
(NT: 1 Corinthians 7:5)

According to the Quran

O you who believe! Fasting is prescribed for you, <u>as it was prescribed for those before you</u>, so that you may guard (against evil).
(Quran translation 2 : 183)

The guarding of evil that is meant by the Quran amongst others is to discipline ourselves concerning eating habits that will lead to all kinds of sickness (physically and mentally) in a long run. How many obese people are there in this world today? Meanwhile, in some other parts of the globe others are dying from starvation! Obesity is often caused by bad and uncontrolled eating habits. If only we all would practice to fast every year, it would never happen.

Today, almost every adult in the West has been on a diet or detoxing program at one time or another, to keep the weight stabile. That is one of the purposes of fasting. On the spiritual side, fasting also trains our sense of discipline, to control our emotion and to be grateful, humble and understanding towards the suffering of poor people, who do not have enough to eat. Many people think that fasting is a torture or punishment. But is it? Let's see what scientist has to say about this:

By Dr. Ben Kim on December 15, 2006

Historical records tell us that fasting has been used for health recovery for thousands of years. Hippocrates, Socrates, and Plato all recommended fasting for health recovery. The Bible tells us that Moses and Jesus fasted for 40 days for spiritual renewal. Mahatma Gandhi fasted for 21 days to promote respect and compassion between different religions. For much of human history, fasting has been guided by intuition and spiritual purpose. Today, our understanding of human physiology confirms the powerful healing effects of fasting.

Fasting is a powerful therapeutic process that can help people recover from mild to severe health conditions. Some of the most common ones are high blood pressure, asthma, allergies, chronic headaches, inflammatory bowel disease (ulcerative colitis and Crohn's disease), irritable bowel syndrome, adult onset diabetes, heart disease, degenerative arthritis, rheumatoid arthritis, psoriasis, eczema, acne, uterine fibroids, benign tumors, and systemic lupus erythematosus.

Fasting provides a period of concentrated physiological rest during which time the body can devote its self-healing mechanisms to repairing and strengthening damaged organs. The process of fasting also allows the body to cleanse cells of accumulated toxins and waste products.Fasting gives the digestive tract time to completely rest and strengthen its mucosal lining. A healthy intestinal mucosal lining is necessary for preventing the leakage of incompletely digested proteins into the bloodstream, thereby offering protection from autoimmune conditions. A healthy digestive tract also helps to protect the blood and inner organs against a variety of environmental and metabolic toxins.

A fast that is appropriate for your situation will allow for you to experience some or all of the following:

- More energy
- Healthier skin
- Healthier teeth and gums
- Better quality sleep
- A clean and healthy cardiovascular system
- A decrease in anxiety and tension
- Dramatic reduction or complete elimination of aches and pains in muscles and joints
- Decrease or elimination of headaches
- Stabilization of blood pressure
- Stronger and more efficient digestion
- Stabilization of bowel movements
- Loss of excess weight
- Elimination of stored toxins
- Improvement with a wide variety of chronic degenerative health conditions, including autoimmune disorders

It is important to understand that the detoxifying and healing processes that occur during a fast are also active when a person is consuming food. A fast can be helpful for people whose conditions are not improving as quickly as they would like, or for people who have health conditions that require a concentrated period of healing to resolve.

It is also important to understand that the most important part of a fast is how a person lives after the fast. Fasting can provide a clean and revitalized foundation upon which you can build and maintain a strong and well-conditioned body by consistently making healthy food and lifestyle choices.

〜ᴓᴕᴏ〜

So: all three monotheistic religious actually command the followers to fast. Hinduism and Buddhism also practice fasting. Fasting alone is difficult, but if a whole nation is doing it together, it becomes easier, satisfactory and even joyous.

PRAYING

The way to pray from each religion (today) is diverse. Basically, there 3 forms of praying (that I know of):

1. By direct silent communication to God, usually we do this in our mother tongue. In Islamic term this is called Do'a – it is a short of meditation (being in silence). This is a direct communication between one and God, it is usually practiced to say gratitude, to ask for forgiveness or/and to ask something from God. Do'a may be done anytime we want. Most Christians practice only this type of praying.

2. By using repeating sound vibration, it can be by repeating God's attribute, or praising God, chanting, singing or using mantra in meditation. The Islamic way is called Dzikir. I believe the purpose of this practice is to clean the passage of chakra (in Hindu term), to clean the soul from all kind of negative energy (such as anger, worry, fear), so we can have better 'contact' with God.

3. By doing a set of movement and fix prayers. This way of praying or worshipping to be more precise, is called Shalat. The Shalat can best be described as the 'contact prayer' (the root word shila means 'to make contact'). Shalat is a daily ritual of making regular contact with God, facing a certain direction, using an ancient formula which begins with washing to purify oneself, and includes the specific acts of standing, prostrating, kneeling and bowing to symbolize total submission to Him. Today it is only Islam that still has this way of worshipping, which is practiced by Moslems all over the world (with the exception of some minority groups in other religions).

At present, every religion has different ways of praying, but I believe that the way to pray (or worship) must have been the same way too originally. I believe the ultimate way of worshipping God is by bowing down, just as the Quran says. This way of worship is then modified through our arrogance of thinking it is a degrading way of worshipping God or in some other case, its movement is exaggerated like the way of some pagan rituals.

Many people mock the way Moslems worship, although Moslems do not bow down to anyone or anything else but God. I think this makes more sense than bowing to some altar or statue of any other human being or creatures. Many accuse this way of worshipping is primitive and pagan-like. Is that so? I believe the pagan way of worship is actually also a corrupted variation from this original universal way of worshipping. How do I come to this conclusion? Let's analyze it.

www.livius.org/a/1/judaea/jehu.jpg

King Jehu of Israel Bows Down Before King Shalmaneser III of Assyria
(the story is told in the Bible, book of 2 Kings)

The mosque – the Islamic house of prayer is empty. There is only a podium for speech during the mass worship, which has to be emptied by the time the worship starts. There is not a single object the Moslems give worship to. The Imam is just leading the worship but he also bows, when everyone else bows. Moslems may pray anywhere, as long as it is clean and to one direction. Now, is it true that Islam is the only religion that decreed its followers to bow down in worship? Let's analyze how the other two monotheistic religions tell us how to worship:

According to the Old Testament

When Abraham's servant heard what they said, <u>he bowed down to the ground before the Lord</u>.
(OT: Genesis 24:52)

Moses <u>bowed to the ground</u> at once and worshiped.
(OT: Exodus 34:8)

Ezra praised the LORD, the great God; and all the people lifted their hands and responded, "Amen! Amen!" Then <u>they bowed down and worshiped the Lord with their faces to the ground</u>.
(OT: Nehemiah 8:6)

As you can see, according to the Old Testament, the prophets (previous to Muhammad) bowed down and worshiped God with their faces to the ground too. There is only one way to bow down with the face to the ground, and it is like the below picture. The picture below is a depiction of how the Samaritan Jews pray and can be found in the book entitled 'To Pray As a Jew: a guide to the prayer book and the synagogue service' by Hayim Halevy Donin.

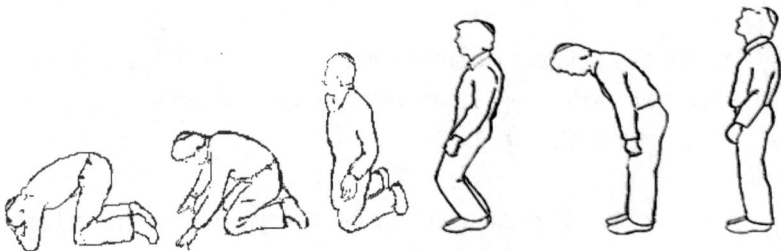

www.answering-christianity.com

Samaritan Jew Way of Worshipping

That sure looks like how the Moslems pray. Now what about the New Testament?

According to the New Testament

And he (Jesus) went a little farther, and <u>he fell with his face to the ground and prayed</u>, saying, O my Father, if it be possible, let this cup pass from me: nevertheless not as I will, but as Thou wilt.
(Matthew: 26:39)

Russian Christian Orthodox Way of Worshipping

Although there are many variations in praying position according to different Gospels, most Christians today only kneel when praying, but in Matthew Jesus also fell with his face to the ground to pray! Above are two pictures that show how the Russian Christian Orthodox prays.

According to the Quran

In the Quran we can still a verse where God commanded Maria the mother of Jesus to bow down:

O Maria! keep to obedience to your Lord and humble yourself, and bow down with those who bow.
(Quran translation 3:43)

And keep up prayer and pay the poor-rate (alms) and <u>bow down</u> with those who bow down.
(Quran translation 2 : 43)

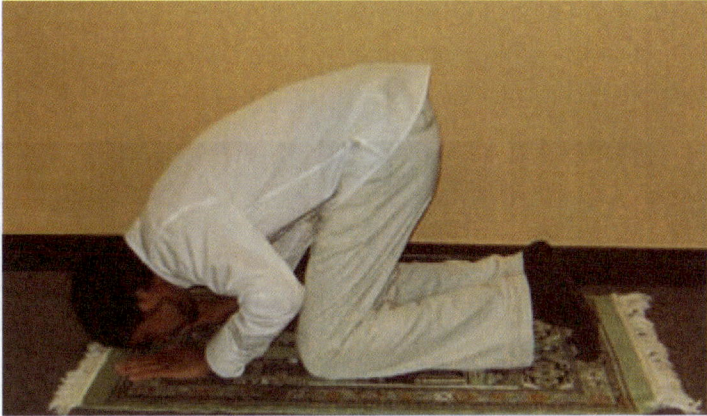

Islamic Way of Worshipping

Clearly this way of worshipping must have originated from one source. If all religions come from one source, is there a Hindu way of praying similar to the above?

'Vandana' A Hindu Way of Worshipping

Yes, Vandana is prayer and prostration. Humble prostration touching the earth with the eight limbs of the body (Sashtanga-Namaskara), with faith and reverence, before a form of God, or prostration to all beings knowing them to be the forms of the One God, and getting absorbed in the Divine Love of the Lord is termed prostration to God or Vandana.

A Buddhist Way of Worshipping and Pay Respect

And what about Buddhism? Yes, Buddhist too bow down to Buddha this way, and sometimes even in front of other honored person, like teachers. Look at the pictures above.

—ɔ⋆ɕ—

SHALAT: THE UNIVERSAL WAY OF WORSHIP?

I think the previously mentioned verses from both the Old/New Testaments and the pictures are enough to prove that originally, the way of worshiping God is the same in Judaism, Christianity, Islam and even Hindu as well as Buddhism. Somehow by time, this practice seems to be forgotten, just as the Quran says:

> *These are some of the prophets whom God blessed. They were chosen from among the descendants of Adam, and the descendants of those whom we carried with Noah, and the descendants of Abraham and Israel, and from among those whom we guided and selected. When the revelations of the Most Gracious are recited to them, they fall prostrate, weeping. After them, He substituted generations who lost the contact prayers (Shalat) and pursued their lusts...*
> *(Quran translation 19:58-59)*

The Shalat has specific rules, as follows:

1. It is to be done at specific times of the day. Moslems worship 5 times a day: at dawn, at noon, late afternoon, at dusk and at night. Each contact prayer last between 5 - 15 minutes.
2. The ritual begins with ablution or washing part of the body for purifying purpose by using water.
3. Facing the Qiblah. Qiblah is the direction where Moslems have to face when praying, which is the direction of the Kaaba in Mecca, Saudi Arabia.
4. Each prayer has a number Rakaah. Rakaah is a set of movements. It consists of standing, prostrating, kneeling and bowing down to the earth - as a symbol of total submission.
5. At every Rakaah the first chapter of the Quran has to be read. It begins with saying the Basmallah (In the Name of God, Most Gracious, Most Compassionate).

Now, so far we have seen that the movement, at least the bowing (and kneeling) part still exist in all 5 religions. As we can see in page 367, in a Judaistic sect the exact same set of movement which consist of standing, prostrating, kneeling and bowing still exist. Let's analyze the other points then to see whether we can still see their traces in Judaism and Christianity.

AT SPECIFIC TIMES OF THE DAY & TO A CERTAIN DIRECTION

In the Old Testament:

> Now when Daniel learned that the decree had been published, he went home to his upstairs room where the windows opened _toward Jerusalem_. _Three times a day_ he got down on his knees and prayed, giving thanks to his God, just as he had done before.
> (OT: Daniel 6:10)

In the above verse we can see clearly how Daniel a Jewish prophet prayed at specific times (three times a day) and facing a certain direction which was Jerusalem. David, another Jewish prophet, also prayed three times every day:

> *Listen to my prayer, O God....... As for me, I call upon God, and the Lord saves me. <u>Evening, morning and noon,</u> I cry out in distress and He hears my voice...*
> *(OT: Psalms 55:1,16-17)*

And the following we can read where Solomon prayed facing the direction of the Temple in Jerusalem:

> *Then Solomon stood before the altar of the LORD in front of the whole assembly of Israel, spread out his hands toward heaven and said... Hear the supplication of your servant and of your people Israel when they <u>pray toward this place</u>.....*
> *(OT: 1 Kings 8: 22, 30)*

In the New Testament:

Today (most) Christians only pray at the church once a week, which is every Sunday. However, the concepts of regular daily prayer times and the central direction faced during prayer still exist in the New Testament as well:

> *At Caesarea there was a man named Cornelius, a centurion in what was known as the Italian Regiment. He and all his family were devout and God-fearing; he gave generously to those in need and <u>prayed to God regularly</u>.....*
> *Cornelius answered: "<u>Four days ago I was in my house praying at this hour, at three in the afternoon</u>. Suddenly a man in shining clothes stood before me..."*
> *(NT: Acts 10: 1 - 2, 30)*

In the above verses, although only implicitly, we can see that Cornelius did not pray once a week in a church. He prayed regularly at home. He could not have prayed once a week, because in the above verse he mentioned that he was praying at three in the afternoon four days before hand. The time of prayer at three in the afternoon must have been the same as the Moslem's late afternoon prayer (i.e. Ashr in Arabic).

In the following verses we can see two different specific times of prayer used to be performed by Peter and John (two disciples of Jesus), which are the three in the afternoon prayer (Ashr in Arabic) and the noon prayer (Dhuhr in Arabic):

> One day Peter and John were going up to the temple <u>at the time of prayer - at three in the afternoon.</u>
> (NT: Acts 3:1)

> <u>About noon</u> the following day as they were on their journey and approaching the city, Peter went up <u>on the roof to pray</u>.
> (NT: Acts 10:9)

WASHING BEFORE PRAYING

The act of washing to purify oneself before facing God in prayer is also mentioned in both the Old and New Testaments.

In the Old Testament:

> Then the LORD said to Moses, "Make a bronze basin, with its bronze stand, for washing. Place it between the Tent of Meeting and the altar, and put water in it. Aaron and his sons are to wash their hands and feet with water from it. Whenever they enter the Tent of Meeting, they shall wash with water so that they will not die..."
> (OT: Exodus 30:17-20)

In the New Testament:

> <u>Submit</u> yourselves, then, to God. Resist the devil, and he will flee from you. Come near to God and he will come near to you. Wash your hands, you sinners, and purify your hearts, you double-minded.
> (NT: James 4:7-8)

The New Testament mentions Jesus' symbolic washing of his disciples' feet, whereupon Peter objected and said he wanted Jesus to wash `not just his feet, but his hands and his head as well'. Jesus answered that a person who has had a bath needs only to wash his feet; his whole body is clean (NT: John 13:9-10).

Although in the story, there is no mention of praying after the washing event, strangely enough the need to wash only the feet when someone has had a bath, is very similar to the Islamic rule on ablution (washing before worshiping).

Baptism with water, as well as the practice of wiping the hands and face with water as one enters a Catholic church today, may very well be an altered practice of ablution before performing Shalat too.

⟬∘⋆∘⟭

Yes, the above verses are certainly not fully comprehensive. Yet it is astonishingly clear that traces of the act of Shalat still exists both in the Old and New Testaments, right?

WHY 5 TIMES A DAY?

When we perform Shalat 5 times every day, we will automatically change our whole pattern of daily rhythm, hence it is a great practice of time management. The first prayer is performed at dawn, so we will automatically start our day early in the morning. Starting the day early in the morning actually can prevent us from depression. Now, the first time I heard this, I remember all the movies about people feeling depressed.. hey, they always lie down so long in bed, right? I also know this to be true from my personal experience. When I feel down, sleeping longer doesn't help me feel better. Only when I force myself to jump out of bed do I actually feel better.

Although sleeping long seems like a privilege, it is actually not necessary and in the long run not good for our health. Sleeping too long can cause arthritis and contribute to laziness if we do it too often. I have read many, many books about successful people (in politics, business and sport), and one thing in common that I have learned about them, is that most of them wake up early and have their days organized. Life can be so hectic that without proper time management, we could easily get overrun by our unorganized schedule. We would feel very tired and stressed out at the end of the day. Time management is also one of the most important topics when we study the business world.

When we perform Shalat in the morning correctly (meaning with clean heart and not feeling forced that it is an obligation), our day will run smoothly, we start the day with a feeling of gratitude.

A true religion is supposed to take us back to our true 'nature', which God intended for us. Every single species in the world has a different form of 'nature'. If we were born as bears, then our nature would be to hibernate for months during winter. But we are not bears nor are we bats. So how do we know our true nature? We can learn our true nature to be in harmony with the universe by watching the behavior of human babies or children. Just observe how healthy babies and young children tend to wake up early in the morning and they go around cheerfully. Many adults forget about that through our own free will and choose to wake up when the sun is high up in the sky. Then wonder why is it so difficult to stay cheerful – and justify this action by telling our selves that we were born as a 'night person'. Many of us have experienced this stage, usually starting from teenage period up to adulthood (the time when our 'free will' can be exercised to the maximum), but as we get older (let's say above 60 years old) most people are 'forced' again to 'obey' our nature. Most old people can not stay up late any longer and they usually cannot sleep too long, so they wake up early again.

The last prayer is to be done around 2 – 3 hours after sunset. This means we can sleep early every night, if we want to. This is also a good way to prevent us from getting the ideas to do 'crazy' things, which are not healthy for our mental and physical health. It is no secret that most 'partying' which ends up making us do unhealthy things is usually done at night. Late night is also the time when the mind usually lingers in negative, dark thoughts. Most heinous crimes are also done at night. That's why most depressed, self destructive people cannot sleep at night until really late, and they end up waking late in the afternoon. This is a destructive cycle.

Many of us are too lazy to move our body after the age of 30, or even younger! Although we know that to have a healthy mind, body and soul a daily physical exercise regime is crucial. We know that there is no pill that can give us that without giving any side effect. And of course, God is aware of this, He is our Creator.

God is the source of Power, Energy, and the Highest Vibration. Only by tapping from the high energy from God can we actually receive some pure energy. Just like electrical equipments need to be plucked into the source of electricity, we also need to do the contact prayer to God to fill our energy. We all know that the less we move, the more tired we get (i.e. less energy).

Research has shown that in average a person has around 40,000 - 60,000 thoughts in a day! From thinking about what clothe are we going to wear that day, what food to eat, what others are thinking about us' up to all the serious and big decisive thoughts. Unfortunately, for many people most of their thoughts are not positive thoughts.

We need to pause a few times a day, just a few minutes each time. This helps to 'shield' negative thoughts. We know how damaging negative thoughts can be to our well being. So Shalat is necessary for success in achieving a healthy body, mind and soul, which will lead us to a successful life here on earth and the hereafter. I know some really powerful non-Moslem businessmen who use this practice of solitude as a secret to their succees.

God does not need us to pray to Him, but we need to pray to Him... it is for our own good. However, the benefit of prayer can only be felt if we are not doing it because we feel obliged to, or we just want to show to others that we are 'good'. It has to be done with clean heart and sincerely.

> O you who believe! Bow down and prostrate yourselves and serve your Lord, and do good _that you may succeed_.
> (Quran translation 22:77)

> O men! You _are they who stand in need of God_, and God is He Who is the Self-sufficient, the Praised One.
> (Quran translation 35:15)

> _If you are ungrateful, then surely God is Self-sufficient above all need of you_; and He does not like ungratefulness in His servants; and if you are grateful, He likes it in you; and no bearer of burden shall bear the burden of another; then to your Lord is your return, then will He inform you of what you did; surely He is Cognizant of what is in the breasts.
> (Quran translation 39:7)

> And whoever strives hard, he strives only for his own soul; most surely _God is Self-sufficient, above (need of) the worlds_.
> (Quran translation 29:6)

> And certainly We gave wisdom to Luqman, saying: Be grateful to God. And _whoever is grateful, he is only_

377

grateful for his own soul; and whoever is ungrateful, then surely God is Self-sufficient, Praised.
(Quran translation 31:12)

Someone said this analogy to me: "Look, we have pets not because we want them to be thankful to us. So why do we have to be thankful to God?" Yes, God doesn't need us to be thankful. We need to do that for our own good. But God does take notice when we are thankful. Yes, we don't expect our pets to be thankful to us, because (some) pets are simply incapable of doing that. But we do, we are capable of being thankful. However, even though we don't expect our pets to be thankful to us, we won't like it if our dogs are friendly to other people and not to us. Would we still keep a dog if it keeps on barking and biting us? Being grateful is an important key to success. Just, ask Oprah... 😊

Unfortunately, this is what we do. We ignore God's existence, we use His name in curse words and some of us actually worship other creatures that He created (i.e. the prophets and saints and statues). Today, the English the word 'holy' is used so often as curse word. Such as: 'holy ---', 'holy ---'. You know what I mean? We feel bad when we talk rudely to our families, bosses, clients, friends but we don't care how we talk about God. We take it as a joke, although this is forbidden by the Bible and the Quran:

Thou shalt not take the name of the LORD thy God in vain: for the LORD will not hold him guiltless that taketh his name in vain.
(OT: Deuteronomy 5: 11)

And God's are the best names, therefore call on Him thereby, and leave alone those who violate the sanctity of His names; they shall be recompensed for what they did.
(Quran translation 7:180)

WHY DO WE HAVE TO BOW?

So now, the question is: why bowing? Why are we commanded to worship God by performing this set of movements?

Professor Muhammad Hembing Wijayakusuma, an expert in traditional healing did an intensive study on the way Moslems worship. He published the result of his research in his book called The Advantage of Shalat for Medicinal and Health Reason (Hikmah Salat untuk Pengobatan dan Kesehatan).

His study shows that Shalat can relax our muscles and help to smooth the blood circulation, especially when our minds are focused to one, which is God. The movement can loosened the nerves and activate the perspiration (sweating) system and the body temperature.

When we bow down to the ground (often and regularly), the oxygen valve to the brain is open and can release all negative vibration in the body, it makes the small arteries that is in the brain to get used to receiving high pressure. Try and bow down a few times like this calmly with focused mind when you have a headache and you will see that your headache could instantly go away. This movement (if done often and regularly) also helps opening the blood arteries in the heart – which in the long run can diminish the risk of having a heart coronary stroke.

When we prostrate calmly, it can maintain the flexibility of our back bones (vertebrate), the central of our nervous system. And I believe psychologists or chiropractors can confirm that a person who is stubborn and rigid with high blood pressure, or just simply stressed usually also have a stiff body (especially on the neck). Look at the following verses in the Old Testament. This is a part of a letter written by Hezekiah to the Israelites who had turn away from their religious practice:

... "People of Israel, return to the LORD, the God of Abraham, Isaac and Israel, that he may return to you who are left, who have escaped from the hand of the kings of Assyria. Do not be like your fathers and brothers, who were unfaithful to the LORD, the God of their fathers, so that he made them an object of horror, as you see. <u>Do not be stiff-necked,</u> as your fathers were; <u>submit to the LORD</u>. Come to the sanctuary, which he has consecrated forever. Serve the LORD your God, so that his fierce anger will turn away from you. If you return to the LORD, then your brothers and your children will be shown compassion by their captors and will come back to this land, for the LORD your <u>God is gracious and compassionate</u>. He will not turn his face from you if you return to him."
(OT: 2 Chronicles 30: 6 – 9)

I believe the above verses were actually a calling to the Israelites who had forgotten to do Shalat. The words 'stiff-necked' and 'submit' seem to point to the practice of Shalat. In fact, the perfect translation for the word Moslem is 'submitter' in English. And even more surprising is the sentence of 'God is gracious and compassionate' which is the exact same Basmallah sentence, the opening prayer Moslems use whenever they perform Shalat (i.e. 'Bismillahi rrahmaani rrahiym – in the name of <u>God most Gracious, most Compassionate</u>).

On the psychological level, Shalat is a way for us to practice humbleness and to remind us of goodness every day. And the main reason is to make us closer to God. At the end of Shalat, only then we are supposed to perform the Do'a - which is the part where we communicate directly to God in our mother tongue, to give thanks, ask for forgiveness and/or wish for a particular outcome. This Do'a is needed for our mental health to communicate and unburden ourselves to God, especially when we feel helpless, alone and powerless. It gives us the sense of serenity, which is proven to be the best immune system against all kind of sickness, most of which are thought to be caused by stress in a restless mind. A sense of peace can be detected in the body by a lower level of the hormone cortisone, which can be achieved when we perform Shalat properly.

In Christianity, it is a common practice to do confession of sins to a priest. I am not surprised if by doing this, a person might feel relieved. But why does God need a mediator between us and Him? A priest is also just human. Is a priest free of sin? OK, put it this way: if doing something like this (confessing, pouring our hearts out) to another human being can already relieve our stress, doing it directly to God must have a greater impact, right?

Yoga Exercise

It is strange how stubborn humans are. Today, Yoga the traditional Indian physical and mental exercise has become very popular worldwide, also in Western countries. This ancient exercise has become a 'new trend' in the West, therefore practicing this exercise is considered 'modern'. Some Indian scholars considered Yoga as some kind of 'moving meditation', where certain set of movement is practiced with a focused mind.

Actually the principal of Yoga is very similar to Shalat. In fact, one of the movement in Yoga also involved bowing down to the ground. Look at the picture on the previous page. So, isn't it strange that we don't have any problem bowing down, but many of us consider bowing down to God is degrading.

The truth is, on the physical level practicing Shalat gives the same impact as Yoga and/or Taichi (a Chinese martial art often practiced for health reasons). Although, actually Shalat still has higher advantage when performed properly, since it involves a true devotion to God and the increased focus and feeling of surrendering to the Higher Power has a tremendous impact on our psyche as well.

Yoga and Taichi practitioners also believe that these movements are good for our joints and nerves. In principal Taichi is expressing the human body as the universe in miniature. The gentle flowing movement of Taichi is done to guide the individual energy to merge in accordance with the law of the universe. When the body is in harmony with the universe, then the physical self will be maintained and the mind becomes clear and stronger.

I am not surprised if Yoga and Taichi also originally came from the practice of the universal worship which had been taught by Indian and/or Chinese true prophets of God. Once again, I will analyze concerning the history in the next books of EarthTrek.

⌐σ⋆σ⌐

Every nation might have different language, but we all share many universal body language. This body language is not taught by society, it is embedded in our body system by 'nature'. Bending or bowing or prostrating is the universal ultimate body posture of humility and gratefulness. We also automatically bow down whenever we feel total desperation, helpless or when natural catastrophe strikes. People of all race understand the meaning of this body posture. Look at the following pictures and translate what you see..

Appropriately, according to Oxford dictionary one of the meanings of the word 'prostrate' is to be completely overcome with distress or exhaustion.

The Quran says prostrating and bowing down in worship was already taught during Abraham's prophet hood. As we can see, most probably all the rest of the prophets after him also prayed this way. Today thanks to scientific studies, we know the reasons and advantages of the movement, but the prophets *most likely* didn't know about any of these during their time. The scientific research was not done yet. And still they did it simply because they were obedient, they did it because they were commanded by God to do so. Bowing is also the ultimate body posture that symbolizes obedience. I know many 'modern' people are already allergic to the word 'obedience'.

But seriously, do you really think it is wise to rebel against our Creator? Just look around, ask any doctor what happen to a cell that grows out of control, disobedient to the signals from its command center (the DNA). The chances are: it becomes a sick cell and will be discarded or it will spread and ruin the whole body, creating cancer and hence destroy itself.

The explanations of the word 'bow' in the Oxford dictionary are:
- to bend the head or upper body as a sign of respect, greeting or shame;
- to submit to pressure or demands.

Now, God is All Powerful, right? So why doesn't He just 'force' us to bow down then? That is because we are on trial in this life time: whether we choose to follow His law or to be rebellious... hence the gift of freewill. The truth is, before we were born, all of us already bowed down to the Law of God. How? Have you seen the posture of fetus in the mother's womb? Well, look at this picture:

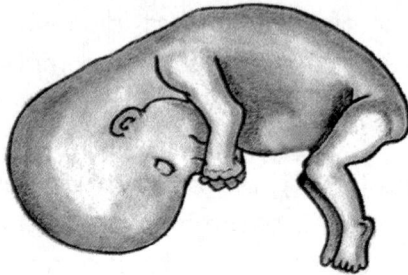

A Fetus Inside the Mother's Womb

Yes, I know a fetus does not always stay in this position, it moves around. But a normal fetus posture is this way; it does not matter whether it face down, up, left or right, it is still bowing the head which is a posture of submission. Is this a coincidence? Or did we actually pledge that God is our Lord before we were born and then we forget about it as soon as walk around on the planet?

> Recall that your Lord summoned all the descendants of Adam, from their loins, and had them bear witness for themselves: "Am I not your Lord?" They all said, "Yes. We bear witness." Thus, you cannot say on the Day of Resurrection, "We were not aware of this."
> (Quran translation 7:172)

So, as observed we can see traces of bowing down in worship in all the (major) religions today. The difference is other religions beside Islam practice also other forms (or ritual) of worship.

Apart from that, sometimes non-Moslems bow down or kneel facing an altar, other objects or even to another human being and non-Moslems do not worship facing one direction. While Moslems only have this form of worship, 5 times a day while facing only towards one direction: the Kaaba. What is the Kaaba?

In the province of Hijaz in the western part of Saudi Arabia, not far from the Red Sea, lies the town of Mecca. In the center of this town is a small square building made of stones. The small, cubed building may not rival skyscrapers in height or mansions in width, but its impact on history and human beings is unmatched. Since thousands of years world travelers have known about this cubed building. Babylonians living around 2000 BCE also knew already about it. This is the Kaaba or Baytullah, the House of God.

Literally, Kaaba in Arabic means 'a high place with respect and prestige'. The word Kaaba may also be derivative of a word meaning a 'cube'. Another name of the Kaaba, is Bait ul Ateeq – which means, according to one meaning, 'the earliest and ancient'.

Apart from being the focal point for the Moslems world wide to pray, the Kaaba is also the place where the yearly 'hajj' takes place.

PILGRIMAGE (HAJJ)

What is hajj?
1.   A Moslem who has made the pilgrimage to Mecca.
2.   In the Near East, a Christian who has made a pilgrimage to the Holy Sepulcher at Jerusalem.
     (The Reader's Digest Great Encyclopedic Dictionary)

The main source of the following text is from The Lost Legacy of Abraham in the West, an article by Gatut Adisoma, Ph D.

To many in the West, the formidable sight of millions of Moslems converging upon the Kaaba in Mecca to observe the Hajj pilgrimage, or their bowing and prostrating in unison during the Shalat prayer, evokes the imagery of a foreign religion. There is no parallel for Hajj today in Judaism or Christianity. But is it really? Is Hajj truly practices unique to the Moslems? Or, is it actually ancient universal practices common to Judaism, Christianity as well as Islam, the religions of Abraham's descendants?

The Quran says that Abraham, together with his son Ismail, founded the ancient shrine known as the Kaaba in today's Mecca. The Quran also says:

> We appointed Abraham to establish the shrine, You shall not idolize any other god beside Me, and purify My shrine for those who visit it, those who live near it, and those who bow and prostrate. And proclaim that the people shall observe the hajj pilgrimage...
> (Quran translation 22:26-27)

It is curious that the concept of Hajj pilgrimage is no longer known in the Western Judeo-Christian traditions, although as pointed out by the definitions, a pilgrimage with a similar name is still practiced by the Eastern Christians.

Actually, the Bible also mentions that Abraham built religious spot. However, as usual, there is a 'slight' difference between the Quran and the Bible. The Quran only mention one shrine (a holy place of prayer) that was built by Abraham, that is the Kaaba. According to the Old Testament, Abraham built several, but the name of Mecca is not mention. Furthermore, according to the Bible Abraham did not built one shrine, but several altars, which means a 'place of slaughter'.

Now, what does the Bible have to say about the Hajj? First of all, there are many words or phrases in the Bible which even

Biblical scholars are unsure of the meaning. For example, the footnotes of New International Version (NIV) Bible, published by the International Bible Society and probably the most widely used version of the Bible, are replete with statements such as 'the meaning of the Hebrew for this word is uncertain'. Then there is the problem of translation itself, from Hebrew or Aramaic to Greek to Latin and finally into modern languages such as English. It has been widely acknowledged that these translation and re-translation processes are fraught with loss or change in the meanings of words and idioms. This is especially true if the translators are not familiar with the Semitic customs and manners of the time, in which the scriptures were recorded originally.

Hajj And Hag: A Parallel
What has this to do with the subject of Hajj? We have to start with the word itself, and its root H-J. The investigation of the original meaning of the root H-J goes no further than hypotheses. The Arabic lexicographers give the meaning 'to betake oneself to' or 'towards an object of reverence' - this would agree with pilgrimage although this meaning is clearly denominative.

According to Genesis' A Hebrew and English Lexicon of the Old Testament, the Hebrew equivalent is Hag. The verb means 'to make a pilgrimage' or 'to keep a pilgrim-feast'. The Hag also refers to the Feast of Booths. The following explanation about the Feast of Booths is quoted from Wikipedia Encyclopedia:

> The Feast of Booths, also known as Sukkot, Sukkos, Succoth, Feast of Booths or Feast of Tabernacles, is a <u>Biblical pilgrimage festival</u> that occurs in autumn on the 15th day of the month of Tishrei (late September to late October). The holiday lasts 7 days. In Judaism it is one of the three major holidays known collectively as the Shalosh Regalim (three pilgrim festivals), when historically the Jewish populace traveled to the Temple in Jerusalem.

A small number of Christians who have revived some Old Testament festivals still celebrate this Feast of Tabernacles (Feast of Booths), which is an eight-day Biblical pilgrimage festival. Among followers, it is one of the most important holy days as it lasts the longest and normally requires a great deal of preparation and travel to be able to attend. It is celebrated on the 15th of Tishrei in the Hebrew calendar (October), the same date of the Jewish festival.

Some Christians believe the New Testament shows Jesus kept the Feast of Tabernacles, as is written in the following verses:

> *After this, Jesus went around in Galilee, purposely staying away from Judea because the Jews there were waiting to take his life. But when the <u>Jewish Feast of Tabernacles</u> was near, Jesus' brothers said to him, "You ought to leave here and go to Judea, so that your disciples may see the miracles you do. ... " Having said this, he (Jesus) stayed in Galilee. However, after his brothers had left for the Feast, <u>he went also</u>, not publicly, but in secret.*
> *(NT: John 7:1-3, 9-10) NIV Version*

An estimated 50,000 Christians observe the Feast of Tabernacles today. The United Church of God is one of the largest groups that observes this festival, as well as the other appointed times of God. Most of those that do observe it were at one time affiliated with the Worldwide Church of God, though some associated with the Church of God (Seventh Day) and even with the Seventh-day Adventist Church (a very small minority) also observe it, though it is not an official practice of those latter two churches. Most ministers do not limit their observance to Jerusalem, but observe it in several hundred places around the world.

Now let's get back to the analysis of the word Hag. It is possible that the root 'hoog' (Hebrew script here = 'to go around', 'to go in a circle') in North as well as South Semitic languages is connected with it. (One may recall that circumambulation, or Tawaf - going around the Kaaba, is an important part of the Hajj). It is a common practice among the Jews to perform circling (hoog) in the temple's sanctuary during the Hag.

It is interesting that the verb Hag can also refer 'to circling in the sacred dance'. Keeping in mind that Hebrew, Aramaic and Arabic the scriptural languages of Abraham's descendants have a common Semitic root, we can easily see that the Arabic characters H and J ('ha' and 'jim') are the equivalent of the Hebrew H and G ('heth' and 'gimel'). Perhaps it is no coincidence that the Arabic speaking Egyptians also make the same substitution. For example, they use Gabal instead of the standard Arabic Jabal for mountain; thus, they also say Hag instead of Hajj.

Let us compare the following passages, which contain the word `pilgrimage,' from the Quran and the Old Testament:

> He said (to Moses), I wish to offer one of my two daughters for you to marry, in return for your working for me for eight pilgrimages; if you make them ten, it will be voluntary on your part...
> (Quran translation 28:27)

> Pharaoh asked him, How old are you? And Jacob said to Pharaoh, The years of my pilgrimage are a hundred and thirty. My years have been few and difficult, and they do not equal the years of the pilgrimage of my fathers.
> (OT: Genesis 47:8-9, NIV Bible)

In both cases, the word `pilgrimage' alludes to the same meaning, i.e. 'years' , which indicates a well-known fact that pilgrimage is an annual event. Other translations of the Bible use the word `sojourning' and `wayfaring' in place of `pilgrimage'. They may have kept the same understanding (i.e. `year') but in so doing, they have inadvertently obscured the fact that pilgrimage already was a well known annual event during the time of Jacob and the Pharaoh.

An Old Semitic Custom

According to E.J. Brill's First Encyclopedia of Islam, 1913-1916 (Vol.III, pp.199-200), pilgrimage to a sanctuary is an old Semitic custom, which is prescribed even in the older parts of the Old Testament as an indispensable duty.

> *'Three times a year shall you celebrate for Me a festival (in Hebrew: hag)'*
> *(OT: Exodus 23:14)*

Another important part of the Muslim's Hajj is the Wukuf, or 'the standing in Arafat'. This has been compared with the stay of the Israelites on the foot of Mount Sinai. To prepare for this, the children of Israel had to purify their garments and refrain from sexual intercourse. Thus they waited upon God (Exodus 19:10-11,14-15). In the same way (Quran 2:196-198), Moslems wear holy clothing, refrain from sexual intercourse and stand before the deity at the foot of a sacred mountain.

While performing the circumambulation of the Kaaba (Tawaf), the pilgrims glorify and praise the Name of God using an ancient formula that predates the Quran (labbayka Allaahumma labbayk = I have responded to You, my Lord, I have responded to You). The Arabic word labbayk (which literally means 'here I am') was the same word used by Abraham and Moses in the Bible, when they responded to God's call (Genesis 22:1,11, Exodus 3:4). In additional, in Exodus 3:5, we can also still see the commandment of taking of the shoes on the holy ground, the same way Moslems take of their shoes whenever they enter the mosque.

And when the LORD saw that he turned aside to see, God called unto him out of the midst of the bush, and said, Moses, Moses. And he said, <u>Here am I</u>. And he said, Draw not nigh hither: <u>put off thy shoes from off thy feet, for the place whereon thou standest is holy ground</u>.
(OT: Exodus 3: 4-5)

In fact, a whole prayer was written around the very phrase 'here I am', solely to be said on the Day of Atonement (Yom Kippur) which follows the Hag.

In the Bible (Genesis 18:16-33), we read that Abraham had a conversation with God where he tried to understand God's forgiveness and mercy. The place where Abraham stood is called 'makom Abrahem' in Hebrew.

Early the next morning Abraham got up and returned to the place where he had stood (in Hebrew: makom Abrahem) before the LORD.
(OT: Genesis 19:27)

The concept of 'makom Abrahem' is also found in the Quran. The place inside the Kaaba in Mecca where Abraham stood and prayed for guidance is called 'maqam Ibrahim' or `the station of Abraham':

*The most important shrine established for the people is the one in **Bacca**; a blessed beacon for all the people. In it are clear signs: <u>the station of Abraham</u>. Anyone who enters it shall be granted safe passage. The people owe it to God that they shall observe pilgrimage (hajj) to this shrine, when they can afford it...*
(Quran translation 3:96-97)

Even more curious, for almost 14 centuries, no one dared to 'correct' the peculiar Quranic spelling of Bacca in the above verse, the city that had been known as Mecca for as long as its people during Muhammad's time could remember. (The advent of the Quran's numerical structure provides an important explanation, as the frequency of the letter M is connected to it). Bacca was the ancient name for Mecca (see historian Ibn Ishaq's view, and editor Ibn Hisham's note, in A. Guillaume's translation The Life of Muhammad, Oxford University Press, 1967, pp. 47, 708). Now we learn that this peculiar Quranic spelling may also shed some light on an obscure Biblical passage. That Bacca is indeed the ancient name for Mecca, the city of pilgrimage in which Abraham founded its shrine, 'Baytullah', the house of God, i.e. the Kaaba. When we read the following verses, it is obvious that pilgrimage to Mecca was in fact known to the children of Israel of ancient times.

> How lovely is Your dwelling place, O Lord Almighty! My soul yearns, even faints for the courts of the Lord; my heart and my flesh cry out for the living God. Even the sparrow has found a home, and the swallow a nest for herself, where she may have her young a place near your altar, O Lord Almighty, my King and my God. Blessed are those who dwell in Your house; they are ever praising You. Blessed are those whose strength is in You, who have set their hearts on <u>pilgrimage</u>. As they pass through the <u>Valley of **Baca**</u>, they make it a place of springs; the autumn rains also cover it with blessings....
> (OT: Psalm 84:1-6) NIV Version

This Psalm is also known as the Psalm of the Pilgrimage. It seems to reflect the children of Israel's ancient longing for the House of God that their patriarch Abraham had built in Baca (Bacca), and their ancient practice of making a pilgrimage there. In a sense, it confirms what historian Ibn Ishaq wrote in the 8th century CE about the ancient Jews who used to make a pilgrimage to their patriarch Abraham's temple in Mecca, centuries before Ibn Ishaq's time. They stopped the practice when the inhabitants of the city turned into unclean polytheists. "Their setting up of idols around the Kaaba, and the blood which they shed there, presented an insurmountable obstacle for them." (Guillaume, op.cit., p.9)

Kaaba View From The Top

So, the Quran as well as the Old Testament say that the House of God in Bacca (i.e. Kaaba) is built as a place for pilgrimage. In addition to that the Quran gives further information that the Kaaba is made as a focal point when praying i.e. direction.

> *We have rendered the shrine (the Kaaba) <u>a focal point</u> for the people, and a safe sanctuary. You may use Abraham's shrine as a prayer house. We commissioned Abraham and Ismail: "You shall purify My house for those who visit, those who live there, and those who bow and prostrate."*
> *(Quran translation 2 : 125)*

Moslems today, face to the Kaaba when they pray. It doesn't matter where they are situated in the world, they all pray to that direction. It is important to understand that Moslems do not worship the Kaaba, the Kaaba is the focal point.

393

Indeed We see the turning of your face to heaven, so We shall surely turn you to a qiblah (focal point) which you shall like; turn then your face towards the Sacred Mosque (the Kaaba), and wherever you are, turn your face towards it, and those who have been given the Book most surely know that it is the truth from their Lord..
(Quran translation 2 : 144)

In the above verse, the Quran repeats again that the Kaaba is made as a focal point, which is already known by 'those who have been given the Book' (i.e. Jews and Christians).

Some people misunderstood and think that Moslems worship the Kaaba, but as we can see again and again it is explained that truly the Kaaba is only for the focal point. Whenever we pray we have to face something – today Christians face the altar; does that mean that they worship the altar? No, right?

It is just a focal point. If Moslems really worship the Kaaba, we will surely find small statues of Kaaba in the Moslems' houses where they worship. However, that is not the case. Amongst all the monotheist religious books, the Quran is the clearest in its explanation concerning the One Unseen God. So where should the Moslems pray to face this Unseen God?

There has to be a focal point. Otherwise everyone will be praying to all different directions. The Quran can not just say: "Face East!" or "Face South!" because the world is round. Hence, the Kaaba.

The Kaaba is 'just' a simple cubicle of around 12 meters tall with a total size of ca. 192 square meter. The inside room is 13 x 9 meters. The walls are 1 meter wide. The ceiling and roof are made out of teak wood and capped with stainless steel. The walls are made of stone. The inside wall and floors are made out of marble.

How does the Kaaba look like? Below is the picture of a replica from Kaaba, so we can have a better understanding:

Replica of *Kaaba*

What is inside the Kaaba? The Kaaba is practically empty. There are only 3 pillars supporting its ceiling, 2 lantern lamps hanging from the ceiling and a table to put items like perfume. There is no window, and there is just one door to go inside. The upper inside walls of the Kaaba is covered with some curtain with verses of the Quran written on it.

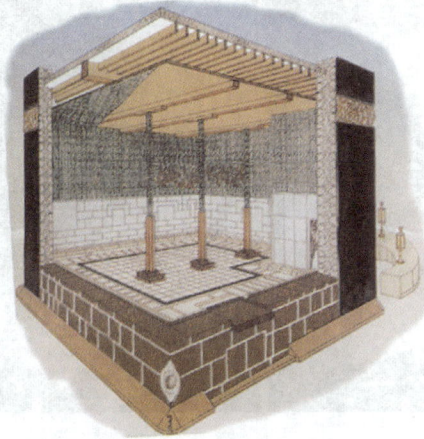

Illustration of the Inside of *Kaaba*

Every year the Kaaba is visited by around 2,000,000 people during the Hajj season from around the world. However, people may also visit and do the ritual out of the Hajj season.

One of the practices that has to be done during the pilgrimage is circumambulations, circling around (Tawaf) with the Kaaba at the center. They circle around the Kabaa 7 times. A black stone (Hajar al Aswad) is cemented on the outside, eastern wall of the Kaaba. This black stone is <u>not</u> an object of worship. The stone measures 16 by 20 cm and is held together by a silver band.

The Quran strictly forbids the worship of any object or being except for God. The Quran does not mention anything about this black stone. This black stone is located outside of the Kaaba. If Moslems were meant to worship the black stone, it would be placed inside the Kaaba. And if Moslems worship this stone, they would surely have replicas of it at home, but they don't.

We can see the picture of the black stone on the previous picture of the replica of the Kaaba. Below is a closer picture of the stone:

www.ezsotech.com

Hajar al Aswad (the Black Stone)

So what is this stone for? It is to mark the counting when the pilgrims are circumambulating the Kaaba. However, many people (as usual) venerated this object too much, by touching and kissing it. It is not forbidden to do that as long as they remember that this stone is only meant as a marker. During the Hajj we are unlikely to see this stone at all, because it is very small and the Masjid Al-Haram (the whole Kaaba area) is just too crowded. There is a line on the floor of the Mosque to tell us where the line of the black stone is.

The Masjid Al-Haram has three levels. So, many pilgrims have to perform the circumambulation on the second and the third level. The second and the third levels are both marks and neon lights (that is in alignment to the black stone) to show us when to start and stop the circumambulation.

In 930 CE the Persian Gulf Qarmatians plundered Mecca and carried the black stone away to Al-Hasa for some 70 years until it was ransomed. In the process, the stone was cracked. It is now hold together by a silver band. The fact that the pilgrimage practice still went on during that 70 years is one of the best illustration that it is a marker for the circumambulation and not an object of worship.

The origin of this black stone is still a matter of debate. Some traditions say that it was a piece of meteor. However, scholars of this subject now believe that the black stone is not meteoric, but may be impact glass, perhaps from the meteor crater at Wabar, about 100 km from Mecca. Wherever it came from, we probably will never find out since the authority will not allow scientists to study it.

～ơ⋆ơ～

So, once again, we have seen that all the major religions in the world still hold traces of 'bowing down to the earth' as one of the movements in their worships. Now, what does the Quran say about worship:

> Hast thou not seen that unto God payeth adoration (i.e. worship) whosoever is in the heavens and whosoever is in the earth, and the sun, and the moon, and the stars, and the hills, and the trees, and the beasts, and many of mankind..
> (Quran translation 22:18)

> And unto God maketh prostration whatsoever is in the heavens and whatsoever is in the earth of living creatures, and the angels (also), and they are not proud.
> (Quran translation 16:49)

The Quran says that everything in the universe prostrates (worship) to God, willingly and not willing. Including the shadows. What does this mean? How do shadows look like? They wax and wane. It is caused by the circular motion of the earth rotating the sun. The 'shadow' on the moon which we call phases is also caused by its circular rotation. Now, a circle is 360 degree. If *that* is how the whole universe worships God, then it sure is true that everything in the universe worship God willingly or unwillingly! Everything in the universe consists of atoms. Let's see how atoms move:

www.geocities.com

Illustration of Atom's Movement

Atoms rotates in circles – that means also for every particle of plants, trees, rocks and every single cells in our body rotates in circles, willingly or unwillingly. We know that this is also true for the heavenly bodies:

Illustration of Planetary Movements in the Solar System

So how are we supposed to worship God? Look at how the Moslems pray:

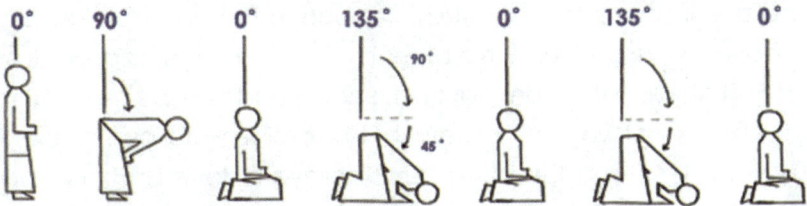

Position of Islamic Contact Prayer (in One Unit)

The above is the set of movements that Moslems do when doing contact prayer (Shalat), this set of movements is called a Rakaah (unit). Probably, many Moslems also do not realize that the total of degree of the above movement is: 0 + 90 + 0 + 135 + 0 + 135 + 0 = 360 degrees! It is also a full circle just like every other 'worship' movement of every single particle in the universe!

Now, do you remember the mathematical code of 19 in the Quran? Here is another fascinating facts concerning this way of worship which even most Moslem are not aware of. The Shalat is supposed to be performed 5 times a day. Each prayer has a specific number of units (Rakaah).

Every unit consists of 360 degree movement. The dawn prayer consists of 2 units; the noon prayer 4 units; the late afternoon prayer 4 units; the dusk prayer 3 units; the night prayer 4 units. Now, if we sum up the numbers of units in a day it becomes: 2 + 4 + 4 + 3 + 4 = 17 units. Hmm... that's not 19, right? But if we join the number of the units together: 24434, it becomes dividable with 19! 24434: 19 = 1268. And if we add the number in 1268: 1 + 2 + 6 + 8= 17! Hey, it is back to the total number of the units. Once again God is using the interlocking system.

Remember how originally the Jewish prayer is supposed to be based on the number 19 as well? Remember the Metonic Cycles that repeats itself every 19 years as well? This also means that the sun, moon and earth are in alignment every 19 years! All of these heavenly bodies also move in circular motion in connection to number 19. So is the Shalat! What is the meaning behind all this? I believe if scientists really study this phenomenon many amazing discoveries will be found. No other form of worship is as powerful as this Shalat – and this is only for our benefit (God doesn't need it). The Quran says that we should establish Shalat to be victorious, successful in this life time and the Hereafter. I believe if done properly, it will. God doesn't lie. Every single alphabet pronounced during Shalat is also based on the 19 numerical coding. A few studies have already proven that sounds do have certain healing or destructive power to our well being. I am not going into the detail; if you are interested you can read it in: www.freewebs.com/tawhiyd/index.htm.

Is it a coincidence that Moslems pray this way? What happens at the center of worship at the House of God, while 2,000,000 people circumambulate the Kaaba?

Kaaba Encircled by Pilgrims

Doesn't the above picture look like this picture of our own Milky Way galaxy circumambulating (worshipping) God?

Rotation of the Spiral Galaxy

God is the Greatest! Now, let's just think about this: 2,000,000 people (and the number keeps on increasing every year) circulating a small cubicle, chanting God's name – like minute particles in an energy field. We know that human mind can radiate very powerful energy, especially when focused. Thus, 2,000,000 million focused minds, praising God, circulating, with a help of the black stone... what a powerful electro magnetic field that creates!

So far we have seen many astonishing scientific facts hidden behind the true religious teaching. I am not surprised if one day scientist will be able to measure the force of the electro magnetic fields created during the Hajj season. I am also not surprised if one day our knowledge in Quantum Physics will be so advanced and finally will be able to confirm that this House of God is an actual portal or Gate of Heaven. In fact, there is a verse in the Old Testament that mentions just that:

> He (Jacob) was afraid and said, "How awesome is this place! This is none other than the house of God; _this is the gate of heaven._"
> (OT: Genesis 28 : 10 – 22)

So, when Jacob said that the House of God is the Gate of Heaven... he was most probably not speaking metaphorically!

CHAPTER SIXTEEN

ONE GOD, ONE MESSAGE, ONE RELIGION

*T*his far, I am almost totally convinced that my study in search of Truth has brought enough evidence that: there is only One Religion with the same message that had been revealed in succession by the One God for the whole of humanity on this planet called earth.

The message is: peace, tolerance, equality, wisdom, goodness, compassion, gratefulness, justice, humbleness, responsibility, honesty, decency, soberness, balance, cleanliness, discipline, patience, respect towards the parents, protection of the unfortunate, bravery against tyranny, believe in the consequence of one's actions on earth impacting the afterlife, above all submission to the One God's will and to worship Him, with periods of solitude for private conversation between one and God.

Many prophets and messengers had been sent to every nation of mankind, yet we keep on altering the message.

Now, I wonder what is the 'true' history behind Hinduism then? Hinduism is the only major polytheist religion that is still influential in the world today. I believe that originally Hinduism must have had the same message too. Although debatable, traces of monotheism still exists in Hinduism, e.g. the Smartha philosophy believes that the Ultimate Power is termed as Brahman or Atman, who is believed to have no specific form and name. Furthermore, the following verses from the Veda sure sound like a monotheist teaching:

> Let us meditate on God, His glorious attributes,
> who is the basis of everything in this universe as its Creator,
> who is fit to be worshiped as Omnipresent, Omnipotent, Omniscient and self existent conscious being,
> who removes all ignorance and impurities from the mind and purifies and sharpens our intellect.
> (Gayatri Mantra, Yajur Veda)

Could this be the authentic teaching of Hindu? If this can be confirmed, that would also be the same case for Buddhism, since some scholars say that Buddhism was originally a sect of Hinduism.

According to Jayaram V: "Both Hinduism and Buddhism originated in the Indian subcontinent and share a very long, but rather peculiar and uncomfortable relationship, which in many ways is comparable to that of Judaism and Christianity. The Buddha was born in a Hindu family, just as Christ was born in a Jewish family. Some scholars argue that Buddhism was an offshoot of Hinduism and Buddha was a part of the Hindu pantheon, a view which is not acceptable to many Buddhists. It is however widely accepted that Buddhism gained popularity in India because it released the people from the oppression of tradition and orthodoxy. The teachings of the Buddha created hope and aspiration for those who had otherwise no hope of salvation and freedom of choice in a society that was dominated by caste system, predominance of ritual form of worship and the exclusive status of the privileged classes, which the Vedic religion upheld as inviolable and indisputable."

"Long ago, over 1500 years ago, Hindu tradition accepted the Buddha as an incarnation of Vishnu. However, strong rivalry existed between both traditions in the subcontinent for a very long time. The followers of Siva and the Buddha could hardly stand each other in the earlier times. There were instances of Buddhist persecution by Hindu rulers, though a great majority followed a policy of religious toleration. Despite the fundamental differences between both the religions, Hinduism and Buddhism influenced each other in many ways."

There is a story in the Old Testament and the Quran that has always made me suspicious, that it might be connected to Hinduism. It is about the worship of the golden calf (i.e. young cow or bull) by Moses' followers when he went for 40 days to Mount (Sinai?) to receive the Ten Commandments (OT: Exodus chapter 32 and Quran : Al Baqarah).

www.artchive.com

The Golden Calf

I have always wondered could it be that the Hindus notion of the sacred cow begins with the above event. Was the tradition of the sacred cow brought by some of Moses' followers who went to India? Or the way around, because according to most scholars the Veda is older than the Old Testament.

Is this too far-fetched? The early religious practice of the Hindu or the Vedas was fire-sacrifices; this also sounds similar to the Jewish animal sacrifice and burnt offerings on the altar. Furthermore, early Vedas also did not build any temple or icons.

In 1935, Dr. Pran Nath published an article in the Times of India that showed that the Rig Veda (one of the Hindu religious books) contains events of the Babylonian and Egyptian kings and their wars. He showed that 1/5 of the Rig Veda is derived from the Babylonian Scriptures.

For example: Brahma (one of the gods in the Hindu Trinity) was actually Abraham – where the initial A in **Abraham** is removed to the end making it **Brahm**a. Similarly, Abraham's first wife **Sara**h is also mentioned in the Veda as **Sara**swati (a goddess who is the co-creator of Brahma).

The prophet **Nuh** or Noah of the flood is mentioned as Ma**nuh** or Manu according to Hindu tradition – who also built a ship or boat to survive a flood!

In 1887, Notovich, a Russian scholar and Orientalist, went to India. At the Zoji-la pass Notovich was a guest in a Buddhist monastery, where a monk told him of the bhodisattva saint called '**Issa**'. Notovich was stunned by the remarkable parallels of Issa's teachings and martyrdom with that of Jesus's life, teachings and crucifixion. Curiously, **Jesus** is also called **Isa** in the Quran!

And here is another connection: in the Bhavishya Puran (another Hindu religious book) verse 5 - 27, Prati Parv III:3,3 that is presented by Dr. Vidyarthi we can read as follows:

> A malechha (foreign) spiritual teacher will appear with his companions. His name will be **Mahamad**. Raja after giving this Mahadev Arab (of angelic disposition) a bath in the 'Panchgavya' and the Ganges water (i.e. purging

him of all his sins) offered him the presents of his sincere devotion and showing him all reverence said, " I make obeisance of thee". " O Ye! The pride of mankind, the dweller in Arabia. Ye have collected a great force to kill the Devi *(goddess)* and you yourself have been protected from the malechha opponents *(idol worshipers, pagans)*". " O Ye! The image of the Most Pious God the biggest Lord, I am a slave to Thee, take me as one lying on Thy feet."

The malechhas have spoiled the well-known land of the Arabs. Arya Dharma *(good moral)* is not to be found in that country. Before also there appeared a misguided friend whom I had killed *(i.e. Abraha Al-Ashram, the Abyssinian viceroy of Yemen, who attacked Mecca); he has now again appeared being sent by a powerful enemy.* To show these enemies the right path and to give them guidance <u>the well-known Mahamad,</u> who has been given by me the epithet of Brahma is busy in bringing the Pishaschas to the right path. O Raja! You need not go to the land of the foolish Pischachas, you will be purified though my kindness even where you are. At night, he of the angelic disposition, the shrewd man, in the guise of a Pischacha said to Raja Bhoj, " O Raja! Your Arya Dharma has been made to prevail over all religions, but according to the commandments of 'Ashwar Parmatma' *(God, Supreme Spirit),* I shall enforce the strong creed of the meat-eaters. <u>My follower will be a man circumcised, without a tail (on his head), keeping beard, creating a revolution, announcing call for prayer and will be eating all lawful things. He will eat all sorts of animals except swine. They will not seek purification from the holy shrubs, but will be purified through warfare. Because of their fighting the irreligious nations, they will be known as Musalamans (Moslems).</u> I shall be the originator of this religion of the meat-eating nation."

Now, this is clearly a prophecy about **Muhammad**. Apparently, there are many verses in the Vedas that contain prophecies about Muhammad, but allegedly, many Hindu translators have removed references to Muhammad's name and while some other replace the names with Hindu terminology. I will also elaborate on this in the next two books of the EarthTrek Trilogy.

It is also interesting to notice that the well-known Hindu mantra for meditation: **AUM**... has the same sound as sh**AlOM** (peace in Hebrew) or **A**ssalmualyk**UM** (may peace be with you) .... As well as the sound of the first and last alphabet of the Greek: **A**lpha and **OM**ega in Greek. One of God's characters: the Beginning and the Last.

Our history is so intertwined... but if we really keep on reading history of mankind from all over the world, we can truly see that there is just One God, One Message, One Religion.

Now that we have seen the possible connection between Hindu and the monotheistic religion, let me show you two similar Hindu and Greek myths :

Hindu goddess Sarasvati

Saraswati was the first being to come into Brahma's world. Brahma began to look upon her with eyes of desire. She turned away saying, "All I offer must be used to elevate the spirit, not indulge the senses." Brahma could not control his amorous thoughts and his infatuation for the lovely goddess grew. He continued to stare at Saraswati. He gave himself four heads facing every direction so that he could always be able to feast his eyes on Saraswati's beauty. <u>Saraswati moved away from Brahma, first taking the form of a cow. Brahma then followed her as a bull</u>. Saraswati then changed into a mare; Brahma gave chase as a horse. Every time Saraswati turned into a bird or a beast he followed her as the corresponding male equivalent. No matter how hard Brahma tried he could not catch Saraswati in any of her forms. The goddess with multiple forms came to be known as Shatarupa. She personified material reality, alluring yet fleeting. Angered by his display of unbridled passion Saraswati cursed Brahma, "You have filled the world with longing that is the seed of unhappiness. You have fettered the soul in the flesh. You are not worthy of reverence. May there be hardly any temple or festival in your name." So it came to pass that there are only two temples of Brahma in India; one at Pushkar, Rajistan and the other in Kumbhakonam, Tamil Nadu. Undaunted by the curse, Brahma continued to cast his lustful looks upon Saraswati. He gave himself a fifth head to enhance his gaze. Brahma's action motivated by desire confined consciousness and excited the ego. It disturbed the serenity of the cosmos and roused Shiva, the supreme ascetic from his meditation. Shiva opened his eyes, sensed Saraswati's discomfort and in a fit of rage turned into Bhairava, lord of terror. His eyes were red, his growl menacing. He lunged towards Brahma and with his sharp claws, wretched off Brahma's fifth head. The violence subdued Brahma's passion. Brahma's cut head seared through Bhairava's flesh and clung to his *hand sapping him of all his strength and driving him mad. The lord of terror ranted and raved losing control of his senses. Saraswati, pleased with Bhairava's timely action, rushed to his rescue. With her gentle touch she nursed him like a child, restoring his sanity. Brahma, sobered by his encounter with the Lord of terror sought an escape from the maze of his own desire. Saraswati revealed to him the doctrine for his own liberation. Brahma sought to conduct a yagna, fire sacrifice, to cleanse himself and start anew. In order to conduct a yagna ritual the assistance of a wife is needed. Brahma chose Saraswati to be his wife and thus they were reconciled.*

Doesn't the story above remind us of this following Greek myth:

Zeus and Europa

Europa was the beautiful daughter of the Phoenician king of Tyre, Agenor. Zeus, the King of the gods according *to Greek mythology, saw Europa as she was gathering flowers by the sea and immediately fell in love with her. Overwhelmed by love for Europa, <u>Zeus transformed himself into the form of a magnificent white bull</u> and appeared in the sea shore where Europa was playing with her maidens. The great bull walked gently over to where Europa stood and knelt at her feet. The appearance and movements of the bull were so gentle that Europa spread flowers about his neck and dared to climb upon his back overcoming her natural fear of the great animal. But suddenly, the bull rushed over the sea abducting Europa. Only then the bull revealed its true identity and took Europa to the Mediterranean island of Crete.*

Yes, the stories are not exactly the same, but we can still see the 'blue print'. Even when we trace back to one of the oldest myths in the world, concerning the creation of mankind from the ancient Sumerian and Babylonian, we can still see the trace of the original story.

For example: according to a Sumerian (modern Iraq) mythology the mother of all living creatures was called as the Lady of the Life/Rib. Isn't Eve, the mother of all human according to the Bible was created from Adam's rib? According to the Babylonian (also in modern Iraq) mythology Adapa was the seed of mankind. Doesn't this sound like Adam?

The similarities between the above myths to the story of Adam and Eve in the Old Testament are so obvious. Therefore, some scholars theorize that the Old Testament copied the story from the Sumerian myth, since the Sumerian myth predates the Old Testament by thousands of years.

Our history is so intertwined... but if we really study the history of mankind we can truly see that there is just One God, One Message, One Religion.

*And surely this your religion is one religion and I am your Lord,
therefore be careful (of your duty) to Me. But they cut off their
religion among themselves into sects, each part rejoicing in
that which is with them.*
(Quran translation 23:52-53)

I believe the Quran is right, when it says that God has sent
messengers to all nations, but we keep on altering the message.
The next question would be: why doesn't God just stop all these
religious fights? Well, this is the answer:

*These messengers; We blessed some of them more
than others. For example, God spoke to one, and we
raised some of them to higher ranks. And we gave
Jesus, son of Mary, profound miracles and supported
him with the Holy Spirit. Had God willed, their followers
would not have fought with each other, after the clear
proofs had come to them. Instead, they disputed
among themselves; some of them believed, and some
disbelieved. Had God willed, they would not have
fought. Everything is in accordance with God's will.*
(Quran translation 2:253)

God's will or God's plan is something that we will never found out,
until we die. This is something that even the angels know nothing
of. One thing is for sure; our life on this planet is definitely some
kind of a trial to enter a better or worse life in the Hereafter. All the
religious scriptures say so. Although after thousands of years, all of
the scriptures had been altered, therefore today they are filled with
discrepancies in the historical, scientific information and the religious
duties, except for the last one, which is the Quran.

*Do they not then meditate on the Quran? And if it were
from any other than God, they would have found in it*

many a discrepancy.
(Quran translation 4:82)

We have, without doubt, sent down the Message; and
We will assuredly guard it (from corruption).
(Quran translation 15:9)

I believe the stories (or histories) of the prophets were real, they were real historical people and real historical events. Most likely all of these stories were also told in all the religious scriptures revealed by the One God, as example how to lead our lives.

There is, in their stories, instruction for men endued with
understanding. It is not a tale invented, but a confirmation
of what went before it, a detailed exposition of all things,
and a guide and a mercy to any such as believe.
(Quran translation 12:111)

These stories have been altered heavily in the ancient pagan religions, as well as in the Old and New Testaments. The prophets miracles had been altered and exaggerated to the point they become totally unbelievable. Instead of keeping the original message of the True Religion, these real histories have become entertaining but empty narrations, and thus misleading all of us.

And from the people, there are those who accept
baseless narrations to mislead from the path of God
without knowledge, and they take it as entertainment...
(Quran translation 31:6)

Many nations exalted the prophets to a divine level, including the saints, although this is the most important message of the only One True Religion: do not worship or idolize anything else besides God. Unfortunately, this religious exaggeration is not only done in the past.

The same tendency to exaggerate was not only done by the ancient Sumerians, Babylonians, Greeks, Romans, Turkish, Jews, Christians, but helas, also by Moslems. Although the Quran keeps on repeating this message some Moslems today also venerate Muhammad as if he was divine. Humans are the same everywhere at all times..

All the prophets and messengers are just human being like you or me. Although, beside the obvious reason that they have amazingly great characters and unshakeable faith, they also received divine guidance from God and were given missions to guide the rest of their races or the whole of mankind. It is totally forbidden to idolize them as divinities.

⟶✷⟵

Now I am fully convinced that my study in search of Truth has proven that: there is only One True Religion with the same message that has been revealed by the One God for the whole of humanity.

The message is: peace, tolerance, equality, wisdom, goodness, compassion, gratefulness, justice, humbleness, responsibility, honesty, decency, soberness, balance, cleanliness, discipline, patience, respect towards the parents, protection of the unfortunate, bravery against tyranny, believe in the consequence of one's actions on earth impacting the afterlife, above all submission to the One God's will and to worship Him, with periods of solitude for private conversation between one and God.

Now, if *that* is the message of religion, how come there are so many people who perform irrational, crazy or mean and down right cruel rituals in the name of religions?

Some people exercise cruel punishment like stoning to death in the name of Islam and Judaism; others make women immolate themselves by jumping into fire to follow their deceased husbands in the name of Hinduism (Sati); some people perform flagellation and even crucify themselves in the name of Christianity (e.g.: in the Philippines); some people mummify themselves in the name of Buddhism (e.g: the Sokushinbutsu in Japan)! I don't have the stomach to share with you the pictures of the bloody 'religious' rituals... so I am only sharing one picture:

Self Mummified Monk in Japan

Many people go into religious frenzy because of ignorance of the true message of religion. Not only do humans like to exaggerate and/or change the detail of real events, we also have a habit to abuse and exceed beyond the limits in what religion has commanded us to do.

We create hardship where it is not the purpose of religion. We like to forbid what is good, and allow what is bad. What is the purpose of doing extreme rituals apart from making others feel apathy towards religion? Of course, God knows that it is human's tendency to exaggerate, therefore the Quran keeps on repeating this message:

> ... (God) has not laid upon you any hardship in religion..
> (Quran translation 22:78)

O you who believe! Do not forbid (yourselves) the good things which God has made lawful for you and do not exceed the limits; surely God does not love those who exceed the limits.
(Quran translation 5:87)

... do not exceed the limits, surely God does not love those who exceed the limits.
(Quran translation 2:190)

... These are the limits of God, so do not exceed them and whoever exceeds the limits of God these it is that are the unjust.
(Quran translation 2:229)

O followers of the Book! do not exceed the limits in your religion, and do not speak (lies) against God, but (speak) the truth..
(Quran translation 4:171)

Call on your Lord humbly and secretly; surely He does not love those who exceed the limits..
(Quran translation 7:55)

CHAPTER SEVENTEEN

THE DIVISION

*N*ow let's answer the question that has been bothering most of non-Moslems about Islam. If truly the teaching of the Quran is correct, why do we hear so many negative things about Islam?

If I feel most uncomfortable towards the Christians when writing Chapter 13 (Son of God?), now I feel most uncomfortable towards fellow Moslems while writing this chapter. I know many Moslems will be surprised, shocked or feel attacked by the following information that I am about to share. Please remember, dear fellow Moslems, that this is not my intention. I truly hope after you have finished reading the whole chapter you will gain something to think about. What I am about to share is based on the facts and information that I have collected in search of the Truth. And if you have different information that can lead to the Truth, I would be very happy and thankful for it. I am sorry for the length of this chapter, but I am not able to shorten it.

(Almost) no Moslem doubts the Quran. But that is not the case for the non-Moslems. It is understandable, when we look at the chaotic world's religious/political situation in the Middle East today. Therefore, many non-Moslems especially in the West doubt the teaching of the Quran, to put it mildly. It is true, that this is due to the lack of information about Islam, but we Moslems should also not close our eyes and realize that many of the Quranic teachings have been practiced incorrectly by many Moslems (including me) and brought to the extreme by radical Moslems.

We have seen in the earlier chapters how amazing and wise the Quran is. All its descriptions concerning the natural phenomena are accurate, and some of the verses can only be explained by recent scientific finding. Could the Quran that is so wise teach Moslems to become terrorists? There answer is a big NO. So, what caused these 'Moslems' to act in such radical ways?

During Muhammad's era, Islam had the reputation as the most tolerant religion: Jews and Christians were allowed to practice their religions; Jews who were expelled by the previous Christian ruler of Jerusalem were invited back by the Islamic ruler. Many verses in the Quran trigger Moslem scientists to do amazing findings in modern science... So how come Islam today is almost identical to militant government style which is oppressive and intolerant? Why do Islamic sects kill each other? Doesn't the word 'Islam' have the same root as the word 'salam' which means 'peace'? I believe these are the reasons:

Reason number 1: Ignorance and/or Fanaticism

The most obvious reason is because unfortunately the majority of Moslems are uneducated people and poor. Although, if we truly study our world's history, we can see that all religions in the world started to recruit amongst the poor in each society. Maybe it is because 'all religions' protect the poor. Therefore, to the poor religion seems to be the only salvation they have. Many Moslems today are still illiterate. So, in many countries reading the Quran – like reading the Old Testament and the New Testament in the past – is mostly done by the so-called religious scholars. Many Moslems do not really study the Quran entirely, and even the ones who read it, most likely do not fully understand the meaning for lack of understanding. And although many non-Arabic speaking Moslems are able to memorize the Quran down to the alphabets, they do not necessarily understand the meaning because of the language barrier. Even I am able to memorize a few chapters from the Quran, I am also able to read the Quran (or sound-out the letters to be more precise) but that doesn't mean I understand the meaning of the Arabic Quran. For the meaning, I have to rely on the Indonesian or English translation – which unfortunately, is not always translated accurately.

Then, there are some Moslems who tend to exaggerate in other word, fanatic. I don't know how it is in other Islamic countries, but in Indonesia several times a day we can hear religious sermons, or tape recorded Quran recitation or the Salawat Nabi (prayers upon Prophet Muhammad) coming through loudspeakers from a number of mosques simultaneously.

A non-Moslem friend of mine; told me that these practices are intrusive towards people of other religions and he said further that there is no Christian priest or Jewish rabbi or any other religious leader who preach via loudspeaker that way. He asked why the sermons coming from the mosques are so loud and sometimes even aggressive. They reminded him of communist propaganda rather than religious calling. Being a Moslem, I was offended when he said that. But then after putting some thought, I realized that he might have a point there. It is true, this way of religious preaching does not sound peaceful, instead of attracting non-Moslems to learn the Truth behind this religion; it actually repels them. I wonder if this was the case during Prophet Muhammad's time, because loudspeaker was not even invented back then, right? He was right! I have never heard sermons from any other religion via a loudspeaker coming from a church, synagogue or temple. Is this really the true teaching of a peaceful religion? How can this be right, when the verses of the Quran say the opposite?

> *And remember your Lord within yourself humbly and fearing and in a voice not loud in the morning and the evening and be not of the heedless ones.*
> *(Quran translation 7:205)*

> And pursue the right course in your going about and
> lower your voice; surely the most hateful of voices is
> braying of the asses.
> (Quran translation 31:19)

> Call on your Lord humbly and secretly; surely He does not
> love those who exceed the limits.
> (Quran translation 7:55)

> You shall invite to the path of your Lord with wisdom and
> kind enlightenment, and debate with them in the best
> possible manner...
> (Quran translation 16:125)

The Quran tells us to lower our voice, to call our humbly and secretly and to invite others in the best of manner. Clearly then, preaching forcefully via several loud speakers several times a day does not fulfill these requirements.

Reason number 2: Division

As any other religions in the world, Islam today is also divided into many sects. This happens because of many reasons, the main reason I believe is because it is just human's nature to transgress (go beyond the limit). Humans tend to exaggerate about everything, especially concerning the divine guidance that is given to us. Also some people who are in authority purposely misguide others in order to gain the power of controlling other people's life. Unfortunately, these same people do not really have the wisdom or purposely refuse to understand the true teaching of Islam. Most people, especially people who are not educated also have the tendency to be superstitious. They tend to think religion has to contain some kind of superstitious teaching; meanwhile there is nothing superstitious about the Quran. Apart from God who is Supra Natural, everything else is 'natural', which is actually the beauty of it... it is telling only the Truth. But many people fail or simply refuse to understand this. So like all other religious people previous to Islam, some Moslems create their own sects according to their traditions, ancient superstitious beliefs and mix them with Quranic teaching.

After the death of Muhammad (632 CE), Islam is divided into 2 major sects: the Sunni (around 80%), the Shi'a or Shi'ite (around 10%) and then there many other smaller sects, today there are around 70 sects exist in Islam. The Shi'a, though a minority in the Moslem world, constitute the majority of the populations in Iran, Azerbaijan, Bahrain and Iraq, as well as a plurality in Lebanon and Kuwait. Allow me to explain this in the most simplified manner: the Shi'a are the supporters of Ali (who was the cousin of Muhammad) and believe that they should be in control of the Islamic society and therefore, they build a kind of religious monarch (so called Imamate). The Shi'a has many traditions that are based on the 'root' of Muhammad's clan tradition, according to them. They have Imams as religious leaders. They also believe that all the Imams chosen are free from committing any sin and have a status directly parallel to those of a prophet, infallibility which is called Ismah (this is the same concept of infallibility of the Catholic Popes on matters of faith and morals). They believe these leaders; especially the Twelve Imams must be followed since they are appointed by God.

Some concepts of it are acknowledged by the Sunnis also. But they differ with as to who is an Imam and what qualities he must possess. The Sunnis totally disbelieve in certain concepts of Imamat. It is not that they believe in Imamat in the sense in which the Shi'as believe but disagree as to the person who holds this assignment.

All these are taught nowhere in the Quran. For a matter of simple explanation, the Shi'a can be compared to the Catholic sect in Christianity, where tradition, hierarchy order and ritual are held high. Imam means 'a leader' or 'one who goes in front'. The word Imam in Arabic does not imply any sense of sanctity. And Imam is the person who has some followers irrespective of the fact whether he is virtuous or depraved. The Quran itself has used the word in both the senses. At one place it says:

> We appointed them Imams who guide with Our permission.
> (Quran translation 21:73)

In respect of Pharaoh the Quran has used a phrase which conveys a sense similar to that of an Imam or a leader. It says:

> On the Day of Judgment he will lead his people down into the Hell fire.
> (Quran translation 11:98)

At another place it says:

> The Imams who invite people to Hell.
> (Quran translation 28:41)

The Quran is against priesthood or monarchy in religion. This can be witnessed also during mass prayer. An Imam during mass prayer is simply the person who leads the prayer, to synchronize the movement. Any Moslem can be an Imam during mass prayer. Moslems pray in rows, whoever comes early may stand in the front row, whoever comes late have to stand at the back row. It doesn't matter what the person's status is in life. Religion is a personal matter; no one can be higher in religious matter (like in Priesthood or Imamhood) – with the exception of the prophets, being the Messengers of God. God is the only One who can determine that.

> Then We made Our apostles to follow in their footsteps, and We sent Jesus son of Maria afterwards, and We gave him the Gospel, and We put in the hearts of those who followed him kindness and mercy; and (as for) priesthood,

they innovated it - We did not prescribe it to them - only to seek God's pleasure, but they did not observe it with its due observance..
(Quran translation 57:27)

Apart from that, just like Christianity and Buddhism, there are also many Moslems who elevate Muhammad's status to an exaggerated degree. There is even a sect in Islam who believes in the Trinity. This kind of teaching is strictly forbidden by the Quran. The Quran clearly states that there is only One God.

This sect (I wont mention the name for safety reason) even has its own religious book besides the Quran. And its Trinity consists of: Allah, Muhammad and Ali! Then there are many Moslems who believe in Imam Mahdi (the 'Guided One') who is prophesied as the redeemer of Islam who will stay before the coming of the Yaum al-Qiyamah (Day of Resurrection). He will rid the world of error, injustice and tyranny alongside Jesus. I know, this sounds like a fairy tale, right?

It is really strange how many Moslems believe in the coming of this Imam Mahdi, when at the same time they believe that Prophet Muhammad was the last prophet. I wonder, who this Imam Mahdi is? If he is a man, he must be some kind of a prophet, right? If not, then who is he? An angel? The tradition of Imam Mahdi is not mentioned anywhere in the Quran. There are many narrations circulating among the Moslems telling future prophecies that were allegedly told by Prophet Muhammad, while the Quran says that Prophet Muhammad can not predict the future:

Say (O Muhammad): I am not the first of the apostles, and I do not know what will be done with me or with you: I do not follow anything but that which is revealed to me, and I am nothing but a plain warner.
(Quran translation 46:9)

Say (O Muhammad): I do not control any benefit or harm for my own soul except as God please; and had I known the unseen I would have had much of good and no evil would have touched me; I am nothing but a warner and the giver of good news to a people who believe.
(Quran translation 7:188)

However, as we have discussed in the Chapter of Astrological Sons of Gods, this kind of religious tempering is not a new thing. None of these are taught anywhere in the Quran.

In Islam (just like in other religions) there are many sects fighting with one another, arguing about various topics, amongst others about the genealogy of Prophet Muhammad. No wonder that our world's religious/political situation is so chaotic today. Unfortunately, that is just human's nature.

He decreed for you <u>the same religion decreed for Noah, and what we inspired to you, and what we decreed for Abraham, Moses, and Jesus: "You shall uphold this one religion, and do not divide it</u>." *The idol worshipers will greatly resent what you invite them to do. God redeems to Himself whomever He wills; He guides to Himself only those who totally submit.* <u>Ironically, they broke up into sects only after the knowledge had come to them</u>, *due to jealousy and resentment among themselves. If it were not for a predetermined decision from your Lord to respite them for a definite interim, they would have been judged immediately. Indeed, the later generations who inherited the scripture are full of doubts.*
(Quran translation 42:13-14)

Most Moslems are taught to believe that the above verses are only directed to the Jews and Christians when it is clear that these verses are also directed to the Moslems as well. Isn't the division in Islam is already proven today?

THE HADYTH

Apart from the Quran many Moslems also believe in the 'Sunna or the 'way' of Muhammad: the Hadyth (read: hadeeth). What is the Hadyth? Hadyth can be translated as 'narrations, sayings and/or deeds'. The Hadyth are various oral traditions contained in specific books, believed in by the majority of Moslems to be the words and deeds of Muhammad. From the first Fitna (First Islamic Civil War) of the 7th century CE people questioned the sources of Hadyth. This resulted in a list of Hadyth narrators or transmitters, for example "A told B, and B told C, then C told me that Prophet Muhammad said...." Despite the doubt, most Moslems still present them as an explanation of the Quran or as an integral part of Islamic law. The two major sects, Sunni and Shi'a have two separate sets of Hadyth, which one sect over the other claim that their own set of Hadyth is authentic.

Sunni generally accept:

Muwatta of Malik ibn Ans, Jamu'us Sahih of Bukhari, Sahih of Muslim, Sunan of Abu Daud Sulaiman, Jami of Tirmidhee and Kitabus Sunan of Muhammad ibn Yazid ibn Majah of Qazwani.

Shi'a generally accept:

Kafi of Abu Ja'fa Muhammad, Man la Yastuhdirahul Fiqah of Shaikh Ali, Tahdhib of Shaikh abu Jafar Muhammad and Najhu'l Balaghah of Sayyid Radi.

Apart from the many Hadyth books there is also a special sub-category of collection which is called the Hadyth Qudsi, meaning 'the Sacred Hadyth'. These Hadyth Qudsi are believed to be the sayings of Muhammad as revealed to him by God. Some scholars mentioned that these Hadyth were revealed by God either by inspiration, insight (instillation in the heart or mind) or a dream. Hence, Hadith Qudsi ranks as a source of Islamic knowledge below the Qur'an but above all other Hadyth. A well-known text among Moslems is the '40 Hadyth Qudsi'.

There is a special science of Hadyth ('Ulum al-Hadyth) which is a method of textual criticism developed by early Moslem scholars in determining the accuracy of reports attributed to Muhammad. This is achieved by analyzing the text of the report, the scale of the report's transmission, the routes through which the report was transmitted, and the individual narrators involved in its transmission. The study is complicated, and here is the widely known category of the Hadyth in a simplified manner:
- sahih (sound, authentic)
- da`if (weak)
- mawdu (fabricated)
- mutawatir (most authoritative)
- hasan (good)
- munkar (ignored)

Growing up as a Moslem, I was also taught to believe in the Hadyth. I never really questioned it, until I came across some Hadyth that are so hard to believe in. I knew that we are not supposed to believe in all of them. I was told that the Hadyth narrated by Bukhari are believed to be as the most authentic. However, after further study I still found many hard-to-believe Hadiyth that were narrated by Bukhari. I know that these Hadyth have no base on Quranic teaching. However, some (if not all) of these Hadyth are still followed by many Moslems.

For a quick Hadyth search visit: www.searchtruth.com/searchHadith.php. Below I am quoting some of the hard-to-believe Hadyth that have no Quranic base. In order for you not to get confuse, I use different fonts when quoting the Quran and the Hadyth, and if you have the color version of this book, the Hadyth are written in blue.

WRITING DOWN OF TEACHING
Hadyth of Imam Muslim (Zuhd 72, Hanbal 3/12, 21, 39) – quote that Prophet Muhammad said that *no one should write anything from him other than the Quran.*

"Do not write down anything of me except the Quran. Whoever writes other than that should delete it".
(Hadyth Ahmed bin Hanbal, Vol. 1 page 171)

I was perplexed when the first time I read this Hadyth. Isn't this Hadyth actually contradicting itself? Prophet Muhammad said not to write what he said, so why is this particular Hadyth not deleted then? Not only that, there is another Hadyth that contradicts this Hadyth as well. Prophet Muhammad is quoted asking, in Hanbal 1/162, Amr bin As, his companion to *write everything he spoke*! I don't understand! So did Prophet Muhammad allow his words and deeds to be written down or not?

From: 'Early Mapping of the Pacific' book by Thomas Suarez

THE SUN AND THE MOON

We have seen in chapter 5: Monotheist Religious Books Versus Science, how accurate the Quran describes the movement of the sun and the moon. And remember, the Quran was revealed hundreds of years before the heliocentric theory was accepted in the West. However, according to Bukhari – Prophet Muhammad tells his companion Abu Darr Ghafari that *the sun goes around the earth* (Hadyth 421, pg. 283, vol.4 of Muchsin Khan's translation of Sahih Bukhari)!

Not only that, another Hadyth by Ibn Kathir (2/29 and 50/1) suggests that *the earth is 'carried on a giant bull'! When the bull shakes its head the earth quakes as a result!*

DOGS

This is also one of the most misunderstood things about Islam – even for the Moslems. Many Moslems believe that dogs are not clean and should not be kept as pets. Where does this notion come from? According to a Hadyth by Hanbal (4/85 and 5/54) *Muhammad ordered that all black dogs be killed because they are devils*! Inspired by that Hadyth, some Moslems consider them unclean and killed hundreds of dogs all over the world. Hadyth Bukhari doesn't even say only black dogs, but just simply dogs.

> *Narrated 'Abdullah bin 'Umar: Allah's Apostle ordered that the dogs should be killed.*
> *(Hadyth Bukhari, Book 54, #540)*

The Quran, contrary to that, talks about the sleepers in the cave having a dog, inside their dwelling place who help keep them safe (surah or chapter 18). And also the Quran allows meat killed by hunting dogs. There is nothing in the Quran which even remotely suggest that dogs are unclean rather than useful animals.

> *They ask you as to what is allowed to them. Say: The good things are allowed to you, and what you have taught the dogs and birds of prey, training them to hunt - you teach them of what God has taught you - so eat of that which they catch for you and mention the name of God over it..*
> *(Quran translation 5:4)*

Although strange enough not all the English translators mention the word 'dog' in their translations. Some of the translators translate the words 'dogs and birds of prey' using: trained hunting animal, beasts and birds of prey trained to hunt, trained hunting animals, or prey of beasts of chase which ye have trained like dogs or hounds. I do not speak Arabic. But when I check the literal translation of the above verse, this is what I see (go to: http://islamawakened.com/Quran/5/4/default.htm).

Transliteration Arabic-English:
Yas-aloonaka matha ohilla lahum qul ohilla lakumu alttayyibatu wama AAallamtum mina aljawarihi mukallibeena tuAAallimoonahunna mimma AAallamakumu Allahu fakuloo mimma amsakna AAalaykum waothkuroo isma Allahi AAalayhi waittaqoo Allaha inna Allaha sareeAAu alhisabi.

Literal translation:
They ask/question you what became permitted (allowed) for them, say: "Permitted/allowed for you (are) the goodnesses, and what you taught from the predatory animals, hunting birds and <u>hunting dogs</u>, training for hunting and retrieving , you teach them from what God taught/instructed you, so eat from what they held/ grasped/seized on (for) you, and mention / remember God's name on it, and fear and obey God, that God (is) quick/fast (in) the counting/calculating."

The word 'dog' is clearly written in the literal translation. So how come some of the English translators go all the way to translate the word 'dog' in such complicated description? It is as if they deliberately avoid using the specific word 'dog'. Why?

Now, we have seen that Hadyth of Bukhari concerning the killing of dogs. Here is another contradictive Hadyth, also from Bukhari!

Narrated 'Adi bin Hatim: I asked the Prophet, "I send off (for a game) my trained hunting dogs; (what is your verdict concerning the game they hunt?" He said, "If you send off your trained hunting dogs and mention the Name of Allah, then, if they catch some game, eat (thereof). And if you hit the game with a mi'rad (a hunting tool) and it wounds it, you can eat (it)."
(Hadyth Bukhari, Book 93, #494)

If Prophet Muhammad really ordered that dogs should be killed, why did he in the above Hadyth allowed his followers to hunt by trained hunting dogs?

VISION OF GOD

The Quran states that 'Vision cannot comprehend God, Who comprehends all vision', yet Hadyth Bukhari (97/24 and 101/129) says that *to prove His identity to Muhammad, God showed the prophet His shin*!

HYGIENE

The Quran places extreme importance on cleanliness and clean eating (tayyab), but look at the following Hadyth:

Narrated Maimuna: The Prophet was asked about a mouse that had fallen into butter-fat (and died). He said, "Throw away the mouse and the portion of butter-fat around it, and eat the rest."
(Hadyth Bukhari, Book 67, #448)

The Quran is accurate concerning any description about biology and hygiene. And yet, the books of Hadyth contain many home remedies, according the ideas prevalent at that time, which are scientifically absurd. The Hadyth narrate that Prophet Muhammad ordered people to drink 'camel urine' as medicine. This is not only disgusting, but urine is toxic stuff that the body discard to protect itself from harm. Here is one example of such Hadyth:

Narrated Abu Qilaba: Anas said, "Some people of 'Ukl or 'Uraina tribe came to Medina and its climate did not suit them. So the <u>Prophet ordered them to go to the herd of camels and to drink their milk and urine (as a medicine</u>). So they went as directed and after they became healthy, they killed the shepherd of the Prophet and drove away all the camels. The news reached the Prophet early in the morning and he sent (men) in their pursuit and they were captured and brought at noon. He then ordered to cut their hands and feet (and it was done), and their eyes were branded with heated pieces of iron, They were put in 'Al-Harra' and when they asked for water, no water was given to them." Abu Qilaba said, "Those people committed theft and murder, became infidels after embracing Islam and fought against Allah and His Apostle ."
(Hadyth Bukhari, Book 4, #234)

What a story! I have such a difficult time believing in this Hadyth. And look at how cruel the Prophet was to them, this is not in accordance to any of the Quranic teachings nor the historical data concerning Prophet Muhammad (even from non-biased non-Moslem historians) that we have discussed previously. Meanwhile the Quran says:

> We have sent you (Muhammad) for no other reason but to be a mercy for mankind.
> (Quran translation 21:107)

STONING TO DEATH

The Hadyth mentions *the punishment of 'stoning to death' for adultery in the case of married couple.* This is not what the Quran says. There is no punishment in the Quran in form of stoning to death! There are around 30 Hadyth of Bukhari concerning stoning to death. According to the Hadyth, the Prophet even stoned monkeys!

Narrated 'Abdullah bin 'Umar : The Jew brought to the Prophet a man and a woman from amongst them who have committed (adultery) illegal sexual intercourse. He ordered both of them to be stoned (to death), near the place of offering the funeral prayers beside the mosque."
(Hadyth Bukhari, Book 23, #413)

Narrated 'Amr bin Maimun: During the pre-Islamic period of ignorance I saw a she-monkey surrounded by a number of monkeys. They were all stoning it, because it had committed illegal sexual intercourse. I too, stoned it along with them.
(Hadyth Bukhari, Book 58, #188)

CRITICIZING AND/OR BELITTLING OTHER PROPHETS
There are even Hadyths narrating stories how Prophet Muhammad criticizing and/or belittling other Prophets!

Narrated Abu Huraira: One day some meat was given to the Prophet and he said, "On the Day of Resurrection Allah will gather all the first and the last (people) in one plain, and the voice of the announcer will reach all of them, and one will be able to see them all, and the sun will come closer to them." (The narrator then mentioned the narration of intercession): "The people will go to Abraham and say: 'You are Allah's Prophet and His Khalil on the earth. Will you intercede for us with your Lord?' Abraham will then remember his lies and say: 'Myself! Myself! Go to Moses."
(Hadyth Bukhari, Book 55, #581)

And look at the following 3 versions (I found 5 versions actually) of Hadyth Bukhari criticizing Prophet Solomon concerning his boastfulness in sexual relationship, and all 3 have conflicting data:

Narrated Abu Huraira: The Prophet said, "solomon (the son of) David said, 'Tonight I will sleep <u>with seventy ladies</u>

each of whom will conceive a child who will be a knight fighting for "Allah's Cause.' His companion said, 'If Allah will.' But solomon did not say so; therefore none of those women got pregnant except one who gave birth to a half child." The Prophet further said, "If the Prophet solomon had said it (i.e. 'If Allah will') he would have begotten children who would have fought in Allah's Cause." Shuaib and Ibn Abi Az-Zinad said, <u>"Ninety (women) is more correct (than seventy).</u>"
(Hadyth Bukhari, Book 55, #635)

In book 62, #169, Bukhari mentioned 'one hundred women' and in book 93, #561 he mentioned 'sixty wives'!

BEARDS
The word 'beard' appears 28 times in 24 Hadyths narrated by Bukhari.

Narrated Abu Ma'mar: We said to Khabbab "Did Allah's Apostle used to recite in Zuhr and 'Asr prayers?" He replied in the affirmative. We said, "How did you come to know about it?" He said, "By the movement of his beard."
(Hadyth Bukhari, Book 12, #744)

Narrated Abu Huraira: Allah's Apostle said, "The Jews and the Christians do not dye (their grey hair), so you shall do the opposite of what they do (i.e. dye your grey hair and beards)."
(Hadyth Bukhari, Book 56, #668)

Why? Meanwhile the Quran clearly mentions (twice):

Surely those who believe, and those who are Jews, and the Christians, and the Sabians, whoever believes in God and the Last day and does good, they shall have their reward from their Lord, and there is no fear for them, nor shall they grieve.
(Quran translation 2:62 **and** 5:69)

Clearly the name of the religion does not matter in the eye of God. The most important is that we believe in Him, the Last Day and do good. The big question is then: what is the criteria of doing good? Well, that we have discussed in length earlier in this book (i.e. the religious duties and laws, etc). One thing is for sure, the criterion is definitely not in the color of our hair or beard. Now, why does the above Hadyth make a distinction between Moslems, Christians and Jews by using such a trivial matter? And what happens if a Moslem man does <u>not</u> dye his hair and beard?

URINATE

There are also Hadyths concerning how the Prophet urinated! Not only I don't understand the importance of these Hadyth, they are also contradictive to one another:

> *Narrated Hudhaifa: I saw Allah's Apostle coming (or the Prophet came) to the dumps of some people and urinated there while standing.*
> *(Hadyth Bukhari, Book 43, #651)*

Meanwhile, another Hadyth narrates that *"The Prophet never urinated in standing position"* (Hadyth Hanbal 6/136,192,213).

CRUEL WAR/FIGHT

We have discussed concerning the rules of war in the Quran, that it is permissible to eliminate tyranny, to defend when being attacked, treaty during war has to be respected, no torturing, no compulsion in religion and captives should be fed with Moslems favorite food.. in short, the ultimate goal is to gain peace on earth and spread the True Religion, but look at the following Hadyth:

> *Narrated Anas: The Prophet cut off the hands and feet of the men belonging to the tribe of 'Uraina and did not cauterise (their bleeding limbs) till they died.*
> *(Hadyth Bukhari, Book 82, #795)*

Narrated Ikrima: Ali burnt some people and this news reached Ibn 'Abbas, who said, "Had I been in his place I would not have burnt them, as the Prophet said, 'Don't punish (anybody) with Allah's Punishment.' No doubt, I would have killed them, for the Prophet said, 'If somebody (a Muslim) discards his religion, kill him.' "
(Hadyth Bukhari, Book 52, #260)

Narrated Ibn Aun: I wrote a letter to Nafi and Nafi wrote in reply to my letter that <u>the Prophet had suddenly attacked bani mustaliq without warning while they were heedless</u> and their cattle were being watered at the places of water. Their fighting men were killed and their women and children were taken as captives; the Prophet got Juwairiya on that day. Nafi said that Ibn 'Umar had told him the above narration and that Ibn 'Umar was in that army.
(Hadyth Bukhari, Book 46, #717)

Dear fellow Moslems, there are many more cruel, non-Quranic based (Shahih) Hadyth by Bukhari alone, please search for yourself, if you will. Imagine the impact of the above Hadyth to the radical Moslems. Especially if this is combined with the Hadyth about the Jihad (in the sense of 'holy war')… the result is disastrous!

MIRACLES
There are several Hadyth about miracles performed by Muhammad. The Quran does mention the miracles performed by other prophets previous to Muhammad, although a lot less in number and less dramatic in comparison to the data found in the Old and New Testaments. However, the Quran does not mention any tangible miracle done by Muhammad, except for the Quran. Don't you think it is strange while it mentions the miracles by other Prophets?

He sent down to you this scripture, containing straightforward verses - which constitute the essence of the scripture - as well as multiple-meaning or allegorical verses. <u>Those who harbor</u>

doubts in their hearts will pursue the multiple-meaning verses to create confusion, and to extricate a certain meaning. None knows the true meaning thereof except God and those well founded in knowledge. They say, "We believe in this - all of it comes from our Lord." Only those who possess intelligence will take heed.
(Quran translation 3:7)

The truth is, the Quran is the perpetual miracle revealed by God through Prophet Muhammad. The verses of the Quran are referred to as 'ayat', which also means 'a miracle' in the Arabic language. However, only people 'well founded in knowledge' can understand and marvel at the miracle of the Quran, for example concerning the natural phenomenon and also to decode and understand the mathematical phenomenon.

But for the people during Muhammad's time (and unfortunately some people today) this is not enough. I believe this is the reason why in the Hadyth, Muhammad is recorded as performing tangible miracles. Some Hadyth is trying to fit the interpretation of certain verse in the Quran (just like what the above Quran verse says) and attribute it to Muhammad.

For example concerning the miracle of splitting the moon. Yes, there is a verse in the Quran about the splitting of the moon.

The Hour has drawn nigh: the moon is split. Yet if they see a sign they turn away, and they say 'A continuous sorcery!'
(Quran translation 54:1-2)

The Hadyth narrations designated to clarify the above verses are as follows:

Narrated 'Abdullah: The moon was split (into two pieces) while we were with the Prophet in Mina. He said, "Be witnesses." Then a Piece of the moon went towards the mountain.
(Hadyth Bukhari, Book 58, #209)

Narrated Ibn Masud: During the lifetime of Allah's Apostle the moon was split into two parts; one part remained over the mountain, and the other part went beyond the mountain. On that, Allah's Apostle said, "Witness this miracle."
(Hadyth Bukhari, Book 60, #387)

You can see, the Quranic verses do not mention Muhammad's name. In fact, without reading the Hadyth, I believe most people will understand the splitting of the moon of the Quranic verses refer to a sign of the coming of the Hour (the Judgment Day). But because of the Hadyths many Moslems believe that the above verses are describing a miracle performed by Muhammad in order to convince the disbeliever of his prophethood.

Virtually all Moslem commentators accept the authenticity of the Hadyth concerning the splitting of the moon. The classical commentator Ibn Kathir provides a list of the early Hadyths mentioning the incident: A Hadyth transmitted on the authority of Anas bin Malik states that *Muhammad split the moon after the pagan Meccans asked for a miracle.* Another Hadyth from Malik transmitted through other chains of narrations, mentions that *the mount Hira was visible between the two parts of the moon (Mount Hira is located in Hijaz).* Moslems believe that Muhammad received his first revelations from God in a cave on this mountain). A Hadyth narrated on the authority of Jubayr ibn Mut'im with a single chain of transmission says that *the two parts of the moon stood on two mountains.* This Hadyth further states that *the Meccan responded by saying "Muhammad has taken us by his magic...If he was able to take us by magic, he will be able to do so with all people."* Hadyth transmitted on the authority of Ibn Abbas briefly mention the incident and do not provide much detail. Hadyth transmitted on the authority of Abdullah bin Masud describe the incident as follows: *'We were along with Allah's Messenger (may peace be upon him) at Mina, that moon was split up into two. One of its parts was behind the mountain and the other one was on this side of the mountain.*

Allah's Messenger (may peace be upon him) said to us: Bear witness to this.'

Al-Zamakhshari, a famous commentator of the Qur'an, acknowledged the splitting of the moon as one of Muhammad's miracles. But he also suggested that the splitting might take place only on the Day of Judgment. The Moslem scholar Yusuf Ali provides three different interpretations of the verse. He holds that perhaps all three are applicable to the verse: the moon once appeared cleft asunder at the time of Muhammad in order to convince the unbelievers. It will split again when the Day of Judgment approaches. Lastly, he says that the verses can be metaphorical, meaning that the matter has become clear as the moon.

Some other Moslem thinkers had difficulties accepting this event and other preternatural events and, according to Annemarie Schimmel (a German Orientalist scholar), sometimes tried to 'de-mythologize' it. For example, Shah Waliullah of Delhi (d. 1762) said that the event "may have been a kind of hallucination, or perhaps caused by a smoke, by the swooping down of a star, a cloud, or an eclipse of the sun or the moon which might be given the impression that the moon was actually split in two."

How can the Hadyth explain the Quran? Obviously, it can not in the above case. Now, according to Rashad Khalifa (the Quranic mathematical code breaker), who studied the Quran without being influenced by the Hadyth, comes to the following conclusion: that the above verses from the Quran are talking about an event <u>after</u> Muhammad's time, because it is talking about the sign of the coming of the Hour (i.e. the Judgment Day). He believes that this event has already happened today. Our modern astronauts, Neil Amstrong and Edwin Aldrin, have landed on the moon in 1969 and brought pieces of the moon to earth (i.e. 21 kg of lunar rocks). This is what the verse means by 'the moon is split' – meaning parts of the moon have left its surface, they no longer are part of the moon. Well, at least this one is factual and it does make sense, right?

There are a few more Hadyth narrating miracles performed by Prophet Muhammad such as ":

> ... *water springing out from underneath his fingers till all of them performed the ablution (it was one of the miracles of the Prophet)" (Hadyth Bukhari, Book 4, #170)* and *"feeding eighty men with a piece of bread" (Hadyth Bukhari, Book 65, #293).*

I wonder why didn't they just perform Tayammum as commanded by the Quran when there was no water for ablution? And doesn't the Hadyth concerning the sharing of small amount of food between many people, remind us of the miracle of Jesus in the New Testament? Once again, how come the Quran doesn't mention any of these miracles?

Now, not only that the above Hadyth have no Quranic base, in fact there is another Hadyth narrated by Bukhari that seems to contradict the above miracles of Muhammad! In the Hadyth below, Prophet Muhammad said that although other Prophets were 'given miracles', but he was 'only' given the Divine Inspiration (i.e. the Quran):

> *Narrated Abu Huraira: The Prophet said, "There was no prophet among the prophets but was given miracles because of which people had security or had belief, but what I was given was the Divine Inspiration which Allah revealed to me. So I hope that my followers will be more than those of any other prophet on the Day of Resurrection."*
> *(Hadyth Bukhari, Book 92, #379)*

I have such a difficult time believing that the above Hadyths truly came from Prophet Muhammad although most of them were narrated by the 'most trustworthy' Hadyth narrators. Yes, I know we have been reminded to be careful when reading the Hadyth, because some of them are 'mawdu' (fabricated) and 'munkar' (ignored). So why aren't the fabricated and ignored Hadyths deleted from circulation then? How are 'commoners' like us supposed to know in which Hadyth we are supposed to believe in then? I read the above Hadyths in a search engine in the Internet, which means everybody in the whole world can also do the same thing.

Some other rules and/or traditions actually make the Islamic teaching becomes 'difficult' and confusing to put into practice. For example: growing beards for men, prohibition of wearing gold ornaments, prohibition of singing, prohibition of drawing, various ruling concerning coloring the hair and recently the Malaysian Government forbids non-Moslems to use the word 'Allah'... although, we have seen earlier in this book that this word was already used by Arab Christians and Maltese Christians before the advance of Islam. So how should they call God then?

Yes, there are many Hadyths that are in accordance with the Quran. Some religious scholars say that the Quran is not detailed enough; therefore we need to follow the words and deeds of Prophet Muhammad to explain the Quran. But.. how can the Hadyth clarify the Quran when there are so many books of Hadyth and many are contradicting the others? After reading the above Hadyth I started reading more. The more I read, the more I doubt the authority of the Hadyth. There are simply too many hard-to-believe Hadyth! Some contradict the Quran, some ridicule the Prophets, some sound too much like fairy tales, many are so cruel.. I felt really uncomfortable reading these Hadyth. Then I started reading books concerning Hadyth versus Quran. I was surprised finding out there are around 200,000 websites discussing this matter in the Internet. It is relatively small for Internet standard, but it is definitely not a small number. Obviously many Moslems are feeling the same as I do.

So please allow me to share with you the information concerning the Hadyth that I have gathered. One of the best websites I can find is: http://www.freewebs.com/tawhiyd/hadiythexposed.htm.

I was truly schocked when the first time I read it. Dear fellow Moslems... please read the following carefully with open mind and open heart. I would like to remind you not to get emotional, although I know this is very tough to swallow, just continue reading until the end of this chapter, only then draw your own conclusion.

HADIYTH COLLECTOR: IMAM BUKHARI

The Hadyth were first written and compiled around 200 years after the death of Prophet Muhammad! So, there were no Hadyth collectors who walked, saw or spoke with Prophet Muhammad at all. Can you imagine how many narrators a Hadyth have to go through in the span of 200 years?

Prophet Muhammad died in 632 CE. Ahmad (Ibn Hanbal) was born in 780 CE in Baghdad. Bukhari, was born in 810 CE in Bukhara (today Uzbekistan). Muslim was born in 817 CE in Nishapur (Iran). Abu Daud was born in 817 CE in Sijistan (Iran). Tirmidhi was born in 824 CE in Tirmiz in Uzbekistan.

I was told that Imam Bukhari – narrator of 'the most authentic book after the Quran' was an upright man, who never lied and had great memory. He had memorized 15,000 Hadyths in 16 days, and memorized 200,000 Hadyths in total!

It might be true, but think about this: 15,000 Hadyths in 16 days is more than double of the Quranic verses! And how many sentences (verses) are there in 15,000 Hadyths?

I always thought the fact that many Moslems are able to memorize the whole Quran is a miracle in itself. As I have mentioned before, there is no other book in the world that can be memorized by thousands of people like the Quran (except for the Veda). And the Quran has around 6,000 verses. That's a lot of verses to remember! There are many factors why many are able to do so: amongst others is because the Quran was revealed little by little, thus it gives time for the memorizer to memorize it; there is no discrepancy in the Quran (it must be very difficult to memorize contradictive statements); the Quran is written in poetic form and rhyming at end of most of the verses; and there is 'only' around 6.000 verses. In short, God has designed or arranged the Quran in such a way that it is humanly possible to be memorized.

> And those who disbelieve say: Why has not the Quran been revealed to him all at once? Thus, that We may strengthen your heart by it and _We have arranged it well in arranging_.
> (Quran translation 25:32)

It took almost 23 years for the whole Quran to be revealed and it takes years for most Moslems to memorize around 6,000 verses of the Quran. The first generation of Moslems during the Prophet's time also needed years to memorize the Quran. So how could Bukhari memorize 15,000 Hadyths in 16 days? And don't forget, unlike the Quran, the Hadyths do not rhyme and many are contradictive! Allegedly, out of the 600,999 Hadyths that Bukhari had collected, he threw as fabrication 592,700 of them and kept only 7,300 as being genuine. They further reduce 2,762 Hadyths after removing repetition (and there are still many repetitive Hadyth in Bukhari's book to be found today). The margin of error in these numbers is so great, that any rational Truth Seeker can see that accepting the book of Bukhari as containing all authentic Hadyths or even majority of authentic Hadyths is very risky, as we can see from the Hadyths quoted above.

The various books of Hadyth that we see in Moslem society today are the same in relation to Prophet Muhammad, as the present

Gospels are to Jesus. They are both similar in that both were compiled (in what we posses today) decades and even centuries after they passed away – unlike the Quran which was written down and memorized at the time of its revelation. Therefore, objectively speaking both the Hadyth and the Gospels do not represent any evidence as to be considered a 100% reliable representation of the words of Muhammad and Jesus.. *in total.*

Some people might think that this is not such a big deal. But let's see it this way: don't we just hate it when people add and/or twist what we said? It is deceiving. And if we are talking about religious teachings, the result can be (and is) disastrous. Because many people can be blind, irrational and down right aggressive when 'defending' their faith.

Dear fellow Moslems, isn't it strange how we can easily point fingers at Christians and say that their present Gospels are false, that they have been altered by men, because they were written and compiled decades or even hundreds of years after the Jesus' departure and yet we Moslems insist to believe in the Hadyth books that were also written and compiled hundreds of years after Muhammad's departure? There is a saying in Indonesian that says: "We can see an ant on the other side of the sea, but not an elephant right in front of our own eyes". In other words: it is easier to see mistakes on others, than our own mistakes. Let's not to be that way, shall we..

THE QURAN:
Complete, Clear, Detailed, Sufficient and Free of Contradiction
The truth of the matter is that Prophet Muhammad of Arabia did not receive any of these so-called sets of Hadyth, not even the so-called Hadyth Qudsi.

The Quran in complete, perfect, fully detailed, it explains all things and nowhere in the Quran is there a single verse where God says we are suppose to follow, believe nor be guided by the so-called Hadyth. Nor is there written that the Hadyth Qudsi was revealed or sent down to Muhammad. God has informed us that the Quran is complete, clear, detailed, sufficient and free of discrepancy.

> ... <u>Nothing is left without a mention in the Book</u>...
> (Quran translation 6:38-39)

> Say: "Shall I seek for judge other than God? - when He it is Who hath sent unto you <u>the Book, explained in detail."</u> They know full well, to whom We have given the Book, that it hath been sent down from thy Lord in truth. Never be then of those who doubt. The word of thy Lord doth find its fulfilment in truth and in justice: <u>None can change His words</u>: for He is the one who heareth and knoweth all.
> (Quran translation 6:114-115)

> Say, "If the ocean were ink for the words of my Lord, the ocean would run out, before the words of my Lord run out, even if we double the ink supply."
> (Quran translation 18:109)

> This (Quran) is a <u>sufficient</u> exposition for the people..
> (Quran translation 14:52)

> ...We have revealed <u>the Book to you explaining clearly everything...</u>
> (Quran translation 16:89)

> ... this (Quran) confirms all previous scriptures<u>, provides the details of everything</u>, and is a beacon and mercy for those who believe.
> (Quran translation 12:111)

> Why do they not study the Quran carefully<u>? If it were from other than God, they would have found in it numerous contradictions.</u>
> (Quran translation 4:82)

Now, please read the above verses carefully. Every Moslem believes that God meant every single word in the Quran. So far we have proven that the Quran is accurate about everything that we have discussed about. The above verses should actually be more than enough for us to understand that we do not need any other religious source of law, except the Quran, right? How can we need additional books as religious source of law, if the Quran is already complete, nothing is left unmentioned in it, sufficient, provides the details of everything and free of contradiction? And these are the words of God! None can change His words. Adding, taking away, contradicting... is changing His words!

So, how could we say that the Quran is incomplete and therefore needs other books to explain it (i.e. provide the details)? Some Moslem scholars even say that 'The majority of the Sharia (Law) in Islam is contained outside of the Quran in the books of Hadyth and Fiqh (Islamic Jurisprudence). Wow... do we Moslems realize that what we are saying is directly challenging God? What are we doing? By saying those words, aren't we actually denying the Quran? This argument is the same like denying the validity of the Quran which claims to contain the complete Law from God.

The Quran says that there is nothing which is neglected in it, everything is already mentioned, all the laws are detailed and sufficient. How could we say that we need Muhammad's words (i.e. Hadyth) to complete God's words (i.e. the Quran)? Yes, Muhammad is our Prophet, but he was still just a human being. How could the words of a human being complete or explain God's word? As we can see by the example of the 'moon splitting', it can not. In reality, almost every law of the Quran becomes a matter of debate among the Islamic sects, *because* of the Hadyth!

Please dear fellow Moslems, stop reading and ponder for a while. It doesn't matter what argumention or explanation we use, if we say that we need the Hadyth to explain the (already complete and detailed) Quran, we are actually challenging God. Point.

OBEY THE PROPHET

Unfortunately, most Moslems, including me have been taught to believe in the Hadyth for too long. Thus, although the above arguments should be the end of the discussion, but most Moslems would ask the following: "But.. aren't we supposed to follow and obey Prophet Muhammad? And the Prophet told us to follow the Hadyth and Sunna."

Once again, the Quran is already complete. So how come there is not a single verse in the Quran that says: we are supposed to follow, believe or get additional guidance from the Hadyth; nor is there a verse that says that Hadyth Qudsi was revealed to Prophet Muhammad? There is not a single record in the Quran that confirms Prophet Muhammad ever said that the Quran and the Hadyth (or the Sunnah) have been inspired (revealed) to me." Why? Because Prophet Muhammad only received the Quran and no other book. God has revealed clear and concise verses in the Quran and told us which Book/ Scripture Prophet Muhammad received:

> Say, "What thing is greatest as a testimony?" Say: "God is the Witness between me and you that this Quran has been inspired to me so that I may warn you with it and whomever it reaches. Do you really bear witness that there are other gods besides God?" Say: "I do not bear witness." Say: "He is only One Creator, and indeed, I am free of what you associate (with Him)."
> (Quran translation 6:19)

Prophet Muhammad only received the Quran and no other Book and that includes the books of Hadyth. Notice that this verse does not say: " ..that these Quran and Hadyth (or Sunna) have been inspired (revealed) to me".

We are not supposed to mix God's Word and words of men. BUT allegedly, before Muhammad's departure, he conveyed a last sermon which is recorded in the Hadyth. The Hadyth claims that Muhammad said: "I have left among you two things; you will never go astray as long as you hold fast to them: the Book of God and my Sunna." But again...the alleged last sermon of the Prophet which is supposed to be witnessed by the thousands has three versions!

The versions are:
1.   *I leave with you Quran and Sunna.*
       Muwatta, 46/3
2.   *I leave with you Quran and Ahl Al-Bayt*
       Muslim 44/4, Nu 2408; Ibn Hanbal 4/366; Darimi 23/1,
       Nu 3319
3.   *I leave you for the Quran alone you shall uphold it.*
       Muslim 15/19, Nu 1218; Ibn Majah 25/84, Abu Dawud 11/56

Look at the contradictions between these three accounts that state Prophet Muhammad allegedly said that he leaves:

1. QURAN AND SUNNA
2. QURAN AND AHL AL-BAYT (THE FAMILY OF THE PROPHET)
3. QURAN ALONE

The contradiction is very obvious. How could there be such contradictions in Prophet Muhammad's alleged last sermon when he was just one man?

Yes, we are supposed to obey the Prophet. But, when the Quran says 'obey the Messenger' it is not referring to the so-called Hadyth. That command simply means that we are to obey, submit, worship God and we only follow Prophet Muhammad in the sense that he was one sent (into this world) by God to reveal the Seal of the Scripture, which is the Quran for all of mankind to follow. Previous to Prophet Muhammad all the Prophets also have brought the same message, unfortunately the Old Testament and the New Testament had been already altered by human's hands, therefore the Quran was revealed.

> ... *We make no difference between any of His apostles;* and *they say: We hear and obey,* our Lord! Thy forgiveness (do we crave), and to Thee is the eventual course.
> (Quran translation 2:285)

The Quran also tells us to obey other Prophets of God. This is not a unique expression for Prophet Muhammad. Let's not forget that the Quran also tells us not to differentiate the Prophets, right? Why would we differentiate the Prophets when the true teaching is the same and from the same One God?

> ... *so keep your duty to God and obey me (Jesus).*
> (Quran translation 3:50)

> *So keep your duty to God and obey me (Noah).*
> (Quran translation 26:108)

> *Keep your duty to God, and obey me (Hud/Eber).*
> (Quran translation 26:126)

> *Keep your duty to God and obey me (Saleh/Shelah).*
> (Quran translation 26:144)

> *You shall keep your duty to God, obey me (Lot).*
> (Quran translation 26:163)

> *Keep your duty to God and obey me (Shuaib/Jethro).*
> (Quran translation 26:179)

When the Quran talks about obeying and following Muhammad it does not mean in a literal sense. It doesn't mean that we have to follow everything that he said and did; especially not the alleged additional religious law, or contradictive actions and trivial habits!

The command is exactly the same for all the followers of the Prophets, obviously what it means is that we have to follow the same guidance from God from the beginning of time.

IS THE HADYTH MENTIONED ANYWHERE IN THE QURAN?

Now, here comes the real shocker! The truth is, the only Hadyth to be followed that God meant in the Quran is the Quran itself. And this is what we are supposed to follow. Do you know that God disapprove of the Hadyth by the exact same name in the Quran? Yes, I know this must come as shock for you, fellow Moslems. So it was for me.

Today Islam is divided into many sects. These sects are created most likely because many Moslems follow other teachings and traditions other than the Quran that appear after the Quranic revelation. Logically, if all Moslems truly follow the teaching of the Quran alone, there won't be any division, right? The Quran clearly forbids sects in religion:

> As for those who divide their religion and break up into sects, you should not be of any of them, in the things they become, surely all their affairs are with God; He will in the end inform them of what they did.
> (Quran translation 6:159)

Many Quran translators belong to one sect or another. From the information that I have gathered, it is very possible that some of them must have purposely translated the Quran vaguely or even mistranslated it to conceal the fact that God disapprove of the Hadyth by name to support their sectarian school of thought.

Please allow me show it to you then...

Let's see the proof with visual/physical evidence in the Quran itself. But before we do that, it is important for us to know how the word Hadyth looks like in Arabic:

حد يث

Next is the same Arabic word 'Hadyth', with each Arabic letter highlighted, remember Arabic is written from right to left:

حد يث

TH   Y   D   HA

Now, please examine the verses below, and when you look carefully you can see the word Al Hadyth ('al' means 'the') is in the Arabic text. Look at the green colored/underlined word.

آللهُ نَزَّلَ آحَسَنَ الحَدِيْثِ

Allahu nazzala ahsana al hadyth ...
God has revealed herein the best hadyth ..
(Quran 39:23)

Huh?! For a non-Arab like me, who is only familiar with the word 'Hadyth' in connection to the Hadyth of Muhammad, it is quite surprising that this exact same word of 'Hadyth' is mentioned in the Quran and obviously not talking about the Hadyth of Muhammad but addressing to the Quran as the best Hadyth!

Yes, of course, the Quran is a Hadyth, it is a scripture filled with narration, deeds and actions of the Prophets of God (not only of Prophet Muhammad, by the way), as well as God's Law.

How come I never read this word in the English or Indonesian translation?? And then I was really shocked when I am informed that there are many more verses with the word 'Hadyth' in it..

لَقَدْ كَانَ فِى قَصَصِهِمْ عِبْرَةٌ لِّأُوْلِى الْأَلْبَابِ مَا كَانَ حَدِيثًا يُفْتَرَى وَلَكِن تَصْدِيقَ الَّذِى بَيْنَ يَدَيْهِ وَتَفْصِيلَ كُلِّ شَىْءٍ وَهُدًى وَرَحْمَةً لِّقَوْمٍ يُؤْمِنُونَ ﴿١١١﴾

Laqad kana fee qasasihim aibratun li-olee al'albabi ma kana hadythan yuftara walakin tasdeeqa allathee bayna yadayhi watafseela kulli shay'in wahudan warahmatan liqawmin yu'minoona.

In their history, there is a lesson for those who possess intelligence. This is not a fabricated hadyth; this (Quran) confirms all previous scriptures, and provides the details of everything. It is a beacon and mercy for those who believe.
(Quran 12:111)

In Quran 39:23, God says that He has (nazala) revealed or sent down the Best Hadyth which is clearly the Quran.

God has told us which Hadyth to follow and that is nothing but the Quran. God has also reinforced this fact when He has said in Quran 12:111, that the Quran is not a fabricated Hadyth.

Why is God underlining that the Quran is not a fabricated Hadyth? Because, of course God knew that confusion will arise amongst the Moslems caused by Hadyth that were fabricated after the death of Muhammad.

How could the so-called Ulamas, Imams, religious leaders whose native language are Arabic miss something as elementary and simple as this?

The above verse clearly says that the Quran 'provides the details of everything'. How could they say the so-called Hadyth is needed to clarify (in other words: to provide the details) to the Quran?? Once again, isn't this a direct denial of the Quran?

Below are the verses that God has revealed in the Quran which challenged us not to believe in other Hadyth by name. Here, again God has made it crystal clear that we are not supposed to believe in nor follow other Hadyth, except the Quran.

تِلْكَ أَيِّتُ اللّهِ نَتْلُوهَا عَلَيْكَ بِالْحَقِّ فَبِأَيِّ حَدِيثٍ
بَعْدَ اللّهِ وَأَيِّتِهِ يُؤْمِنُونَ ٦

Tilka ayatu Allahi natlooha aa'alayka bialhaqqi fabi'ayyi *hadyth*in ba'aada Allahi waayatihi yu'minoona.
These are God's revelations that We recite to you *truthfully. In which* **hadyth** *after God and His revelations* *do they believe?*
(Quran 45:6)

The 'revelations' here is the Quran and God is challenging in which Hadyth they (we?) are going to believe in after the revelation of the Quran. So any Hadiyth that came after the revelation of the

Quran is not approved by God and remember the men-made Hadiyth came to existence <u>after</u> the revelation of the Quran.

God repeatedly told us in His Book (the Quran) that He is the All Knowing and that He is the only One who knows the future (of course!) and God has disapproved of the Hadyth before they fabricated them, thus this is a prophecy fulfilled right in the Quran. God knew one day some Moslems would fabricate their innovations: HADIYTH and God had warned us in the Quran.

وَمِنَ النَّاسِ مَن يَشْتَرِي لَهْوَ الْحَدِيثِ لِيُضِلَّ عَن سَبِيلِ اللهِ بِغَيْرِ عِلْمٍ وَّ يَتَّخِذَهَا هُزُوًا أُولَٰئِكَ لَهُمْ عَذَابٌ مُّهِينٌ

Wamina alnnasi man yashtaree lahwa al<u>hadythi</u> liyudilla 'aaan sabeeli Allahi bighayri 'aailmin wayattakhithaha huzuwan ola'ika lahum 'aaathabun muheenun.

Among the people, there are those who uphold baseless <u>hadyth</u>, and these divert others from the path of God without knowledge, and take it in vain. These have incurred a shameful retribution.
(Quran 31:6)

فَبِأَيِّ حَدِيثٍ بَعْدَهُ يُؤْمِنُونَ ۝

Fabi'ayyi <u>hadeethin</u> ba'adahu yu'minoona?
Which <u>hadyth</u>, other than this, do they believe?
(Quran 77:50)

Here is another verse which I am sure many Moslems are very familiar with:

فَلْيَأْتُوا بِحَدِيثٍ مِّثْلِهِ إِن كَانُوا صَادِقِينَ ﴿٣٤﴾

Falya'too bihadythin mithlihi in kanoo sadiqeena.
Let them produce a hadyth like this, if they are truthful.
(Quran 52:34)

I am sure many of non-Arab Moslems are surprised reading the above verses, as I was. How come I never realize these? Could it be because these translators believe in the men-made Hadyth, therefore they purposely use other words to translate the word Hadyth so we won't be able to detect God's disapproval of it? How can we dispute the above facts from the Quran? The Arabic Quran is right and exact. The men - made Hadyth is disapproved by God; therefore we should not use it as guidance in God's prescribed way of life. We do not have to be an Arabic scholar to comprehend this; it only takes an elementary level of Arabic knowledge to see it.

It is truly intriguing, how some translators keep many Arabic words as is in their English translation, such as Allah (God), Hajj (pilgrimage), Ramadhan (fasting month), Qiblah (focal point when praying). So why don't they leave the Arabic word 'Hadyth' also?

Please check for yourself, and you will see the translation of the word Hadyth in the Quran varies from: speech, discourse, announcement, recital, statement, scripture, saying, message or phrase, etc. Not only that, when you compare various translations from the same translators, you will see that they are not even consistent in using the same word to translate the word Hadyth! Below are the English translations of the last verse that I have just quoted (52:34) done by several Quran translators:

Yusuf Ali
*Let them then produce a **recital** like unto it..*

Ibn Kathir
*Let them then produce a **recitation** like unto it ..*

Shakir
*Then let them bring an **announcement** like it ..*

Sarwar
*Let them produce a **discourse** like it if they are true..*

Hilali/Khan
*Let them then produce a **recital** like unto it ..*

H/K/Saheeh
*Then let them produce a **statement** like it..*

Malik
*Let them produce a **scripture** like this..*

Maulana Ali
*Then let them bring a **saying** like it..*

Qaribullah
*Let them produce a **phrase** like it..*

Asad
*.. let them produce another **discourse** like it..*

No wonder non-Arab readers can hardly get the proper context and understanding to know that God has disapproved other Hadyth than the Quran. I am sure, most Moslems just like me, thought that God in 52:34 was challenging non-Moslem disbelievers to produce other Quran-like scripture.

If I knew that the word used in that verse was Hadyth I would have understood right away that it was not only directed to other books than the Quran, but also to the so-called Hadyth of the sectarian Moslems. Wow! It took me quite sometime to digest this shocking information. God clearly disapprove us of producing a Hadyth. Can you believe that the Hadiyth writers, who no doubt understand these words without any difficulty, deliberately produced their own Hadiyth?! They don't even bother to give it a different name! And many

Moslems (including me) just follow their steps ignorantly. Oh, no...!

FOLLOW THE QURAN ALONE

Apart from that, God also mentioned in the Quran for us to follow the Quran ALONE:

وَجَعَلْنَا عَلَىٰ قُلُوبِهِمْ أَكِنَّةً أَن يَفْقَهُوهُ وَفِي آذَانِهِمْ وَقْرًا وَإِذَا ذَكَرْتَ رَبَّكَ فِي الْقُرْآنِ وَحْدَهُ وَلَّوْا عَلَىٰ أَدْبَارِهِمْ نُفُورًا ۝

Waja'aalna 'aala quloobihim akinnatan an yafqahoohu wafee athanihim waqran wa'itha thakarta rabbaka fee alqurani wahdahu wallaw 'aala adbarihim nufooran.

And We placed shields around their hearts, to prevent them from understanding it (the Quran), and deafness in their ears. And when you preach your Lord, using the Quran ALONE, they run away in aversion.
(Quran 17:46)

After finding out this information, I tried to share it with other Moslems. I said, we should only use the Quran as religious guidance. It's really amazing, how the reaction of my fellow Moslems was exactly as the above verse: .. when you preach your Lord, using the Quran alone, they run away in aversion. Sadly, most of them wouldn't even listen until the end of the explanation..

The above verse says 'Quran ALONE', which confirms that we should not follow other Hadyth than the Quran. The Arabic word WAHDAHU means 'ALONE' and this word come directly after the

Arabic word AL QURAN. Please examine the order of appearance of the three Arabic words and remember we read Arabic from right to left:

رَبَّكَ   RABBAKA (Lord)

الْقُرْاٰن   AL QURAAN

وَحْدَهٗ   WAHDAHU (alone)

Isn't it obvious that **WAHDAHU (ALONE)** is mentioned directly after **AL QURAAN** and not after **RABBAKA (Lord)**? This is why this verse says 'QURAN ALONE'. This means, we are supposed to follow only ONE source and that is the: QURAN alone.

So why do the following translators mistranslate this verse? By putting the Arabic word WAHDAHU (ALONE) after the Arabic word RABBAKA (Lord), the right message that is telling us to follow only one source of law (i.e. the Quran) becomes vague, and at the same time still leaving room for those to follow another source of law: the Hadyth.

> *Yusuf Ali:*
> .. when thou dost commemorate thy Lord and **Him alone** in the Quran, they turn on their backs, fleeing (from the Truth).
> *Ibn Kathir:*
> .. And when you make mention of your **Lord Alone** in the Qur'an, they turn on their backs, fleeing in extreme dislike.
> *Shakir:*
> .. when you mention your **Lord alone** in the Quran they turn their backs in aversion.

Sarwar:
*... We deafen their ears. When you mention **your Lord in this Quran as One** (Supreme Being), they run away.*
Hilali/Khan:
*.. And when you make mention of your **Lord Alone** (La ilaha ill-Allah; none has the right to be worshipped but Allah; Islamic Monotheism) in the Quran, they turn on their backs, fleeing in extreme dislikeness.*
H/K/Saheeh:
*.. And when you mention your **Lord alone** in the Quran, they turn back in aversion.*
Malik:
*.. When in the Quran you mention **His Oneness**, they turn their backs in disgust.*
Qaribullah:
*We lay veils upon their hearts and heaviness in their ears, lest they understand it. When you (Prophet Muhammad) mention your **Lord alone** in the Quran, they turn their backs in aversion.*
Asad:
*... And so, whenever thou dost mention, while reciting the Quran, **thy Sustainer as the one** and only Divine Being, they turn their backs (upon thee) in aversion.*

ISLAM - THE RELIGION OF ABRAHAM

Most Moslems (including me) do not really pay attention that Islam is called as the 'Religion of Abraham' (Milla Ibrahim) throughout the Quran – instead of the Religion of Muhammad.

> *...   He has chosen you and has not laid upon you an hardship in religion; <u>the faith of your father Abraham</u>; He named you Moslems before and in this...*
> *(Quran translation 22:78)*

> *Who would forsake <u>the religion of Abraham</u>, except one who fools his own soul? ...*
> *(Quran translation 2:130)*

... Say, "We follow the religion of Abraham - monotheism - he never was an idol worshiper."
(Quran translation 2:135)

Say, "God has proclaimed the truth: You shall follow Abraham's religion - monotheism. He never was an idolater."
(Quran translation 3:95)

... "And I (Joseph) followed instead the religion of my ancestors, Abraham, Isaac, and Jacob...
(Quran translation 12:37-38)

Who is better guided in his religion than one who submits totally to God, leads a righteous life, according to the creed of Abraham: monotheism? God has chosen Abraham as a beloved friend.
(Quran translation 4:125)

The above verses clearly state that Abraham – God's chosen 'beloved friend' was the original Messenger of the True Religion, the only monotheist religion ever delivered by all the Prophets that are mentioned in the Old Testament, New Testament and the Quran. A True Religion does not need a name. The name is not important for God. The monotheist religions we presently call Judaism and Christianity; are in fact the exact same religion of Abraham. The main teaching is 'to submit to the will of God', and this definition in Arabic word is Islam.

Thus, Islam is not really the 'name' of this True Religion, the only religion and guidance ever given by God to mankind, but it is a definition.

Say: We believe in God and what has been revealed to us, and what was revealed to Abraham and Ismaeel and Isaac and Jacob and the tribes, and what was

given to Moses and Isa (Jesus) and to the prophets from their Lord; <u>we do not make any distinction between any of them, and to Him do we submit.</u>
(Quran translation 3:84)

Previous to Muhammad's time, other Prophets had been exalted to an exaggerated status. So is Muhammad in Islam today. I was told that Prophet Muhammad was the highest in rank amongst other Prophets. However, this is stated nowhere in the Quran. Instead, the Quran repeatedly say not to make distinction between any of the Prophets. If we claim to be a Moslem, a Believer, we have to be really, really careful not to insist on elevating Prophet Muhammad, higher than any other Prophets. This is clearly forbidden by the Quran:

Surely those who disbelieve in God and His apostles and (those who) desire to make a distinction between God and His apostles and say: We believe in some and disbelieve in others, and desire to take a course between (this and) that. These it is that are truly unbelievers, and We have prepared for the unbelievers a disgraceful chastisement. And <u>those who believe in God and His apostles and do not make a distinction between any of them - God will grant them their rewards</u> ...
(Quran translation 4:150 – 152)

.. He (Muhammad) was a messenger of God and the final prophet...
(Quran translation 33:40)

Muhammad was no more than a messenger like the messengers before him...
(Quran translation 3:144)

Those messengers We endowed with gifts, some above others: To one of them God spoke (i.e. Moses); others He

raised to degrees (of honour); to Jesus the son of Mary
We gave clear (Signs), and strengthened him with the
holy spirit...
(Quran translation 2:253)

The Quran repeatedly informs us not to differentiate the Prophets. Although, some of them do receive gifts above another, in the above verse the examples given are not of Muhammad but of Moses and Jesus. God spoke directly only to Moses, and strengthened Jesus with the Holy Spirit. These Prophets are still not higher than Muhammad, right? Yes, Muhammad was the last Prophet, but Adam was the first Prophet. Why should the last be higher than the first?

Please don't get me wrong, these are not my statements.

Furthermore, Abraham was called 'beloved friend of God'. Meanwhile Muhammad and the rest of the Prophets were called 'servants of God'.

Yes, Muhammad's special gift is the Quran, the divine Book from God which will be guarded until the end of time. But it doesn't mean because this Book (the Quran) Muhammad is higher than the other Prophets.

In fact, in the following verse God repeats again that He bestowed other gifts to different Prophets, and the example given is the Book given to David, which is the Psalms:

.. We did bestow on some prophets more (and other)
gifts than on others: and We gave to David (the gift of)
the Psalms.
(Quran translation 17:55)

I was also taught that Muhammad is higher than other Prophets, because Muhammad brought Islam, which is the perfected religion. This common 'teaching' amongst Moslems actually comes from the following Quran translation 5:3:

> Forbidden on you is the animal whose death was caused by suffocation or strangulation, and the blood, and the pig's/swine's flesh/meat, and what was declared/praised the name of whom the sacrifice was made for to other than God with it, and the strangled/choked to death, and the beaten to death/dead due to sickness, and the fallen/destroyed/perished (to death), and the animal whose death was caused by another's horns , and what the beast or bird of prey ate (from), except what you slaughtered, and what was slaughtered on the slaughter places, and that you seek oath with the featherless arrows , that (is) debauchery ; today those who disbelieved despair from your religion, so do not fear them, and fear Me, <u>today I completed for you your religion, and I completed on you My blessing , and I accepted/approved for you the Submission (Islam) (as) a religion</u>, so who was forced in hunger, not deviating from righteousness/justice to a sin/crime, so that God was/is forgiving, merciful.

I quoted the above verse from the literal translation. Here, you can see that the word used is not even 'perfected' but 'completed'. This gives a totally different meaning, don't you think? If the word used is 'perfect' it would imply that the 'previous religions' were somehow inferior than Islam. But the word 'completed' does not give that implication, right? And if we read carefully, it is kind of odd how the sentence is inserted in between this long verse concerning the rule of haram (forbidden) meat! Why?

We have analyzed about this topic in Chapter 9: In Vino Veritas. Do you remember how in the Old and New Testaments the rule of forbidden meat has been exaggerated? In the Old Testament this rule becomes pages long. So, I believe with this single verse

(5:3) the Quran is bringing the rules back to the original state, and even in the case of hunger, it can be overruled. That's *probably* what God means with the completion of His blessing as well as the completion of the religious teaching. One thing is for sure, obviously, this verse can not be used to justify the elevation of Muhammad's rank above other Prophets.

WHERE CAN WE FIND THE RULES OF SHALAT IN THE QURAN?
I think by now, most Moslem readers are already shaken by this information. We know we should believe in the Quran, but (at least) one big question still lingers in our heads: "So where can I find the rules of Shalat (worship) in the Quran then?"

Moslems (including me) are so much used of being told that Prophet Muhammad was the highest and most important Prophets; Muhammad was the one who taught us the religious practices in Islam; that Muhammad received the commandment of the 5 times daily worships during the Isra' Miraaj (Night Journey and Ascension), right? But this is not what the Quran says! Actually, the Quran says that all religious practices of Islam were already established before the Quran revelation:

> We appointed them (Abraham, Lot, Isaac and Jacob) as leaders to guide the people _through Our command and sent them revelation to strive for good deeds, **worship their Lord, and pay religious tax.**_ All of them were Our worshipping servants.
> (Quran translation 21:73)

The above verse clearly says that the commandment of worship (i.e. Shalat) and religious tax (i.e. Zakat) was already revealed previous to Muhammad's time. On the contrary to the Hadyth that says Shalat was first commanded during Muhammad's time, the Quran actually tells Muhammad to follow the religion of Abraham. Let's read the following verse once again:

Then we inspired you (Muhammad) to follow the religion of
Abraham, the monotheist...
(Quran translation 16:123)

The above verse is direct proof that all religious practices commanded by the Quran were intact when Muhammad was born. Muhammad was enjoined to "follow the religion of Abraham." Logically, if I ask my friend to follow my car, it is assumed that my friend already know what my car is. Similarly, when God enjoined Muhammad to follow the practices of Abraham, such practices must have been well known.

Another proof of divine preservation of the Quranic practices given to Prophet Abraham is the 'universal acceptance' of such practice. There is no dispute amongst Moslems concerning the number of units (Rakaah) in all 5 daily worships. This should be enough for us to believe that the religious practices had been given by God to Prophet Abraham and passed on to us generation after generation ever since. If we truly believe in the Quran, we should trust that God Almighty is able to preserve His own religious practices to give to us pure, clear and complete.

Why do we Moslems today have such a difficult time in believing that the Shalat have been kept intact since Abraham's time up to Muhammad's time? We can even still see the traces of those religious practices in the Old and New Testaments as discussed in Chapter 15: Gate of Heaven.

Even the pagan Quraisy during Muhammad's time also still practiced the Shalat but in a distorted form around the Kaaba.

And their (pagan Quraisy) worship at the House (of God –
i.e. Kaaba) is naught but whistling and hand-clapping...
(Quran translation 8:35)

.. and when they (pagan Quraisy) observed the worship (Shalat), they observed them lazily, and when they gave to charity, they did so grudgingly.
(Quran translation 9:54)

I think it is difficult for many Moslems to 'remember' these facts from the Quran itself, because we have been taught to believe again and again (through the Hadyth) that Muhammad has higher in status in comparison than other Prophets. Therefore, many Moslems (including me) dare to 'challenge' God by asking: " If the Quran is complete and fully detailed (as claimed by God), where can we find the rules of worship (Shalat)?"

Oops! After gaining all this information, I realize how absurd I had been for asking this question. Many Moslems (including me) know that not all Hadyth is authentic, and we say that we know that a Hadyth is not authentic when it is in contradiction with the Quran. And yet, when we are truly faced with this exact dilemma, our belief in the Hadyth supersedes our belief in the Quran!

Instead of searching in the Quran further, we insist on questioning it. Actually, all the five prayers times, all the movements and what to say are mentioned in the Quran.

The Five Times Worship Are Specified in the Quran:
  (1) The dawn worship (Fajr) is mentioned by name in 24:58.
  (2) The noon worship (Zuhr) is specified in 17:78.
  (3) The afternoon worship (Asr) is in 2:238.
  (4) The sunset worship (Maghrib) is mentioned in 11:114.
  (5) The night worship (Isha) is in 11:114, and is mentioned by name in 24:58.
       *O you who believe, permission must be requested by your servants and the children who have not attained puberty (before entering your rooms). This is to be done in three instances - before the Dawn Worship (**Fajr**), at noon*

when you change your clothes to rest, and after the Night Worship (Isha). These are three private times for you. At other times, it is not wrong for you or them to mingle with one another. God thus clarifies the revelations for you. God is Omniscient, Most Wise.
(Quran translation 24:58)

You shall observe the Worship (Salat) at both ends of the day (Fajr and Maghrib), and during the night (Isha). The righteous works wipe out the evil works. This is a reminder for those who would take heed.
(Quran translation 11:114)
You shall observe the Worship (Salat) when the sun declines from its highest point at noon, as it moves towards sunset (Zuhr). You shall also observe (the recitation of) the Quran at dawn. (Reciting) the Quran at dawn is witnessed.
(Quran translation 17:78)

You shall consistently observe the Worships, especially the middle prayer (Asr), and devote yourselves totally to God.
(Quran translation 2:238)

However, many Moslems still argue that the above is not clear enough, because it is scattered and intertwined. But we have to remember that everything in the Quran is written *that way*. The stories of the Prophets in the Quran also seemed scattered and unorderly. Are we also going to say that the stories of Prophets are incomplete in Quran? Oh no, they are complete! There are many hidden clues behind the seemingly scattered stories and definitely behind the numbers. God willing, I can share with you more insight concerning this topic in the next books of this EarthTrek Trilogy.

If we truly observe, we will see that this is how God has designed the whole world for us: everything is intertwined and nothing seems to be in orderly manner. Only when we truly study, ponder and search then we can see that everything is designed in an orderly manner. Why? I think God purposely made it that way, because we are on this planet to be tried. Yes, the Hadyth mention about the 5 times worships a day. But many Hadyth also mention other worships. In fact, if we follow the Hadyth, this is what we will come up with:

Name	Prescribed Time	Voluntary before fard		Fard	Voluntary after Fard	
		Sunni	Shi'a		Sunni	Shi'a
Fajr	Before sunrise	2	2	2	-	-
Zuhr	When the sun declines	2-4	2-4	4	2	-
Asr	Between noon and sunset	2-4	2-4	4	-	-
Maghrib	Immediately after sunset	2-4	2-4	3	2	2
Isha	Sunset til before sunrise	4	4	4	2 +3	2, 8 (4x2)

The above is only a simplified chart of the Shalat ruling according to the Hadyth. 'Fard' means obligatory. The numbers are the total unit (Rakaah) to be performed each Shalat. Allegedly, the red color ones are the voluntary Rakaah done daily by the Prophet. The green ones are the so-called Mustahab (praiseworthy) to be done everyday according to the Shi'a. As we can see, there are disagreements between the rules of these two main sects.

In fact, the only agreements that they have are: the total number of the Fard worship (5 times) and the Rakaah of the Fard. The chart is only referring to the name and numbers of Rakaah. I am not even going into further detail concerning what to say during the prayer according to the Hadyth, it is even more confusing!

The Quran tells us to do the Shalat at specific times, and then God tells us what these times are. There are 5 specific times mentioned in the Quran, which means we are supposed to worship 5 times a day, as have been 'universally' inherited since Abraham's time. Do we still consider the Hadyth explanations to be clearer than the Quran, when in fact everything else that is not mentioned in the Quran is made even more confusing? And if we read the Hadyth further there are still many more different ways of how Muhammad allegedly worshiped, for example Muhammad was even recorded of performing a 5 Rakaah worship!

> ... *Then he (Muhammad) got up for the prayer and I stood up by his left side but he made me stand to his right and offered five Rakaah followed by two more Rakaah...*
> *(Haydth Bukhari, Book 3, #117)*

THE MISSION OF MUHAMMAD

Each Prophet has a specific task or mission from God. Abraham's mission was to teach the practice of religious practices; Muhammad's was to deliver the Quran.

> ..Your only mission (O Muhammad) is to deliver (Quran), while it is We who will call them to account.
> (Quran translation 13:40)

> ..You (O Muhammad) have no duty except delivering (Quran).
> (Quran translation 42:48)

> ..The messenger (Muhammad) has no function except delivering (Quran)...
> (Quran translation 5:99)

I was really surprised to be 'reminded' of the above verses. Furthermore, unlike what most Moslems assume, actually the Hadyth and Sunna books do not have complete information about how to perform Shalat, the number of Rakaah, or what to say in them. And since the Hadyth and Sunna books are full of contradictory statements instead of explaining, actually we just get confused when trying to follow them. Not a single time, was Prophet Muhammad reported in the Hadyth as telling the people; "Let me tell you how to perform your Shalat", or

"Let me tell you the number of Rakaah in the Shalat." Had Muhammad willed or was of his mission to teach the community their worship and the number of Rakaah, he would have done such that, and in the public arena for everyone to witness it. It never happened, because Muhammad and the people before him were already given the ways to worship, handed down from Abraham through generations of believers who kept the worship intact as God promised. God would not have told Muhammad to follow the religion of Abraham if no one knows or practices that religion.

The task of Muhammad was 'only' to deliver what was in the Quran. God explicitly forbid Muhammad to add (delete or change) any teaching stated in the Quran and this warning from God is quite harsh, which shows that this is not a warning to be taken lightly:

> ... It is a revelation from the Lord of the worlds. _And if he (Muhammad) had fabricated against Us some of the sayings, We would certainly have seized him by the right hand, Then We would certainly have cut off his aorta._ (Quran translation 69: 40 – 46)

The above verses clearly explain that we should only practice the teaching which is in the Quran, without any additional from Muhammad (i.e. the Hadyth).

So: once again, everything we need to know about Shalat is also already written in the Quran. I am not going to go into the detail, this chapter is getting far too long as it is. For there rest of the additional rules, you can check it yourself if you really want to verify at: http://www.freewebs.com/tawhiyd/findsalaatinquraan. htm.

However, there is one thing in particular closely connected to the worship that I really think is needed to be shared here. At first, I was really hesitant whether to share this information or not. Finally, I decided to do it, because this is the single most important thing to know if we claim to be a true monotheist, God-fearer: the Shahaada - confession of faith.

We need to remind each other when we stray from the Words of God, especially concerning the ascribing of partner to God without being aware of it. Remember when syaitan said:

> He (Syaitan) said: As Thou hast caused me to remain disappointed I will certainly lie in wait for them in Thy straight path. Then I will certainly come to them from before them and from behind them, and from their right-hand side and from their left-hand side; and Thou shalt not find most of them thankful.
> (Quran translation 7:16-17)

Syaitan already promised to God that he will make most of us unthankful and he will seduce most of us to create partners (idolize) others than God. And he has succeeded! Syaitan has seduced our ancestors (Adam and Eve) and made them expelled from the Garden. He has defeated the people of Noah, Saleh, Hud, Abraham, Moses and Jesus to deny God as the ONLY GOD. So what about us? Moslems? Can we escape from Syaitan's evil work? Or have we fallen too without realizing it?

> Say, "Shall I tell you who the worst losers are? "They are the ones whose works in this life are totally astray, but they think that they are doing good."
> (Quran translation 18:103-104)

The Quran already states that people who ascribe partners to God are unaware, that they are doing it.

> They worship beside GOD idols that possess no power to harm them or benefit them, and they say, "These are our

intercessors at GOD!" Say, *"Are you informing GOD of something He does not know in the heavens or the earth?" Be He glorified. He is the Most High; far above needing partners.*
(Quran translation 10:18)

Moslems can see straight away that it is a wrong notion for Christians to believe that Jesus can intercede on behalf of Christians, yet many Moslems believe that Muhammad can intercede on our behalf.

> And the Day We gather them all, then We say to those who set up partners: "Where are your partners whom you used to claim?" Then, their only excuse was to Say: "By God, our Lord, we did not set up partners!" See how they lied to themselves; and that which they invented deserted them.
> *(Quran translation 6:22-24)*

Look, how they will TESTIFY by God that they do not set up partners! So are we really sure that our confession of faith is correct?

SHAHAADA/TASHAHHUD – CONFESSION OF FAITH

The Shahaada is the confession of faith, the first obligation in the True Religion. Moslems mention this Shahaada everytime they perform the Shalat. This confession of faith, can also be found in the Old and New Testaments.

The Sunni confession is as follows:

> *"Ashhadu anla illaha illa Allah, wa ashhadu anna Mohammedan Rasulullah."*
> *"There is no god but God, and Muhammad is the Messenger of God."*

I had also been uttering the above confession for as long as I could remember. Until one day, a non-Moslem friend of mine said to me: "How can you claim to be a monotheist when your confession of faith consists of two sentences – there is no other god but God AND Muhammad is His messenger? Wasn't Muhammad just a human being?" Wow! I was so angry at that friend of mine... for days! But then I thought about what he said, and I realized that he has a point. In Indonesian the common 'Islamic' term for the confession of faith is called 'Dua Kalimah Shahaada' the literal translation is the 'Two Verses of Confession'. Suddenly it hit me like a brick!

Moslems condemn Christians when they say 'In the name of the Father, Son and Holy Spirit'. Moslems can see right away that it is a corruption of the monotheistic confession, because basically it is a trinitarian confession. But by that logic, the Islamic 'Two Verses of Confession' must also be a corruption of a monotheistic confession then, right?

Yes, most of Moslems (including me, in the past) argue that putting Muhammad's name in the same sentence as God does not mean they are equal. But as we have analyzed, actually the 'name' of Islam (i.e. Submission in English) as the pure monotheistic has been given since the time of Abraham. Furthermore, Islam teaches us to believe in all the Prophets of God and the Revelations that were given to them, and not to make any distinction between any of the Prophets. And Islam is called Milla Ibrahim (religion of Abraham).

So how did Abraham declare his Faith? Did he say "There is no other god but God, and Muhammad is His Messenger?" Of course, not. Muhammad was not even born yet back then.

What about the followers of the Prophets previous to Muhammad? Did they state their confession according to the Prophet they follow at their time? "I confess that there is no other god, but God

AND that Abraham/Jacob/Moses is His Messenger"? If this is not wrong, so why do we Moslems condemn Christians for saying 'In the name of the Father, Son and Holy Spirit'?

Most Moslems would be surprised if they learn that the confession of a certain Sufi (Islamic mystical sect) is: "There is no god but God and Jesus is His Messenger".

Then later on I learned that the Shi'a confession is follows:

> "Ashhadu anla illaha illa Alllah, wa ashhadu anna Mohammedan Rasulullah aliyun waliullah wa ashhadu an amireeul momineen wa imam al mutaqeen, Ali an Waliullah, wasiyeh Rasulullah, wa kalifatahu bila fasl."

> "I testify that there is no god but God, and I testify that Mohammed is his Messenger, and I testify that the Commander of the Faithful, the Pure Leader, Ali, is the friend of God, the successor of the Messenger of God, and nothing can come between them."

What? Yes, I know that uttering the above doesn't mean that we are worshipping Muhammad or Ali. But isn't that still some kind of ascribing partners to God? This can not be right!

If this was OK, then Moslem should also be allowed to say the Basmallah like this: "In the name of God and Muhammad", right? Which means the Christian way of saying "In the name of the Father, Son and the Holy Spirit" should be allowed as well.

Clearly then, no matter what our arguments are, placing the name of Muhammad in the confession after God is associating partner to Him. In many mosques in Indonesia, there are the Arabic writing of God (Allah) then, below it, or even next to it is Muhammad's name.

Caligraphy of Allah and Muhammad

Besides that, if we keep on putting such high importance in what Muhammad said and did (the Hadyth), we believe the alleged words and deeds of Muhammad as reliable sources of religious law (to explain the law of God in the Quran) and repeat daily chanting of the Salawat Nabi (prayers upon Muhammad).. are we Moslems sure that we are not already idolizing Muhammad? Are we sure that we are not ascribing Muhammad as God's partner? And when the verses from the detailed Quran are quoted concerning certain religious practice, we say: "But the Hadyth (i.e. Muhammad words or deeds) says differently." Aren't we doubting God's Word in comparison to a human's word? Are we sure this is not idolizing? Are we sure we are not ascribing Muhammad as God's partner? Everyday we hear in Indonesia people chanting the Salawat Nabi (prayers upon Muhammad) at the mosque. Meanwhile the Quran clearly says:

> *The places of worship belong to God; do not call on anyone else beside God.*
> *(Quran translation 72:18)*

Oh nooo...!
So what are we suppose to utter in our confession?

Before we go to the Quran let's see what God said to Moses in the Ten Commandments and what Jesus said in the New Testament:

> *"You shall have no other gods before Me."*
> (OT: Deuteronomy 5:7)

> *'"You shall love the Lord your God <u>with all your heart, and with all your soul, and with all your mind."</u> This is the greatest and first commandment."*
> (NT: Matthew 22:37-38)

We do not see in Deuteronomy, Moses' name being mentioned or Jesus' name in Matthew 22:37-38. Muhammad was commanded to follow the religion of Abraham, the same religion followed by Moses and Jesus. Like the rest of the Prophets, Muhammad would not have uttered his confession of faith by mentioning his own name. Jesus specifically said that it is the greatest and first commandment! So yes, Christians today are making a great mistake, and so are most Moslems.

Why aren't true believers of the One God supposed to add the name of any prophet in the confession of faith? The answer is: because the name of the prophet should not have any impact in our faith to the One God. Every monotheist person only needs to declare that 'There is no other god than God' it doesn't matter whether he or she is a follower of a specific Prophet at his or her lifetime. All the Prophets were 'just' human beings that taught us the same message of <u>total</u> 'submission to the One God' <u>not</u> 'submission to the One God and a specific Prophet'.

A simple analogy is this: let's say a king of a country has many messengers (ambassadors). When this king makes a decree, does he need to mention the name of his messenger(s)? No, right? Prophets are Messengers of God. They are 'only' mediators. Besides, when we mention the name of Muhammad, aren't we implying that we are following a different religion than the religion of Abraham/Moses/Jesus?

And just like the Old and New Testaments, the confession of the monotheistic faith in the Quran is also the same. Islam is a pure monotheistic (belief in the One God) religion, the true and correct Shahaada is supposed to be:

> La ilaha illa Allah
> There is no other god beside God

The above is stated in verse 37:35 and further in 59:22-23, 6:102, 6:106, 5:73, 16:51, 3:62, 3:64, 23:116, 39:64-65, 17:22-23, 12:108, 7:85 and 64:13.

Muhammad's name (excluding the ones inside the brackets) is only mentioned 4 times in the Quran. Just like in the Old and New Testament, there is nowhere in the Quran can we find the Shahaada of "There is no god but God AND Muhammad is the Messenger of God" written in one sentence!

So where does the Sunni Shahaada come from? Actually the Sunni Shahaada is a merging of two separate chapters and verses together. It is a joining of "There is no god but God" (37:35) from one part of the Quran, and "Muhammad is God's messenger" (48:29), from another part of the Quran.

> Muhammad, the Messenger of God...
> (Quran translation 48:29)

But actually the above verse is not unique for Muhammad only, read the following:

> ... Jesus the son of Mary, the Messenger of God..
> (Quran translation 4:157)

The Quran condemns certain Jews during Muhammad's time for altering the Word of God by changing the words, moving them from one place to another, joining parts of two different verses, distorting the interpretation and context of the scriptures. Refer to (4:46 and 5:41). So why do Moslems do the same thing? The sentence of 'Muhammad, the messenger of God' is just a regular statement, not a confession of faith. In fact, it is only a part of an unfinished sentence. It is not even finalized with a dot. This (part) of a sentence, is just another statement such as the following:

> Muhammad was no more than a messenger like the messengers before him...
> (Quran translation 3:144)

The above verse is also reminding us that the second part of the Shahaada "I testify that Muhammad is a messenger of God", is not even true, grammatically and factually, because Muhammad has passed away, just like the rest of the Prophets. So the sentence should be '.. Muhammad <u>was</u> a messenger of God', right? Please don't get me wrong, like all Moslems **I respected and loved Prophet Muhammad,** but I also respected and loved the rest of the Prophets, but they are all no longer alive in this world, only God is truly Alive.

Apparently, the second verse 'Muhammad is God's messenger' of the Shahaada, can be found in the following verse. Now let's analyze this verse, below is the Latinized Arabic verse and the literal translation:

> _Transliteration Arabic-English:_
> _Itha jaaka almunafiqoona qaloo **nashhadu** innaka larasoolu Allahi waAllahu yaAAlamu innaka larasooluhu waAllahu **yashhadu** inna almunafiqeena lakathiboona._

Literal translation:

*If/when the hypocrites came to you, they said: "We testify/witness, that you are God's messenger (E)." And God **knows** that you are His messenger (E), and God witnesses/testifies that truly the hypocrites (are) liars/ deniers/ falsifiers (E).*
(Quran translation 63:1)

The word 'testify' is used two times in the above verse in: one is used by the hypocrites who said "We testify that you are God's messenger", the other 'testify' word is used by God, when He testifies that the hypocrites are liars. Notice, the above verse mentions: "God **knows** that you are His messenger" and NOT "God **testifies** that you are His messenger". Here, God didn't even mention Muhammad's name. We have to remember, the Arabic Quran is accurate about its selection of word, and every word is meant to be.

Isn't the above verse clearly saying that only a hypocryte would use the name of God's messenger in his/her testimony/ confession? Besides, why do we insist on adding the Prophet's name in our confession? Isn't our confession sufficient just by mentioning God's name? How can it not be enough for us, when God Himself states in the Quran:

Say: God is sufficient as a witness between me and you..
(Quran translation 29:52)

In fact, the word 'witness' in the above verse is 'Shaheedan'. The same root of the word 'Shahaada', i.e. confession, witness, testimony!

I would like to remind you to verify the translation of the Quran that you read. Even when you can not speak Arabic (like me), God willing there will be a way to do so. Because, as we have seen, sometimes the translators 'adjusted' their translations according to their beliefs. I am sure many Moslems are shocked as I was, But after gathering all the above information (and more) and thinking back and forth whether to share this information or not, finally I decide to do it. Eventhough you can't and won't accept the information, it is my duty as a Believer, as a Moslem to at least make you aware of it. The decision is of course in each individual hands to search further information about it. I hope I am not sharing the wrong information. My God forgive me..

As for myself, although I had a difficult time in accepting this information, finally I feel relieved because no other sin is more grievous than considering others equal to God.

> *God forgiveth not that partners should be set up with Him; but He forgiveth anything else, to whom He pleaseth; to set up partners with God is to devise a sin most heinous indeed.*
> *(Quran translation 4:48)*

This is the way how I see it, even if I make a mistake by not mentioning Prophet Muhammad's name in my shahadat... surely a sin towards a human being can still be pardoned. But, if I am making a mistake by mentioning Prophet Muhammad's name, who is a Prophet but still a human being, and therefore I am ascribing partner to God, the sin will not be pardoned. So to me, uttering the confession mentioning Muhammad's name is waay more riskier than without.

Apart from that, I believe that the Quran is complete and I do not find a complete two verses of confession without joining two separate verses. I realize now, that if I keep on doing that, I will keep on invoking other human being's name (Muhammad) every time I worship! Thus, clearly I have violated verse 72:81 every day! Oh, may God forgive me..

HADIYTH AND MIDDLE EASTERN MYTHS
To me, it is already clear how the Hadyth is misleading many Moslems from the true teaching of Islam. We have seen and will

still see further Hadyth mentioning additional rules which are not mention in the Quran. Strangely enough, many of these Hadyths are actually very similar and even have the same writing style to some (also distorted) verses from the Old and New Testaments.

How come? I believe this is the explanation. Today the majority of populations in the Middle Eastern countries are Moslems. But this was not the case during the Prophets previous to Muhammad. First of all, there were many pagan religions born in ancient Middle East: ancient Egyptian religion, Assyro-Babylonian religion, Hittite mythology/religion, Mithraism, etc. And there were the dualistic religion of Zoroastrian (in Iran today) and the monotheistic religion of Aten in Egypt.

Then, although at the beginning Judaism was only for the Israelites or Hebrew of the ancient Middle East, later converts are also included. One of the groups is called Mizrahim (Easterners Jew) that is, the diverse collection of Middle Eastern and North African Jews. Among Mizrahim there are Iraqi Jews, Egyptian Jews, Berber Jews, Lebanese Jews, Kurdish Jews, Libyan Jews, Syrian Jews, Bukharian Jews, Mountain Jews, Georgian Jews, and various others. The Teimanim from Yemen and Oman are sometimes included.

Christianity was also born in Israel. By the 4th century CE it had become the dominant religion within the Eastern Roman Empire or the Byzantine Empire, with its capital in Constantinople (today Istanbul, Turkey). Thus, being subjects of the Roman Empire, some community in the Middle East and North Africa also adopted Christianity as their religion. Here we can see, that actually the Middle Eastern people were not always Moslems, they have gone through many 'religious conversions' throughout the ages. This means many of the Moslems ancestors today were either polytheists, or Jews or Christians. In fact, the Council of Nicea, an important Christian historical event was held in Nicea (today Turkey – a predominantly Moslem country).

Is it not possible that the Hadyth collectors' forefather's traditional teachings, previous religions and ancient myths became intermingled with whatever religion they adopt later? I think it is not only possible, but it is already proven. For example: according to one version of Bukhari's biography (among the many versions) Bukhari's grandfather was a believer of Zoroastrianism of Persian origin. Please don't be offended, my ancestors were most likely polytheists too. And traditions are hard to die...

> And when it is said to them, Follow what God has revealed, they say: Nay! we follow what we found our fathers upon. What! and though their fathers had no sense at all, nor did they follow the right way.
> (Quran translation 2:170)

Allow me to give an example of this case. There is a Hadyth which is telling the story about the Isra' Miraaj travel of Muhammad. Isra' Miraaj can be translated as the Night Journey and Ascension which refers to the miraculous journey that prophet Muhammad experienced - which is mentioned in the Quran as follows:

> Glory be to Him Who made His servant (Muhammad) to go on a night from the Sacred Mosque to the remote mosque of which We have blessed the precincts, so that We may show to him some of Our signs; surely He is the Hearing, the Seeing.
> (Quran translation 17:1)

Like any other Moslems, I was already familiar with this story since I was a child. I have no doubt that this event really took place, since it is mentioned in the Quran. The Quran is not giving further detail concerning this event, at least not on the first glance. Most Moslems however know the detail of this event through the Hadyth. According to the Hadyth in this event Muhammad traveled on a Buraq (a white animal smaller than a mule, bigger than a donkey), met other Prophets (i.e. Adam, Jesus, John, Joseph, Idris (Enoch), Aaron, Moses and Abraham). At the end of this journey Muhammad was given the commandment to perform the daily worship (Shalat) of 50 times a day. And at the end he negotiated with God to reduce the commandment into 5 times a day. Here is the Hadyth:

Narrated Malik bin Sasaa: The Prophet said, "While I was at the House in a state midway between sleep and wakefulness, (an angel recognized me) as the man lying between two men. A golden tray full of wisdom and belief was brought to me and my body was cut open from the throat to the lower part of the abdomen and then my abdomen was washed with Zam-zam water and (my heart was) filled with wisdom and belief. Al-Buraq, a white animal, smaller than a mule and bigger than a donkey was brought to me and I set out with Gabriel. When I reached the nearest heaven. Gabriel said to the heaven gate-keeper, 'Open the gate.' The gatekeeper asked, 'Who is it?' He said, 'Gabriel.' The gate-keeper,' Who is accompanying you?' Gabriel said, 'Muhammad.' The gate-keeper said, 'Has he been called?' Gabriel said, 'Yes.' Then it was said, 'He is welcomed. What a wonderful visit his is!' Then I met Adam and greeted him and he said, 'You are welcomed O son and a Prophet.' Then we ascended to the second heaven. It was asked, 'Who is it?' Gabriel said, 'Gabriel.' It was said, 'Who is with you?' He said, 'Muhammad' It was asked, 'Has he been sent for?' He said, 'Yes.' It was said, 'He is welcomed. What a wonderful visit his is!" *Then I met Jesus and Yahya (John)* *who said, 'You are welcomed, O brother and a Prophet.' Then we ascended to the third heaven. It was asked, 'Who is it?' Gabriel said, 'Gabriel.' It was asked, 'Who is with you? Gabriel said, 'Muhammad.' It was asked, 'Has he been sent for?' 'Yes,' said Gabriel. 'He is welcomed. What a wonderful visit his is!' (The Prophet added:). There I met Joseph and greeted him, and he replied, 'You are welcomed, O brother and a Prophet!' Then we ascended to the 4th heaven and again the same questions and answers were exchanged as in the previous heavens. There I met Idris and greeted him. He said, 'You are welcomed O brother and Prophet.' Then we ascended to the 5th heaven and again the same questions and answers were exchanged as in previous heavens. there I met and greeted Aaron who said, 'You are welcomed O brother and a Prophet". Then we ascended to the 6th heaven and again the same questions and answers were exchanged as in the previous heavens. There I met and greeted Moses who said, 'You are welcomed O brother and. a Prophet.' When I proceeded on, he started weeping and on being asked why he was weeping, he said, 'O Lord! Followers of this youth who was sent after me will enter Paradise in greater number than my followers.' Then we ascended to the seventh heaven and again the same questions and answers were exchanged as in the previous heavens. There I met and greeted Abraham who said, 'You are welcomed o son and a Prophet.' Then I was shown Al-Bait-al-Ma'mur (i.e. Allah's House). I asked Gabriel about it and he said, This is Al Bait-ul-Ma'mur where 70,000 angels perform prayers daily and when they leave they never return to it (but always a fresh batch comes into it daily).' Then I was shown Sidrat-ul-Muntaha (i.e. a tree in the seventh heaven) and I saw its Nabk fruits which resembled the clay jugs of Hajr (i.e. a town in Arabia), and its leaves were like the ears of elephants, and four rivers originated at its root, two of them were apparent and two were hidden. I asked Gabriel about those rivers and he said, 'The two hidden rivers are in Paradise, and the apparent ones are the Nile and the Euphrates.' Then fifty prayers were enjoined on me. I descended till I met Moses who asked me, 'What have you done?' I said, 'Fifty prayers have been enjoined on me.' He said, 'I know the people better than you, because I had the hardest experience to*

> *bring Bani israel to obedience. Your followers cannot put up with such obligation. So, return to your Lord and request Him (to reduce the number of prayers.' I returned and requested Allah (for reduction) and He made it forty. I returned and (met Moses) and had a similar discussion, and then returned again to Allah for reduction and He made it thirty, then twenty, then ten, and then I came to Moses who repeated the same advice. Ultimately Allah reduced it to five.* When I came to Moses again, he said, 'What have you done?' I said, 'Allah has made it five only.' He repeated the same advice but I said that I surrendered (to Allah's Final Order)'" Allah's Apostle was addressed by Allah, "I have decreed My Obligation and have reduced the burden on My slaves, and I shall reward a single good deed as if it were ten good deeds."*
> (Hadyth Bukhari, Book 54, #429)

Even as a child I thought the part of the story where Muhammad negotiated with God concerning the number of daily worships seems odd. I had a difficult time imagining God could be so inexact, not firm and hesitant. And I also had a difficult time imagining Muhammad could be so daring and disobedient to God.

Now, after the previous information that I have shared with you, I realize that this story is even odder; because now I 'remember' that the commandment of Shalat was already given since Abraham's time, long before Muhammad's night journey. In fact, the Quranic verse doesn't mention anything concerning the meeting with other prophets, the mythical Buraq nor the commandment of worship, let alone the negotiation.

I also wondered why did Moses weep because more of Muhammad's followers will enter Paradise than his? Is Moses jealous? And isn't Muhammad's and Moses' religion supposed to be the same? Now... after reading both the Old and New

Testaments, I was really surprised to read stories which are so similar to the above Hadyth. Could these stories be the base of the above Hadyth?

Four Rivers of Eden
And a river went out of Eden to water the garden; and from thence it was parted, and became into four heads. *The name of the first is Pison…. And the fourth river is Euphrates.*
(OT: Genesis 2: 10-14)

The Transfiguration
After six days Jesus took with him Peter, James and John the brother of James, and led them up a high mountain by themselves. There he was transfigured before them. His face shone like the sun, and his clothes became as white as the light. Just then there appeared before them Moses and Elijah, talking with Jesus.
Peter said to Jesus, "Lord, it is good for us to be here. If you wish, I will put up three shelters—one for you, one for Moses and one for Elijah." While he was still speaking, a bright cloud enveloped them, and a voice from the cloud said, "This is my Son, whom I love; with him I am well pleased. Listen to him!"
When the disciples heard this, they fell facedown to the ground, terrified. But Jesus came and touched them. "Get up," he said. "Don't be afraid." When they looked up, they saw no one except Jesus….
(NT: Matthew 17: 1-9)

Abraham Pleads for Sodom
Then the LORD said, "The outcry against Sodom and Gomorrah is so great and their sin so grievous that I will go down and see if what they have done is as bad as the outcry that has reached me. If not, I will know." The men turned away and went toward Sodom, but Abraham

remained standing before the LORD. Then Abraham approached him and said: "Will you sweep away the righteous with the wicked? What if there are fifty righteous people in the city? Will you really sweep it away and not spare the place for the sake of the fifty righteous people in it? Far be it from you to do such a thing—to kill the righteous with the wicked, treating the righteous and the wicked alike. Far be it from you! Will not the Judge of all the earth do right?" The LORD said, "If I find fifty righteous people in the city of Sodom, I will spare the whole place for their sake." Then Abraham spoke up again: "Now that I have been so bold as to speak to the Lord, though I am nothing but dust and ashes, what if the number of the righteous is five less than fifty? Will you destroy the whole city because of five people?" "If I find forty-five there," he said, "I will not destroy it." Once again he spoke to him, "What if only forty are found there?" He said, "For the sake of forty, I will not do it." Then he said, "May the Lord not be angry, but let me speak. What if only thirty can be found there?" He answered, "I will not do it if I find thirty there." Abraham said, "Now that I have been so bold as to speak to the Lord, what if only twenty can be found there?" He said, "For the sake of twenty, I will not destroy it." Then he said, "May the Lord not be angry, but let me speak just once more. What if only ten can be found there?" He answered, "For the sake of ten, I will not destroy it." When the LORD had finished speaking with Abraham, he left, and Abraham returned home.
(OT: Genesis 18: 20-33)

Surprisingly similar, aren't they? What do you think? Do you really believe that the Prophets dared to 'argue' with God that way? Do you really think God needs 'input' from humans in executing His commands? Do you really think God would change His words because of that? Meanwhile the Quran says:

... there is no changing the words of God...
(Quran translation 10:64)

WHY ARE WE MAKING RELIGION DIFFICULT TO PRACTICE?
Allow me to bring up a story in one of the longest surahs (chapters) in the Quran: Al Baqarah (Chapter 2: The Cow). Here is a story concerning the followers of Moses who were commanded to sacrifice a cow. That was all what was commanded. Then his followers kept on asking all kinds of detailed questions, again and again, until finally God told them to sacrifice a cow that was not old nor young, yellow in color, without blemish and had never been used to work in the farm! All these details finally were required since they kept on asking God to clarify and detail the commandment! At the end, they made it complicated for themselves, right? Isn't this exactly the same thing what Moslems are doing? The Quran says repeatedly that we are not allowed to forbid things that are not forbidden by the Quran, however there are many Hadyths that forbid or imposing things that are not even mentioned at all by the Quran:

> *O you who believe! do not forbid (yourselves) the good things which God has made lawful for you and do not exceed the limits; surely God does not love those who exceed the limits.*
> *(Quran translation 5:87)*

Now here are some more non-Quranic religious rules mentioned in the Hadyth, the Old Testament and the New Testament that are obviously based on the Middle Eastern tradition:

CIRCUMCISION
Now here is flash news: there is not a single verse in the Quran that mentions about circumcision. Circumcision is a Jewish tradition that says it is a mark of covenant between the Jews and God. It is also a tribal Arab as well as many other secluded tribal people's tradition today. This tradition actually exists in almost all ancient

pagan religion, even in the ancient Greco-Roman world. However, since Moslems are supposed to follow the religion of Abraham, according to the Hadyth then Moslems should also follow Abraham who was circumcised according to the Old Testament.

I do not dare say whether circumcision is wrong or right. Apparently, although it sounds scary, it can be good for health. I just would like to point out that many people in the West judge Islam as being primitive amongst others because of this practice. Although, actually whenever a practice is not mentioned in the Quran, that means there is no absolute ruling whether it's an obligatory or allowed (halal) nor forbidden (haram). That means we have to use our common sense to practice it or not. Remember, God doesn't forget to mention anything in the Quran.

In accordance to this topic, I would like to add an article that I read in the Internet concerning circumcision in Islam that made my goose bumps stand. This is just to prove how easy it is for others to twist around a teaching that is clearly not mentioned in the Quran. I believe what I am about to write here is one of the first sources of misinformation about Islam that made the Westerners hate and fear Islam in the past. (Of course today is the continuation which is added by the extreme actions of the radical Moslems).

There were 5 different versions of the speech made by Pope Urban to the first calling of the First Crusade (1095 CE). They are all different but the contexts are the same. Let me just quote the worst one of them which contains something about circumcision. The following is the version by Robert the Monk: he said that..

"<u>They (Moslems) circumcise the Christians, and the blood of the circumcision they either spread upon the altars or pour into the vases of the baptismal font</u>. When they wish to torture people by a base of death, they perforate their navels, and dragging forth the extremity of the intestines, bind it to a stake; then flogging them lead the victim around until the viscera having gushed forth the victim falls prostrate upon the ground. Others they bind to a post and pierce with arrows. Others they compel to extend their necks and then, attacking them with naked swords, attempt to cut through the neck with a single blow. What shall I say of the abominable rape of the women? To speak of it is worse then to be silent... "

Wow! No wonder the West hates Islam so badly if this was the 'introduction' of Islam to the Western Christians. You know how story always evolved after sometime? Even to the third person already a story could change so much. Imagine what happens to a story like this after many generations, it becomes more and more dramatic – if it is still possible. Imagine what the impact of such a story to the next generations can be.

You can watch one of the Crusade stories in a Hollywood movie by producer Sir Scott Ridley: Kingdom of Heaven, which is surprisingly, quite accurate historically. But that's not the end of the war. The history continues and even more romanticized especially during the Christian leadership of King Richard – which became also the beginning of the search of the Holy Grail.

Anyways, who won the 'holy war'? Probably a more appropriate question would be: has the 'holy war' ended? I believe the war... has not stopped. Just switch on CNN and see the continuation of the 'holy war' in modern day. The war gets more complicated and it still goes on. Just look at the suspicion, enmity and misjudgment between the three monotheistic religions today. I hope we all can see that it's not the religion that is causing all this but it's just the people. It doesn't matter which race. Humans are the same everywhere.

Don't get me wrong... I am quoting the above purely to show the irony. I know that many so-called Moslem preachers today are just the same. I know that some Imams in Holland preach that Moslems should kill any Christians that they meet! I know that

92% of the world's opium circulation is planted in Nangarhar, Afghanistan, because the farmers have no other choice since opium is the only plants they can sell to the Taliban to be sold further in order to finance the 'holy war'! (Ref: CNN TV reportage 'Narco State' September 30, 2007). Although, opium like any other intoxicant is strictly forbidden in the Quran. This is another good example that shows corruption in a religious teaching caused by the people in power.

So, let me get back to the Hadyth again: so there is not even a single verse in the Quran that tells the Moslems to circumcise! Many Moslems do not even know about this.. On the contrary, read the following verses from the Old Testament:

> And ye shall circumcise the flesh of your foreskin; and it shall be a token of the covenant between Me and you. (OT: Genesis 17:11)

What does the Quran say about God's covenant with the children of Israel?

> And when We made a covenant with the children of Israel: You shall not serve any but God and (you shall do) good to (your) parents, and to the near of kin and to the orphans and the needy, and you shall speak to men good words and keep up worship and pay the poor-rate. Then you turned back except a few of you and (now too) you turn aside. (Quran translation 2:83)

> And when We made a covenant with you: You shall not shed your blood and you shall not turn your people out of your cities; then you gave a promise while you witnessed. (Quran translation 2:84)

There is no circumcision in the above verses! Dear fellow Moslems, are we going to say again: "But the Hadyth says..." Are we going to doubt God's Words again in comparison to the men-made Hadyth and accuse God of being incomplete and forgetful?

According to Wikipedia encyclopedia: male circumcision began as a religious sacrifice, as a rite of passage marking a boy's entrance into adulthood, as a form of sympathetic magic to ensure virility, as a means of suppressing (or enhancing) sexual pleasure, as an aid to hygiene where regular bathing was impractical, as a means of marking those of lower (or higher) social status, as a means of differentiating a circumcising group from their non-circumcising neighbors, as a means of discouraging masturbation or other socially proscribed sexual behaviors, to remove 'excess' pleasure, to increase a man's attractiveness to women, as a symbolic castration, as a demonstration of one's ability to endure pain, or as a male counterpart to menstruation or the breaking of the hymen (a membrane which partially closes the opening of the vagina and whose presence is traditionally taken to be a mark of virginity). It has been suggested that the custom of circumcision gave advantages to tribes that practiced it and thus led to its spread regardless of whether the people understood this. It is possible that circumcision arose independently in different cultures for different reasons. So, should it be obligatory? I believe not. The Quran doesn't say so, or else it would have mentioned it.

Now, let us see what the New Testaments has to say about this topic:

> Yet, because Moses gave you circumcision (though actually it did not come from Moses, but from the patriarchs), you circumcise a child on the Sabbath.
> (NT: John 7:22)

> Circumcision has value if you observe the law, but if you break the law, you have become as though you had not been circumcised...
> The one who is not circumcised physically and yet obeys

the law will condemn you who, even though you have
the written code and circumcision, are a lawbreaker.
A man is not a Jew if he is only one outwardly, nor is
circumcision merely outward and physical. No, a man is a
Jew if he is one inwardly; and circumcision is circumcision
of the heart, by the Spirit, not by the written code. Such a
man's praise is not from men, but from God.
(NT: Romans 2:25, 27-29)

What advantage, then, is there in being a Jew, or what
value is there in circumcision?
(NT: Romans 3:1)

Circumcision is nothing and uncircumcision is nothing.
Keeping God's commands is what counts.
(NT: 1 Corinthians 7:19)

Wow, I think now I am even more confused. There are so many
contradictions between the Old and the New Testaments. I can
understand if the New Testament is supposed to correct the
Old Testament, but unfortunately there are also contradictions
in the New Testament as well. And why are these two books
presented together in one book (Christian Bible)? Isn't it just
confusing us?

This is just the same as the Hadyth. Many Hadyth are contradicting
and some are even talking about something that is clearly not
mentioned in the Quran. Here are the Hadyths concerning
circumcision:

Narrated Abu Huraira: Allah's Apostle said, "Abraham
did his circumcision with an adze at the age of eighty."
(Hadyth Bukhari, Book 55, #575)

Ouch! With an adze? Really? An adze is a tool similar to an axe,
with an arched blade at right angles to the handle. I don't know

exactly how Moslems today do the circumcision, but I don't think they still use an adze! I know that most Moslems do it at the hospital. So, if we really have to follow the Hadyth, why don't we still do it with an adze then? After all it is clearly mentions on the above Hadyth, so it must have some significance, right?

> *Narrated Abu Huraira: I heard the Prophet saying. "Five practices are characteristics of the Fitra: circumcision, shaving the pubic hair, cutting the moustaches short, clipping the nails, and depilating the hair of the armpits."*
> *(Hadyth Bukhari, Book 72, #7791)*

Apart from circumcision, the above Hadyth also talks about personal grooming which is supposedly in accordance with the Fitra (natural state). Does that mean we commit a sin if we forget to depilate the hair of the armpits?

THE VEIL

Finally, let us shed some light on what is considered in the West as the greatest symbol of women's oppression and servitude in Islam: the veil or the head cover. Actually, this topic should be discussed in the chapter of 'Daughters of Eve' – however since it is very closely connected to the Hadyth rules, I have decided to analyze it in this chapter. Before we go into the veil topic in particular, allow me to quote some Hadyths concerning women in general. The following is a shocking one which is quite well-known in the Moslem society:

> *Narrated Imran: The Prophet said, "I looked at Paradise and saw that the majority of its residents were the poor; and I looked at the (Hell) Fire and saw that the majority of its residents were women."*
> *(Hadyth Bukhari, Book 62, #126)*

Meanwhile the Quran says that Prophet Muhammad did not know what would be done to him or us. How could Muhammad 'looked at Paradise' when he didn't even know what will be done to him (and us)?

> *Narrated Abu Said Al-Khudri: Once Allah's Apostle went out to the Musalla (to offer the prayer) o 'Id-al-Adha or Al-Fitr prayer. Then he passed by the women and said, "O women! Give alms, as I have seen that the majority of the dwellers of Hell-fire were you (women)." They asked, "Why is it so, O Allah's Apostle?" He replied, "You curse frequently and are ungrateful to your husbands. I have not seen anyone more deficient in intelligence and religion than you. A cautious sensible man could be led astray by some of you." The women asked, "O Allah's Apostle! What is deficient in our intelligence and religion?" He said, "Is not the evidence of two women equal to the witness of one man?" They replied in the affirmative. He said, "This is the deficiency in her intelligence. Isn't it true that a woman can neither pray nor fast during her menses?" The women replied in the affirmative. He said, "This is the deficiency in her religion."*
> *(Hadyth Bukhari, Book 6, #301)*

Which is even more surprising, many Moslem women believe that this Hadyth is telling the truth! I would like to analyze it though. Maybe it is true that many women are ungrateful to their husbands; however isn't the other way around also true? Is there prove that women curse more then men? I think the opposite is more likely.

Is there prove that men are more intelligent than women? We already analyzed that the above ruling concerning the evidence of two women equal to a man in the Quran is only concerning financial matters. Not due to the difference in intelligence level, but difference in emotional level. What this Hadyth conveniently forgets is that there is an opposing ruling concerning men accusing their wives in matter of adultery, which turns out to be more lenient towards the women. (Read: Chapter 10) Is there prove of women's deficiency in religion? What does this mean? If by definition women are less ethical than men, can someone explain to me why there are way more men then women imprison world wide? If it is because women are considered as seducer, well aren't men also responsible for not being able to control their lust?

Why is that only the women who are responsible in such case? Concerning the menstruation, we have also discussed in the chapter of 'Daughters of Eve'. There is no such restriction written anywhere in the Quran, except for having sexual intercourse (which is a restriction for both genders benefit). And to make matters even worst, read the following Hadyth:

> *Narrated 'Abdur-Rahman bin Al-Aswad: (on the authority of his father) 'Aisha said: "Whenever Allah's Apostle wanted to fondle anyone of us during her periods (menses), he used to order her to put on an Izar (any covering or lower garment tied to the waist covering the lower half of the body). and start fondling her." 'Aisha added, "None of you could control his sexual desires as the Prophet could."*
> *(Hadyth Bukhari, Book 6, #299)*

What is the moral of the above Hadyth? Now the Hadyth is even ridiculing Prophet Muhammad himself! If you still think that the above Hadyth is true, tell me what do you think of the followings?

> *Narrated Abdullah bin 'Umar: Allah's Apostle said, "Evil omen is in the women, the house and the horse.'*
> *(Hadyth Bukhari, Book 62, #30)*

> *Narrated Usama bin Zaid: The Prophet said, "After me I have not left any affliction more harmful to men than women."*
> *(Hadyth Bukhari, Book 62, #33)*

Narrated 'Aisha: It is not good that you people have made us (women) equal to dogs and donkeys. No doubt I saw Allah's Apostle praying while I used to lie between him and the Qibla and when he wanted to prostrate, he pushed my legs and I withdrew them.
(Hadyth Bukhari, Book 9, #498)

The Quran honors women and lifts up their status, it states that men and women are equal (although not the same), as we have discussed in the chapter about women. Now look at the following Hadyth:

Narrated Sahl: The men used to pray with the Prophet with their Izars tied around their necks as boys used to do; therefore the Prophet told the women not to raise their heads till the men sat down straight (while praying).
(Hadyth Bukhari, Book 8, #358)

Clearly, all of these Hadyth have nothing got to do with Islam. And although shockingly, many Moslem women believe that these Hadyths are true.

www.news.wisc.edu

Veiled Women in Many Traditions and Religions

So now let's analyze concerning the veil. Before learning the Quranic perspective concerning the veiling, let's see the history behind the veil and what do the Old and New Testaments say about it.

The first recorded instance of veiling for women is recorded in an Assyrian legal text from the 13th century BCE which restricted its use to noble women and forbade prostitutes and common women from adopting it. Greek texts have also spoken of veiling and seclusion of women being practiced among the Persian elite and statues from Persepolis depict women both veiled and unveiled, and it seems to be regarded as an attribute of higher status. For many centuries, until around 1175, Anglo-Saxon and then Anglo-Norman women, with the exception of young unmarried girls, wore veils that entirely covered their hair, and often their necks up to their chins. Only in the Tudor period (1485), when hoods became increasingly popular, did veils of this type become less common. More pragmatically, veils were also sometimes worn to protect the complexion from sun and wind damage (when un-tanned skin was fashionable), or to keep dust out of a woman's face. Today there are still many societies where the women are still wearing veil, like in India, Russia or even in Western Christian women during the wedding.

According to Rabbi Dr. Menachem M. Brayer (Professor of Biblical Literature at Yeshiva University) in his book, 'The Jewish woman in Rabbinic literature', it was the custom of Jewish women to go out in public with a head covering which, sometimes, even covered the whole face leaving one eye free. He quotes some famous ancient Rabbis saying," It is not like the daughters of Israel to walk out with heads uncovered" and "Cursed be the man who lets the hair of his wife be seen....a woman who exposes her hair for self-adornment brings poverty." Rabbinic law forbids the recitation of blessings or prayers in the presence of a bare headed married woman since uncovering a woman's hair is considered 'nudity'. Dr. Brayer also mentions that "During the Tannaitic period the Jewish woman's failure to cover her head was considered an affront to her modesty. When her head was uncovered she might be fined four hundred zuzim for this offense." Dr. Brayer also explains that veil of the Jewish woman was not always considered a sign of modesty. Sometimes, the veil symbolized a state of distinction and luxury rather than modesty. The veil personified the dignity and superiority of noble women. It also represented a woman's inaccessibility as a sanctified possession of her husband.

Today, most pious Jewish women do not cover their hair except in the synagogue. Some of them, such as the Hasidic sects, still use the wig. Thus, the veil can be traced back to early civilizations. It can be found in early and late Roman and Greek art. The evidence can be seen in archeological discoveries whether in pottery fragments, paintings or recorded civil laws. In Greco-Roman culture, both women and men wore head covering in religious contexts. The tradition of wearing the veil (by women) and the head cover (by men) was then adopted by the Jews who wrote it in the Talmud, then the Christians adopted the same.

A well-respected Rabbi once explained to a group of young Jewish women, "We do not find a direct command in the Torah mandating that women cover their heads, but we do know that this has been the continuing custom for thousands of years." After the Prophet Muhammad's death, the writers of the Hadyth books adopted and encouraged the ancient tradition of head covering. Hadyth book' writers took after the Jews as they did with many other traditions, and alleged them to Muhammad since the Quran does not command it.

Thus, the traditional Arabs, of all religions, Jews, Christians and Moslems used to wear head cover, or 'Hijab', not because of Islam, but because of tradition. In Saudi Arabia, up to this day most of the men cover their heads, not because of Islam but because of tradition. North Africa is known for its tribe (Tuareg) where the Moslem men wear Hijab instead of women. Here the tradition has the Hijab in reverse. If wearing Hijab is the sign of the pious and righteous Moslem woman then Mother Teresa would have been the first woman to be counted. The cloak and hood is also an ancient European tradition. In brief, Hijab is a traditional dress and has nothing to do with religion.

What about the Christian tradition? It is well known that Catholic nuns have been covering their heads for hundreds of years, but that is not all. St. Paul in the New Testament made some very interesting statements about the veil:

> *Now I want you to realize that the head of every man is Christ, and the head of the woman is man, and the head of Christ is God. Every man who prays or prophesies with his head covered dishonors his head. And every woman who prays or prophesies with her head uncovered dishonors her head - it is just as though her head were shaved. If a woman does not cover her head, she should have her hair cut off; and if it is a disgrace for a woman to have her hair cut off or shaved off, she should cover her head. A man ought not to cover his head, since he is the image and glory of God; but the woman is the glory of man. For man did not come from woman, but woman from man; neither was man created for woman, but woman for man. For this reason, and because of the angels, the woman ought to have a sign of authority on her head. (NT: I Corinthians 11:3-10)*

St. Paul's rationale for veiling women is that the veil represents a sign of the authority of the man, who is the image and glory of God, over the woman who was created from and for man. St. Tertullian in his famous treatise 'On The Veiling Of Virgins' wrote, "Young women, you wear your veils out on the streets, so you should wear them in the church, you wear them when you

are among strangers, then wear them among your brothers..."
Among the Canon laws of the Catholic Church today, there is
a law that requires women to cover their heads in church. Some
Christian denominations, such as the Amish and the Mennonites
for example, keep their women veiled to the present day. The
reason for the veil, as offered by their Church leaders, is that "The
head covering is a symbol of woman's subjection to the man
and to God", which is the same logic introduced by St. Paul in
the New Testament. There are many Hadyth concerning the
instruction of wearing the Hijab, below is one of them:

> Narrated 'Aisha: The wives of the Prophet used to go to
> Al-Manasi, a vast open place (near Baqia at Medina) to
> answer the call of nature at night. 'Umar used to say to the
> Prophet "Let your wives be veiled," but Allah's Apostle
> did not do so. One night Sauda bint Zam'a the wife of the
> Prophet went out at 'Isha' time and she was a tall lady.
> 'Umar addressed her and said, "I have recognized you, O
> Sauda." He said so, as he desired eagerly that the verses
> of Al-hijab (the observing of veils by the Muslim women)
> may be revealed. So Allah revealed the verses of "Al-
> hijab" (a complete body cover excluding the eyes).
> (Hadith Bukhari, Book 4, #148)

Thus, according to this Hadyth, God revealed the verses
concerning the Hijab upon a (trivial) protest made by Umar
against Sauda. This is a strange story, don't you think? And there
are different versions of the stories too (from the same Hadyth
narrator Bukhari) although this one is connected to another wife
of Muhammad named Zainab:

> Narrated Anas bin Malik: The Verse of Al-Hijab (veiling
> of women) was revealed in connection with Zainab bint
> Jahsh. (On the day of her marriage with him) the Prophet
> gave a wedding banquet with bread and meat; and she
> used to boast before other wives of the Prophet and used to

*say, "Allah married me (to the Prophet in the Heavens."
(Hadyth Bukhari, Book 93, #517)*

The Quran is clear about the dress code for the believers. To understand a topic like the dress code for Moslem women, we need to review quickly some of these rules established in the Quran. Every rule is important and every rule is meant to be. Let's verify what does the Quran say concerning women's dress code.

THREE RULES FOR WOMEN DRESS CODE IN THE QURAN

Rule 1: the best garment

*O children of Adam, we have provided you with garments to cover your bodies, as well as for luxury. But the best garment is the garment of righteousness. These are some of God's signs, that they may take heed.
(Quran translation 7:26)*

This is the basic rule of dress code in the Quran.

Rule 2: cover your bosoms

The second rule can be found in 24:31. This verse clearly orders women to cover their bosoms whenever they dress up. But before quoting this verse let us review some crucial words that are always mentioned with this topic, namely Hijab and Khimar. Hijab is the term used by many Moslems to describe the head cover that may or may not include covering their face except their eyes, and sometimes covering also one eye. The Arabic word Hijab can be translated into veil. Other meanings for the word 'Hijab' include, screen, cover(ing), mantle, curtain, drapes, partition, division, and divider. Can we find the word Hijab in the Quran? The word Hijab appeared in the Quran 7 times, 5 of them as Hijab and two times as Hijaban, these are 7:46, 33:53, 38:32, 41:5, 42:51, 17:45 and 19:17. None of these Hijab words are used in the Quran in reference to what the sectarian Moslems call today (Hijab) as a dress code for the Moslem women. Hijab in the Quran has nothing to do with the Moslem women dress code.

<u>The word Khimar in the Quran</u>:
Khimar is an Arabic word that can be found in the Quran in 24:31 - where the second rule of the dress code for women can be found. Some Moslems quote this verse as containing the commandment to wear the Hijab, or head cover, by pointing to the word, Khomoorehenna, (from Khimar). However this word can be found several times in the Quran which do not mean as Hijab or for head cover. In the Quran translation those words are usually written in brackets (head cover/veil) after the word Khomoorehenna, because it is addition to the verse not the original text of the Quran. So here is the verse:

> And tell the believing women to subdue their eyes, and maintain their chastity. They shall not reveal any parts of their bodies, except that which is necessary. They shall cover their chests, (with their Khimar) and shall not relax this code in the presence of other than their husbands, their fathers, the fathers of their husbands, their sons, the sons of their husbands, their brothers, the sons of their brothers, the sons of their sisters, other women, the male servants or employees whose sexual drive has been nullified, or the children who have not reached puberty. They shall not strike their feet when they walk in order to shake and reveal certain details of their bodies. All of you shall repent to God, O you believers, that you may succeed.
> (Quran translation 24:31)

The translation of the word Khimar has been done differently according to many Quranic translators. Some left untranslated in its Arabic word of Khimar, other translate is as 'veils' , 'shawls', 'headcovers', some adds the information in brackets and leave other word in its Arabic form such as 'veil all over Juyub', etc.:

Yusuf Ali:
.. they should draw their **khimar over their bosoms ..**
Ibn Kathir:
to draw their **veils all over their Juyub..**
Rashad Khalifa:
.. **cover their chest** *..*
Pickthal:
.. draw their **veils over their bosoms** *..*
Shakir:
.. let them wear their **head-coverings over their bosoms..**
Sarwar:
.. let them cover **their breasts with their veils** *..*
Hilali/Khan:
.. to draw their **veils all over Juyubihinna (i.e. bodies, faces, necks and bosoms, etc.)** *..*
H/K/Saheeh:
.. *to wrap (a portion of)* **their headcovers over their chests..**
Maulana Al:i
.. let them wear their **head-coverings over their bosoms..**
Free Minds:
.. let them cast their **shawls over their cleavage..**
Qaribullah:
.. let them draw their **veils over their neck ..**

Obviously, there is no unity in the above translation. Some translation using the half English-half Arabic translation is the most confusing of all. Why don't the translators just translate the word Juyub or Juyubihinna (plural form) in English? Yes, we have discussed previously that they should leave the word Hadyth in Arabic. The point is, I think we can see clearly now how the translators choose to translate or not translate some Arabic word whenever it suits their purpose, in order to match the translations according to the Hadyth that they believe in. The word Juyub refers to the chest area or bosom... as you can see, most of the translators correctly use the English word of: bosom, cleavage or chest. But the translation of Hilali/Khan not only leaving the word Juyubihinna in Arabic, there is also additional information in brackets that not only refers to the bosom, but also to bodies, faces and neck. Information in brackets is not the original message of the Quran. Thus, Khimar is an Arabic word that means cover; any cover. A curtain is a Khimar, a dress is a Khimar, a table cloth that covers the top of a table is a Khimar, a blanket can be used as a Khimar, etc. The word Khamra used for intoxicant in Arabic has the same root with Khimar, because both covers, the Khimar covers (a window, a body, a table, etc) while Khamra covers the state of mind. Most of the translators, obviously influenced by Hadyth translate the word as veil and thus most people believe that this verse is advocating the covering of the head. The above verse, God is asking the women to use their cover (Khimar) albeit a dress, a coat, a shawl, a shirt, a blouse, a tie, a scarf, and yes, it may also be a veil ... to cover their (Juyub) bosoms, not their heads or their hair. If God so willed to order the women to cover their heads or their hair, nothing would have prevented Him from doing so. God does not run out of words. God does not forget. There is not a verse in the Quran that orders the women to cover their heads or their hair explicitly.

Rule 3: lengthen your garments

O prophet, tell your wives, your daughters, and the wives of the believers that they shall lengthen (let down) their garments. Thus, they will be recognized and avoid being insulted. God is Forgiver, Most Merciful.
(Quran translation 33:59)

It is clear from the above verses that the dress code for the Moslem women according to the Quran is righteousness and modesty. Being a Moslem doesn't mean that we have to dress like an Arab. We can dress according to the style of each culture as long as it is modest and according to the rule of the Quran. Why would it be wrong if it is God Himself who has created us in various colors, i.e. races? The Quran is universal. Every race has its own distinct taste for certain aspect of life, right? We should use our own sense and knowledge to know how to dress according to the rule from God.

> *Also, the people, the animals, and the livestock come in various colors. This is why the people who truly reverence God are those who are knowledgeable. God is Almighty, Forgiving.*
> *(Quran translation 35:28)*

Thus, the basic rules of dress code for women in Islam are:
(1) The best garment is the garment of righteousness,
(2) Whenever you dress, cover your chest (bosoms),
(3) Lengthen your garment.

For me personally, this veil topic had been a very confusing matter. When I came back from Europe to Indonesia around 2002, I was going through a very rough personal experience. I was very confused concerning the relation between man and woman. So I thought wearing veil (as in head covering) must be one of the solution to that problem. So, I wore it out of my won will and because I thought it was commanded by the Quran. But then as you can see, there is no explicit verse in the Quran saying that God commands women to cover their head or hair. And when I read the verses of the Old Testament, the New Testament and the Hadyth, I realize like many other rules, this one was also just fabrication made by men in order to keep women under their control. Covering the head is an ancient tradition of the Middle Eastern people. This is another example of how (illogical) tradition is hard to die. If this is truly a commandment imposed by God, the reasoning would not be as flimsy as all the verses that we have read in this chapter.

Please allow me to remind fellow Moslems not to be judgmental towards women who are not wearing the head-cover, especially when they are already dressed modestly. Why? Because this kind of behavior will be counter productive to the spread of the true message of Islam. Just imagine this, let's say a female Truth Seeker finally decided to embrace Islam, but she is not really sure about the ruling of the veil (i.e. head-cover). And she couldn't find any rational explanation to the purpose of the head covering. And not only that, what if this woman is an executive who works in a Western country where wearing head-cover will be subjected to discrimination. She might decide not to pursue the study of this true religion, right? Then, won't we be responsible for this unfortunate decision due to our exaggeration in practicing religion? The same reasoning goes for circumcision for men. These two rulings are amongst the most restricting non-Quranic rules that can repel many potential Truth Seekers to find Truth in the Quranic teaching.

On the other hand.. I know many people; especially in the West who criticize Moslem women who are wearing veil. I can fully understand when they are criticizing the ones who are wearing black Burkha - a covering from head to toe and only let their eyes show. That scares me too. They do look scary, not only the Hijab has no shape, why do they have to pick the color black for it. Remember in verse 7:26 the Quran also mentions that the garment may also be used as a luxury/adornment/beauty. Where is the beauty in a Burkha? If that is classified as oppression, I couldn't agree more. We have seen from our study above that it is just men invention to keep women under their power.

However, in principal as a woman I have to say that there is nothing wrong with the veil. In fact, I agree that some women do look more elegant and gracious with long dress and veil. I would like to add that most of the veiled Indonesian women that I know choose to wear the veil out of their own free will. Why else do Christian women still choose to dress this way when getting married? It is because wearing long dress and veil can also be done tastefully. Most little girls, also like to wear long gown and veils, it makes them feel like princesses. But to force women to wear veil all the time, is not right. If they want to do it freely themselves, that is their right too – these women should not be judged.

Now, let's be honest... which one do you think is better: women wearing long, decent clothes or what most women wear today in the West? I am talking about the mini skirt, almost bare bosoms and showing the belly button. Sure, if you are a man you would probably say... the sexy one, right? Well, I am sure you like that kind of outfit on female strangers or probably you don't mind if your wife wears this kind of outfit outside of the house. You might even feel proud. But what if it is your mother? Sister, grandmother, aunt or daughter? If you are a woman, you probably say the sexy one as well, right? But think about this: do you honestly feel secure when your husband is surrounded by women who dress scantily, especially when you are not around? We should not forget that every woman is a daughter, sister or mother of some other person. So, don't you think the world would be a more peaceful place if all women just dress modestly? And of course, all men should also be modest when dealing with women.

> Say to the believing men that they cast down their looks and guard their private parts; that is purer for them; surely God is Aware of what they do.
> (Quran translation 24:30)

⟨०⋆०⟩

I know, that many Moslems will be surprised or even feel attacked when reading this chapter, like I did when the first time I gather this information, but please bear in mind that these are not my words, I merely refer to the Quran. Isn't all the above enough to prove that Hadyth books are fabrications which has nothing to do with God, Islam nor Muhammad?

Dear fellow Moslems, don't you think we should stop dividing the True Religion, stop the arguments concerning the Sunna practices and other non-Quranic based Hadyth, especially when most of us haven't even fulfill the extra voluntary religious practice clearly commanded by the Quran (i.e. reciting the Quran). Does adding worships make us a better person? Haven't we seen enough so-called religious people who constantly practice religious rituals but is not kind towards others? What is the point of all the religious rituals when we do not really study the whole teaching of the Quran concerning humanity, kindness and other wisdom?

> ... You shall also observe (the recitation of) the Quran at dawn. (Reciting) the Quran at dawn is witnessed.
> (Quran translation 17:78)

If only all Moslems really recite, read and study the Quran everyday.. we probably wouldn't even have any topic to argue any longer. Yes, we will discuss but not argue. The Quran says that it 'explains everything'... wow, imagine how much knowledge can we gain from studying it? Then maybe, God willing, instead of being known as backward and intolerant people, Moslems can become scientific inventors again just like during the Golden Age of the early Moslem generations. In fact, the medieval Madrasah known as Jami'ah (university in Arabic) founded in the 9th century was the first examples in the world of an institution of higher education and research which issues academic at all levels (bachelor, master and doctorate) like in the modern sense.

This alone should be a proof that in the past the true teaching of Quran (amongst others) was studied in a logical research instead of dogmatic teaching intertwined with illogical ancient traditions that we see in most Islamic world today. If we truly obey Prophet Muhammad, above all obey God, let's not forsake the Quran..

> (On the day of judgment) the Prophet will say: O my Lord! surely my people have treated this Quran as a forsaken thing.
> (Quran translation 25:30)

I am not a religious scholar; however I can see that the Hadyth is clearly one of the reasons for division and distortion in Islam. Imagine how scary, backward and oppressive a nation would become if it practices the religious law from the Quran which is added and exaggerated by the law from the Hadyth. I suggest you read a very disturbing yet touching novel called 'A Thousand Splendid Suns' about the oppressive life of the people in Afghanistan by Khaled Hosseini.

Yes, I believe some of the Hadyth came from reliable sources that really lived during Prophet Muhammad's time. Of course, some of the Hadyth maybe useful as reference to learn the history of Islam. Just like the Bible, although it is heavy altered, some of the verses maybe useful for the same purpose. But clearly no Hadyth maybe used to create a new religious rule, except the Quran.

For that matter, the Quran is very clear. Although Moslem might have the opinion that the Quran is 'only' clear about the religious law, I am almost convinced that in fact, it is complete about everything. It never states specifically that it is clear only concerning religion, but it is complete. Another reason that makes me come to this opinion is the challenge of God in the Quran as follow:

> And if you are in doubt as to that which We have revealed to Our servant, then produce a chapter like it and call on your witnesses besides God if you are truthful.
> (Quran translation 2:23)

The above verse is indirectly telling us, that every single chapter of the Quran is impossible to be copied. Some of the chapters in the Quran are very short. The shortest is chapter 108, which only consists of 3 verses and 10 words! Yes, the Quran is written in poetic form, it is also accurate scientifically.. but I am sure a human can still make 3 verses that consists of 10 words that fits into the criteria.

Apart from the mathematical coding, I believe there is more to each chapter of the Quran that we are still unable to decode. I am not surprised, that when the Quran says that "nothing is left without a mention"; "explaining clearly everything"; "provides the details of everything".. that is exactly what it means. For example, I have found a website that explains the calculation of the Speed of Light in the Quran. This has got nothing to do with religious law, right? We just have not been able to reveal all of them. Isn't it exciting?

～ᴏ⋆ᴏ～

Do we have to be an expert in religion to study and have an opinion concerning our own faith, to ponder and search for the Truth? Isn't religion the first and most private right of a human being? Won't we all be judged individually for each of our actions? Aren't the choices of our Hereafter destinations the same? Does it make sense then if laymen, non-expert in religion are not allowed to search the Truth individually? I believe not only that we are allowed to, but we are commanded to verify every piece of information we see, hear or read.

> And follow not that of which you have not the knowledge;
> surely the hearing and the sight and the heart, all of these,
> shall be questioned about that.
> (Quran translation 17:36)

CHAPTER EIGHTEEN

THIS IS RELIGION

*B*y now, I realize that my study about the Truth will never be finished, the more I learn the thirstier I get. Of course, what could be more fascinating than a study of our own Source? However, I feel that at this point I have already gotten the big picture of the Truth. Because now, not only do I believe that there is One God but I also know it to be true. So what to do about that? Shall I stick with Islam or convert into another religion? Is it necessary to believe in religion?

I know now that the teaching of all the Prophets, from Adam to Muhammad is intended to free human from ignorance, backwardness, superstition, immorality and the wrong pattern of thinking.

Although the Quran says that we are free to 'choose any religion' we want, we have to be careful that we practice the right one.

> *There is no compulsion in religion; truly the right way has become clearly distinct from error..*
> *(Quran translation 2:256)*

From our previous study it is obvious that originally there is only one teaching, hence only one religion. Although some of the practices might differ, the main message remains (more or less) intact.

My analogy is this: religion is like coughing syrup. Its purpose is to cure the sickness (the cough). There are many coughing syrups with different flavors. Now to cure the cough, we can choose any coughing syrup with the flavor that we like, as long as we do not forget that the flavor is not of importance here. It is the medicinal ingredients that are the ones that will cure the cough, not the flavor. We should also be careful and make sure that the ingredients to make the flavor are not giving any chemical reaction that will make us even sicker instead of curing us.

Thus, in choosing religion we have to be careful that it fulfils its purpose. Religion is not tradition. In the analogy above, religion would be the ingredients and tradition is the flavor. Many people today are too busy arguing the traditional aspect of religion, instead of the main message that is the ingredients, the cure itself. A true religion is beyond tradition (i.e. the origin, the race that a particular religion is connected to, the symbols, the myths connected to it, etc). Religion is knowledge of the meaning of life, knowledge to the Ultimate Reality, a guidance to gain happiness, peace and success in this life and the hereafter.

A true religion cannot contradict science. Because what is science? Science is the result of observation concerning the regularity of the nature's law. If there is no regularity in nature, science would not even exist. Mathematics would not exist if 1 + 1 sometimes equals 2 or 3 or whatever. Physics would not exist if 2 atoms of hydrogen + 1 atom of oxygen sometimes becomes water, sometimes becomes other substance.

Many of us still believe that the universe is created by chance, that we are born in this world by chance; there is no purpose in anything. And the same people say that they only believe in science. In fact, science exists because there is order in the universe. If everything happens by chance, if there is no order in the universe, what can we study? We cannot study anything which has no pattern.

So in essence, science is a part of religion... the study of the law of God. Thus, a true religion must be in accordance with science, and beyond.

If we truly study the law of nature, we will see regularity in the universe, we will see Gods law everywhere. Science actually has given proof to us, that there is an Intelligent Designer, a Creator of the universe, and yet we still keep on guessing just in order to avoid admitting God as our Lord; to avoid being in harmony in His law and to avoid submissision to His will.

> And they disbelieved in it before, and they utter conjectures with regard to the unseen from a distant place.
> (Quran translation 34:53)

> And they say: There is nothing but our life in this world; we live and die and nothing destroys us but time, and they have no knowledge of that; they only conjecture.
> (Quran translation 45:24)

On the personal level, the laws of God also apply. There is regularity in consequences to our actions, for example if we do not learn to control our appetite, we eat whatever we want, we consume liquids that may act as poison in our body, we will become imbalance (i.e. obese, sick or become an addict). This will lead to suffering, etc, etc.

We know today with the technology that we have, it is not impossible for any government to monitor every single (electronic) communication that we make. In fact, we can find any information that we want via the Internet, we can communicate and see anyone we want wherever he/she may be on the planet via the Internet. And yet, we still have difficulty in believing that God sees, hears and keep records of every action and thought that we have. The Quran calls this record the Lauh Mahfuz – the clear book:

... nor do you do any work but We are witnesses over you when you enter into it, and there does not lie concealed from your Lord the weight of an atom in the earth or in the heaven, nor any thing less than that nor greater, but it is in a clear book (Lauh Mahfuz).
(Quran translation 10:61)

Some of us might believe that there is a Force, which is greater than us, but refuse to believe that this Force is involved in our lives. If God is really detached from our lives, why do we have dreams when we sleep? Who gave humans the ability to have the sense of right or wrong? Where do our feelings of compassion stem from?

Why are there so many people talking about the existence of Afterlife after they had near death experiences? Where does the feeling of guilt come from? Do we really think that God doesn't really care about us? Do we really think that our lives have no purpose at all? Do we really think that our action has no consequences at all? Do we really think that the heavens and earth will be here forever?

Do they not reflect within themselves: God did not create the heavens and the earth and what is between them two but with truth, and (for) an appointed term? And most surely most of the people are deniers of the meeting of their Lord.
(Quran translation 30:8)

Animals do not have the qualities that we have, at least not on the same level. Qualities such as: guilt, sense of right and wrong, and the drive to better their lives. Animals do not ponder about life and the purpose of life. But we know deep down that we are supposed to take care of the planet. That's why we also learn about the animal kingdom, we are concerned when animals are treated badly; we want to preserve endangered animals. Why?

It is because we are placed here by God to be the caretaker of the planet. This is what God said before He created Adam:

> .. *your Lord said to the angels, I am going to place in the earth a khalif (ruler, care taker) ...*
> *(Quran translation 2:30)*

We keep on educating ourselves in order to become more sophisticated, to become more 'modern' and to create the 'perfect' society. Many of us are convinced that religion is going to be obsolete, because religion is primitive. Nothing could be further than the truth, actually a 'sophisticated modern' man is the closest to the teaching of religion.

A nation that upholds God's law is guaranteed prominence among the nations of the world, prosperity and happiness.

> *Now surely the friends of God - they shall have no fear nor shall they grieve. Those who believe and guarded (against evil). They shall have good news in this world's life and in the hereafter; there is no changing the words of God; that is the mighty achievement.*
> *(Quran translation 10: 62 – 64)*

On the other hand, a nation that violates God's laws incurs a miserable life.

> *And whoever turns away from My reminder, his shall be a straitened life..*
> *(Quran translation 20:124)*

A nation that upholds God's law is guaranteed to be a great nation. This is not a mere idealistic dream; since God is in full control. His guarantees and promises are done. A nation that upholds God's laws is characterized by:

- Freedom for the people – freedom of religion, freedom of expression, freedom to travel and freedom of economy.
- Guaranteed human rights for all the people, regardless of their gender, race, color, creed, social status, financial situation or political affiliation.
- Prosperity for all the people. God's economic system is based on constant circulation of wealth, productive investment and no usury. Non-productive economy such as gambling, human exploitation and high interest loans are not permitted.
- Social justice for all. Because of the obligatory charity, no one will go hungry or unsheltered.
- A political system that is based on unanimous consensus. Through mutual consultation and freedom of expression, one side of any given issue convinces all participants in the discussion. The end result is a unanimous agreement, not the opinion of 51% majority imposed to the 49% minority.
- A society that upholds and maintains the highest standards of moral behavior. There will be a strong family, no alcoholism, no illicit drugs, no illegitimate pregnancies and ideally no divorce.
- Maximum regard for people's loves and properties. Therefore, there will be no crime against the people's lives or properties. Prevalence of love, courtesy, peace and mutual respect among the people, and between this nation and other world communities.
- Environmental protection is guaranteed through conservation and prohibition of wasteful practices.

Disasters have spread throughout the land and sea, because of what the people have committed. He thus lets them taste the consequences of some of their works, that they may return (to the right works).
(Quran translation 30:41)

...and do not squander wastefully.
(Quran translation 17:26)

A true religious person, a true God believer by definition is a person who is highly conscious, intelligent (at least logical), sober, balanced, peaceful, optimistic, patient, responsible, healthy, polite, humble, decent, protector of the poor and weak, caretaker of the earth and therefore modern and successful. Most importantly a true religious person is not someone who is judgmental against others who are not well-informed about religion. Instead a religious person should be the living example of goodness.

Some people might say that we don't need religion to know all that? That it's all common sense. Well, if that is truly so.. why do we keep on adjusting our laws? Why is there not one single nation in the world that can fully apply the above category? Why is there so much oppression in the world? Why are we still fighting against one another? Our earth is corrupted with dictatorship, (material) colonialism and slavery (still not fully abolished), racism, prostitution, drug and food abuse, continued oppression towards women, abuse of earth's resources, etc, etc…

Once again, a nation that upholds God's law is guaranteed to be a great nation. Now: "Where is the proof?" you might ask. On this note I would like to give a comment about my own country: Indonesia. As I have mentioned at the beginning of this book, Indonesia is the largest Moslem population in the world. Ironically, according to some polls, Indonesia is also the most corrupted country in the world! So what does this mean? Is the Quran wrong? No. The truth is, in fact this is an indication that Indonesians must have done something wrong here. I have observed that in the past 20 years or so, most Moslems in Indonesia have become more fanatic. I believe this fanatism comes along with the tendency of too much focus on imposing rules which are not in accordance with the Quran, but instead coming from the Hadyth. What I have seen is that Indonesian Moslems have become more and more concern with the exaggerated 'HabluminAllah' (the vertical relation between human and God) and neglecting the 'Habluminannas' (the horizontal relation between humankind).

The English term for Hablumninannas is probably 'human rights'. Sadly, human rights in Indonesia and in many (or even most) Moslem countries in the world have been so neglected. I believe Indonesia is still one of the richest countries in the world when it comes to its natural resources, and yet around 50% of Indonesians live below poverty line!

In Indonesia, the internationally agreed minimum wage is totally ignored, tolerance between religions has become scarce, bribery is practiced by almost everybody in all different level, the people in the government is so busy filling their own pocket, nature is totally abused, meanwhile so many religious people are busy condemning others instead of giving good example.

Obviously, we are doing something wrong here. If Indonesians are truly as religious as we claim to be, we would not be in this situation right now. So, allow me to remind my fellow Indonesians, especially Moslem Indonesians, if we do not study the Quran properly, we will never be prosperous as the Quran promised and we will also be responsible in giving a bad name to the True Religion to the outside world.

If we do not do change our attitude concerning human rights, we could never make non-Moslems realize that religion is truly necessary in life. We would never remind the world how our scientific development was way behind what the Quran already said around 1400 years ago. And only God knows what other scientific knowledge is still hidden in the Quran.. while we are still searching for it.

We always ask for guidance, we complain about the bad things that happen in this world, but when we are given guidance, we disobey or we change it because it is not to our liking... And we still refuse to believe despite the proofs God has given us.

Previous to Muhammad, all the prophets were given the ability by God to perform physical miracles. And now the Quran is supported by abundance miracles of science, and we still do not believe it.

> And when Our clear communications are recited to them, those who hope not for Our meeting say: Bring a Quran other than this or change it. Say (O Muhammad): It does not beseem me that I should change it of myself; I follow naught but what is revealed to me; surely I fear, if I disobey my Lord, the punishment of a mighty day.
> (Quran translation 10:15)

On the other hand, disbelievers of God simply do not like to hear any prohibition or being told to practice any religious duties imposed by God, although the practices are imposed for our own good. We want excessive freedom; we don't want to have restriction in our consummation and social ethic. Although, if we are truly intelligent, we should already know by now that everything which is excessive always end up bad for us.

If God doesn't exist, why do humans from all ages keep on asking about His existence? Could it be because there is a memory or radar in each of us that keeps on reminding us about Him? If religion is such a nonsense; how come there are many prophecies concerning the coming of the next prophets which are written in thousand years old scriptures and many are coming true? Who made these prophecies?

Religion is guidance, since we are given the free will by God, we need His guidance. Whether we follow it or not, it is up to us... but surely, like everything else in this lifetime... there will be a consequence to whatever we choose.

Well, put it this way... whether we believe in religion or not, we know for sure that we will all die one day. There are certain laws of the universe that none of us can escape, willingly or unwillingly. It doesn't matter whether we understand it or not.

A good example is when someone throws a ball in the air. This ball will surely fall down. Why? Because of the law of the universe called the Law of Gravity. It doesn't matter who throws the ball, whether it is a young girl or an old man, rich or poor, or whether the person understands this law or not.

There is another Law of Physics, which says that matter and energy can not be destroyed. It can only be transformed into another form of matter or another form of energy. We all know that there is another matter or energy inside each one of us, which we call the spirit or soul. When we die, this soul or spirit leaves our body. Now, where does the spirit go to? The law says that it cannot be destroyed, so it must go somewhere! But where?

Another Law of the Physics says that action equals reaction, or call it the Law of Consequence. The New Testament says: "We reap, what we sow.."

(Almost) all of the religions talk about two destinations after we die. If we are good, our destination is Paradise, the Kingdom of Heaven, Jannah, Tian, Swargaloka, Firdaus, Asgard, Valhalla... whatever it is called, it is a beautiful place where there is no more suffering. If we are bad, our destination is Hell, Naraka, Di Yu, Niflheim, Tartarus, Jahannam, Gehenna, Hades, Elysium... whatever it is called, it is an ugly place where suffering prevails. Hinduism and Buddhism are slightly different; they believe that we will keep on reincarnating. However, it still follows the same principle, i.e. if we are good, we reincarnate into a better state of being and if we are bad, we reincarnate into a worst state of being.

Now, how do we know what is 'good' and what is 'bad'? This is where religion comes in. Which religion then? The Quran and this study has shown me that there is only One God, so that rules out the Polytheist religion and the Atheist believe. Now, which guidance shall I choose: the Old Testament, the New Testament or the Quran?

We have seen from the previous chapters, the Quran is the only one amongst the three books which is flawless and free of contradiction. Although God says we can 'choose' whichever religion to enter Heaven, we still have to choose the 'guide book'. If all three books are free of contradictions I would pick all... but we have seen how the Old and New Testaments are heavily altered. Meanwhile, not only is the Quran consistent, it is also accurate in its explanation in Natural Science (i.e.: mathematics, biology, physics, chemistry) as well as in sociology and psychology. Although some of the Quran translation might use different choice of words, (most of) the message stays the same and the Arabic Quran is intact for our main reference when in doubt.

This is how I see it: I have to go to a destination. I am presented with 3 maps that can guide me to that destination. Although the three maps originally point to the same destination, some people have been writing notes, adding different alleys and erasing some streets on the 2 of the older maps. Meanwhile, the newest map has been proven clean from any adjustment. Which one do I choose? Of course, I choose the clean one, especially if this is the map that can guide me to Heaven! And the other alternative is Hell!

We all know a little deviation of the straight path will take us to a different place, that's for sure. Look at the illustration on the next page. Let's say we are on A (earth) and we want to go to B (Heaven) and instead of going straight, we take a little turn to the right or left. Before we know it we might end up in C. Who knows what C is? And worst yet, what if we end up in D? If we are 'lucky' we might just go back to square one. What if we end up below D (i.e. Hell)? Well, we could also go the zigzag way. But what wouldn't it just waste our time? And what if we die while we are on our detour to D? Oh, nooo.....! I am not taking any risk for that.

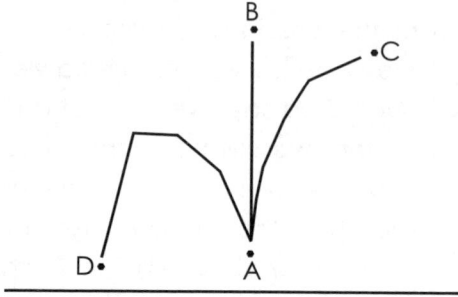

B

•C

D•   A

Yes, there are many ways to Rome... but if the *direction* is already wrong... we will surely end up in a different city. And when it comes to principle of right or wrong, there is no half way. Look at science, there is only 1 theory which is right for everything. For example... either the theory of geocentric is right or heliocentric... only one of them is right, it can not be both right. In fact this is the main prayer that the Quran teaches us:

> In the name of God, the Gracious, the Compassionate.
> All praise is due to God, the Lord of the Worlds.
> The Gracious, the Compassionate.
> Master of the Day of Judgment.
> Thee do we serve and Thee do we beseech for help.
> <u>Keep us on the straight path.</u>
> The path of those upon whom Thou hast bestowed favor, not (the path) of those upon whom Thy wrath is brought down, nor of those who go astray.
> (Quran translation 1: 1 – 7)

DOES HELL REALLY EXIST?

Now, how can we prove whether Hell really exist? Almost all religious books talk about punishment in the form of fire. But only the Quran explains this punishment in connection to the skin:

(As for) those who disbelieve in Our communications, We shall make them enter fire; so oft as their skins are thoroughly burned, We will change them for other skins, that they may taste the chastisement..
(Quran translation 4:56)

That's scary! Does the Quran mean it as allegory or literally? And it is even scarier, because science today has proven that full thickness burns destroy nerve endings so that further burning does not cause pain. The pin prick test is used to verify full thickness loss! So in order to feel constant pain, the skin has got to be renewed, exactly like what the Quran says!

The Quran has been proven accurate in everything it says. So the above must be correct too! It couldn't have been made up by Muhammad, because the knowledge of the nerve system was not known back then.

What do we do with this kind of information? Shall we just not believe it, ignore and 'wish' that it is not true? Or change it into something nicer? Well, we can do all that (and in fact we do), but if this is truly how Hell is, it won't help if we just ignore it.. I think the wisest thing to do is: make sure we don't end up there! Don't you think?

Some people say that God is love and believe that God would never punish us that harshly. That's a nice wishful thinking. But is this true? I want to find out the Truth and not just a fairy tale, doesn't matter how nice that fairy tale is, it wont help me to find out about the Truth. Yes, love comes from God too. But that doesn't mean that God cannot be angry with us.

We don't know what God's plan is by creating us. No one knows that, not even the angels. But God must have something wise planned for us. However, we are fooling ourselves if we say that God would never be that angry to us. Just look at the violence in the animal kingdom. Look at how violent the turbulences in our nature can be!

There are other verses in the Quran that say many ancient polytheist nations that have been ruined because they wrong themselves by rejecting God's guidance. In reality, there are hundreds of ancient ruins of old kingdoms or temples around the world. Archeology study has confirmed that some of those civilizations were quite advanced. Now, most of those civilizations lay in ruin. Accordingly, (almost) in all the ruins we do found statues of idols.

Today we scoff at these notions. We know that catastrophes happen, whether we are 'good' or 'bad'. Well, the Quran says there are two reasons for such catastrophes: one is as punishment and the other one is to try our faith.

> You shall certainly be tried respecting your wealth and your souls, and you shall certainly hear from those who have been given the Book before you and from those who are polytheists much annoying talk; and if you are patient and guard (against evil), surely this is one of the affairs (which should be) determined upon.
> (Quran translation 3:186)

> Do they not travel in the land, and see what was the end of those before them? They were superior to them in strength, and they tilled the earth and populated it in greater numbers than these have done: and there came to them their Messengers with clear proofs. Surely, God wronged them not, but they used to wrong themselves.
> (Quran translation 30:9)

Could this be right? After all the Quran also says that God will preserve the 'houses of God' which are places where His name, the only One God is mentioned, just like the following verse:

> Those who have been expelled from their homes without a just cause except that they say: Our Lord is God. And had there not been God's repelling some people by others, certainly there would have been pulled down cloisters and churches and synagogues and mosques in which God's name is much remembered; and surely God will help him who helps His cause; most surely God is Strong, Mighty.
> (Quran translation 22:40)

Well, look at these devastating and yet amazing pictures, which are mostly taken from Sumatra in Indonesia after the Tsunami. Look at how the mosques survive this catastrophe, and not only one mosque but many! There are many more pictures like the below pictures all over the world.

Tatler Magazine & www.stagmancreations.co.uk

Mosques That Are Not Destroyed by Tsunami in Sumatra

What amazing, scary and yet awesome scenes! Once again: coincidence? One thing is for sure: the Quran doesn't lie.

WHAT ABOUT THE 'NEW AGE' THEORIES?

Many 'modern' people, especially in the West already lost their faith completely in religion. However, it is interesting to note that in fact there are many occult sciences flourishing in the West. Although some do not specifically mention that they are in fact occult teachings. Some of them use the term 'self-improvement' or the most popular term is the 'New Age' teachings.

The New Age teachings cannot be defined into one simple definition.

There are so many New Age gurus, there are so many terms and names for the teachings, and some refuse to be called New Age gurus, although they are. The New Age teachings can vary from the usage of physic powers, crystal powers, meditation, natural healing and most common is the power of the mind.

Many of these teachings talk about how to get what we want in life by visualizing. I know that this principle works, because I have proven it myself. But in order for the visualization to give the result that we want, there are certain conditions that we have to follow. Such as: asking for what we want, think positive, visualizing, being patience, grateful and the main condition is an unwavering faith that we can get it.

Please allow me to remind you to be very careful in accepting any belief just like that. It has already been widely known that our mind is a very powerful tool; it can manifest anything that we believe in strongly. So if we believe that certain crystal can help us better our lives, most probably it will. This is even confirmed in the field of medicine, it is called the placebo effect.

Many 'New Age' self help books about getting what we want in life have become big hits. One the most popular today is 'The Secret'. These teachings do not consider themselves as religious teachings, so most of them do not talk about God and the Hereafter. They just talk about the principles of the universe.

I know that many influential, famous and rich people, especially in the Western world believe in this. They say that this is not a religion but just a philosophy that works. So how come it works? This one sounds so simple and it sounds like a guarantee of a successful life.

Why bother believing in the 'old fashioned religion' then? The New Age teachings say that all we need is to ask, trust in the universe (which most of them consider as equivalent of God), think positive and we will get whatever we want.

Meanwhile, it seems most religious people are so somber, unimportant and have difficult lives, right? They walk around in strange clothes. And either they are meek or they are fanatic to the point of aggressive. It seems like they are only concern about the Afterlife (which can not be proven to exist) and sacrifice the joy of this life. This however, is not entirely true. Just look at the samples of the prophets. Solomon was a very rich, wise king (in the Bible version he became an unbeliever towards the end of his life, but not according to the Quran); Abraham, Joseph and Muhammad were all powerful, successful and brave leaders. And just look how famous and influential are all these prophets up to this day. Many of these prophets were rich also, but they all used their wealth and power in the right way.

Well, actually the Quran does teach all the principals that are used in the New Age as well. I believe that this New Age philisophy also originally came from the wisdom of the only True Religion brought by all the prophets. In fact unwavering faith in the goodness of God is the true essence of religion (i.e. the ultimate positive thinking). Unfortunately, although so-called religious people do have unwavering belief in God, many of them fail to think positive about God. Many are too focused on avoiding 'sinful' things, too focus on the baseless traditions, many are too scared of visualizing abundance. Many are so focused in questioning God concerning their miseries, instead of saying positive things only in their prayers. And since one of the Laws of the universe is: what you focused on expands, therefore, these somber thoughts materialized in their lives. Many do not realize that it is their own negative thinking and whining (even during prayers) that bring the miseries. Many so-called religious people fail to understand that the essence of religion is not some kind of superstitious, meaningless rituals. Religion is also not a tradition; it should not belong to one particular race. A true religious principle should be universal and true for everyone. It is a guide to a victorious life on the Hereafter and ... on earth!

Being religious doesn't mean that we have to suffer in life. We have to strive in life. If we are not happy with our 'fate' right now, we should change it. But we should not forget about the Hereafter and also about the well-being of our fellow humans. To get what we want we must ask God positively, and that is what true praying is all about. This is what the Quran says:

.. God has never changed a favor which He has conferred upon a people until they change their own condition..
(Quran translation 8:53)

Human being often prays for something that may hurt him, thinking that he is praying for something good. Human being is impatient.
(Quran translation 17 : 11)

Whatever benefit comes to you (O man!), it is from God, and whatever misfortune befalls you, it is from yourself...
(Quran translation 4:79)

And that was your (evil) thought which you entertained about your Lord that has tumbled you down into perdition, so are you become of the lost ones.
(Quran translation 41:23)

And when My servants ask you concerning Me, then surely I am very near; I answer the prayer of the suppliant when he calls on Me, so they should answer My call and believe in Me that they may walk in the right way.
(Quran translation 2:186)

And when your Lord made it known: If you are grateful, I would certainly give to you more..
(Quran translation 14:7)

That is how powerful our prayer can be. I would like to remind everyone that some of these New Age philosophy teachings sometimes go as far as saying that we are all creators.

Some even say, that the universe is our 'genie' (like the genie in Aladdin's lamp, this word comes from the Arabic word 'jinn').. that whenever we ask something this genie will fulfill it since 'our wish is the genie's command'! Wow, hold on back here! Now, this is a very dangerous territory. It is ironic that these philosophies are termed as New Age, when actually this kind of belief is one of the oldest in the world... it was just called by a different name: pantheism!

This is the same teaching of the ancient pagans. We should never say that all is God, because the truth is: we all belong to God. No matter what; the Creator is not the same as the creation or creature. Sure, we can connect to the Creator; in fact we are commanded to connect to the Creator. Yes, God grants us what we ask with determination:

> ..and whoever desires the reward of this world, I shall give him of it, and whoever desires the reward of the hereafter I shall give him of it, and I will reward the grateful.
> (Quran translation 3:145)

But we should never ever equalize ourselves with God or worst yet say that the 'universe' (i.e. God) is our *genie* (i.e. servant)..

> And they set up equals with God that they may lead (people) astray from His path. Say: Enjoy yourselves, for surely your return is to the fire.
> (Quran translation 14:30)

Flash news: this is not a new theory; many pagans practiced this philosophy since millennia. How else did the Egyptian Pharaoh who chased Moses became so powerful and rich? Because he thought only of abundance, he thought extremely high of himself... so high that he also believed that he was a god! And see what happened to him in this life time... I don't even want to imagine what will happen to him in the Afterlife.

It is sad to see, that in a different form this kind of idol worshipping actually still exist in our modern day. We use the word 'idol' so lightly today. Don't get me wrong, I love watching entertainment program on TV, especially the American Idol. I am just saying we should be really careful using these 'blasphemous' terms lightly. We do use these exaggerated terms in many TV programs today. We call our celebrities 'divas' and 'divos'... this word derives from a Latin word 'divus' meaning 'divine'.

Yes, it's just a word, we might say... but in reality many of us truly idolized them, some behave obsessively copying them, some are hysterical when they see their 'idols'. We idolize the celebrities, we are mesmerized by their abundance of wealth and extravagant life style. Yes, some of them truly have managed to reach some great achievement, but we should really be careful not to exaggerate in adoring them. These celebrities should also be careful not to be so decadent. They should also realize that their success are also a trial. Some of them truly lead extravagant life like the royalties of the ancient civilizations. I remember how amazed I was when hearing how Queen Cleopatra used to bathe in milk. Today some of these celebrities even spray real gold on their bodies to have the appearance of a 'gold goddess'! Some of them adorn their dogs with diamonds! Come on... that's too far! Meanwhile many people are starving to death!

> The life of this world is made to seem fair to those who disbelieve, and they mock those who believe, and those who guard (against evil) shall be above them on the day of resurrection; and God gives means of subsistence to whom he pleases without measure.
> (Quran translation 2:212)

So yes, of course we should think positive about our lives, in order to have a successful life on the earth... but we should never forget to bow down on our Creator for a successful life on the Hereafter also.

> But when the prayer is ended, then disperse abroad in the land and seek of Gods grace, and remember God

much, that you may be successful.
(Quran translation 62:10)

Life is short. No matter how long it seems to us, especially when we are still young. But just ask any older people.. they will tell us how fast life goes by. Before we die, we will see how unimportant the rivalry of the world that we are competing in, i.e. fame, fortune and all the life's vanities. Well, there is nothing wrong with having fame and fortune, but not if that is the single goal of our lives and not when we use them in the wrong way.

The Quran says:

> *O people! This life of the world is only a (passing) enjoyment, and surely the hereafter is the abode to settle.*
> *(Quran translation 40:39)*

> *Know that this world's life is only sport and play and gaiety and boasting among yourselves, and a vying in the multiplication of wealth and children, like the rain, whose causing the vegetation to grow, pleases the husbandmen, then it withers away so that you will see it become yellow, then it becomes dried up and broken down; and in the hereafter is a severe chastisement and (also) forgiveness from God and (His) pleasure; and this world's life is naught but means of deception.*
> *(Quran translation 57:20)*

> *Who created death and life that He may try you – which of you is best in deeds; and He is the Mighty, the Forgiving.*
> *(Quran translation 67:2)*

JUDGEMENT DAY

Most people think that Islam is the hardest, most rigid of all the religions. I used to think that way too. But after a thorough comparison study I found out, that it is not true – Islam is the most realistic of all the existing religions. Now, let's analyze the doctrine of Judgement Day and Hell in the three religious books.

According to the Old Testament

The Judgment Day appears in several prophetic books: such as Amos, Isaiah, Joel, Obadiah, Zephaniah, and Ezekiel. Other phrases, such as "on that day" and "the day of God's wrath," are considered synonyms for the Day of the Lord. All these phrases refer to a time in the future when God will manifest His Divine rule over all by a series of destructive judgments over the other nations and Israel. There will be frightening changes in the rules of nature: a day of darkness; a day when the lights of the heavenly bodies will be dimmed; a "day of trouble and distress, a day of devastation and desolation".

Day of the Lord

Blow the trumpet in Zion; sound the alarm on my holy hill. Let all who live in the land tremble, for the day of the LORD is coming. It is close at hand - a day of darkness and gloom, a day of clouds and blackness.

Like dawn spreading across the mountains a large and mighty army comes, such as never was of old nor ever will be in ages to come.

Before them fire devours, behind them a flame blazes. Before them the land is like the garden of Eden, behind them, a desert waste - nothing escapes them. They have the appearance of horses; they gallop along like cavalry. With a noise like that of chariots they leap over the mountaintops, like a crackling fire consuming stubble, like a mighty army drawn up for battle.

At the sight of them, nations are in anguish; every face turns pale. They charge like warriors; they scale walls like soldiers. They all march in line, not swerving from their course. They do not jostle each other; each marches straight ahead. They plunge through defenses without breaking ranks.

They rush upon the city; they run along the wall. They climb into the houses; like thieves they enter through the windows. Before them the earth shakes, the sky trembles, the sun and moon are darkened, and the stars no longer shine.

The LORD thunders at the head of his army; his forces are beyond number, and mighty are those who obey his command. The day of the LORD is great; it is dreadful. Who can endure it?
(OT: Joel 2:1-11)

The Day of the Lord will bring about the destruction of God's enemies, who are the enemies of Israel (Isaiah 13:6-11; Ezekiel 30; Joel 3:1-8). Almost all of these books tell about the punishment of the other nations on the Day of Judgment/the Lord, except for the book of Amos that extends the judgment to Israel as well: "Woe to you who desire the Day of the Lord! For what good is the Day of the Lord to you? It will be darkness, and not light" (Amos 5:18). If the wicked nations come to ruin, so will Israel (Isaiah 2:12; Zephiah 1:7-16). Ezekiel (13:5) regards the destruction of the Temple as the Day of the Lord. Certain prophecies of the Day of the Lord were directed against specific hostile nations: Babylonia

(Isaiah 13:6, 9, 13); Edom (Isa. 34:8, 63:4); and Egypt (Jeremiah 46:2-12). Later Jewish literature extends the Day of Judgment even further. Before the advent of the day, all the dead will be revived, so that they too will be judged on that day. Judaism does not have a specific doctrine about the afterlife, but it does have a mystical tradition of describing Gehenna. Gehenna is not Hell, but rather a sort of Purgatory where one is judged based on his or her life's deeds, or rather, where one becomes fully aware of one's own shortcomings and negative actions during one's life.

According to the New Testament

Jesus on Judgement Day

Probably the most complete story of the Day of Judgement in the New Testament is told in the prophecy of John, a servant of Jesus in the Book of Revelation. The story is really long, detailed and the timeline is somewhat confusing. Below, a short *simplified* compilation of the beginning of the prophecy.

On that Day a sound like a trumpet will be heard, then Jesus will come from the clouds, dressed in robe, his head and hair like wool, white as snow, his eyes like blazing fire, his feet like bronze glowing in a furnace, and his voice was like the sound of rushing waters. In his right hand he held 7 stars, and out of his mouth came a sharp double-edged sword. His face was like the sun shining in all its brilliance.

There are symbols of 7 stars representing 7 angels, and 7 candlesticks representing the 7 churches. Jesus will judge the churches according to their deeds: Jezebel, a female false prophetess who performed sexual immorality and eating food sacrificed to idols, will be cast to a bed of suffering and her children will be strike dead. Jesus will punish liars who claim to be Jews to come and fall down at the feet of Christians. Jesus will spit lukewarm believers out of his mouth.

Throne of Lord in Heaven

In heaven, the Lord sits on a throne, He has the appearance of jasper and carnelian. A rainbow, resembling an emerald, encircled the throne. Surrounding the throne are 24 elders dressed in white, wearing gold crowns, also sitting on thrones. These 24 elders praise and worship the Lord God Almighty non-stop.

In the center, around the throne, are four living creatures, and they were covered with eyes, in front and in back. The first living creature was like a lion, the second was like an ox, the third had a face like a man, the fourth was like a flying eagle. Each of the four living creatures had six wings and was covered with eyes all around, even under his wings.

Then the 7 angels will sound 7 trumpets. When the 1st angel sound trumpet, hail and fire mixed with blood will hurled down upon the earth. A third of the earth, the trees and grass will burn.

On the 2nd sound of the trumpet, an ablazed huge mountain will be thrown to the sea. A third of sea, the creatures in it and the ships will be destroyed.

On the 3rd one, a blazing great star will fall from the sky and turn a third of the waters bitter and many people will die from that water.

On the 4th one, a third of the sun, a third of the moon and a third of the stars will turn dark. A third of the day will be without light, and so will a third of the night.

On the 5th one, a star will fall from the sky to the earth, goes to an abyss and smoke will rise from it as if from a gigantic furnace. The smoke will cover the sun and the sky. Out of the smoke locusts will come upon the earth. These locusts will have power like scorpions. These locusts will look like horses prepared for battle. They wear crowns of gold, faces like human, hair like women and teeth like lion's teeth. They wear iron breastplates, and the sound of their wings like the thundering of many horses and chariots rushing into battle. They have tails and stings like scorpions, and in their tails they had power to torment disbelieving people for 5 months.

On the 6th one, 4 angels and 200 million horsemen riding on lion headed horses will kill the rest of men.

Then the 7th angel will sound his trumpet, and loud voices will appear saying: "The kingdom of the world has become the kingdom of our Lord and of his Christ, and he will reign for ever and ever."

⌐∘*∘⌐

Although scarry, both the above descriptions concerning Judgement Day in the Old and New Testaments, also sounded like a fairy tale and not accordance to science. Obviously, whoever wrote the story do not have the understanding that the stars are the same like our sun.

These stories of final battle of good and evil, or the well-known Armageddon in both the Old and New Testaments must have been the sources of inspiration for the Hadyth concerning the coming of the Imam Mahdi. Now, below is the description of the Judgement Day in the Quran which is radically different then any of the above descriptions.

According to the Quran

The Arabic word for Judgement Day is Yaum Al Middin, in the Quran sometimes it is referred to the Hour. Since the beginning of time, humans had been skeptical concerning the Hour, as described in the following verse:

> Those who disbelieve have said, "The Hour will never come to pass!" Say, "Absolutely - by my Lord - it will most certainly come to you. He is the Knower of the future. Not even the equivalent of an atom's weight is hidden from Him, be it in the heavens or the earth. Not even smaller than that, or larger (is hidden). All are in a profound record."
> (Quran translation 34:3)

> If We give him a taste of mercy after suffering some adversity, he says, "This belongs to me. I do not think that the Hour will come. Even if I am returned to my Lord, I will find in Him better things." Certainly We will inform the

538

disbelievers of all their works and We will afflict them with severe retribution.
(Quran translation 41:50)

When is the coming of the Hour? People of all ages have been asking the same question. The Quran anwers:

And verily the Hour is coming, no doubt about it, and that God will resurrect those who are dead.
(Quran translation 22: 7)

The description of the Hour in the Quran is totally scientific rather then fairy tale like, and is universal.

When the earth will be shaken up.
(Quran translation 56: 4)

When the Hour comes, the entire earth will be shaken by a terrible earthquake(s). The Quran says that the tremor will cause mountains to be pulverized, and men will run to and fro in panic. As for the sea, we have the following indications:

When the seas boil.
(Quran translation 81: 6)

When the seas are suffered to burst forth.
(Quran translation 82:3)

An earthquake(s) will pulverize mountains, hot lava will burst forth from many corners of the earth. Volcanoes will erupt and lava will rise from the sea. It is unlikely that the depiction of the end of the world was an exaggeration of natural disasters that Muhammad experienced in his lifetime. The area where Muhammad lived was not on a major earthquake fault-line, and those who spent most of their lives in the middle of desert, most likely, never witnessed the eruption of a volcano in mid-ocean..

When the wild beasts are summoned.
(Quran translation 81: 5)

The Quran draws our attention to the herding together of animals. We know today that animals react to a tremor even before we, human beings, realize it. For instance, in the zoo in Seattle Woodland, the odd movements of elephants and the restlessness of gorillas were observed before the earthquake was felt by human beings. This is a domain in which further research studies are being conducted. In view of this statement of the Quran, I think this research should be intensified.

And when the earth is flattened out. And when it throws out whatever it contains and is empty.
(Quran translation 84:3-4)

The contents of the earth, the magma, the molten rock, will rise to the surface as lava, as described in the verses quoted. The Quran would like us to turn our attention to the most serious event of earth history to come. Advanced science has demonstrated that the end of the world and the universe is inevitable. No one can assert any longer that the stars and the sun will shine forever, and that the universe and the earth will abide to eternity.

When the sun is rolled.
(Quran translation 81:1)

The Arabic word 'takwir' refers to the wrapping of the turban around the head in a spiral form; it also means the rolling or winding of a thing into a ball or round mass, or around something. The scene describes how the end of the sun will come. Like all the other stars, our sun also consumes Hydrogen atoms by transforming them into Helium atoms and releasing energy in the form of radiation, heat and light. The transformation of Hydrogen into Helium stops with the exhaustion of the Hydrogen. Even without the effect of other potential causes, the sun will have to come to an end for this reason. Before their extinction, the stars, according to their sizes, pass through such phases as red giant, white dwarf or black hole. In view of its magnitude, our sun must turn first into a red giant before dying.

> When the stars are put out.
> (Quran translation 77:8)
>
> When the planets are scattered.
> (Quran translation 82: 2)

At the time of the descent of the Quran, people believed that the light of the stars would last forever. This at a time when the inner structure of the stars was a mystery and the fact that the energy of the stars would, one day, be exhausted was not known.

While the verses speak of the putting out of stars, the planets, not light sources, will scatter. The Arabic word for a star is 'najm', while 'kavkab' is a planet. Given the fact that the planets are dependent on a central star, when this star is no more, the planets will necessarily scatter. (There have been translators who translated both words as stars without heeding the difference between them.) Planets are not light sources; therefore their extinction is out of question.

The description of the end of the universe in the Quran relating to the end of the sun and of the world is given in striking colors. What the people at the Prophet's time knew about astronomy could not possibly have permitted them to describe such occurrences. Moslems who lived at the time of the revelation of the Quran believed in all these, not because of scientific deductions but because they had faith in the fact that it was easy for God, the Creator of the heavens and the earth, to destroy them. All the statements of the Quran about the disappearance of the stars, the sun and the earth are corroborated today by scientific discoveries.

Then, when the universe is torn, and turns like a rose coloured paint.
(Quran translation 55:37)

Many English translations of above verse mistakenly added the word 'red' in the translation. God never said that the explosions will look like Humr or Ahmar (red) rose coloured paint. He just said 'like a rose coloured paint' without any specific color. It is worth mentioning that dynamites, bombs and explosions, in general, weren't known to man during Muhammad's time, and certainly, not the explosions of galaxies, and nor were they even known to us until very recently. Explosion of galaxies can not be seen with the naked eye. It also can not be seen with regular telescopes. We need the special NASA owned Hubble Space Super Telescope.

Now, look at the following photo taken from the NASA web site : http://antwrp.gsfc.nasa.gov/apod/ap991031.html:

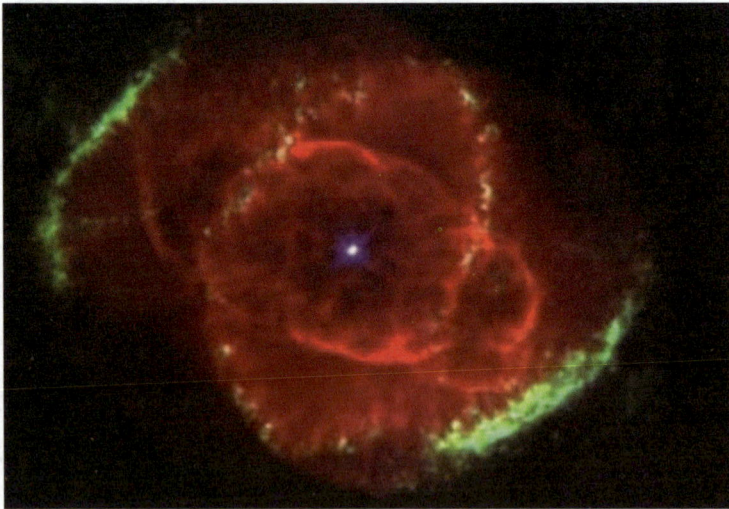

In the above verse, God Almighty in the Quran is telling us that the universe will all turn into exploded galaxies looking like roses when the Day of Judgment happens. Look at these fantastic following pictures and notice the amazing resemblance!

Natural roses:

The rose-like explosions of galaxies:

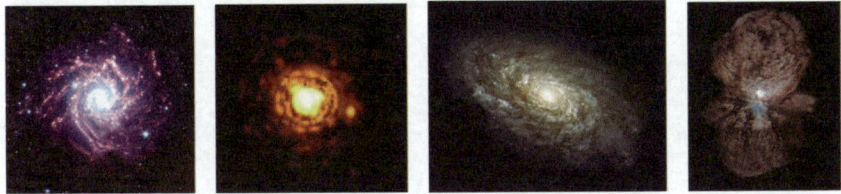

Below, more pictures of rose-like explosions captured by NASA!!

Wow! God Almighty! Isn't that amazing? What argument do we still have not to believe? Are we still waiting until the Hour comes suddenly? By that time, surely it is already too late...

Are they waiting until the Hour comes to them suddenly? Its signs have already appeared. How can they benefit then when it has come upon them?
(Quran translation 47:18)

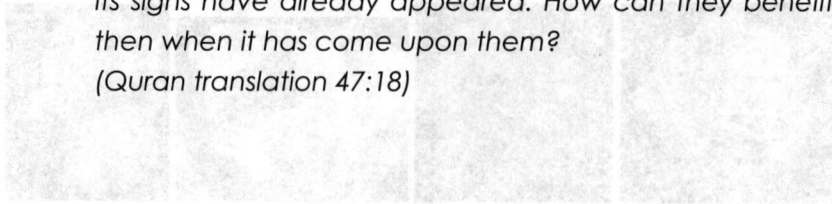

CHAPTER NINETEEN

UTOPIA

Illustration of a Peaceful and Beautiful Place

W e have talked about the scary part of religion, now let's talk about the nice part, shall we? The main purpose of a True Religion is to build an ideal community in this world. It must promote moral, political, economical and social harmony, as well as good health (mentally and physically) for its believers or followers...and above all Peace.

Although the nature can be vicious, the good news is that it is also awesome and breathtaking. So our today's world already reflects the two extreme natures of God's destinations for us. In other words, Heaven and Hell are already reflected in this life time.

Now, the purpose of religion is to guide us to create the ideal community on earth and to go to Heaven after we die. Some of us might think that the message of religion is primitive, rigid, no fun and even pointless. Well, is that so? What do we want in life? Don't we all strive to be happy, successful and experience love in our lives? Who else can make us truly successful, happy and experience love if not God? Some people say that God is love, but I believe this is not entirely true. God is beyond everything, also beyond love. God is the Source of everything. Where do the feeling of love, laughter and tears truly come from? So love must originate from God too. Try to remember when you fall in love. Where does that feeling come from? Thousands of books try to explain what that is... none has truly succeeded, right? It is unexplainable, it is just given.... By whom? Who else, but God.

True love can only come from goodness, i.e. true kindness and compassion. This includes in a romantic love between a woman and a man. True love can only be found in a good relationship, where the couple are truly God-fearing people, meaning both understand the right moral ethic, which includes amongst others: kindness, tolerance, forgiveness, sense of fairness, equality, etc. Not in fleeting, lustful, unethical, over emotional elicit love that ultimately always lead to suffering. So is true happiness. True happiness can only come from doing good deeds. I don't think anyone can truly be happy, even after receiving, let's say a great amount of money by deceiving others.

> Surely (as for) those who believe and do good deeds for
> them will God bring about love.
> (Quran translation 19:96)

Whoever does good whether male or female and he is a believer, We will most certainly make him live a happy life, and We will most certainly give them their reward for the best of what they did.
(Quran translation 16:97)

So, what is the connection to all that with religion? Actually above happiness, there is one state of mind that is should be the ultimate goal of any human's struggle... that is Peace. Peace is freedom from disturbance. When we are only in state of happiness, it can easily turn into sadness, anger or anxiety when some disturbance appear. Peace can only be attained by true submission to God. What does this mean?

I read an excellent (Buddhist) book written by Elkhart Tolle: The Power of Now. He explains very well concerning the concept of acceptance and peace. In short, only when we accept everything that comes to us, can we truly be in the state of peace. We are only angry, anxious or disappointed when things are not going according to our way. Hence, we are subject to a roller coaster of emotion, from ecstatic to depression. Although, this doesn't mean that we simply accept and do not do any effort to change whenever we don't like a situation. The difference is, in acceptance we do something to change it, without letting the situation influence our emotion.

Submission is a higher form of acceptance, in submission (to God) not only do we do something to change the situation while accepting it, we also have unwavering faith that God is able to change it for us. Now, how can we stay optimistic, how do we stay grateful, how do we maintain the faith and keep our patience? By practicing the 3 main religious practices: worshiping God, fasting and giving alms.

Apart from that, we need to attain a certain attitude to be successful in live and the Hereafter. Ask anyone who is truly successful in life, they will tell you the same thing: the right attitude is the key to success (so much more important than talent, for example). These certain attitude is what characterized a so-called Believer. Now, let's see what are the criteria of a believer in the Quran:

> O you who believe! Be patient and excel in patience and remain steadfast, and be careful of (your duty to) God, that you may be successful.
> (Quran translation 3 : 200)

> And follow not that of which you have not the knowledge; surely the hearing and the sight and the heart, all of these, shall be questioned about that. And do not go about in the land exultingly, for you cannot cut through the earth nor reach the mountains in height. All this – the evil of it – is hateful in the sight of your Lord.
> (Quran translation 17:36 - 38)

> Say: Come I will recite what your Lord has forbidden to you–(remember) that you do not associate anything with Him and show kindness to your parents, and do not slay your children for (fear of) poverty–We provide for you and for them–and do not draw nigh to indecencies, those of them which are apparent and those which are concealed, and do not kill the soul which God has forbidden except for the requirements of justice; this He has enjoined you with that you may understand. And do not approach the property of the orphan except in the best manner until he attains his maturity, and give full measure and weight with justice–We do not impose on any soul a duty except to the extent of its ability; and when you speak, then be just though it be (against) a relative, and fulfill God's covenant; this He has enjoined you with that you may be mindful.
> (Quran translation 6 : 151 – 152)

Who are humble in their prayers,
And who keep aloof from what is vain,
And who are givers of poor-rate,
And they maintain their chastity, only with their spouses,
or those who are rightfully theirs, do they have sexual
relations; they are not to be blamed.
(Quran translation 23 : 2 – 6)

And what will make you comprehend what the uphill
road is? (It is) the setting free of a slave,
Or the giving of food in a day of hunger
To an orphan, having relationship,
Or to the poor man lying in the dust.
Then he is of those who believe and charge one another
to show patience, and charge one another to show
compassion. These are the people of the right hand.
(Quran translation 90 : 12 – 18)

Have you considered him who calls the judgment a lie?
That is the one who treats the orphan with harshness,
And does not urge (others) to feed the poor.
So woe to the praying ones,
Who are unmindful of their prayers,
Who do (good) to be seen,
And withhold the necessaries of life.
(Quran translation 107: 1 – 7)

God does not love him who is proud, boastful.
(Quran translation 4: 36)

Now, that doesn't sound too difficult, right? There is nothing superstitious, complicated, irrational nor impossible. The Quran is sober and totally makes sense. Some people might think that being spiritual or religious is not cool and boring. Is that so? But let's see how is the characteristic of people that most of us think is cool? Let see how Hollywood movies picture the character of our heroes (I am not talking about how they do the religious practice, just the characters, ok..).

Hmm, who then... ?
Let's say: Superman? That guy in Matrix? Luke Skywalker? Maximus in Gladiator? Angelina Jolie in Tomb Rider? All those people are upright, sober, honest, keeping their words, not arrogant, determined, purposeful, logical, tolerant, discipline, brave against tyranny, compassionate, just, not vain, etc, etc, right?

Just imagine if everyone is like that... The earth would definitely transforms into Utopian world! Yeah, I know... it would be called Paradise then. Let's see what the Quran say about the ultimate promise of the Utopian world that God has reserve for us, if we do good:

> The gardens of perpetual abode which they will enter along with those who do good from among their parents and their spouses and their offspring; and the angels will enter in upon them from every gate.
> (Quran translation 13:23)

> These it is for whom are gardens of perpetuity beneath which rivers flow, ornaments shall be given to them therein of bracelets of gold, and they shall wear green robes of fine silk and thick silk brocade interwoven with gold, reclining therein on raised couches; excellent the recompense and goodly the resting place.
> (Quran translation 18 : 31)

> Blessed is He Who, if He please, will give you what is better than this, gardens beneath which rivers flow, and He will give you palaces.
> (Quran translation 25 : 10)

And convey good news to those who believe and do good deeds, that they shall have gardens in which rivers flow; whenever they shall be given a portion of the fruit thereof, they shall say: This is what was given to us before; and they shall be given the like of it, and they shall have pure mates in them, and in them, they shall abide.
(Quran translation 2 : 25)

Ah, isn't that nice? I wish I could find a picture of the description of this Paradise. Unfortunately the pictures of Paradise that I come across are mostly so somber. I do find a cartoon picture that really looks like the description above, just in case you really want to have visualization of it. Guess where? In the movie my 3 years old daughter watch everyday: Barbie – the 12 Dancing Princesses ☺. Have a look at it, it is soo beautiful!

Some people say that the above description is made by the desert Arabs, who are always lacking greenery and water, hence the description of the gardens with the rivers flow. But, I think we all love water. Most of us love to spend holiday on the beach or a lake. And even if we just spend it in a hotel, we make sure the hotel has a nice swimming pool, right? And isn't the description of the garden of Eden of Adam and Eve the same?

Some also say that the promise of having pure mates is also only a typical Arab's dream. I don't think so. I think ultimately we all dream of having easy lives with nice houses, nice clothing, nice surroundings and nice companions. If a couple are both good in this life time then there are lucky and will be together in heaven.

Enter the garden, you and your wives; you shall be made happy.
(Quran translation 43:70)

But what if the other spouse fails to go to Heaven? What is wrong if God promising us nice, pure mates? How many of us are truly lucky enough to find nice mates in this life time? We all know what a misery it is having a bad mate in this life. So if we are lucky enough, maybe we can meet our earth mate again in Paradise, but if not ... for sure it is fair enough that God promises one to get a pure mate, right? What else do we want? Above all, when we enter Heaven, God will give us peace.

> *And those who are careful of (their duty to) their Lord shall be conveyed to the garden in companies; until when they come to it, and its doors shall be opened, and the keepers of it shall say to them: Peace be on you, you shall be happy; therefore enter it to abide.*
> *(Quran translation 39:73)*

The way how I see it: life is like a school. It is a big learning process, with tests. If we pass we graduate, if we don't we fail. I was not a diligent student, but my grades were always good, several times I came out as top student in my class. I was accepted in three prestigious universities in Indonesia and I turned down a chance of getting a scholarship in Japan. But I was lazy and I wanted to have as much fun as I could in college. Yes, I got my Swiss hotel management school diploma, and I was just one year away from getting my master degree in the Netherlands, but I blew it! Do I regret it? Yes, sometimes I do. If I would have an impressive doctoral degree, my words would have more credibility, right... I know many people feel the same way I do. Just imagine how we will feel in the Hereafter? The Quran is correct and accurate about everything we have discussed so far. What if it is right about Heaven and Hell?

So, I see no negative side at all of being a Believer. In fact, I can only see loss if I don't. Let's say the Quran is wrong about Heaven and Hell. Well, I don't loose anything by being good, and being correct. Like I said, upright people (not pretentiously righteous and judgmental though) are liked by most people. And history has proven that upright people are the truly victorious ones. I don't see any loss in that, in fact striving for perfection in one's character is already a victory in itself. Yes, some evil people can be successful, but their success usually don't last long. And I believe most likely, they can not attain peace. How could they feel peaceful when they have wronged other people?

So: what if the Quran is right, and we choose not to believe? Then we are surely at a big loss.

> Say: What if it (this Quran) is from God, and you disbelieve in it...
> (Quran translation 46:10)

> We have not revealed the Quran to you that you may be unsuccessful.
> (Quran translation 20:2)

> Serve then what you like besides Him. Say: The losers surely are those who shall have lost themselves and their families on the Day of Resurrection; now surely that is the clear loss.
> (Quran translation 39:15)

So, I choose to be a Believer, a Submitter... and in Arabic, the word is 'Moslem'. Once again, Moslem is not a name, it is a definition. And the religion I choose to practice is the same and the only religion that has been revealed by God through all the prophets: Abraham, Ishmael, Isaac, Jacob, Moses, Jesus and finally Muhammad. Unlike 'other religions' whose names points to a specific location or race, this religion has no 'name'... in Arabic this religion is called 'Islam'... i.e. 'submission to God's will'.

> Say: We believe in God and (in) that which had been revealed to us, and (in) that which was revealed to Abraham and Ishmael and Isaac and Jacob and the

*tribes, and (in) that which was given to Moses and Jesus,
and (in) that which was given to the prophets from their
Lord, we do not make any distinction between any of
them, and to Him do we submit.
(Quran translation 2:136)*

I am not writing this book to 'convert' anyone.. I wrote this book
to share my spiritual journey and give food for thought for anyone
who is searching for the Truth.

As I have explained in Chapter 15, page 361.. in the Quranic term
there is no such thing as 'to convert' but only 'to revert' or 'to
incline to the Truth'. And as we studied this far, even if, let's say I
was born in a Christian family, and I decide to practice Jesus' true
religious teaching… I would have to bow while praying, perform
fasting and even do the pilgrimage like he did, right?

The Quran also says that the definition of Moslem i.e. 'submitter'
was also used during the time of Abraham and Jesus, <u>maybe</u> not
specifically in the Arabic language, but it could be in Hebrew or
Aramaic language. In fact, the term 'God willing' (or InshAllah
in Arabic or Im Yirtzeh Hashem in Hebrew) is still commonly used
in the Jewish and Christian community, right? Isn't that term
indicates a statement of 'submitting' to God's will?

*Abraham was not a Jew or a Christian but he was (an)
upright (man), a Moslem (a Submitter), and he was not
one of the polytheists.
(Quran translation 3:67)*

Some Jews and Christians might feel offended because of
the above statement. But think about this: not only do we see
traces of the same Islamic religious practices that began with
Abraham still mentioned in the Old Testament; historically also,
it is proven that Abraham originally came from a land out of
Israel (most likely somewhere in Iraq today), during the time

when the term Israel, Judah and Jew had not even existed yet. So it is more precise to give the adjective of a Moslem (i.e. Submitter to God) to Abraham rather than a religion with a connotation to a certain race which had not even come to existence during his life time yet, right?

> *And they say: Be Jews or Christians, you will be on the right course. Say: Nay! (we follow) the religion of Abraham, the Hanif, and he was not one of the polytheists.*
> *(Quran translation 2:135)*

And in the above statement, Abraham is addressed by the term 'Hanif' which means 'to incline towards a right state'. This is also means that whatever 'name' of religion we choose, is not a matter of importance, after all the Torah and the Gospel were also revealed by the One God. It is our belief in God and good deeds what counts. Let's not sacrifice our search of Truth just because of our prejudice towards a certain language...

Allow me to quote the following verse, once again:

> *Surely those who believe, and those who are Jews, and the Christians, and the Sabians, whoever believes in God and the Last day and does good, they shall have their reward from their Lord, and there is no fear for them, nor shall they grieve.*
> *(Quran translation 2:62 and 5:69)*

> *... among the followers of the scripture (i.e. Jews and Christians), there are those who are righteous. They recite God's revelations through the night, and they fall prostrate. They believe in God and the Last Day, they advocate righteousness and forbid evil, and they hasten to do righteous works. These are the righteous. Any good they do will not go unrewarded. God is fully aware of the righteous.*
> *(Quran translation 3:113 – 115)*

I am writing this book out of love, care and concern. I won't gain anything by 'converting' anyone. My purpose is also not preaching. Who am I to preach? I am sooo far from being pious, I make so many mistakes and hurt many people. I am merely sharing the information that I have gathered, while striving to be a better person, a better human being, to give something back to the society (i.e. knowledge)... now, that you know what the real meaning of Jihad is... I dare to say: this is my Jihad... ☺

Why am I sharing all this knowledge? Because although the world is advancing in terms of technology, other issues such as: violence in the name of distorted religion, racial prejudice, women oppression, slavery (child labor), economic injustice, drug abuse, teenage illegitimate pregnancy are getting worst... and I know the Quran can guide us away from all these miserable things.

Allow me to quote once again, what Goethe said: *"It is undeniable that all the prophets of the world have powers to bring goodness for mankind, like sunshine, rain and wind that revive the dry earth into green earth. We should acknowledge their prophet hood. The prove of their goodness can be seen by the fact that they all lived in faith, peaceful and harmonious soul, with passion and strong will, devoted and patience through all kind of diversity, strong against the mental corruption and the decreased moral of the people. They believe that these will disappear when we fight against the corruption and do daily prayers. If all that is taught in Islam, then by definition we are all Moslems."*

So, once again this book is not about 'converting'... Yes, I wish I could, but I know that I cannot even do it... religion is a very personal matter; it is a matter of the heart. It is the first human right. No one can force any religion to anyone; no one can truly succeed forcing anyone to change a belief anyway. As the Quran says:

You shall have your religion and I shall have my religion.
(Quran translation 109:6)

There is no compulsion in religion, truly the right way is
clearly distinct from error..
(Quran translation 2:256)

Once again, Islam and Moslem are not names, these are definition that is universal that can be applied for every single children of Adam, for all of us. Therefore, in the Quran there is no calling for a specific race, the callings are universal as follows:

O children of Adam! if there come to you apostles from
among you relating to you My communications, then
whoever shall guard (against evil) and act aright-- they
shall have no fear nor shall they grieve.
(Quran translation 7:35)

However, before you close this book, please allow me to give an advice, from one human being to another. Most of the time we are too comfortable in leaving important matters in other peoples hands. We leave it in the hands of our parents, teachers or society. We just believe whatever they say without pondering any further the truth behind it. If they are right, then we are lucky. But what if they aren't? Our life on earth and after is our own responsibility. Do we really want to leave it to pure luck? Most of us just leave the reading and analyzing to the religious scholars or simply believe what our parents say to us. Most people in this world do not read any of the religious books. At least not entirely. How risky is that? The answer is very risky – if truly the price for that is either Heaven or Hell. I am not taking that chance.

Therefore the least I can do is read and try to find out the Truth. I hope that this book can give you food for thought. Please keep on reading, learn, educate and search for the Truth. The least we can do is search for it ourselves... so, as the first verse of the Quran, allow me to suggest:

Iqra..
Read..
(Quran translation 96:1)

Assalamu 'alayna,
May peace be upon us,

Anita Herawati Moormann

BIBLIOGRAPHY

Quran
Translation by Yusuf Ali
Translation by Rashad Khalifa
quod.lib.umich.edu (English search engine)
http://quran.al-islam.com/ (Kingdom of Saudi Arabia search engine)
http://islamawakened.com/Quran/default.htm (English search engine)

Bible
King James' Version
New International Version
www.biblegateway.com (English search engine)
www.einjil.com (Indonesian search engine)

Gospel of Barnabas
www.barnabas.net

Rig Veda
www.meluhha.com (search engine)

Talmud
www.huc.edu (search engine)

Ecclesiasticus (Catholic Bible)
www.drbo.org (search engine)

History of Myths Retold
Chancellor Press

Books of Hadyth
www.searchtruth.com (search engine)

Sejarah Indonesia (Indonesian History)
www.indo.com

Manifest Your Destiny
Wayne Dyer

In Quest of God
P.P. Arya

Mengenal Tuhan (Getting To Know God)
H. Bey Arifin

History Testifies to the Infallibility of the Qur'an
Sejarah Bangsa Israel dalam Bibel dan Al-Quran
Dr. Louay Fatoohi
Prof. Shetha Al-Dargaselli

Jerusalem: One City, Three Faiths
Karen Amstrong

The Magic of Thinking Big
David. J. Schwartz

Geheim en Wijsheid van der Jezuiten
Herman Somers

The Celestine Prophecy
James Redfield

Mencari Jejak Evolusi Dalam Quran
Searching For Traces of Evolution In The Quran
Harun Yahya

Europe in the High Middle Ages
William Chester Jordan

The Story of the First Crusade
www.brighton73.freeserve.co.uk

Rahasia di Balik Penggalian Al Aqsha
Secret Behind the Al Aqsa Excavation
Abu Aiman

The Epic of Gilgamesh
Pinguin

The Myth of Aryan Invasion of India
David Frawley

Mahabharata
www.indiaoz.com.au

Ancient Cities of the Indus Valley Civilization
Kenoyer J. March

Atlas Al Quran untuk Anak
Al Quran Atlas For Children
Zuhriyah Hidayati, Setya Bhawono, Mansur Oka Usmani

Mystic Places
Time Life Book

Riwayat Kehidupan Nabi Besar Muhammad SAW
The Biography of Great Prophet Muhammad
H.M.H. Al-Hamid Al Husaini

Chariots of the Gods
Erich von Daeniken

Agama Agama Dunia (World Religions)
en.wikipedia.org

Big Bang – Olbers Paradox
en.wikipedia.org

Annie Dillard
Pilgrim at Tinker's Creek

History of Akhnaten and Zoroaster
en.wikipedia.org

African Involvement in Atlantic Slave Trade
Kwaku Person-Lynn, Ph.D

Le Bible, Le Koran et La Science
Dr. Maurice Boucaille

The Bible in Encyclopedia Universalis
J.P. Sandroz

The Foreign Vocabulary of the Quran
Arthur Jeffery

The Unifying Theory of Everything
Muhammad A. Asadi

Lighting The Dark Ages
Deane Morrison

Statistical Miracle in Quran
Prof. Tariq Swaidan

Matematika Alam Semesta
Mathematic of the Universe
Arifin Muftie

Matematika Alam
Mathematic Science
KH Fahmi Basya

Studies in Jewish Mysticism
Joseph Dan

Esquisse de l'Histoire Universelle
Dr. Armanazi

Whither Islam
Hamilton Gibb

The Genuine Islam
George Bernard Shaw

The Preaching Islam
A History of the Propagation of the Moslem Faith
Sir Thomas W. Arnold

The 100:
A Ranking of the Most Influential Persons in History
Michael H. Hart

The History of Christianity in the Light of Modern Knowledge
Harcourt Brace and co.

Islam: The Straight Path
John L. Esposito

Muhammad: Prophet of Our Time
Karen Amstrong

The Heirs of the Prophet Muhammad
Barnaby Rogerson

Civilization of the Arabs
Dr. Gustav LeBon

History of the Crusades
Michel Michaud

Islam: Impressions and Studies
Count de Castri

Bonaparte et L'Islam
Cherfil

Dari Penjara Taliban Menuju Islam
From the Taliban Prison to Islam
Anton Kurnia

Quantum Ihklas
Erbe Sentanu

Prison Dilemma
Roopal Patel and Peter McMurray

Do You Eat Unhealthy Pork?
Heather Moore

Facts About Pork Meat
Dr. Mohammed Nezar Al-Dakr

Polygamy Reconsidered
Father Eugene Hillman

Jesus's Family Tombs
Simcha Jacobovici dan Charles Pellegrino

Apologia ad Autolycum
Theopilus of Antioch

The Holy Fire:
The Story of the Early Centuries of Christian Churches in the Near East
Robert Payne

Jesus
Lisa Spray

The Myth of God Incarnate
Michael Goulder

Zeitgeist the Movie
www.zeitgeistmovie.com

The Fifth Tablet of Enuma Elish
B. Landsberger & J.V. Kinnie Wilson

The Power of Now
Eckhart Tolle

Mythologies
Roland Barthes

Mysteries of the World
www.crystalinks.com

The Handbook of Christian Apologetic
Kreeft & Tacelli

Islam en Democratie
Fatima Mernissi

The Ultimate Frontier
Eklal Kueslana

The Complete Guide to Astrology
Julia and Derek Parker

World's Sixteen Crucified Saviours
Kersey Graves

A Documentary Survey of the French Revolution
John Hall Stewart

Article about Muhammad in Bhavishya Puran
Dr. Vidyarthi

Bangkitnya Bangsa Yajuj dan Majuj di Asia
The Rise of Yajuj and Majuj in Asia
Syeikh Hamdi bin Hamzah Abu Zaid

Article about Fasting
Dr. Ben Kim

The Secret
Rhonda Byrne

Secrets and Mysteries of the World
Sylvia Browne

The Jewish Woman in Rabbinic Literature
Rabbi Dr. Menachem M. Brayer

To Pray As a Jew:
a guide to the prayer book and the synagogue service
Hayim Halevy Donin

Hikmah Shalat untuk Pengobatan dan Kesehatan
The Benefit of Worshipping For Medicinal and Health
Profesor Muhammad Hembing Wijayakusuma

Ternyata Akhirat Tidak Kekal
Apparently The Hereafter Is Not Eternal
Agus Mustofa

Dibalik Pusaran Kabah
Behind the Circumambulation at Kaaba
Agus Mustofa

What Everyone Needs To Know About Islam
John L. Esposito

The Power of Intention
Wayne Dyer

The Power of Karma
Mary T. Browne

De Tao Van Het Geld
Walter Luebeck

The Discovery of Early Pottery in China
Zhang Chi

Who Is A Jew?
Rebecca Weiner

Serpent in the Sky
John Anthony West

The Great Wall of China: From History to Myth
Arthur Waldron

Essentials of Hinduism
Swami Bhaskarananda

The Bible Unearthed:
Archeology's New Vision of Ancient Israel and the Origin of its Sacred Texts
Israel Finkelstein and Neil Asher Silberman

The Lost Legacy of Abraham in the West
Gatut, S. Adisoma, Ph.D
(www.submission.com)

Finding God
Salmawy

Reply To Robert Morey's Moon-God Allah Myth:
A Look At The Archaeological Evidence
M S M Saifullah
Mohd Elfie Nieshaem Juferi and
Abdullah David

Hadyth Exposed
http://www.freewebs.com/tawhiyd/hadiythexposed.htm

General References:
www.wikipedia.com

Anita Herawati Moormann was born on June 25, 1968 in East Java, Indonesia. However, as an ex-Ambassador's daughter she spent a long time living outside Indonesia. For about twenty years she traveled and lived in several countries – starting from Malaysia, ex-Yugoslavia, Switzerland, Germany, Czechoslovakia and the Netherlands.

After her education in a Swiss Hotel Management School, she started working in various jobs - starting as a restaurant waitress, Garuda Airlines and going on to own travel and international trading companies in Germany and the Netherlands. In 2002 she came back to Indonesia and worked as a Public Relations Manager with various international companies in Jakarta. Her life and working experiences, involving many contacts with foreigners, have led Anita, who likes to read, socialize and ponder about life to write several books - especially concerning her autodidact observation in religion, philosophy and cultural comparison study.

Anita is currently living in Jakarta with her Dutch husband, and a daughter.

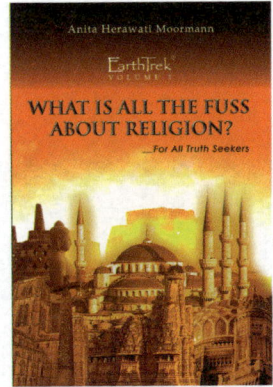

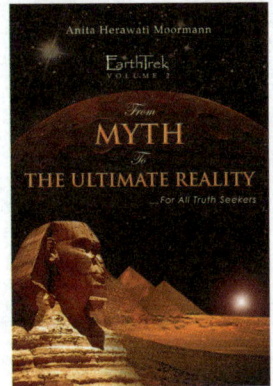

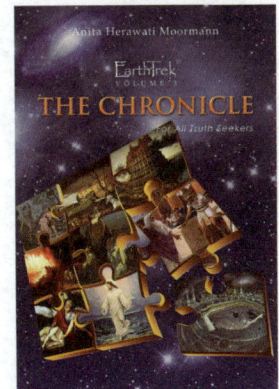

THE
REICH INTRUDERS

Pip Fioretti has a professional background in visual arts, both practice and teaching, and took up writing fiction in 2008. She has published three women's fiction books with Hachette Australia and Pan Macmillan. Her first crime novel was *Bone Lands*, published by Affirm Press in 2024. Pip lives in Sydney and likes reading, looking at art, bushwalking and hanging out with friends and family.

SKULL RIVER

A GUS HAWKINS MYSTERY

PIP FIORETTI

affirm press

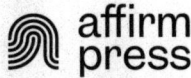

affirm press

First published in Australia in 2025 by Affirm Press,
a Simon & Schuster (Australia) Pty Limited company
Bunurong/Boon Wurrung Country
28 Thistlethwaite Street, South Melbourne VIC 3205

Affirm Press is located on the unceded land of the Bunurong/Boon Wurrung peoples of the
Kulin Nation. Affirm Press pays respect to their Elders past and present.

New York Amsterdam/Antwerp London Toronto Sydney/Melbourne New Delhi
Visit our website at www.simonandschuster.com.au

AFFIRM PRESS and design are trademarks of Affirm Press Pty Ltd, Inc.,
used under licence by Simon & Schuster, LLC.

10 9 8 7 6 5 4 3 2 1

A Cataloguing-in-Publication entry for this book is available from
the National Library of Australia

NATIONAL LIBRARY OF AUSTRALIA — A catalogue record for this
book is available from the
National Library of Australia

9781923046788 (paperback)
9781923293854 (ebook)

Cover design by Blue Cork Design/Luke Causby
Typeset by J&M Typesetting in Garamond Premier Pro
Proudly printed and bound in Australia by the Opus Group

FSC — MIX
Paper | Supporting
responsible forestry
www.fsc.org FSC® C001695

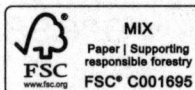

For my father and his books

To ravage, to slaughter, to usurp under false titles,
they call empire, and where they make a desert,
they call it peace.

Tacitus, *Agricola*, c. AD 98

Autumn 1912

Colley, Central West,

New South Wales

1

I heard gunshot. Startled awake, heart thumping, waiting for the next one. Nobody sounded the alarm. The officer of the watch must be down. Very deep shit.

I groped for a light. As the candle toppled to the floor alongside a spill of matches, I realised I was not in a tent on the Transvaal. I was in a bed, in a lean-to at the back of Colley police station. I sat up and pushed the curtain to one side, letting in a sliver of starlight; rubbed away the condensation on the glass and peered out into the night, just to be certain, then sank back onto the bed, waiting for my nerves to settle.

Outside, two foxes called to each other in a gravelly yap. I was so cold I debated getting up to put on my greatcoat but could scarcely muster the energy. The autumn air was bitter as wormwood and the meagre police regulation blanket a match in meanness. *Welcome back to the New South Wales Mounted Troopers, Gus, you rash and reckless fool.*

I'd ridden into Colley from Bathurst last night, arriving close on midnight. After I found the police station and banged on the door of the private quarters for five minutes, Trooper Scanlon answered, bleary and befuddled, in his nightshirt; yet he was ready to vacate his bed for me, his

new sergeant. I couldn't have that, so I gave him my firearms to lock up, took a lantern, put my horse in the stable, rubbed him down and left him some tucker, then let myself into the lean-to out the back.

Wasn't much to look at, just a sagging old mattress on a rickety iron bedstead, a couple of cats curled up on the blankets, and a heap of dust. I could have slept leaning on a gatepost after an eight-hour journey on a horse who had ideas of his own. I kicked off my boots, swept the cats away and dropped like a stone, eyes closed before I hit the mattress.

Now I was awake, and with no idea of the time I just lay there, eyes closed, telling myself I was resting and that's as good as sleeping. It's not really but I always like to keep my self-deception skills polished and ready. Then I heard a voice outside and just about sprang up to the ceiling.

'Sorry to wake you, sir.'

Trooper Scanlon. I swallowed, took a breath. 'What is it?'

'Sorry, sir, but I just had a message. Trouble up at Gibbet Hill – Trooper Murphy's sent for help.'

'Details?' I said, sitting up and swinging my legs out of bed, planting my bare feet on the cold, gritty floor.

'No, sir. Reckon we should get up there quick-smart, but.'

I sighed and rubbed my face, then stared at my uniform, freshly issued yesterday, lying in a tumbled heap on a spindly chair. I'd hoped for a slow day and did not relish the prospect of getting back on a horse. Gibbet Hill, high in the hills to the west, was a goldmining town where the gold was tucked away in underground reefs. A lot of mine shafts, a lot of grog, feuds, sudden wealth and long, drawn-out failure. Not a good combination for public order.

4

'Give me a moment,' I called out. 'I'll meet you in the stable. What time is it?'

'Quarter to six, sir.'

The pitcher in the washbasin was empty. I ran my hand through my hair, stretching and wincing as the muddle of scars around my chest and underarm pinched and puckered. Fresh shirt, buckskin breeches, navy tunic; do up those buttons, son, smarten up. Tucked my warrant card, notebook and pencil in my tunic pocket, cap on my head and stepped out into the gloom. Light in the east above the darkened mountains signalled dawn.

I had no idea where the outhouse was so I went around the back, through the long grass, and pissed against the wall, steam rising, shoulders stiff, my entire body aching. Feeling eyes on me, I looked over my shoulder to see, in the neighbouring paddock, a flock of horned white goats in the grey half-light. They'd all paused in their grazing and were watching me with those unnerving devil eyes. In the corner of the police block was a stand of pine trees laden with white cockatoos, which flew away like screeching demons at first light.

I went back around through the damp long grass past the police station private quarters, noticing wisps of smoke rising from the chimney. I tried the front door of the station. Scanlon had locked up already. I could have murdered some porridge. Even a crust of bread would have done.

I trudged back up to the stable and found my horse. He was knackered from the ride yesterday and had a mutinous glint in his eye. While I was saddling up, Scanlon appeared and began to saddle his horse: another bay, with three white socks, name of Tosser, by the sounds of it – not one to inspire confidence. Scanlon was a young, lanky bloke, fair, ruddy-cheeked,

5

clean-shaven, an open face and a broad smile that had a curl of mischief to it. My first impressions were that he'd be easy to work and live with.

'Had breakfast?' I asked him as he tightened the girth on his horse.

'No, sir. When we get to Gibbet Hill, they'll do us something at the Criterion. Gotta good cook there. I've got your guns here too.'

I took my Martini–Henry carbine and a Webley revolver, a .455 Mark II, which the British complained had no stopping power. But we in the colonies still used them. These were the old, mounted trooper standbys that were issued to me yesterday in Bathurst. I loaded them and took some spare ammunition for my saddlebags.

We led the horses out into the subdued light, mounted up and clattered through the town. I'd spent a week in Colley about six years before, but most of that week had been spent blind drunk so my recall was not good. I glanced around: huts and cottages, some in good repair, others abandoned, a general store, a blacksmith's, the huge, two-storey pub with a balcony all prettied up in iron lace. The cold morning air was thick with the smell of burning grease. A woman swept the front of her house, the ostler at the coach turnaround raised a hand in greeting; kids ran about in their school pinafores, clutching thick chunks of damper smeared with dripping.

'Five hours to Gibbet Hill, sir,' Scanlon said, flexing his back and yawning. 'Whatever trouble they're having should be over by then.'

Five bloody hours. As we left the town, I looked over at the river on our right, heard the water rushing over pebbles. The Bull wasn't a transport river: it was shallower, faster, narrower, and had large river stones and gravelly banks pitted with mounds and holes from past gold diggings. It was scattered with broken wood cradles, picks and shovels, pans and assorted rubbish that had been left to rot by the diggers who'd had a gutful

of cold, wet work and nothing to show for it. There were pools of yellow water so thick you could stand a spoon in them. It was the colour that astonished me, like a stream of piss trickling across the pavement, but opaque and stinking of rot.

'River usually like this?' I asked.

'Yes, sir,' Scanlon said. 'Dump's full so people chuck their rubbish in the river.'

'Why don't they organise a new dump?'

'Don't know, sir.'

I'd have to speak to the mayor about that. Put it on my checklist, which was growing longer by the minute. I'd been told that at the height of the gold rushes the town's population was around forty thousand. Now it was three hundred and dropping. The rush was over, the town's vigour and optimism spent, its buildings losing the battle to stay upright; its bleary occupants waking as if from a fever dream, only to find their pockets empty, their gold gone. That gold is now deep inside the government pocket and spent on the wages of mounted troopers like me, who lock up those bleary drunks who smash up the place after finding no gold. This was the grand circle of existence; it had a pleasing symmetry if you thought about it.

To our left was a steep hill studded with rocky outcrops and a few saplings. Wattlebirds and parrots flitted about, calling in the fresh morning air. At the base of the hill, down beside the road, lay mullock heaps, great piles of stones taller than a man, heaped up in endless testimony to the gold diggers' backbreaking work. Creeks ran off into gullies choked with billowing blackberries, tall grasses grew on either side of the road, but rabbits were around, busy as ever gobbling down some other vegetation.

Scanlon was a neck ahead of me as we clopped along, his broad

shoulders pushing at the seams of the navy-blue tunic. He'd have to get a new one soon.

'Did you hear gunshot this morning?' I asked.

'You hear them all the time just before dawn. Farmers or hunters going after rabbits, foxes, pigs, wild dogs. Usually it's—'

Scanlon suddenly jerked to the right and a spray of blood spurted from his head. The echo of the gunshot bounced around the valley. He slumped forward on his horse. Another shot – coming from the slope to my left. Scanlon's horse took off with him collapsed over his neck.

The crack and whiz of another shot, again from the left. Hit my horse's neck with a thud. He screamed and reared up. My training kicked in. I slipped my feet out of the stirrups and, as he went down, I jumped off and hit the road just as he did.

Fumbling for my pistol, I dropped beside my horse as he screamed and thrashed. He wasn't going to survive, by the look of the blood gushing from his neck and pooling beneath us. I hesitated but his terrible screams cut through me. I placed the muzzle of the gun behind his ear and pulled the trigger. He jerked and stilled while the beat of the call to arms drummed through my veins.

My rifle, in its saddle holster, was pinned under him. Another crack and whizz echoed around the valley. Sheltering behind a dead horse, eyes scanning the hill, lying in a spreading pool of blood. What the fuck was going on?

My mind raced back to my sweaty, grimy years on the veldt as a young subaltern, making decisions under fire, getting it wrong, getting it right, trained to do this, so do it. I rolled onto my back, still sheltered by the horse's body. Checked out the lower riverbank. A ditch ran along the side

of the road – I could roll into that. Had to – no choice. My heart was hammering like a piston in a threshing machine.

Birds were silent. Frogs, insects, all holding their breath, curled up, small targets. Just the river rushing over stones. Scanlon's blood spurting through my mind, horse's blood spreading from beneath his body, pooling around my body, wet and ferrous, his screams ringing in my head.

The gunman was up there with a good view of the road – of me – and he was waiting, he had all the time in the world. I grimly counted to three and then rolled and slithered across the stony road and into the ditch, which was deeper than I thought. Panting and nauseous, I lay still, pushed my face against the grass, the acrid, fresh smell bringing the thwack of leather on willow, pretty girls, strawberries and cream in the tea tent. Then more bullets thudded into the earth, sending tufts of grass and gravel flying up, the echo of the shots ringing out across the valley.

From my new vantage point, I could think. Someone was trying to kill me – that much I knew. Killing police troopers was a one-way trip to the gallows with a few well-aimed smacks along the way, as was widely known among our usual customers. It had to be that way or they'd be shooting us left, right and centre. So what was his game?

Did he want to take out as many troopers as he could before shooting himself? That was not unheard of. Maybe his missus had left him, and he was so angry he wanted to kill? Also not unknown. Wanted to stop us getting to Gibbet Hill? Maybe. Which meant that if there was trouble up there, it was very big trouble. Mail coaches. Gold transport. Prisoner transport. A grudge. Or all of them, crammed into a bullet.

A breeze blew along the river, coming from the east, from Colley. Horse blood dripped down my face. A haze had fallen across my eyes.

9

I was dying. He'd hit me somewhere. I frantically ran my hands over my chest, tugged my tunic up, looking for holes. I knew you could be shot and not feel it in the chaos of the moment.

Church bells rang in the distance. Smoke on the breeze. Looking up, I saw billowing clouds of smoke rising from the town, great thick, grey plumes of it. I wasn't shot. But try as I might to orient myself to whatever the hell was going on, I couldn't. Unless Germany had invaded and were ahead of the newspapers. Clever Hun bastards.

I slipped and slithered down the riverbank into the stinking, shallow water. Bastard fired again. Crept along, keeping my head low, sloshing, sinking into sandy gravel, muddied hands, visions of Scanlon's head exploding. Gunshot screaming out across the valley. Church bells ringing the alarm.

Closer to town, I clambered up the muddy slope onto the riverbank, then staggered onto the road. Smoke was thick. Dogs barking, people shouting. I ran towards the main street, but the fire was coming from higher up in the town. A crowd of people milling about.

It was the police station, burning like a bonfire on Guy Fawkes Night.

2

The entire structure of the police station was ablaze, flames leaping, roaring in my ears, air thick with smoke. I stopped running, took in the sight, panting, hands on hips. All the files and records from sixty years, the incident book, the weapons, the private quarters, stable and the lean-to with my barely unpacked bag, spare boots, uniform, books, all gone. People staring in fright. At me.

'Where's Trooper Scanlon? And who the hell are you?' some bloke shouted at me.

'And who the fuck are you?' I shouted back in his face.

He took a step back, eyebrows raised as if he'd confronted a wild man.

'Is anyone in there?' I yelled over the roar of the flames, pointing at the burning station. The crowd silent, staring, huddled. 'Is there anyone in there? Answer me'

There was no time to wait. I marched towards the flames. A hand grabbed me, tried to drag me back. I shook it off, but the hand yanked me back again. I struggled against his grip. Women were crying, coughing, kids clutching their skirts. Burning farms over their heads. The girl, her body suspended above the flames in an infinitesimal moment. Then she

falls through the fire and into eternity.

'The blood on your breeches, man, whose is it?' a man asked.

I turned away, rubbed my eyes, then jumped out of my skin as the roof of the police station caved in, the sparks dancing into the sky. This wasn't Ventersburg and the girl had been dead for ten years, only she died again and again in my night terrors.

'Trooper Scanlon?' the same man asked, louder this time. 'Where is he?'

'Dead – he's dead on the river road,' I shouted back at him. 'An ambush.'

I heard people gasp and took a deep breath, coughed from the smoke, the scars on my chest pinching and tightening. A tremble in my hand and the small muscle beneath my eye twitching like a maddened earthworm.

'Davy's dead?'

I whirled around to see who'd spoken. He was a slight older man, a ring of white hair around his skull and horror in his eyes.

'But how?' he said. 'Who? Was he shot?'

'Who are you?'

'Bill Pomeroy, local doctor. You sure he's dead?'

'Of course I'm sure – you don't survive a bullet to the skull from a hundred and fifty yards. Why? You think you can use your pills and potions to revive him?'

The word that Scanlon was dead went around the crowd. Exclamations, horror and fear on all the faces. At the edge of the crowd a woman dressed in mourning paced in circles, her hands pressed against her mouth, eyes closed, while a young lad followed her, step for step, wailing and sobbing, reaching out to grab her dress.

Questions shouted at me. Who did it? What happened? Who are you?

A babble of voices in the smoke haze. All of us confused. I undid a couple of buttons on my tunic and took out my warrant card, which was all I had left, apart from my filthy reeking uniform. A man took it and passed it around.

'Rode in last night arrived after dark,' I said. 'Call Bathurst if you don't believe me. I have to speak to them anyway. Who's the telegraph operator?'

'I am – Harry Barker.'

I turned to see a middle-aged man, lock of dark hair falling across his face, unshaven, puffy around the eyes. He looked down at my breeches. I looked too, shocked to see the pale buckskin breeches half-sodden with horse blood, my navy tunic too, my shaking hand gripping my pistol.

'Maybe a brandy first, eh?' said the first bloke as if he were trying to humour a madman.

'Listen, Mr Whoever-you-are,' I said, getting right in his face. 'I'm the new sergeant in town and we have a bloody serious situation to deal with.'

Without waiting to see if anyone was going to come with me, I strode off towards the post office. Couldn't miss it. A two-storey red-brick building at the entrance to the town, beside the coach exchange.

Barker caught up with me, panting. 'Mate, you can't just ring up the cops in Bathurst. You have to wire them, and only I can do that.'

'Then do it,' I said, striding ahead.

'Where's Scanlon now?'

'His horse took off when he was shot. Body's probably on the road somewhere. How many houses are there along the river?'

'A few, yeah, just labourers, stockmen, all law-abiding, respectable.'

Someone wasn't abiding by the law, I knew that much – but no more. I watched myself walk along the road in bloodstained clothes, a man in

fragments, the chilling echo of gunshot bouncing around inside my skull.

'Reckon it's bushrangers?' Barker said.

I couldn't answer. We reached the post office. He unlocked the front door and I followed him inside. Then he lifted part of the countertop, put it back down and grabbed his official cap, put it on and struggled into his official jacket, saying, 'Gunna take a few minutes to get through to the operator and the police. How's about Mrs Barker gets you a cup of tea, eh?'

'Got a smoke?'

'Yeah, yeah, sure,' he said, and he fished a packet of cigarettes from his pocket. I took one and he lit it for me, saying, 'You know it's not a secure line, mate.'

'It's not "mate" – I am not your mate. It's Sergeant Hawkins.'

He looked up at me and blinked rapidly, nodding, 'Yes, Sergeant.'

'Do it. Put the call through. Now.'

'Are we … is this?'

'Do it.'

He went to the telephone and dialled a number, holding the earpiece to his ear, and was told by the operator to wait. Then she came back on the line and said the duty sergeant in Bathurst would not accept a telephone call. That we needed to wire them or write.

I could feel the tremble resume, the muscle under my eye pulsing madly, my hand, soon my arm would shake. I dropped the fag and took hold of the back of a chair. Barker gave me a nervous look.

'Tell her,' I shouted, slamming the chair. 'Tell her now'

Barker stammered out that the situation was urgent. In a few moments I was speaking to a Sergeant Crawford in Bathurst.

'Better not make a habit of this, Hawkins.'

'Officer shot, Trooper Scanlon, an ambush—'

Suddenly I could barely speak, tears pricked my eyes. The sergeant on the other end of the line was yelling something at me.

Barker carefully took the telephone from my hand and spoke into the mouthpiece. 'Trooper Scanlon has been shot and ...' He looked at me. 'Yeah, gone off, and Sergeant Hawkins' horse was shot from under him, and the police station, been a fire. We ... ah ... we could do with a bit of help.' I heard Crawford murmur some obscenity.

By now I'd collected myself and I took the phone from Barker. 'Hawkins here. Scanlon and I were riding on the western road to Gibbet Hill after a report of trouble in the town. You need to contact them. And stop all scheduled traffic on that road until further notice.'

'Bushrangers, you think?'

'Don't know, but all troopers must be armed and capable.' Then I rang off. Not all troopers were capable. I was not capable, not anymore. I slumped into the chair and put my head in my hands while Barker fussed over his telephone logbook. Footsteps on the stairs. A woman peered around the door, hair tightly wound in a bun, eyes wide in a lined face.

'You alright, love?' she said. To me, to Mr Barker, to nobody in particular.

'Yes, I'm fine,' I snapped, too harshly, and she disappeared like a rabbit to its burrow.

'Oi, Sergeant,' Barker said. 'I know you've had a nasty shock ...'

That's what he called it. Seeing a man's brains blown out only a few feet from me. Feeling my horse give way beneath me while it screamed in terror. I was as far from fine as north is from south, and terrified of myself, of reactions I couldn't get a grip on. The screams of my horse, his coarse

15

mane in my face, a single hair pricking my eye, pressed against his body as I killed him, felt his life gallop away.

'I had to shoot him,' I said, shaking my head, looking to Barker for absolution.

Barker carefully put down the pen he'd been using.

'My horse. The bullet hit him in his neck. He went down and there was nothing I could do. I had to shoot him.'

'Yeah, you had to. Awful thing to do, but you had to. Got no choice when a horse is down.'

'Only assigned to me yesterday.'

'Poor bugger,' Barker said, wiping his chin with his hand. 'That scar on your face—'

'Bayonet, Boer War.'

'Yeah? Had some blokes from Colley fight over there. Australian Commonwealth Horse. Did alright too. Was you in that?'

'New South Wales Mounted Rifles.'

'So you went over before Federation, eh?'

I nodded.

'Listen, Sergeant, I—'

The telegram machine started up. We both looked at it. Barker put his headset on and noted the message, then put it in an envelope, handed it to me and noted it in his book. I signed for it and ripped it open, hand shaking. I couldn't read it and handed it to Barker.

He read it out. '*Reinforcement coming STOP*' Barker looked up, then passed the telegram to me.

'That's all those fuckers have to say?' I shouted, and I screwed the paper into a ball and hurled it at the wall. 'Put another call through.'

16

Barker shook his head. 'I can't, it's a party line. Cops in Bathurst'll have my guts for garters.'

I slumped back into the chair, exhaustion crashing down on me. Closed my eyes, saw Scanlon's head explode.

'Gonna leave Scanlon out there?' Barker ventured.

My eyes snapped open. I was in a small post office, with the postmaster gazing at me, wearing a bloodied uniform, only it wasn't the Light Horse uniform, I was back in the traps.

'I mean, could we get his body, d'you reckon?'

'He's dead,' I said. 'If you can shoot straight and want to provide cover, I could probably get his body.'

He blinked a few times, then shook his head. 'Ah, no.'

'When does the mail coach come in?'

'Twice a week, Mondays and Thursdays, and then I deliver around the place. Goes up to Gibbet Hill, turns around, comes back. It's Friday, so we aren't expecting a coach today.'

'Did you take a message from Gibbet Hill this morning and deliver it to Trooper Scanlon?'

'Nope, not me.'

'Your wife?'

'Nobody touches the telegraph machine but me, and nobody delivers the messages but me.'

Was this my madness or something else? Who had told Scanlon there was trouble?

'Who's the mayor?'

'That's Ray Fitzgerald, but he's not in town today. His uncle's the publican at the Commercial and Ray sorta runs it. It's just along by the

17

river, you can't miss it, big white timber place with iron lace.'

'But he's not there?'

'No, he's got business in Bathurst.'

'But the pub's open for business?'

'Yeah, I reckon you could do with a cuppa too.'

I followed him out into the day, and as we walked down the road to the Commercial, all I could think of was the moment my horse went down and the bullets flying over me and how it felt so right and perfect. I knew what to do, met the chaos like an old friend, the familiar smell of gunpowder and blood. And a feeling so familiar, yet so long past, of being alive.

3

The morning sun shone as if nothing had happened. A dog wandered the street sniffing, lifted a leg against a wall. Men milled around outside the pub, a sea of weathered faces, grim eyes, strong arms, men who worked long hours. I knew none of them, yet I knew them well. They looked to me as I approached, falling silent. One grabbed my arm and I nearly put my fist in his face, then I hurried inside the pub, desperate for drink.

The inside of the Commercial was big enough to handle large groups of men who'd come in for the light and warmth after a day digging in a cold river. It had a large fireplace, a battered billiards table, windows at the back looking across the river, tables and chairs, a long bar and plenty of room. The man behind the bar had a stoop and long, greasy hair and was drying beer glasses. One or two old men were sitting with shandies, their old eyes widening at the sight of me.

'Welcome to Colley, mate,' one of them croaked.

'Sergeant, yeah?' the man behind the bar said, nodding at the three bloodied chevrons on my jacket arm. It was the man who'd challenged me at the fire, asked who the hell I was. I'd worked it out by now and could answer.

'Yes, Sergeant Augustus Hawkins, replacement for—'

'Sergeant Barrett,' he said.

I nodded, looked around. I glimpsed my confronting reflection in the mirror behind the bottles on the shelf behind the bar. 'Your name?' I asked, a touch too testily.

'Mr Septimus Watt,' he said, hard-eyed and equally testy. 'Manager of this hotel.'

I closed my eyes for a moment. *Steady on, Gus, mate, go slow here.*

'And deputy mayor,' he continued. 'Might please you to know I've set some blokes on wetting down the station, to stop stray embers blowin' about, cool it down a bit.'

'Good work,' I said, nodding. I should have thought of that.

'Have some breakfast, Sergeant. I reckon you need something in yer belly.'

'And coffee, strong, thanks.'

'No coffee out here, mate. Chicory essence or tea.'

'Tea.'

'Leila, tea and a breakfast,' Watt bawled through an open door.

'A packet of cigarettes too, please.'

He put a packet of fags on the counter and I suddenly realised I had no wallet or money.

'I can't pay you for this today, Mr Watt ...'

''Cause you're police, I'll do youse credit, but if you don't pay up by the end of the month Ray'll come after yer.'

I shook a cigarette out of the pack with shaking hands, lit it and inhaled with relief. My head was in fragments. Watt pulled out a ledger and a stubby pencil, wrote down what I owed him, then turned the book around and showed me. I signed, grateful.

'No credit on alcohol,' he said, reading my mind. 'But I think you could do with a medicinal brandy. Just the one.'

He took a bottle from the shelf behind him, poured the spirit into a glass, a double. I tossed it down and felt it swim through my veins, soothing, pacifying. I could have drunk the bottle dry and welcomed the oblivion.

The maid came back with a sugar bowl in one hand and a plate piled high with blackened sausages, scrambled eggs flecked with char and what could have been mushrooms, cooked to exhaustion. I shovelled in the food, methodically working my way from left to right, not tasting it, just getting it in, ignoring the nausea as my stomach screamed refusal. As a soldier you learnt to eat when food was available, no matter what state you were in, because you had to keep going and were less likely to screw up if you were fed and thinking straight.

Then Harry Barker ran in, pale beneath the stubble on his cheeks, postie cap sitting awry on his head. A chunk of sausage caught in my throat. The drumbeat quickened.

'Leila, bar, now,' Watt shouted, draping his wiping cloth over his shoulder.

I pushed my empty plate to the side, gulped down the tea. 'Mr Barker?'

'Just got a wire from Bathurst.' He handed me an envelope and made me sign for it in a little book he carried. I tore it open and read, then looked up at Barker and Watt.

'Gibbet Hill did not call for assistance,' I said. 'They've had no trouble.'

One of the old blokes gave a short laugh. Watt took out two more glasses, splashed the brandy into them and handed one to Barker, then he refilled mine. We all drank and it was not yet eight in the morning. It was an ambush. Somebody had set it up in order to kill us. An icy hand

clutched my innards. There were no japies here. We weren't at war, or not that I was aware of.

'More troopers coming?' Watt asked.

I looked up at him, Barker and the old blokes, my heart pounding. 'On their way, but they won't arrive until dark.'

'Do you think the fire was deliberate? Set by these bastards?'

'Too soon to draw conclusions.'

'I'll have a beer, thanks, Sep,' Barker said, putting his brandy glass down with a sigh, 'seein' as I'm here. You do what you think is best, Sergeant. If you fought in South Africa, then you know what way is up with this sort of thing.'

'Ah, Boer War injury,' Watt said, nodding at my face.

I nodded as a wave of weariness washed over me. By the time I copped a bayonet in the face and chest, I was a twenty-one-year-old captain with sixty-odd soldiers to hand, a commanding officer to advise and direct, and a brace of junior officers and non-commissioned officers to help shoulder the load, and half the time nobody knew what was going on. We operated in the midst of major fuck-uppery, day after day, but we were in it together. Here, I knew nobody and had no idea who I could trust. I was like a man washed ashore on an island, half-mad and with only my warrant card and blood-soaked uniform to vouch for me. But I had to act as if I knew what the hell to do.

'I'm going to have a closer look at the remains of the police station.'

'Your tunic,' Watt said. 'Take it off.'

'Why?'

'It says you're in the traps, and somebody's shooting them today.'

Good advice. I took it off; it was stiff with blood.

'Leila,' Watt bawled, and the woman scuttled back in. 'Take the sergeant's tunic out the back, put it in the laundry.'

She took it, holding it at arm's length, and left. My white shirt was also soaked in drying blood and sticking to me, as were my breeches.

'Could do with a wash and brush, Sergeant,' Watt said with a cheerful smile.

But I didn't have time for that. I stepped outside, looked up and down the empty street. The men had dispersed. Smoke hung over the town. The main river road, High Street, ran east to west. West was the way to Gibbet Hill; east followed the river for several miles to the foothills and rugged cliffs of the ranges. Two more streets ran parallel, like the layout of a theatre, joined by a steep crossroad. The police station was on the furthest street back, next to a small white cottage and surrounded by paddocks. There had probably been more houses but they were gone now, their materials reused or burnt. I spotted other buildings dotted here and there on the low hills to the east: what looked like a brick schoolhouse and a couple of churches. I'd get to know them, but not today.

As I approached the police station, the stench of ash and burning wood filled the air. The timbers of the building had collapsed inwards, taking the iron bars of the lock-up with them, leaving a pile of unsalvageable debris.

Files, records, forms, all the saddlery and kit in the tack room, all of Scanlon's personal possessions, and mine too. A few broken teacups and plates, shattered by the heat and scorched, lay amid the acrid ruin. The whole thing had gone up so furiously it was hard not to suspect some sort of accelerant, kerosene or the like. Then again, when a fire gets its fangs into dry timber, it burns hard and fast.

I stank like a corpse, flies buzzing around me in delight. Waving them away, I poked about at the edges where I judged the lean-to that I'd slept in to be, vainly hoping to find my bag with a clean uniform inside it, unscathed. But it was all gone. The enamel jug and washbasin lay disfigured. Water pooled where men had thrown buckets of it. The station tank was charred and twisted. There was a water tank by the trough in the horse paddock but they'd probably emptied it. Put it on my list.

The acrid smell was underlaid by another scent, something familiar. A closer look revealed that the bars of the lock-up had fallen against some beams and rested on a pile of burnt, indistinguishable mess. I took a few steps and from a different vantage point saw what it was. I shut my eyes, took a deep breath. Someone had been in the lock-up. But we had no record of who it was.

I kept expecting to hear the crack of a rifle, all my senses straining to detect danger before it got to me first. I heard somebody come up behind me and jumped like a terrified cat. I reached for my pistol as I turned but came face to face with a grinning lad. I'd seen him earlier, crying at the shock of the fire. On closer look, it was clear he was a mongol kid. Ginger hair, red-faced, plump around the middle, carrying a toy of some sort.

'Hello,' I said, voice shaky. 'What's your name?'

'Percy.' He held up a battered wooden soldier, with a red jacket and blue pants. 'This is Tommy.'

Boys love soldiers. Matches too.

'Where do you live?' I asked.

He pointed across the road to a block with a couple of grazing sheep tethered by long ropes. Beyond them was the rear of a shabby two-storey

house, a corrugated-iron washhouse, a long washing line and some white chickens wandering about pecking and scratching.

'That's my house.'

'Is that the back of the dry goods store?'

He nodded, and together we walked down. He nipped in the back door. I paused and looked back south to the police block and the smoking ruin. The second-storey windows would have had a perfect view of it.

The store on the main street had the usual sort of window display, canned goods set up in carefully constructed pyramids, bags of dry goods arranged around them, some notices in the windows. When I walked in a bell was tripped and a woman came out from the back. It was the woman I'd noticed earlier, wearing mourning. Thin shoulders, black hair sprinkled with grey, dark eyes surrounded by a matrix of lines, a long, sharp nose, jutting cheekbones and not even the shadow of a smile. Just a combative stare, daring me to buy a boiled humbug or a packet of salt.

'Percy, where have you been?' she said.

'We met out the back,' I said. 'I'm Sergeant Hawkins, the new—'

'I'm Mrs Lennox.' She picked up a dirty cloth and began to wipe the counter, faster and faster, round and round, unable to stop. Percy's face crumpled, as if her distress was going to engulf him.

'Poor Davy,' she said, suddenly closing her eyes, her hand stilled.

'He's dead,' Percy said, his eyes wide and guileless beneath ginger eyebrows. 'Will we put him in the ground?'

Mrs Lennox looked up, watching me carefully, crouched like a lioness, those sharp cheekbones ready to strike.

'We will find him,' I said. 'And send him home to his parents and they'll bury him.'

'Bury him,' Percy repeated.

'Now, do you wish to buy something?' Mrs Lennox said. 'Some new breeches maybe? Or do you like the slaughterman look?'

A pert comment.

'I have no money, at present.'

'I don't give credit.'

'Mr Watt has generously extended credit to me, given the circumstances.'

'He did, did he? Yes, well, the Commercial isn't his business. But as you're a trap ...' She ran an expert eye up and down me. 'Percy, find the sergeant a pair of the tall canvas trousers and a large shirt.'

Percy grinned and scuttled off. Mrs Lennox rummaged behind the counter and produced a woollen spencer with long sleeves and matching long johns, some boxer shorts and thick socks. Percy returned with the trouser and shirt; I tossed in a buckskin jacket, a notebook and pencil, matches and a ball of twine. I had some vague idea that if I caught the gunman, I could tie his hands with the twine. Mrs Lennox wrapped it all up and made me sign the ledger.

'First day on the job, eh?' Mrs Lennox said, a trace of sympathy in her voice. 'Shocking thing to happen, just shocking.'

She handed me the parcel, then came out from behind the counter and walked me to the door and out into the dusty, deserted street. The day was still and the terrible sound of a female crying and wailing floated across the street, through the smoke, from a large house beside the hotel.

'Poor Hilde,' Mrs Lennox murmured. 'It's too much for her, too much for all of us.'

'Who is Hilde?'

'She was married to the publican's son, William Fitzgerald. He drowned a couple of years ago, and now poor Davy ... They were so close, the three of them.'

The unseen girl's distress was too much, and memories of Flora wailing and screaming, her grief like a savage beast, rushed at me. Mrs Lennox patted my shoulder and disappeared inside her shop. The touch of her hand made me want to weep.

Clutching my package close, I scurried across the road into the Commercial and organised a room on credit. I dumped my goods on the bed, then ran a bath in the large, shared bathroom. I stared at myself in the mirror, the steam from the hot water lending my reflection an unnerving ghostliness. My hair and heavy beard, usually the colour of a parched wheatfield, were dark with matted blood. The bayonet scar ran across my face, from hairline to jaw, although it was beginning to fade to white and was partially hidden by my heavy beard. Still, it was a confronting sight at the best of times, and this was far from the best.

I tore off my bloodied shirt and saw my chest, the frenzied mass of scar tissue from midline to underarm. I ran my fingers over the gristly welts and thought of that day, the shouts of the medics, then the hushed voices, *No, you're not dying, mate*, and the gauze bandage slapped on my face so they wouldn't have to see the light leave my eyes as I died.

I soaped and scrubbed, submerging myself and sloshing water onto the tiled floor, scouring my skin over and over until I was raw. Then I emptied the tub, refilled it and lay there smoking, watching the steam rise and the drip from the tap send ripples across the surface of the water. I tried not to think but it was no good: my mind would not be fooled. It was ramped up, ready to fight, and startled at every slammed door, every shout.

It was a blessed relief to be clean and smell clean. I bundled up all my bloodied clothes and padded down the stairs, boots in hand. The laundry was in a brick building by the river, out the back of the hotel. Half a dozen clotheslines were draped with various linen items, men's drawers, tablecloths and the like. Inside the small building I found a bench and set my clothes down beside a heap of grated soap flakes. Two huge coppers sat over their fireplaces, both full of water but still and cold. I found a cloth, wiped my boots, put them on and got out of there.

4

To the west, thin white wisps of cloud streaked across the blue sky. It was a dry autumn and there was no rain in those clouds. The main street was deserted, smoke hanging in the air, stray dogs having a scrap.

Back at the post office I found Harry Barker hunched over the telegram machine. He looked up at me in alarm.

'At ease,' I said. 'No telephone calls. But do you have a rifle I can borrow?'

He nodded, disappeared and came back with a Lee–Enfield .303. 'What are you gunna do with it?'

'Just precautionary,' I said, checking it was loaded.

'Listen, Sergeant,' he said, giving me an earnest look. 'I was wrong to ask about retrieving Scanlon's body. If he's dead, he's dead and he don't care anymore. You don't want to end up like him.'

Didn't I? I couldn't answer that question.

'I heard gunshot this morning, before dawn,' I said. 'Who'd be out shooting?'

Barker shrugged. 'There's foxes and wild pigs around here, always somebody shooting them.'

'A licensed hunter?'

'Dunno, mate, you'd have to ask ... well ...'

'The local police?'

'Yeah.'

I took the rifle and set off, walking west along the road Scanlon and I had taken, and arrived at the crossroads. My heart was thumping blood through me, but one bullet and out it would spurt. I could scarcely breathe. I scanned the treeless hills for signs of the shooter. I was out in the open with no idea what the hell I was doing, and that's the way you die.

If I went out to retrieve Scanlon's body, there was a good chance I'd be killed too. It was an old and trusted way of taking out the enemy. Kill his comrade and wait for him to come for the body, then bam, bullet in the head, two for the price of one.

A sudden noise off to the right saw my mind give way like an old bridge that had one too many carts go over it, and I dropped to the ground. Nothing happened. An axe falling on wood. The rasp of my panicked breath. I got back to my feet, shaky. I couldn't go after Scanlon's body – at least, not on my own.

I made my way back up to the large block on the low hill where the police station had been. Up in the south-east corner was a small grove of Monterey pine. Nothing grew under these trees but there was a soft bed of pine needles. I found the best tree to lean against, one where I had sight lines everywhere except behind me, where there was a small, whitewashed timber cottage with a goat paddock at the back. The resinous scent reminded me of walking to school past pines on a hot summer's day as a child.

Hidden in the trees' shadows, I closed my eyes and saw Scanlon as his head jerked to the right and his blood spurted to the left. I opened my

eyes quickly and watched the smoke rise from the ruined police station as despair settled over me like sticky grey ash.

~

There were no reinforcements by dusk, but there should have been. It was an eight-hour ride from Bathurst but they had been alerted before seven. I suppose they had to run around in circles for the requisite two hours, then get everything in triplicate, shine their brass buttons and sort out the formation – but an officer had been murdered, in uniform and on duty, the station was a heap of ash, and as far as I knew there was no greater emergency on the fucking agenda.

I waited at the stone marker at the crossroads. The road south back to Bathurst intersected the western river road to Gibbet Hill and ran across a narrow low timber bridge and north up to Ilford. I kicked stones around as I scanned the darkening hills, waiting for the Zulu hordes to sweep down, banging their shields and chanting insults, or for a dozen japie fanatics to slither through the long grass and take me out with a shot to the head. Or maybe a spear in the chest from some hidden Wiradjuri warrior. You hear the spear a second before it hits, so I've been told. A second to panic or say a quick prayer, and then you've got six foot of sapling piercing your lungs.

Tired of kicking stones, I picked one up and hurled it at the fence across the road. The sky was now a dark blue, the stars out and the shadows holding a ghostly menace I had to face alone with just a stone in my hand. If I'd been back in the Bourke Police District there would have been a bloody horde of troopers riding in from all points, looking for a fight because one of our

own was down. They did things differently in the Western Police District.

I hurled another stone, heard a satisfying thud as it hit the fence. Then I heard the sound of horses and riders coming down the hill at a pace.

They emerged from around the hill, five troopers, weapons holstered, bridles jingling. They rode right past me, not even a greeting, just five grim faces. One was an inspector, the others just juniors, and I did not recognise any of them. They came to a halt outside the Commercial, dismounted and tethered their horses, their breath misting in the cold, smoky air. A couple of oil lanterns hung from the pub verandah, casting a golden light on the horses and the dirty road. I walked down and introduced myself.

The inspector looked me up and down: the wild hair, the miner's shirt and that damn scar. Then he grunted, a short nod.

'Inspector Ian Northrup, Bathurst. You signed on yesterday, I understand. Where's your uniform?'

'In the Commercial's laundry. All spares and everything I had went up in flames.'

'Trooper Scanlon has been shot, so I was told,' he said. 'Is he with the doctor? Have you apprehended the shooter?'

So much for telephones. If it wasn't written down, the messages were scrambled into gibberish.

'Trooper Scanlon was killed by a single shot to the head early this morning in an ambush,' I said as steadily as I was able. 'He fell on his horse, which ran off with the body. My horse was killed by a single shot to the neck. While this was taking place, the police station burnt down with the loss of everything in it. I have not searched for Scanlon's body as I have no backup, sir.'

Silence as he took it all in, the blood draining from his face. The four troopers lined up behind him showed a range of expressions, from shock to astonishment to fear. All good, healthy reactions.

Northrup was compact, smooth-shaven, neat uniform, medium build. He looked more like a prosperous accountant than a mounted trooper. But then again, I was used to the traps from the Bourke division, who were a dustier, more dishevelled lot. The four juniors were also all neat and polished, their horses clipped and groomed, coats gleaming in the lamplight.

Some of the town's men came out of the pub and stood about. Some women came out of their homes, kids pushing in front of them to get a look at the troopers. It wasn't a big town and everyone knew what had happened.

'Back to your homes, please,' Northrup said to the townsfolk. 'We are here to ensure your safety. We will hold a town meeting tomorrow.'

There were mumbled questions and slurs at our expense as they dispersed. To be expected. Nobody liked the traps, but they squealed like piglets if we weren't there when they wanted us. In these parts, gold towns, they called us the demons – that was the traditional level of animosity.

Northrup turned to me to speak, but at that moment we heard a lone horse approaching from the west. It was too dark to see, but the horse was trotting towards us.

'Arms to the present,' Northrup ordered, and four rifles swung up and aimed at what was probably some poor bloke hurrying home after a back-breaking day. But all of us were keyed up.

The horse entered the circle of light outside the hotel, coming through the smoke like a survivor from battle. Northrup swore softly and ordered

the troopers to lower their weapons. The body of a man in the uniform of a mounted trooper was draped over the saddle, head and arms dangling over one side, legs sticking out the other.

It was Scanlon's horse – I recognised his three white socks. I approached him slowly and he let me take his bridle. I noted the rifle holster was empty.

'Get him off,' ordered Northrup.

I held the horse steady while a couple of troopers went around to pull Scanlon off by the arms.

'Bloody hell,' one of them cried, jumping back as if he'd seen a snake.

Northrup and I looked to where the trooper was pointing. Scanlon's arms were dangling but his hands were gone. The six of us stared in horrified silence, transfixed by the sight of what wasn't there.

5

Septimus Watt, the barkeep with the stooped back, came out of the pub, fag in the corner of his mouth, and saw the body of Scanlon draped across the horse. 'Ah, you found him.'

'Is Bill Pomeroy still the town doctor?' Northrup asked.

'Yes, still here,' Watt said, scratching his balding head. 'Four doors down, but you won't get much sense out of him at night. You can put Scanlon in our cellar until morning. Won't be the first body we've had down there.'

Two troopers were put on watch, and the other two pulled Scanlon's body off the horse and carried him in through the pub's side entrance, grunting and puffing, poor Scanlon's handless arms dangling, blood spotting the weathered floorboards. Watt opened a large trapdoor, lit a lamp and hung it on a hook above the rough wooden steps leading down into the musty gloom. The cellar was long and damp, with seepage from the river on the walls, which were lined with old railway sleepers. It smelt of hops, mould and earth.

Rumbles from the bar upstairs echoed down the stairs. Scanlon was laid on the floor alongside beer barrels. Watt clumped off up the stairs and

the four of us gazed down at the body. His face was mottled and almost white, but his bare feet were livid where the blood had settled. He was muddied and his uniform was torn about, consistent with being dragged by a horse.

I looked up at Northrup, who was almost as white-faced as poor Scanlon, blinking rapidly as he tried to take in the implications of a murdered and mutilated trooper. Not a common occurrence, or not these days. Colley was situated in what was known as the settled areas – as opposed to the unsettled wastelands of the west. But for my money, the more people, the more unsettled a place could be.

Watt stomped back down the stairs, a yellowing sheet in hand.

'Hang on, let's just inspect the body,' I said, as he prepared to throw the sheet over it.

The two troopers exchanged looks, as if I were a ghoul. Even Northrup blanched at my suggestion. Mounted troopers were a simple lot: forms and force were our stock in trade. In rural areas, we were outposts of government as well as keepers of the peace. We had our duties and liked to stick firmly to them. But having been in a one-man station for three years, I knew we had to venture out of that safe little corner when there was no one else.

'There could be some evidence on him,' I said, and Northrup reluctantly agreed.

Scanlon's pistol was missing from his holster, a fact I recorded in my notebook along with the absence of the rifle. His notebook was also missing, which meant our chances of discovering the identity of the body in the lock-up just diminished. His warrant card was gone too.

Then I examined the stumps of Scanlon's arms. 'His hands have been

sliced off with a very sharp blade,' I said, gesturing at the white of the bone glowing in the light. Watt, his eyes bright with interest, leant over to get a better look.

I checked the outside pockets of Scanlon's tunic and felt something odd, like the body of a hairless mouse. I took it out and held it up to the lamplight.

'Fucking hell,' I yelled, dropping it like I'd just grasped a burning coal.

'Jesus, it's his cock,' a trooper cried. The other trooper promptly heaved his guts up onto the beaten-earth floor.

'You'll have to clean that up,' Watt snapped.

'Holy mother of God,' Northrup murmured, his face now drained of all colour. 'Who would do such a monstrous ...' He turned away, hand at his face.

'Steady now, gents,' Watt said, kneeling beside the corpse and undoing the flies on the breeches. He took a look, then got to his feet nodding. 'It's his todger all right.'

'Put the ...' Northrup said. 'Put it ... in there.'

'The undertaker's gunna stick it on again?' a trooper said, horror in his eyes.

I wasn't going to pick up a dead man's cock, and I didn't think I'd ever forget the feel of it. Nobody wanted to touch it. Finally Northrup took out his handkerchief, picked up the orphaned organ and stuffed the pathetic bundle into Scanlon's breeches.

'A man has a right to be buried intact,' he murmured.

The troopers watched, no doubt thinking about their own equipment and how much they wanted to keep it. I know I was.

'An axe on the hands but I reckon he used a knife on the todger,' Watt said, cool as the dank cellar. 'Can't take a man's dick off with an axe, now, can yer?'

'Thank you, Mr Watt,' I said, glancing at the two junior troopers. 'You can go now. And not a word to anyone about this.'

'Yes,' Northrup said. 'It is vital we keep this secret and confidential, Troopers.'

'Yes, sir.'

'Mr Watt?'

'You have me word,' he said. 'When you're ready, gents, you can have a drop of brandy, on the house.'

'Not you two,' I muttered to the troopers, and we slowly moved to follow Watt up the stairs. As I turned down the lantern, I looked back, Scanlon's shroud visible in the gloom. He was my junior officer, and as such had been my responsibility, and I wanted to promise him justice. Or something. But I was losing the struggle to hold back the puke, such was the stench in the cellar, so I hurried up the stairs, leaving Scanlon's shade to the underworld.

~

Northrup and I downed a medicinal brandy in silence. A dozen men behind us were on the scoot, playing billiards, smoking, talking softly among themselves.

'You'll have to put in claim forms for your possessions and the destroyed uniforms,' Northrup said. 'Some kit should arrive with MacKerras in the morning.'

'I'd like to request a transfer, sir.'

'What? Now?'

'Yes, sir.'

Watt poured two more shots of brandy and they went down easily. Northrup shook his head as he replaced his glass on the bar.

'No. Since Sergeant Barrett passed on, we've been at half-strength in this district. And with Scanlon gone we're still at half-strength. There are four other stations under your command, and I need you here to supervise them. We've only got one more trooper and he has to stay in Bathurst. There's fourteen foot police and one detective to service Bathurst, but only the detective will come out at this stage. He'll be with MacKerras probably. All troopers in Capertee, Gibbet Hill, Hargreaves and Rylstone are all under orders to stay put and keep their wits about them. They report to you. So you simply cannot bail out.'

I knew I could bail out, by resigning. I wasn't expecting a bloody ambush, and I didn't want to deal with this aftermath, not while my hand shook and only brandy loosened the clenched fist in my stomach. Justice for Scanlon could be another man's mission.

'With the police quarters gone, where are you bedding down, Hawkins?' Northrup asked, as if the matter of my transfer was settled.

'Here, for now.'

'I know the station quarters are gone, but we can't have you spending the King's coin on hotel rooms,' he said with a frown. 'We have tents with us – pitch them near the station. They should do you.'

'Not tonight, sir. I am not sleeping outside while a gunman with mounted troopers in his sights is out there. And if you're up for that, then I strongly advise you have two men on watch, changed at three-hourly intervals. Sir.'

He gaped at me. But what of it? It was what I would have done if I were camping out tonight, and I'd have been negligent not to suggest it, rank be damned.

'It's not a coincidence that Scanlon's horse came back just after you arrived, sir,' I added. 'They probably mutilated him and slung him over the horse, and they've been waiting for the reinforcements they knew would come before sending the horse back. Sending us a message.'

His surprise changed to unease. As it should have. Unless he wanted to wake up to a paddock full of dead troopers, he'd do well to take my advice.

'Another drink, gents?' Watt said, appearing in front of us. 'On the house, given the circumstances.' He splashed the brandy into our glasses and Northrup tossed his back without a moment's hesitation.

'On close inspection of the lock-up of the destroyed police station,' I said, dropping my voice and leaning towards Northrup, 'I found the remains of a body, burnt beyond recognition. Scanlon must have locked him up, but the records have gone up in smoke and Scanlon's notebook is missing. Could be connected to the shootings. Until we know more, I'd be very careful out there.'

Northrup stared at me for a moment, then nodded. He'd come out here thinking he'd find a wounded trooper and a kitchen fire, but what we had on our hands was very nasty indeed.

'Keep that to yourself for now,' he said, almost inaudible.

He left to organise his men and I went up to my room with its narrow bed and mouldy wall. Then I came downstairs and had another double brandy, then another, until the world was blurred and softened and I could pass out into blessed oblivion.

~

I thrashed about in the narrow bed, seeing Scanlon's blood bursting forth from his head. I'd put my hopes in the brandy but it was not earning its keep. When I opened my eyes, there was the grimy wall of the hotel room. Closed them, the blood spurts. Open my eyes, grimy wall.

I got up, wrapped myself in a blanket, pushed the rickety French door open, stepped onto the balcony and lit a fag. From here I could see across the roof of the general store to the wreck of the police station. A waning moon rode high above the dark hills, the paddock beside the station dotted with sleeping goats, their white coats glowing in the moonlight. Over to the west, beyond the pale dirt crossroad and further into the darkness, lay the river road soaked in blood.

The bitter cold air nipped at my ears and cheeks, and for the hundredth time today I wondered what the hell I was doing here. It had been a rash and reckless decision to come back to the traps after resigning only six months ago. My own stupid fault, and contrary to all sane and well-meaning advice. *But bail out now, Gus, and you will look even more unstable than you already do.*

I flicked my cigarette over the balcony and put myself back to bed, but lay staring at the ceiling, the day refusing to let me go. My mind raced back to that dirt road, soaked in blood, my horse screaming, a more God-awful sound you cannot imagine. He fell to his knees, artery pumping his life onto the dirt, and Scanlon's head jerked to the right, blood spurted to the left.

I lit a candle and lay on my side, watching the flame burn down, watching the flying ants circling. Next thing I knew, I was in darkness

and Septimus Watt was banging on the door and telling me to shut the hell up.

'Yes, I'm sorry,' I called, shamed yet again by the night terrors I could not shake. I had to get away from here. Nobody stayed on a battlefield after the slaughter.

6

I was up and dragging on clothes when I heard noises from the street. I stepped onto the cold floorboards of the verandah and looked down. In the gloom of dawn I recognised Superintendent MacKerras, who I'd met in Bathurst when I signed on only the day before yesterday. Looked like he'd ridden through the night to get here. He was standing with Harry Barker and Septimus Watt, nodding his head as they talked and gesticulated. He had two troopers with him, one a young black, probably a tracker. There was an undertaker's van, a closed wagon and some spare horses.

I had no water to wash in and I probably still reeked of brandy, but I raced down the stairs, still getting the buckskin jacket on when I came face to face with MacKerras and Watt by the hotel entrance. MacKerras's pockmarked face was like a gravel pit, his eyes like two grey stones. He was tall, grim and had the air of a man who'd been raised in a Scottish stone bothy.

'Where's Northrup?' MacKerras asked.

'They camped by the burnt-out station, sir.'

He turned to the young trooper with him and told him to fetch them down here quickly. 'And where's Scanlon?'

I led him to the cellar where Scanlon lay under the sheet. After twenty-four hours, the awful smell of bodily decay had begun, no matter that the cellar was cold. It mingled with the mould and dank in a way that made my gorge rise.

'Where's your uniform, Hawkins?'

'It was covered in blood, sir,' I said, looking up at him in surprise. Of all the matters we had to attend to, this was hardly top of the list.

'And your horse?'

'Dead on the Gibbet Hill Road, sir.'

'Why didn't you retrieve it?'

I gazed at him for a short moment, all sorts of insults lining up to be lobbed at him. 'I judged it unsafe with no troopers to provide cover.'

After an ambush, you can't stop and let everyone have a cry and a fag – you have to complete the mission. But you might just place a hand on a man's shoulder or give him a nod, let him know he's done well. Not this joker.

'And the police station?' he said.

'Burnt to the ground, sir, along with everything in it. The fire started while Scanlon and I were riding out to Gibbet Hill.'

I told him about Scanlon's penis. He looked incredulous for a second. I lifted the sheet and showed him Scanlon's handless stumps and his jaw tightened. I resolved to wait for the right moment to raise the issue of a transfer.

'Cover him,' he said, then he marched up the stairs and out into the street. I followed him and found Northrup rushing about in the pub hallway outside the dining room.

'Ah, Hawkins – no time for breakfast this morning. Does the Super know about the body in the station?'

'I haven't told him yet.'

'We're to assemble by the burnt-out station – now.'

~

Three tents flapped in the early-morning breeze. Pairs of white corellas fussed in the branches of the huge manna gum in the horse paddock. The goats in the adjoining paddock all raised their heads and stared. An old woman, a tiny thing in a long skirt, lugged a bucket of mash up from her cottage. Ignoring the assembled police force next door, slopped the mash down and watched as her goats jostled and gobbled.

'Sergeant Hawkins,' MacKerras barked.

'Sir.'

'Remove the dead horse and dispose of it. The Gibbet Hill Road needs to be cleared for traffic – there's coach services waiting for the all-clear from us.'

'Sir.'

'Northrup, retrieve Scanlon's body. Dismissed.'

Northrup glanced at me and then gave the burnt-out police station a pointed look as he walked off.

'Sir, there's a body in there,' I said. 'Looks like he was in the lock-up.'

MacKerras looked up, blinked a few times. 'Where?'

I pointed out the body, unmistakeable now, given the rising smell. 'We have no record of the deceased's identity, sir.'

He stared for a long moment, probably cursing the shit pile that had landed on him. 'Get him out. All of you – this is police business and not to be discussed with anyone.'

'Yes, sir,' the troopers all snapped.

Mounted troopers were considered elite, and the possibility of demotion to the lowly foot police always hovered over their performance. But there was nothing elite about the three young troopers in front of me. They were typical young blokes: all muscle and high spirits, eat their own bodyweight in mutton pies and sleep the sleep of a puppy at day's end. Mind you, they were subdued in the presence of the Super.

I hadn't taken in their names yet, but I gathered the black tracker was Trooper Scott. He was a handsome young fella with hair slicked down and a magnificent cavalry moustache, and the stillness that, in my experience, most Aboriginal men possessed. Not fidgeters or leaners. Getting the measure of these men would take time, and frankly I didn't want to do it. But I had to, at least until I could persuade Northrup to let me go. I sent them down to the Commercial to ask Septimus Watt where we'd find a man with a hoist and dray.

This left me alone with MacKerras, who'd produced a map from his pocket and was scowling at it. He ignored me. I waited, looking past him to the police horse paddock on the slope. We had to get a new stable up quickly, it occurred to me, as winter was on the way.

'Hawkins, I understand you recklessly used a telephone to convey crucial and confidential police intelligence,' MacKerras said sharply. 'We in the Central West do not use a party line to mewl for help. Every scoundrel west of the Dividing Range now knows that discipline has broken. You will not bend the rules and regulations to fit your idea of how things should be run.'

I was not expecting this, given the crisis we faced.

'Yes, sir,' I managed to say. 'At this point I must inform you of my

unwillingness to proceed with this posting. Given the nature of the incident, I would like to put in for a transfer.'

The goats snorted in amused disbelief. A breeze swirled through the wreckage, sending ash our way.

MacKerras's jaw muscle tightened and the hard eyes narrowed a fraction. 'Request denied. You will find your uniform and put it on, whatever state it may be in. You will use Scanlon's horse and be ready to retrieve your dead horse in ten minutes. Dismissed.'

Using the telephone had been a mistake. I hadn't thought through the implications – I was too ... there wasn't even a word for how I was. I wasn't even sure where I was, South Africa or my last posting out west. Was it some bastard japie commando shooting at us, burning our buildings as we had burned theirs?

In that blur of terror, I had not reacted as I once would have, calmly assessing the situation, making sound decisions, issuing orders. I wasn't that young soldier anymore. I was thirty-two, young for a sergeant but too old, as I saw it, for this crisis, or any crisis. I was one of those most pitiful of creatures: a man out of his depth.

~

In the laundry behind the hotel, I found a teary girl wiping her face on her apron, catching her breath, still ragged with sobs.

'Augustus Hawkins,' I said, coughing and trying to keep myself together. 'New sergeant in town.'

'Oh, I'm sorry – Mrs Hilde Fitzgerald,' she said.

The girl who'd been wailing yesterday. She was very young and thin,

all elbows and collarbones, her thick golden hair tied up and pinned in a plait across her head, much like I'd seen on some of the Afrikaner women. Her pale face was blotchy from tears, and she had a small red prayerbook clutched in one hand.

'I need my uniform, Mrs Fitzgerald.'

She scurried around retrieving the shirt, breeches and tunic, all still damp, stained and smelling of rotting flesh.

'I can't put the breeches in the copper, Sergeant – they'll shrink – and the tunic too.'

'Not to worry,' I panted. I rushed out and upstairs to change, then thumped down the stairs and ran into Northrup in the hallway. A whiff of burning mutton chops from the hotel kitchens floated past.

'Sir, request permission to retrieve Scanlon's body and complete the paperwork,' I said.

'But you're going to get the horse off the road, aren't you?' he said, frowning. 'No, I want you there because you know where the gunman was positioned.'

'Yes, sir. But it's not essential for you or MacKerras to see it.'

'That's not for you to say, Hawkins,' he said, eyes hardening.

'A rocky outcrop, one hundred and fifty yards up from the bloodstains, sir.'

'All right,' he nodded. 'I want to see it for myself. You do the bodies.'

I couldn't face going out there only twenty-four hours later, and thank God he didn't ask why.

~

Getting Scanlon into the van was easy. Getting the body from the ruins of the police station was not. The corpse came apart as the troopers lifted it, then one trooper threw up and the other let fly a string of curses that echoed around the valley. The undertaker gave me a disapproving sideways look, but he was used to corpses. When the body was finally in the van, I sent the troopers off to steady themselves with a fortifying fag and ordered them eat breakfast, whether they wanted it or not, then followed them down to the pub.

In the dining room, a plate was thumped down in front of me: fried eggs swimming in grease and with brown rills around the edges where they'd been given the old thermal treatment by some heavy-handed cook. I manfully sawed through them, washing them down with cups of stewed tea, bitter and bracing.

As I finished up, an old man entered the dining room. He stopped on the threshold and stared at me as if I were the bad fairy at the christening. He looked to be in his seventies, with a large nose like a toucan's beak. He cocked his head and stared down the length of this appendage at me, his jaw tightening and eyes narrowing, hands moving to his skinny hips. No weapon, just that stance, legs apart, and a look that said, 'Who the fuck are you?' It brought on both indigestion and weariness in me.

'Look what the cat dragged in,' he said in a high-pitched, nasally voice. 'And all dressed up like a trap, for the love of Christ.'

'Pleased to meet you, Mr ...?'

'Fitzgerald. Mr Len Fitzgerald, owner of this establishment, and it is not a pleasure to meet you – again, may I add.'

'Maybe you haven't been appraised of the situation vis-a-vis the killing of—'

'Don't you vis-a-vis me, mate. I've had you here before and I'm still paying off the damage. And here you are, all tricked up like a fucken' Christmas bauble in yer brass buttons, eatin' my eggs like a cat with the cream. Well, I won't have it. I'll tell MacKerras, I won't bloody have it.'

He turned to leave, then swung back, waving his finger like a sabre. 'There's no forgettin' a man with your face. Pack your bags and bugger off!'

He stomped off down the hall. I pushed my plate away, lit a fag and tried to recall my last visit to Colley.

Not long after coming back from South Africa on a hospital ship in 1905, I'd turned my back on my father and gone off to drink myself to death. I swung between fury and melancholy for several years, drinking and generally living the life of a returned soldier: bedding every girl who'd let me, fighting every man who looked sideways at me and being run out of towns. Colley was one of them.

Now that Mr Fitzgerald had refreshed my memory, I did recall a bit of a smack-up in the front bar. Broken glass everywhere, glittering in the lamplight, some prick with rotten teeth, smashing chairs over each other, the usual melee. The details of my misdeeds in Colley would be recorded in the station log, which was probably stashed in a dungeon under the Bathurst head station. But I was sure Len Fitzgerald would enjoy letting MacKerras know all about it.

After breakfast, I nipped down to the post office.

'Morning,' Harry Barker said, looking at me over his spectacles. 'I'm not to let you near the telephone – Superintendent MacKerras's orders. I did tell you.'

'I need to send a telegram.'

He nodded at the forms on the bench. I filled one in with a brief

message to my father that I was alive and in good nick. If MacKerras was right, Scanlon's killing and the fire would be in all the papers, but they would not identify the troopers by name. My father knew where I was stationed, and over the years I'd put him through more than enough paternal worry. He had not wanted me to go back to the traps; if I'd been killed on my first day back, he'd have said, *I warned you, Augustus*, as my coffin was lowered into the ground.

~

There were meetings all day – MacKerras, Northrup, talking, speculating, going in circles while I said little, all my efforts being spent on holding myself together. In the late afternoon I walked up to the wreckage of the station. The two tabby cats from the stables were sitting in the long grass, enjoying the afternoon sun.

During the worst of the rabbit plague – which we were still living through, and would be living through for centuries to come – some bright spark came up with the idea of releasing hundreds of cats into the bush, as they would catch the rabbits. Seemed like a good idea at the time. And yet in all the years I'd spent in the bush, not once had I seen a cat take a rabbit. A cat had no need to kill a rabbit when there were so many other smaller tasty creatures around. But this was what humans did. It was what I did. Have a good idea, act on it and then, after a few drinks and a lie-down, wake up to the consequences. That I was back in the traps only illustrated my point.

I ran my eye over the ruins. Was it arson or accident? And if it was arson, how could we know? Even the leatherheads in the city found

it hard to determine, unless the place was awash with kerosene. They rescued people, contained the fire and tidied up – that was it, job done. A warehouse by the Darling Harbour docks went up in flames not so long ago, and word was it was German or Japanese spies. Then a cooler head said it must have been copra, dried coconut flesh, which was notorious for self-combustion; the warehouse had been full of it. But there was no copra in the Colley police station.

The sound of kids playing filled the air as Colley's two schools let their charges go free for the rest of the day. A small Catholic school up on the hill to the west, and a small public school closer to town. The racket of harmless play took on an edge, and I looked down the road to the east and saw a small bunch of boys throwing things. I strolled down to see what they were up to.

'*Catholic dogs jump like frogs, in and out of the water,*' chanted three ruffians in their short pants and scabby knees, hurling rocks.

Two other boys cowered by a bush, too young or too scared to throw back.

'Oi' I shouted. 'There'll be none of that.'

The five of them looked up and saw me. That should have been an end to it, but no, one little devil picked up a rock and glared at me defiantly.

'You throw that, son, and you'll be in a world of trouble.'

'But they're Catholics,' he said, as if he were explaining the obvious to the dim-witted.

'Off you go,' I said to the alleged Catholic boys, who poked their tongues out at their attackers and ran.

'Names?' I said, getting out my notebook.

The three of them scuffed their worn shoes in the dust, heads hanging,

furtive glances at each other. 'Sergeant Barrett let us do it.'

'I am Sergeant Hawkins, and I won't let you do it.'

'They do it to us.'

'Names. Now.'

They murmured their names, but the ringleader, one Frank Simmons, said his with a wisp of a sneer. He'd be one to watch.

'If I catch you at it again, your fathers will be hearing from me. Now get out of here.'

They galloped away, leaving a trail of dust. I went back to the burnt-out station and stood, legs apart, arms folded, frowning at where the body had been found. No records had survived, but if he'd been drunk and disorderly and Scanlon had to remove him from the pub, then there would have been witnesses. Or somebody would have come forward to tell us their mate or son or husband was missing, last seen at the bottom of a bottle.

~

The river road had been cleared of my dead horse. A trooper told me wild pigs had been at the carcass, and as the dray hoisted it up the guts fell out and onto the bloodstained road. As he told me this, the lad's face was a pale green. Just a youngster, no more than nineteen. Mopping up after a crime is never an easy job.

There was a town meeting that night, where fear crackled through the room like an electric storm on its way. MacKerras charmed the local population and introduced me. When the meeting broke up, we were suddenly surrounded by men wanting details, wanting to raise suspicion about their mate, or their mate's mate, or a work colleague they hated. Even

the Catholic priest was accused of having an unsteady temper and a liking for big fires.

The town took on the look of an army camp, with rows of tents pitched on the police land alongside the burnt-out station, small campfires where the troopers gathered to talk, troopers on watch at both ends of the town. Horses everywhere, being walked or rubbed down. Since old Mr Fitzgerald had turfed me out, it was a tent for me, shared with Northrup. He was a reasonable man, a little distracted, and not as experienced at the gritty side of the job as he could have been.

I was familiar with canvas tents and bedrolls but never enjoyed them, and ours was barely more than a bivouac tent so we were shoulder to shoulder. We hung a lantern from a pole while we sorted our kit out and climbed into the bedrolls. It was freezing cold on the ground. I asked what he and MacKerras had done that day.

'Haggling with Len Fitzgerald, owner of the Commercial. A temporary station is going to be set up in one of their rooms. Troopers stay in the bunkhouse, Detective Kennedy – he's the Bathurst station detective, very good, very thorough – in your old room. There's the necessary furniture on the way, all the forms and so on.'

'And Scanlon's murder?'

'Kennedy is in charge of that,' he said, smoothing his bedroll. 'Ever been in an ambush like this before? I've read the Boer were underhanded like that.'

'Yes, they were, and the British didn't play fair either. But Scanlon and I were not in a war; we were just doing our job in a country town. We had absolutely no idea what was coming.'

'We'll catch them.'

'You think?'

'Oh, yes. Maybe not immediately, but we will. And there is nothing to be gained by taking a soft approach. We carry a big stick and we use it. These gold towns can be unsettled.'

'I thought the mining days were over.'

'There are two gold dredges on the river, mostly downstream to the west. The dredging crews are a rough mob, and there are still lone prospectors here and there. They've no stake in these towns so they muck up and it can get nasty.'

'I suspect the killer is cleverer than your average digger or labourer.'

'Let's hope Kennedy will crack it quickly.'

'And the police station here?'

'They're sending a clean-up gang and surveyors – important we do that quickly. Don't worry, nobody wants this to fail or we'll all be feeling the bullet in the head every time we ride out.'

This was the moment to explain to him that he was bunking in with a man who screamed in his sleep, but I just couldn't bring myself to speak.

'MacKerras reckons the mutilation is sending us a message, that we're impotent,' Northrup went on.

'Impotent?' I looked over at his solemn face in the lamplight.

'He says this is a challenge to the mounted troopers. Cut off a trooper's hands and he can do nothing, cut off his private parts and he can generate nothing, burn down his station and he knows nothing.'

We lapsed into silence. I suspect he was measuring his ability to take on such a challenge. As was I.

~

55

Colley was nestled in a river valley amid steep hills and cliffs on the western side of the Great Dividing Range. It had been built on the southern bank of the Bull River, which started in the mountains and joined the Macquarie River just south of Gibbet Hill. It was higher, wetter and hillier than the plains to the west, but not as wild and craggy as the mountains to the east. The land was suited to dairy, wool, mutton and beef cattle. Too wet for cropping, but good for orchards and market gardens.

It was a tricky district to police, so I was told, there being some rugged bushland. At about a hundred miles square, there were long distances to cover between its stations, and I had four of them to supervise: two to the west and two to the east. And then there was an eight-hour ride to the head station at Bathurst. No nearby railways, no paddle-steamers, just horse, coach or ox teams to get produce to the rail hubs in Bathurst. And there were stock routes down to the slaughter yards. The high transport costs meant this was not a wealthy area. If it hadn't been for gold, the town would not exist.

I was aching from a night on the cold ground, and in low spirits. Northrup had woken me several times to tell me to shut the hell up. I briefly explained my malady, but he didn't care – he wanted to sleep. So I lay there, willing myself to stay awake until dawn, feeling the uneven ground beneath me like a cheap mattress, only harder. There was no place for me, it seemed, not even the traps.

It was a relief to get away from Northrup in the morning. I went down to the pub, had a wash and joined the troopers in the pub dining room, where my plate was piled high with greasy sausage and eggs. I was a taciturn bastard in the mornings, but the maid, Leila, who was at the

buffet filling up dishes with more sausage, had a joke for every one of the troopers. She went quiet when a well-dressed man entered.

'The boss?' I asked.

She nodded. Ray Fitzgerald, nephew of the Commercial's owner, old Len of the toucan nose, looked to be in his forties, muscular and trim with a clipped grey moustache and clipped grey hair. I wondered about his look of prosperity. What did a well-dressed man do for a quid out here? He and his uncle wouldn't be making much from the hotel – although having a pack of troopers eating and sleeping and working under their roof for the foreseeable future would be a nice little earner. MacKerras got up and approached him. Looked like they knew each other. They shook hands and disappeared.

~

Our temporary police office was to be set up in a large room with two windows facing the Fitzgerald house next door. The room was sandwiched between the front office of the hotel and the bunkroom where the troopers were sleeping. It opened onto the hallway with the trapdoor leading down into the cellar and the staircase up to the accommodation. We could make it work, but we'd have to have a secure rifle chest as an armoury. What we were going to do with anyone we arrested was beyond me. Make them stand in the naughty corner with their face to the wall?

The back door at the end of the hall opened outwards – a clever bit of carpentry – to a path leading to the outside bathroom, which was a bit grim but would do. There were a couple of outhouses, the laundry block, a woodshed and then about ten feet of grass, which appeared to be an

unfenced access strip running the length of the town riverside.

Young Mrs Fitzgerald was sweeping the floor of the empty office room. She looked up as I entered and gave me a piercingly sweet smile, then continued to sweep.

'My condolences, Mrs Fitzgerald,' I said. 'Mrs Lennox told me of your friendship with Davy Scanlon.'

My attempt at sympathy caused her to break down in tears. 'First Will, now Davy, and I've been left behind,' she said, her voice breaking.

I remembered Flora saying much the same thing when her brother and two sisters were murdered. There was nothing I could do to fix it for her. Now this girl, with her golden plait like a crown and the tears glistening on her eyelashes, made me feel equally useless, or worse. Having caused her pain, I could offer no comfort.

Then Mr Fitzgerald the younger appeared. 'Go to the kitchen, Hilde. Don't let the guests see you carrying on,' he snapped.

Head bowed, handkerchief at her face, she hurried out.

'Sergeant Hawkins?' he said, shaking my hand. 'Ray Fitzgerald. I apologise for my daughter-in-law, and indeed for my uncle's rudeness earlier.'

Fitzgerald's face was lightly tanned and his movements brisk and efficient. Firm handshake, tight smile.

'Thank you, Mr Fitzgerald. I understand my troopers will be in your bunkhouse?'

'Yes, very cosy, and they can take their meals in the dining room. There's a bathroom outside they can wash up in – but take care, as the back door opens outward. The front door by my office will be your entrance; this side door to the bar will be locked at all times.'

'We should be out of your hair in a month or so.'

He smiled. 'Not much experience of builders, eh?'

'No, not really.'

'Ex-army?'

'Yes, New South Wales Mounted Rifles, Boer War.'

'We're honoured to have you in Colley, Sergeant Hawkins. I served in South Africa too; I'll tell you about it one day.'

Something to look forward to. He studiously avoided the subject of a room for me. Obviously, neither MacKerras nor Northrup had gone in to bat for me with Fitzgerald senior, or arranged a billet.

Thanks, chaps, very decent of you.

The closed wagon that accompanied MacKerras yesterday contained boxes of forms, binders, paper, handcuffs and so on. I grabbed a requisition form, sat in the empty dining room and made a list of everything I wanted, including a large tent with a wooden floor, an officer's tent I could stand up in, a camp bed, a small table and chair, a washbasin and jug, and various other sundries. I reviewed the list, rounded up a few numbers and signed the requisition form with a firm flourish, dotted it with vigour. *Stick that in your bleedin' pigeonhole.*

~

The shooter's position, Northrup told me, the rocky outcrop with a view of the road, was on Fitzgerald land, and he wanted to see it. That meant we had to escort him and I had to return to that terrible moment.

Two troopers by the names of Vogel and O'Malley were close at hand. I grabbed them, and we waited out the front for Northrup and

Ray Fitzgerald. Vogel, a thin, lanky fella with wingnut ears, and O'Malley, muscular, mouthy and a little disorganised, were busy arguing in hushed voices. It seemed to be getting heated: when I turned around, I saw O'Malley push Vogel. I gave them my *don't-fuck-with-me* look, which all sergeants had to master. These two troopers were not a good combination, their animosity so thick you could punch it. As soon as my back was turned, they were at it again.

When we were all mounted, I turned my horse and rode closer to them. 'You stop the bickering or you'll both be returned to Bathurst with a mark on your record,' I snapped. 'Are we clear?'

'It's him,' Vogel said, jerking his chin at O'Malley.

'It's him, *sir*,' I said. 'I throw the ball, you catch it.'

They weren't finished with each other so they had to be separated. Truth was I couldn't send them to Bathurst because we had no replacements. Two bloody idiots, a spooked horse and no bloody room at the inn.

ΩWe proceeded down the western road. I rode out the front with O'Malley, both of us with rifles out, scouring the hill, the road, the river, while at the back I'd put Vogel, and in between Northrup and Fitzgerald. We were all tense and jumpy. As we neared the spot where it happened, the bloodstained road a stark reminder, Tosser, Scanlon's old horse, began to dance and carry on, as you'd well expect. I felt it too, the surging terror, the sweat and nausea, and maybe he picked it up from me. Both of us were on high alert, ready to make a run for it.

We passed several creeks in gullies to our left, overgrown with blackberries and surrounded by stones and debris, as if the whole landscape had been turned over again and again as men dug for what they called 'the colour'. Soon we came to a road off to the left, which led us to a

farmhouse and an array of sheds and pens, nestled in a low valley. Men emerged from these buildings, some to stare and one who walked over as we dismounted. Fitzgerald shook his hand and introduced him as Mr Bluey Rankin, overseer.

Rankin was a thin, wiry man wearing moleskins and a sheepskin coat, his white hair buffeted by the wind, face like weathered timber. 'Aye, Cemetery Hill, no use for grazing,' he said when Northrup told him we wanted to examine the location of the shooter.

'What's the best way to get access?' Fitzgerald asked. 'I haven't walked these paddocks in a while and the land between here and there is covered in mullock.'

'Aye,' Rankin said. 'No walking it, blackberry all through gullies. And pig up yon creeks, no walking it.' He took out a tobacco pouch and expertly rolled a fag in silence, stuck it in his mouth, lit it, then spat out a shred of tobacco. Fitzgerald looked disconcerted.

'Blackberry,' Rankin repeated, like an oracle gazing into the mysteries of the universe.

'What about it?' Northrup said.

'Birds eat berries, shit seeds out. Pig likes a nice blackberry.'

'A bit dangerous, then, to walk the gullies because of the wild pigs?' I tried.

Rankin nodded.

'We'll go back and up the road to the cemetery, access it from there,' Fitzgerald said.

Rankin nodded again and took a deep drag of his fag. As he exhaled, he said, 'Boars kill a man if he looks t'other way.'

We stared at him for a moment.

'Right, well, carry on,' Fitzgerald said at last.

We rode back to the crossroads and then proceeded up the Colley Road, which wound around the hill up onto the plateau and continued to Bathurst. At the top of the hill was a dirt road on our right, and we followed that to a flat area. On the left was the town cemetery, shaded with manna gums thick with kookaburras bunched up together and magpies swooping around, and on our right was the fence surrounding the area we wanted to see.

I left O'Malley and Vogel with the horses and a warning, while Fitzgerald, Northrup and I jumped the fence and tramped down the hill to the rocky outcrop. Fitzgerald stared around at his land, as if seeing it for the first time. A brace of kookaburras let loose a round of maniacal laughter.

At the rocky outcrop, we looked down on the road, to where the stain of my horse's blood was still visible. We gazed about, squinting into the sun, vaguely hoping insights into the crime would come.

'If this is the best way in,' Northrup said, 'then maybe that indicates the shooter had local knowledge.'

'He picked his ambush position with care,' I admitted, 'but he could have come from anywhere, sir.'

Northrup nodded. He really wasn't cut out for this.

'It's a bit late but I think Trooper Scott needs to have a good look at this hill and the ways in and out,' I said.

'The black tracker?' Fitzgerald said.

'Yes,' Northrup said. 'Best thing to do in these situations.'

As if he'd know. Northrup was a townie, an officer who could run a ceremonial parade of troopers and relish it – all stray hairs in place

on both men and horses, everything shiny, hoofs, buttons and boots – but aid a murder investigation? No. It wasn't a mounted trooper area of expertise because it called for patience, subtlety and – as Detective Arty Baines, who I worked with on the Kirkbride case, said to me – an ability to think horizontally. We traps liked to think in a forward-moving line, not straying into the scrubby thickets of the unknown. Hunt down the offender, hold him captive, offload him to the more cerebral types, then go back to smacking the drunk and disorderly around and keeping ourselves looking nice.

'I don't want blacks nosing about my land,' Fitzgerald said.

'Of course, but we do have to do it, and it's better to have your permission,' I said.

Fitzgerald reluctantly agreed.

On the way back to town, Northrup and I were riding two abreast, and as the horses clopped along and the sunlight sparkled on the river, I asked him about my predecessor, Sergeant Barrett.

Northrup stretched his back, sitting as if he had an injury, then said, 'James Buckland Barrett, sergeant at Colley for thirty years and a good, solid officer was Old Buck. Didn't like itinerants, blacks, Chinese, Irish or Catholics, but he applied the law fair and square.'

I glanced across at Northrup to see if he was having me on, but he wasn't.

'Buck ran all the travelling prostitutes out of town, along with the fortune tellers, travelling theatricals and tent preachers. If a man needed entertainment after a day's work, he said, he wasn't working hard enough. A drink at the local is all any bloke needs – that and a copy of *The Bulletin*, read cover to cover. Kept this town quiet, which is what we like.'

'Managed his juniors without complaint?'

'Mostly. Why?'

'The bullet that Scanlon took could have been meant for Barrett.'

Northrup gave me a hard look, like I'd brought this calamity on the town. 'Could have been meant for you, Hawkins.'

7

MacKerras and Northrup returned to Bathurst in the afternoon, leaving me with five troopers and an assurance that Pat Kennedy, the detective, was on his way. Not long after they left, more carts arrived from Bathurst, with all the new furnishings for the police office, and a fresh uniform for me. I binned my old stinking uniform. Forcing me to wear the blood-soaked rags was obviously MacKerras's way of boosting morale and endearing himself to those under his command. It was a relief to see the back of him.

We crammed two large desks into the back corners of the room, then came filing cabinets and shelves, pinboards and a chest of drawers, with its back facing the entrance door, which would serve as our counter. This would be where the incident book was kept and where our customers filled in their forms.

Along the wall beside the door were placed several chairs for people to wait, and between the two windows there was enough space to hang a lithographic portrait of King George V, looking splendid in uniform with gold epaulets and sash, badges and stars, his moustache waxed and virile, so all-comers could see by whose authority we gave them a good thrashing.

As we arranged ourselves, the charming Len Fitzgerald walked back and forth in front of the door, peering in, scowling. Finally, I had a moment to sit and write a coherent report of the events of Friday. Then I heard his nasally voice addressing me.

'Did you get permission to put a picture up there?' he said, cocking his great beak to the side. He wore a checked shirt tucked into baggy trousers pulled up way above his waist and held there with suspenders and force of will.

'Mr Fitzgerald, how nice of you to stop by,' I said, putting my pen down and blotting the paper. 'As I understand it, we have been given permission to arrange our room as we see fit, with any damage to be paid for when we leave.'

'That's a supporting wall,' he said, jabbing his finger at His Majesty. 'Should have asked first. You'll have to take it down and put the nail in a post beam.'

'I'll see to it,' I said, not moving. 'Thank you.'

'You'd better,' he said with a frown. 'This is my pub – my father built it and I own it, every inch of it.' He glared for a moment, waiting for a bit of lip, but I gave him none so he moved on.

I resumed the task before me, the words unwilling to be written, the times refusing to be recalled. There'd be an inquiry and I had to get my account written down before I forgot crucial details. But the words on the paper became blood spatters. Scanlon's head jerked to the right, blood spurted to the left.

A thump and gust of laughter interrupted my thoughts. The police room shared a wall with the bunkroom where the troopers were to sleep. I could hear them now, horsing around: laughter, the odd crash and groan,

more laughter. I'd been in boarding school and lived in barracks, so I knew exactly what they were doing. Animal spirits let loose, jumping each other, wrestling, testing their strength, their reaction times, their friendships, while having a laugh. But it sounded like it was getting out of hand.

Mindful of old Len, I presented myself at the door of the bunkroom to find Trooper Lawlor on his back on the floor, Trooper O'Malley about to leap from the top bunk and Trooper Jackson somewhere in the middle. Trooper Vogel was reading. O'Malley landed with a thump and they all scrambled to attention, panting, their hair and uniforms askew.

At that moment, Hilde Fitzgerald walked along the hall past the doorway, her golden head bowed, eyes lowered, and to a man the troopers craned to get a glimpse of her. Their heads were so drawn by an invisible string that they forgot that their sergeant, me, was standing in the room preparing to bark at them.

I moved around and blocked their view. 'Keep it down. We are guests here, and you do not want to camp out for however many months we'll be here.'

'Months?'

'Could be. Could be a day and a half. Our job is to complete the mission, and until that's done, we stay.'

'You served in the Boer War, didn't you, sir?' Lawlor asked. Lawlor was a fair, ruddy-faced lad with a habit of leaning against anything to hand. Horse, fence, wall, gate.

'I did, yes.'

'A captain, they said, sir?' Jackson added. He looked like a gypsy, all five o'clock shadow and sleek black hair. He liked to chew – a straw, a matchstick, whatever passed near his mouth, he'd snap it in and champ away.

'I was, yes.'

They waited. I was being prodded for the whole 'war is glory, lads' spiel, but it actually isn't.

'Soldiering is a job, like this one.'

An underwhelming statement if ever there was one. Thousand-mile horse treks across the veldt in blistering heat; ambushes along the way with scheming japie commandoes; horses dropping dead beneath us; army biscuit for dinner, if we were lucky; lice feasting on our exhausted bodies nightly; losing comrades to typhus almost daily; whisky as rough as a pig's breakfast; and witnessing human actions so horrific, so at odds with the dreams and ideals of youth, that my mind still stared in shocked disbelief all these years later.

I heard noises outside in the hall and looked around the doorway. Three men in suits had arrived, two of them lugging typewriters. The man with free hands had to be Pat Kennedy, the detective. I excused myself and went to greet him.

Kennedy was in a grey suit, at the back of his head a homburg, which he removed and put on the nearest hatstand as casually as if he'd walked in his own front door. Medium height, in his fifties, thickened around the middle but still muscular, hooded eyes, a fag in the corner of his mouth, salt and pepper hair swept back, a relaxed air but a crusher of a handshake.

'Sergeant Hawkins,' he said as he broke my fingers. 'I've heard about you. Did well sorting the Kirkwood murders out west. Nasty business, eh?'

'Yes, sir.'

'Now you've got another nice little murder on your hands. You seem to attract them like flies, eh?'

'Sir.'

'Don't you worry, son, we'll sort it out in no time,' he said, and he slapped me on the back so hard I tried not to stagger. 'Let's wet the whistle, eh?'

'The door to the bar is permanently locked as our office is just there,' I said, pointing. 'Have to go out into the street and in through the western entrance.'

'Bloody awful coach trip,' he said, as we made our way outside and back in.

'It's a long journey.'

We settled at the bar and he bought the first shout, a couple of beers. He downed his in a single swallow.

'My word but that's better,' he sighed, wiping the froth from his lip.

Septimus Watt observed us from a distance. I bought the next shout and Kennedy lit up a fag. We drank. I can put the grog away, but keeping up with this bloke was going to be a challenge.

'You worked with Arty Baines and John Denning on the Kirkbride case, I heard,' he said. 'Arty Baines, now he's a rising man. But Denning, he's on the wrong side of the grass now, and headed down, not up.'

'Dead? How? Choke on his own bile?'

Kennedy laughed, ashed his fag. 'The way I heard it was he told his men he was nipping up to the hospital to see a sick friend, but he was actually paying a visit to Madame Jeanette, over in Crown Street, whereupon his exertions caused him to expire, as it were.'

'Died on the job, eh?'

'Yeah, lucky bastard. That's the way to go. Smothered by her massive jugs, probably.'

'You're acquainted with Madame Jeanette's chest?'

69

'She does a special price for the detective branch, mate, one of the perks. I'm a married man, but I've heard of Netty's legendary knockers. I was doing my training and us mugs from the bush couldn't believe the life these city cops led – free drinks, a bit of horizontal refreshment, you name it. All hush-hush, mind.'

I took a sip of my beer, feeling like a wide-eyed naif. How little I knew about the world, despite my world-weariness.

'Been stationed in Bathurst a long time?' I asked.

He nodded as he ordered another round. 'Senior sergeant on the beat, then I did the detective training in Sydney about ten years ago. They'd just opened the Fingerprint Section then, and all our training was based on Scotland Yard methods – even had some of their blokes visit once. But yeah, we don't get the sort of crimes they get in London. We mostly worked on horse theft and armed robbery.'

'And in Bathurst?'

'Ooh,' he sighed, ashing his fag again. 'Manslaughter at closing time, wife bashing, the usual. Just blokes coming unglued. Nothing clever or premeditated.'

'Any thoughts on Scanlon's murderer?'

'Cop killer.'

'Not personal, then? I mean, he's taking out the uniform, not the man?'

'Ezackerly.'

'The mutilation after death?'

He glanced at me, bushy eyebrows bunched in a frown. 'That's not normal.'

'What does your Scotland Yard say about that sort of thing?'

'That it's not normal,' he laughed. 'Killing a cop isn't normal neither.

70

He's gotta be a fucken' mongrel or a lunatic, and I've seen a few lunatics in my time. Blokes who think they've been given the green flag by the Almighty to slice and dice. But we'll find him, find the evidence, hand him over to the courts, justice done.'

Ray Fitzgerald appeared, shoulders squared. He walked over and slapped Kennedy on the back. 'Good to see you, Pat,' he said.

'You too, mate. How's the canning business, eh?'

'Not up and running yet, but you'll be the first to know when it is.'

'Yeah, my missus reckons opening a can of stew for dinner will suit her.'

Fitzgerald bought us yet another round, then looked at me and said, 'Old Killer Kennedy, he'll have Scanlon's murderer locked up before you know it.'

'Killer Kennedy? Alarming nickname for a copper.'

Kennedy laughed. 'Don't shit your daks, mate. I only kill targets, bull's eye, right in the centre.'

'We're both in the Bathurst Rifle Club,' Fitzgerald said. 'Kennedy's our champion marksman. He received a trophy from Lord Kitchener himself in 1910.'

'When he was here to open the Boer War Memorial,' Kennedy said. 'What a day that was. Thousands of people. He gave a full inspection of all the Boer War veterans and there was a parade, the police and mounted troopers, the rifle club, the militia regiments. So much brass it hurt your eyes. You must have heard about his visit to Australia?'

'I was out west then, and not reading the papers. Is your rifle club part of the militia?'

The two men looked at each other.

'The new army blokes,' Kennedy said, 'they wanted us in, but that

would mean shooting under service conditions, not for money prizes, which is how we shoot. They wanted full control, and yeah, we have some top marksmen, and if they were needed in defence they'd lend a hand, but we keep to our rules.'

'Are you a sporting shooter, Sergeant?' Fitzgerald asked. 'We have a wild pig problem in this area and constantly need to cull.'

'I'm usually too busy for such activities.'

'You must have done a fair bit out in the Western District. I heard they hold some magnificent kangaroo shoots.'

'No, no, I left the sport to others.'

'We'll take you shooting,' Kennedy said. 'It's good practice, keep your aim up, get some tips from the experts.'

Patronising pricks. I didn't need a couple of greying chocos teaching me how to shoot. Yes, they could shoot a bull's eye on a still, sunny day, but could they do it on two hours' sleep, with their guts cramping from dysentery and a brace of murderous japies swarming on both flanks and closing in fast?

These rifle clubs had once been supported by the government as being crucial to Australian defence interests. There had been a rifle club in every town at Federation – after all, the Germans were on our doorstep in the Bismarck Archipelago and we had to be ready. But if I were a betting man, I'd have put my money on the Huns.

~

Before heading for my tent, I went to the bathroom out the back of the hotel and saw that Trooper Scott was sitting on the grass outside his tent.

72

As a black, he was not allowed in the hotel – not to sleep, to eat or to drink, even in uniform.

'Can't sleep, Scott?'

'Just looking at the stars, sir.'

'Oh. Find anything important up at the cemetery?'

'I did, sir – or at least I think it could be important. The one track that I thought was curious leads from outside the cemetery, where we tethered our horses, but this horse, instead of going back the way it came in, his tracks lead west, down into the mullock heaps and blackberry.'

'Excellent work – show me tomorrow.'

'Thank you, sir. Might not be the killer but I reckon that if you want to take a horse to the west, you're not going to do it over stony mullock, where they gunna slip. It's not a short cut because you'd have to get off and walk 'em through, sir. I reckon he could have been hiding the horse there.'

'We'll look at it tomorrow. Good night.'

I left him looking at the stars, and they were worth looking at tonight– a glorious band of brilliance. On Earth, the acrid smell of the burnt-out station hung in the night air. A fox ran across my path, stopped and stared at me, his green eyeshine unearthly, then walked into the shadows.

My tent was visible in the darkness, a small bivouac tent under the pines. I crawled in and lay there thinking about what a feeble barrier a sheet of canvas was. If the killer was out there, he could shoot me, set fire to the tent, anything. There was nobody on watch and Bathurst didn't give a shit about a half-mad officer whom they didn't really want. If I died tonight and my cock was parted from my body, it'd be hushed up. At least then Bathurst would really know they had something dreadful on their hands.

8

I woke at dawn, hips aching from the hard ground, muscles tight and a grey mood blowing in. The pain in my shoulder like someone was pushing it through a band saw, turning it and pushing it through again. Wincing and groaning, I rolled onto my back, reluctant to get up and start the day.

My first job was to build some trust between me and my new horse, which had been Scanlon's horse– the ominously named Tosser. I'd checked him over, but just to be sure I took him to the blacksmith, who examined his hoofs and legs.

'Any chance you know his real name?' I asked.

'Davy used to call him worse, but "bloody tosser" was the standard – said with affection, mind. I got him in me records as the Duke of Marlborough, but that's for billing the cops. Now, I never had no problem with him, but he can, when the mood takes him, be a bit of a humourist, likes to pull hats off heads and so on. Davy and Toss were a team, bit like me and the wife. We like to bicker but don't much like being apart.'

'I'll stick with Toss, then.'

'Yeah, I would. He's had a terrible fright too, ain't yer, Toss, old lad,' he

said, stroking the horse's neck. 'Lost his master, lost his stable, probably near lost his wits with fear, so be kind to him, Sergeant.'

'No worries, he's safe with me.'

I took him for a walk up the eastern river road, walking beside his head, chatting away, telling him all about my home and my horse, Felix, who now lived with my father and spent his time gorging on the rich pasture of the Monaro. Toss's ears flicked back and forth, showing an interest in descriptions of rich green grass. But it was me and my voice he had to get used to.

The farmhouses were few and far between along here, and soon the treeless paddocks were replaced by great mullock piles of stones, huge and rolling, like a small mountain range. Just bare grey stones piled everywhere, left by the prospectors.

High, rugged cliffs loomed over the other side of the river, rocks jutting and eucalypts clinging on in places too hard for a timber cutter to get to. In the first light they looked dark and forbidding. They appeared to run east into even more rugged country. The river ran between these cliffs and the shoals and beaches of river stones on the side close to the road.

Toss suddenly startled and pulled away. My nerves sent a burst of fear hurtling through my veins. Gunshot any moment. Then a brown dog appeared, coming up the road on our left, intent on his journey and scarcely looking at us. We kept walking, me taking deep, soothing breaths, but still rattled. The dog ran ahead, then stopped and waited. When we got closer, he ran ahead again, then stopped and waited, looking back to check that we were coming. He looked to be a mix of kelpie and possibly labrador – young, sleek, bright-eyed – and he'd been fixed, which meant somebody cared about him.

The river, on our left, was losing its yellow look, although there were an awful lot of pebble shoals up this way and I suspected the dredges had been through, digging up the riverbed, sifting through it and dumping the sieved waste on the side of the river. We kept walking, and soon the filthy river eased into clearer waters with more life around.

We rounded a bend and saw an extraordinary sight. The dog saw it too and barked. A man, possibly Dr Pomeroy – we were too far away to tell for sure – was sitting in front of an easel, working on a sketch or painting, beside a wall of bullrushes. He appeared to be sitting in the middle of a shoal of skull crowns, the hairless bone crammed beside yet another smooth grey bone, glowing in the strange dawn light. An army buried standing, only the tops of their heads visible. I faltered for a moment, and then the sun emerged from behind a cloud and the skulls became large, rounded river stones. The man behind the easel turned and waved. The dog ran over to him.

I had to coax myself to step onto the river stones, and I crunched and slipped as I made my way, leading Toss. Pomeroy was a slight man, maybe around sixty. From a weathered face under a knitted cap a couple of clear grey eyes peered out. He was rugged up for the dawn air, a vacuum flask sitting in a basket beside him.

'Good morning, Sergeant,' he said, putting down his paintbrush and reaching out to shake my hand.

'Dr Pomeroy,' I said, aware of the shakiness of my voice. 'This your dog?'

'No, he just appeared last week. I'd say he's run off and can't find his way back to wherever he's come from.'

I let Toss go and he wandered down to the river's edge with the dog.

They sniffed each other and the water and waded around.

'I apologise for my poor behaviour when we met. I was—'

'You were in shock,' he said, eyeing me kindly. 'No offence taken. I've had patients curse me black and blue over the years, and they're all sheepish about it a day later.'

I didn't like the word 'shock', which was too close to 'weak' for my taste. It was galling to admit it, but he was right. I looked at Dr Pomeroy's painting. It was a watercolour of the river, the rugged cliff reflected in the still water, and very competent it was too.

'A good likeness.'

'Yes, hmm, but I'm wanting more than a likeness,' he said.

'What more is there?'

'A feeling. A place has feelings, you know,' he said.

'Left by the people who were there or have been there?'

'Mm, yes. This is a well-known swimming hole,' he said, nodding. 'See that rope hanging off the gum down there? Kids love to play about here in the summer if we've had good rain.'

'Would you mind if I watched for a bit?'

'Not at all,' he said.

I rolled an old driftwood log over, perched on it, lit a fag and stared at the river stones, hoping they'd continue to be river stones. Dr Pomeroy gazed at the sky then dabbed at his paint, gazed back at the picture, back at the sky and in a quick, streaking motion painted in the wispy streaks of cloud above us.

'You aiming for a happy feeling?' I asked.

'What do you feel when you look at the painting?'

'Accuracy.'

'You feel accurate?' he laughed.

I felt a wistful sadness, actually, as if the swimming hole had once been a place of joy but never would again. I grew up beside the Molonglo River and my mates and I had a waterhole, a place with a rope where we'd swing out over the water, bellowing and then dropping into the depths below. We spent hours at it, swimming back to the muddy bank to line up and do it again. Laughing, the water glittering on our sunburnt skin, the river water still cold from the snow melt. Back then a glorious future lay before me. I didn't know what it would be, but I was certain I'd feel as I did on those days, alive and full of energy.

'Dr Pomeroy, I know you can't betray a patient's confidence, but can you fill me in a little on Percy Lennox?'

'Percy's got a heart problem – a lot of kids like him do,' he said, dabbing at the painting. 'He won't make old bones. If Mrs Lennox had the money, she could probably get him an operation. No guarantees it would work, though.'

'Has he lit fires before?'

He turned and frowned at me. 'He's not a criminal, just unfortunate.'

'Sometimes unfortunate people do lash out at an unfair world.'

A look of disgust passed across his face as he turned back to his painting. But it was my job to ask these uncomfortable questions.

'May I ask you about Davy Scanlon? Did you know him well?'

He glanced at me, then returned to staring at his painting. 'I knew him well and I grieve for his passing. It's shocking – and we don't get many shocks like that around here.'

'Any notion of who would like to see him dead?'

He shook his head. 'No. He was good at his job, friendly and helpful,

78

and after old Buck dropped dead, Davy just took over. He would have made sergeant himself one day.'

'How did Barrett die?'

'Heart gave out. Fifty-six, he was, so he was getting on. Davy found him in the stable, face down. It was a hot summer and it got him.'

'He must have had some young troopers pass through the station in thirty years.'

'Most of them stayed a couple of years and were transferred out to other stations. Davy stayed the longest – three years, I think.'

I considered Pomeroy's observations. Sounded like the usual setup.

'Davy was looking forward to you coming,' he said.

'Me? Why?'

'He said you'd been an army officer and fought in the Boer War and were a bit of a hero. And we all followed those awful Kirkbride murders. Terrible business. Davy was over the moon when he heard you were going to be stationed here.'

'I'm not and never have been a hero, Dr Pomeroy. That's the papers making up stories. I did not catch those killers single-handed.'

'Well, Davy was young, and we don't get heroes out this way very often, made-up or otherwise. Except for Lord Kitchener – not here, but he came to Bathurst, can you believe it? A hero of the empire walking around Machattie Park.'

'He didn't burn any of the town's houses, then?'

He frowned and gave me a quizzical look. 'Why would he do that?'

'Just a little habit he picked up in South Africa,' I said, getting my watch out and checking the time. Pomeroy picked up his paintbrush.

'I'll take the dog back to town – somebody might come looking for

him,' I said. 'He'll get a bullet in him if he's on the loose for too long.'

'Good idea. If anyone asks me, I'll tell him to ask the traps. Oh, Sergeant, I suppose you know it's Empire Day next month?'

'I wasn't aware, no.'

'We usually do a big bonfire, firecrackers, speeches, cakes and flags, the whole thing – for the kiddies, of course. Sergeant Barrett was always on the committee. We need the local cop on the committee.'

I took a deep breath, exhaled and nodded. A committee and a bonfire. What an enjoyable prospect.

~

I walked Toss back, wondering how this day might have unfolded if there'd been no ambush. Scanlon would be showing me the beats and the books, where to eat, where to get clothes washed, introducing me to the townsfolk, and we'd have a beer and a few laughs. Or I wouldn't be laughing because I'd sensed he was bloody useless.

In the two brief moments we'd encountered one another – when I arrived in the dark, and when we set out in the morning – Scanlon had struck me as a likeable fellow, at ease with people, unlike me. I was told he was a diligent and reliable officer. An orphan who'd been sent from St Annes, in Liverpool, to work in the police stables in Moore Park as a youngster, and who had worked his way up to mounted trooper. Then got killed because he was a mounted trooper. His inescapable fate, or some random evil run amok? Evil did a lot of that, hurtling down roads, setting fires and screeching with excitement. It was my job to corner the vicious little sucker. But I just didn't feel up to it after the ambush.

I'd expected to be working daily with one trooper and overseeing the other nine scattered around the district. Wrangling the five junior troopers was a challenge I'd rather not have faced, in my current state. All of them looking to me for direction and protection, while my nerves were fraying, my eye twitching and my thirst for strong drink so intense it took me by surprise.

I put Toss in the paddock and looked up at the corellas perched in the branches of the manna gum. They mated for life and liked to sit close to their partner, heads touching and in a state of perfect peace. Just the sight of them made me yearn for Flora – a sudden shaft of longing to smell her hair, rest my forehead against hers in a moment of tenderness. We two, together on a branch, the late dusting of pale gum blossom surrounding us.

~

Kennedy was in the dining room, making short work of a stack of mutton chops. I ran a practised eye over the breakfast offerings; everything was greasy and charred, even the porridge. I slopped some into a bowl, covered it with golden syrup and sat opposite Kennedy.

'Mornin', sunshine,' he said.

'Good morning. I want to take Trooper Scott back to the where the killer waited,' I said, startling as someone dropped a plate. 'He thinks he's found a track that could be of interest.'

Kennedy put down his knife and fork, dabbed at his greasy chin and said, 'Later. First we're going to take witness statements. Get a picture of that morning before people forget what they saw.' I was about to disagree

when he cut in. 'I have to ask you this, so don't get narky about it, but is there anyone you know who'd like to take you out?'

'No.'

'No angry husbands?'

'Nope. Kill me as a trap, yes; kill Gus Hawkins, no.'

He nodded, tore a hunk from his toasted damper, lavished it with butter. 'Do you know who knew you were coming and when?'

'Scanlon knew, and he knew about the Kirkwood murders and the part I played in catching the killers, according to Dr Pomeroy. Apparently he was keen on serving with me.'

'Bit of a coincidence, don't yer think? If the killer just wanted to kill Scanlon, he could have done that when Scanlon was in the station or riding about on his own. But he set this up, probably knowing he'd get two for one. So who was the target? You or Scanlon, or both of you? You might be his next target. Have you thought of that?'

I thought of it every moment I was out in the open, like a lamb crossing a paddock alone. I was on the killer's agenda and it was not a good feeling. Kennedy had a boiled egg in an eggcup, its smooth, pale surface like a river stone. He picked up a teaspoon and whacked the egg several times until the shell cracked.

'What about the fire?' he said, scalping the egg. 'You could have set that.'

'Me?' I felt my pulse rise, those shrewd eyes trying to see into my soul.

'Yeah, you. Got a name as a mad bastard.'

Grease pooled on the plate in front of me. I put my fork down, took a moment.

'Detective, I may be mad, but it's a private madness, and one that takes no joy whatsoever in fires. And if I am on this man's kill list, then I should put in for a transfer. In fact, I will put in for one.'

'Don't waste your time,' Kennedy said, 'because they won't give it to you. Not until we catch 'em. You have experience in this sort of thing and the dicks in Phillip Street have vouched for you. You're here, matey, and you'll stay until we're done.' He got up and slapped me on the shoulder. 'You could take a shit on MacKerras's desk and he wouldn't sack you.'

9

Trooper Scott was in the office, hands on hips, gazing at the map on the wall. He kept gazing as I walked in, then turned and said, 'Permission to speak, sir?'

'Yes, go ahead.'

'This creek here, Insolvency Creek, runs south from the western road and is the closest one to Cemetery Hill. Those hoof tracks I found, I reckon they lead down to the creek. Once he's in the creek, he can get to the road without being seen.'

I had a look. 'He'd have to go through all the mullock piles, then through yards of dense blackberries into a gully infested with wild pigs.'

We both stared at the map in silence. Kennedy came in behind us.

'We should go look up this creek,' I said, tapping the map.

'Yeah?' the detective remarked. 'In the notes Northrup gave me it says all creeks along there are infested with wild pig. Nobody in their right mind would go up there except a gang of experienced hunters.'

I could have sworn he and Fitzgerald saw themselves as expert riflemen.

'Anyway,' Kennedy said, looking around for a pencil, 'we gotta get statements before we do anything else.'

Outside the pub, a trace of the smoke still lingered in the morning air. Women swept porches and the troopers lined up in front of the hotel, squinting in the autumn sunlight. Vogel stood apart with his arms folded, O'Malley had egg stains down his tunic, Lawlor was holding up a post while cracking a joke, Jackson was holding up the other post while chewing a matchstick and Scott was fiddling with his fingernails. Add me and Killer Kennedy to the mix and you had a crack team looking for action and answers.

'Rightio, witness statements,' Kennedy said, hitching up his trousers. 'All got your notebooks? I want names, addresses, where they were between five and seven on the Friday morning, what they did the rest of the day and whether they saw anything out of the ordinary.'

The troopers were madly scribbling this down in their notebooks while Kennedy went on, barely giving them time to write. I noticed Percy staring at us through the shop window.

'I want to know how well they knew Scanlon,' Kennedy said. 'And if they know of anyone who had a grudge against the coppers. You'll work in pairs and Sergeant Hawkins will supervise. You've all done this sort of thing before, but are there any questions?'

Silence.

'Sergeant, you want to add anything?'

I did, because I'd been through this business before and knew the pitfalls.

'You may come up against a person, male or female, who's had dealings with us and resents having to answer questions,' I said. 'If you get a feeling they're resisting, or holding back, or being difficult, come and get me. Don't nag or push – we want to get maximum cooperation, and all their sympathies are with us right now, so we need to use that.'

Kennedy looked at me askance, as if I was asking the troopers to namby-pamby around when they could be smashing answers out of the recalcitrant with a pistol butt.

I sent Vogel and Lawlor to the western sector and O'Malley and Jackson to the eastern sector, while Scott and I took the main street. I suspected people of the town might not care for telling their business to a black tracker, despite him being in uniform, so he and I would work together.

The ostler at the coach turnaround and stables, a cheery man, rubbed his chin, folded his arms and looked thoughtful for a moment. Some people loved being questioned. Soon enough we were being treated to a detailed account of how his wife hogged the blankets.

Next was Harry Barker. In his office, at his desk. He looked up with alarm at the sight of Scott. 'You know I don't know anything,' he said. 'Why ask me again?'

'A formal statement is required. As one of the vital links in the police communications chain, you'd know the rules and procedures, right?'

'Yeah, of course,' he said, looking over his spectacles at me.

'As would Trooper Scanlon.'

'Yeah,' he replied, flicking another uneasy look at Scott.

'Scanlon received an order, so he said, to go to Gibbet Hill. It must have been on an official form, signed by you. But you say you never got the order, never transcribed or delivered it. I doubt Scanlon would have made the order up. So where did it come from?'

'How would I know?'

'Ever used others to deliver messages?'

'No, I have not. I'd lose me job.'

'He received that message from someone in this town, someone he trusted to be carrying messages from you, Mr Barker.'

'I don't know who that would be, and you're accusing me of doing something I would never do. And I wasn't even awake then – you ask the missus. We weren't up until we heard the church bells.'

Jackson and O'Malley appeared at the door, and we left Barker to his duties. I wasn't convinced but had to leave it. Maybe Kennedy could put the screws on him.

'Woman in that house there told us to sod off, sir,' O'Malley said. He took his cap off and rubbed his hair irritably, then jammed his cap back on. 'I told her this is an official investigation, but she just shut the door in our faces.'

'Which house?'

'That one, right next to the post office, with the vine on the gate.'

I took a note of it, told them to keep moving, and to take Scott with them and I'd deal with her alone. If the woman was already uncooperative, she'd be even less so if a black was with me.

A few minutes later I knocked on the door. A young woman with a grumpy infant attached to her side yanked it open and was about to flay me alive when her mouth fell open and her eyes widened.

'Gus? Oh my lord, it is. Gus Hawkins,' she said, her surprise turning to a smile, which quickly turned to anger. 'You've got a bloody hide, turning up here.' Another child galloped down the hall behind her and poked his head around his mother's skirts, saw me and ran off again. It was the little bugger from the stone-throwing episode, Frank Simmons.

'Mary, is it?'

'You don't even remember me, do you?'

'I do, I do, it's just the context,' I stammered, trying desperately to recall that week in Colley back in whenever it was. She adjusted the baby on her hip, who stared at me with a frank and fearless gaze, a rusk clutched in a small fist. I did a quick and panicky calculation. It was 1906 when Mary and I must have become acquainted, and it was now 1912. That kid looked to be eleven or twelve. Not mine.

'Is he your kid?' I asked about the boy.

'Frankie? I'm his stepmum, so you could say he's mine. Got no other mum. His father, and my husband, is Jack Simmons, but he's away from home right now. So if you've come to have a word about Frankie, I don't care to hear it.'

As she spoke, the memories returned. Mary Brennan, very young widow of the parish, glorious carroty curls, pearly skin in the candlelight and me passed out beside her, reeking of whisky and vomit. My God, what a charmer I was in those days.

'Pretty as ever, Mary.'

Mary smiled, 'Full of blarney as ever, Gus. And who would have thought a man like you, set to take on the world with his fists, would sign up for the traps, eh?'

'Only safe place for me.'

'Stationed here?'

'Yes.'

'Then I'd ask you to pretend you don't know me, and to never breathe a word of the past to my Jack or any of his mates. He works away as a water diviner and well digger, and gets awful jealous when he comes back.'

'I won't say a word, I promise. Can I ask where you were the morning the station went up?'

'Here – where do you think? I was busy getting Frankie ready for school and this one fed. I didn't even know poor old Davy had been killed.'

'Know him well?'

'No. He'd come around about Frankie now and then, but he knew to stay away. Most of the men around here know Jack don't like me talking to them. So off you go, and don't even nod to me in the street.'

She closed the door in my face, and I took out my notebook and jotted down what she'd said. Mary had been just eighteen when I met her, a widow for a year, and yet life coursed through her lovely blue veins. She looked a little thinner now, and the dark circles under her vivid green eyes could be attributed to the infant attached to her, but by God, she could still stir the loins.

Lawlor and Vogel reported resistance from a man in Mrs Lennox's shop who told them to fuck off.

'That's using offensive language against an officer of the law, sir,' Vogel said, all huffy. 'He can't do that – got no respect for authority.'

'Did you get a name?'

'No, sir, he just pushed past us,' Lawlor said. 'And he went out of his way to shove me aside.'

We went into the store and found Mrs Lennox behind the counter, arranging a wall display of jars of boiled sweets.

'What now?' she sighed, turning around.

'A customer of yours refused to speak to the troopers. Know him?'

'Mr Edmund Wallace, dairyman on the Topknot Road,' she said. 'I can't say I'm surprised, and it wasn't these two's fault, he just isn't a terribly pleasant man.'

I jotted this in my notebook while Lawlor and Vogel stood there, arms

dangling. About as useful as a pair of glass hammers.

'I thought of something I didn't tell them,' Mrs Lennox said, nodding at the troopers. 'My bedroom upstairs overlooks the empty block, and I can see the police station clearly, or I could. On Thursday night, late, I was woken by a man on Cullen Street shouting. I looked out and saw Scanlon manhandling him up the road towards the station. Probably went into the lock-up.'

'Anything distinctive about him?'

She shook her head. 'Just another drunk. I hope Scanlon let him out before the fire.'

I thanked her and we got away quickly before we could explore that topic further. Kennedy and Ray Fitzgerald were yarning in the hallway when we returned. Hilde Fitzgerald, her golden head bowed, long skirt rustling, walked past.

'Get us a cup of tea, love, will you?' Kennedy said. 'Couple of biscuits too.'

'I'll put this lot on your desk,' I said, holding up the notebooks the troopers had written in.

'Ta,' he said. 'Done the dredgers yet?'

'Now they're a rough mob,' Fitzgerald added. 'Brace yourselves on a Saturday night.'

'We'll go down there now.'

~

Vogel, Lawlor, Scott and I rode along the western road for several miles, all of us jumpy as cats, rifles out, scanning for the sharpshooter. The two

dredges in operation were in the deepest and filthiest part of the river at Ringer's Rocks. The sound of steam engines rattling and grunting, of metal clanking, rhythmic and regular, could be heard, growing in irritating intensity the closer we came. We rounded a bend and found, on the banks of the river, the remains of the earliest settlement in the gold rush times, which had had a school and cottages. Now it was just a jumble of dilapidated hovels, huts and debris, all muddy tracks, smouldering campfires and scurvy-ridden, listless old men.

Shoals of pale grey river stones lay on the edges of the river, smooth and unnerving. The dark yellow water lapped at them as the noise from the dredges echoed off the rugged cliff on the other side of the river. The racket was so deafening I had an urge to shoot one of the monsters just for a bit of peace. Each dredge looked like a small cottage on a barge. On the inside of each cottage was a great machine with buckets that scraped the riverbed, brought up the soil and gravel and any gold, which was then extracted using mercury, then the remaining gravel and mercury was dumped on the riverbanks. There were great mounds of it everywhere, which had to explain the colour of the water. These things went up and down the river, digging, sifting and dumping. The four of us stared at them as if their hunger for gold included men. Our horses were well and truly unhappy being near these dark satanic mills.

A soot-covered bloke emerged and pissed over the side, into the river. I waved at him, he waved back and went inside, and the din stopped. Then the other dredge, taking its cue, also stopped. The silence was startling.

A motley bunch of men who looked like piratical, grimy figures from an unspeakable hellhole – which in fact they were – emerged from both dredges, clambered into dinghies and rowed over. A marginally better-

dressed bloke sauntered over to me and introduced himself as the foreman in charge of both dredges.

'Sergeant,' he said, with an unfriendly nod. 'Replacement for old Buck, eh?'

'That's right. My men are going to take statements from your crew.'

'What for?' he said, and lit a fag.

'The murder of a mounted trooper on the Gibbet Hill Road on Friday morning.'

He took a drag on his cigarette and squinted back at the shoreline, where his men were lined up and talking, or not, to mine. 'Won't talk to no coon,' he said, nodding at Trooper Scott, who was standing alone. 'And we dunno nothing about it.'

'Had you met Trooper Scanlon?'

He nodded, his unshaven jowls and cheeks smeared with black grease.

'In town at the hotel?'

Another nod.

'See anyone around who looked suspicious?'

Shook his head. He was the sort of man who'd dance a jig at the news of the death of a demon. As for cooperating with us, well, that would be too close to admitting there was anyone at all who had authority over him.

Over by a row of shabby tents, an enormously fat woman sat on a log, taking the watery sunlight. She wore a dirty blue satin evening gown with puffy sleeves and a very low bodice out of which ballooned most of her substantial bosom. Her hair was not a colour normally seen in nature and she had a large fan open and flapping around at the flies.

'Morning, luvvy,' she said, as I walked over. 'Got a special on today for

the demons. Two for one, or one for two, however you like it. Girls, come on out and meet the gentlemen.'

'That won't be necessary, Mrs—'

'Madame La Foufoune,' she said, with an extravagant wink. Four girls clambered out of the tents. Two were Chinese, one looked like she was from some island in the Pacific – dark skin, hair like a puffball – and one was white. All of them were wearing torn and dirty petticoats and corsets. Their faces were masks of indifference, but when Mrs Foufoune clapped her hands, they smiled and swished their petticoats back and forth.

'It's disgusting,' I heard Vogel mutter. He'd obviously finished questioning the workers and thought it'd be a good idea to come over and breathe down my neck.

It was not only disgusting, it was also indescribably sad. I had been, in my ignorant, callous youth, a brothel customer, although not at this squalid level. But with the zeal of a reformed man I loathed these travelling outfits, with their steady supply of opium for the girls and money for the madam. But we weren't here to right this particular wrong today.

'Pack up and get out, Mrs Foufoune. If you're still here tomorrow, you'll be very sorry.'

'We're here because the men on the dredges want us here, luvvy, so you'll have to sort it with them,' she said with a hard look.

'Been in the business long?'

'Longer than you've been alive, luvvy.'

'It's not luvvy, it's Sergeant Hawkins of Colley Station. Leave this area today, or you will find yourself in deep trouble.'

She looked me up and down slowly, from boots to cap, and no doubt she saw the same randy, drooling beast inside me as she saw in every man:

pitiful, chained to our idiot cocks, which led us hither and yon, providing a never-ending supply of horniness for her to make money from.

'Come on, girls, time to pack up,' she said, having calculated the odds.

The dredging foreman, who'd been about to row back to his boat, came back over. 'You moving Kiki and the girls on, eh?'

'Kiki?'

'Madame Kiki La Foufoune,' he said with a leer. 'Foufoune's French for pussy – yer know that, Sergeant. She serves only the best foufoune too. Get a taste of it while yer can, eh?'

'She's not serving it on my beat.'

That earned me a sneer and his crew sniggered in support, and what a mucky lot they were. Barely one tooth between the lot of them and that was a blackened ruin begging to be pulled. The girls in the tents had to suffer their stench, their rough hands, their breath as fragrant as their greasy balls.

Old Foufoune whispered to the white girl, then said, 'Little Rosebud here reckons she knows something about the murder.'

Rosebud looked more like a daisy that had been trampled on by a carthorse, poor kid. I asked her what she knew.

'It'll cost you,' old Foufoune said.

'The police do not pay witnesses.'

'Let us stay, then.'

The dredgers watched closely, sensing their evening's entertainment at risk.

'Charge them, then close them down, sir,' the righteous Vogel hissed in my ear.

'What do you know?' I asked the girl.

She glanced at her boss, then said, 'I'd been with a customer in the town and—'

'When?'

'Thursday night. We had a bit to drink and when I woke up I dunno what time it was, but I had to get back or I'd be in trouble, so I walked back along the river road in the dark and I saw a man on a horse. On his way south up the Colley Road. It was real dark and I looked because I heard it and got frightened because I was on me own, but he didn't see me and was just riding up the hill. I ran all the way back.'

'Notice the colour of the horse, or what the man was wearing, anything like that?'

'Too dark – it was like a bit of moonlight and then gone.'

I scribbled all this down. Nobody carried a watch besides police and doctors, so there was no telling what time this was.

'Name of the client?'

'Now, Sergeant,' old Foufoune said. 'We pride ourselves on discretion. No names, you understand, as the gentlemen want to feel safe.'

'Whereabouts of his house?'

Foufoune shook her head. 'It was dark when we dropped her there.'

'Did you know Trooper Scanlon, Mrs Foufoune?'

'He wasn't a customer, if that's what you're asking. He'd pop in now and then, ask us to leave, that sort of thing.'

'I'm not asking, I'm ordering you. Move on or I'll come back and arrest you.'

The wily old bag folded her arms across her chest, a feat of flexibility that pushed her great knockers even higher, and smiled the sort of smile that said *the hell you will.*

As we walked back to our horses, I pulled Vogel to one side. 'Do not tell me what to do unless you want instant dismissal. I am your sergeant, and I tell you what to do.'

'Maybe you don't think what they're doing is wrong, sir, but it's a sin.'

'Maybe I think you are impertinent, Vogel,' I snapped, astonished. 'The state of their souls is not our concern. We apply the law as it stands. How long have you been a mounted trooper?'

'Seven months, sir.'

'Then you will know that backchat to a senior officer is not tolerated.'

'Yes, sir, but—'

'There is no "but" when you speak to me. Dismissed.'

We rejoined the others. No wonder O'Malley had a problem with him. Vogel stood apart, dancing to his own peculiar tune, and God knows what it sounded like. Sharing a bunkhouse with him was probably an ordeal – no doubt he gave unwanted commentary on the others' varying standards of cleanliness and lack of prayers before bedtime.

I was never all that fussed about following orders when stationed at Calpa. It was a one-man station, and I expanded to fill the command vacuum, ordering myself around wherever I saw fit. The Bourke Super lived in a state of dyspeptic fury because of me, but it was a hard posting to fill so I stayed. Now I was getting a taste of my own maddening medicine.

10

I rode out the front on the way back, irritated by what we'd just seen and by Vogel's insubordination. But the sight of the western river, so recently dredged, held no cheer either. The entire river valley and river bottom had been dug up in search of alluvial gold, overturned and dumped on the riverbanks over decades. I knew from school chemistry lessons that when you expose certain minerals to air, you start a chemical reaction that produces sulphuric acid. That had to be what was happening here with the yellow water.

Wave after wave of prospectors had come in and dug over everything in a frantic search, like a locust plague, taking everything and leaving a ravaged landscape and a dying river. The timber was all gone, except for some trees on private land, used to build cradles and hold up dugouts, then burned to make steam for the dredgers, whose bosses probably lived in Melbourne and spent their gold on the granite columns with gold inlay that propped up the nation. There was no local prosperity or even any level of security. The gold was gone, the party over, and the rich men could get on with being rich. Only the blackberries and wild pigs were doing well.

As we passed what appeared to be the last creek before Cemetery Hill, the mournfully named Insolvency Creek, I remembered Scott's hunch. We had to get up there somehow.

~

Back in town, I'd come off the boil. I pulled Vogel aside again. 'If you have something to tell me, I will hear it,' I said. 'Just pick your moment and respect the rank.'

'Why didn't we arrest her? She's breaking the law, sir.'

'She is,' I said, with all the patience I could lay hold of. 'But our job is to complete our mission, which is the investigation into Scanlon's murder. We don't have the time or resources to arrest and process them, so we kick them into someone else's patch. But I expect they'll drag their feet, so what I want you to do is go upstairs to one of the court clerks, get this account by Miss Rosebud typed up, and then go back and get her to sign it. Then remind them they have to move on. Take Jackson with you.'

He didn't want to go back; his face looked like I'd offered him a slice of dog turd. But he had to learn. Most of our usual customers had complicated moral lives; we simply had to get on with applying the law fair and square, the Bucky Barrett way. And Jackson had a bit of menace running through his veins – I reckoned he could turn it on at will – whereas Vogel would just yap out rules and regulations plus a bit of God-bothery and everyone would have a good laugh.

I wrote it all up at my desk, pleased that Kennedy wasn't around. O'Malley approached my desk. I put my pen down, blotted the paper, looked up.

'Excuse me, sir, but I reckon ... ah, I don't know,' he said, shifting his weight from foot to foot. I waited. O'Malley seemed to have a good head on his shoulders, despite the egg yolk on his uniform. 'One of those dredgers,' he said at last. 'I reckon we need to have a closer look at him, sir.'

'Because?'

'The others were sorta avoiding standing next to him and he was all nervy.'

'Name?'

O'Malley whipped out his notebook, flipped through the pages. 'Josiah Mutkins, sir.'

I jotted the name down. 'Good work, trooper. Dismissed.'

He strutted out of the office, pleased with his pat from the boss. It was the sort of initiative I wanted, not Vogel's pious impertinence.

I returned to my paperwork but soon I felt eyes on me and my skin prickled. It would be sudden oblivion, no pain. I looked up and around. Len Fitzgerald was standing in the doorway, his usual scowl in place.

'Yes?' I said.

He looked away down the hallway and back at me, opened his mouth, thought better of it and disappeared, much to my relief. Old Len was like a wizened ghost from Dickens, haunting the hallway, his scowl hanging in the air long after he'd disappeared.

~

Late afternoon, when a wagon arrived from Bathurst with everything I'd asked for, I rummaged around in the crates, ticking it all off, then told

the carter to take it all up to the ruined police station. The block was at least an acre, and the ruined station had been built to one side on the only levelled area.

I roamed around, looking for a good spot to pitch the large bell tent, and picked a flattish spot beside the pines, the only trees left, and close to the adjoining fence. Maybe too close to the neighbouring cottage, but flatter ground won out. Ferrying it all up from the cart would be laborious, and I spotted a wheelbarrow in the adjoining property. I knew a Mrs Owen lived there but not much more. I walked down the block and up the path to the front door of the tiny cottage and knocked.

The door opened and the pungent smell of boiling milk and lye just about felled me. A diminutive elderly woman stood there, her weathered face covered in a sheen of sweat. Deep vertical lines above her top lip led like sheep trails to her mouth. On her head she wore a thick, knitted tam-o'-shanter the colour of wood ash. The matching shawl around her thin shoulders was fastened with a dolly peg. She stared at me, her hands working a pair of knitting needles, clicking and clacking in a ceaseless rhythm, the skein of wool leading to a bulging pocket in an apron made of old flourbags.

'Mrs Owen?'

'Who wants to know?'

As I was in a mounted trooper's uniform, I hesitated. Was she blind too? Small, dark eyes like apple pips. No, she could see. Probably saw everything.

'Augustus Hawkins, new sergeant in town.'

'From where?'

'I'm from Queanbeyan.'

'Hawkins from Queanbeyan,' she said. 'Don't know them.'

'Do you know Queanbeyan?'

'No,' she said. 'What is it you're after?'

'I'm setting up my tent next door and I saw your wheelbarrow – wondered if I might use it for a couple of hours?'

She left the front door, walked past me, around a large lemon tree covered in fruit and up the side path of her house. As I watched, she yelled over her shoulder, 'Do you want it or not?'

I hurried after her, along a narrow path beside an ancient post-and-rail fence, rotting here and there and covered in blue-grey lichen. At the back of her cottage she had a large vegetable garden, mounds of dark earth like freshly dug graves, some covered in silverbeet, celery and onion shoots, others lying fallow. Beyond the garden was the goat paddock, full of long-haired beasts grazing.

The wheelbarrow was parked beside a pile of goat dung. She shoved her knitting in her pocket, took the wheelbarrow handles and tipped out the contents.

'There you go,' she said. 'But bring it back.'

From where we stood, the burnt-out wreckage of the police station was only about two hundred yards away. She must have seen or heard something.

'Mrs Owen, were you on friendly terms with Trooper Scanlon?' I asked.

She nodded, looking up across her garden to her goats, a couple of tears rolling down those lined cheeks. She took a handkerchief from her apron and wiped them away.

'Did anyone have a grudge against him?'

She looked down at the paved path. A very foolish snail was slowly

creeping towards the cover of a parsley thicket. She raised her skirt, revealing a man's heavy working boot, and slowly crushed the snail beneath it, so slowly I could hear the cracking of its shell breaking. Then she shook her old head: no, she didn't know of any grudges.

'Did you see anyone approach the station yesterday morning, just before dawn?'

She shook her head again, not looking up. She took the knitting from her pocket and resumed the ceaseless clack, then walked down the path to the front of the house. Wheeling the barrow in front of me, I followed her bird-like frame.

I set to finishing my campsite. The brown dog appeared again and watched all the activity with interest. I packed my spare uniform into the tent, along with my red shirt and the canvas pants, squaring it all away and tying it down. To hell with the Fitzgeralds and MacKerras.

~

A long day ended with a meeting of the Empire Day committee. I had no reasonable excuse for avoiding this chore, as town troopers had to be seen to be part of the life of the district. We met in the dining room of the Commercial after the supper service. It was a cavernous room on the western side of the hotel, crammed with tables and chairs and with a timber floor that creaked with age. Its windows looked out to the river, and a large fire crackled in a black iron fireplace in the far wall. All the heat went up the chimney. I noticed a soot-stained painting of what could have been a half-naked woman having a bath in a stream while a bunch of old men peered through the bushes at her.

'*Susanna and the Elders*,' Ray Fitzgerald said, walking into the room. 'My grandfather wanted a painting of a nude woman to hang behind the bar, as he'd seen one in a pub in Melbourne he admired. But he didn't want to pay for a decent one so we got this instead, and there it will stay, as long as Len is around.'

I had some dim recall of Susanna's plight: she'd been bathing in a stream, watched by some old blokes who decided they wanted a taste, and when she said no, they accused her of adultery. What the point of this Biblical story was I did not know, other than as a warning to women not to bathe naked in streams.

I took a seat at the long table. The committee consisted of Ray Fitzgerald as mayor, myself as representative of the law, Mrs Lennox as president of the Colley Progress Association, Dr Pomeroy, a teacher whose name I couldn't remember and the Church of England minister, whose name likewise escaped me.

Empire Day had started in 1905. I knew very little about what the protocols were, and I'd have preferred to stay in that state of ignorance. But here I was, with the minutes of the last meeting in front of me and listening to the others argue over who should address the town at the ceremony.

'I wrote to the president of the Bathurst Branch of the Empire League and he, once again, has sent his apologies,' Mrs Lennox said. 'Third year in a row. And he's left it so late to reply to my request, I doubt we can find anyone else.'

'It's almost like they don't care about us,' the teacher said. 'They want a bigger stage to strut.'

Fitzgerald looked at me. 'You fought for the empire. I'm sure you could do a very stirring speech for the children.'

'But you did as well, didn't you say?'

'Yes, but I speak most years. Time for new blood.'

'Thank you, but no. As you know, we are very busy with a murder investigation, and I really don't have the time to write a speech. My first priority is—'

'The town,' Mrs Lennox broke in, 'and what better way to show yourself to the local population than by giving the main speech? The sooner you are known around here, the easier your job will be in the long run.'

'That may be, but I am no cheerleader for the British Empire and would be a poor choice as speaker.'

The fire crackled and hissed. From the kitchen came the sound of crockery and cutlery being handled. Surprise and disapproval showed on all their faces.

'Catholic, are you?' the teacher asked.

'No. Is that why the Catholic minister isn't here?'

'He's not interested. He wouldn't be, would he? Catholics want to see the empire fall, Sergeant.'

'Sergeant Hawkins has been out bush for a long time,' Dr Pomeroy said. 'Maybe they don't celebrate out back of Bourke, eh?'

'Not that I ever saw.'

That raised a few smiles. They could forgive ignorance, but not disloyalty, and certainly not difference.

'Then this is your chance, isn't it?' Mrs Lennox said, looking around at the others, who all nodded.

'You know, I think Detective Kennedy might be a better choice,' I said. 'He received a shooting trophy from Lord Kitchener. He may have something to say.'

'Good idea,' Fitzgerald said. 'He'll be an excellent speaker.'

Smiles, nods and noted. I should not have spoken my private thoughts on the matter, just pleaded business. As a paid-up minion of the British king, I needed to at least pay lip service to common loyalties.

The meeting broke up and people hurried away, keen to get home to their hearth fires. After the stampede, I pushed my chair in and made my way towards the door, but Ray Fitzgerald appeared with a whisky bottle and two glasses.

'Have a nightcap, Sergeant,' he said. Without waiting for me to agree, he splashed the spirit into the glasses. I got a whiff of whisky and sat back down again, bracing myself for old war stories.

'I was thirty-two when I tried to join up,' Fitzgerald said as he slid my glass across the tablecloth towards me. 'My wife had died, William was fine with Len looking after him, so I went to join up in Sydney, but they wouldn't have me. Too thin, they said. So I got myself to Cape Town and what did I see? The British fighting man, raised in the slums of Manchester or Bristol on bread and jam, narrow-chested, thin-armed weaklings.'

'Weaklings with Maxim guns,' I said.

'Ah yes, the Devil's paintbrush.'

'Did you sign on with an irregular?'

'Steinaecker's Horse. Heard of them?'

'Steinaecker was a Prussian, wasn't he?'

'Yes, and not the full quid either. Led us into endless scrapes just for the fun of it. We lost men to lions, crocodiles, japies and each other, blue on blue or just plain dislike.'

He refilled our glasses and we drank.

'Did you see much of Cape Town?' I asked.

'Not much. I went up to Witwatersrand and got a job as an overseer in a goldmine, just past Jo'burg. Very good wages for white men. I came home with a small fortune and bought back all the Fitzgerald land my feckless father had gambled away,' he said. 'I built the house next to the hotel where Len, Hilde and I live, and I'm building another to the north, overlooking the Bull River valley.'

'Nice.'

'Do you own any land?' he said, warming to his theme.

'Not personally, no.'

'You should get started. A young man like you could go far if you get the right soil beneath you. Build it up from there.'

'Got a nice little block you want to flog, eh?'

'I do, Sergeant,' he laughed. 'Been buying up around here for a long time now. My family were one of the earliest settlers on the Bull River. The Fitzgeralds of the parish of Roxburgh. We own much land between here and Bathurst. I grow beef and mutton for processing into canning. Canning, that's the future.'

'Canned what? Bully beef?'

'Of course, a man of your background wouldn't know what goes on in a kitchen,' he laughed. 'We grow much of own produce around here, so why not put the excess in a can and send it to all the markets around?'

'Indeed,' I said.

'I'm building a cannery on the outskirts of Bathurst. We'll make stews, soups. It will revolutionise the kitchen and we'll be leading the charge. And ironically, all of it stems from the goldmines of Witwatersrand, not local gold.'

I listened to him talk about how clever he was for a little longer, then prised myself away. He could have kept going until the small hours, but I was worn out and not up for a night of reminiscing about the war, South Africa and canned stew.

~

The brown dog had waited patiently for me outside the hotel. I stopped and gave him a pat and he followed me up the hill to my tent. He was well trained and at a loose end, much like me. I grew up with dogs. As I was an only child, it was considered that I needed a companion. Often I had two dogs, and at one time three. My father always had a dog too, and we often spent Sunday afternoons walking our pack, throwing balls and putting them through obedience drills, and just enjoying their company.

There was a forlornness to this dog that matched my own state of mind, so I let him into the tent and threw a towel down for him, and he settled on it as if it were where he always slept.

I lit the lantern and placed it on the small table, then sat and opened a packet of letters my father had forwarded to me. Not much of interest, but my father wrote to thank me for my telegram. 'It's always gratifying to hear one's only child is still alive,' he wrote. No mention of my utter foolishness in going back to the traps, or of the precarious state of my mind, or even of what he thought I should actually do with my life. For that I had to be grateful. But I could read between the lines.

He'd thoughtfully sent a replacement coffee grinder and pot and a packet of the coffee beans I had sent to me from South Africa. The Dutch know their coffee, and my hoard was like gold, jealously guarded.

I climbed into my rickety camp bed, pulled the blankets up, blew out the candle and lay in the darkness thinking about Flora. She was constantly in my thoughts when I laid my head down at night – unless she was chased out by murderous ambushes, killings or fires. As a schoolboy, in the science laboratories, we'd been shown what happened when a strip of magnesium touched the flame from the Bunsen burner. It flared into a dazzling light, too bright to look at. That was how I felt when I first saw Flora. A bright light burning inside me, and I still burnt for her. I was terrified of that flame going out, because then I'd be hollowed out, my heart a blackened ruin, forever mourning the girl I couldn't have.

I'd caught the men and the woman who'd murdered her sisters and brothers. Her wild grief had prompted her father to lock her up in a sanitorium in Katoomba. She was still there, almost a year later. I know this because my father, a doctor, had made some discreet enquiries through his sawbones chums. Still there and quite unwell.

Those words, *quite unwell*, were almost unbearable in their vagueness. I could not write to her or visit, as I had been blacklisted by her wretched father. We loved each other, were going to elope. And then the chaos struck, and I'd failed her in ways that shame me. I didn't know now if she still loved me. Nothing was resolved, or not in a way I needed it to be resolved. And in that no man's land I swung from unworthiness, to fury, to the need to act, to get her out, to hold her and keep her safe, then back to despair. *Should I let go of the love?* I asked myself every night. It was like walking a labyrinth of unanswerable questions, only to find myself every morning back at the beginning.

I heard a voice outside the tent. Or I thought I did. The dog growled and leapt up off the floor. There was somebody there.

11

I heard it again. From outside the tent came a faint female voice calling my name. I fumbled for matches, lit the candle on the chair beside my camp bed. Whoever it was, she was trying to undo the tent flap.

I struggled to my feet, pulled the flap aside. A woman stood there, a dark scarf over her head, starlight brilliant on the frosty grass.

'What is it?' I said, rubbing my eyes. 'Is somebody hurt?'

The moonlight was behind her face in the shadows. She placed a hand on my chest and gently pushed me back into the tent. I swiped the hand away and she laughed, low and cheeky.

'Mary? What the hell? Something happen?'

She slipped past me and into the tent, let the flap fall behind her. The candlelight threw our shadows onto the wall of the tent, a golden light within. The dog was carefully watching but taking his cues from me.

'I can't have you in here,' I said. 'Whatever it is, just say where and I'll be there in a tick.'

Then she was at me, all lips and hands running all over me. Her fingers found their way under my nightshirt and I pushed her away.

'You have to leave, Mary. Now,' I said.

'Oh, come on, let's have a little fun, like we used to do.'

I was gobsmacked. Only a day or so ago she said she was married and warned me not to even look at her, and now she was here trying to tear my nightshirt from me. Her hands were back at my face, holding me, and she stood on tiptoe to kiss me, her ample bosom pressed against my chest, warm and firm. Crimson flickers of lust stirred in my entrails.

I gently pushed her away, and in the dim light gazed at her. Cheeky Mary, the young widow who took me in hand for a week, back when I was hellbent on doing myself permanent damage.

'You better go,' I managed at last. 'You're still a bonny lass but you're also married.'

'Oh, so what? He's never here! What does he expect me to do? And since when has Gus Hawkins denied himself the flesh of a willing woman?'

She undid the buttons on her bodice and pulled it down from her shoulders, revealing two sumptuous, creamy white breasts, heavy and veined and yearning towards my hands. She gave me a saucy look I remembered well, head slightly turned away, a half-smile on her lips. The flickers of lust sprang into flame, my gaze on what she offered, mesmerising, so warm, so soft.

I swallowed hard, caught sight of the dog in the corner watching everything, a look of disgust on his face, as if to say, *You're not a horned-up stripling ready to rut at flag's drop, are you?* I wasn't, but I could be, given a few seconds.

'Mary, you go home now, and we'll forget you came.'

'You chased me around the waterhole, remember? Buck naked, you were.'

'I do.'

She took a step closer and looked up through her eyelashes. 'Remember what you did when I let you catch me?'

What a sight she was, naked as the day she was born, skipping over the pebbles light as a nymph, every curl glinting in the sun, every inch of her luxurious flesh wobbling and jiggling, her arse, my God, the sight of it bouncing away out of reach, and her peeping over her shoulder, giggling, the glorious shamelessness of her. And here she was, offering me another taste.

'I do remember, Mary, and it's a vision I will draw on when I'm an old man sitting by the fire, but—'

'You're so full of it, I remember now,' she said, pushing me away with both hands. 'To hell with you.'

'Your husband will kill me, or you, or both of us, by the sounds of it. And it's not the end I'd choose for myself. Go home to your children.'

Mary buttoned up her dress, groaning. 'Children. Always hanging off me and whining for this or that, and there's no time for myself and no man to put his arms around me. I'm fair sick of it. Go home to me children, ha!'

Without another word she yanked the tent flap open and flounced off silently. I settled back onto my cot, suddenly aware of how cold I was. Thinking of her breasts jouncing away from me in the night, I cursed myself for a fool with a wowser of a dog.

'It's alright for you, mate, you don't know what it's like, and you're never going to know.'

The dog raised an eyebrow, shuffled around so his back was to me, curled up and gave a long-suffering sigh.

I rolled over, my face to the wall of the tent. I had the solace of virtue. I was a man of principle, a man who swore he would never bed a woman

111

whose husband was alive. Not because it was the act of a blackguard to do so, but because it invariably ended in violence, for her or the lover. I'd seen it too many times, heard about it too – women with the life punched out of them for offering to another man what belonged to their husbands. I was, in fact, saving Mary from herself. There, conscience squared, manliness restored.

~

I woke with a bone I needed to pick with Mary, or with any nubile and willing female, come to that. I flung back the covers, filled the basin with icy water and splashed my face, reciting *incipio, incipiebam, incipiam, incepi, inceperam* ... By the time I arrived at the future perfect I could get on with my day.

But it wasn't just that Mary was married that prevented me from falling on her like a grunting beast. It was me – I wanted to be a better man than I had been these last ten years. Better than the shambling womaniser with whisky breath who had so hurt Flora when she was already in agony. I might never see her again, but I wanted to redeem myself anyway, to be worthy of her, and to know that I was, deep in my viscerals. I wanted to wash my stained soul in a bucket of abstinence, and for God to look down and see the glistening soap bubbles of purity. Until I'd paid for my sins, it was self-restraint for me.

That restraint had been untested, mind you, until now.

While I brooded on virtue, the dog shot out of the tent and over to a hole he'd been digging by the fence. It looked as if he were planning to bury a horse. But at that moment he was busily sniffing a grey bundle in

the grass. I called him off and had a look. It was one of the tabby stable cats, dead, its body contorted in agony. Had to have taken a bait, but there was no telling where it had picked it up. I took note and, with the dog running alongside, hurried down to the butcher to get food for him so he wouldn't be tempted. Labradors would eat anything, I knew, whereas a kelpie would rather have a word from the boss, then his tucker. Had to hope he was more kelpie.

We were too early, because the butcher had only just killed a sheep. Told me to come back in half an hour, so we kept going east along the road, my mind racing, barely noticing where we were. The gunman was still at large and I was in the open, an easy target. Then the dog took off, barking like mad. Somebody in the bushes?

The high escarpments and rugged foothills were in close distance, and the bushland was thick on either side of the road as it swung south away from the river. I was on alert, straining to hear the threat before it found me. I hoped the dog would jog back looking sheepish but he didn't. I took my sidearm out of its holster as unease crept up into my chest and began spreading into my veins. A sharpshooter with a penchant for mounted troopers and all I had was my sidearm. I stopped, about to hurry back to safety, when the dog shot out of the undergrowth and barked at me, then ran ahead, stopped and waited.

I followed him off the dirt road to the left and along a bush track to a wide, grassy clearing with the remains of some old piece of goldmining equipment, half rusted away. A hobbled horse, a pretty grey mare, looked up and walked towards me, her liquid eyes full of relief. I kept the sidearm in my hand, because in the centre of the clearing was a tent and the dog was barking at it.

My heart raced. I scanned the surrounding scrub, hoping I wouldn't see an armed man coming at me. The dog ran over to the horse, who lowered her head and snuffled him. She knew him. I walked a little closer to the tent, heart in my mouth.

'Hello? You in the tent – do you need assistance?'

No reply. There was no evidence of a campfire, which was odd.

'This is Sergeant Hawkins, Colley Station. Are you in need of assistance?

No reply. I was reluctant to undo the flap and look inside. There was no smell of death or blood, but there could be a man with a gun waiting to blow my head off.

'Come out, if you can.'

Nothing. I undid the flap, whipped it aside and sprang out of the way. Nothing.

The dog lolloped over and went straight into the tent, sniffing all over it. He knew the tent. Then he came out and followed some scent around the place, I watched him but there was no pattern. I glanced into the tent. A bedroll was laid out but looked unslept in; there was also a saddle and saddlebags and a bridle. I dragged them out of the tent and looked around. The mare watched, eyes gleaming in the early-morning light.

My mind raced. Scanlon's killer, come into the district meaning to do harm, camped here. And he was somewhere out there now. Or he was the body in the lock-up. Dr Pomeroy said the dog had only been around a few days, which tied in with the fire. I looked in the saddlebags. In one, a knitted cap, some twine, a hunk of stale bread and some filthy postcards. Nothing but a half-empty cardboard packet of ammunition in the other. If he was out there, he had the rifle with him, and I only had a pistol. Like a fool.

I searched the tent for anything that could identify the owner, then tied the flaps, leaving the bedroll in it. I saddled the horse and strapped the saddlebags on, mounted up and whistled to the dog, who ran over, and we quickly left.

~

As we approached the outskirts of the town, I heard something thumping or hitting a hard surface, then a smash and tinkle, then more thudding. I rode towards the sound, which was coming from the side of the hill not far from the Church of England school. As I got closer, I saw a couple of boys beside an empty cottage. They were laughing and mucking about, throwing rocks, having such a grand time they didn't see me.

The dog ran over and they looked up.

'Master Simmons,' I called, recognising one of the lads.

He took one look, eyes widening in horror, and took off, his mate racing after him. Little buggers. Vandalising empty cottages and huts was a fine old pastime for kids with time on their hands. But I wanted a closer look, because Frank Simmons struck me as a budding master criminal.

The small timber cottage's windows were smashed in and the padlock on the door had been jemmied open. Flies were thick in the putrid air. I took out my sidearm and stepped inside. The walls had been papered with old newspapers, yellowing and peeling away. Rat droppings, fox too, maybe cat, on the wooden floor, parts of which had been ripped up. The lean-to kitchen with its sturdy brick chimney still had a massive old woodburner stove, doors open, covered in rat droppings, broken windows with a tall shrub of some sort coming in through the window.

115

The buzz of flies intensified. At the western end of the kitchen there was a door. Probably a bedroom. Terrible smell wafting from it.

I gagged at the smell – or was it the fear? I had to stop and take a deep breath, steady myself. *This is the job, so do it.*

I pushed the door open, heart pumping, sweaty hands clutching my gun. Nothing except two bunks. But lying on the floor between them was the body of a cat with its head blown off and the remains of penny bungers scattered around. Little shitheads. I stepped out the back door for some fresh air. You heard about this sort of thing every time there was a cracker night. Little brutes tying bungers to dogs' tails, or blowing their own hands off, blinding themselves or their mates. This town was no different.

Bungers, tom thumbs, flowerpots, Catherine wheels, all of them and more. What exciting creations they were to children, all their barbarian tendencies hemmed daily and then let out on cracker night. I was never allowed near fireworks, as my doctor father had seen what they did to small hands and faces. But I was allowed to hold a sparkler. Probably why I went off to war.

~

Back in town, I went to the store. Coming out were two of Mrs Foufoune's girls, threadbare coats over their petticoats, heads bent over their waxed paper bags, examining their sweets, giggling and chaffing each other. They took no notice of me. Anywhere between thirteen and sixteen, but they'd claim to be eighteen if challenged, and proving they weren't was a long and laborious procedure that only the most zealous officer would pursue.

Inside, I found Percy carefully building a pyramid of canned soups in

the window display, and Mrs Lennox rearranging her stock to make room for packages of fireworks.

'Mrs Lennox.'

'Sergeant,' she said, briefly glancing at me.

'Sell many of those fireworks to kids?'

She snorted. 'Who else? Why? It's not against the law.'

'No, but—'

'It's Empire Day in a few weeks, as you know. And we celebrate with a bonfire and fireworks, as does every other town in this country.'

'Have you sold any to Frank Simmons?'

'Yes, and to Nobby Lougher, Billy Compton, Lizzie Greer ...' She went on, ticking the names off her fingers.

No point in badgering her. As she said, it wasn't against the law to sell firecrackers. I thanked her and turned to go, then noticed a tall bookshelf in a dark corner of her shop.

She followed my gaze. 'The remnants of the town library, left after the Institute for the Arts shut down. Pay a coin into the tin when you take one, get it back when you return it.'

I went and looked over the spines, hoping to find something I hadn't read. But they weren't going to have the latest Jack London in this neck of the woods. I settled on a battered copy of Homer's *Odyssey* that had washed up on this faraway shelf. I was enthralled by the *Iliad* and the *Odyssey* as a kid, knew the stories off by heart. Given the other choices, I decided, it couldn't hurt to sail to Ithaca with Odysseus again.

12

I led the grey horse down to the pub and tied her up outside, then went over to the ostler at the coach turnaround and fetched one of our nosebags. I filled it with oats, went back and hung it around her neck. Then I headed inside, the dog at my heels.

Immediately I ran into old Len, who'd no doubt been lurking in a dark corner, brooding on the injustice of the positioning of the King's portrait in our office. 'Watch where yer goin', he snapped at me. If only the name Tosser hadn't already been taken.

Vogel was in the office, arms folded as he stared into space, thinking clean and sober thoughts. He returned to this world when he saw me.

'Excuse me, sir, but Mrs Hilde Fitzgerald—'

'What about her?'

'I know her, sir, she's from the same Lutheran congregation as mine in Wagga Wagga. We all thought she was going off to marry a rich man, but she's no better than a servant girl here.'

'She's widowed. Has to live.'

'She should go back home, sir.'

'Mrs Fitzgerald and her circumstances are none of our business, and

you and all the other troopers will treat her with respect and courtesy at all times. And do not even think of playing up with her or you will be dismissed immediately.'

'I wouldn't, sir,' he said, looking injured.

No, he wouldn't; he wasn't that type of young man. But I'd seen Jackson staring after her, O'Malley too, and they were that type of young man. But staring was not a crime, and they were young males, and she was a young female, and all was right in the world. But, by crikey, I'd be putting some stick about if it went any further.

'I have a job for you,' I said.

He stood a little straighter, eyes and ears alert.

'I need you to be my proxy at the Empire Day celebrations committee's weekly meetings. It's vitally important the law be consulted. But I have my hands full with the investigation. I'll need you to read the minutes and take notes, and run all suggestions pertaining to our role by me.'

'Yes, sir,' he said, pleased to be given this vital role – as pleased as I was to offload it. There'd be no whisky or talk of land grabs with Vogel in attendance.

'Now, come and have a look at this,' I said.

Before we could walk out, Kennedy came down the stairs. 'Found something?'

I showed them the horse, told them what I'd found. 'I don't know if the horse had been hobbled for a while, and the dog appeared very familiar with the campsite, sniffing and barking. We can keep her tethered out here, ask people if they've seen the horse before, or if they remember the rider, that sort of thing. Vogel, that's your job.'

'We'll go back up there after breakfast,' Kennedy said, then he disappeared into the dining room.

I nabbed the newspaper from Kennedy's desk and sat perusing it while drinking a cup of tea. I always hoped for any news of Captain Scott's Terra Nova expedition to the South Pole, an endeavour that fascinated me. A team of Manchurian ponies were on the expedition, taken to haul supplies through the Antarctic. I considered it a bad decision and was certain I'd be proved right. But, as ever, there was no news.

A headline caught my eye: 'Germany's Navy'. As usual, the British government was whining about how much money the Germans were spending on naval armaments. It was a destructive arms race, the paper thundered, that if unchecked threatened to submerge civilisation and wreck society. I snorted and turned the page.

My interest was piqued by a picture of a distinguished older man, his beard tapered to a point. Too heavy on the moustache, though, too old-fashioned. Then I realised this man was Alfred Deakin, our off-and-on prime minister, whom my father greatly admired. Father's dog, Barty, was named after Sir Edmund Barton, Australia's first prime minister after Federation, so it made a kind of sense for me to have Alfred Deakin.

'Alfie.'

He turned at the sound of my voice, tail wagging.

'Alfie, eh? That'll do you.'

He'd thrown his lot in with me, but if the owner of the grey mare also owned him, I'd have to let him go. Unless his owner was the cop killer, and was somewhere out there on this bright day making plans to bag himself another trooper.

~

Kennedy wanted to get an alibi from Edmund Wallace, the man who'd been rude to the troopers in Mrs Lennox's shop. 'He's to the east – you can check that tent site again on your way.'

I left Alfie behind as I didn't want him alerting the tent's owner. O'Malley, with the usual flecks of porridge on his tunic, and I rode up there, tethered our horses on the road, took our rifles out and eventually found the path through the thick scrub to the clearing. The tent was gone; there was nothing now but old horse droppings to say anyone had been there. I knew the tent had been there – I'd been in it. But now it was gone.

A nearby kookaburra, a snake in its beak, bashed the life out of it against a branch, rhythmic bangs that shuddered through me.

'Nothing there, sir,' O'Malley said. 'You sure it was this track?'

'Yes.'

He said nothing but I knew what he was thinking. I had a reputation as being a bit mad, a reputation that no doubt had spread among the Bathurst mob when they heard I was coming. I was a fool to come back to the traps, a bog-standard, brown-paper fool. You could not step into the same river twice, but you sure as hell could fall in and drown.

'We'll go and see Wallace.'

We rode along the eastern road until I couldn't bear the silence. Just to stop my own brooding, I asked O'Malley what he and Vogel were always arguing about.

'Hilde. Mrs Fitzgerald. He thinks just because he knows her from Wagga that he has a better chance than me or Jackson.'

'Ah. You like her?'

'Yeah, and I met her when Davy was alive, so we like to swap stories,

you know? Because Davy was my mate. I met him at Moore Park when we were training. He knew everything about horses, and when we had leave, he'd come with me to my parents' farm near Camden because he didn't have a family. Then he was posted out here. He wrote and told me how lucky he was because he'd made friends, and his sergeant was a good bloke.'

'You came out here to see him?'

'After I was posted to Bathurst. He took me on a picnic to the waterhole with Hilde and her husband. So why shouldn't I talk to her?'

'Indeed.'

'When I first saw her, you know, she was married and all, but she was as pretty as a princess, all that golden hair, and always smiling. She's so sad now, and, well, Jackson and I try to joke with her, to lift her spirits sort of.'

'Fair enough.'

'Vogel goes spare when she laughs at our jokes,' he said with some satisfaction. 'She doesn't laugh at his because he's about as funny as a fart at a funeral.'

'Did you come out here after her husband died?'

'Went to his funeral in Bathurst with Davy, who was real cut up. Then I came out here whenever I could get away to give him a bit of company. Hilde, Davy and I, we'd walk up this road, but if we got near the waterhole she'd start crying.'

'He died at the waterhole, did he?'

'Yeah, they reckon he was working his claim, slipped, and went under the water and that was it, drowned. Must have knocked his head on something. That's what Sergeant Barrett told me.'

'You met Sergeant Barrett?'

'Yeah, he was an old-school demon, knocking heads together, chasing the Chinamen, always looking for trouble so he could have a bit of fun. Kept him young, he reckoned.'

~

We'd arrived at the turn-off to the Wallace home and rode up the long dirt road. A large farmhouse was set in the shadow of some rugged cliffs and hills. To one side there was a thick cypress tree windbreak. The house had a verandah all around, with washing strung under cover, flapping in the breeze. A dog on a chain went berserk as we rode up.

I noticed a stable with a massive Clydesdale parked inside, a cart and half a dozen tin milk cans, and a six-stall dairy open to the elements but under a broad roof. Over to the side there were more outbuildings and odds and ends, including a large aviary with dozens of green budgerigars flitting about, a large chook run and a cat stretched out in the sun on the verandah. A short, thickset woman came onto the verandah, wiping flour from her hands.

'Mrs Wallace? I'm—'

'Who is it you want?' she said. 'I'm the cook, Mrs Delamere. If it's Mr Wallace, he's out on the southern boundary, at the slaughter pits.'

Another woman appeared, younger, slimmer, in a shabby long white dress. After a moment I realised she was blind.

'A couple of troopers to see your husband, Mrs Wallace,' Mrs Delamere said. 'Nothing to worry about.'

'I'm not worried,' she said, clutching the verandah post. 'What is it you're after?'

'Just wanted to speak to your husband regarding the death of Trooper Scanlon, to see if he can help with our enquiries.'

Mrs Delamere had her hands on her considerable hips and glowered at us. As I spoke of Scanlon's death, Mrs Wallace appeared to shrink back, like a sea anemone being touched, turning in on herself and folding her arms for protection.

'If you want Mr Wallace, best come back tonight after he's had his supper,' Mrs Delamere said.

'Mrs Wallace?' I said, ignoring the cook.

'Follow the dirt road by the creamery and keep heading south,' she said. 'You'll find him there.'

O'Malley and I set off, passing hills covered in Scotch thistle, Bathurst burr and Paterson's curse, the latter a pretty purple flowering weed that would kill your horse quickly, your cow moderately quickly and your sheep slowly. Wallace hadn't got his weeds under control; the Agriculture Department would be onto him if they knew. He had what looked like a feed and malt barley crop growing in one paddock, but there was nothing about the place that said prosperity.

'There's Wallace, sir,' O'Malley yelled into the wind, half an hour later, pointing at a shed in the distance. A man was moving about outside, and cows in a pen were making a hell of a racket. The closer we got, we were able to see what he was doing. He'd dug a pit and was leading a cow to the edge of it, shooting it and letting the carcass fall into the pit. Tough job, killing off your stock.

'Must have the pleuro,' O'Malley said.

'What's that?'

'Like cow pneumonia. Spreads quickly, and if you have it on your

property, you're in quarantine until you get rid of it. Getting rid of it means killing the herd.'

'A bad business, then.'

'Oh yeah, really bad. My uncle ran a dairy farm, went through the pleuro and came out of it as a travelling salesman.'

Was it the right time to be questioning this poor sod? And if we rode down there, we'd be breaking quarantine. Which begged the question: why didn't the women tell us? Maybe farm matters weren't discussed with them. We rode closer. The ridge we'd followed gradually dropped away to the pasture. We rode down, tethered the horses, dismounted and were about to walk over when a shot rang out.

There was no cover anywhere. We both swung our rifles up and pointed them at the man striding across the paddock, his rifle aimed at us.

'Police. Put down your weapon.' I shouted, hands sweaty, mouth dry. The man kept coming while the cows bellowed in fear, jostling to get away but trapped by the fence. I trusted the uniform to protect me, but my heart was pounding like an engine piston.

'Drop your weapon,' I repeated, but he kept advancing. I fired over him. That stopped him.

'Get the fuck off my land,' he shouted, but his rifle was down. Tall, lean, leathery, a long face with a broken nose in the middle of it and two fierce eyes on either side, unblinking and full of fury.

'Mr Wallace?'

'I said get off my fucking land.'

'Put your gun on the ground. Now.'

'Get the hell off my land or I'll shoot you,' came the response.

'Do not threaten a police trooper, Mr Wallace, there are stiff penalties—'

'I'll shoot both of you – now fuck off.'

Bastard was digging a huge hole for himself every time he opened his mouth.

'Mr Wallace, we can take this road, but I promise you will not like the destination when you get there.'

'I don't give a fuck. I said, get off my property,' he said, and fired over our heads again.

This was escalating too fast. I had to retreat. He stood like a rock, gun aimed at us as we backed away, mounted and got out of there. Tired and tetchy, I wasn't in the mood for being scared out of my wits. We'd come back later and lead him gently to the realisation of his errors.

~

We rode back in silence, past the dairy buildings and the chook run. I noticed Mrs Wallace on the front verandah, holding onto the post and carefully taking a step down. Once she was on the ground, she ran a few steps with her arms out in front of her.

'Sergeant? Is that you?' she cried out. 'I heard gunshots.'

I stopped and dismounted, then walked over to her. Lank fair hair, her face drawn and hollow, dry lips and rough skin, misery embodied. Her eyes were unseeing, and the eyeballs had turned up, just two half circles of blue amid the bloodshot whites. She had a crochet hook and some wool in her hands and fingered them restlessly.

'Nobody hurt, Mrs Wallace. Your husband wants us to leave, so we are.

126

But we will be back. You can tell him that.'

Her fingers ran up and down the crochet hook, fiddling with it and pressing the end of it into the palm of her other hand.

'Why would he shoot at us, Mrs Wallace?'

'My husband is a very angry man,' she said.

'Is it standard practice for a dairy farmer to kill his herd without another herd to replace them?'

'I don't know,' she said. 'I milk the cows, we all do, but my husband makes the decisions.'

'He didn't mention disease?'

'Ma, come inside.' A girl of about ten in a stained pinafore ran down and took her mother's hand. 'Don't talk to them – you know you're not allowed to.'

'Did your husband say anything about the murder of Trooper Scanlon when it happened?'

Mrs Wallace swiftly bent her head as if ashamed.

'Was your husband on this property on the morning of the nineteenth of April?'

'Yeah, he was,' said the girl. 'Ma wouldn't know.'

I looked at the girl's pinched and bitter face. A kid, but one who'd seen more than she should have, no doubt. Mrs Wallace again pressed the pointed end of the crochet hook against her palm, almost willing it to go through the flesh.

'Mrs Wallace, are you in need of help?'

'Go away,' the girl said. 'She's doesn't need anything.'

The girl tugged her mother along back to the house. Mrs Wallace turned her head as if she were looking over her shoulder, but her eyes

could see nothing. There was not much I could do, given Wallace had threatened us. If he found us here, I had no doubt he'd do something even more reckless.

13

O'Malley was silent all the way back to the town limits. We rode along the main street to the coach turnaround, unsaddled the horses and took them back up to the police paddock and turned them loose. I closed the gate and started down the block.

'Permission to speak, sir,' O'Malley said.

I nodded, kept walking. He'd stopped so I turned back, already irritated by what I knew he was going to say. 'What is it?'

'Why did you let Wallace get away with it, sir? Shooting at us, threatening us?'

'He hasn't got away with it. We'll get reinforcement and go back, and he'll be charged.'

'He was coming at us with a loaded shotgun. You should have stopped him, fired at him, aimed for his legs. Sir.'

'Been in an altercation with an armed and angry man before, Trooper?'

'No, sir, but we looked like cowards. Scanlon's dead and other blokes will think we're a bunch of pansies, that they can take us out whenever they want because we don't fight back.'

'This is not a playground fight, O'Malley,' I said, trying to stay calm.

'We are the law and have all the advantage, therefore we avoid unnecessary confrontation where people may die.'

'Yeah, people like us,' he said. He was frightened and angry. I was too. That was even more reason to do things by the book, but I overlooked his last comment.

When we were back in town, I sent him off to go back through all the gazettes and bulletins we'd received and never read to see if there'd been an alert put out about this cow disease. Because if there wasn't, an angry man shooting his own stock was a bloody huge red flag for more violence. Or previous violence, like shooting Scanlon.

I went to our office and slumped in my chair, a headache growing by the minute – like someone was using a log splitter on my head. Then Kennedy trotted in, tense and irritable.

'Heard about Wallace. Why didn't you arrest him?' he said.

'Not my day to die, mate,' I said, leaving him to think through the obvious.

'O'Malley reckons it would have been easy, that Wallace was all bark and wouldn't have shot you.'

'That'd be junior Trooper Sean O'Malley, just out of short pants but with extensive experience in handling armed men? I'm the sergeant and I don't shoot men in the leg when I go to check on a fucking alibi.'

'No need to do your block, mate, just asking.'

He said this with a mystified look on his face, as if I really were a cowardly nut job. Stupid prick.

I found Septimus Watt behind the bar, fag in hand as he chatted to the old men who were bolted to their stools, their shandies, which they never appeared to drink, in front of them. I had a mighty thirst for a

slug of whisky. It was a way out: drunk on duty. But I'd feel worse if they booted me out, worse than I did already. Still, my eyes lingered on the bottle behind Watt.

'Sergeant,' Watt said. 'Bit early for the brandy, but—'

'Edmund Wallace – what do you know about him?'

'Dairyman, on the Topknot Road,' said one of the old fellas. 'Keeps the town in milk.'

'Good bloke.'

'Too right he is.'

They both nodded, while Watt picked up his polishing rag, flapped it, then folded it neatly into fours, as if it were a fine linen handkerchief.

'Wallace aimed a weapon at me and Trooper O'Malley today, and threatened to shoot us if we didn't get off his land,' I said. 'He's got a grudge against the uniform, so it would appear.'

'Yeah, probably,' Watt said. 'Lot of people do. You lot were called the demons for a reason, and Sergeant Barrett wasn't a pushover.'

'Wallace is shooting stock. Looks like his dairy herd. O'Malley mentioned pleuro.'

Ray Fitzgerald emerged from the door to the side of the bar that led to the kitchen, his clipped moustache almost bristling with apprehension. 'Did I hear you say pleuro, Sergeant?'

'Yes – is it in the district, do you know?'

'Damn well hope not. I've not heard anything, but ...'

'I've got a trooper checking now.'

'We'll have to go into quarantine – the whole district – if it is. You mentioned Ed Wallace, the dairyman? He's killing his herd?'

'Yes.'

Fitzgerald looked worried. Killing off infected stock could break a man if he was on a financial edge, and seriously damage a man who was doing well.

'It's not common this far south, but it's been through here before so you can never feel a hundred per cent safe. I'll contact the Department of Agriculture in Bathurst, they'll know.'

~

I left the bar and went out the back to get a breath. Stood staring at the river, dammed up here and there with snags. As a boy I often dammed the creek at the bottom of my father's garden, kicking the rocks and sticks away when I was ready and standing back to watch the debris washing away, revelling in my control over nature.

The muscle under my eye had resumed its pulsing twitch. No one could see it, but I felt it – had been feeling it since the war, a fluttering beat I sometimes wanted to rip from my face. A fox, only yards away in broad daylight, with something in its mouth, saw me and trotted away.

I found Kennedy in our office trying to reattach the map which kept falling off the wall.

'We'll get him tonight,' I said, dropping into my chair. 'He'll be at home, shitting himself no doubt. Can't shoot us all. But we have to wait for the all-clear from Agriculture.'

With the map secured, Kennedy said, 'I want to know who told Scanlon you were wanted at Gibbet Hill. If Wallace is the killer, how did he organise the note to go to Scanlon?'

'Harry Barker swore black and blue that he is the only person who

delivers telegrams, and you'd know the police are great sticklers for protocols around communications.'

'Yeah,' he said, lighting up a fag. 'That's why we don't use telephones, sunshine.'

'The sky didn't fall in, did it?' I said, pinching the bridge of my nose in an attempt to ward off the headache. 'The Central West hasn't been overrun with a resurgence of bushrangers – or have I missed that crime wave?'

'Listen, smartarse, you don't use a party line to communicate sensitive information. There are fucken scribblers everywhere, thanks to you. But worst of all is we look like a bunch of pussies – again thanks to you, Golden Boy.'

'Golden Boy?'

He shook his head, looked down at the papers in front of him. Maybe my getting the nod from the Phillip Street detective branch got up his nose. Probably had half a dozen resentments jammed up in those cavernous nostrils.

'The important fact is that Scanlon trusted whoever gave him what he thought was an official order,' I said. 'So it had happened before. We need to put the screws on Harry Barker.'

'Thank you, Sergeant, I really had no idea where to turn to next.'

O'Malley could find nothing in the last month's newsletter or alerts from the Department of Agriculture Bulletin. But that didn't mean the dairy farm was in the clear. An inspector could have made his visit and declared quarantine and mandatory destruction of the herd, and the paperwork just hadn't made its way back to Bathurst and then out to us. Or the inspector could be the now-dead man in the lock-up – which would

be a bad look for us, burning hapless government employees.

Kennedy and the troopers were all in the office. I called for their attention. 'Until we know why Wallace is killing his stock, we can't go onto his property.'

'He could just be killing off the spent cows, sir,' Jackson said, a straw at the corner of his mouth.

'Why wouldn't he sell them on for beef?'

'Cost too much to send them down to the saleyards, for what you'd get for them. Cheaper to kill them off and buy new ones, sir.'

The map on the wall suddenly dropped to the floor.

'We have to wait for Agriculture to give the all-clear,' I said.

O'Malley and Jackson exchanged a look. I knew what they were thinking.

'Wallace is not a suspect – yet. Not until we clear up his alibi. His threats to us can wait. We won't let him get away with it, but we don't want to spread this disease around the district and take the blame for it.'

I left them to grumble about me, as if this caution was the excuse of a man who'd lost his nerve. Maybe it was? Terror-filled dreams assailed me every night, to the point where I preferred to work late. Or I'd get into bed and pick up the *Odyssey*, but instead of the page I'd see Scanlon's head exploding and I'd be back on the western road, sheltering behind a dead horse, waiting to die.

In this world there was compassion for a spooked horse, a mistreated dog, a frightened child, but a grown man had to move towards the danger, to grapple with it and best it, regardless of his feelings. Or he was not a man.

~

That night I crawled into my tent, let Alfie in, pulled the cork out of a full brandy bottle and drank long and deep. Scanlon's head jerked to the right, blood spurted to the left. Wallace aimed at my head and fired, my skull was breached and my head jerked to the right and blood spurted to the left. Tears welled up. Brandy in, tears out. I couldn't stop weeping, but there was no one to see my shame, just Alfie, and he shoved his nose in my face, whimpering and licking me as if trying to make me feel better.

I pulled him onto the bed, drank some more and cried into his warm fur. Must have passed out. I don't know what time it was when I got up for a piss. I staggered outside into the darkness and straightaway hit a stinking dog turd. Unsteady, I tried to wipe it off my bare foot on the damp grass, lost my balance and fell into the dark pit the dog had been preparing.

I don't know how long I slept in the cold, damp earth, but through fitful snatches of wakefulness I assumed I was in my grave, and what a relief it was to have reached the end. I was woken by Alfie barking and somebody shaking my shoulder. Lawlor's voice asked me if I was all right. A muttered exchange between Lawlor and O'Malley. They hauled me back into my tent and onto my bed and left me there. When I woke, the dog was curled up next to me on the narrow bed, his gaze full of love.

14

In the morning, I cuddled up to Alfie, aware I'd had some terrible dreams. I could set up a shop for bad dreams, oh yes, nightmares, ten a penny, come and get them while they're fresh and screaming. They deceived me in their content but never in the feelings they provoked, and I'd wake panicky, full of horror and helplessness and a deep sense of having failed the young black servant girl I saw raped and tossed into the flames by a British soldier.

Now I also saw Scanlon's head jerk to the right and his blood spurt to the left only a couple of feet away, and the same acute helplessness engulfed me. I took those feelings around with me all day, and took them back to sleep at night. And then I screamed like Mr Rochester's mad wife in the attic as another version traipsed through my skull.

I'd heard of the activities of Steinaecker's Horse and wondered if Ray Fitzgerald suffered night terrors too, as he was always exercising by the river. I would never ask, though, because I'd have to reveal my own weakness. Maybe he was locked in to his frantic push-up count in an attempt to build his muscles up, day after futile day.

I crawled out of the tent, feeling storm-damaged and no doubt looking

it. I'd assembled some rocks and put together a fireplace out the front of my tent. I brewed up a strong coffee on my campfire and drank it in a state of numbness, staring at nothing. Then my brain, addled as it was, suggested there was something not quite right about what I was looking at. Soot and burn marks streaked up the side of the tent. There was a hole where the fire had burned through the canvas, and a half-burnt bit of cloth lying beside it. I drained my coffee, squatted down and had a closer look. I sniffed the rag, soaked in kerosene.

I stood up and looked around, slightly breathless. The goats ignored me. The corellas in the giant manna gum chattered and smooched in the morning sun. The fact that I had a spectacular hangover was not helping me make sense of what I'd discovered.

I made my way down to work, all the while suffering the sensation that someone had driven a railway spike between my eyes. The troopers tiptoed around me as I stalked in, surly and smelly, brown dog at my heels.

'How did you know to come up to the police paddock?' I asked Lawlor, who was on the desk.

'The dog – he came down here barking his head off, sir. Fitzgerald wanted to shoot him, but me and O'Malley, we followed him because we knew he was yours. Or sort of yours.'

'What time was this?'

'About half-nine.'

I went into the dining room and found Kennedy having a laugh with Ray Fitzgerald over a plate of greasy bacon and toasted damper.

'You look like you're on the arse end of a bender, mate,' Kennedy said. 'Drop a chop and you'll feel better.'

Fitzgerald wandered off and I told Kennedy he had to come with me to the police block.

Having heard that the tent I'd reported was not actually there, he gave a great sigh. But to humour me, mad bastard that I was, he got up and we walked out into the morning sun, which wreaked havoc on my delicate eyeballs, and up to the police block.

'What am I looking at?' Kennedy asked as we stood near the tent. 'Apart from dog turds.'

'Look at that,' I said, pointing at the scorched canvas and tamping down a surge of nausea.

He crouched down, picked up the rag, sniffed it. 'This yours?'

'Nope.'

'Not an ember attack? Your tent's pretty close to the fire.'

'The rag's been soaked in kero, used as a fire starter. The dog went down to the hotel around nine-thirty, barking the alarm. Someone was watching or saw the dog had gone and knew I was unprotected.'

'Why?' he asked.

'Why? That's your department, mate. You're the chief investigating officer, so you tell me.'

'No – why did the dog go for help?'

'I'd had an unfortunate incident while relieving myself.'

'Toppled arse over tit, did you?' he said with a grin.

'Something like that.'

'Then why not kill you as you lay in the dirt?'

I couldn't answer that. Kennedy rubbed his chin, looked around, hitched his trousers up. Neither could he.

'Kids, probably, up to mischief,' he said at last. 'Didn't you see a

couple throwing rocks at a cottage?'

'Or maybe linked to the station fire?' I said. 'Although that could have been a coal falling from a stove door.'

'The rag says this is a deliberate arson attack.' Kennedy stared around. 'Wallace? He's a loose cannon. Shooting at traps is a serious offence, but maybe he's done this as a warning to stay away from him.'

'I found a dead cat up there, where the dog's been digging,' I said. 'One of the police stable cats, taken a bait.'

'Yeah, poor pussy, but hardly an assault on law and order, mate. We need to talk to Wallace. Want to have another go today?'

I nodded, too weary to care, and we walked back to the pub in silence, although I longed to crawl back into bed amid the dog hair and mud from last night. Just lie in the stinking mess as a moral curative. But I had to push on, lest my troopers see that they had not just a coward as their boss but a drunk as well.

~

Instead of going back to the office, I went to Dr Pomeroy's. I let myself in and a bell tinkled somewhere in the house.

'Feeling a bit crook, eh, Sergeant?' he said, walking down the hall towards me.

'Self-inflicted, but that's not why I'm here.'

My attention was caught by the watercolours on the wall. I recognised the river. In some of the paintings there were figures swimming, in others they were fishing or sitting.

'The waterhole?' I asked.

'Yes. I keep going back,' he said. 'It's a pleasant place to sit of an evening. There's a few of us like to paint there.'

'But the same view all the time?'

'There's this French painter. Paints the same thing over and over, like poplars or haystacks, but always the light is changing, clouds, time of day, that sort of thing. You get your details in, but capturing the different light is the challenge.'

'Oh. Dr Pomeroy, are there any Chinese healers in town anymore?'

'No, not since Sam Hong left – why?'

'I bought several jars of ointment from a Chinese bloke back in 1906 and it did wonders for this scar,' I said. 'Smelt like cat's piss – no idea what was in it.'

'Cat's piss, probably,' he said with a smile. 'Urea is top-notch for treating scar tissue, keeps it soft and supple. It's what they tan hides with. Do you mind?' he said, taking a closer look at the facial scar. 'Yeah, he's put some of their herbs in it, too, keep the scar from contracting. Sam moved to Bathurst. If you can find him, he could probably make you up some more. He works in the Chinese vegetable gardens in Hereford, down by the Macquarie River. Not exactly sure where he lives, though.'

'I'll try to find him next time I'm in Bathurst.'

'Whoever did that made a good job of it,' he said, nodding at my face.

'The man who cut me or the man who sewed it back up?'

'Both of them, I reckon.'

The man who worked on my face was different to the one who worked on my chest. The chest surgeon was younger, but the older one was a Scot. He said he didn't hold with sutures in the face. There were a lot of bandages for a long time, and no talking, smiling or laughing, just

darkness and silence as people moved about. I hardly felt like laughing, except with hysteria perhaps. A nurse sometimes read to me in the evenings, but otherwise I was left in a gauze shroud to ponder my lot. And when the night terrors came and I screamed in my sleep, it was considered better to sedate me for weeks to allow the scar to heal, but still she read to me. The story I recall was, of all things, 'The Man Who Would Be King', by Kipling. And through the susurrations of morphine, I found myself hallucinating into my bandages that I was Danny, falling to my death in an icy ravine in the Hindu Kush, and crying out.

There were no more book readings after that; the patient needed silence.

~

I couldn't face Wallace today. I was not at my best and couldn't be sure I wouldn't lose my temper and fire back at him; I might actually enjoy it. I stayed at my desk all afternoon, trying to wedge myself into a safe position with sight lines running everywhere. I even pulled down the blind so I couldn't be shot from outside.

Alfie slept at my feet, his nose resting on one. I reached down and patted him occasionally, soothed by his presence. There was a summons from Bathurst to a preliminary enquiry into Scanlon's death. I had to attend, much as I didn't want to. But maybe they'd take one look at me and see that I was unfit for duty.

Kennedy was in his corner. A door slammed and we both jumped out of our skin. Harry Barker came in with the dispatch bag, O'Malley signed for it and gave it to me. I upended it on my desk and out came the autopsy

reports on Scanlon and the man in the lock-up. Kennedy and I took one each and read. As Watt and I had surmised, a heavy bladed instrument had been used to sever the hands, and a knife or machete to sever the penis – a very sharp blade, done post-mortem. Not much there that we didn't already know.

'Have you got the burned body?'

'Yeah,' Kennedy said, and handed it to me as I handed him Scanlon.

Died of smoke inhalation. A blessing. A male aged between twenty-five and forty-five: our usual customer, a man in his prime years lacking in self-restraint. There were plenty of us around. The coroner noted that the penis stump had been detected; the rest had probably burnt away. That at least confirmed the body was more likely a drunk-in-the-lock-up-bad-timing-sorry-mate instead of the victim of a nutter obsessed with cutting off hands and cocks.

'What do you reckon?' Kennedy asked.

I reckoned I wanted to go and sit on the balcony of some convalescent home for broken warriors, a pretty nurse massaging my temples while another perched on my lap and coaxed me into eating another spoonful of broth.

'The body in the lock-up was just some poor bastard,' I said. 'Mrs Lennox said she saw Scanlon dragging a man along Cullen Street towards the station late Thursday night. Said he was shouting and sounded drunk. But no one has come forward to report a missing person. I did see a tent and found the grey horse hobbled beside it.'

Kennedy nodded. 'Nobody said you didn't, mate.'

'What we know about Scanlon's death is it was planned,' I said. 'The alleged trouble at Gibbet Hill, the mysterious note, the sighting of a man riding up towards the cemetery at night, the horse tracks going down the

western side of Cemetery Hill and stopping behind a stand of she-oaks, well hidden from the road. It was a planned killing. Why? What if it's personal and not the uniform?'

'How many blokes of twenty-three have a personal life?' Kennedy said, stabbing out his fag.

'Plenty – Scanlon could have knocked up another young bloke's wife. Could have got in over his head with a card shark, or smacked the wrong drunk around, or run up a billiards debt. Plenty of ways for a young man to bring trouble on himself.'

Kennedy leant back in his chair and stretched. 'I was married with two kids by age twenty-three, walking the beat to support a family, sober as a judge at night, too.'

'At twenty-three I was in a military hospital in Cape Town being weaned off morphine.'

'Yeah? The nurses – were they pretty?'

'Some of them. We all hoped to be sponge-bathed by this one girl: well-developed chest, brushed against you as she wiped you down.'

'Jesus, you poor bastards, reduced to longing for a brush past.'

'If you got a bit frisky, they'd give you a bromide,' I said. 'Nobody wanted one of them.'

'Bloody hell,' he murmured. Then he held up a letter. 'Scott's being recalled to Bathurst to track an escaped prisoner.'

We exchanged a look. What was Northrup thinking, if indeed he was thinking at all?

~

After being seen to be a serious and competent officer, I gave myself the rest of the day off. I was not a well man, aside from being hungover, and needed to pull myself together in private. I found a hooked needle, twine and a patch of canvas in the police kit and spent an hour sitting in the dirt patching the tent and trying to keep Alfie from getting in my face.

I had another packet of letters. I undid the buttons on my tunic, got a fire burning, lit a fag and shuffled through the letters quickly, hoping for something, anything, from Flora: forgiveness, love, hope. She'd have to smuggle it out and maybe I was just too much bother. As usual, there was nothing.

I came to the last letter and stared at it, my heartbeat drumming. The rampant lion contained in a girth strap shaped into an oval, and beneath it a scroll with the words *Pro Gloria et Honore*. The Light Horse. Like a stab from a past knife fight puncturing time and space. With a shaky hand I ripped it open and read, feeling my heart skidding to a halt. Still being a commissioned officer, I was being recalled to active duty.

I put the letter down and stared at the ruins of the station, stunned, then reread it to make sure I'd got it right. How the hell had this happened? I should have been medically discharged years ago. I assumed that it had gone ahead because I'd never heard a damn thing from them after I got back to Australia, no get well cards, no flowers. But as my father told me, when I blithely took a commission straight out of school, once they'd sprinkled you with holy water they had you for life. But did I listen to him? No, I did not.

Maybe this was a way out? Second time around, maybe I'd get that longed-for bullet, an end to the pain and then glory ever after, a man's death on the battlefield.

'But we're not at war, are we?' I said to Alfie.

He wagged his tail and looked at me adoringly. *Dunno, mate.*

And there wasn't going to be a war I wanted any involvement in, because Australia, seated on her three-legged stool at the bottom of the world, drab skirts modestly tucked around her feet, swiping away flies as she mixed her suet pudding, had no enemies. She was no prize beauty to be carried away and ravished, just a fat and slightly stupid scullery maid.

So what the hell did they want with me?

I looked around for someone to blame and landed on a reliable old stand-by: my father. I went into the tent, snatched a piece of paper and sat at the tiny writing table, dashing off a letter demanding to know if he was behind this.

~

That night I woke to a paddock of dead horses, their blood seeping down the hill and filling my tent until I woke with a shout of terror. Panting in the darkness, sweaty, my heart drumming against my chest.

I fumbled about, lit a candle with a shaky hand and welcomed the light. With the blanket wrapped around me I let myself out of the tent, Alfie beside me, my feet on the frosted grass, the chill glaze of starlight illuminating the cluster of our police horses under their thick blankets. Sounds from crickets and frogs, a chorus of bells and clicks, the eerie cry of a mopoke owl across the paddock.

Unnerved and wary, I climbed back into bed and lay staring into the dark until sleep overcame me.

15

Autumn had been very dry west of the mountains, but a thick fog had settled over the town during the night. In the morning, I couldn't see as far as Mrs Lennox's sheep across the road, nor the tops of the manna gum. Even the goats had such a spectral cast they could almost be a herd of satyrs. I made my coffee and communed with it in peace.

Alfie shot off and sniffed something down by the messy ruin of the old station, a ghost dog barely visible in the mist. I called to him but he wouldn't come. I walked down, and as I got closer, he went all silly, jumping about, barking, rushing back to whatever he'd found and squirming with joy and guilt.

'What have you got, you great nong?' I muttered.

His head was down, nose pointing, wriggling with excitement. I squatted down and took a look. Got up and took a few steps away, some deep breaths. Hot tears welled up and I swiped them away angrily.

It was one of Scanlon's hands, rotten and decayed. Lying on the green, motley flesh was the small red and gold badge of the Crown: the badge on every mounted trooper's cap.

Confronting this horror was a test I suddenly failed, retching on the

wet grass. The sick fuck who had mutilated Scanlon was playing with us.

'Get out of it, Alfie,' I shouted, and wiped my mouth. He was prancing around the hand as if it were something to play with. I'd have to fetch Kennedy and find a sack or something. What I wasn't sure about was whether to tell my troopers. They were all young lads, on the cusp of manhood and at the peak of their physical energies, but they were new to the horrors of humanity. Then again, they'd signed on to do this job.

I fetched a towel from the tent, folded it and covered the hand, weighting the edges down with stones from the fireplace; then I jogged down to the station.

~

Kennedy and the others stood staring down in horror at the hand in the grass. I took my notebook out and made a quick sketch of the position of the hand and the badge. Trooper Scott had left town earlier, just as we could really have used him.

O'Malley walked away, his face to the fence, his shoulders shaking. Poor lad. Jackson and Vogel were white-faced; Lawlor looked at me like a dog who'd been whipped, needing me to make sense of this atrocity for him, but I couldn't. Jackson couldn't take his eyes off it, and when he finally did he shouted, 'Fuck' at the top of his voice and stamped away. Vogel was busy praying.

'This is some bloody grudge,' Kennedy murmured. 'You have to sleep at the hotel, mate.'

'No, I won't be chased away,' I said. 'This is police land and we don't take a step backwards.'

'Then arm yourself,' Kennedy replied. 'Rifle and pistol.'

O'Malley came back over, eyes a little watery. 'What are we going to do, sir?'

'Our jobs, son,' Kennedy said, with a grim look.

Mrs Owen had been watching, her head barely visible above the fence railing in the thick mist. 'Sergeant, everything all right?' she called.

I walked over to her while the others went back to the station with the hand in a sack.

'Yes, nothing to worry about,' I assured her. 'Just routine police business.'

'I didn't come down in the last shower,' she said with a wry smile. 'But I wanted to ask a favour of you. I need some kindling chopped.'

'I can do that.'

'I do struggle a bit now Davy's gone.'

'He chopped your wood, did he?'

'Yes, after my Clyde passed away last spring. Davy were a good lad, kind and helpful.'

The woodshed was on the eastern side of her cottage, beside the chook run. Where Clyde did the business, as she called it: killing a chook on a Sunday and chopping the wood for the stove. He'd built a strong corrugated-iron shelter for the chopped wood directly opposite the chook run. What a place for a chook shed, right opposite the place where the birds could listen to the fall of the axe on the stump day in, day out, wondering when their time was up.

'I'll get this sorted out for you in no time,' I said, taking off my coat and tunic and picking up the axe. I was relieved to be doing something routine again.

I'd taken to chopping wood to help me cope with the pain of my extensive scarring. Raising the axe stretched the scars under my arm and along my chest, preventing them from seizing up. It hurt like nobody's business at first, so agonising I thought I'd pass out, particularly if I'd not chopped for a while. But I knew that if I kept at it, relief would come.

Mrs Owen watched with her tam-o'-shanter on and a thick knitted blanket around her shoulders. Alfie sat by the chooks, staring in at them with intense interest.

I brought the axe down, split the log into two. Placed a half on the stump and whacked it into halves again.

'You look like you've done this before,' she said.

'Oh yes, and I can keep doing it if you like.'

'I could do your meals in return – that's what Davy did. He always ate with me and Clyde. Buck ate at the hotel because he liked to see who was in town and so on.'

'Did you know Buck well?'

'He was our neighbour for thirty years. He and Clyde had their differences, mind, and they both liked to be right.'

'That's a failing with most men, I reckon,' I said, panting and putting the axe down. 'I'll stack these while I'm here.'

'Come in for breakfast when you're done,' she said, and pottered off.

First I sorted through Scanlon's mess, piling everything according to size, feeling a little shamed by the obsessive pleasure it was giving me given the recent shocks. The tent burning, Scanlon's hand and the letter from the Light Horse. Those words, *recalled to active duty*, shocking in their confidence, their command, their imperative. I wasn't being invited back, I was being recalled. As if I'd always been theirs and just didn't know it.

149

I inspected the axe. It needed sharpening and I couldn't see a whetstone anywhere. I was poking about behind the chook shed when I sensed somebody nearby. My hair stood on end. The fog was still heavy and visibility low. I peered around the side. Alfie was licking the hand of young Frank Simmons, who was wrapped in an enormous coat. My heart gave a jolt. Had Frankie found Scanlon's hand and left it for us?

'If you need a trooper, Lawlor's on duty,' I called out. 'Down at the Commercial. You'll see the signs telling you how to find our office.'

'Nah, I just saw your dog. He is your dog, right?'

'I think he's lost, but I'm keeping him until someone claims him.' I returned to sorting through the chopped wood. The chickens stopped their muttering and came over to the wire to watch boy and dog. All Orpingtons, the standard Australian chook that did for eggs and meat.

'Do you know my mum?' Frank asked.

'Yeah, she lives just down the road, opposite the post office. White cottage, vine on the fence, can't miss it.'

He rolled his eyes and giggled. 'I know where she lives, I live with her. But are you friends?'

'No, we're not. I met Mrs Simmons some years ago when I was in Colley, back in 1906. But we aren't friends. Acquaintances, more like.'

'What's acquaintance?'

'Means you know someone, maybe see them every day, but you don't know them well enough to use their Christian name or invite them into your home.'

He nodded as though that seemed reasonable. I picked up a chunk of wood that needed splitting and tossed it onto the pile.

'Why do you ask – is your mum all right?'

150

He nodded.

'When does your dad get back?'

'Another two weeks, he reckons. He's going to take me on one of his jobs, when I'm a bit older. We'll sleep under the cart and have a campfire.'

'That'll be fun.' I kept sorting, occasionally glancing at him and the dog.

'I want a dog but Mum says they cost too much to keep.'

'You have to be able to do right by them.'

'Yeah, Dad says that too. But I think if we had a dog, he could protect us, Mum and my little sister. Dad says I have to protect them, and a dog would help me do that.'

'Protect them from what?'

He shrugged, then Mary came around the corner out of the mist, curls bouncing, little one on her lovely hip, avoiding my eyes.

'Get home this instant, Frank, right now, or I'll give you a dose of castor oil. Full of worms, you are.'

He got up and ran, and I looked over at Mary.

She put the infant on her other hip, raised her chin defiantly. 'I love my kids, Gus. I didn't mean what I said ... the other night, all right? I just ...'

'Must be tough on your own, Mrs Simmons,' I said, looking away at the chooks.

'But I'm not on my own,' she said, her voice breaking. 'He's never here, and when he comes home, he can't wait to get away, because this one screams and carries on and Frank won't leave him alone. What if he doesn't come back one day? What then? I'll have to put them in an orphanage, and I won't have anywhere to live and ...'

'He sends you money?'

151

She nodded.

'Because I can charge him for failing to support his family, Mrs Simmons.'

'No, he sends money, never enough but,' she said, and took a closer look at me. 'What's this Mrs Simmons business? It's Mary. Where's the old Gus gone?'

'He's not here anymore.'

Mary gave me a mocking smile. 'He's in there, I see him hiding, smacking his lips at the sight of me. Men don't change, so don't be kidding yourself you're a buttoned-up copper, because they're the worst of it, using their badge to get under a girl's skirts. Is that why you're a demon now? Straight to the front of the queue, eh?'

'Mrs Simmons, I have to get on with my chores.'

'To hell with you then, Sergeant Hawkins.'

She flounced off into the fog. I called after her, then joined her on the road, panting.

'What?' she snapped, tossing those fiery curls, all damp with moisture. God almighty, but she was voluptuous, like a vivid red hibiscus in full bloom. Deciding not to have sex meant it was all I could think about. Sex with Mary.

She gave me a lazy, knowing smile. The white, smooth skin of her neck led to the white, smooth skin of her breasts, and there was a bright curl blowing against her cheek.

'Mary, are you thinking of anyone specifically when you talk about the demons and ...'

She tossed her head with impatience. 'What a bore you turned into, mate.'

'Do you mean Buck Barrett and Scanlon? Or just Barrett, using his badge to ...?'

'Seduce women?'

'Yes.'

'I never had anything to do with them beyond them picking on Frankie. But I know what the demons get up to. You ought to take a broom to that lot up at Gibbet Hill.'

She left and I watched mournfully as her sumptuous hips sashayed away from me. But if I let that principle out of the iron box of my conscience, I would return to being the man who shamed himself, who traded his *arete* for the grubby state of *kakos*, which was basically unworthy shittiness.

I trailed back to my woodheap. Alfie trotted along beside me, spry and pleased, looking up at me with approval. *Virtue is its own reward, Gus.*

I picked up a chunk of kindling and tossed it onto the right pile. With Scanlon's murder crowding my mind, there was no way I could get out and inspect the other stations and troopers. God knows what louche pastimes they got up to at the Gibbet Hill station. I imagined troopers, humming 'Let Me Call You Sweetheart' while dancing cheek to cheek with scantily clad barmaids on their afternoons off.

16

Mrs Owen called me in for breakfast. I had to take my boots off and put on a pair of thick knitted bootees before she'd let me in. She gave the dog a dirty look and insisted I tie him up outside so he wouldn't go after the goats. As I did this, I noticed the surviving tabby stable cat from the station sitting among the orange nasturtiums, unconcerned by his mate's death.

'He had a friend, another tabby,' Mrs Owen said, looking at the cat. 'Wonder where he's got to?'

'I found him on my block,' I said. 'Looked like he'd taken a bait.'

She shook her head and tut-tutted. 'Not baiting season. That's spring, when all the vixens have their kittens. And they have to tell you lot and you have to put a sign up in Mrs Lennox's window.'

Mrs Owen's kitchen was quite large, almost the largest room in her cottage, by the looks of it. She had a sagging scrubbed pine table pushed up against the wall, a couple of chairs, a huge woodstove, a dresser with a full dinner set in pale green, shelves crammed with preserves and, sitting on a crocheted lace doily, an old daguerreotype of Mr Owen. Beside him was a small pale blue vase of pink and yellow snapdragons.

'That's my Clyde,' she said when I entered the kitchen. 'Pay him no mind.'

She nodded at a chair, and once I was settled she ladled a mass of steaming porridge into my bowl and put a tin of golden syrup in front of me. She went back to the stove, where she broke eggs, the crack of their shells startling me. I shovelled the porridge in; it was made with goats' milk with an underlying taste of straw.

'Aren't you eating?' I asked.

'Had mine. Go on, go for your life,' she said, staring down into the frying eggs. 'Davy had a good appetite, like you, God bless him.'

'Did you know a Sam Hong, a Chinese healer? Left town a couple of years ago?'

'Oh yes, I knew Sam. He was a much better healer than old Bill Pomeroy. My Clyde would go to him and he'd fix all his aches and pains just like that. He was the last of the celestials. They aren't welcome round here. There was a white woman, married to the last butcher before the one we got now, she ran off with a Chinaman.'

'Really?'

Mrs Owen nodded. 'She did. Scandalous, it was. Elsie was her name, and she said to me, "Oh, Meggie, he treats me so kindly." Can you imagine?'

'Caused a stir?'

'Did it ever. My Clyde liked the Chinese too. He ran a team of Chinese timber cutters for years. He reckoned they were hard workers, and they'd still smile and have a laugh at the end of each day. He made sure they had their rice each day and vegetables from the garden. That's when I started to grow the vegetables, to keep the Chinamen happy. Clyde said they'd add their dried odds and ends to the rice and sit around the fire on their hams eating and laughing. Yeah, he had a lot of time for them Chinese, but I warned him, I said, "Don't you bring them back here, not them nor

that muck they eat." He laughed, said he wouldn't bring them back here because maybe I'd take a fancy to one of them, like Elsie did, and run off to China. "Not on your nelly," I said.'

She came over and slid a couple of eggs onto a plate, pushed a plate of fresh damper at me and then sat down and took her knitting out. Now she lapsed into silence, just the clack of the needles and the bleats from the goats drifting down the slope and through the open back door, where the dog sat sniffing the scents from the kitchen as they wafted past.

'When did Clyde pass away?'

'October last year. Then Buck in January and now poor Davy. Been some sadness on this hill.'

'My condolences,' I murmured, and drank my tea. 'Mrs Owen, do you know of anyone who might have benefited from Trooper Scanlon's death?'

'Me?' she said, looking up in surprise. 'No, I mind my own business. I never gossip. Hear no evil, speak no evil.'

Never gossiped indeed, having just told me all about the butcher's wife Elsie.

'Did Davy have any girls he was sweet on? Any visits, any jealous blokes in town, that sort of thing?'

She shook her head. 'I don't know his personal doings, but he was a good neighbour, and he didn't deserve this.'

Not many people deserved a bullet in the head. I sensed she knew more than she was prepared to say, but now wasn't the time to push her. I got up to leave.

'Thank you for a delicious breakfast,' I said, bringing a smile to her wrinkled old face.

After the horror of the hand and the rush of realisation that the killer

156

was out there watching, being invited into this warm, cosy home was like balm on a blister. Full of simplicity and order, a place where old Clyde had eaten his supper and they'd shared a laugh at the end of the day, the goats bleating and the sizzle of frying onions and the grasses turning gold in the long summers of the west.

As I left, Percy arrived at the back door, a basket on his arm. 'Come for the veggies, Mrs Owen,' he said with a grin.

'All right, love, let's go and see what we've got.'

She tucked her knitting away and I paused and watched the two of them wander up to the vegetable garden. Mrs Owen filled his basket with a huge bunch of bright green spinach and some crimson beetroot. A willy wagtail sat on the old timber fence. I untied Alfie, who wriggled with happiness. The world was not full of monsters: it was simply that I'd put myself in the way of them by my own stupid choices. I walked with Percy down to his mother's shop.

'Mum said you'd been a soldier,' he said.

'Yes, I was.'

'I've got some lead soldiers,' he said, pulling a few little figures out of his pocket. 'They wear red coats. Did you wear a red coat?'

'No, that was the British, and they don't wear red anymore. Makes you a target for the enemy.'

'Percy, enough dawdling,' a voice called. 'The sergeant's got a lot to be getting on with.' It was Mrs Lennox, her black skirts swept against her legs by the wind, sharp eyes watching me like a cat. Percy hurried towards his mother and disappeared into the house.

'Mrs Lennox, have you seen anybody approaching the police block in the last few days?' I asked. 'Anyone at all?'

'Nobody comes up here,' she said. 'The station is only here because there used to be, back last century, more pubs and a gaol up here. The Commercial's the centre of town now.'

'So anyone up here, apart from Mrs Owen and myself, has no business being here?'

'You could say that. I rarely see anyone up here. But I'm not looking, either. Good day to you, Sergeant.'

~

I had to go to Bathurst for the enquiry – a day in, a day there and a day back. I suggested to Kennedy that Wallace could keep until I got back, as he was a dangerous man.

'You think I can't deal with him?' Kennedy said. 'I was a beat cop for years, a dab hand with a truncheon. And I can shoot straighter than a die.'

'Not doubting your abilities, but I'd rather be present. I'm supposed to be in charge of field operations, after all.'

'Suit yourself. I've got more than enough to keep me busy. I want to take the lads up to the cemetery, have a look at how the gunman got in and out.'

'Go up Insolvency Creek, see what you can find.'

'Yeah, like a wild boar. You know what they do? Bastards will charge you, slash your calf with their tusks, and when you're down they come back and finish you off. I'll leave that job for you, sport.'

The grey mare was still in the police paddock – nobody had claimed her. I had to do something about it because our paddock could barely sustain the five horses we already kept. I'd ride her into Bathurst for the enquiry, I decided. They could sort her out and I could take Alfie with me.

No dogs on the coach.

I went to the tack room in the coach station to fetch her saddle and the saddlebags, dusted them off and went through the contents again. Took out the dirty postcards, six in all, shuffled through them, flipping them over to see if there was any clue as to where they came from. I'd looked through them before, but hastily, as I was in the mysterious tent and expecting a bullet at any moment. There wasn't anything until I came to the fifth card. Some faint pencil marks.

I took the card out into the sun, held it this way and that, and deciphered the words *pretty mary colley opp p.o.*

~

Mary answered her door, face flushed, the sound of a screaming infant echoing down the hall.

'Whatever it is, it'll have to wait,' she said.

'It can't wait.'

'Then you'd better explain to her that you want to speak to her mother now. I'm sure she'll oblige,' she yelled at me. 'And I said not to come to the house.'

'I need to speak to you urgently about a police matter.'

'Bloody Frank, right?' she said, turning away and pacing down the hall to where the infant was howling.

I followed her into a small, sunny kitchen with a woodstove and scrubbed pine table, a few stuffed toys on the floor and a half-eaten bowl of porridge on the table. Mary picked up the kid and soothed her, rocking her back and forth patiently while glaring at me. Eventually the grizzly little

girl's eyes drooped, and her head dropped onto her mother's shoulder.

'You want to put her down before we talk?'

'Ha. If I put her down, she'll go off like a strip of bungers. What is it?'

'The dog you've seen me with. Seen it before?'

'No.'

'Frank seems familiar with it,' I said.

She shrugged. 'Just likes dogs.'

'The dog seems to know him.'

'And? And? Is that why you're here?'

'Mary, do you see this?' I took the postcard out of my pocket and showed her the writing on the back.

She stared at it, swallowed, then shrugged again. 'What of it?'

'What's his name?'

'Don't know,' she said and, turning away, picked up the porridge bowl with her free hand and placed it by the sink.

'You do know. He's some fellow you've been dallying with.'

'That's my business. He's long gone anyway, and his dog's run off.'

'He's dead, Mary, and I need to know who he is.'

She froze, her back to me. 'Charlie ... I don't know his last name. Had a grey horse and that dog. He paid a visit and left, and I never saw him again.'

'He was thrown into the lock-up. Why?'

'How would I know?' she snapped. 'All I know is that my girl can't eat. She screams after every meal, and Dr Pomeroy says she needs an operation but Jack won't hear of it, says to give her gripe water because he's not paying for an operation.'

She turned to the child, kissing its sleeping head, leaving her mouth there as her tears ran into her daughter's dark curls.

'I'm sorry.'

'Yeah, so am I,' she said softly. 'Sorry I ever came into this wretched world. I had two baby boys before this one, buried them myself only weeks after they were born, and where was Jack? Digging his stupid wells, and both of them dead in their first month. Jack blames me, says I'm a rotten mother and that's why my babies died, and now I'm going to lose this one. So I don't care about Charlie or what happened to him.'

'Can the church raise the money?'

'Don't go to church anymore. God's got no time for us women.'

Her voice was raised, and the child stirred and whimpered. I noticed a movement by the door. Young Frankie. I wondered how long he'd been listening. I turned to speak to him but he ran off.

'When did you last see him?'

She looked up in surprise. 'You still pestering me about Charlie when I told you my baby's going to die?'

'I'll have a word to Dr Pomeroy. He may know of some charity that can help get the operation for your girl.'

'Jack won't take charity.'

'He's going to have to or, like I told you, I'll charge him with failing to provide for his dependents.'

'You can do that?'

'Yes ... It's not terribly helpful in the long run, but as a threat it might work.'

'Charlie came to visit the night before the fire. He only stayed a few hours and then left around midnight.'

'Did he say he'd come back?'

'No, because I told him not to. That's all I know. Now, go out the

back door – you can get through to the lane, less people to see you. And please, ask Dr Pomeroy.'

~

A cart trundled into town carrying long planks of wood, followed by another cart laden with bricks and workmen. I watched them head up to the police block. Shortly after, the foreman found us tucked away in the pub, announced he'd brought the materials to build the new stable and asked where I wanted them placed.

'The clean-up crew hasn't been through,' I said. 'Stable can't be built yet.'

He pulled a scrappy bit of paper out of his pocket, flicked it and said, 'My schedule says deliver today. Not here to build it, matey.'

Matey. I didn't like the sneer in his voice. Probably been in a lock-up a dozen times or more.

I called Vogel over and said, 'I am deputising this officer, Trooper Wilhelm Vogel, to oversee delivery and placement.'

'Hmph. Don't need him,' the foreman grumbled.

I took Vogel aside and handed him the file with all the invoices and paperwork for the building supplies, which had been sitting in my in-tray. 'Your job is to match all goods delivered with all goods ordered and to ensure what we are paying for is what we get.'

He stood a little taller. 'Yes, sir.'

'They can place it all on the far western side of the block. And nobody is to touch my fireplace. Tell them it's a police fireplace if they argue.'

'Yes, sir.'

I unleashed him and off he went to make their life hell.

~

It was a relief to be on the road again next morning, despite the inquiry waiting for me. It had to be done, but tell my nerves that. Up here on the plateau, the wind blew, the air was as fresh as cold water. There were no troopers hanging off me waiting for me to give the order, no townsfolk giving me blank looks or hostile stares. I had a horse and a hound – all I needed was a falcon on my wrist.

The grey mare was an easy, willing creature. Alfie ran along beside, game for adventure. The sky was bright, and once we'd toiled up the hills and were on the plateau, I set the mare to a canter and then a gallop to see how she'd run. I brought her to a halt and turned, panting, to see Alfie way back on the road, racing towards us, tongue flapping, determined not to be left behind.

There was a small hotel at the hallway mark where I fed and watered the three of us, and then we set off on the slog to Bathurst through untold miles of sun-dried paddock. By the time we arrived at the mounted troopers' barracks, Alfie was sitting awkwardly on my lap, I was slouching like a chaff bag with my mind emptied of thought, and the mare was plodding, head down. The sun was almost at the horizon.

~

I could have slept in the barracks, but I would've preferred to sleep in a ditch than bunk in with a gaggle of farting, snoring troopers. Instead I found a room at a hotel near the police station, one that was indifferent to the dog. I ate a quick supper in the crowded dining room, then took a

long walk to allow the wind to clear my head. A couple of girls came out from the shadows, offering to make me happy. They'd have a job doing that: a quick knee-trembler with another despairing human certainly wasn't going to work.

I walked for an hour, dodging brawls outside pubs and more come-ons from the town streetwalkers. The clear sky above was crammed with stars. I inspected the gardens of some worthy citizens, noting the shops and businesses. After the three-street town of Colley, it felt like a metropolis.

I returned to my room, stripped off, washed and fell on the bed, rolling down into a ditch in the middle of the mattress. The bed stank of cigarette smoke; on the wall hung a framed lithograph of Landseer's *Stag at Bay*, sagging behind its glass. I rummaged in the drawers of the bedside cabinet and found a Bible, which, when held by the spine, automatically opened at the well-thumbed page of the Song of Solomon. I was surprised the pages weren't stuck together with the rapturous essence of travelling salesmen.

It was certainly a page in the Bible that enthralled us boys at school. The line that so intrigued us was: 'Let my beloved come to his garden and eat its choicest fruits.' We breathlessly speculated about the masculine possessive pronoun, surmising with schoolboy logic that she – the possessor of the garden – belonged to us, that her garden was actually ours, to cavort in as we pleased. It was heady stuff.

The scripture master was ready for our bold questions about the Song of Solomon and put on a long-suffering air as he answered: 'Boys, it is to be read as an allegory of the marriage of the Christian soul to Christ. And the "hill of frankincense", since you ask, is merely a reference to the eminence of those who crucify earthly desires, as they shall be exalted.'

Boyish sniggers faded to dumbfounded silence. I put the Bible back

in the cabinet drawer, blew out the candle, pushed and pummelled my pillow into shape, dropped my head onto it, yanked the blanket up and tried counting backwards from a thousand.

~

I woke to Alfie frantically licking my face. I pushed him away mumbling threats, rolled over and sighed and dozed a bit longer until daylight filled the room. I sat up, relieved the night was over. Alfie was looking at me as if we'd shared a tryst during the night.

'Try licking my face again and see what happens, matey.'

He thumped his tail and grinned at me. He'd done it the night before we left too, as if he could see the terror in my dreams and had to rescue me. It was uncanny.

The head station was across the road from the barracks, not far from the hotel. I tied Alfie up outside, went in and waited on a chair in the hallway, looking around at the polished floorboards, the whitewashed walls and mahogany chairs, the portraits of past police on the walls, the low noise echoing through from the offices, the soft clatter of typewriters.

I'd taken care with my uniform: everything that could be polished had been, all creases banished, beard trimmed, boots immaculate. But my heart was galloping, swerving, bucking, and I found it hard to get a breath. They were going to ask me to go back to that moment when the bullet breeched Scanlon's skull. Then I was called.

17

Three men sat at a long table in front of two large windows. I sat on a chair a couple of yards away from them in the middle of the room, almost unable to see their faces because of the glare. A couple of stenographers perched at desks to one side, and there was a uniformed officer by the door. The three were Northrup, MacKerras and another senior officer from the mounted trooper offices in Sydney whose name I could not recall. He had to be the reason the enquiry was being held on a Saturday. He could be back at his desk Monday morning, having got this provincial unpleasantness out of the way.

I gave them an account of what happened and then they asked questions. As with most enquiries, everything seemed so clear and obvious, and all was calm: papers neatly stacked, pencils sharpened, voices restrained.

'Your behaviour on return to the town was described as being "erratic" and "undisciplined".'

That was MacKerras. I blinked a few times. The three men with the light behind them. Cowards hiding their faces. I knew what they were up to.

'I was not erratic or undisciplined, sir,' I said as calmly as I could. 'I observed the station fire and reported the shooting of Scanlon and the fire to Bathurst immediately and asked for reinforcements. Sir.'

'I have reliable witnesses whose accounts are solid,' MacKerras said. 'You were expected, as a senior officer, to calmly take control of the situation and reassure the populace, not swear at them, cry ... and use the telephone.'

I had the urge to get up and walk out, and on the way tell them all to fuck off to hell. But that was no way to end this miserable episode in my life.

'Sir.'

'Well? What have you to say in your defence?' MacKerras persisted.

'Nothing, sir.'

'Your explanation,' Northrup quickly added. 'For the record.'

I couldn't give it. Why were they forcing me to speak of my shock and terror? Who were these shiny-arsed pen pushers who'd probably never experienced the terror of ambush? I stared at them, and they stared back at me.

'The body in the lock-up,' Northrup said eventually.

'Scanlon said nothing to me about him. All records pertaining to his identity have been lost. Sir.'

Then we reached the subject of Scanlon's mutilation.

'What do you make of it?' asked the officer from Sydney.

'That's not for me to say, sir.'

'But your personal opinion, off the record,' he said, nodding at the stenographers to stop. This was a bit unorthodox and made me uncomfortable, but what the hell.

'The shooter plans the ambush,' I said. 'He aims for and kills Scanlon.

167

Then Scanlon's horse takes off with his body. Nobody can factor that in – it's entirely random and unusual. The shooter keeps shooting at me, but I escape back to the town. But the shooter, he's just murdered a police officer – he's crossed into some dangerous territory, but he's not afraid. In fact, he sees more opportunity to enact his anger and contempt when Scanlon's horse takes off. He goes in search, finds the body. He doesn't stab it in a wild frenzy of rage; he cuts, deliberately, coolly. This is not an act in the heat of the moment. Then he waits for us to get reinforcements so he can rub our noses in it, as if he needs us to see how powerful he is. Or believes himself to be.'

Nobody said anything for a moment. A deep hatred for mounted troopers wasn't unheard of, but acting on it was. We were all suddenly in someone's gun sights.

'The arson on your tent and the hand left on the police block?' Northrup asked.

'Taunting us to disrupt morale, maybe? Or a threat. I'd like to recommend an alienist look at this. The Detective Branch in Sydney would know somebody. Because, to my mind, the mutilation is the key to this case.'

'An alienist?' MacKerras said, as if I'd recommended a circus clown.

'A psychiatrist, I think they call them these days,' Northrup said. 'What can they tell us?'

'Why he's doing what he's doing, and what he might do next?'

'We don't need those quacks,' MacKerras said. 'Kennedy knows what to do.'

I was dismissed and went straight to the nearest hotel and had a double whisky. Northrup came in just as I tossed it down.

'I'll pretend I didn't see that. Not the right time or place.'

'Sir.'

'You handled the enquiry well.'

'You mean MacKerras's uncalled-for attack on me, sir?'

Northrup was taken aback at my boldness. But I wasn't going to cop a dressing-down from a pen pusher, no matter his rank.

'Put in a complaint if you like, but I will hear no more of that sort of talk.'

'While I'm in town I'd like to look through the records of the Colley station,' I said. 'Those that have been kept. See if I can pick up some clues about who may have had a problem with Scanlon.'

'Such as?'

'Men who have been frequently arrested. Names would all be in Scanlon's incident book.'

'Go and get some lunch and I'll have the files ready for you.'

'And a plan of the burnt-down station, please,' I said.

'Why do you want that?'

'I can't recall it, and I want to know, if it was up on stumps, if the cavity was boarded up.'

'It had been, when it was first built, but Barrett pulled the boards off. He got permission to replace them but never did. He stored his copies of *The Bulletin* in the cavity. Great piles of them, stashed under there, and he was in that station for thirty years. I spoke to him about it many times.'

Poor bastard in the lock-up paid for every single one of them.

~

169

After lunch, I waited in the wide hallway for Northrup to find a desk and the records and whiled away the time looking at the framed photographs on the wall. All taken in 1910, during the visit of Lord Kitchener to Bathurst to unveil the Boer War memorial. There he was, Lord K of K, with his dress sword and sash, stern and upright, the hero soldier of the British Empire, the man who ordered the burning of farmhouses over the heads of Boer women and children. The flames still flickered inside my skull each night.

Northrup appeared. 'Ah, Bathurst's finest moment. See this one?' he said, nodding at a photograph. 'The parade was magnificent – and look there, the mounted troopers. That's me out the front. Everything went smoothly, no spooked horses, every man upright and solemn.'

The line of traps in dress uniform were in front of the lines of mounted militia, chocolate soldiers who took themselves too seriously and liked to prance about in feathered hats and gold epaulettes. Then they'd move on to the more serious business of mingling and mutual back-scratching. But Northrup's eyes shone as he recalled that day when the hero stepped down from Olympus to be among the mortals. I'd suspected Northrup was a shiny boots man.

'And see here? That's our new memorial for all the Bathurst and district men who served in South Africa. You might want to take a look while you're in town, it's very stirring.'

I flicked a glance at him. He was still gazing at the photographs, remembering the glory of it all. Men who actually fought would fall about laughing if they saw this happy day. I'd do my best to avoid the memorial because the war was not over for me. I was dying of wounds, slowly but surely. The recall to the Light Horse was a handful of salt in those wounds, and yet I hadn't dismissed the idea completely.

Northrup found me an empty desk and a clerk to fetch whatever I needed, and brought me the last incident book on hand and copies of the reports Scanlon had returned. The police station had burned down on the nineteenth of April. The incident book I was looking at stopped about two months before then, and the reports, regular as clockwork, stopped a week before.

I made my way through the incident book, finding that the disturbances followed a celestial rhythm: the gravitational pull of the pub. They reached a crescendo on a Saturday night, then ebbed away, only to crash over the pub again the following Saturday night.

The same names did show up with monotonous regularity: drunk and disorderly, dragged to the lock-up and sent on their way the next morning. I assumed these men were the dredging crew. Josiah Mutkins was one, the bloke O'Malley had sniffed out. Jack Simmons appeared every couple of months, drunk and disorderly. I briefly speculated on Mary and Scanlon having a dalliance and Jack Simmons taking out his fury on Scanlon with a bullet to the skull. It was plausible, as it appeared I was not the only man she'd shared her charms with.

There were no random shootings, no murders, no manslaughters, plenty of rounding up truants – again wee Frank Simmons appeared – gun licences renewed, shooting licences renewed, pig culling requests, rabbit shooters going through the town, doggers selling scalps. Just the usual rural business of a small-town station.

A couple of incidents stood out. There'd been picnic races held at the town racetrack, which I had yet to find, last November. There was a report of Edmund Wallace attacking Buck Barrett in front of the crowd. Barrett was off duty and a serious brawl ensued. Wallace only got a warning. I jotted this down in my notebook.

Next I sifted back through the years, looking for the report on William Fitzgerald's death. Found in the river by Trooper Scanlon, body retrieved by Scanlon and Barrett, water in the lungs, consistent with drowning, ruled as a suicide. No wonder poor Hilde was miserable. To lose a young husband is a terrible loss, but to think he was so full of despair while married to her was another entirely.

I did notice one more thing to follow up. About five or six weeks before he was killed, Scanlon had three days' leave. At no other time in his three years of service had he applied for leave, which in itself was unusual.

As I was scribbling in my notebook, I was approached by a young uniform who said I was to report to Superintendent MacKerras's office immediately.

~

MacKerras's room was spartan. No fire in the grate, no carpet, window partly open on a bitterly cold day. Desk with the bare minimum: no ashtrays, no teacups, photographs or bowls of goldfish like the Bourke super's desk. MacKerras was obviously a man who luxuriated in self-denial.

'There's been an incident in Colley,' Northrup said, interrupting my thoughts. 'We've just had a wire from a Trooper Jackson. It appears that Detective Kennedy, along with Troopers Vogel, Lawlor and O'Malley, attended the Wallace farm, whereupon the man in question, Mr Edmund Wallace, fired a weapon and shot Trooper Lawlor, seriously injuring him. Wallace then absconded, with his weapon, into the dense bushland to the south-east of his property.'

It took me a moment to digest this, it was such a massive blunder. I could scarcely believe Kennedy had been so foolish. They were all panicky at the appearance of the hand. The loss of Lawlor was a blow. He was steady, reliable, could turn his hand to most things and had the driest of wits.

'When was this, Sir?'

'Early this morning. We've dispatched an ambulance,' Northrup said.

You are to return immediately to Colley and lead a manhunt,' MacKerras said, giving me a stone-eyed look. 'Apprehend Wallace and place him in custody.'

'Why did Kennedy go after Wallace?' Northrup asked. 'Was he onto something?'

'I don't know, sir. I went to Wallace's property with one trooper in an attempt to question him about his alibi on the morning Scanlon was killed. We found him slaughtering his dairy herd and he threatened to shoot us if we didn't get off his property. We retreated as I considered it unsafe.'

'So Kennedy went back to follow up on the alibi and Wallace's threats to you and O'Malley?' Northrup said.

'It would appear that way. I decided not to follow up until we could determine why he was killing stock, in case it was a transmissible disease. Kennedy has ignored my decision.'

'He is your senior officer.'

'Sir.' *Then he can clean up the mess, not me.*

'I recall some business between Sergeant Barrett and Edmund Wallace,' MacKerras said.

'Buck Barrett was having an affair with Wallace's wife, sir,' Northrup said.

That was a surprise. No wonder her kid was dragging her away from us

– and no wonder Wallace was furious at the sight of the traps on his land.

MacKerras's jaw muscle tightened. It was the most expressive thing about him. 'Blasted fool.'

'Barrett was certainly misbehaving, sir,' Northrup said. 'But I see no connection there with Scanlon.'

'Vengeance,' MacKerras said. 'Men in mounted troopers' uniform. Kennedy's got the right man. Your job is to retrieve Wallace from the bush, Hawkins. Dismissed.'

~

I walked down the polished floorboards, cap in hand, the daylight beckoning to me through the open door, when I heard Northrup call me back.

'Word from Agriculture is there was no disease on Wallace's property that they know about,' he said. 'They suggested he was clearing out spent cows.'

'I took the precaution I thought was correct, sir.'

'Noted. This investigation must take precedence, though.'

'Over the economy of the district? I think you'd find farmers disagreeing with that assessment. And if it's so important, and the cold-blooded murder of a serving officer is important, why are we being left to do this on a shoestring, sir?'

'Because shoestrings are all we have. It's up to us to do our best. If we pull mounted troopers from their stations, we just don't know if the criminal element will take advantage of that. They know we're wounded – it's in all the papers.'

'I don't need more troopers, sir, I need Trooper Scott back and a uniform to run the station while we hunt down Wallace.'

'Scott has been deployed on another job – an escaped prisoner, dangerous man – and there are no other black trackers available. But I'll send you a uniform to run the station. See the quartermaster and get what you need for the manhunt. He can have a horse packed and ready. I need you to leave today, so you can take a mount from the stables. We have what we have, Hawkins. Crimes like this don't happen often, and we aren't equipped or manned for it. If you can get some local men to assist, we can pay them a daily stipend.'

'Sir, I noted that Scanlon took three days' leave six weeks before he was killed. Do you know what that was for?'

'Personal leave, very run of the mill. We sent one of the men from the Capertee station to fill in. There were no problems.'

'Except he has no family to visit.'

'Probably came into town to buy personal items. Now, I have to be getting on,' Northrup said. 'My wife's due to have a baby any tick of the clock.' He had his hands on his hips and looked down at the floor, shaking his head as he murmured, 'I don't know how that happened.'

'Want me to explain it to you, sir?'

He laughed, slapped me on the shoulder and left.

I had a natter with the quartermaster. He was an old hand and knew exactly what we'd need, so I left him to it and went in search of Sam Hong, the man Pomeroy reckoned would have the ointment for my face.

18

The police barracks and stables were not far from the Macquarie River. Looking north-west, I could see acres of land under cultivation, with neat rows of cabbages, spinach, pumpkin vines, broad beans and more. This had to be Hereford, where Sam Hong now worked. Obviously not much money in Chinese healing if he had to do the back-breaking, filthy and cold work of toiling in vegetable gardens.

I made my way there along a levee, where a gang of kids, boys and girls, were chanting: *Ching-chong Chinaman, sitting on a rail, along came a white man and chopped off his tail.* They scattered as I strode towards them and regrouped once I'd passed. I made a mental note to think carefully if ever I had the urge to reproduce. The Chinese men ignored them.

A Chinaman in shabby trousers and an ancient bowler hat, wearing a shoulder yoke with two baskets either side, walked towards me. He nodded and kept going, ignoring my request to talk to him. I was in uniform, and that was enough to blow the wind up the arse of a man who wanted no trouble, and the Chinese had had enough of that.

The soil smelt rich and damp, watered by a donkey whim and human toil. I noticed a tin shed some way along and made my way there. The

Chinese could grow vegetables on a piece of corrugated iron and not much more: the vigour of the rows of vegetables was testament to their skill. Still, some people wouldn't eat their produce, and no government agency would buy from them.

By the tin hut, two ancient Chinamen sat beside a brazier playing mahjong, long clay pipes in their pursed mouths. They looked up at me for a moment and returned to their game.

'Sam Hong – do you know him?'

That got me nothing. A man who looked to be in his sixties, in a shabby coat and muddied trousers, came to the doorway of the hut, saw me and faded back into the darkness.

'He's a healer,' I said to the old men, pointing at the scar. 'He has some ointment I want to buy, for my face.'

The man came back out of the shadows and a smile spread across his wrinkled face. 'I remember you – you came through Colley five or six years ago. Drunk all the time. And you're still alive?'

'I seem to be,' I replied with a laugh. 'Sam Hong?'

He nodded and we shook hands. He had a broad Australian accent, as I remembered from years ago.

'I religiously apply the ointment you sold me, and chop wood whenever I can. It does help keep the scars from contracting.'

'Good, good. May I see your face closely?'

He came over and peered at my face, turning my head and nodding to himself. 'Very good, very good. Makes you very handsome, ha-ha.'

'You're from Gulgong, aren't you?' I asked.

'That's right,' he replied with a broad smile. 'Born on the goldfields. Sam Hong from Gulgong, ha-ha.'

'Got a family in China?'

'Never been to China, mate,' he said with a laugh. 'But the people here look at me and think I'm a coolie. I don't mind, it's easier to hide.'

'Why would you want to hide?'

A look of uncertainty flickered across his eyes and the bright smile faltered for a second.

'I wanted to buy some more ointment from you. If you have any, that is.'

'Not here, but I have a small barber shop in Furness Street – you can buy some there.'

'Could you post me some?' I asked. 'I'll pay now, but I'm stationed at Colley now and not in Bathurst all that frequently.'

His smile faded.

'Bill Pomeroy told me the two of you painted together at the waterhole.'

'Yes,' he said, clearly unhappy. 'We had many evenings painting together, talking shop.'

'Talking shop?'

'Healing, Chinese way or white devil way,' he said with a forced grin. 'Did Bill tell you where to find me?'

'Yes,' I said, getting my wallet out and handing him some money. 'Send it to Sergeant Augustus Hawkins, Colley Police Station.'

He nodded and tucked the money away. 'You work with Davy Scanlon, then?'

I gave him a close look. 'Davy Scanlon passed away a few weeks ago. Murdered in an ambush. We're looking for the killer now.'

Hong was silent for a long moment. 'I will post you the ointment. But you have to go now.'

'Mr Hong, do you know something about Scanlon's death? You won't be in any trouble if you tell me.'

'Ha. We're always in trouble in this country, whether we do anything or not.'

~

The quartermaster had tents, bedrolls, billies, cans of bully beef, nosebags and all the paraphernalia that four men and five horses would need while searching the bush, all packed and loaded onto a horse.

A spare horse was saddled and waiting, with extra saddlebags full of kit for him and two waterbags for me for the long ride ahead. I managed to talk the quartermaster into issuing me with a greatcoat and scarf, as I'd not expected an eight-hour ride on a cold night. I purchased some fruitcake at a bakery, had it wrapped up and packed it in my saddlebags, along with a couple of raw mutton flaps for the dog. I also bought a billy and a packet of tea, and some matches. After supper at the hotel, I set off around five pm, hoping to be tucked up in my tent by one am.

We set off, past neat cottages and paddocks, and soon there was only the occasional farmhouse and the creak of saddle leather. A dog barking somewhere inspired a volley of insults in exchange from Alfie, who trotted along beside my horse. It was a moonless night but the brilliant starlight in the clear sky helped. The dirt road to Colley, a well-used road, wasn't too hard to follow.

We stopped around eight and I pulled a fire together in a small fireplace obviously used by other travellers. I made a cup of tea and broke off a chunk of fruitcake, eating it while the packhorse and saddlehorse nosed around

the verge and Alfie tackled his mutton flap with gusto.

I lit a fag and looked at the stars, thinking of Sam Hong and his unease. He would have known Scanlon, but he'd asked no questions about how he died, as most people did, and he appeared more frightened than shocked and saddened. He needed to be officially questioned. I took out my notebook and jotted down the conversation. His reference to hiding was curious too. Hiding from whom, or what? There was not much local sympathy for the Chinese, of course. They took all the gold, they said, took it back to the Celestial Kingdom, and now there was nothing for the Australian working man to find.

I kicked over the coals, mounted up and on we plodded through the night. I encountered the ambulance carrying Lawlor back to Bathurst but didn't stop to talk. He needed a hospital more than he needed me. Colley was hidden away in the folds of the river valley, and it wasn't until you rounded a steep hill and looked down that you saw the lights of the town. It being past midnight, there were none, but I could see Mrs Owen's goats, their white coats glowing in the starlight to guide me home.

I unsaddled the horses, put them in the paddock and covered our manhunt kit with a tarp, ready to sort through it tomorrow. Alfie and I stepped into the tent. I secured the flap, stripped off and crawled onto my unsteady camp bed with a sense of acute animal pleasure. My last thoughts were about what fresh new screw-up awaited me in the morning.

~

In the morning, before hitting the chaos of the station, I dropped into Dr Pomeroy's rooms. He came out of his surgery wearing a brown suit vest

and fob chain and watch, white hair neatly combed and looking more doctorish than down at the waterhole. He peered over his spectacles and asked what he could do for me.

'My trooper, Ralph Lawlor. Can you tell me how bad his wound is?'

'A .22 bullet through both cheeks. Not good, but better than a .303. It took a few top molars but missed his tongue. Must have had his jaw open at just the right moment.'

'How was he?'

'In shock. I stopped the bleeding, got Clara Lennox down to give me a hand settling him down. She's good in a crisis. He went to Bathurst last night. They sent a nurse, too, for the long journey. Only the cops get a nurse.'

'He'll have bad scarring, and he was a handsome lad,' I said.

'Not too bad with a .22, but he'll probably go down to Sydney for the patch-up. I've seen much worse facial injuries on farmers, and they don't have the money for nurses or Sydney surgeons.'

'What can you tell me about Edmund Wallace, the man who shot him?'

He folded his arms and sighed. 'A bad-tempered man, always has been, even in good times.'

'His wife appears to be blind.'

'That was Ed's handiwork. He found out she'd been carrying on with Buck Barrett.'

'And he bashed her to the point of her losing her sight as punishment?'

'Had a go at Buck, too, at the picnic races, only last November. It was an ugly business. Ed called me out after he'd done Anne over. Can't say he was remorseful, but he didn't want her to die. Got two daughters.'

181

This was the man we were going to hunt down. Angry and violent with a grudge against the mounted troopers. *Thanks, Buck*, I thought, *for dragging the rest of us into your affairs.*

'I also wanted to ask you about Dawn Simmons.'

'She's got a hernia. Needs to be fixed with an operation. I told Mrs Simmons, I can't do it here – she has to go to Bathurst. I used to do the operations here when we had the hospital but that closed around ten years ago. Couldn't get the nurses to stay.'

'Mary doesn't have the money.'

'Jack Simmons has money; he just prefers to spend it on women he's not married to.'

'Is there a charity like the Benevolent Society that could pay for the operation?'

'They could give her a loan for the operation, but she won't qualify because she's married to a man who earns a living. If they pay for Dawn's operation, then Jack can carry on happily buying drinks for the dollymops in Mudgee or Gulgong. They won't have that, and nor should they.'

'Looks like I'm going to have to speak to him.'

'You can try. And if you can, tell him to fix his water tank. Mary has to get water from the river, and it's bad water. She boils it, but you can't boil the mercury or arsenic out of it. People don't believe me when I tell them. Never, ever drink from this river.'

~

O'Malley, Vogel and Jackson were all in the office when I walked in, huddled together as if they'd been talking. They had that look, the look

of a junior officer who knows one of his seniors, whose word he hangs off, has done something wrong. Not getting plastered and passing out in dog's diggings, but really wrong, like charging into an already inflamed situation and making it worse, plus getting a junior nearly killed. A very, very bad look.

Seemingly relieved that it was me and not Kennedy, they talked over one another in an effort to offload their unease. I was full to the brim and could take no more, as I had to sort the bloody mess out now.

O'Malley had no idea why Scanlon would have gone to Bathurst for a day. He hadn't stayed at the barracks, he hadn't logged in at the stables, so he must have taken the coach. A day in, a day there and a day back and no contact with a mate. But my immediate problem was the manhunt.

Kennedy walked in, and the troopers – except for O'Malley, who was on the desk – disappeared. I had to take these three on a manhunt with no black tracker, and they were not a happy lot at all.

'Need a word with you, Hawkins,' Kennedy said. 'In private.'

Off we went, out the back and onto the grass by the clotheslines to stand amid the stained sheets and threadbare towels blowing in the breeze. The back door opened outwards, so we always had to be cautious, lest we slam it into Hilde or some hapless customer coming in from the lavatories. Ray Fitzgerald was on the grass, dressed in shorts and singlet, doing his calisthenic exercises. His physique was impressive for a man his age.

'Wallace made a run for it, stupid bastard,' Kennedy said, lighting a fag, his face puffy and the bags under his eyes looking even roomier, if that were possible. 'He saw me, knew we'd come for him and slammed the door in my face. I went after him, shouted at him to stop but he didn't. I sent the lads after him and he shot Lawlor. He wouldn't have run if he wasn't guilty

as hell. Now he's off in the bush somewhere.

'After he ran, I had a nose around his house,' Kennedy continued. 'I've got all his financial documents, bills and receipts, that sort of thing. Looks like Ray Fitzgerald owns the land and Wallace was a tenant farmer. The rent was raised late March.'

I glanced over at Fitzgerald, who was lost in his quest for physical perfection and didn't appear to be listening.

'Why did he raise the rent? Have you asked him?'

'He's entitled to raise capital by raising rents, but it might have put Wallace under pressure. But you won't have any trouble catching him. He's got a bullet in him, so that'll slow him down.'

'What? Who shot him?'

'I did, because he needed to stop, bloody fool. Guilty as hell,' he said.

'Did you give warning?'

He paused before answering, which suggested he didn't. 'I reckon I did.'

'Where did you shoot him? Trunk or limb?'

'Yeah, ah, yeah, in his back,' he said, sucking on his fag as if it were going to save his life.

His back. Could it get any worse? He was looking at me, waiting for my reaction.

'Right, well, maybe it will make our job easier,' I said.

'I'm in a heap of shit,' he said, looking over at the river as he flicked ash from his cigarette.

'It's at your ankles and rising, but let's go back and search the outbuildings. I'll talk to the Wallace women, then we'll go after him. Bathurst is sending a uniform to mind the shop while we're up there, so you can sort through the evidence while we're gone.'

'What did MacKerras say?'

'Ordered me to catch him. What else is he going to say?'

'But he thinks he's guilty, doesn't he?'

'What would MacKerras know? Miles away in his comfy office, reading what we send him. He's not investigating this, we are. Or you are.'

~

I found Hilde poking sheets as they boiled in the coppers, a sheen of sweat on her face, her golden hair tied up and across her head, steam billowing around.

'Mrs Fitzgerald?'

She looked up, startled, then smiled. 'You have some laundry for me, Sergeant?'

'Ah, not with me but there'll be a bit of a deluge in a few days. We're going out on an operation, and it'll be mucky. I just wanted to ask you a quick question about Davy Scanlon.'

She took the paddle out of the copper, leant it against the wall and pushed a lock of hair from her face. She really was a bit of a sweetie, like a buttercup growing in a cowpat.

'I understand Davy took three days' leave around five or six weeks before he died. Do you know where he went?'

The light faded from her eyes and she looked away through the doorway. 'Oh, he was ...'

I waited, willing her to reveal it, as I could see her grappling with indecision.

'He had some business in Bathurst, so he needed three days, to get to there and back.'

'Do you know what his business was?'

She looked down at her feet, plucked at her apron and shook her head. 'He said he had to go. He went and he came back. But when he came back, he was really angry – he wouldn't say why.'

I didn't pester her any more in case I provoked tears. She was as fragile as glass, despite her endless toil. The troopers and I all saw and felt it. She provoked, in the masculine breast, a strong urge to rescue and protect. Although not in Fitzgerald's muscular and expanding chest.

19

The packhorse was laden with equipment, about as much as he could take, and we divided the rest between our four horses. I debated taking spare horses but, after a thorough check of the maps available, decided they'd only be a burden. We'd be doing much of this manhunt on foot.

Vogel, O'Malley and Jackson were all keyed up and looking for action, like a pack of hunting dogs. But often manhunts are futile plodding for miles with a dead body at the end of it, or a lunatic who's naked and dancing about with a sheep skull. As Wallace had a bullet in his back, my money was on finding a dead body. Then again, he might have enough hatred left in him to stay alive long enough to take one of us out.

While we waited for the coach bearing the uniform, I gathered the troopers outside the pub and spoke. 'Wallace is angry, unpredictable and armed. Our job is to find him, capture him and bring him in. To be successful at this, you wait for the order and you follow the order.' My eyes slid over to Vogel. 'We rely on each other, keep tight and act boldly, and we will succeed.'

It wasn't Leonidas at Thermopylae, but it would do.

Jackson took a match out of his mouth and said, 'What if he takes a

knife to our ... you know?'

It was a good point, one that had obviously lodged itself in their minds – as it had in mine. If it was an act designed to frighten the horses, it was doing its job.

'It won't hurt because you'll be dead,' I said.

'Yeah, but I don't want my girl to hear that's what happened. What'll she think of me? Unmanned and—'

'If one of us is killed, we retrieve the body, no matter how long it takes, no matter how dangerous. We will not allow our fallen comrades to be unmanned in death. We may die but we die as men doing our duty.'

They nodded and glanced at each other. I hoped I hadn't promised the impossible.

'Anyway, you're not going to need your dick if you're dead,' Vogel said. 'So don't worry about it.'

The others rolled their eyes at this typical contribution.

'We don't know what goes on after we die,' I said, 'and, personally, I'd like to keep my options open. There may be some pretty angels waiting for us to slip those white robes off and blow our heavenly trumpet, and we would not want to disappoint them.'

'Oh yeah,' Jackson said, his face brightening. 'An angel with brown eyes and big tits.'

'I want one that blushes,' O'Malley said, all dreamy.

'Blushes?' Vogel said, incredulously.

'Yeah, it shows she likes you, so you have a chance with her.'

As they argued over what an angel would or wouldn't do if she liked you, I left them and went inside.

The uniform sent to cover the station was so young he was trailing his

umbilical cord behind him, tripping over it in his awkward eagerness to run a station on his own. *Big responsibility, son, don't muck it up.* Such a big responsibility they sent an infant. Couldn't be helped.

I showed him where everything was inside our office, then Vogel, O'Malley and Jackson swaggered in, smelling of yesterday's socks, horse and sweat, glanced at him, got their weapons out of the armoury and clattered out, oblivious to his calls for them to sign for their rifles.

'They'll do it when they get back,' I said. 'Remember, if you leave this room, it must be locked.'

'Yes, sir.'

'Detective Kennedy will return tonight.'

'Yes, sir.'

'You right? Any questions?'

'Yes, sir. No, sir.'

~

We rode out to Wallace's, armed and bristling, but the place had an awful air of defeat, as if the life had been drained from it. Kennedy, O'Malley and Jackson searched the dairy and other outhouses, Vogel was put on watch, while I walked up to the house. The girl I'd seen before came to the door. I asked her why she wasn't in school, and she just stared in silence, then showed me in.

Mrs Wallace sat alone in a shabby, barely furnished drawing room, a small fire in the fireplace, a wedding portrait of her and Edmund Wallace hanging over the mantel. Both of them looking grim, as if the business of marriage held no joy for either of them. Her daughter, hair plaited down her back and a scowl on her thin face, sidled in and stood near the door.

'Edmund Wallace has absconded into the bush at the south of your property. He has been wounded and it's imperative we find him quickly. Is there anywhere he'd go? A cave, a creek?'

'I wouldn't know,' Mrs Wallace said quietly.

'There's a cave,' the girl said. 'Down by the slaughter pit, there's a path you can follow, winds up the cliff to a cave. It's got red hands in it.'

'Red hands?'

'That the blacks did, paint their hands red and press them to the wall. Pa showed me one time.'

'Can you show us?'

'No.'

'It might save your father's life,' I urged.

'Find him yourself,' she said, and left the room.

'I apologise for Alice, she's ...'

'No need, Mrs Wallace.'

'That man just charged through the kitchen,' she said. 'Never told Ed to stop, just raised his gun and fired at him.'

'Mrs Delamere told you this?'

'Yes, but I was in there too. The detective was panting hard, he never spoke, he was too out of breath, and afterwards he cursed my husband for running. Cursed him, as he runs off bleeding.'

I verified this with Mrs Delamere, who pretty much said the same as Mrs Wallace, only with more colourful language. If we managed to capture Wallace alive, and if we subsequently found he was innocent of everything except wounding Lawlor, then maybe there'd be some compensation. Funds Wallace could clearly use. If he died from that bullet wound, then Kennedy had a lot of explaining to do.

But Kennedy had found a jacket covered in twigs, a clean machete and a .303 rifle, and he looked like a cat who'd been at a dish of cream.

'Told you. It's him,' he said, holding the blade up to the sunlight.

'Every man in the bush has a .303, and every farmer has a machete and a dirty jacket,' I said.

'I'm going to send the gun to ballistics in Sydney,' he said, putting it in a sack.

I looked back at the craggy escarpments sweeping north to south, the rugged bushland, the unstable ground and myriad caves and scrub where a man with a gun and a grudge could hide.

'He's up there somewhere, sunshine, and you better hope my bullet's done its job,' Kennedy said, slapping me on the back.

~

I took the lead and felt the old familiar clutch in the stomach, a mix of fear and excitement, an addictive brew. O'Malley came next, then Jackson and Vogel leading the packhorse. We found the path that started near the slaughter pit, which led through an undulating series of wooded foothills. Without a tracker, we only had the Wallace girl's word to go by, and her father could of course have gone in the opposite direction. But this was what Bathurst wanted, and it was our only lead. I had checked it out on the map and estimated a couple of hours to get up there.

The terrain became increasingly rugged as the path followed the contours of the hills. The scrub got thicker, the trees bigger and the low buzz of insects louder. The sky above was bright and clear, the air cool. The familiar sound of creaking saddle leather, a couple of black cockatoos

flying overhead, the clod of horse hoofs on earth. All of us had our rifles out, scanning up and down, in front and behind, waiting for the gunshot that would kick things off, almost begging for it so the fear would ease.

I had a pair of binoculars, and I called a halt now and then so I could check out the surroundings. No glint from a rifle barrel, no movement, but a feeling of being watched. That could be imagined, or he could be watching and waiting, drawing us into the terrain where he wanted us to be when he made his move. Or he could be dead – but we'd be foolish to assume that.

On we climbed, past rugged sandstone boulders and outcrops, a gully way below us and the odd eucalypt clinging to the escarpment. According to the map, the cave was near the top of a switchback track, with a couple of small plateaus at the track's elbows. We'd aim for one of them, tether the horses and approach the cave on foot.

I'd prepared as well as I could, but we had some handicaps. Apart from having no black tracker, we were what it said on the box: mounted troopers, with boots made for riding and slipping quickly out of stirrups, not for climbing gravelly scree. Our navy wool tunics, with their row of brass buttons that glinted in the sun, would give any killer a nice fix on our vital organs. But we looked good – which was, apparently, a key concern of the Spartans, who spent time combing their long hair as they prepared to hold Thermopylae on a narrow path. We too would arrive in the underworld looking smart.

Birds were making a racket, which usually meant all was in order. It's when they're silent you'd get chills up your spine. We pressed on, slowly climbing, in a vulnerable position, open to fire from above or below. Just as that thought occurred to me, a shot rang out.

The pack horse was hit. He was screaming. I twisted in the saddle to see him topple over into the deep ravine on our left. Another shot rang out. I shouted the order to return fire at will. We were all dismounted now, crouching down beneath our frightened horses – not a clever move, but there was nowhere else to go. The packhorse was still in agony and screaming, a sound guaranteed to shred your nerves. I shouted at O'Malley, crouched under his horse, to give me cover; he looked blank for a moment. I realised with an awful clarity that these lads had never been soldiers. They had never experienced an ambush and were relying on me alone.

'Fire up at him, all of you, now,' I shouted, ice pumping through my veins. 'Keep hold of your horses too.' The wounded packhorse's screaming echoed from the ravine.

Police horses were picked for their steady temper, but they were not war horses, and they were not used to the dying screams of one of their herd. The bond between horse and rider was paramount now. Toss was dancing around, and so were the others. O'Malley and Jackson managed to fire upwards. Screaming and gunshot echoed around.

I let go of Toss and slithered over to the edge of the path, praying the lads would keep firing up at Wallace. I sighted the dying packhorse on a ledge and shot him. Then I scrambled back and retrieved Tosser, who was up and down and all over the place. This was sticky, but I knew what to do, how to do it. The scene was unfolding slowly, vividly, yet I was as calm as a man could be, estimating distance, time, angles, odds, chances.

Then Vogel's horse took a bullet and toppled over the side in a haze of spurting blood and screams. Vogel pressed against the side of the cliff, clutching his rifle, white with fear. Bloody lucky that it was just the horse

and not him as well. Three horses left and they were ready to get the hell away: O'Malley had his by the head, Jackson too, and Vogel just stared. Toss was pulling, and I had to come up with something quick.

'Keep firing up at him,' I shouted. 'Vogel, get over here and take my horse up the track out of range.'

He got on his hands and knees and crawled over the stony path beneath and between the horses, got to his feet, eyes wide, but I talked him through it. I shouted at O'Malley and Jackson to cover him, and Vogel pulled an eager Tosser up and away along the path.

With a volley of shots coming at him, Wallace didn't dare shoot back at us, so next I sent O'Malley with his horse. Jackson and I were left firing upwards, with only Jackson's horse to get out. He was rearing up, dislodging stones that dropped into the ravine. I shouted at Jackson to go, then I carefully backed away up the trail and out of Wallace's range.

Suddenly I heard a shout above me, and a second later a man and a shower of gravel landed on the edge of the path. He scrabbled madly at the earth and I lunged forward to grab him, but he went over into the ravine. The bullets stopped. A beautiful stillness under the bright sky.

The troopers came running back. Vogel looked down into the ravine, then looked up at me, eyes wide with shock. I was laughing.

'You all right, sir?'

'Yep – that was a bit of fun, eh?' I said, still laughing.

It's exhilarating to survive an attack, to best your enemy, to win. Made me feel young again, like my first time under fire, like winning a rugby match. The shockwave would thump into me later.

Vogel peered over the precipice again. 'It's Wallace, sir. I think he's

dead. Or maybe not – he's stuck in a tree.' Then he began calling out his horse's name.

'He's dead, you idiot,' O'Malley yelled. 'Berryman is dead. Do you hear him? No? Because he's fucking dead.'

Vogel got to his knees and shouted back, 'It's not Berryman, it's Berry Man.'

'For fuck's sake' Jackson shouted. 'Berry fucking Man is dead.'

'I can't leave him there; we have to bury him,' Vogel said.

'Vogel,' I said. 'We cannot bury ...'

I stopped, hands on hips, looking down at the gravel. I was afraid I might laugh, and I knew how he felt. I took a big breath and said, slowly, 'We cannot bury ... Berry Man, all right?'

He nodded, head hanging. Who called a horse Berry Man, for God's sake?

I got to my knees and looked over the side. The packhorse lay dead, half the kit spilling out about a hundred yards below us. Berry Man wasn't far from him, his body on a boulder, his head hanging like his neck was broken. Wallace, meanwhile, was splayed out in a sapling, partly resting on thin branches. He could be dead or he could be alive; either way, we had to get him down. We also had to retrieve Berry Man's saddle and kit, and retrieve everything the packhorse had on him – and all before sunset.

I stood, shaky now the exhilaration had ebbed away, and grabbed my fags, lighting up with relief. 'We rejoin the horses for now,' I said.

'But what about—'

'Vogel, do not question my fucking order' I roared. The thrill had passed, and I was on my way down to the rocks in the ravine inside my skull.

'Yes, sir,' he said meekly.

We made our way back up along the trail and found the plateau, a small area with some trees at the edges, some boulders and a bit of grass. We had no feedbags and no way of watering the horses, but at least they could move a little more freely and nose the ground for the sparse grasses. I suspected the cave was at the top of the next trail leading up. It had to be where Wallace had been shooting from, and he'd lost his footing somehow. He'd probably watched us coming through the foothills and waited until we were in range.

We off-saddled and spent some time calming ourselves and the horses. They felt less trapped, and we felt less trapped too. As we all settled down several notches, the situation became clearer to me.

I left the troopers, walked back down the track and had another look with my binoculars. Wallace was alive – he was moving a leg.

'Mr Wallace,' I shouted down to him. 'We are going to get you out of that tree and get you medical attention. Don't try to move. Can you hear me?'

He raised his hand. Poor bastard. I had no idea how we were going to get him down, and with sunset coming on fast he was in danger of exposure, as we all were. What a bloody fuck-up this was. And yet no more troopers had been wounded or died. A low bar, but we'd cleared it.

I sent Vogel and O'Malley back to Colley with a note to give to Bluey Rankin requesting men, horses and a stretcher. I'd also written out a telegram that Harry Barker was to send to Bathurst verbatim. 'And organise some food and flasks of hot tea for us and Wallace, because we won't see you until dawn and we'll have been exposed all night.'

I kept Jackson's horse with us. I was planning to tether a rope to the horse and then loop it around a tree to use as a pulley and go down the

cliff to retrieve Wallace, then use the horse to pull him up. But no matter which way we looked at it, getting Wallace out of the tree and pulling him up a rocky cliff was too much for two men and a horse. We risked injury to either me or Jackson getting down to Wallace, while getting him out of the tree and dragging him up the cliff face risked injury to him.

I had to call down to him that we'd get him in the morning, to hold on as his daughters needed him. His wife didn't, obviously – or not in the way a wife needs her husband – so I left her out. He didn't respond, but that didn't mean he was dead.

Jackson and I gathered as much firewood as we could find in the fading light and managed to get a campfire lit, which was some comfort. We had water, matches, cigarettes and some grasses for the horse, but not shelter. We had the cliff wall behind us but were exposed to the north and east; it was not going to be a comfortable night. Jackson and I lay down, one on each side of the fire, smoking and staring at the night sky.

'Was what happened on the track – him shooting at us – like it was in the Boer War?' Jackson asked.

'Sometimes. Except there might be six of them above you and another five waiting further along. They were expert riflemen, too.'

'How do you ...?'

'You train for it.'

'We didn't train for something like that in the traps.'

I looked over at him, his face in the flickering shadow, staring up into the stars. He'd be thinking about this day for the rest of his life. Had he lived up to his own expectations? Or had he faltered?

'What matters is that you act,' I said, looking away. 'Not how you feel. You could have shit running down your leg, but you step up and shoot back.'

'I wasn't afraid.'

I knew that having no fear meant only that you died fairly quickly, but there was no point in talking about it. After a long silence, I assumed Jackson had fallen asleep, or just didn't feel like talking. He was a saturnine fellow whose contempt applied to all humanity, I realised, not just me. I could accept that – I even had some sympathy for such an outlook – but I worked hard at keeping it at bay.

Sleeping on the dirt with a cold wind whipping around was hard. I'd done it many times on the veldt, but I lived then, as we all did, in a state of endless exhaustion, and passing out on the dirt was a moment we all hankered for. A decade later, my body having accumulated injuries like sports trophies and my mind cluttered with traces of horror, sleeping on the dirt in the cold wind was torment.

Jackson was out to it, on his back with his cap over his face. Only about twenty-one, he slept like a pup. I got to my feet, grabbed my fags and matches and looked out to where the bright starlight illuminated the river valley to the north, where Colley lay, like a gold nugget inside clenched knuckles of hills. I turned and walked past Jackson and made my way carefully up the last of the path that led, according to my map, to the cave.

I came to what looked like an impassable rockfall, but on closer inspection I saw a well-worn path leading around a boulder and into the mouth of a cave, dark and forbidding. As my eyes adjusted, I saw it was not much more than a shelter with an overhanging ledge but protected by the boulders. It didn't go very far back. On the ground I found a blanket and ammunition. I searched for the rifle, but Wallace must have been holding it when he fell. I lit a match and looked around.

On the back wall were a couple of dozen handprints, either red or

yellow ochre or stencilled and surrounded by red ochre. The match went out and I lit another and gazed at the hands. It was as if the owners of the hands were on the other side of the rock, pressing their hands up against it like a window.

I kept relighting the matches, seeing the hands in the momentary flare of the flame, then darkness. I only had a short moment to make some sense of it – like life, really – but I could never know why they put these marks here. I had the eerie thought that they were standing beside me, waiting for the flame to die out, so they could place their hands back against the cave wall.

I took the blanket and walked back down the path, keeping close to the wall of the cliff, slipping on scree and gravel. At the clearing, Jackson was flat on his back still. One blanket, two men. Logic said share the blanket, but I doubted Jackson would want to wake cuddled up to his hairy sergeant, so I covered him and made my way down to where Wallace had gone over.

I called his name, and I couldn't be certain but I think I heard him answer.

'Mr Wallace, we'll have you out of that tree as soon as a stretcher arrives at first light.'

I definitely heard him this time, a hoarse, 'Help me.'

'We are going to get you out, first light, I promise. Just hold on.'

That poor bugger. I settled myself against the wall of the cliff, knees up, stones biting my arse. Whirring around in my head, stopping me sleeping, was the memory of Wallace's ambush, of coolly and methodically working through it, saving the horses, saving the men. I could still do it, and do it under fire. I felt no pride, just satisfaction, a longed-for sense of mastery returning. I wasn't a washed-up country copper, not yet.

These thoughts slowly dissolved into replays of Scanlon's death, head jerking to the right, blood to the left. Dozing and fitful, confused as to where I was, red hands reaching into the darkness, shivering and drowsy, aching in every scar, every joint. I knew I was in danger of exposure, but my scarring pains tethered me. Once I was numb to it, I'd be in trouble.

And I was wearing a woollen tunic. Wallace was hanging in a tree, exposed on all sides, in a shirt and threadbare coat. I called down to him whenever I could remember what the hell I was doing there on the side of a cliff under the stars.

20

Jackson woke me. There was the faint glow of light in the east, the birds stirring. He had the binoculars.

'Is he alive?' I said, struggling to my feet.

'No. He's gone.'

'Gone where?'

'Dead, sir.'

I took the binoculars and looked myself. Wallace's head faced west, eyes open and staring, shirt tails stirring in the updraft, skin as white as milk.

Jackson got the fire going again and gave me the blanket, thanking me for covering him during the night in a terse, didn't-really-need-it tone of voice, as if the act unmanned him. I crouched by the fire, smoking, stifling the urge to yell at Jackson that I covered him because he was my fucking responsibility, because that's how the rank structure works: it goes up and because of that it must also go down. If he died of exposure while I was cosy and warm under the blanket, it'd be my arse that would be kicked over the horizon.

He took off down the path, probably to get away from me and the discomfort my act had aroused, returning later to say he saw a long line of

men and horses crossing the Wallace land. I grunted an acknowledgement at him. I was not in a good mood.

When the reinforcements finally arrived and O'Malley handed me a hunk of mutton gristle sandwiched between two slaps of week-old damper, I tore into it, then swigged from the vacuum flask of hot, sweet tea. After scoffing down a wedge of pound cake, I could finally manage to speak without hurling abuse at everyone.

Bluey Rankin had taken over and had men on ropes going over the side. Vogel and O'Malley, who'd slept and been fed, funnelled orders from me as I watched and smoked and cultivated a sour mood. I was brooding mainly on the Light Horse recall, a directive I still could not dismiss.

Australia didn't have the money to keep a large number of regulars on hand. Therefore, wanting me, banged up as I was, didn't make sense. I'd had a fast climb up to the rank of captain and had been mentioned in dispatches several times, but that was before I was cut to pieces by a bayonet-wielding japie. Serving in a frontline unit was exciting but that was not what I was being recalled for. They might have wanted me to be a staff officer, those despised creatures who risked nothing yet came up with the most absurdly dangerous missions. In peacetime I'd probably be deployed to drill militia units. Swagger up and down with a riding crop under my arm, barking, 'Stand to your horse. Prepare to mount. Mount. Not fast enough. Dismount. Stand to your horse. Prepare to mount ...'

It took us all day to get Wallace's body up and the saddle off Berry Man, and to retrieve the packhorse kit. It was made a whole lot easier by Wallace being dead. I was last off the cliff, riding behind the grim column of men and horses. Wallace's body was on a stretcher slung between two horses, with Bluey Rankin riding alongside. The Wallace women stood silently on

the verandah in the dusk, watching as their father and husband, their sole source of income, was carried away. He had to go to the coroner, so they couldn't even have his body yet.

I dismounted and approached them. The dog on the chain carried on and a couple of gimlet-eyed kookaburras watched in indifferent silence.

'Killed him, did you?' Mrs Delamere shrieked. 'You murderers, you bloody murderers.'

'That's enough, Mrs Delamere,' I said. Wretched old harpy that she was. 'Mrs Wallace, I need to speak to you. Alone.' I was nearly dead from exhaustion, but we'd just presided over the death of this woman's husband, and clearly nobody else was going to explain it to her.

'Come inside,' she said, her voice shaky.

I stepped onto the verandah. The two daughters disappeared, one of them crying noisily. Mrs Delamere, hands on her hips, opened her mouth to screech again.

'Don't you have a floor to scrub?' I hissed at her.

'Mr Wallace employed me to look after Mrs Wallace, and that's what I intend to do,' she shot back, 'even though he's dead because you lot killed him.'

I closed the parlour door in her face. Mrs Wallace stood by the feeble fire in the grate, wearing her long shabby white dress. She picked up a Bible and held it to her chest with her arms crossed over it. A card fell out. I picked it up to find it was a memorial card from Buck Barrett's funeral. All she had left of him, and she couldn't even see it.

'My condolences, Mrs Wallace. Mr Wallace fell from a cliff edge near the cave with the red hands. He was caught in a tree overnight and died of exposure.'

'But couldn't you get to him?'

'Not safely, no. That's why we had to send for more men to help. I and another trooper stayed with him overnight. I called out to him periodically, but he was dead by first light.'

'That other man shot him.'

'He did. The cause of death will be established by the coroner.'

'Will we be compensated?'

'I don't know what will happen, Mrs Wallace. It depends on the outcome of the investigation, and unfortunately these things take time. Can you ask your church for aid and assistance until then?'

She didn't reply. A coal from the fire toppled over, revealing bright embers beneath. I took her left hand. She flinched and tried to pull it away, then I put the memorial card in it. She felt it, running her finger along the bevelled edge.

'It slipped out of your Bible,' I said softly.

'Thank you,' she whispered.

'I am sorry. I know what's it's like to love someone you can't have.'

She gasped in surprise at my words, then raised her chin and said, 'I did love Buckland, and I still do. He was very kind to me, kinder than anyone ever has been.'

This cold, grim room, with the window looking out to the escarpment where Wallace died, the peeling paint and heatless fire. It was no wonder she was drawn away by another human's kindness, because there wasn't a trace of it here.

'Did you know Davy Scanlon well?' I asked.

'Not terribly well, but he was always friendly to me. He never sneered

or was rude when I visited. He accepted our arrangement. Buckland said Davy was a good sort.'

'What arrangement was that?'

A bright blush crept up her neck and fanned out to her cheeks, and she bowed her head. I waited, and heard Mrs Delamere screeching at the daughters out the back like a malevolent galah.

'He was ... Davy watched out,' she said to the floor.

'Kept a lookout when you visited?'

She nodded.

'Did your husband ever refer to Scanlon in an angry manner to you? Share an opinion of him?'

'I was the last person my husband would share his thoughts with. I shared a bed with him, that's all.'

What hell that must have been. Sharing a bed with a man who'd beaten her half to death, a man who she could no longer see. No wonder her nerves were shot to pieces.

'Mrs Wallace, thank you for speaking with me, and again, my condolences for the loss of your husband. And Buckland. We have your husband's records of his financial affairs, and will have them for some time. If any of his creditors harass you in any way, please let me know. I will keep you informed of the progress of the investigation.'

I left her clutching Barrett's memorial card in that cold room.

~

Back in town by nightfall, I was desperate for sleep, but went to see how the young uniformed officer had got on. Outside the pub, I found two

unfamiliar mounted troopers' horses and a trooper standing by, hands in his greatcoat, nose red from the cold, breath pluming in the night air.

He saluted and I asked him where he was from, in case he was one of the mystery troopers I'd not yet met but was actually supervising.

'Bathurst, sir. Come in with Superintendent MacKerras, sir.'

'And where is he?'

'Inside, sir.'

Come to praise or blame – the latter, no doubt. In the office I found the young uniform at the desk looking worried, like he'd shat himself but couldn't leave his post to clean up.

'Is MacKerras here because of me, sir?' he whispered.

'What have you done, son?'

'Nothing, I just—'

'Unless you shot Trooper Scanlon, I'd say no, he's not here for you. Now, go and have your supper. Dismissed.'

I hauled Vogel out of the bunkroom, put him on the desk and went to the front bar. If MacKerras wanted me, he'd find me soon enough; but I found him having a whisky with Kennedy, amid the usual suspects quietly drinking and playing billiards. I ordered and drank a double, and spotted the undertaker, who'd come for Wallace, sitting alone with a glass of sherry.

'Your office, now,' MacKerras said, with his usual grace and charm.

I wearily trudged after him and Kennedy out the front and back in, down the hall and into the office, where MacKerras closed the door and put Vogel on the other side of it to keep watch.

'Wallace is dead?' MacKerras said.

'That's right, sir. A bullet wound in his back,' I said, glancing at Kennedy.

'His back?'

'I fired when he ran away, sir,' Kennedy said.

'At the farmhouse, before he absconded?'

'Yes, sir,' Kennedy said, looking like he was sitting on a pile of prickles.

'It weakened him,' I said. 'But he may well have died of exposure without the bullet wound. Spent all night in the open at altitude.'

'This does complicate matters,' MacKerras said, looking around with distaste at the cramped clutter of the office, almost as if he wasn't aware of the conditions we worked in.

'Despite being wounded, he fired on us, killing two horses,' I said. 'He had enough energy to do that and kept it up until he fell. Hit the path in front of me, then went over the side and into a tree.'

'The coroner will find the bullet,' MacKerras said, allowing himself a small frown.

Kennedy had a green tinge to his face by this time. A bullet in the back could not be ignored. The sound of raised voices from Fitzgerald's office came through the thin wall. Len and Ray at each other's throats, as usual.

'I stopped in to speak to Mrs Wallace on our way out,' I said. 'She told me Davy Scanlon used to keep watch while she and Barrett met.'

MacKerras's eyebrows righted themselves and a faint glimmer of relief shone from the gravel pit of his face. Kennedy looked like he'd been dragged alive from a lion's mouth. He'd put a bullet in a cop killer. From murderer to hero in seconds.

'Looks like I'm in the clear,' he said, cautiously.

'It does, Pat,' MacKerras said, nodding. 'Your good instincts, as usual. Get the reports done, evidence logged, and we can call an end to it.'

'There is no evidence, sir,' I said.

'Kennedy will take it from here, Hawkins. But I want you to emphasise to the troopers in your district that any immorality with local women will not be tolerated. Now, I want our horses stabled for the night. Trooper Benson can bunk in with your lot, and we'll leave before dawn tomorrow.'

'There are no stables, sir.'

'What do you do with your horses?' he said. As if he didn't know.

'Blankets overnight and in the paddock, sir. I've sent several requests for urgent stabling, even a temporary shed would do, but—'

'I'll look into it. Dismissed.'

He went off and Kennedy and I looked at each other.

'Good work, mate,' Kennedy said, and shook my hand.

Wallace's death was a poor outcome, but I brought the lads back alive and we had an answer. It was enough, but I wouldn't have called it good.

'MacKerras is a hard-nosed bugger,' I said, and lit up a fag.

'Yeah, Terry's always been a bit frosty, but he's been a good boss to me. When it was decided to park a detective in each head station, he tapped me on the shoulder, asked if I wanted to do the training. I've got seven kids, so I said yes. Better pay than sergeant on the beat. He's loyal to his men, protects us.'

'From what?'

'Sydney brass – what else, mate? Always making cuts, the usual malarkey that goes on. You better put his horses to bed. He's fussy about his horses.'

'But not ours, obviously,' I said. 'You can sleep easy tonight, sport.'

'My word, I will.'

There was a packet of letters on my desk. I tucked them into my uniform and found Fitzgerald, who lent us two horse blankets. I led the

horses up to the paddock while Benson found himself a bunk. These two were beautiful animals, perfectly formed, soft-eyed and willing, used to the finer things in life, like warm and dry stables. I turned them loose in our frosty paddock and they looked at me as if to say, *Surely not – there must be some mistake?*

I shut the gate and let myself into the tent, then lit the lamp and tied the flap. Alfie went straight to his blanket and groaned with pleasure as he curled up. He'd been on the chain at Mrs Owen's since I left for the Wallaces' farm. I sat on my rickety camp bed, listened to the owls calling and thought of poor old Ed Wallace, slowly dying in his tree, the wind whipping around him, the two dead horses lying below. This was what his life had amounted to. A more mournful scene you could not picture.

Turning to the letters, I found one from my father.

Dear Augustus,

It is very unfair of you to accuse me of manoeuvring to get you back into the military. Having nearly lost you to that wretched war, the last thing I want is your return to uniform. When we got you back, I was not thinking of your future because, like as not, you didn't have one. Then, when you could stand unaided, you told me to go to hell, and that's it, for six years. One day you will understand that a parent is damned if they do and damned if they don't. When that day comes, I hope you will spare a thought for me.

He thought it would be madness to go back to the military, et cetera and et cetera, and something looming on the horizon in Europe, shaky Ottomans, bellicose Kaiser, British and German naval race, blah and blah.

And with your injuries, you don't have the stamina for frontline work – you'd be a liability. Yes, your current position can be physically taxing but you are getting fed three times a day, sleeping lice-free somewhere warm, having time to read and rest, filling in forms and inspecting diseased sheep. What do you think a return to frontline service would be like? You wouldn't last a day. You are no longer robust enough for the arduous demands of the military.

A liability? No stamina? I was as fit as a mallee bull.

You need to get out of any sort of military or policing employment, not run recklessly towards risk, violence, guns and chaos. Give your nerves a rest, give yourself time to heal from what was a profoundly damaging experience in every regard.

I knew what he wanted – he wanted me back home and trying my hand at breeding horses. Put me out to grass breeding Shetland ponies for kiddies' parties. Become the town invalid, the doctor's half-idiot son who tucked a daisy behind his ear and got about in harlequin pantaloons, and all the kids would run screaming when I went near them.

I crunched the letter with both hands and hurled it across the tent. *A liability, no stamina, shattered nerves, no longer robust.* The words sliced through me. How dare he? I'd just spent the last two days in a frontline situation and I was perfectly fine. More than fine, I was on top of it. He knew nothing. I began pacing back and forth, the dog wearily watching me.

'My state of mind, he says,' I complained to Alfie. 'Am I in need of a

straitjacket? Should I be fed gruel and subjected to enemas all fucking day long?'

The dog raised a quizzical eyebrow. *Maybe, yeah?*

'You're an idiot,' I snapped at him. 'And so is my father.' I undressed, fell on the bed and conked out immediately.

21

I gasped awake, Alfie's warm, wet tongue on my face, and whipped back the blankets, panting, searching for the blood that had seeped down the hill and into my bed, engulfing me. With a shaky hand I lit a candle. Just me, dirty and sweaty, but no blood. I slumped back, pulled the blankets up and then, like a fool, let Alfie up close to me, the warmth of another living creature holding me steady.

With my hand on Alfie's warm body, I thought of my father's letter. I was an only child of a widowed man; he'd been my father, my mother, my everything, and what he said I heard, even if I pretended not to. At this moment, shaken by the dream of a blood deluge, my arm around a dead man's dog, living in a draughty tent, I heard him.

~

In the morning Alfie hopped down, stretched and stood wagging his tail, nose to the flap, happy as a lark with the new bed-share arrangement. I let him out, found my father's letter and unscrewed it, flattening it on the table. There was an undertone of panic to his words, and indeed an uncharacteristic

wordiness, as if he'd blurted out his fears. He was usually cagier, trying not to appear the dictatorial father, knowing it usually backfired.

I folded the letter and placed it with the Light Horse letter and stood the lamp on top. The Light Horse had waited ten years to tap me on the shoulder; it wouldn't hurt them to wait a bit longer.

Outside in the cool morning air, I got the fire going, prepared my coffee and drank it while hanging on the paddock fence having a chat with the horses, Alfie beside me chewing his bum or whatever it was that needed doing. A blue fairy wren hopped along the fence in his cobalt suit, hoping to find a lady wren to impress. The corella pairs up in the manna gum fussed and smooched, and over in the goat paddock the male goat, Zeus, with his splendid curving horns, gazed with smouldering desire through the gaps in the fence at his females. And I thought of Flora.

Flora loved to roam her father's property. Almost in defiance of the death all around, she would sometimes find birds with broken wings or legs that she could nurse and then release back to the wild. Often they were these small parrots, corellas, and she wore them on her shoulder, where they nibbled at her ear. Sometimes she'd put seed in her hand and the birds would sidle down her arm and feed, and her lovely face would glow as she watched these wild creatures, hers for a brief moment, before they returned to the sky. Birds were just birds before I met Flora; now I noticed their colours, their behaviour, their strange beauty. That was one of her many gifts to me.

One day out west, before Christmas 1910, Flora and I were sitting on the homestead verandah in the wicker chairs, a pot of tea and scones on the table between us. Suddenly a rosella slammed into the window beside us, then dropped down on the floor of the verandah.

I went to pick him up, but Flora stopped me. 'If his neck isn't broken, he'll come good,' she said. 'They often do.'

The rosella, a few moments later, got up, rustled his feathers and flew off, no doubt feeling a little addled.

'They remind me of you,' she said, her brown eyes laughing at me. 'You slammed into a window, but you've come good.'

But would she? The deaths of her siblings, to whom she was so close, was a hell of a catastrophe to slam into ... would Flora get up and fly again? She might try to take her life again. And she might succeed, and then I would never again get the chance to tell her how much I loved her.

~

After breakfast I walked down the hill to the pub, passing a clutch of boys scuffling about in the dirt not far from the butcher's. Three girls were trying to get on with a game of hopscotch while the lads chanted, '*Girls are weak, chuck 'em in the creek.*' Like a bloody Greek chorus, bobbing up here and there with their chants.

I sat at my desk and began to compose my report of the manhunt, chewing on a pencil. Could I use a split infinitive or not? A grammatical error of monstrous proportions, said my old English master, whacking the desk with a cane. No, I could not.

Jackson, on the front desk, called out to me. 'Dr Pomeroy to see you, sir.'

'Morning, Sergeant,' Bill Pomeroy said.

'Come through,' I said, getting up. 'Take a seat.'

He settled in the chair in front of my desk, looking very dapper in his brown suit.

'How can I help?'

'I saw a little china doll the other morning, she was scurrying along toward Ringer's Rocks. I suspect Madame Foufoune's back in the district.'

'I told her to move on a few days ago.'

'Buck used to make them leave, slapped them around. It's all she understands.'

'I'm not hitting women or burning their possessions.'

'Fair enough, but Foufoune is a health hazard, spreading disease, and then the men come to me and it's too late, they've given it to their wives, who've given it to their babies. When you get a minute, you have to run her out of town, however you want to do it. She's testing you. Buck never allowed them to stay, so maybe she thinks she can now he's gone.'

'I'll check them out this morning. Thanks for the tip. I saw your friend Sam Hong in Bathurst the other day. He's going to post me some of the ointment.'

'Good – it obviously does work.'

'He was keen to get rid of me. Seemed disturbed by the news of Scanlon's murder.'

'It is disturbing. More than disturbing, it's a tragedy,' he said. 'Sam knew Davy Scanlon and they always had cordial relations.'

'Why did he leave?'

Pomeroy was silent for a moment, then got up to leave, saying he had a busy day ahead. I couldn't imagine his surgery was crammed with patients. More likely he just did not want to talk about Sam Hong.

~

I didn't have the time to be running up and back to Ringer's Rocks to try to dislodge Madame Foufoune. She was a horrible old slag and had been in the game for so long she knew all the tricks. That she had a white girl working for her said that the girl was really down on her luck.

The girls were usually Chinese or Islander, very young, sold into the business by family or, in the case of the Islander girls, kidnapped and then smuggled into Australia through Singapore in the bilge sections of ships. Unable to speak much English and terrified of their pimps, they never lasted long, or so I'd been told. Just turned their faces to the wall and died.

I saw Malay and Indian girls in brothels in Port Elizabeth – same situation but legally shipped in by the British for their soldiers. But that was the British for you: spreading the light of Christian civilisation wherever they went. I wasn't having that sort of business in my district. I rounded up O'Malley and Vogel and sent them out to Ringer's Rocks to read the riot act to that mangy old Foufoune.

'Charge her with suffering a child under sixteen to be in a brothel, keeping a brothel, living off immoral earnings, and failure to comply with direction given by an officer of the law. And if she argues, hit her with being an idle and disorderly person and resisting arrest. Bring her back here and chuck her in the woodshed and call for a van to take her to Bathurst for processing. Clean the woodshed out before you go, and she can sit there and think on her sins. And don't hurt the girls. They can take their cart to Bathurst and sort themselves out there.'

Vogel's eyes lit up. Finally, a Godly mission.

'And don't shoot anyone or make any decisions that can't be undone.'

A package from Bathurst had been delivered for me, and I tore the wrapping off to find four porcelain jars of my beloved scar ointment. I took

one and scurried into the bleak bathroom out the back, dabbed my finger in that familiar cat's piss smell and, while looking in the mirror, smeared it up and down the facial scar, from hairline to beard, back and forth, the soothing ritual gathering up the fragmented pieces of Gus Hawkins and fitting them back together.

~

Over the next few weeks, I heard it said around the town that if Mrs Wallace hadn't strayed, Ed Wallace would still be alive. This came from men gossiping while playing billiards, men gossiping at the bar, men standing around the smithy forge waiting for a horse to be shoed, men outside the general store – all of them blamed her. Even Mrs Lennox, who disliked Ed Wallace, said Anne Wallace killed her husband even though she hadn't meant to.

Edmund Wallace, dairyman on the Topknot Road, bashed his wife and blinded her, planned and carried out the cold-blooded murder of a police trooper, mutilated his body, left his hand to spook us, fired at police troopers in the course of their work, and deliberately shot and killed two police horses while trying to take us out, and everyone in town had sympathy for him? That showed the level of animosity people carried towards the demons. Or it showed what a bloody-minded lot of halfwit bigots the burghers of Colley were.

Now we had Scanlon's killer sorted, Kennedy and I faced the long and arduous pile of paperwork that documented the what, where and how of the investigation: the inventories of kit, the loss of the horses, the description of the engagement at the cliff and so on. While we smoked and

scribbled, stretched and yawned, I felt the soporific effects of paperwork calming my overstretched nerves. With Alfie at my feet, Mrs Owen dishing up nourishing food, and a chance to tidy my tent and get my washing done, I felt I was returning to humanity.

While Kennedy and I were busy in the office, Vogel, Jackson and O'Malley cleaned every weapon in the armoury, oiled all the saddles and leathers, fixed the water trough, rode out on the beat, organised the forms and filing systems, sharpened the pencils, polished their boots and kicked a ball around in the street with the local boys. I'd be sending two of them back to Bathurst soon, now the show was over. Bathurst would decide who they'd leave with me, and I begged the gods to let it not be Vogel. I could work with him, but share living quarters? No. Sarcasm was the great consolation of a senior officer, but while intensely pleasurable in the moment, it led to bad blood. I had no doubt I'd use it on Vogel like a cudgel, with predictable results.

The coroner finally released Scanlon's body and the funeral was arranged in Bathurst at the All Saints' Cathedral. We were all suitably rested, the blood had cooled, and we could face what would be a very emotional day with suitable mounted trooper stoicism. Once the funeral was done, I'd be free to consider my options for my future, limited as they were.

Vogel, Jackson and O'Malley were to be pall bearers, along with a few other mounted troopers. Our horses were tidied up, hoofs oiled, manes clipped. We wore our dress uniforms, and other troopers, including me, formed a guard of honour. The head of the mounted troopers from Sydney, Ted Buchanan, was there, and he made a point of seeking me out, shaking my hand and congratulating me, again, for capturing the Kirkbride killers.

MacKerras watched on. Having Buchanan shake my hand in public was like being anointed: protection against the internecine brawling the police force enjoyed on a routine basis.

Ray Fitzgerald was there with Hilde, who wore a mourning dress that was too big for her and clutched her little prayer book as she trailed around in his shadow like a lost girl. Mrs Lennox and Percy came, as did Dr Pomeroy and others I was familiar with from Colley. Not Mrs Owen, though; she found Bathurst too busy, she said – it upset her digestion. She felt Davy would have understood.

Only the most senior officers went to the wake, held at the head station. The police had been his family, so there was nowhere else to hold it. But there were too many men in the small room, clashing scents of shaving creams and brilliantine, leather, conceit and ambition, despite the sadness. There was always an opportunity for scheming, even at a funeral, and even more so because all your allies and enemies were there mouthing pieties while looking for an opportunity to stick the dagger in.

I would have been left to my tea were it not for Buchanan's handshake, and sure enough MacKerras cornered me, a plate with a buttered scone in one hand. Was he going to offer it to me? I noticed Northrup watching from the other side of the room, deploying a slice of sponge cake.

'The Light Horse have been sniffing around your file, Hawkins,' MacKerras said. 'What have you to say to that?'

'Nothing, sir. I'm as surprised as you are, sir.'

'They tell us nothing,' he said.

'Maybe they're organising a reunion dinner?'

He snorted. 'Your loyalty is to us. You're not still on their books, are you?'

'No, sir. I am a New South Wales Mounted Trooper and my job, as it currently stands, is to conclude the murder investigation of Trooper Scanlon.'

He grunted and wandered off.

That the Light Horse had been perusing my police file without saying why must have been driving them insane. There was nothing so affronting than the self-importance of the military, which saw the police as a working man's organisation: uncouth ruffians who bashed vagrants for sport, unlike the warrior gentlemen of the military officer class, who had Great Concerns and the National Interest to think about as they gazed at themselves in their shaving mirrors each morning.

Northrup slipped into the space vacated by MacKerras. 'A sad day, Hawkins.'

'Yes, sir.'

'But the investigation is at an end.'

'Yes, sir.'

'It's a relief for all of us who wear the uniform, eh? No stray bullets from unknown assailants,' he said with a small laugh.

'Yes, sir.' *Good joke, sir. Certainly no stray bullets in the comfortable Bathurst police station, sir.*

He wasn't looking at me as I spoke, but towards Superintendent Buchanan and the rest of the brass. It dawned on me that this seemingly mild and affable man was as ambitious as the rest of them. He was far away, kicking MacKerras's head around a football field and laughing gleefully as it rolled about.

'Will you be attending the send-off tonight, sir?'

He looked at me for a moment, as if he didn't know what I was referring to.

'One drink, that's all. The troopers don't need me spoiling their fun.'

~

The send-off was held at the pub all the troopers drank at, close to the head station. Much alcohol was drunk and many songs were sung. I knew plenty of soldier songs but there were not many songs about the traps – none, in fact. But when, during 'Waltzing Matilda', the words 'up came the troopers, one, two, three' came around, they were bellowed so loudly the windows shook. Then there was the perennial filthy favourite 'The Good Ship Venus', and from there it descended into rugby songs of an extremely earthy nature. Everyone thoroughly enjoyed themselves.

The troopers and I rode back to Colley early the next morning, a sorry lot with our throbbing heads and bleary faces. But Scanlon had been sent off in style, and that was what mattered. Halfway back to town, with another four hours to go, we stopped at a small pub. When we got back in the saddle it began to rain.

We had heavy oilskin capes but it rained as we climbed the hills, it rained as we crossed the plateau and it rained as we rode down to the river valley. By then we may as well have been wearing cotton sheets as capes, because we were all wet and cold to the bone. We had to get the horses into the ostler's stable, which he was none too happy about, walk them around, rub them down, feed them and lay out all their kit to dry while cold, wet and hungover.

The troopers trickled off to their bunkhouse while I set off for my tent, which was sagging under the weight of a dozen pinecones the cockies had gnawed off the tree. Where they sat against the canvas a

drip had formed, right onto my pillow. Welcome home, trooper.

Mrs Owen had kept Alfie for me tied up on her back verandah. Silly bugger was overjoyed to see me and be let off the chain, and he raced around up and down the paddock in the rain, bouncing off me with his muddy paws and streaking along like a brown bee. When he'd finished, I let him into the tent and rubbed him dry, then he threw himself at the tent flaps, barking furiously.

I opened them and looked outside. Vogel, O'Malley and Jackson were marching up the block in the drizzle, carrying a lantern. Alfie raced out to greet them.

'You better come down, sir,' Jackson said, his voice full of suppressed rage.

'What's happened?'

'It's his other hand,' O'Malley said. 'It was left in our room.'

'While we were giving him a send-off, some fucking mongrel got in there—'

'It stinks something bad.'

'His hand, his fucking hand!'

Talking over each other, upset, angry, exhausted. A sense of dread filled me, icy and low in my guts. I was still wearing my sodden uniform, as were they. Two green fox eyes shone from the darkness, watching us.

'Where's the uniform who relieved us?'

'On the desk, sir, the fat toad.'

'And the pub is kicking off. Full of those mangy dredgers, sir.'

'Could be they did it, sir.'

I peeled off my wet tunic, found my dry greatcoat and put it on over my sodden shirt, then I got my fags and matches. 'Right, let's go.'

The four of us marched down, and an angrier, colder, more hungover and exhausted bunch you couldn't hope to find. Alfie took the lead, trotting ahead of us like a regimental mascot, tail in the air, as I tried to quell my fury and fear.

The lights of the hotel were ablaze. It was only around seven and the pub was full. The laughter had a threatening edge to it, the shouts and bangs indicating some pent-up steam. It was a wet night, and wet nights brought in the dredging crews, when they weren't being serviced by the sad girls old Foufoune had under her yoke.

Whiffs of the decaying hand gusted up the hallway as somebody went out the back door. The uniform who had relieved us while we were at the funeral was a fat old bastard, not long from retirement. Should he have been faced with an emergency, he would have done fuck-all.

The skeletal hand, with shreds of browning flesh clinging to it, sat in a corner. I stared at it, recalling the absence of Scanlon's hands when his body was draped over Toss. We'd buried the man yesterday, sang him out of this world, if not with songs of his bravery, then at least with lusty, strong voices. Then this. By God, it was an insult – to Scanlon, to us, to me, to the uniform.

'Vogel, go into the bar and ask Watt for a clean linen napkin.'

He ran off and I went back into the police office, where the dullard constable sat, working up a fart and needing all his fucking brainpower to do so.

'Sir. How'd the funeral go, eh?'

'Come with me,' I said.

He followed me into the hall without shutting the office door or locking it. I demanded the keys and did it myself.

'Relieved of duty. Look there – see that? Smell that? How did it get there on your watch?'

The man scratched his scrofulous head, blinking, looking at the assembled troopers with their haggard faces. 'Wasn't there this mornin' when I got up, sir. Musta got in there today.'

'Crawled in on its own, did it?' I snapped. 'The room should have been locked if no one was in there.'

Vogel returned with a white napkin. I entered the room, wrapped the hand and sent the troopers to get carbolic and hot water from the laundry. The din from the front bar echoed through the building, laughter long and loud. Laughing at us.

'You're on report for failing to follow procedure, Constable. This outrage happened on your watch and Bathurst will know it.'

He didn't care. His comfy pension was only months away.

'Go out to the woodshed and make sure it's clear and ready to take any arrests. Now.'

He waddled off to find a lantern, muttering and complaining. The troopers set to scrubbing the smell out of their bunkroom. Ray Fitzgerald appeared at the end of the hallway, agitated, in his clipped, efficient manner.

'Terrible smell out here,' he said, distracted. 'A dead rat in the cellar maybe. I'll get Mr Watt onto it, but right now there's a bit of a disturbance in the bar.'

As he spoke there was a rise in the clamour, more bangs and thumps. Just what I felt like doing, wrangling drunks. I sent Jackson and O'Malley in and raced up the stairs, two at a time and thumped down the hall to Kennedy's room. I banged on the door until he finally answered, a bit worse for wear, breath of a distillery, bags under his eyes.

'What?' he snapped.

'Another hand. In the troopers' bunkroom.' I held up the linen-wrapped bones.

'What did you bring it up here for?' he said, recoiling.

'It's Scanlon's hand. We buried him yesterday, remember? And we've collared Wallace for his murder. To me this looks like Wallace has got out of the mortuary, put the hand there and is having a fine old fucking laugh at our expense as he trots back to his marble slab. Or it wasn't Wallace.'

Kennedy rubbed his face with both hands, dropped them in exasperation. 'I'll talk to you in the morning. Listen to the flaming racket in this pub. It could have been one of the dredgers found the hand and put it there to fuck with us. You have been needling that old banger Foufoune.'

The din from the bar beneath us took a turn to the serious.

'Better go and sort that out, sunshine,' he said, then closed the door in my face.

I raced down the stairs, Scanlon's hand in mine, unlocked our office, put the hand for the moment just inside the door, locked the door, then ran out and around and into the bar. Two men with broken pool cues were facing off. O'Malley and Jackson were keeping the other blokes away, all of them heckling and calling for one or the other to beat the shit of their opponent.

Watt and Fitzgerald stood behind the bar. They must have seen a lot of this sort of thing, and I was surprised that a muscular man like Fitzgerald, so keen on fitness and an ex-Steinaecker man to boot, wasn't willing or able to stop them.

'Let it run its course,' Watt said, polishing a glass. 'Simmons needs a good beating, just to remind him he's home.'

I assumed Simmons was the younger one: black hair, stocky build, fire in his eyes and trouble, just like his kid. The other looked like a dredger.

My blood raced, every sense alert, scanning the scrum for the dangers: guns, knives, the men who'd step in if we pulled Simmons and the dredger apart, the men who lived for fighting as I had once done, so angry at a broken world that I'd smash my fist against it until it was broken and bloody too. But I was tired and wanted to go to bed, so I took the rifle from behind the bar and strode over and inserted myself between the two aggressors.

Simmons took the moment to nip around me and bash his opponent with the broken pool cue, and then all hell broke loose.

22

Assaulting a police officer is a serious offence with a very stiff penalty, but when a pack of dopy dredgers get on the turps, it's odds-on that cold, hard fact gets thrown against the wall along with chairs and other blokes. A brawl ensued, locals against outsiders, punches flying and landing all over the place. Vogel, who turned up to help when he heard the racket, Jackson and O'Malley were in there, subduing, handcuffing, taking the blows, maybe landing one or two punches themselves, just to stun the offender before getting the cuffs on. Amid this uproar, Fitzgerald stood behind the bar and watched. Didn't bring out a rifle, didn't get in there and lend a hand.

When the worst of it was over, I stepped outside, wiped the blood from my face and found Madame Foufoune standing by her cart. She was wearing a large man's overcoat and had a shawl knotted under several of her chins, and her breath was pluming in the lamplight.

'You still here?'

'The men paid my bail, luvvy,' she said with a grin. 'I've come to pick them up.'

'They can kiss goodbye to their money if we find you've been peddling your girls to them while on bail.'

'Is that your dog?' she said, bending over and holding out a hand to Alfie. He, being a friendly chap, wagged his tail and sniffed her.

'Get away, Alfie. I'll have to wash your nose.'

Foufoune found that very funny. 'I like dogs. Always happy, aren't they?'

'Seen this one before? With a man on a grey horse?'

'Can't say I have, luvvy,' she said, crouching down to smooch with Alfie. 'I like dogs better than people.'

Jackson came outside and whispered in my ear.

'You'll go back without your scaly mates, Mrs Foufoune. They're locked up, every one of them. You can stand them bail, if you care to.'

She hauled her great bulk up with a groan. 'Ooh, he's a darlin', that dog. If the men are off to Bathurst, then the girls can have a good wash in the river.'

'The river's full of mercury – you know that, don't you?'

'It's what keeps my girls clean,' she said with a wheezy laugh. 'Don't need injections when you can wash in it.'

'That's not how salvarsan works.'

'Don't wet your pants, luvvy, we're all clean as new pennies,' she said. She climbed, grunting, up to the cart, then looked me up and down. 'A strapping young man, you are, fine as there ever was. I reckon I could make a lot of money from you.' She winked, gave the reins a shake and trundled back to her cesspit.

She'd dug in up at Ringer's Rocks, a walking fortress of flesh and wile, but a bit of sweet talk with me and my dog would not deter the law. I would win this battle.

~

The rain had cleared by morning. I'd snatched only a couple of hours' sleep and was running on low spirits, waking to the awful memory of Scanlon's hand in the bunkroom, and feeling the bruises from the settling of the pub last night. I'd tapped a nail into one of the pine tree trunks and hung a shaving mirror there so I could see what I was doing when I trimmed my beard. I took my ointment and stood, gazing into the mirror, rubbing it into the scar tissue, feeling myself reassemble for the day.

If Wallace was dead, who had left the hand for us? Maybe, as Kennedy suggested, the dredgers had found it and thought it would be a lark to leave it in the bunkroom. Which meant Wallace had left it wherever he'd carried out the mutilation. A location we had not found. Or it wasn't Wallace at all, and the killer had kept the hands, along with Scanlon's rifle, sidearm, warrant card and notebook. None of which had been found either.

I'd taken the hand with me up to the police block in the early hours of the morning, dug a deep hole and placed it in, backfilled and covered the diggings with heavy river stones from the fireplace. It could stay there until Bathurst decided what to do with it. Scanlon had been cremated, his remains interred in a cupboard out the back of the head station, no doubt, while somebody tried to find a regulation on *Officer body parts – disposal of.*

At breakfast, Mrs Owen remarked on my seemingly peaceful nights. 'You don't scream anymore,' she said. 'Getting better, you are. It's probably the goats.'

'The goats?' I said, knife and fork paused above a plate of sausages and eggs.

'Soothing, they are. Animals, that is. I like to sit with the goats of a summer evening, always makes me happy.'

'It's the dog,' I said, returning to my food. 'He senses my distress and wakes me before ...'

'They can tell,' she said, nodding sagely. 'My dad had fits, but one of our dogs used to get all whimpery, and ten minutes later Dad started to see spots. Mum knew it was going to happen, so she got the stick for him to bite down on and she'd clear us kids from the room, and sure enough, it happened.'

'I don't mind telling you what an enormous relief it is,' I said. 'Having him wake me before I make a racket.'

'Not all dogs can do it, mind. But your Alfie, he's got the power.'

Alfie heard his name and poked his nose over the threshold of the back door, taking a rare liberty with Mrs Owen. She commented on my black eye and offered a cold cloth, but it was past that. We agreed that I would give her a detailed account of Davy's funeral after supper, and I headed off to work.

~

I ran into Jack Simmons' evil spawn on the way, young Frankie, standing in the mud, idly banging a stick against a fence in the lane behind the ostler.

'Master Simmons,' I said, coming towards him.

'Sergeant Hawkins,' he replied, still banging his stick. 'Still got the dog?' he asked.

'Yes, and I think I know who owned my dog. Belonged to a man called Charlie, but I can't find him. He visited your mum, then he disappeared.'

'She's not my mum. She's a slut and I wish she was dead.'

I was taken aback for a moment, then said, 'She's looked after you half your life. You show some respect.'

He gazed up at me, bold as brass, and said, 'No. I won't.'

We stared at each other. I didn't know what to do with unruly kids, or even with good kids.

'You called Scanlon on Charlie that night, didn't you?'

He looked down, started banging the stick again. 'Had no business in my dad's house and he was drunk. He wouldn't leave he was so drunk, so I ran and got Scanlon. He was smacking my mum around when we got back, and Scanlon took him off and I don't know what happened to him.'

'You saw me on his horse. I saw the look in your eyes – like you'd seen a ghost.'

'You were coming for us, and we weren't doing anything wrong.'

'Just wrecking someone's else home. You put the bungers around the cat's neck too, didn't you?'

'Put 'em around your neck if I want,' he said.

'Watch yourself, son, you're talking to the law,' I snapped back, despite the thud of alarm.

He looked up, like a dog sniffing the breeze. 'Gotta go.'

He ran off with me staring after him. Bungers around my neck, bloody hell. He was a hard case at twelve. A few more years and he'd be dangerous.

He slipped through a gap in the fence, and I realised it was the back of Mary's property. I could hear her daughter screaming like a banshee. She was doing it all on her own, waiting for Dawn to die while her feckless husband sat in our locked laundry picking scabs off his knees.

~

Kennedy was re-pinning the map to the wall, squinting through the smoke from the fag in his mouth. O'Malley was on the counter doing the daily paperwork, his split eyebrow swollen and scabby. All the others sported evidence of last night's smack-up too. I dropped into my chair and looked over at my senior officer in all his glory, waiting for his direction, his assessment of the awful discovery of Scanlon's hand and its implications for the investigation. Hilde walked past and Kennedy yelled out an order for a cup of tea, then he lit another fag from the one in his hand.

'You know she doesn't work for us,' I said.

'Don't get your knickers in a knot. I'll get her to bring you a cuppa next time, all right?'

'I'll get my own tea, thank you.'

'You know what your problem is?'

I couldn't wait for him to tell me, like so many before him. Bloody-minded, neurasthenic, up myself, too hard on myself, a malingerer, a nutcase, stuck up, letting the side down, reckless, cowardly, boring, a pedant, ambitious, lazy, lacking ambition, violent, a drunk, a womaniser, a cur – that one was from a woman – and so on. I was a man with many facets: some glowed, some were dull.

'You're an arsehole.'

'C'mon, you can do better than that,' I laughed.

'Don't tempt me, mate,' he said, returning to his desk and stabbing the ashtray with his fag. 'Got to let Bathurst know about the ... thing.'

'The thing in the troopers' bunkroom. Placed there while they were attending the owner's funeral. The only reason they slept in there last night

232

was because they were exhausted, but I have a serious morale problem now.'

'Send 'em back. We're done here.'

'It wasn't Wallace. It's someone else in this town.'

'Probably one of those dredgers put it there. Found it out bush. Wanted to make a point.'

'I'll make a bloody point for them, all right.'

Vogel had wired Bathurst for two police vans last night to take the worst of last night's offenders there, because we had no facilities to keep them until a magistrate showed up. They'd all spent the rest of the night crammed in the woodshed – it was like the Black Hole of Calcutta, except they could sit, had blankets and a bucket to piss in. Now, having sobered up, they were waiting to be processed by the troopers.

I hauled the foreman aside, dug out his statement and set to questioning him again.

'You said in your statement that Scanlon visited regularly to try to move Mrs Foufoune on. Did you ever see any argument between her and Scanlon, or with any of your crew?'

He blinked rapidly, dazed from being hungover and tired. He'd been hit on the scalp with something and his face was streaked with dried blood. All of us, troopers and dredgers, looked the worse for wear, as we recovered from the eternal dance in which we were locked.

'I didn't see it, but I heard about it. Mutkins, one of mine, came into town on his day off, took young Pearl with him—'

'One of the Chinese girls?'

'Yeah, she's gone, but.'

'What happened?'

'Mutkins was havin' a drink, minding his own business, and Scanlon

put him in the lock-up, and while he was there Pearl went off with another bloke. Mutkins blamed Scanlon.'

'Scanlon just pulled him off his barstool and put him in the lock-up?'

'He'd bought a few beers for Pearl, taken them out the back so she could have a drink, and he got a bit punchy when Scanlon turned up.'

'When did this happen?'

He screwed his face up with the effort of recall, then said, 'This woulda been the week before the trap was shot.'

'Never thought to tell us before?'

'Nuh, not a dobber.'

If it happened the week before Scanlon's death, then we had no record of the incident. I found Watt in the bar, polishing glasses as he liked to do, and asked him.

'You can't have women drinking in a pub or on the pub property,' he said. 'And you can't have girls of fourteen drinking at all, let alone prozzies. I sent for Scanlon and Mutkins had a go at him, and guess what? Into the lock-up he goes.'

Jackson was at the woodshed and extracted Mutkins for me. Mr Josiah Mutkins of Ophir, a queer-looking bloke with small eyes and a mouth that he appeared to be unable to close, age thirty-seven, he reckoned, been on the dredges since Christmas, so he was a blow-in. I asked him about Pearl.

He shrugged. 'She went off somewhere while I was locked up.'

'Why were you locked up?'

'Dunno.'

'Did the girl go back to Foufoune?'

'Nuh,' he said, slurping up some drool.

'Did you try to find her?'

234

'Nuh.'

'Did Foufoune?'

'Dunno. Gotta new girl from Bathurst.'

'Were you sweet on Pearl?'

He bridled at that, wiping his mouth, half-embarrassed, half-incredulous that I would ask him such an emasculating question.

'Pearl was all right, yeah. If Scanlon hadn't locked me up, she'd have been safe with me.'

Funny definition of safe.

'Scanlon was an arsehole,' he went on. 'Demons is all arseholes.'

There was a glint in his eye I did not like. Pearl was probably in a shallow grave somewhere, brutalised to death. There was no way for a young Chinese prostitute to get away from Colley, dressed in petticoats and with no money. The coach wouldn't take her, and not many men driving carts would give her a ride without expecting payment in kind.

'Do you own a rifle?' I asked.

'Yeah, we all do, 'cause of the wild pigs.'

I got Jackson to process Mutkins with the rest of them. He'd go to Bathurst, and the plods in Bathurst would carry on about having no space in their lock-up and the magistrate is flat out and why can't we hold them, and on and on until they remembered we had no lock-up at all, and we were off the magistrate's circuit until we did. And that therefore I would shunt all my customers their way just to annoy the hell out of them. After all, they weren't going to send them back.

~

Jack Simmons had spent the night secured in the laundry. I went to haul him out while Kennedy feigned deep analytic thought on the appearance of the second hand.

Simmons was bleary and bruised, a state he was probably familiar with, sitting on the floor between the cold, empty coppers.

'Come on, out,' I ordered.

'You've been talking to my wife,' he said, giving me a menacing look. 'Frankie told me. Said you know her.'

'I was in this town in 1906 when I met her. She is an acquaintance only. I am here to do my job, and that doesn't involve getting at other men's wives.'

'You'd better not.'

'Threatening my safety will bring a shitstorm down on your head, Simmons. A mounted trooper was killed here only weeks ago, and we take any threat to our safety seriously. What do you know about his murder?'

'Nothing. I wasn't here.' He got to his feet, a little unsteady, feeling the punches from last night. Out in the sunlight, he squinted and looked around. Vogel was escorting a dredger over to the back door. Fitzgerald, clad in singlet and shorts, was on the grass whirling a pair of Indian clubs around his head.

'Now that you're here, we need to have a talk about your daughter,' I said. 'Come inside.'

He traipsed into the office, me behind him getting a whiff of grimy body odour. I sat him in a chair. Kennedy had his newspaper up, his shield against the world.

'Your daughter—'

'Dawnie? What, has Mary been whingeing again? The kid's alright, just got a tummy ache.'

'She has a serious medical condition, Mr Simmons, one that could kill her if it's not fixed by an operation.'

'She's my kid and I say what happens, right? Not you, not the doctor and not any interfering busybodies.'

He wanted to toss his little girl into the flames. Let her die for his pride.

'Let me bring your attention to Section 43A of the *Crimes Act*, "Failure of persons with parental responsibility to care for child". Section 2. "A person: (a) who has parental responsibility for a child, and (b) who, without reasonable excuse, intentionally or recklessly fails to provide the child with the necessities of life, is guilty of an offence if the failure causes a danger of death or of serious injury to the child. Maximum penalty: Imprisonment for 5 years."

'Dr Pomeroy has declared that the child may die if she does not have the operation. And when she does, I will charge you and plead for the maximum penalty due to your wilful and persistent neglect.'

His mouth sagged, then his whole face did. I'd practised that section of the *Crimes Act* on the ride into Bathurst for the funeral and was well pleased with my delivery. Nothing like a good bludgeon with the book to bring a man to heel. I charged him for last night, processed him and said a court date would be fixed and he'd have to get himself to Bathurst to attend. If he came to my attention in the meantime, I went on, he'd go to Bathurst in a prison van, and possibly a little worse for wear too.

'Feisty little bastard,' Kennedy said as Simmons stomped out.

'One of Scanlon's frequent customers, according to his logs.'

'Married to that redhead with the big knockers, yeah? No wonder he's mean. Keeping the blowflies away would be a job and a half.'

'He's probably going to go and smack her about,' I said, getting to my feet.

'You can't interfere,' Kennedy said. 'Maybe she needs a few smacks to bring her into line.'

I wrote out a search warrant, got Kennedy to sign, picked out a sidearm from the armoury, holstered it and said, 'The hand, Kennedy, the hand.'

23

The Simmons' house was right by the western entrance to the town, a neat, freshly painted cottage with jasmine growing along the fence. I knocked on the door. Mary answered, infant draped over her shoulder, and a look of panic shot into her eyes.

'He's home,' she whispered. 'Got home yesterday.'

'I know. Didn't he tell you where he was last night?'

She shook her head and the man himself appeared at the end of the hall.

'What is it now?' he yelled, advancing.

I showed him the warrant.

'Why? What's she done?'

'I'll start around the back,' I said.

The backyard had a large shed and a wide gate to get a horse and cart through. The water tank, up on stumps, had a rust hole big as a fist near the bottom. Infant nappies flapped on a clothesline, and that wailing, my God, it set your teeth on edge. I could feel the irritation and impatience. Surely Mary could get the child to sleep. As I stood there, Frank came out the back door, saw me and ran off.

Mary came out, the screaming infant draped over her shoulder. 'Want a turn with her?'

'Where's Frankie's room?'

'Frankie doesn't have a bedroom; he sleeps on the back verandah.'

The verandah was partially enclosed and separated from the main house by a sturdy back door. Up one end was a narrow iron bedstead holding a thin mattress, made up all neat with blankets and sheets.

As I stared, Mary said, 'What are you looking for?' Before I could answer, she made an impatient noise, said she couldn't hear herself think and had to get on. She left me and went back inside.

I looked under the bed and found only boxes with tools and odds and ends, a cricket bat and some balls. The shabby chest of drawers beside the bed held nothing more than a few clothes and an extra blanket. I looked around the side of the house, then opened the shed, which held a cart laden with Simmons' digging tools, tins of kerosene for the lamps and a few dead mice.

After finding a sturdy horse in a neat stable, I looked down the narrow gap between the stable wall and the fence and saw something shoved in there. I couldn't get into that gap but Frank could. I took a rake from inside the shed and pulled and scraped the bundle towards me, half an inch at a time. Little Dawn was still carrying on inside the house.

I got the bundle within reach and pulled out a heavy canvas roll. Once unrolled, it revealed the tent and bedroll that had gone missing from the campsite. Frankie had seen me riding Charlie's grey horse and run off. No wonder he was so curious about the dog, as he knew it was Charlie's too. In the folds of the tent lay a handful of red papers, bunger wrappers that had been peeled off the cardboard tubes that had been full of black powder.

I knocked on the back door. Mary flung it open. 'I just got her down – what is it?'

'Charlie, who visited you the night before the fire.'

'Don't, Gus, please,' she whispered, looking over her shoulder with a look of terror that caught at my heart. 'I was lonely, that's all.'

'He died in the lock-up.'

She stepped outside and quietly shut the door behind her.

'He burned to death in the fire,' I told her. 'Your Frankie called Scanlon to deal with him because he wouldn't leave here. They returned to find him smacking you about.'

Her face was pale. 'He was in the lock-up? Jesus Christ, no.'

'He wouldn't leave?'

'No, he wanted to sleep over,' she said, dragging me away from the house. 'He'd had too much brandy and didn't want to walk back to his tent. I told him he'd had his fun, but he had to go. Then Scanlon turned up. I didn't know, at first, how he could have known, because I thought Frankie was asleep out the back, but he went and got him.'

'I think he set fire to the police station.'

'Frankie? No, he wouldn't do that, he's just a kid.'

'I'm going to have to officially question him.'

'But you can't,' she said, suddenly fearful. 'What if his father finds out I had a man here? He'll leave me and he'll take Dawn and give her to his mum. Don't, please don't. I just get lonely on my own, that's all it is.'

'Mary, Frankie has been sadistically killing cats, throwing rocks. And if I'm right, and I think I am, he's purposefully set fire to government property in an attempt to murder a man. And he succeeded. You can't let a kid like that run wild.'

'He's not running wild—'

'I'm sorry, Mary, I have to question him.'

'Jack'll beat me black and blue,' she said in a suddenly dull voice, as if all the fight had gone out of her. 'He'll kill me this time, and I won't have to wake every day to this hell.'

'He won't touch you, I promise.'

'Oh, you promise, do you?' She turned back inside and quietly closed the door.

~

Kennedy intercepted me in the street outside the pub. 'I've sent a wire about the hand. They'll tell us how to proceed.'

'You're the chief investigating officer, the detective who knows how to proceed. They're just desk jockeys.'

He scratched his neck, sighed. He was way out of his depth and so was I.

'Right, for starters, I reckon the positioning of the hand, like in the troopers' bunkroom, is sending a signal,' he said.

'He didn't just position it there to see if it suited the colour of the walls?'

'Ha bloody ha,' Kennedy said. 'First he shoots at you, then he sets fire to your tent, then he leaves the hand with the Mounted Trooper badge near your tent, and then he puts the other hand in with the lads. If we go back before Scanlon's death, maybe the firing of the station was part of it?'

'I'll be making an arrest this afternoon for setting fire to the police

station. That was Frank Simmons, all of twelve years old. Had nothing to do with the ambush and murder of Scanlon.'

'Maybe his mum was shagging Scanlon and Simmons?'

'Thought of that. But Simmons has been digging a well at Eurunderee, and has been there since before Scanlon's death. I checked he was there after the firing of my tent.'

The sound of a drumbeat floated across the town, loud and insistent, beating the alarm. We both looked around in bewilderment.

'What the hell is going on in this town?' Kennedy said.

The drumming seemed to be coming from the next street up, behind Mrs Lennox's shop. I left Kennedy and walked along the street, glancing up to check my tent was still standing. Alfie loped along beside me as my nerves cringed in horror, my mind all over the place.

It was Percy Lennox, sitting on the grass of his long block, drumming on an upturned galvanised-iron bucket. A quick glance around for the enemy made me feel foolish but it was almost automatic. Not that we used the drum in the Light Horse, but everyone knew the signals.

Mrs Lennox was pegging out washing on a long line held up by saplings, her black skirts flapping in the breeze.

Percy saw me and stopped. 'Sergeant Hawkins, I'm a drummer boy, listen.' He beat again on the bucket, doing Advance, Retreat, Prepare.

Mrs Lennox peered around a red shirt she'd been pegging up. 'Percy, stop that, please. Sergeant Hawkins might not like hearing it.'

I was amazed at her comment. How could she possibly know?

'I have to train, though. Drill myself,' Percy said.

'They don't use drummer boys in the Australian military,' I told him. 'Maybe the British still do, but it's the bugle now.'

'The British stopped using drummer boys after Isandlwana. I've told Percy this,' Mrs Lennox added, shaking out a wet apron and hanging it.

'How do you know? If you don't mind me asking,' I added.

'My father was a drummer in the 79th Cameron Highlanders at Sevastopol,' she said, leaning down to her wash basket and picking out another wet garment.

'Under Field Marshal Campbell?'

'Yes, "Die Where You Stand" Campbell. But Father lived and came to Australia. Taught my late brother, Dan, all the drumbeats, and Dan taught Percy as a boy. Dan and I grew up hearing about the Crimea every day of our lives. The old man went over it and over it and sometimes thought he was still there. He was like a parrot who could only say a few lines,' she said brusquely, flapping a tea towel. There was a world of anger behind that tone, and I decided to ask no more.

'But boys like soldiers,' she said with a sigh, putting her hands on her hips. 'I took this one to see Lord Kitchener when he was in Bathurst a few years ago. The great soldier hero of the empire, up there with God and the King. The whole town put on an afternoon tea for him, the day he opened the Boer War Memorial. Women baking for days, putting on their best dresses, and the men all clean and sober, and he didn't turn up. The great Lord Kitchener said he couldn't be bothered. Of course, Percy didn't know, but some of us think differently about Lord Kitchener now.'

'I'm not surprised.'

'No?' she said, with a bleak laugh as she pegged up a long pinafore apron with frills on the bodice.

'That apron, it's the same as Mrs Fitzgerald's,' I said. 'She wears it every day.'

'Hilde? Yes, we made them together when she first arrived in town. She stayed with me before her wedding, and we spent our evenings stitching. Hilde does love a frill.'

'I'm not trying to be a do-gooder, Mrs Lennox, but Hilde does seem very despondent.'

'You've noticed.' She pegged up a pair of socks, then said, 'Percy, love, run inside and put the kettle on.'

'Is she happy?'

'Really, what sort of question is that?' she said, picking out some more socks. 'Is anyone happy? Do the faces in the street look as if people are full of joy? Life is hard, Sergeant, and Hilde's life is no exception, except it's probably worse than it should be.'

'Why is that?'

'I'll say no more,' she said, shaking her head. 'Now, let me get on with my chores.'

'Nobody in this town will speak the truth.'

'Sometimes there's no fixing the truth, so better to let it lie. And you would surely know that, as a lawman.'

'I'm sworn to the truth, Mrs Lennox, it's the basis of the job.'

'Still a young man, aren't you, love?' she said, with a mirthless laugh.

'Apart from early widowhood, why is Hilde so unhappy?'

Mrs Lennox tucked a lock of hair behind her ear, looked around and said in a low voice, 'Hilde Fitzgerald works, unpaid, from before dawn until late every day, cooking, mending and cleaning for those Fitzgerald men, as well as doing the hotel laundry. He won't even let her go up to the church on a Sunday morn – says Len needs her to bathe him and fix his lunch. And she, being the kind-hearted lass she is, feels she can't say no.'

'But she's a maid, isn't she?'

'No, she is not. She's his daughter-in-law, under his protection, if you can call it that. Ray doesn't believe in women working for money. Says it's vulgar. But women slaving from dawn to dusk for family is not vulgar, to his mind. She's used as an unpaid beast of burden with no rights. No eight-hour day for her.'

'She could leave.'

'With what money?' she said, impatient with me. 'And besides, Hilde has been a modest and obedient girl all her short life, raised to put others before herself, and has never done anything without her father, husband or father-in-law telling her to do it. By the time she gets to my age she'll be alone, exhausted and poverty-stricken, and they'll wash their hands of her.'

I must have looked bemused, because she shook her head impatiently and said, 'Stick to sorting out pub brawls, Sergeant, do-gooding is obviously not your forte.'

Maybe Mrs Lennox was a socialist or a suffragette or something like that. I was wrapped up in my own concerns for so long that I hadn't caught up with these ideas. I had meant happiness in a different sense, but now I wasn't sure what I meant.

I wandered back to the station. Best to leave do-gooding to those who knew better. I had a weapons search to carry out. That was a task a man could get his fist around.

24

After that perplexing talk with Mrs Lennox, I took a moment to go to the bathroom and apply ointment to my scar, dabbing and running my finger up and down it from hairline to beard, soothing and reassuring. I had a fear of the scar returning in all its livid ugliness if I didn't apply the ointment several times a day. My father had reassured me that this could not happen, but I dismissed his comments. It was my face, not his.

Thus anointed, I took Vogel and Jackson and we rode up to Ringer's Rocks. As we got closer, we saw figures splashing about in the river, the rugged cliff behind them, sheltering the two dredges. The bend in the river here was quite pronounced, leaving a stony isthmus as a sunny beach on which somebody had lit a fire, while across the road, higher up, lay the ramshackle remains of the town.

We rode closer and Vogel gasped. I called a halt. The girls ran from the river onto the shore, completely naked in the cold afternoon air, and began to taunt us, waggling their skinny arses, lifting their breasts and bouncing them, yelling foul curses like sailors carousing in the Rocks in Sydney.

'That's obscene,' Vogel spluttered, bright red. 'We have to arrest them, filthy little strumpets.'

Jackson was silent, gazing at the bare female flesh in a primal daze as he chewed on a stalk of straw.

'We have to arrest them, sir,' Vogel said.

'Trooper, what did I say about telling me what to do?'

'Yes, sir, but—'

Conjunctions like *but* make me want to hit something. Vogel shut his mouth just in time.

'Permission to speak, sir.'

'No. They are provoking us and it's working. Learn this lesson now and learn it well, Vogel. Your facial expression must be as a rock, hard, impassive, unmoved. Or they will shit all over you.'

A titanic inner struggle played out across his face, then he emitted a strangled, 'Yes, sir.'

Foufoune appeared wearing a vast, magenta flowered kimono. She strolled across the road and picked her way down the stony beach as if she were on the sands at Coogee. She gave us a wave, then dropped the kimono. Both Jackson and Vogel groaned and carried on as she stood there, her great pink belly hanging down to her bulging, dimpled thighs, her arms akimbo, flesh hanging and wobbling, two bags of bosom quivering, her brassy hair tied up on top in a coquettish bow.

This was too much for Vogel and he began spluttering his outrage.

'Stow it, Trooper,' I snapped. If ever there was a time for the rock face, this was it.

Then the old doxy raised her arms and held them out to the side, threw her head back and shimmied her great dugs in an act so brazen it was all I could do not to laugh. She was like Scylla in the *Odyssey*, eating living men, using our weakness to survive. Vogel, burning with fury, repelled her

onslaught with a barrage of moral fire. She laughed at him, all her ragged succubi joining in, dancing around her, screeching with laughter. Vogel had broken the square and now we were for it.

I ordered the troopers to fix in place the mask so essential to this sort of work, then sent them off to search huts and tents for weapons, noting where they'd been found. I dismounted and went over to Mrs Foufoune. The girls were skipping around the troopers, still naked, poking out their tongues, making lascivious gestures, whipping their wet, ropy hair around, squealing like imps.

'Call your girls off, Mrs Foufoune,' I said, watching Jackson watching the girls. Vogel spat insults, assuring them brimfire would rain upon them all the way to the eternal flames of Hell, and then they'd be sorry.

Meanwhile, Foufoune, her kimono open, displaying her corpulence to great effect, said thoughtfully, 'The dark one – looks like he might come back for a taste. He going to be stationed at Colley for a bit?'

'Not if I can help it. Now, call them off or we'll charge them and lock them up.'

She clapped her hands and screeched, 'Girls, get dressed, you'll catch your death.'

'Thank you,' I said, nodding and keeping my eyes above the neck. 'A dredger called Mutkins – what can you tell me about him?'

'Don't take much notice of them really, as long as they pay and don't get too rough.'

'Was he one to be rough with the girls?'

'You want to know about Pearl,' she said with a sigh. 'It happens in this game, sometimes a john takes to a girl and doesn't want to share her. He doesn't understand or he doesn't care to. Mutkins was like that with Pearl.'

'Do you know where she is now?'

She shook her head. 'I heard that Mutkins got himself in trouble buying grog for her. She hung about town while he was locked up. Some fella was seen groping her behind the post office, and next day Mutkins got out and that was that.'

'What do you mean?'

'He went asking around for her, heard about the other fella copping a feel, got angry and we never heard from Pearl again. I'm not saying he killed her or anything, but if he found her, he wouldn't have been happy with her. But what else was she supposed to do? Anyway, that's what I heard.'

'And Scanlon?'

'Just doin' his job. But Mutkins reckoned it was his fault Pearl had to fend for herself.'

'Was he angry enough to kill Scanlon?'

'Wouldn't know, luvvy. I'm not interested in them and their ways, to be honest. Been in the game too long, probably. Pearl was picked before she was ripe, her English was bad and she'd go with anyone who gave her a pat. Girls like that don't last long.'

'Did you report her missing?'

'Cops wouldn't give a rat's bum about a china doll, you know that.' She waddled off up the stony shoals, kimono flapping in the breeze.

'Aren't you supposed to keep them safe?' I called after her.

'Can't do much if they run off,' she yelled back.

I turned and looked at the dredges, silent and ugly. The river like a sallow gutter. Could be anything stashed inside the dredges: guns, illegal alcohol, maybe even Pearl's clothes.

I followed Foufoune up the stony incline to the ragged settlement. The huts were a jumble of timber slab, bark and corrugated iron. Vogel and Jackson worked their way around, taking notes, piling up rifles. Two old men, not dredgers and not with Foufoune's travelling brothel, and so weathered they looked like tree knots, nodded at me, said g'day. Both wore striped shirts and ragged waistcoats, stiff with grime, stained old daks, shoes with toes sticking out.

'Blackie McGeehan,' one of them said, holding out a wizened hand, which I shook.

'Mr McGeehan, excuse me asking, but were you aware that the state now pays an aged pension? Your camp looks as if it could do with a flush of funds.'

'Next year, officer, I'll be sixty-five, and me brother, Bundy,' he nodded at the other old fella, 'the year after. Then we'll get ourselves some dancing shoes, eh?'

The two of them laughed, croaked and coughed, hacking up phlegm. Poor old buggers, with their blackened teeth and scurvy spots. Hopefully they'd have a few decent years on the pension, if they lasted that long.

We had a haul of half a dozen rifles, mostly .303s. We'd send them off to Ballistics in Sydney, and we might get a match with the bullet that killed Scanlon or we might not. The doors to the cabins on the dredges were padlocked so we couldn't search in there. At least, not yet.

Jackson was speechless as we rode back to Colley, but not Vogel. On and on he went about how he never thought he'd see Sodom and Gomorrah here, right here on the Bull River, of all places.

'Just see it as part of the rich tapestry of policing, Vogel,' I said, swatting at a fly.

'We've told them twice to move on and they haven't, and we just ride away, sir?'

'Complete the mission,' I said. 'One day, when we have nothing else demanding our time, we will have another go.'

'I want to be there when we do, sir. Put that woman in the woodshed with a Bible for a few days. Do her good.'

Given a few more years, I mused, Vogel would be a formidable law enforcer. Or he'd be exhausted from trying to clean an uncleanable world and would become a quartermaster.

When we got back to town, I wired Bathurst and requested they provide an alert when they released the dredgers. I wanted to enter those dredging cabins at the same time as them.

~

With another hour before dusk, O'Malley and I returned to the Simmons house. We knocked on the door and Mary opened. She had bruising around her neck already and looked like one eye was on its way to turning black. She wouldn't look at me.

Jack Simmons was at the table having a meal with Frank. Dawn was sitting on the floor with a shabby knitted doll. Frankie jumped to his feet, his chair falling back, and his father roared at him to sit down. I don't know who he was more frightened of, us or his father.

Simmons took a gulp of tea and said, 'What is it?'

Mary stood at the sink, her back to us, like she didn't care anymore.

'We've come to question Frank Simmons for arson on the morning of the nineteenth of April. We believe he deliberately lit a fire beneath the

252

police station knowing a man was inside, with intent to murder said man.'

Frank tried to run again but his father was too quick, and he lunged from his chair and caught the boy by the ear, twisting it. 'What the fuck have you done, boy?'

The poor kid had tears rolling down his cheeks as his dad twisted harder.

'That's enough, Mr Simmons.'

'You telling me how to discipline my own son?'

'Like you discipline your wife, by the looks of it,' I said.

'Don't, Gus, please,' Mary said, turning around.

'Oh, it's "Gus", is it? You been whoring around with a copper now?'

'No, she hasn't,' Frankie cried, and he pulled himself out of his father's grasp, ran to Mary and threw his arms around her. She hugged him tight, cradling his head while the baby cried.

'Been away working my arse off for months and this is what happens when I'm gone? You, slut, fucking a demon?' Simmons went for her, but O'Malley got there first, slamming him back against the wall.

'She wasn't fucking a demon,' Frankie cried, 'He was a—'

'A stock and station agent, in the district for work,' Mary said in a dull voice. 'Name of Charlie.'

'And I killed him, Dad, I didn't want him here in our house, and he wouldn't go and so I called the cops and burnt down the lock-up in the morning.'

The four adults in the room looked at him with astonishment. Twelve years old and he had done that.

'You stupid little bastard,' Simmons said.

Frankie winced. Probably thought his father would approve.

'You emptied out the black powder from some bungers and used it to set fire to a stack of magazines under the station,' I said.

He nodded, his face against Mary's shoulder. 'Yep,' came a muffled reply.

'This is your fault, you faithless bitch,' Simmons said. O'Malley braced himself but Simmons confined himself to verbal abuse.

'See what I have to deal with?' he said to us. 'She's always whining or crying, and then she goes out whoring.'

'And what do you do on your long stints in other towns, Mr Simmons? The only difference here is that the boy saw her being unfaithful. He doesn't see you whoring around.'

'He never,' Frank shouted.

'What happens now?' Mary asked.

'We'll take him to the station and charge him. One of you will have to accompany him while he's being charged, then he'll go to Bathurst on remand, unless you can bail him, and then, like as not, he'll be sentenced to a boy's reformatory.'

Frank cried harder as I spoke, clutching at Mary as if she could save him.

'You go with him, and take her with you,' Simmons said, nodding at Dawn on the ground as if she were a bag of flour, nothing more.

Mary scooped her up, prised Frank from her skirts and took his hand, and we walked in silence to the station. We completed the paperwork while Frank and Mary sat in front of my desk, both silently crying. Then O'Malley took Frank out to the woodshed after Mary kissed him goodbye.

She turned back to me and shook her head. 'What good will it do,

Gus? A reformatory will turn him into a hardened, angry man, and he'll probably go on to even worse things.'

'Worse than deliberately burning down a police station in order to kill the man inside? At age twelve? No, as I said, I'm sorry but I can't look away.'

I pulled open a desk drawer, took out a cheque I'd written and gave it to her.

'What's this for?'

'Take the next coach,' I said. 'Get to Bathurst and get that kid her operation.'

'I can't take this,' she said, trying to hand it back.

'Please, take it. Just for once I'd like to do some good instead of cleaning up after the bad.'

Mary hesitated.

'I'm lending you this as an old friend, because you need to keep Dawn alive. Once she's stopped screaming, you can think about what to do next.'

'It's an awful lot.'

'I don't spend my pay on anything other than Mrs Owen's knitting.'

'You buy her things?'

'Got a nice tam-o'-shanter for sitting outside on a cold night, and I bought a blanket from her and one for the dog, and some of that soap she makes. I use it when I have my bath upstairs and smell all dainty and fresh when I'm done.'

Mary laughed, then looked down at the cheque. 'Jack won't be happy. Because if I go to Bathurst, I'm not coming back.'

'His problem.'

'I used to love him, you know. But not anymore,' she said, tucking the

cheque away. 'And what about Frankie? I'll never see him again, and I'm the only mum he knows.'

'You write to me at this address,' I said, giving her my father's address. 'He'll forward it to me, and I'll tell you where they've taken him. Come on, I'll walk you back and stay while you pack a bag. Then stay here in the hotel until the coach comes tomorrow. Jack won't come after you here, not with all of us troopers loitering about.'

We walked down the street in silence until we came to their house. Mary hitched Dawn up on her hip, looked up at me, took a deep breath and we went inside.

I didn't want Mary's gratitude, or the money paid back; I just wanted to see right being done, to feel as if I could do some good in the world. As if I could atone for the bad done in South Africa. I'd thought I was going there to fight for an Empire that needed me, an Empire under threat, but it wasn't that at all. It was to satisfy the Empire's rapacious appetite for gold, and it was us soldier fools who did the digging.

25

I made my way back to the pub, a wave of weariness crashing over me. I felt as if I had not recovered from the convivial refreshment of Scanlon's farewell yet, let alone the dredger smack-up. In that swamp of fatigue, I saw myself wandering up and down this main street over the years to come, administering, thumping, warning, nipping the heels of the recalcitrant like a sheepdog. And for no thanks, from above or from the townsfolk. No wonder Barrett amused himself with other men's wives – women who might make him feel better or wanted or simply more than just a uniform.

This train of thought led straight to Flora, dwelled there for some time, then flowed towards the Light Horse. Surely a military career would be better than this? Staff in Remounts, lunching at a fine club with other officers, robust arguments on how the Japanese military managed to give the Russian army a good thrashing, whisky and billiards afterwards, regimental dances with pretty girls all wide-eyed and breathless at my swagger and dashfire.

I stepped over a dog conked out in the sun, flies swirling around him, and pushed open the door to the pub.

'Why is Frankie in the woodshed?' Fitzgerald asked as I made my way down the hall.

'Been a naughty boy,' I said.

'He's a terror all right, always up to no good, lying and getting into scrapes. His father needs to take a strap to him.'

'I'm sure he does.'

Kennedy was where I usually found him: drinking tea and reading the paper.

'Been following this *Titanic* sinking?' he said, slurping his tea.

'My mind has been otherwise occupied.'

'Fifteen hundred people,' he said, shaking his head. 'It wasn't an iceberg. Couldn't have been. All of those Irish travelling steerage; it's the Fenians, put a bomb together and blew a hole in the ship. Y'see, they knew there was millionaires on board.' He turned the pages, frowning as he read. 'And my Joan agrees.'

'Joan is Mrs Kennedy?'

He nodded. 'She is, and has had that pleasure for thirty-two years.'

'I think we need to follow up a dredger called Josiah Mutkins. Had a grudge against Scanlon and a run-in with him only the week before he died. Foufoune says Mutkins was stuck on a china doll called Pearl, subsequently missing, whereabouts unknown, and—'

'Wallace is Scanlon's killer,' Kennedy said with an impatient sigh. 'Done and dusted. If you want to investigate some local matter then go ahead, but I'm wrapping up the Scanlon case.'

Vogel appeared and asked to have a word. I followed him into the bunkroom, where the others were sitting on the lower bunks.

'We've been talking, sir,' Jackson said, looking around at the others.

258

'And, well, we think the three of us should be rotated out. They could send the troopers from Rylstone and Capertee, and we could man their stations.'

'Hand got you spooked?'

'We got Wallace, so isn't it time, sir? For us to leave?'

'The hand suggests we made an error, or that he had an accomplice,' I said.

'But Detective Kennedy shot him, sir – and didn't Superintendent MacKerras say it was him?' Vogel said. 'He congratulated us on bringing Scanlon's killer in.'

The bunkroom was small but slept six. It was cold and stank of their filthy kit, which, while regularly washed, was given a beating every day. The food was garbage, they hadn't had a day off in weeks, and they'd been shocked to the core by the murder of their mate. And now the hand's appearance seemed to suggest that one of them, or all of them, was next. I know I'd had enough. I'd lost any faith I had in Kennedy and was as shocked by the appearance of the hand as they were. I was tired of the hard-faced townsfolk, who looked at us with antagonism; tired of the brass in Bathurst, who were out of their depth; tired of our ramshackle office, whose constant disorder physically pained me.

'I'll send a request in immediately. Make sure your door is locked tonight.'

'What about you, sir?'

O'Malley. Asking about me? Nobody asked about me or how I was managing, and I was touched.

'I'll stay, but you make your own decisions. Now, get on with your duties until we hear from Bathurst.'

Bathurst would take their time, no doubt, despite the second hand's

appearance, assuming it was just dredger mischief. Kennedy and I could sit at our desks and flick paper clips at one another and speculate about the *Titanic*. Frankie would go to Bathurst and be charged. Wallace was dead. Mission complete, and I had to have a hard think about my future.

~

Mrs Owen and I had moved beyond the kitchen, and after supper, if I wasn't busy, we'd retire to her parlour. One side of the room had sacks of goats' wool and a spinning wheel, the other side had two comfy chairs in front of the fire and a koala fur rug between them. Clyde held pride of place on the mantle, alongside a commemorative plate of Queen Victoria's Diamond Jubilee. Our feet were encased in goats' wool socks, the fire crackled, and young Alfie had ingratiated himself with her to the point that he lay in the prize position in front of the fire, fast asleep.

'What do you do with all your knitting?' I ventured.

'I've got forty-seven grandchildren,' she said with a laugh. 'Some great-grandchildren too, I think. Got a list somewhere. Always knitting blankets, hats, mittens and so on. My two girls in Bermagui have twenty-two between them. That's a lot of kids to keep warm. And I make the soap to send too. I can't be there for 'em so I do my bit here. They're good girls, my two. Had their own aprons as soon as they could walk.'

Alfie got up, a bit groggy from sleep, staggered away from the fire and dropped onto the cool floorboards.

'Why don't you have a wife, love?' she asked. 'You could have married quarters when the new station goes up. You'd be nice and cosy in there.'

'Can't have the woman I want, so there's no reason to marry.'

260

'She married someone else?'

'No, it's just ...'

'Pretty?'

I thought of Flora, her dark brown eyes so soft and clear, her slender neck, the thrill I felt when I saw her, that explosion in my chest sending glowing sparks through my soul. Flowers were pretty, butterflies were pretty, but Flora was full of grace and spirit. But I couldn't find all that she was in just one word.

'Can she cook?'

'I don't know. I don't think so.'

Mrs Owen raised her eyebrows at that. 'Can she sew?'

'She embroiders, yes, but her sister was renowned as an expert needlewoman.'

There they were, glossy dark heads bent, sitting in the wicker chairs on the homestead verandah, a soft breeze blowing from the Darling, Nessie laughing while she stitched and Flora reading aloud, changing her voice with each character.

'She's a rich man's daughter, then. Because only a rich man's daughter has time to embroider, not mend. Makes her more attractive so she can find a husband.'

'Is that all there is to life?'

'For a woman? Yes, you mark my words, love. Even a rich man's girl has to marry. And then the time for samplers and dainty handkerchiefs is over and she'll be giving her husband a family and sorting the servants and the linen cupboard and whatnot.'

Alfie got up from the cold floor and returned to the rug in front of the fire, settling down with a grunt. I rummaged around in the biscuit tin.

'What do you make of young Hilde Fitzgerald?' I asked, dunking a rock-hard gingernut in my tea.

'You don't want to marry Hilde,' she said, looking shocked. 'Skinny little thing. Got no hips, and you'll be wanting babies.'

'I don't want to marry her, but I see her every day down at the pub and she's always wiping tears away. She seems miserable. Mrs Lennox says she works from dawn until way after dark and isn't paid.'

The needles clicked and clacked, and Mrs Owen shook her head sorrowfully. 'Poor little love. When Ray Fitzgerald brought her home from a business trip to Wagga for William to marry, she was only sixteen and as giggly and sweet as they come, a laugh like a magpie, all warbly and high. She stayed with Mrs Lennox and made a nice white blouse for her wedding day, like a good girl, with lace and frills. She went up to the church, even though she's a Lutheran, and sang in the choir. William and her were always hand in hand, whispering and giggling, like youngsters do. Then after they got married, you could see the happiness just draining away, day by day.'

'Did he hit her?'

'Oh no, William wasn't like that,' she said, looking up, taken aback.

'Then what?'

'Didn't take to married life,' she said with a shrug.

'You mean the marriage bed?'

'How would I know that?' she said all indignant. 'No, it was Davy, he and William were thick as thieves, two young lads going out pig shooting, yabbying or fishing or whatever, and Hilde was left out.'

'That would be a common story,' I said, looking at the fire, remembering all the isolated women I'd come across in the Bourke division, left in shanties while their feckless men were off drinking.

262

'Men have their pastimes and women have theirs, and to my way of thinking that's a good recipe for peace and quiet,' Mrs Owen said. 'But when you're just married you want your groom to be paying you attention, at least for a few months.'

'I wonder why she doesn't go back home?'

'She's the eldest of twelve brothers and sisters, that's why. Her parents can't afford another mouth to feed. No, she has to find herself another husband – that's all she can do. Or she can keep house for one of her brothers, if they'll have her.'

Alfie staggered over to the cold floorboards again, dropped, stretched out and sighed. The flickering flames and glowing logs gave the room a golden cast, and on the mantelpiece, the porcelain plate picture of my old queen, Vicky, long gone. I remembered her portrait in every schoolroom, and in the school chapel, where on the occasion of her jubilee we recited lines from Kipling's poem: '*God of our fathers, known of old, Lord of our far-flung battle line, Beneath whose awful hand we hold, Dominion over palm and pine ...*'

I certainly had dominion over the pines on the police block, but it wasn't the vision my mind conjured at the time. I was part of that far-flung battle line, as I sat wedged into a pew with my schoolmates, my inflamed imagination seeing me leading a cavalry charge in all its power and glory, enemies scattering as I thundered towards them, sword to the ready to smite down every foe of Her Imperial Majesty, Queen Victoria, then drinking a toast to her in the mess and tucking candied rose petals between the creamy breasts of some luscious courtesan and fishing them out with my tongue.

I was eighteen when I took a commission, and, as lads that age often

are, convinced of the rightness of my decisions and the moral soundness of my convictions. My father was set against the military. I had no need of paternal advice and asked my father why, if he wanted me to be a coward, did he send me to a school where we learnt that to lay down our lives in sacrifice was just about the most manly and noble thing we could do?

When my father retrieved me from South Africa, cut to pieces and hovering between life and death, he hired nurses and sat beside me all night in the darkness, in case I should need him. He never said, *I told you so*, and I never said, *Why didn't you stop me?* But we probably both thought it.

~

The police van to take Frankie into Bathurst was arriving sometime in the morning. And the coach to Bathurst was leaving, too, taking my request for the troopers' reassignment to the bosses. I went down to the coach station to make sure Mary and Dawn got away. I heard my name and turned to see Mary, all smiles and her curls all shiny, and that haunted, fretful look gone.

'Good morning,' I said. 'You look well.'

'That's because I am well. Dawn's booked in to have her operation the day after tomorrow. Can't tell you what a weight that is off me. Once I'm free of this town and Jack, I'll look even better.'

'Before you go,' I said, 'tell me about Charlie. I have his dog and he's taken to me as if Charlie never existed.'

'Charlie was tall like you, had a beard like you, same deep voice, I suppose, but not as much fun. He wanted his needs met and to drink, that's all.' Mary rubbed her eyes. 'He wasn't even any good.'

'Unlike me, of course?' I said, giving her a hopeful glance.

She smiled and shook her head wearily. 'You men, you need to be praised for just putting your pants on in the morning.'

'We had fun, I do remember that.'

'We did,' she said with a cheeky smile. 'Made each other laugh, didn't we, like a couple of clowns. You told me all those stories of Africa and we sang the soldier songs, remember? Charlie would make a burnt log seem like better company. Sorry he's dead, but.'

'Could have been me, if Frankie thought we'd been at it.'

Her smile faded and she shook her head again, this time in sorrow. 'Got the devil in him, poor kid.'

'Do you have a place to stay in Bathurst?'

'My Aunt Beryl and Uncle Reg – he's an engine driver for the railways – live in Milltown, and they said I could come and live with them. Beryl's my mum's sister. She's got six kids and said we'd be no bother.'

'Welcome news.'

'It is, oh, it is, Gus. Aunty Beryl's been at me to leave Jack and move to Bathurst for years. But how could I leave Frank behind? He'll have a lawyer, won't he?'

'Of course. But you'll have to be with him whenever they speak to him. Unless his father shows up.'

'Jack's not much use. Just lies on the bed and stares. His world has fallen apart, but I can't stop to put it back together for him. I've got to see Dawn through her operation, and Frankie through what he's going to go through.'

'Jack's a fool for not looking after you, Mary.'

'Don't start the blarney, Gus Hawkins,' she laughed, her green eyes shining like polished jade, her flame-coloured hair blazing in the morning light, that appetite for life rekindled. No wonder Jack felt sorry for himself.

He had her and he lost her, and it was his own stupid fault.

'Good luck,' I said. 'I'll be thinking of you.' We had a brief hug, nothing that others would see and wonder about. Then she was in the coach and rattling up the hill with her little girl, her back to this town for good, and the hem of my soul was cleansed of a few grimy spots.

26

I went out the back of the pub, nodded at poor Hilde, who was up and at work already, dragging a heavy bucket along as she mopped the hallway, and opened the door to the woodshed. A flood of light illuminated the scene. Frankie was curled up on a horse blanket with a pillow and covered by two police blankets. He raised his head and flopped it back down when he saw it was me.

'Go away,' he said. 'I hate you.'

'Fair enough, but what you did is very serious.'

'I'm glad I killed him,' he said, sitting up. 'I'll kill everyone.'

'Don't go saying that to anyone. Tell the magistrate and the lawyer and the judge that you're sorry, you weren't thinking straight.'

He gazed up at me, his sleepy, tear-stained face full of fear. 'Will they whip me?'

'In the reformatory, yes, possibly, so hold your tongue,' I said, feeling pity for the lad. 'First you have to get through remand and the trial. You'll have a lawyer, and they'll do their best for you, plead youth and provocation or something like that, and if you behave yourself, you might get out early.'

'Can't I stay here?'

'No, sorry, mate.'

I sat beside him on the horse blanket. 'Your dad been to see you?'

He shook his head.

'Then you listen to me, Frankie. When they put you in the reformatory, you do everything they tell you to do. Keep your head down, don't answer back, and if they whip you, do not cry or yell out.'

Poor kid. His lip began to tremble and a couple of tears appeared, but I had to prepare him, because no one else was going to.

'Other boys will give you trouble at first. You give it right back, so they know not to mess with you. Any whiff of weakness and they'll come for you.'

'But I'm just a kid,' he said, head against his knees, sobbing.

'Frankie, you killed a man,' I said, putting my hand on his shoulder. 'It's wrong, but it takes some balls. You've got it in you to survive this.'

He raised his head, looked at me. 'I wasn't going to do it, you know. I was awake early, and I had a jar full of the bunger powder and I really wanted to go and do it, but I was afraid too.'

The tears flowed as the enormity of what he'd done sank in. I couldn't sit with him all day, and nor should it have been me preparing him for what lay ahead. I went down to see Jack Simmons.

I barged in, found him sitting at the kitchen table, a bottle of brandy in front of him, unshaved, a picture of misery.

'She's gone?' he said, not looking up.

'Yes, her and Dawn, safely on the coach.'

He splashed an inch of brandy into a tumbler and drank.

'You have to come and stay with Frankie, go with him in the police van to Bathurst.'

'Nuh.'

'He's your kid – you have to be there.'

He shook his head slowly. 'Can't.'

'Why the hell not?'

He said nothing, just turned the brandy bottle around and around as the sun streamed in onto the table. I snatched the bottle up from the table and put it on top of a cupboard. Simmons did nothing.

'Go and wash, and pack a bag. You are going with Frank to Bathurst.'

He drained the remains of the brandy from his glass, put it down and glared at me. 'What do I say to him? Little runt ruined everything. Nah, he can go by himself.'

'They'll make him a ward of the state and then you'll never have any say.'

He shrugged. 'Never did anyway. Didn't listen to me. Nobody listened to me. I told her, I told Mary to watch out for him, but did she? No.'

I grabbed him by the scruff of his shirt and shook him, and the chair fell back with a clatter. He took a swipe at me but I pinned him back against the wall and got in his face. 'Get yourself down to that fucking kid now or I will break both your arms.'

Simmons looked shocked at that. I was too – it came out of nowhere. But he washed his face, walked into the bedroom, me one step behind him, threw some clothes into a knapsack, found his wallet and a coat.

'What do I say to him?'

'Just stand beside him – that's all you have to do. All the way through this, because nobody else is going to.'

In silence we walked back to the pub. The police van had arrived and the driver was standing around waiting for me. I took Simmons out

the back and there was Vogel, standing firm in front of the woodshed, stalwart as a mule in a blizzard.

'Let him out,' I said.

Vogel opened the door and Frankie came out into the sunlight, blinking at the brightness. He saw his father and ran over, throwing his arms around him. Simmons put his hand on the boy's head and then took his hand. They walked back through the pub and across the road to the van, with me right behind them.

The general store had a large window, and in its reflection I could see Ray Fitzgerald at his window, watching as the driver locked the van door, got in his seat and flicked the reins, and the van rolled away along the main street. I crossed the road and walked into the pub.

'Good riddance to Frankie,' Ray Fitzgerald said, standing in the doorway of his office. 'Been a bloody nuisance in this town.'

'There's always one.'

Kennedy was in our office, slurping his morning tea, reading the papers that had come through on the coach. Did this man do anything else? The troopers were with the horses, having their shoes checked over, and would be gone for at least half an hour.

'I need to talk to you,' I said in a low voice.

'Talk away, sunshine,' Kennedy said, his eyes still on the papers.

Ray Fitzgerald walked in. He stood beside me in shirtsleeves and braces, his arms firm and strong, his clipped moustache looking like brushed steel.

'Investigation winding up?' he asked.

'Yeah,' Kennedy said. 'I reckon by next week we'll be back in Bathurst, get those typists out of your rooms too. They might even send two of the troopers back?' he said, looking at me.

'I'm not so sure we'll be winding up,' I said.

'Oh, for God's sake,' Kennedy said. 'Yes, we are, Ray. It's done and dusted.'

Fitzgerald smiled. 'I'll leave you two to argue the toss. Still on for Empire Day, Pat?'

'Yeah, of course. It's this Friday, isn't it?'

'It is, yes. Bunting's ready, we have the trestles and the dais for out the front. I think the children are going to march in formation too. Pity we don't have any cadets here, that would be a nice touch.'

He disappeared and Kennedy glared at me, a fag burning between his fingers. 'What now?'

'I would not rule out one of the dredgers. We've sent all the rifles from their camp to Sydney, so we at least have to wait for the all-clear from Ballistics. And even then, I want to search their dredging cabins.'

'And this is because? Wait, don't tell me – you want to be the hero again.'

'This is because a dredger called Mutkins has a strong motive for killing Scanlon.'

I got to my feet, went over to the door and shut it. Fitzgerald could still hear our voices but not the words.

Kennedy lit another cigarette from the one he'd been smoking. 'Look, mate, you stay out of it. It was Wallace – MacKerras is happy with that. Now you need to let me get on and do what I have to do.'

'I can't stay out of it. Davy Scanlon was my junior officer, and I owe it to him to find the truth. I'm not about to pin it on Wallace because it's expedient.'

'Worried about your honour, are you, Captain? Come on, the military

271

throws officers under a bus if it suits them. What about them Australian officers they executed in South Africa, eh? What was that if not fuckin' expediency? They were told to shoot prisoners, so they did, and when the shit hits, the higher-ups cut them loose and say, "Oh, you bad boys for shooting prisoners," and put them in front of a firing squad to keep the War Office happy.'

'That was the British.'

'And what are we, mate, if not the sons of the Empire? The Empire that taught us everything it knows about expediency?'

'You want to hang this around Wallace's neck to justify shooting him.'

'Ah, fuck you,' he said.

'Fuck you too,' I yelled, then stalked out and slammed the door.

I walked around the block, calmed down and approached the station from the west, then entered the office again. Kennedy and I exchanged a wary glance, then he hid behind his newspaper. Harry Barker walked in with the dispatch bag and another bundle of mail, leaving both on the front counter. As he turned to go, I said, 'Mr Barker, a moment, please.'

Kennedy put his paper down. Barker startled but turned around, eyes wide. 'Yes, Sergeant?'

'Are you not supposed to sign over the police dispatch bag?'

'Oh. Yeah, I forgot.' He took a notebook out of his pocket, flipped through the pages, then passed it to me to sign. The date was correct, so I signed.

'Ever had a burglary at the post office?' I asked.

'Yeah, once. Took the petty cash and lots of stamps.'

'When?'

'Easter weekend, just past.'

'You reported it?'

'My word, I did. But any record of that report would have gone up in the fire when Davy died.'

'Any stationery taken? Maybe the official forms that police communications are transcribed onto?'

'Yeah, I think so.'

'Did you tell the police?'

'Yeah, I told Scanlon, and he said that until a replacement pad came, he'd accept a note signed by me.'

I wanted to slap his puffy face. 'Why didn't you tell us this when we interviewed you? And why didn't you refuse Scanlon's suggestion? You could have had Bathurst send another batch of forms in the next coach.'

'Yeah, but then they'd know we'd been broken into.'

'They are the police, Mr Barker, they are supposed to know. Look, just get out. And just so you know, I'll be recommending you be relieved of your duties as postmaster.'

He gazed at me in disbelief. 'But we don't have anywhere else to go, me and the missus.'

This cowardly, lazy old bastard had told MacKerras I'd been crying and out of control. He'd broken the sacred trust put in him by His Majesty's Postal Service, as well as the trust of the New South Wales Police, and now Davy Scanlon, who should have known better, was dead.

'Not my problem, Barker. You do your job until you're relieved, and that will be any tick of the clock.'

He left and Kennedy quickly raised his newspaper again.

'Mutkins, or Wallace, must have heard about the break-in, or organised

it, and seen a way to lure Scanlon onto the western road,' I said softly to Kennedy's newspaper.

Bastard ignored me.

'Detective, did you hear me?'

'You telling me how to do my job?' he said, slamming his paper down. 'Don't think you can do a better job than me just 'cause you were born with a silver fucken ladle jammed in your mouth and all yer fancy schoolin' and hi ho, off we go on yer cavalry, and fuck me if it isn't a working man, let's ride over the poor bastard, show him who's boss. Well, I'm the boss here, Lord Fuck-All of Police Paddock 6A, understand?'

We were all unravelling. To hell with it. I stomped off to my camp, leaving the ox-brained chump who called himself a detective to his own devices.

27

A light breeze stirred the pines. A mob of galahs under the manna gum foraged for seed, their pink breasts glowing in the dappled sun. Above them in the branches sat a dozen or so pairs of smooching corellas, more interested in each other than in the galahs muscling in on their food. I leant on the fence watching them as I brooded on Kennedy's firm decision that it was all over. I wanted it to be over too, but I also wanted to get it right. I shared his belief it was Wallace, but we had a duty as policemen to close down the other possibilities.

Alfie didn't care: he was having an enthusiastic dig over by the fence, dirt flying, tail wagging. I wandered around, picking up twigs to use as kindling, and piled them near the fireplace. After I'd lit the fire and got the flames leaping, I took my seat and my notebook and scribbled away in it, trying to make sense of what I'd learnt, trying to wrestle the mess of human crime into a neat timeline with motive and evidence and all the other procedure the detective handbook went on about. Procedure was essential but so was the 'golden gut', as Detective Arty Baines told me. Had to entwine the two, make a rope out of them, and never assume. Which is what we were doing.

Alfie, tired of digging, came and sat beside me, blinking at the fire. I looked over at the cluster of smooth round river stones marking where I'd buried Scanlon's hand for safekeeping.

'We'll get him,' I murmured. 'And I promise you, he will swing for this.'

Vogel suddenly appeared, probably wondering why I was talking to stones. But then again, maybe not. We were all under strain.

'These came for you, sir,' he said, handing me a packet of letters. 'Jackson's on the desk until ten, but I'm relieving while he has his supper.'

'Good,' I said, nodding as I looked at the letters. 'You have it all sorted.'

He went off and I tossed a bit more wood on my campfire. I had an hour or so before supper, so I settled myself and opened the first letter from my father. He'd enclosed a clipping from a newspaper. I scanned the paper and felt ill.

Mr and Mrs Robert Fraser Kirkbride of Inveraray Station via Cobar are pleased to announce the engagement of their daughter, Miss Flora Jean Kirkbride, to Mr Bernard Alvin Baillie-Hamilton of Tanidgee Downs via Darwin.

I screwed up the cutting, threw it aside, swore like a bullocky, then jumped up, roamed around the block, picked up a stone and hurled it as hard as I could at the pile of timber planks, where it hit and bounced away. Alfie went scuttling after it. I found another and slammed it at the timber, and another, and another, hit that bastard, hit that plank, hit that man, hit that stupid, useless Gus Hawkins.

I stood there panting as Alfie ran about, picking up stones, dropping them, sniffing out another.

'Going to cram them all in your mouth, you dopy dog?'

I flopped back down and picked up my father's letter. He expressed his deepest sadness as, he said, he knew how much I loved her. Tears rolled down my cheeks, blurring the words on the page. I wiped them away and went on reading. He said he'd made enquiries and Tanidgee Downs was a big cattle station near Darwin. The Baillie-Hamiltons were rich and had extensive landholdings in the new Northern Territory, South Australia and the west of New South Wales.

Well done, Robert bloody Kirkbride. You've beaten me, you greedy old bastard. It would never be me to stand with Flora at the altar.

As hard to fathom as it was, this was not about me but about land and the Kirkbride legacy. It obviously wasn't about Flora either. She'd barely had the embrace of anyone who loved her since the murders of her siblings. She had been told she was mad, had been sent away from her home to be locked up among strangers, and was now to be married off to a strange man in exchange for his land and fortune. My only hope was that this Bernard joker would love and care for her as she deserved. Or, better still, that Bernie was ancient and impotent, and they would sleep in separate rooms.

I tossed a stick onto the fire. Alfie leant against me, and we sat staring into the fire, numb with cold and despair as the dusk settled around us.

~

Mrs Owen called out, asking me to cut some wood before supper. I went around to the woodshed, and Alfie, forever on duty like a canine praetorian guard, followed me. I'd sharpened the axe and pulled a log out of the pile, named it Bernard Alvin Baillie-Hamilton and brought the axe smashing

down on his skull, watching it split into two halves, his rich cattleman's brains spilling everywhere.

'Not dead yet, mate? Want another go?' I panted at the half-log, and then whack, through his Baillie-Hamilton neck. I set up the other half, raised the axe. 'You touch her, and this is what will happen.' Thwack, right through his miserable spine. I kept going, my eyes and hands on fire, chopping Bernie Big Cattle into tiny pieces, finding it frighteningly enjoyable. I stood there panting, my chest heaving. Even Alfie was glancing warily at me. *Steady on, mate.*

'How can I be steady when she's been taken from me?' I cried, hurling the axe away.

I dropped down, sat on the dirt. Alfie, never missing an opportunity for a good lick, came over. I gave him a pat and looked over into the woodpile. I reckon we had enough for tonight and tomorrow morning. I noticed a red glint in the woodpile, something wedged between a log and the corrugated-iron wall. I was reluctant to thrust my hand into a dark woodpile, but any self-respecting snake would have taken off by now, after the massacre of Baillie-Hamilton of Tanidgee bloody Downs.

Whatever it was, the thing was wedged between a couple of rounds up the back. I reached in, my fingers closed around it and I brought it out. A Prince Albert Crimp Cut Pipe and Cigarette Tobacco tin. Probably old Clyde's or Scanlon's.

I opened it, and inside, neatly folded, was a piece of paper. I took it out and saw my own name written clearly on the white paper. I felt like Alice tumbling down a rabbit hole. I glanced around but there was nobody watching or lurking. The paper with my name on it had been folded, and enclosed an onionskin carbon copy of a letter.

The letter was dated the fifteenth of March 1912, and marked urgent and confidential.

Dear Superintendent MacKerras,

I, Constable David James Scanlon of the New South Wales Mounted Troopers, currently stationed in Colley, wish to inform you of a serious threat to my life made by Mr Raymond Fitzgerald, proprietor of the Commercial Hotel, Colley, on the twelfth day of this month.

I have uncovered, through my diligent efforts, that the death of Mr William Gordon Fitzgerald, on the tenth of February, 1910, was not suicide but murder. Mr William Fitzgerald was murdered by his father, the said Mr Raymond Fitzgerald, who held his son's head underwater until he was deceased. I have spoken to a reliable witness who saw this happen.

When I confronted Mr Raymond Fitzgerald with this information, he declared it to be untrue and that he would kill me. I believe he is serious in his intent, and therefore I request an immediate transfer away from Colley, as well as the arrest of Mr Raymond Fitzgerald for the murder of Mr William Fitzgerald.

Bloody hell. I read it again and again, questions flooding my mind. Davy wanted out of Colley, and he knew I'd end up chopping Mrs Owen's wood so he left this copy here for me – he had to have. *It's addressed to you, idiot – of course he put it here for you.*

I looked back through my notebook until I found the dates Scanlon had taken his three-day leave. The eighth, ninth and tenth of March, only days before Fitzgerald allegedly threatened him. I shoved the letter back in

the tin, and the tin in my pocket, picked up an armful of wood, my mind galloping, and went to the back door. Boots off, goat slippers on, the fire in the woodstove crackling and hissing. The scent of mutton stew filled the kitchen. I put a load of wood in the basket.

'Supper's ready,' Mrs Owen said. 'Go and wash up.'

'I found something in the woodpile.'

'Not more kittens, I hope.'

'No, a letter, addressed to me – from Davy Scanlon.'

'That's odd. What's it say?' Mrs Owen said. 'Sit down and I'll dish up the stew.'

I sat down and read the letter aloud. Mrs Owen gaped at me, an old wooden spoon loaded with mutton stew held halfway between pot and plate.

'Why would he drown his own son?' I said.

She put down the spoon and the old pot and sat down heavily in her chair.

'Why did Davy write this?' I asked. 'Was he not well in his head or something?'

'I thought Will was ashamed and that's why he took his life,' she said.

'Of what? Not being a good husband to Hilde?'

She didn't speak, and I poured myself a glass of water, drank it noisily.

'Will wasn't a good husband to Hilde because he was too busy being a husband to Davy,' she said at last.

I spluttered my water everywhere, coughing and carrying on, and managed to croak, 'You mean they were ...'

She nodded. 'Yes, but—'

'How do you know?'

'Clyde told me. I only found out when he and I saw William sneaking up there at night. Anyway, the lights never went on, and Clyde said, "They aren't playing chess in the dark, Meggie." He had to explain it to me.'

'For how long? I mean, was it just the once?'

She shook her head.

I gazed at the letter, reading it over and over. Davy was reaching out to me from beyond the grave. He left this for me because he must have worried that MacKerras wouldn't investigate and wouldn't transfer him before Fitzgerald made good on his threat. I thought back to his body wrapped in the white shroud on the floor of the cellar the night his horse brought him back, the horror of it, the pitiful mutilation.

Mrs Owen said something but I didn't hear it. I raced out the back, struggled into my boots and ran down to Pomeroy's surgery, rapped on the door, then let myself in.

I looked at the watercolours on the wall. The heat in the air, the joy of the two animated figures, splashing each other while their horses waited in the shade. Then at the end of the row I saw an ink-and-brush sketch. It looked to be Chinese, a painting of the river with some sort of calligraphy in a vertical line.

Pomeroy came through from his private quarters, smelling of drink but still dapper. 'Is it urgent? An emergency?'

'You paint at the waterhole every evening, and Sam Hong used to sit and paint with you, didn't he?' I demanded.

'What's this about?'

'You and Sam saw Fitzgerald drown his son.'

He said nothing but his face had paled.

'There's a witness – I know there is – and I think it's you.'

'I saw nothing. We were behind the bullrushes and heard a noise. Sam stood up and looked over. That's all I can tell you.'

'Did he tell you what he saw?'

'You'd better leave now, Sergeant,' he said, herding me towards the door.

~

The light was on in Fitzgerald's study. Jackson was on duty. Kennedy was upstairs. I sent Vogel to saddle Toss for me and took the steps two at a time, barrelled down the long, dim hallway and rapped on Kennedy's door.

He yanked it open, saw me and went to close it in my face.

'I have to show you something,' I said, pushing the door open.

He was shirtless, just his braces over a woollen undershirt, a fag burning in the ashtray on the small table, bottle of whisky and a tumbler beside it. He had been writing a letter and it lay there, pen beside it, near a small, framed photograph of the woman who was probably his wife. He wanted to go home to her, and I had some sympathy.

'What is it?' he said.

I closed the door behind me and showed him the letter.

He read it and looked up at me. 'Where'd you get this?'

'Scanlon put it in a tin in Mrs Owen's woodpile, knowing I'd be chopping her wood for her.'

'But why?' he said. 'Why would Ray do that?'

'Because Scanlon and his son, William Fitzgerald, were lovers.'

He stared at me for so long I thought he'd turned to stone. 'Hang on – you mean homos, right?'

I nodded.

'Filthy bastards,' he murmured, looking down at the letter and rubbing his chin again. 'Nah, it was Wallace who killed Scanlon. You can't take what a pansy says seriously. He's had a fight with Ray, there's a bit of bad blood and he wants to transfer away from Colley – that's what this is about. I'll go and talk to Ray, find out what happened.'

'No, do not show him this.' I tried to take the letter back, but he snatched it away.

'I see you, Hawkins, you're coming up on the outside. You think you can win this when I've done all the work.'

'You? I didn't see you sleeping on a windswept cliff or retrieving Wallace's body or talking to the townsfolk. You sit around reading the paper.'

'MacKerras says it's over, so it's over. Full stop. It's my collar and the dicks in Sydney will know it's mine, so sod off. I'm closing it down and going home.'

'MacKerras has seen this letter. There's no way he wouldn't have, and yet he let us set up shop under an accused cop killer's roof. Your mate Terry MacKerras, who cares so much about his men.'

He gave an exasperated sigh. 'All right. Who's this witness?'

'I think it's Sam Hong, a Chinese healer who used to paint at the waterhole with Bill Pomeroy. Pomeroy reckons—'

'Hang on – paint, did you say?' he said, screwing his face up.

'Watercolours.'

'Oh.'

'Pomeroy says they were there that night and he saw nothing, but that Sam did, although he won't say what. Days after William dies, Hong closes his shop and moves to Bathurst to work in the vegetable gardens. I went

to see him on another matter. He was fine until I told him Scanlon was murdered. Wanted me out and away. He was really spooked.'

'You want to back a Chinaman's shiver against Ray Fitzgerald's reputation? Because no jury would. Besides, Fitzgerald has a cast-iron alibi for Friday morning.'

'Give me back the letter.'

'What are you going to do with it?' he said, handing it back.

'Show Northrup. I'll ride to Bathurst tonight.'

'In the dark?'

'Yes, in the dark.'

'You watch Northrup,' he cautioned. 'He looks like a nice, footy-playing dad from suburban Bathurst, but he's got the morals of a sewer rat. Been choking this investigation at the source, wanting it to fail so he can stick the knife into MacKerras.'

'Then he'll like this,' I said, holding up the letter.

I left him staring at the wall and raced downstairs. Jackson was on duty; the others were in the bunkroom.

'I'm riding to Bathurst tonight,' I told him. 'I have to speak to Northrup urgently.'

His mouth fell open in surprise. 'Yes, sir.'

I lowered my voice and said, 'Kennedy knows where I'm going. Only you, O'Malley and Vogel are to know. Anyone else asks, I'm unwell and having an early night, not to be disturbed.'

'Yes, sir. Early night.'

'While I'm gone, the three of you are to be vigilant at all times. And keep the bunkroom door locked at night.'

A flicker of fear arose in his eyes.

'Just a precaution, no imminent threat,' I said.

I hurried outside to the front of the hotel to find Toss saddled and ready to go. He was blowing plumes of steam into the air as the golden light from the lanterns pooled around us. I could see MacKerras standing in the dawn light, listening to Harry Barker slander me. No wonder he was such a cold bastard when he came out here. He'd failed in his duty, spectacularly, and he knew it.

~

Riding up that Colley hill and past the cemetery turn-off was eerie. Shadows jumping at me, a scattering of silent flying foxes, black against the sky, heading out for the night. But my mind closed in on the shock of discovering Scanlon and William had been at each other. It was a hellish risk. And a man like Fitzgerald – his obsession with his muscles, with expanding his landholdings, with his record in South Africa – would not likely tolerate such vices in his only son.

At the halfway mark there was a small pub, but it was closed by the time we got there. Tosser had a drink in the trough, while my breath misted in the cold air and I jumped at every noise. Alfie was with Mrs Owen, but I could have done with his protective instincts. With the long, flat ride ahead, I settled into my coat, wrapped my scarf tight and pulled my knitted cap down.

A half-moon rose over the paddocks. Fences hung with dead foxes, their hind legs tied to the barbed wire, their gaping muzzles grazing the long grass. In the night shadows it seemed as if they were smiling through the stench of their own ending.

28

The gas lights of Bathurst gave off a golden glow in the distance. Only the city centre was lit, but it was enough to restore a small measure of cheer in a man. I rode straight to the barracks on William Street, as they'd have the night watch and a stable for Toss.

It was nearly three am and I was exhausted, but so keyed up I couldn't think of sleeping. The officer of the watch let me in, and I took Toss to the stables, walked him around to cool down, took his kit off, rubbed him down and put him in a stall with a manger full of hay. He'd done a brilliant job and had earned all of it.

I was assigned a bunk and just lay on it, fully clothed, waiting for dawn when I could go and find Northrup. I must have slept, though, as the next thing I knew it was light and the smell of sizzling bacon fat was dancing up my nose. I went to the mess, grabbed a chunk of bread and wrapped it around a thick slice of bacon, gulped down some hot, sweet tea and went across the road to the head station, chewing madly.

Northrup wasn't expected until nine am, the officious desk officer informed me, and my business would have to wait. Then I saw Jack Simmons sitting in a chair, head back, snoring loudly.

'What's he here for?'

'His kid's out the back in the cells – has to wait for the solicitor, who's held up.'

I swallowed a mouthful of bread and bacon and said, 'I really have to see Northrup. It's an urgent matter, one he'd want to be informed of immediately.'

He relented and a runner took a note and shot off into the early-morning light.

Simmons woke up, saw me, blinked and stretched. 'Need to talk to you,' he said. 'Frankie's got something important to tell, but we don't know who to tell it to.'

'He has to have a solicitor with him.'

'He reckons you lot will really want to know, and he wants to tell somebody important,' he said with a yawn.

'Right. I have to see someone, but I'll come straight back and see if we can get Inspector Northrup to hear what he has to say.'

The runner soon returned a with a reply from Northrup to meet him at his home as soon as possible. Northrup lived close by in a red-brick cottage with iron lace, arched windows and a good-sized garden strewn with balls, hoops and other evidence of his offspring. I knocked and he answered in his dressing gown, telling me to meet him around at the back door.

A water tank, vegetable garden and chook run marked it as the same as most other rural and suburban homes. He came down the stairs in the morning light looking cross and dishevelled, though not as dishevelled as me.

'What is it, Hawkins? What the devil is it that's so important you'd ride through the night, for God's sake?'

287

'A letter, sir, that I believe you must read.' I took it out of my pocket and handed it to him, aware of the bacon grease in my beard. 'Note my name scrawled on the envelope.'

'Why couldn't you just put it in the dispatch bag?' he grumbled. Then he read it, rubbed his unshaven chin, glanced up at me and read it again. In that glance I saw the fire of ambition. Northrup really needed to work on his poker face. 'Well, well, well,' he said. 'How did you come upon this?'

I explained how it had unfolded. He stood listening in his red plaid woollen dressing gown, which was neatly fastened with a shiny cord, his blue and white striped flannel pyjama pants beneath, feet in leather slippers – the very picture of a mild suburban man. Yet beneath those flannel pyjamas beat the heart of an ambitious man, one with the gnawing hunger of a second-in-command.

'But why would he drown his son?' he asked. 'Fitzgerald has always been an upright and respectable citizen. We'll have a hard time convincing a jury without a good motive.'

'I suspect it may have something to do with the fact that his son, William, and Trooper Scanlon were lovers.'

Northrup just about fell over. He pulled me away from the house so we could not be heard. 'Good God – are you saying ...?'

'They were lovers. Homosexual lovers, and had probably been for several years.'

His eyes were as wide as his mouth. Maybe they don't have them in Bathurst.

'But Scanlon wasn't a moral degenerate? He was an excellent officer, tough and reliable.'

I shrugged. 'Sir, rumour has it Lord Kitchener plays on the same team, and he's nothing if not tough.'

'Kitchener? Oh, now you really are having me on, Hawkins.'

'His aide-de-camp is rumoured to be his lover, and they like arranging flowers and drapery.'

Northrup laughed, then looked incredulous, then frowned. 'Soldier talk, that's all it is, badmouthing the boss.'

'I think Kitchener is a war criminal, you think he's a hero, and I've no doubt his ADC thinks he's his very own darling.'

He looked at me like I'd dropped into his yard from another planet. The back door opened and a small child appeared in a nightgown, hair all tousled. A pair of female hands reached through the doorway, snatched the child back inside and closed the door.

'Scanlon left you the carbon copy in case MacKerras failed to act,' Northrup said, returning to the safer, more enjoyable topic of his superior's culpability.

'It's dated almost five weeks before he died,' I added. 'It would have been a simple task to swap postings with Capertee or Mudgee. But MacKerras didn't. Why didn't he act to ensure the safety of his junior officer, sir? Or take steps to investigate his claim about Fitzgerald's murder of his son?'

'We don't know that he got the letter. Just because Scanlon took a copy of it doesn't mean the original got through to MacKerras.'

'Doesn't it? Are the police communication lines between Bathurst and Colley so unreliable, sir?'

'No, they're secure. But it may be that someone, his clerk perhaps, read it and—'

'Filed and forgot? If that's the case, then there is something seriously

wrong with this station,' I said. 'The letter is addressed to him. If it came in and was processed by the clerical staff, there must be a record of it. I know how police files work. It would be logged, dated and filed.'

'Who is the witness Scanlon's referring to?'

'A man called Sam Hong. He used to live in the town and paint by the waterhole each evening with Bill Pomeroy—'

'You mean ... paint pictures?'

'Yes, sir. They were there that evening. Pomeroy declares he saw nothing, but Hong may have. Hong left town soon after.'

'A Chinaman?'

'Yes.'

'Oh, you can't trust them, and no jury would convict on the say-so of a Chinaman. Can you imagine, a Chinaman giving evidence against a man of Fitzgerald's standing? No, we need more than that. And as for Scanlon's death at the hands of Ray Fitzgerald, we only have this letter. None of the evidence points to him.'

'None of the evidence points to Wallace, either. It may be a dredger called Mutkins – I've sent a case of the dredgers' rifles to Sydney to see if there's a ballistics match. He had a solid grudge against Scanlon.'

'Ray Fitzgerald,' Northrup murmured, staring into the distance. 'Mayor of his town ... No, it's impossible.'

'Also, you may be aware we have the police station arsonist in the cells, Frank Simmons, a minor. He says he's got something to say and wants to say it to someone important.'

'He can say it to the judge,' he said, snapping back into the moment with a scowl. 'That boy has cost us a lot of money, and a man his life.'

'I request your presence at the station as soon as possible to hear what

290

he has to say, sir. Then I will go and investigate Fitzgerald's alibi. The watchman at the building site of his factory says he saw him on the Friday morning. I want to question him about that.'

'Hold off for now. There may be another reason, or reasons, for Scanlon's letter.'

'Such as?'

'Malicious mischief making, overwrought nerves, lying or misinterpreting Fitzgerald's words. If Scanlon was so certain Fitzgerald murdered his son, why didn't he arrest him?'

'A young trooper of twenty in his first posting, no senior with him, arresting a well-connected man like Fitzgerald on his own? Would you have done that as a young trooper? At twenty you're still tucked under a sergeant's wing, except Scanlon was on his own. He's asking for backup from his superiors, or at least to get him the hell away from Fitzgerald. It should have been acted on immediately.'

'But Ray Fitzgerald is—'

'You do know Fitzgerald's war experiences?'

'Not in detail – and what do they have to do with anything?'

'He was a scallywag. Some men the Australians wouldn't touch with a bargepole because of their bad character, so they bought passage to Africa and joined whatever irregular unit was looking for men, and all of them bloodthirsty cut-throats who were happy to get their hands dirty. In fact, they longed for it.'

'Ray's not like that.'

'He told me he served with Steinaecker's Horse. If that's the case, then he's capable of killing and mutilating, because that's what they got up to, doing the British dirty work. And not content with that, he ran a team

of black Africans in an underground goldmine, where they were regularly whipped and beaten. They died by the dozen.'

'I don't believe it. Ray wouldn't do that. And besides, that's not evidence. Can't convict a man because of his unfortunate past. Dismissed, Hawkins. I'll see you at the station in half an hour.'

~

Frankie Simmons sat at a table beside a solicitor, a big man with a grey beard, half-moon spectacles and the air of an impatient schoolmaster, casting disgusted looks at his dirty little client. Northrup and I sat opposite, and Jack Simmons sat on a chair in the corner, arms crossed, black circles under his eyes. In the other corner sat a clerk stenographer. Frankie appeared smaller, younger and more lost than ever.

'Now, Master Simmons,' Northrup said, deepening his voice. 'What is it you want to say to me? And remember, I am the law, and you cannot tell lies to the law or you'll be punished. Where do boys who tell lies go?'

'To hell, sir.'

'Speak.'

Frankie looked at me. I tried to lose the stone-cold law-enforcement look and replace it with the face of a kindly local trap. Gave him a small nod.

'I know I done wrong. I wasn't going to do it, even though I'd got the bunger powder out.'

'This was on the morning of April nineteenth?'

'Yeah. I sleep out on the back verandah and it was still dark, but I got dressed and then a man appeared. It was Ray Fitzgerald.'

'In the backyard of your home before dawn?' Northrup said.

'Yeah, and he said he had an errand for me to run and offered me a shilling, a whole shilling, if I would take a note to Trooper Scanlon.'

'And you said yes?'

'For a shilling, yeah. I can't read too well so I didn't look at the note. I just thought while I was there, after Scanlon took the note, I may as well set the fire, so I nipped around the side and did it. I'm really sorry. I didn't mean to.'

'Did Fitzgerald say anything else?'

'Yeah, he said he'd hurt my mum and sister real bad if I told anyone. But he can't now, can he? Can he?'

'No, he can't,' I said. 'They're safe, and you did the right thing telling us.'

'You should have bloody well told him no,' Simmons cried, casting a dirty look my way. 'Stupid kid. Always doing the wrong thing.'

'Had you delivered notes and letters around the town for Harry Barker before the nineteenth?' Northrup asked.

'Yeah, he's got a bad hip, and he always gave me a penny.'

'Scanlon was used to you delivering police telegrams, then?'

'Yeah, he'd give me a lolly from a jar, same as Sergeant Barrett.'

Northrup pushed his chair back with an angry clatter. 'Hawkins, outside.'

He was pacing up and down the hall, angrier than I'd ever seen him. He stopped and snapped, 'Harry Barker, that treacherous ... This is going to look very bad for us. And that wretch Buck Barrett was a damned fool.'

'We also set the police office up under Fitzgerald's roof. At Len's insistence. Another foolish move.'

'That was MacKerras,' he said, giving me a sharp look. 'Not me. I wanted our own premises.'

'Right now, we have to arrest Ray Fitzgerald, stop him killing anyone else. At the very least I need to confirm his alibi – or not.'

'I'll do that. I have copies of the alibi and I know the building site,' Northrup said. 'If it doesn't add up, I'll send an arrest warrant to you immediately. And I'll put in a report on Harry Barker. He'll have to be suspended, pending the outcome of an enquiry. You get back to Colley.'

My shoulders sagged. Get back on a horse and go another eight hours?

'Ride through the night, did you?' he said. 'Go and have a feed and get a fresh horse. And regarding Scanlon's hands and his … manhood. Be very careful around Fitzgerald. He's obviously deranged, and I do not want to explain any more troopers' deaths to Sydney.'

I walked away and tried to find a place to eat. I'd have to leave Toss here – I couldn't ask him to do another eight hours. Which meant a spare horse, which meant a hard mouth and a grumpy nature, which meant a long and tiring ride. But O'Malley, Vogel and Jackson were all under a cop killer's roof, and in danger.

29

I didn't get away until past ten am, and with an eight-hour ride ahead, and a stop here and there, I'd be getting into Colley well after sunset. We made steady progress on the flat, watching the clouds build up to the west. Maybe they'd bring rain; I just hoped it wouldn't fall until I reached Colley because I didn't want another soaking.

The sun set before I reached the climb up to the plateau, and I took it slowly, conserving the horse's energy. Once I'd reached the top of the plateau I had to ride through a large holding of thick wooded scrub on both sides of the road, said to belong to a local crank who had a liking for native animals. Good for him, but in the not-too-distant past, it had been a prime ambush spot for the gold coaches. So the half-moon, its brightness visible through the tree canopy, was a welcome sight.

A shot rang out, thudding into a tree about ten feet ahead of me on my left. My nerves shattered and then quickly reformed, calling on reflexes developed years ago. Blood coursing, pounding in my ears, I grabbed my rifle, fired into the air and shouted, 'Police! Hold your fire!'

Another shot came my way. Not fox hunters. No cover but the bush. I raced the horse into the dark, urging him on through the tearing scrub.

Out of range, I dismounted, tethered him, grabbed my rifle and hurried away, pushing through the scrub, panting, sizzling with nervous energy. I moved closer to the road, found some cover and fired at the scrub across the road, drawing his fire away from my horse.

The gunman fired back and I got a fix on his location. For now. It had to be Fitzgerald, or somebody sent by him. And it had to be his factory watchman that wired an alert to him. Northrup could have held the watchman until I reached Colley, but that would have been too logical, too clever and too farsighted. Thucydides said he was more afraid of his side's blunders than of the enemy's plans. We had that in common.

He fired again, now about a hundred yards north, moving silently. Just my luck to fall foul of a veteran of one of the roughest, most deadly units ever deployed in South Africa. I dug up a handful of dirt and rubbed it over my face to take the shine off. He was waiting. I was waiting. Nerves stretched tight as piano wire. He wanted to kill me and I wanted him alive. The hair on the back of my neck was up. He could be behind me, stealthy, armed with a sharp knife. I wouldn't know until the blade touched my throat. A crashing in the bush behind me caused a moment of terror. Kangaroos getting away.

Above us, the clouds were moving quickly on a westerly wind. I thought I caught a glimpse of a horse rump in a moment of moonlight. I aimed my rifle in that direction. The clouds parted again and I fired. Hit the horse over the road. Heard him scream. Fired again, a crash, thump and he was down. I shifted position quickly. Bullets hit the tree where I'd been crouched only seconds before.

I kept moving, stealthily, so alert that the shape and shadow of every leaf appeared impossibly vivid and lovely. Crouched down, eyes straining

to detect movement. If he killed me, he'd chop my cock off, maybe wear it stuck in his hatband like a feather.

After a time, my legs got pins and needles. I heard mopokes and rustlings in the ground cover. Maybe the bastard had moved on. He'd have a fair walk to get home, or he might have two horses. I waited and waited. Then I found my horse, led him to the road and waited in the shadows.

'Sorry, mate, used you as bait,' I said, mounting up. I set him at a canter and then a gallop, and only slowed when the lights of Colley were close. It was a huge relief to be back, and alive. I wanted to hug someone.

~

Mrs Owen's cottage was in darkness. I untied Alfie and we both wriggled with pleasure at being reunited. I refused to lick his face, however. I badly needed a drink, but did not want to come face to face with Fitzgerald. I had no idea how he'd get back to town, where he stabled his horses or if he would go for me in public. But I was safer in a crowded pub, with troopers nearby, so Alfie and I scurried down the hill, my senses on heightened alert.

I went straight for the front bar, where Watt was polishing his glasses and men caroused and washed away the day's sweat. I knocked back a double and, by crikey, there was nothing like a belt of strong drink after getting close and personal with death. I decided to come back for another once I'd checked the offices.

Fitzgerald's office was in darkness, the door locked. Vogel was on the desk and Kennedy, fag in his mouth, in shirtsleeves with his tails hanging out, had his shoe in both hands and was hammering the hell out of the pin holding up one corner of the map, and swearing at it like a bullocky.

297

On his desk was a half-empty bottle of whisky and a cigarette burning in an ashtray. Vogel cast a disapproving glance at him.

'You can go, Vogel,' Kennedy called out. 'The boss is back.'

I nodded at Vogel and he signed off, gave the keys to me and left.

'Shut the door,' Kennedy said, taking a swig from the bottle.

'We don't close until ten.'

Kennedy gulped some more whisky and grimaced. I shut the door. Something had happened.

He tried to light the burning fag in his mouth from the burning fag in the ashtray, squinting and spilling ash everywhere. 'You know I'm shit at this job, right?' he muttered eventually.

'Yeah, mate ... Look, you need to stub out one cigarette and then ...'

He mashed them both out in a rage and lit another with a match.

'I reckon Scotland Yard would be hard-pressed here,' I said.

'I'm shit at this job, and –' he lowered his voice – 'that is why I am here. That's why MacKerras insisted to Sydney that Scanlon was one of our own and we could handle it. Knowing we couldn't. He's played me for a fucking mug.'

'What's happened? Did Northrup get back to us about the alibi?'

'Nope,' he said, dropping his voice to a whisper. 'But what I do know is a fox hunter, by the name of Nig Parsons, was working in the early hours of the nineteenth, and he saw ...' He gestured to the wall dividing Fitzgerald's office from ours.

I grabbed an empty teacup from my desk, gave it a wipe with the corner of my tunic and held it up so Kennedy could splash some spirit in it.

'MacKerras played me for a mug, all this time,' Kennedy continued, a little unsteady on his feet. 'Lying bastard. All these years I've covered for

him, and he thinks he can stick his hand up my arse and use me as a puppet.'

'When did you speak to this fox hunter?'

'Early this morning. Took Jackson with me and we rode down to Ringer's Rocks. I thought I'd better question Mutkins, like you said – just to rule him out, mind. But he'd run off because, the dredgers claim, he killed one of Foufoune's Chinese girls. Anyway, on the way back we came across Nig Parsons finishing up a night's work. He's an old mate of mine from way back and we had a bit of a yarn.

'Before dawn, on the morning Scanlon was shot, Parsons was crouched behind the stone distance marker in the dark – he reckons the foxes come to town to get at the garbage and it's a good hide. Anyway, reckons he saw a moll, a white girl, running west along the road. Then a horseman appeared from the Ilford Road and crossed the bridge. The girl crouched in the shadows, the man on the horse went up the hill on the Colley Road, and the girl reappeared and ran off into the dark.'

'Miss Rosebud.'

Kennedy nodded, took a deep drag on his fag. 'Parsons recognised that sorrel horse Ray rides and it was him. He knows it was him, as anyone around here would, because he sits on a horse like a broom stick is up his arse. Bit like you, actually.'

'Coming from the north, where he's building his house.'

'Yeah, it's not finished yet, but he could shelter there and nobody would know if he was in Bathurst or not. Parsons reckons he'll stand up in court too.'

'Northrup checked Ray's alibi today,' I said. 'And I'm pretty sure the factory watchman alerted him, because somebody, probably Fitzgerald, tried to shoot me on the road tonight.'

'Bloody hell,' he murmured.

'I shot his horse and got away,' I said, holding out my teacup for another splash, my hand a little shaky. 'As far as the alibi goes, I would have thought we'd hear by now.'

'Didja? Yeah, me too, once upon a time. But Northrup and MacKerras have to slug it out first. Useless bastards. And then a judge has to sign the warrant, and Ray's in the rifle club with most of them, and meanwhile we're under a cop killer's roof.'

He lit another cigarette from the one he'd only half-smoked, took another mouthful of whisky.

'He was my mate,' he said, shaking his head. 'But I didn't know him from a hole in the ground. Joan will be shocked. He's been to tea at our place, eaten off her Royal Doulton.'

There was a knock at the door and we both jumped. I got to my feet, walked over and unlocked it, then peered out.

'Heard you two in here,' Fitzgerald said, an amiable look on his face. 'Come into my office – it's warmer, and I've got a bottle of the good stuff.'

I opened the door wider, striving for the face of stone while my pulse reared and bucked, eye muscle twitching madly, a bird wing beating beneath the skin. This man just tried to kill me. Killed my junior officer, sliced off his hands and his penis, and he was now asking me to have a drink with him? I was face to face with the sort of lunatic that makes your blood run cold, and by God my blood was flowing like the snowmelt in spring, pooling in my guts – which were already clenched tight from the encounter on the Colley Road.

'Got a bit of dirt on your face, Sergeant,' Fitzgerald said. 'Might want to wash up first.'

'I have to see to my horse.'

'Long day?'

'Another time, Mr Fitzgerald,' I said, a little unsteadily. 'Haven't had any supper yet either.'

'Shepherd's pie on tonight, or rabbit stew if Mrs Owen can't do for you,' he said, all hail-fellow-well-met. 'Better hurry before the kitchen closes.' *Or I shoot both of you point-blank and take your dicks for doorknockers.*

Suddenly the pin holding the map gave way and the damn thing fell to the floor, startling us all. I shot off to the dining room and left Kennedy to sort it out. He was three sheets to the wind and as such could blurt out anything. But it would look wildly unusual if Kennedy begged off, and I could only hope he'd be able to play along. I shovelled in a serve of shepherd's pie, downed another whisky and, with a sense of foreboding, walked through the darkness to my tent.

The exultation that came with survival had drained away and I was on my way down, shaky despite the whisky and more than spooked by Fitzgerald. He could come up here, cut Alfie's throat in silence and then go for me, tucked up in bed and dreaming of Scanlon's murder.

I applied some ointment, smoothing the line across my face, waiting for the calming ritual to kick in, then got inside my tent. A light rain began to fall. With the lamp burning, Alfie on his rug and me at the narrow table, I started a letter to my father. I reassured him that while I was desperately angry and unhappy at the news of Flora's impending marriage, I would not do anything rash. I knew I was beaten. I folded the letter and slipped it into an envelope.

Alfie gave a low growl. Someone was outside the tent. He was on his feet and barking now. This was it. Fitz had come to finish me off. I grabbed

301

my pistol and checked it was loaded; my heart was thumping so hard I nearly fired through the canvas.

'Shut that stupid dog up,' a voice growled. It was old Len Fitzgerald. He could be as mad as his nephew, so I kept the pistol in my hand. 'I need to talk to you, Sergeant.'

I opened the flap and looked out to see the old man in an outsized old coat, raindrops sparkling on his knitted cap in the lamplight.

'Can't it wait until tomorrow?'

'No, let me in.'

He barged inside, and I let the flap drop and we stared at each other. I gripped the pistol.

'No one can hear us?' he asked, giving the gun a nervous glance.

'They can if they're out there,' I said. 'This is not secure. But the dog will give us some warning.'

He looked around, a sheepish cast to his grizzled features, and said, 'It's snug in here. You got it all nice and orderly.'

'What is your business, Mr Fitzgerald?'

'I'm sorry about the room at the hotel,' he said, his cap in his hands, thinning hair all messy. 'That was wrong of me. I wasn't meself that day, not after Scanlon's murder.'

'Do you know anything about it?'

'Can I sit a moment? It's a long walk up here.'

I nodded and he perched on the edge of the camp bed. This was a Len I'd not seen before.

'I don't know anything,' he said, still looking around. 'But Davy Scanlon was my William's best friend.'

'Your William?'

'Yeah, mine. Ray sired him, that's all. But I raised him after his mum died and Ray went off to Africa. Walked him to school each day, did his numbers and letters with him, tucked him in at night, told him a story. He was a lovely kid.'

He sat there, gazing into the past with a half-smile on his face, cap in his gnarled hands.

'Then Ray came back with all this money and packed William off to the fancy school in Bathurst. It would've been better if Ray'd never came back, because we were grand without him. I didn't have no say at all about the fancy school.'

Len trailed off into a reverie again. It wasn't hard to see there was bad blood between Len and his nephew, but I'd put it down to Len being a querulous old bugger. Which was probably how Fitzgerald wanted the world to see his old uncle.

'And William and Scanlon were good friends?'

'Best mates, oh yeah, my word they were. They'd go gold panning up at the waterhole all the time. Looking to be rich, they were, so they could buy an orchard together. Set up an apple orchard at Hartley, grow table apples and brew cider, the two of them and Hilde, because Hilde knew how to do all that sort of thing. But Ray didn't want his son toiling in an orchard like a coolie, no, not a Fitzgerald, as if we weren't a family of hard workers from nowhere. He wanted Will to be a toff, so put his foot down real hard. My Will was a soft-hearted lad. He'd had enough of his dad badgering him, you see. That's why ...'

A couple of tears trickled down his face, and he swiped at them and looked down. I gave him a moment. Len was clearly another of Fitzgerald's victims, but if he knew about Davy and William, he wasn't going to tell me.

'What I wanted to see you about was these,' he said, pulling an envelope from inside his coat and handing it to me. I took a couple of documents out of the envelope and laid them side by side on the table in the lamplight. They looked like loan papers from the Bank of New South Wales.

'What am I looking at?'

'That there,' he said, poking at a signature with a grimy finger, 'is a forgery. I never signed this. Ray forged my signature because I said no to this loan. I've been trying to get your attention for weeks now.'

The arguments between Ray and Len that I overheard. Always heated. Slammed doors. This was what it was about.

'It's my pub, left to me by my father,' he said. 'Not to my brother Gordon, but to me. I say whether it gets mortgaged, and I said no. And Ray's gone ahead and forged my signature. Taken a loan out in my name to put into his bloody cannery, which is never gunna be finished, and he's off buying up more rubbish land.'

'This is a serious matter, but—'

'Go and arrest him. He's in the office.'

'Does he know you have these documents?'

'Nope, I found them while he was at Scanlon's funeral in Bathurst. Just checking on things, I was. And lucky I did. Who wants to buy canned meat? He's mortgaged all his rubbish land to get the cannery up, and he'll lose the lot and they'll take my pub. And it's mine, left to me by my father. Ray's dad, my older brother, Gordon, was a wastrel, a drunk who gambled away half the family land, and now his son's doing the same. With my hotel.'

'Leave them with me.'

'No, I'm not leaving the deed with anyone.'

304

'I'll make an official report which you can show a solicitor, but if I'm to do that, I'll need the documents. Then you'll have to get yourself to Bathurst, notify the bank—'

'Can't you arrest him for forgery?'

'To arrest him I'd have to have the forgery verified by a third party, the bank or your solicitor, and I can't do that tonight, so I can't arrest him tonight.'

'It's my pub.'

'Yes, it is your pub, Mr Fitzgerald.'

'And one day it's going to be Hilde's, not Ray's, because she needs a good dowry to catch another husband. It's in my will that it goes to Hilde. It's mine to leave to her. She'll get a good husband, one who'll work the pub.'

I got to my feet, bone-weary and drunk. 'We will sort through this tomorrow, Mr Fitzgerald. Goodnight.'

This was not the immediate action he wanted and he grumbled off into the wet night. As I retied the tent flap, I had the horrible realisation that we'd been looking to Wallace as the man at the end of his tether when it was actually Ray Fitzgerald.

If he was thinking straight, he would never have tried to take me out on the Colley Road. He reacted to the telegram he'd received. When he came for me, it would be silent, sudden and with no trail leading back to him. Or we'd get him first.

30

It was Empire Day. Rain hammered my tent – loud and relentless and dripping through the canvas onto my heavy goats' wool blanket. I was snug enough and wasn't looking forward to the kerfuffle of arresting Fitzgerald. But maybe he had a cast-iron alibi that would send the investigation into a death spiral, where it would land in the basket marked *Too hard*. I could just stay here, in bed, with Alfie for company and my book. The town would be a muddy swamp, too wet for tables laden with fruitcake and scones. Until Northrup fired the starter's pistol, there was not much I could do.

Then a voice, frantic in tone, cut through the din of the rain. 'Sir You have to come quickly, sir. It's an emergency.'

Vogel. Not given to hyperbole. 'What?'

He scrabbled at the tent flap. I sprang up and opened it. He was standing there in his oilskin, rain streaming off his shoulders, hood up and his face white with shock beneath it. My heart beat a bit faster.

'It's Ray Fitzgerald – he's taken Hilde and Kennedy hostage and locked himself in the police office.'

'He's done what?'

'Barricaded himself, sir. And he's refusing to come out. He woke us up, had a rifle in his hand and told us to get dressed and get the hell out. He'd been through all the guest rooms saying the same thing to the guests, and they're all in their pyjamas over at the store and nobody knows what to do.'

'Fucking hell,' I murmured.

'Yes, sir.'

'Did you get your weapons out of the office?'

'No, he wouldn't let us, sir. Jackson and O'Malley are waiting out the front of the hotel, trying to keep people calm, but nobody knows what the hell he's gunna do.'

'Right. Remember Bluey Rankin?'

'Yes, sir.'

'Get up there fast and requisition all his guns and ammunition. The traps will pay for them in time, but we need all he's got, right now. Has Bathurst been alerted?'

'No, sir. We thought you—'

'I'll be there in a few minutes.'

He took off in the rain. I found my uniform, muttering, 'Shit, shit, shit,' as I yanked it on, staggering about. I strapped my sidearm in its holster, shoved my fags into a pocket. Alfie was up and ready. I pulled my cape on, stepped out into the hammering rain and jogged down to the pub. The downpour was so heavy I could scarcely see.

'Sir,' I heard Jackson shout.

I made my way over to them, noticing a cluster of faces at the window of the store. People coming out to see what was happening, then scurrying back in because of the rain. Bunting saturated and trailing in the mud, the red, white and blue of the Union Jack dissolving into rivulets.

'How long has he been in there, Jackson?'

'Twenty minutes, maybe. He's got Hilde with him – she's crying and only in a nightgown. Kennedy was going to hit him but Fitzgerald was pointing a gun at his chest so there was only one thing to do.'

'Yes, right, good,' I muttered, frantically sorting through options. 'I've sent Vogel to requisition some weapons from Bluey Rankin. Stay here until he gets back. I'm going to wire Bathurst for backup. I'll be back in a tick. Nobody goes in or out, not Len Fitzgerald or any guests, nobody. Got it?'

'Sir.'

I splashed down the road to the post office and rang the bell several times before Harry Barker appeared, not too happy to see me.

'We're not open yet.'

'Yes, you are,' I said pushing past him. 'This is an emergency, and I need to send an urgent wire to Bathurst.'

'Yeah? Why don't you ring them again, eh? They'd like that.'

'Are you going to wire the telegram for me or do I have to charge you with obstructing an officer of the law?'

'Yeah, yeah,' he said, shuffling over to his machine and pressing buttons and whatever. Then he took a telegram form and a pencil. 'What do you want to say?'

'For Northrup and MacKerras STOP Ray Fitzgerald holding hostages Commercial Hotel STOP Threatened officers and guests with firearm STOP Request urgent assistance STOP Hawkins.'

Urgent meant in eight hours' time.

'What's he doing that for?' Barker asked.

'Just send it, and don't leave this building. And, by the way, I know you gave errands to Frank Simmons.'

'Frankie's a liar.'

'I've no doubt, and so are you.' I sloshed over to the door, turned and said, 'Bathurst knows.'

Then I splashed back through the heavy rain to the front of the hotel. Septimus Watt was pacing back and forth, huddled inside a massive coat, a fag in his mouth.

'Do you have any idea why he's doing this and what he wants to get from it?' I asked.

'He got a telegram yesterday arvo. Went a bit strange after that. He's had a bit of strife with Len too.'

'Is Len about?'

'No, haven't seen him. Probably lying low. Ray and Len aren't fond of each other. Let me go around to the police window at the side. I'll knock on the glass – he might open the window and say something.'

'No, I don't like the sound of that. He could shoot you.'

'Not gunna shoot me, he's my mate.' Watt quickly walked away and down the side of the hotel, between the Fitzgerald home and the pub. I followed him and watched from the street. He stood to the side of the window, knocked and a second later a shotgun blast shattered the glass, blowing lethal shards everywhere. We could hear Hilde screaming. Watt was crouched down, a look of astonishment on his face.

I signalled to him to get back to the front of the hotel, and he scuttled along as fast as he could, panting when he got back. 'Got a fag?' he said, all shaky.

'Is everyone out of there that you know of? The cook and kitchen staff?'

He nodded, rain pouring down around us. Thunder boomed overhead.

'Do you know if all the guests went across the road?'

'Yeah, I reckon.'

I hurried over to the store and went inside, water pouring from my cape onto the floor. About five men in nightshirts, the cook and two kitchen hands were huddled at the back, with blankets draped around their shoulders. Mrs Lennox came through when she heard the door open.

A man with a grey moustache and bald head called out, 'When can we fetch our belongings, officer? I have to leave town today.'

'Not until we sort this matter out, and I don't know how long that will take,' I said. 'Mrs Lennox, would you take the names and addresses of all the guests and staff, please?'

The man with the moustache was muttering about delays and appointments; the others just looked cold and miserable. Percy trotted into the room.

'Hello, Sergeant,' he said. 'We've got people over.'

Mrs Lennox stopped taking names and watched the group in that lioness way she had. Mock her Percy and she'd rip your throat out. But they ignored him. I looked out the window, at the front of the hotel.

As I went back outside, Vogel galloped into town, an oilskin swag of rifles and ammunition on his back. He dismounted and set down the swag beneath the shelter of the pub verandah.

'Troopers, arm yourselves,' I ordered. 'Not you, Mr Watt. Vogel, how was Bluey Rankin?'

'Shocked. Said if we needed men just to give him a cooee, otherwise he'd stay out of our hair.'

Then Harry Barker appeared through the grey sheets of rain, clutching an umbrella and wearing his official postie's cap.

'Urgent. For you.'

I signed for it, tore it open and read the words, but they didn't make sense.

'R. Fitzgerald has no alibi STOP Warrant coming STOP.'

That was handy. Fucking incompetent bastards. I looked up from the flimsy paper at the men watching me.

'Thank you, Mr Barker, please return to your post. It may be a busy day.'

Now what? I'd never been in a siege before, other than at Elands River. But that was different: we were armed and refused to surrender, and I was way down the chain of command and almost wetting myself. But Kennedy and Hilde had nothing, and a man who was at ease with killing and mutilating was holding them against their will. If I wanted to put my endurance, stamina and abilities to the test, this was it.

I was painfully aware of Jackson and Vogel waiting for me to act, to order, to do something. I told them to wait and sidled down the side of the pub to the shattered window, staying well out of range.

'Mr Fitzgerald,' I shouted. 'Put down your weapon and let Kennedy and Hilde go and we'll talk. Tell me what you want, what I can get for you.'

Nothing but rain.

'Mr Fitzgerald?'

I could hear Hilde crying over the heavy rain.

'Let her go, mate, she's just a girl.'

'I'll decide what to do with her, not you, not anyone else.'

The thought went through my head: *Bugger negotiation, slay him*. An ancient solution to a man run amok. But the traps didn't run along those lines, or not in 1912 and not when a wealthy white man was the problem.

'Is Kennedy there?' I asked.

311

'I'm here,' he shouted.

Fitzgerald told him to shut up. 'And you can fuck off, Hawkins,' he added.

'Is there someone you'd rather talk to?'

'I want to speak to Terry MacKerras. You get him out here, today.'

'He's on his way. Stay calm, he'll be here.'

Thunder rumbled overhead. A flash and crack of lightning close by. I looked back up the narrow gap between the two-storey hotel and the two-storey Fitzgerald home. On the second floor of the Fitzgerald house were two sash windows that looked straight into the windows of the hotel rooms on the second floor of the pub. The gap between the buildings was about three or four feet.

I sidled back up to the street and beckoned the troopers over. 'I want to see if we can get a look at what's going on from a second-storey room in Fitzgerald's house. O'Malley, you come with me, and Jackson, you go around the back and keep people out. Vogel, stay here and do not allow anyone in, no matter what.'

I didn't knock on the Fitzgerald front door, just pushed it open, and we silently went through the lower floor checking for people. We crept up the stairs and along the landing, inspecting each room. One was thick with the smell of an old man, and Len was there in bed. Either he was deaf or dead. I crept closer, expecting him to spring up at any moment and shoot me. Pulled the blanket away from his face.

Dead. His face was an awful puce, his tongue out. A cord around his neck had been used to strangle him. I covered his face and we moved on to the next room.

'Is he dead, sir?' O'Malley asked.

'Yep. Which means Hilde and Kennedy are in serious danger.'

We found the room with the windows facing the hotel. One of the windows was open. Maybe the occupant, terrified by his landlord appearing with a rifle, had opened it hoping to escape. The rain was falling steadily, splashing off the windowsills.

We looked down, careful not to make any movement that could startle Fitzgerald. We could see my desk, Kennedy's desk and a little of the floor. At regular intervals Fitzgerald would appear and then disappear, like he was pacing back and forth. Getting the hostages out with minimal loss of life was what I had to do, but there was no handbook for this sort of operation, or not that I'd ever seen.

O'Malley and I positioned ourselves at a window and aimed our rifles down and into the police room.

'If I get a good sight, do I shoot, sir?' O'Malley asked.

'Not unless you get an order from me,' I murmured.

'But—'

I turned to look at him. 'But what?'

'Yes, sir.'

These youngsters. I would no more have questioned the order – aloud – than taken to the air with wings. While I was marvelling at the upstart youth of today, another part of my mind was at work. The gap between the two buildings' windows was no more than four feet. If we could get a plank long enough, we could cross over and into the hotel.

And then what? The minutes ticked over. The rain fell. If I forced the situation, Fitzgerald might kill his hostages. Getting into the hotel, if he heard us, would alarm him, and he was unpredictable.

'Permission to speak, sir?'

'Yes?'

'If we could get through that window and into the hotel, we might be able to get Hilde and Kennedy out,' O'Malley said.

'How would we do that?'

'Well, there's those planks of wood up at the police block, we could bring one down. You'd need a six-footer at least. We crawl across and get in that room, then go down the stairs. First station Vogel or Jackson by the open window, ready to take Fitzgerald out.'

'Vogel shoots, misses and we two are the mugs in the firing line.'

O'Malley nodded, crestfallen.

'It's a good idea, Trooper, we just need to fine-tune it. In the meantime, you nip downstairs and find Vogel, tell him to fetch a sturdy six-foot plank and bring it to us.'

'Yes, sir.'

Alone now, I could better think through the consequences of getting into the hotel. It could end in a shootout, and nobody could predict the outcome of such an event. We could just let the hours slip by until MacKerras and reinforcements arrived and I handed him the mess to sort out. Yes, I liked that one – then we would see how old Gravel Face worked under pressure.

O'Malley returned, sodden but bristling with excitement. He and Vogel carefully handled the plank up the stairs, then Vogel hurried back to his post. In O'Malley's absence I'd made a decision.

'We go in,' I announced. I know you're sweet on Hilde, but you must act on my orders and not be distracted. We have to get Fitzgerald under our control before anything else. That's best for her and everyone.'

'Yes, sir.'

Carefully we hoisted the plank up, and as quietly as we could slid it across the gap until it was resting firmly on the windowsill of the hotel room window. There was no sound from below. Fitzgerald didn't come to the window to check, so I took off my cape, slung my rifle on my front and clambered up onto the plank, and with my heart in my mouth I inched my way along, rain pelting my back and every sense straining to hear gunshot.

I made it to the other side and managed to get down from the plank silently. Then I turned around and motioned for O'Malley to come across. He was up and on the plank, then was halfway across when I heard it, loud and clear: the long roll of the alarm beaten on a galvanised-iron bucket.

O'Malley froze. He didn't know what was going on. I hissed at him to hurry and reached for him at the moment a shotgun blast blew the plank apart, sending shards of wood flying. I had the sleeve of O'Malley's tunic but he was dangling, struggling to get purchase on the wall. Another shotgun blast. I leant down, grabbed the scruff of his tunic, put every sinew into it and hauled him in, dragging him over the windowsill. We both fell to the floor then instantly jumped up, swung our rifles around and pointed them at the door.

I looked to O'Malley, who was wild-eyed but raised a shaky hand to give me a thumbs-up. Good lad. Thank God Fitzgerald was an amateur rifleman.

31

Once we were in the hotel, I smelt kerosene. There were great puddles of it in the hallway. Bloody hell – we'd crawled into our funeral pyre. We crept silently to the top of the long staircase. Kero on all the steps. Fitz was ranting abuse at Hilde, who was crying, almost hysterical, her sobs echoing in the dark cavern of the hotel. O'Malley was straining at the leash to get at the bastard, but we could not act on our feelings, even though I too wanted to blow Fitzgerald's head off, hold it up by the hair and roar victory.

Kennedy yelled at Fitzgerald to shut up. Gunshot. Hilde screaming, incoherent with terror. Kennedy cried out in shock, moans of agony.

I sprinted down to the landing, O'Malley a step behind me. Fitzgerald appeared in the hall and I fired, but he darted back inside the police office. If Jackson came in now from the back and Vogel from the front, we'd have him. But they didn't because I'd told them not to.

'Fitzgerald,' I yelled, going down a step or two, rifle trained on the doorway, O'Malley giving cover. 'Let's stop this and talk. Let Kennedy and Hilde go.'

He half-emerged from the doorway and fired up at me just as O'Malley fired down at him. He disappeared again. We moved a few steps closer,

both of us with our rifles trained on that door, every sense on high alert and only one objective. Nothing else existed or mattered. O'Malley was rock-solid; we were doing this together.

Then Hilde came through the door and into the hallway, her golden hair streaming down her back, her white nightgown splattered with blood and matter from Kennedy's wounding, her face blank with terror. Fitzgerald, behind her, was gripping her arm, and with his other hand he had one of our Webley service pistols against her head.

O'Malley shouted to her. I heard Kennedy groan, heard the crackle of flame coming from the police room, smoke creeping along the floor.

I took another few steps, my rifle trained on Hilde and Fitzgerald. 'Let her go, Ray,' I said. 'Let her go and we can sort this out.'

He backed away down the hallway, past the bunkroom and towards the back door, using Hilde as a shield. We heard him drag her to the back door, where Jackson waited. Fitzgerald pushed the door open and I heard a loud thud as it slammed into Jackson. Then Fitzgerald and Hilde were gone. I shouted at O'Malley to get Kennedy out and raced out into the rain.

Fitzgerald was over by the riverbank's edge, which was crumbling into the racing water, the level rising every moment. If he threw Hilde in, she'd drown.

Alfie appeared around the corner, barking like a maniac. I couldn't see Jackson anywhere, then I saw his legs: he'd fallen and was lying behind the open door. Mrs Lennox ran around the corner, an ancient Winchester in her hands, her black eyes steely. By God, she was her father's daughter.

'Let her go, Ray,' she shouted, raising the rifle to her shoulder and training it on him.

Fitzgerald slipped the safety catch off the Webley. Hilde shivered violently, her white nightgown clinging to her thin body, her pleading eyes fixed on Mrs Lennox. Fitzgerald was almost smiling. I knew that smile. The power, the control – he was revelling in it.

Alfie, brave little bugger, ran at him again, barking and snarling. I told him to leave off but he wouldn't. The river was rushing past, a deluge of brown water moving at unbelievable speed. Alfie rushed at Fitzgerald, who took a kick at him. Alfie retreated, then went for him again, and Fitzgerald kicked him into the river. He was swept away, his brown head visible and then gone.

In that horrendous moment, Fitzgerald threw Hilde at me and then ran west along the riverbank. I couldn't stop for Hilde; Mrs Lennox would take her. She shouted after me to get the bastard. I took off after Fitzgerald along the riverbank as it crumpled and fell into the torrent.

He was running for his life through the rain, and I was right behind and closing, pain wrapping itself around my chest as I pushed. I wanted him like a dingo wants a rabbit; nothing mattered except the hunter and his prey. We were on waterlogged ground but fear was giving him speed.

The water level was rising above the bank now and spreading across the road, and soon the low, single-lane bridge would go under. He was trying to get across it first.

I heard gunshot but couldn't stop to work out who it was or where. I was gasping for breath, and then I realised O'Malley was behind me, shouting.

Fitzgerald made it to the bridge, paused for a moment, chest heaving, to see where I was, his look of triumph visible through the pouring rain. But before he got across, I gave one last mighty push, hurtled along the

bridge, launched a desperate tackle and landed on my chest, my hands gripping his ankle.

He was down and kicking and I couldn't get a breath. I yanked on his leg. He was panting, clawing at the sodden timber, the rain so hard it felt like someone was beating me. I yanked him towards me again. Fitzgerald twisted on his back, his other leg kicking out at me, at my head, spurring my fury. He gave an almighty kick that loosened my grip on his ankle, then he sprang up and pushed me into the flooding river.

The water slammed me into a timber pylon with enough force to empty my lungs of air, and my head banged into a strut. I managed to loop my arm around it and pull my head clear of the rising water. *Not in the mouth*, was all I could think. *Mouth shut, keep it shut*. Rubbish swirled around me, timber, rats and lizards clinging on, branches and muck, the force of the water against me almost unbearable.

There was about a one-foot gap between the water and the planks of the bridge that rested on the crossbeams held up by the pylons. I needed to get myself up and around the edges of the planks, which jutted out beyond the crossbeams, and onto the bridge. All the while the water was hammering me. My left arm was looped around the strut, my right reaching back and up for the edges of the planks. My hand gripped the sodden timber. If I took my left arm from the strut and couldn't get a grip on the planks, I knew I was dead.

I heard the thumps of people running along the bridge above me. Shouts, gunshot. I transferred my left hand to the planks and held on for dear life, my body being swept along, my grip on the wet wood slipping. I hauled myself up, teeth gritted, eyes blinded by water, every tendon strained, my fury burning as fuel. Up and onto the bridge.

When I lifted my head I saw a trooper lying motionless at the northern end. O'Malley, with a bullet in his shoulder, fading fast. The river was still rising, and the last thing he needed was filthy water in that wound. I grabbed his rifle and slung it around me, then put my hands in his armpits and dragged him off the bridge and as far up the muddy road as I could, all the while him screaming in agony. Then a surge of nausea washed through me, and I threw up from the effort of getting onto the bridge and dragging a full-grown man in the rain. I heard more gunshots from further up the road.

Saying I'd be back, I left O'Malley and ran up the muddy slope, my hair plastered to my skull. Through the sheets of rain I saw that Vogel was down, too, his blood trickling in a rivulet towards me. He'd been shot in the thigh. Fitzgerald was somewhere, with a bead on me. With a mighty rage surging in me, I spat the sour taste of vomit onto the mud and wiped my mouth with my sodden sleeve.

'Where'd he go, Vogel? Did you see?'

'Up the road,' he said, grimacing as he spoke. 'Go after him.'

I had nothing to use as a tourniquet, no way of getting either of them to shelter and an armed nutjob on the loose, and still Vogel was giving me orders.

I pushed on up the muddy road. Slogging along in the rain and mud, waiting for the bullet to put an end to it. Killed doing my duty. I could live with that. I'd have an afterlife as a heroic police martyr, my photograph staring out at the new recruits, an officer with dashfire, fallen in pursuit of evil. I was losing my mind, I realised, slipping into fatal exposure after my dunking in the river and not thinking straight. Fitzgerald couldn't be far ahead of me. But I saw nothing, just water, mist, boggy paddocks and this dirt road heading north into the steeply wooded slopes.

A shot rang out, echoing around the hills. I dropped to the mud. No idea where he was. Nothing but rain and the sound of my rasping breath. I got to my knees, then to my feet. Pushed myself forward. Cold rain in my face, mud holding to my boots – and then he loomed out of the mist, a figure indistinct, the revenant of Scanlon, his handless arms outstretched, reaching for me. Fitzgerald was standing where Scanlon had been, pointing his pistol at me.

'Turn back or I'll shoot you,' he shouted.

I stopped, panting, hands on hips, my lungs burning from the effort. We faced each other, cold and exhausted, and time seemed to slow. I wiped the rain from my eyes, spat on the mud, took a step towards him. He gripped the pistol tightly with both hands, aiming at my chest. If he'd had any ammunition left, he'd have shot me by now, I was certain. The odds suddenly surged in my favour.

I stepped towards him again. That would provoke a bullet. But he didn't have any. Another step.

'I told Barrett what I'd found his junior officer doing to my son in the lean-to,' he shouted, standing his ground. 'To my son! But Barrett was busy tupping Anne Wallace and didn't care. That police station was a moral wasteland, and we all rejoiced at the news that an army man was coming to put things right. But look who we got. You.'

He laughed and laughed, bent double with it. The rain beat down and I laughed along with him. I could see the joke, after all. An off-his-chump veteran with a head full of madness and a taste for strong drink sets himself up as a trap. And to show him exactly how funny I found it, I stepped towards him and gave him an almighty fistful, which sent him sprawling into the mud.

The violence sent a surge of fire through me. I grabbed him by the neck, pulled him up and gave him a solid gut punch, which sent him flying into the water streaming down a ditch to join the river. He tried to raise his head and keep it above the water, but I put my boot on his neck, pushing him under the current. He thrashed about until, having decided he'd had enough, I released him. His nose gushed blood, joining the water racing down to the river.

I leant over him as he coughed and spluttered. 'It's terrifying to be held underwater, isn't it? Makes you panic. What if it's your own father doing it to you, eh? The man supposed to protect and guide you, but he's killing you instead?'

'He seduced my son,' he gurgled. 'And I'll tell everyone.'

'You think anyone will care about what you have to say? You murdered a police trooper in cold blood. That's it for you, mate, you'll be dancing at the end of a rope while you shit yourself.'

He bared his teeth and got to his feet. I had some fire left. If I really put my back into it, I could end him. Now, that was a feeling of power and control, one to relish. All he needed to do was make a run for it.

32

We heard it at the same time. The jingle of bridles, the fast clop of hoofs, and then out of the misty rain rode a couple of sodden mounted troopers I'd never seen before, leading two spare horses.

'Sergeant Hawkins?'

'Yes?'

'Troopers Wilson and Torrance, Rylstone Station, sir,' one of them shouted over the rain. 'Bathurst notified us of the siege in the Commercial. The troopers from Capertee, Gibbet Hill and Hargreaves are on their way to Colley too.' The trooper nodded at Fitzgerald. 'Looks like you've caught him.'

'The river's up, may be impassable, and I have two wounded officers – they need urgent medical attention.'

The troopers dismounted. Fitzgerald sat down in the mud, head between his knees. The rain continued. I never thought I'd be grateful to see a couple of traps again, but I was. We shook hands, despite the absurdity of it all. They took battered vacuum flasks from their saddlebags and handed one to me and one to Fitzgerald.

'Don't give it to him,' I said, taking a swig and handing mine back.

'Troopers Vogel and O'Malley – we have to get them out of here. They'll need the tea.'

Vogel lay in the mud, lips blue, face white. I shook him and he opened his eyes. We got him up onto the spare horse and gave him a hot drink, then put a rain cape around him. Next we found O'Malley, who was in worse shape but conscious. We lifted him onto the horse and put a cape around him too.

'How long to Rylstone?' I shouted to the troopers.

'Three hours. Got a doctor there.'

'Ride in a four formation – take one man each and watch them closely.'

O'Malley and Vogel were drooping over their horses' necks. 'This is going to hurt like a bastard,' I shouted at them. 'If you feel you're going to let go, tell the man beside you.'

O'Malley was near to passing out. He wasn't going to last three hours in the rain.

Then one of the Rylstone troopers, who'd been staring at the swollen river, spoke. 'I reckon it's peaked, sir – the river, that is. I reckon we could get across the bridge. Get 'em out of the rain and to the doctor in Colley, twenty minutes, tops.'

'It's too risky,' I said, looking at the brown, rushing water. 'The bridge has taken a hammering and could give way with any extra weight.'

Or it might hold. Pomeroy was just over there. He could stop the bleeding, get those bullets out. But if it didn't hold, the bridge could plunge four horses and their troopers into an icy, flooded river and certain death.

The Rylstone troopers looked at me. My decision. No one else was going to shoulder the risk. It was what the chevrons were for.

'All right,' I said. 'Two at a time. I'll wait here with Fitzgerald.'

'There's an old drover who lives in a hut by those she-oaks over there,' Trooper Torrance shouted. 'There's the track. He'll have a fire going.'

I watched the first two cross, holding my breath. They made it. Men in oilskins appeared in the mist on the road on the other side of the river, swarming around the troopers. Maybe it was Bluey Rankin's men, thank God for them. The next pair went across and the bridge held.

Now Fitzgerald and I could walk across. But as we watched, one of the planks, loosened by the surging water and the vibrations of the horses, shifted and then gave way, washing downstream. Another followed, then another. There was nothing for it but to locate the drover's hut and wait it out.

~

I found the rickety wattle-and-daub hut nestled by a grove of she-oaks and rapped on the door, holding the rope that was tied to Fitzgerald in my other hand. The door opened a crack, and a yellowing eye set in a crumpled face looked out.

'Sergeant Augustus Hawkins, Colley,' I announced. 'We need shelter.'

He opened the door and let us in.

The hut was just a small room. A single iron bedstead with a sagging mattress stood on one side. There was a roaring fire with an iron cauldron hanging above the flames, a table made of kerosene tins and bit of scavenged timber, and upturned kerosene tins as stools. An old .22 Winchester stood in the corner by the door, and a galvanised-iron bucket in another corner caught drips from the ceiling. Apart from the leaks it was as neat

as a new pin and reminded me of the cattlemen's huts in the Snowy. Everything in its place.

'I'm Shep Thompson,' he said, shaking my hand. 'You look like youse need a cuppa, eh? Get over by the fire and I'll sort one out.'

I untied Fitzgerald's hands and he slumped against the wall. I threw a blanket over him and slumped opposite him, my rifle pointed in his direction, mindful too of the sidearm on my hip.

Thompson was a stringy old bloke, wearing what looked like two woollen checked shirts, his scrawny neck poking through, a bald brown skull like an egg above wrinkled eyes, lined cheeks and a rich, hacking smoker's cough. He squatted down and placed a billy on some coals and gave me a sideways look.

'You know that's Ray Fitzgerald,' he said quietly.

I nodded. 'Under arrest. We may be here for a few hours, until the troopers can get back, then he'll go on to Bathurst.'

'What's he done?'

'Murder.'

Thompson thrust out his lower lip and nodded, as if he wasn't surprised. Soon he had hot water and tea-leaves in a chipped teapot, three battered enamel mugs lined up and a tin of condensed milk. Our sodden clothes gave off steam and stink. I didn't think I'd ever feel properly warm again in this lifetime, but the blanket and the fire were helping.

He poured the tea and handed a mug to me and one to Fitzgerald. My icy hands closed around the hot mug with relief. Hot and sweet, flooding my frigid insides. Fitzgerald did the same, breathing into the steam with relish, staring at me over the rim of his mug, eyes full of calculation, blood congealing under his nose. I had the rifle beside me

but felt a bone-weariness stealing through my veins.

'I should have finished you off, Hawkins,' Fitzgerald said with a laugh. 'I underestimated you.'

Laughing at me. I could imagine him laughing with his mates in Steinaecker's Horse as they thought up nasty ways to kill the Boer. I could imagine him in the goldmines of Witwatersrand, Zulu and Xhosa men slaving in the dim, dusty underground gold reefs, lashed, starved and dying beneath their own land while Fitzgerald laughed with the other white overseers.

'But we should talk,' he went on, 'because I have powerful friends. You don't want to fall foul of them.' He gave a sly smile. 'Perversions in the police force? Nobody wants that, and I'll have their sympathy.'

As I listened to his delusions, a thunderhead of rage roiled up in my chest. This man had murdered my junior officer, my brother in arms, on my watch, and he'd mutilated his body and insulted his memory. By God, I would happily take this man apart with my bare hands and feed his remains to the dogs for that. Fitzgerald was the first man to call for a trooper when his pub was full of fighting trash, expecting us to take a fist or a bullet for his profits. Like the British, exchanging our lives for African gold and calling it honour. And we, the rough colonials, so fucking dazzled to be part of the Imperial sweep, we almost thanked them for letting us die of the shits under a British flag.

Fitzgerald's sly smile, his implicit belief that he could buy his way out of this. He raised a questioning eyebrow and I sprang up with a roar, Martini–Henry rifle in hand, and went to smash it down on his skull so hard it would shatter. He grabbed it and pushed back at me, and the bastard was strong, the look in his eyes pure hatred. We grappled and then I was back

against the wall, the rifle to my neck, the pressure of it, the terror – and a shot rang out. Thompson and his .22 – he'd fired into the ceiling.

I kicked at Fitzgerald's leg and he went down, clutching the Martini–Henry. Quick as a snake he rolled and shot at Thompson, hitting him smack in the chest and sending him out through the door. Rain blew in as Fitzgerald wheeled around and fired at me but there were no bullets left. Both of us stood shocked, but only for a second, then he grabbed the .22 and ran into the rain.

I remembered the loaded Webley on my hip. It had been submerged in the floodwater and so would be unreliable, but I'd killed a man with one of these before. A bullet to the guts – there was your stopping power. I raced out the door and along the grassy path to the muddy road, rain pelting down. Fitzgerald would be going uphill, away from the broken bridge. I couldn't see him, but I would hunt him down and kill him. Nothing would stop me.

Visibility in the heavy rain was almost nil. I had to be gaining on him. Teeth-clenching fury spurred me on. I heard gunshot and felt a thud in my arm. He was up ahead. I stopped and fired. I missed, but he now realised I was armed and began running in a zigzag motion, wasting energy when distance was the only thing that could save him. I was at the far end of my Webley's range, but I raised it in both hands, sighted him, held my breath, squeezed the trigger and dropped him like a rabbit.

Silence. Only the beating rain.

I went over to Fitzgerald, half-expecting him to jump up and laugh. But I'd blown the top of his head off and he was not going to laugh again. I staggered back to the hut, walking like an infant, one foot in front of the other, slowly, painfully. I dragged Thompson's body in out of the rain,

closed the door, stepped over to the table, scraped a few mouthfuls of condensed milk from the tin, gulped down Thompson's cold mug of tea, wrapped myself in a blanket, kicked off my boots, fell on the sagging old bed, closed my eyes and slept.

I stayed at the Rylstone station that night, lying in the darkness listening to the racket of frogs outside in the dark, reliving the day's events. Alfie's absence, apart from anything else, meant I had no defence against the terrors I knew would come. The flutter under my eye, that reliable barometer, had intensified. Falling into the river, that terrifyingly long fraction of a second before I hit the water, then the battering ram of floodwater, Fitzgerald's face as he pointed the Martini–Henry at my chest, and all I'd thought was, *Oh, shit*. No review of my life, no yearnings, no quick prayers, just an eerily calm recognition that he'd bested me.

But the bullet meant for me wasn't there. When Trooper Torrance handed me his rifle, he didn't check and neither did I. An unforgivable lapse in procedure, but I was alive because of it. The irony was that a lapse in procedure led to Scanlon's death.

~

I stayed in bed the next day, and nobody at Rylstone thought I should get up, so I dozed and fretted. There was a hard little Alfie-shaped knot in my chest that I dared not undo. Flora was to be given to another man, and I was so worn out that I almost believed I would never stand up again. I felt like I'd been fighting the Russians at Austerlitz single-handed. Every muscle ached; my arms, my good shoulder, even my hands and wrists all hurt to move.

Northrup wired that night. I was to attend the Bathurst station for debriefing. No mention of my wounding. It was a deep graze more than a bullet wound, but it had still been incurred in the line of duty. No congratulations. Nothing from MacKerras.

~

I refused an ambulance and rode into Bathurst slowly, leaving well before dawn. From Rylstone the journey was twelve hours, and then there were stops along the way to rest and eat, light a fire and boil a billy. Trooper Torrance's wife had packed mutton pies and a stack of buttered pikelets for me – to fill in the cracks, she said.

My spirits rose as the sun did. I was still sore as hell, the tremor under my eye was still there, but I revelled in the simple pleasure of being well fed, warm, astride a fine horse, travelling through pastures that had turned from gold to green with the rain, and sprinkled with the brilliant purple flowers of Paterson's curse.

Farm workers in their cabbage-tree hats, their ladders against the rows of apple trees, waved as I rode past. If they were near the road, I stopped and had a yarn. Yes, I was the new sergeant, replacement for old Buck ... Yes, this was my district now, a domain of a hundred square miles and five stations ... Yes, I was at the siege in Colley and thank you for the apple.

I crunched my way through their offerings as magpies swooped and burbled, hopping along the verge of the dirt road amid the dandelions and flowering vetch. I was alive, bloody sore, but alive and eating an apple, fresh and crisp. Add to that marvel the satisfaction of finishing

that murdering blatherskite off with a Webley pistol at fifty yards. A fine bit of shooting, if I did say so myself.

~

I found Northrup taking a telephone call from Sydney. He grinned when he saw me, gave the thumbs-up. As I waited outside his office, I wondered where MacKerras was. It was a win for the traps – and, more importantly, it would be seen as a win by the public. Kill one of us and we'd hunt you down. Even if we trampled another bloke to death while we were hunting ... but we'd put that to one side. I'd assumed MacKerras would be here to shake my hand at least.

Northrup poked his head out of his office door and beckoned me in, beaming like he'd got first prize for his runner beans at the local show. He pumped my hand, almost with tears in his eyes. 'A great day for us, Hawkins, a great day. What heroes, the four of you. You all acted in the finest traditions of the Mounted Troopers. Commendations for all. Shame about the injuries, but you're all tough – we knew you'd come through.'

'Len Fitzgerald dead, Shep Thompson dead, a girl half lost her mind, a detective and two troopers seriously wounded. Hardly a great day,' I replied. 'A great day would have been if MacKerras had acted sooner. He didn't, and the day he decided not to was a very bad day for the entire Western Police District.'

Northrup's happy look faded and he took a deep breath, then exhaled slowly as he considered me. *Going to be like that, are you, Hawkins?*

And why not? Somebody had to.

He swung back and forth in his swivel chair, elbows on the armrests,

fingers steepled. Then he stopped, got to his feet and closed the door.

'MacKerras says he knew Scanlon was a homo and therefore didn't believe what he said in his letter. He knows Ray Fitzgerald well and thought Scanlon was being hysterical. That's what he says. Which I think is reasonable.'

'I don't.'

'You're not in charge. I am. Acting Superintendent. That's who you're talking to.'

'Sir.'

'As you probably know, your men are in hospital. Kennedy's lost a leg, O'Malley had a hard time of it but he's come good, Vogel may have a limp and Jackson still has bad concussion.'

'Kennedy lost his leg?'

'The bullet shattered his shinbone, so they had to amputate. But he's cheery enough – he'll get good compensation and take early retirement with a decent pension.'

'MacKerras tried to push Kennedy into birdliming Wallace for Scanlon's murder,' I said. 'That's why he came out to Colley after Wallace's death. Kennedy won't stay quiet.'

'Then we'll have to have a discussion about Kennedy's compensation,' Northrup said, smooth as a king's oily courtier.

'Has MacKerras been stood down?'

'He's being relocated to Deniliquin, to head the South Western District.'

'Relocated? Does Buchanan even know about MacKerras's wilful disloyalty?'

'These matters do not concern you, Sergeant,' he said, rearranging the

pencils on his desk. 'We are all relieved you shot Fitzgerald, however. An outstanding job under very difficult conditions. And while seeing him brought to justice would have been the best outcome, we do see this, under the circumstances, as ... protective.'

'Protection from what?'

Northrup closed his eyes and furrowed his brow as if he had a headache. 'Public disgrace. Homosexuals in the ranks, seducing the locals. Terrible for our reputation.'

'Fair go, sir – it sounds to me as if it was mutual.'

'I don't give a damn if it was love or a master and slave arrangement, Hawkins,' he said, slamming a pencil down. 'Acts of sodomy taking place under the roof of an official police station is outrageous. We are sworn to uphold the law, remember? What the hell was Buck Barrett doing while this was going on?'

'Reading *The Bulletin* on the verandah, sir.'

The brow furrowed again as the pain in his head seemed to reappear. *Welcome to the world of the police superintendent.*

'Who's on duty in Colley?' I asked.

'I've sent a team of uniforms to search the Fitzgerald home, the pub, his building site, all the buildings on his property holdings, looking for evidence, for the weapon used and so on. There's a detective from Parramatta in charge of that. There's a young uniform in the station office, and when you go back, he'll join the searchers. You are to concentrate on local matters: the other stations in your district, and all the business that's been put on hold.'

Very strange that Northrup could suddenly find all these resources that were so scarce only a couple of weeks ago.

'And Hilde Fitzgerald?'

'Can barely speak, so we won't be interviewing her anytime soon.'

'Where is she?'

'Under sedation in the hospital, but I daresay she'll go to the asylum in Newcastle.'

'She has family in Wagga Wagga. They should be notified.'

'Someone will do that, the hospital or somebody – not our problem,' he said, waving a girl towards the flames.

'I want to recommend Percy Lennox for a bravery award. Can you see to that?'

'I thought he was a bit slow?' he said, cocking his head to the side. 'What on earth did he do?'

'Saved O'Malley's life. He saw Fitzgerald come out of the hotel and drummed the alarm on a metal bucket. Gave us a second to get him out of range.'

'How extraordinary,' he murmured. 'Well, put it in your report. Make the case for him. We found the widow of Charles Graham, the fellow who died in the lock-up. Now she'll get compensation for her husband's death, unlike Mrs Wallace, even though Mrs Graham said he was a faithless pig who she'd shed no tears for. She didn't want his possessions, so you can keep the dog if you like. We'll sell the horse.'

'The dog was killed by Fitzgerald at the siege. He kicked him into the river.'

'Oh. Sorry to hear that.' He straightened the blotter so the edges were parallel with the edge of the desk. 'You will be assigned another trooper. Probably one of the three you've been working with, after they've recovered. What are your thoughts on their performance?'

'All three are solid, reliable officers. You could deploy them anywhere and rely on them, sir.'

He noted that down, then stood up. We shook hands and I was dismissed.

~

O'Malley lay in bed in a long ward in Bathurst Hospital, shoulder bandaged and the remains of his breakfast scattered over the blankets. Jackson and Vogel were sitting on either side of the bed in their pyjamas and dressing gowns. Jackson's head was bandaged and Vogel had crutches nearby. The three of them were playing poker for matches on the bedcovers. I shook each man's hand, pleased to see them alive and intact. I brought out a flask of whisky and some tumblers I'd swiped from other bedsides and splashed a little in each.

'To a job well done,' I said, and raised my glass.

We all drank, and a grim-faced nurse swooped down on us, skirts rustling, eyes narrowed. Like a starched white hawk, she'd spotted alcohol on her ward and was coming in talons first.

'What's that you're drinking?' she snapped.

'Iced tea, Sister,' I said, staring up at her innocently.

Before she could gather her wits, we all downed the whisky.

'I think you'd better leave, Sergeant.'

'Yes, Sister.'

She bustled off after running an eye over us, in case she'd missed a distillery under the bed. If it had been a military hospital, I'd have been frogmarched off the premises by the matron herself, with a swift boot to the arse on my way out.

'Now that we've drunk to our success, I'd be failing in my duty as your supervising officer if I did not point out a few ... errors of judgement,' I said.

Two glum faces. Jackson had been stretchered off at half-time, so he was in the clear.

'You are not going on report, but when a senior officer tells you to do something, it's an order and you do it. O'Malley, you were to stay with Kennedy, and Vogel, you were posted out the front. You should have stayed there until relieved.'

'Mrs Lennox told us to go after you,' O'Malley said, glancing at the others. 'She came running in with Hilde and told Leila to take her and clean her up and put her in Percy's bed, and she sent Percy to fetch the doctor and a stretcher. She was barking orders left and right, and when she cracks the big whip you don't muck about.'

'Yes, sir,' Vogel said, the words tumbling out over O'Malley's. 'We got Jackson in out of the rain and over to a bed in the store, and I went to call Bathurst for ambulances while Watt and O'Malley took Kennedy down to the doctor. Mrs Lennox was running about the town commandeering hot water bottles to pack beside the three of them, to get them warm, and when I got to the post office, Barker told me to eff off because I wanted to put a telephone call through and he wouldn't do it. Well, I said, you cannot use offensive language with me, and I will charge you unless you do as I order you to.'

'Good, good,' I said, nodding my approval. 'Complete the mission using a minor misdemeanour to leverage cooperation.'

'Bathurst wasn't happy about the telephone call, but I said I would accept a reprimand because of the urgency, sir. Detective Kennedy's leg was in pieces. Anyway, then Mrs Lennox yelled at us to go in pursuit.'

'Running towards an armed and angry man who has nothing to lose takes courage. Well done, both of you. However—'

'Mrs Lennox is not our senior officer, sir,' Vogel said.

'Exactly, and I don't want you saying to your future seniors, "Oh, but Sergeant Hawkins let us run about doing whatever we like."'

'Understood, sir.'

Smiling faces.

'How's Hilde?' I asked.

'She's in a bad way,' Jackson said. 'When I came to, I was in a room with her at Mrs Lennox's, and Hilde was curled up in the corner in her nightie, face to the wall, and no amount of coaxing could get her back into her bed. I put a blanket around her shoulders and she flaked out again. Poor thing, she's in the hospital here.'

'I'm going to go and see her when they let me get up,' O'Malley said.

'I'm going to see her too,' Vogel said quickly, glancing at O'Malley. 'She's from my hometown, my Lutheran congregation, and I thought I'd go and sit beside her, sing some of our favourite hymns. She'd like that, I reckon.'

The three of us looked at him in badly disguised horror. If I woke to the sight and sound of Vogel sitting beside my bed humming 'Abide with Me', I think I'd relapse.

'That's a very kind thing to do, Vogel,' I said, keeping a straight face. 'Another act of kindness would be to write to her family, or her church minister. Tell them what's happened and where she is, so she can go home and not be sent to a lunatic asylum. Will you do that for her?'

'I'll write tonight,' he said, and sat back, satisfied, glancing at O'Malley as if he'd already bought the ring. O'Malley would win hands down if

Hilde got to choose, but Vogel was the man she'd be able to rely on. If the marriage vow said love and cherish, by crikey, that's what Vogel would do. Still, the competition had a fair way to run yet. Hilde might even decide she'd had enough of men.

'How was that kid, Percy, doing the drum thing?' O'Malley said. 'I'd be dead if it weren't for him. A hero, I reckon. I'm going to come back and shake his hand.'

'Not bad for a little drummer boy, eh?'

The nurse loomed on our left flank, looking for a fight. I shook their hands and told them how proud I was of their performance. And I was, because I knew how easily courage could be stripped from a man. A few more lessons to learn and they were on their way to solid careers.

As I walked out, O'Malley called me back. 'Why did he kill Davy, sir? No one told us.'

What could I say? Such matters were never discussed in polite society, or in impolite society, for that matter. I could say that Davy batted for the other team ... and William was on that team too ... and they were caught batting balls to each other. But you could only push a euphemism so far before it fell under the weight of its own absurdity.

'They'd had a disagreement, and Ray Fitzgerald was a dingo,' I said eventually. 'Couldn't sort his differences without shedding blood.'

'And the mutilation?'

'That's what a dingo does. Tears out a piece of sheep just for the pleasure of it.'

Before I left the hospital, I looked in on Kennedy. Given he'd just lost half a leg, he wasn't in too bad a shape; a bit groggy from morphine. He raised his hand off the bed and said, 'Told you it was a lunatic.' Joan

Kennedy was by his bed, her guarding instincts matching those of the nurses. She got up and yanked the curtain around his bed, leaving me on the outside.

The horses had all been brought back to Bathurst for a check. They'd been in a waterlogged paddock for over a day, in sodden blankets over a cold night, with little fodder, as we were all wounded. They were in stalls in the same row as Toss, who had his head out over the stable door, ears forward, looking at me with bright eyes. He was saddled for me and we set out for Colley. My arm wound was healing well but gave me a bit of strife on that ride, but there was no way on earth I was going to arrive back in my town as an invalid on a coach.

~

Back in Colley, I tethered Toss outside the hotel, went in and told the uniform on duty to find a trooper to sort Toss out for me, as I was not up to lifting saddles. Outside, I heard a door slam and Mrs Lennox appeared outside her shop, Percy beside her.

'Sergeant Hawkins,' she called, her black skirts fresh and trim, those sharp cheekbones supporting a rare smile.

I went across the road and shook Percy's hand. 'You saved Trooper O'Malley's life, Percy. You're very brave.'

Percy, overwhelmed, hid his face in his mother's arm.

'I am very proud of him,' she said, beaming down at him. 'More than I can say.'

'Thank you for dealing with the wounded here. The troopers told me of your magnificent effort,' I said.

She gave a brisk nod by way of acknowledgement.

'You could run for mayor.'

'Do you really think this country is ready for women mayors? We may have got the vote ten years ago, but I can assure you, men will not vacate the halls of power for us.'

'Men are fools, and I speak as one.'

She laughed heartily at this, and said, 'Congratulations for killing Fitzgerald. He deserved what he got, and I'm glad it was you who gave it to him.'

'Why so?'

'Because Scanlon thought you were the ant's pants, long before he met you. Now, before you blush and flutter your fan, I have some good news for you. Alfie's alive.'

'Really? How? Did someone find him?'

'Good to see a smile on your face, Sergeant. You're always so stern and forbidding. You look like a human being now.'

So did she, for once.

'He was swept downriver and got caught in a snag, and you wouldn't think it possible, but that awful Foufoune woman tied a rope around her waist and the dredgers held on and she waded in and saved him. Then a dredger put him in a haversack and walked into town with him on his back. Took him to Bill for a check-up.'

'Is he there now?'

'He's with Meggie, being fed warm goats' milk and honey. Always does the trick.'

33

I rushed up the hill to Mrs Owen's. The back door was unlocked, so I crept in and found her, sitting in the parlour, in her chair by the fire. On her lap she had a bundle all wrapped in a thick, white goats' wool blanket with a brown nose poking out.

She looked up at me and smiled. 'Here he is, the man you've been waiting for.'

I sat on the koala-skin rug in front of the fire. She put him down and Alfie slowly walked over, licked my face, lay down and flopped his head on my thigh and gave a great sigh, as if all was finally right with the world. A great lump rose in my throat as my devoted friend, my mate, my guardian was restored to me. Yet again, young Alfie had fallen butter-side-up.

'He's a love,' Mrs Owen said, looking at him fondly. 'Bill reckons he'll be all right as his lungs is clear. A miracle, I reckon. I've been dosing him with my special tonic, and he's onto meat broth now.'

'Thank you,' I managed to say. 'I thought I'd lost him.'

'I bet you did. One of them young policemen from the pub brought him up here, said I had to keep him alive or the sergeant would go mad.'

I laughed at that. 'Which one?'

'I dunno, but I think he was pulling my leg,' she said. 'Leave him with me for a few more days. It's too cold for him to be in that tent.'

I ran my hand over his warm coat and fondled his soft ears as he lapped up the attention. *More of the scratching, Gus, over to the left ... Aah, that's it.* Incredible that he'd survived. Madame Foufoune had won herself a long reprieve. Not a permanent stay, but I'd give her a few more weeks.

'Have you seen Hilde?' Mrs Owen asked.

'No, but I've asked someone who knows her family to write to them.'

'Poor lass – Mrs Lennox told me what she went through. There'll be no tears for Fitzgerald in this town. He killed Len, too. Len was crotchety but he was a decent man, underneath.'

'He told me he helped raise William.'

'A proper mother hen, he was, and William adored him.'

'He left the pub to Hilde in his will. He told me the night before he died. She'll have something from this ordeal and she's still young.'

'Good old Len. William would have approved of that because he really did care about her. But she won't want to live in this town again.'

'Well, she's the publican now, and Watt will run it for her. But I'd say she needs a long spell at home first, some peace and quiet. Two of my troopers are very sweet on her so she'll be married again in no time.'

'That's what she needs, a wedding and a few babies and she'll be so busy she won't even think about Will and Davy,' Mrs Owen said. 'Did Len know Davy and William were ...'

She shook her head. 'Only us up here, I think. They were very careful. When Clyde explained to me what they were doing, I said it was wrong. But he said people say God says it's a sin, but how do they know? God doesn't have a body. He's floating around up there like a bit of old thistledown,

and he never even had conjugals with Mary, so how could he know what's right for every man?'

'Clyde must have been quite the free thinker,' I said.

'Oh, he was,' she nodded, picking up her knitting. '"Take people as you find them," he used to say. "Davy and William don't have to answer to us, Meggie. That's for God to sort out." After William died, well, Davy was beside himself. Because you see, they loved each other, they really did. Davy stopped eating, and Clyde and I, we thought we'd lose him. After a bit he put the weight back on. I had to dose him with my tonic, though. And then when I lost Clyde, Davy was real kind because he knew, you see. The two of us, up here on our hill, mourning our men.'

'What did Buck Barrett make of all this? Did he know?'

'Can't share small living quarters and not know. I don't know what Buck thought, but when Anne Wallace paid her weekly visits to Buck, Scanlon kept a lookout. When William visited Scanlon, Buck kept a lookout. Buck may not have approved neither, but he was a practical man too. But then Ray found out.

'He came looking for Will, and Buck had fallen asleep reading his magazine, and Fitzgerald found them out the back. Called them both names you wouldn't hear a sailor using. Buck tried to shut him up. I was here, putting in the onions. Nobody saw me but I heard it all. Clyde told me to never say anything about it to anyone, because we pay rent to Fitzgerald. William killed himself a few days later from the shame of having his father call him those names. Or that's what we thought. Nobody tells us anything.'

'Ray Fitzgerald drowned him. Then he shot Davy.'

She was silent for a long time, just staring at the dancing flames.

I thought of Davy, young and alone in the world, losing his beloved William and losing the desire to live. But he'd had Clyde and Meg, who wrapped him in warm goats' wool and tended him with plain, unadorned kindness. That was something to be grateful for.

I stroked Alfie, who gave soft little groans of pleasure, probably thinking about how he could prolong this new world of meat broth, thick rugs and ear scratching.

'I got some letters for you,' Mrs Owen said. 'Have a look while I fix supper.'

The usual letters, none of them outstanding. The last letter was in a hand I didn't recognise, with cramped, uneven script and no return address. I ripped it open and found just one sheet of paper.

Dear Mr Hawkins,

I am writing to you because I think you should know that Miss Flora Kirkbride, who is a patient where I used to work, the sanatorium in Katoomba, told me only last week how much she loves you. I think you should know because it's not fair that you don't. She really loves you and doesn't want you to ever forget her even if she is there forever, which some of our patients get stuck here. I don't work there anymore because they sacked me because they said I made Miss Flora cry, but she cried because she's sad, not because of me. She lost two sisters and a brother, so she got every reason to be sad.
Yours faithfully
Miss Dolly Neil

I read it again and again, tears welling up and spilling down my cheeks.

344

Soon I was weeping into my hands, unable to stop as the river of pent-up pain burst its banks. In that warm, stuffy room smelling of goat and dog and woodsmoke, I realised that after the hell Flora and I had been through, the thread had not snapped and the love still held.

I felt Mrs Owen place a hand on my shoulder. 'More bad news, love?'

I handed her the letter without looking up, trying to stem the tears that came from almost a year of silence, of regret, of longing.

''Course she loves you,' she said, crouching beside me and patting my arm. Alfie was trying to get at both of us now, licking and waggling about. 'It's what keeps her goin', no doubt. Now get off me, yer silly dog.'

'But she doesn't know that I've never stopped loving her and never will,' I said fiercely, wiping my eyes. 'I want her to know, so she doesn't ever feel alone again. They shoved her away, shut her up with strangers ...'

Mrs Owen sighed and slowly stood up, her old knees cracking. 'You go off and have a ... I'm not going to say it, because his nibs here will want to go with you. Go and settle your tears, they won't do neither of you no good.'

I extricated myself from Alfie and slipped out the back door and closed it. I walked along the old dirt road up to the waterhole. The river was still fat and swollen, the bushes and grasses all flattened, but there were ducks and herons and finches and wrens, and the deafening sound of frogs. Life had come back to the river.

Whoever Dolly Neil was, she'd given me a raft to hold on to. I took great deep breaths of the late-afternoon air, cold and damp and soothing. The tears had settled but not the rush of the underground river of despair. Flora loved me but had to marry another. The Fates would not even grant her the solace of a being loved by a man she loved in return.

The Lord gave and the Lord hath taken away, that's what it says in the Bible. *Get used to it, Gus,* I told myself. *You can be cut down on the dusty plains of the Transvaal, but you will be denied a hero's death, living on, damaged in mind and body. You will love a girl deeply, but you cannot marry her. This is your lot.*

I rounded the river bend, pleased to see those river stones beneath water. Bill Pomeroy, his painting spot underwater, sat on a log on the riverbank, rugged up in coat and woollen cap, watching the rushing river, quietly smoking as the crickets in the bullrushes clicked and the frogs croaked, and skeins of mist drifted down below the craggy cliffs.

'No painting tonight,' I called out.

He turned around and waved. 'No, but I can't help myself – this is where I like to be around dusk.'

I sat beside him. Neither of us spoke for some time. Clyde must have been thinking about these cloud fragments when he spoke of God floating about like thistledown. I could see it, the transient vapour, ghostly and fleeting, like the interest God took in our affairs. Swamped with sins needing to be punished or excused, he'd washed his hands of the lot of us and gone for a beer and a yarn with Satan.

'You know,' Bill said, 'Clara Lennox found Percy along here, only hours old, wrapped up in newspapers like a parcel of fish and chips.'

'She's not his mother?'

'She is, just not of the blood. Not married, neither. Just stuck a Mrs on her name and wears a black dress to keep men away. Old Buck used to pester her something rotten. He couldn't understand why she didn't want a fella.' Bill laughed. 'Buck was a stupid bastard.'

'Did she ever look for the real mother?'

346

'Nope. I think wrapping a baby in newspaper and leaving it to die said clearly that she didn't want it. Clara brought the baby to me, and I said let him go – he was blue and half-dead, and he'd only end up in a home for the retarded, and that's a terrible life. But she wouldn't. She took that baby home and raised him and loves him more than life itself. He was a lucky kid that day he was found.'

'Like a little gold nugget, eh?'

'Yeah, some of us find them.'

'I found one, her name's Flora. She loves me, she still does,' I said, looking at him half in wonder. 'There's a speck of gold in that, in the middle of a sea of muck.'

'Where is she now?'

'Locked up in a madhouse in Katoomba. She's not mad, she's grief-stricken, and that's not madness.'

'Grief does terrible damage to some people. It's what killed Davy.'

'Fitzgerald killed Davy,' I said, taking out my fags and lighting one.

'I told Davy what really happened to William,' he said. 'He'd pestered me for nearly two years, and I kept saying we didn't see anything, and then—'

'So you did see Fitzgerald drowning his son?'

'Sam saw it. I wasn't game to stand up and look over the bullrushes, but he did. And he wasn't sticking around for Ray to find out he'd seen him. If you'd seen a man in a rage like that, heard him hold his own child underwater until he was dead, and you had to see him every day, you'd have said nothing too. You can get transferred out, but I can't start again, not at my age.'

'Why did you end up telling Davy?'

'He just couldn't believe Will would leave him like that. He was in agony, thinking William had rejected him, rejected their life together, and it wasn't true. I thought he needed to know. I thought it was in the past and it might help him to know that William hadn't left him, hadn't taken his own life from shame, hadn't stopped loving him.'

'How did he take it?'

'He cried for a long time. I thought it would ease his pain. I didn't realise ... I know grief makes a person angry, but I didn't expect Davy to go to Bathurst to see Sam. Sam wrote to me afterwards and said he'd told Davy the truth, and that I should keep an eye out for him, and I didn't. He had it out with Fitzgerald and a few weeks later he was dead too. If I'd kept my mouth shut, none of this would have happened.'

'At least Davy died knowing William never left him,' I said.

'Rubbish. You can get over loss, but you can't get over death.'

'Never been in love?'

'Only once, and I didn't like it.'

'But you know what it looks like.'

'I do,' he nodded. 'Sam and me, we'd set up our easels and sit in the evening peace. In early summer, the river has water in it. Starts up there, in the mountains, and flows west, all those specks of gold churning and turning. William and Davy would be on their claim, digging and rocking the cradle, peering into the gravel for specks of gold, they'd laugh and chatter, splash water at each other, and sometimes they'd stop and look at each other, as if in astonishment, as if they were saying, *I found you*, and then they'd kiss.'

I glanced at him.

'That's what it looks like,' he said, nodding his head slowly.

34

A detective from Parramatta, Stan Boxworth, sat at Kennedy's old desk. He was balding, with thick glasses, and smoked a pipe that he clenched between his teeth when he spoke. And he wasn't much given to speaking, which suited me. He had all the files, great piles of them, and ran the young uniforms ragged, as well as sending a couple of mounted troopers to get out and about.

I'd developed a bad cough and was happy to sit in a warm office while Boxworth ran the end of the investigation. I used the time to write a report on the missing Pearl. It wouldn't help her, and maybe she was beyond help, but her probable death mattered, at least to the law. If her remains were found, they could be placed in the Chinese cemetery up at Burying Ground Gully near Tambaroora, where she'd lie with her own people. Maybe one of the living would one day light a joss stick for her spirit, as the celestials liked to do.

Then I sorted through local matters, reading reports from the other stations in my beat, the usual paperwork. The incident book, which should be a homage to the orderly administration of justice, with no blots, spelling mistakes or random apostrophes, looked like a bunch of chickens had

dipped their claws in ink and danced the foxtrot across it.

As we toiled at the paperwork one afternoon, we were startled by the galloping arrival of a couple of mucky mounted troopers carrying a bundle in an oilcloth and looking like they'd just won a grand final.

Boxworth sat back, puffing on his pipe, utterly calm. 'Well?'

'We found Trooper Scanlon's weapons, or we think they are, because we also found a—'

'Where?' I asked, getting to my feet.

'I'll deal with this, Hawkins,' Boxworth said.

The troopers laid the bundle on the front counter and unwrapped it. A horrified silence came over us. The Martini–Henry rifle was there and the Webley service pistol, all muddy with leaves and grit, but there was also a long, sharp blade attached to a wooden handle, one side of which still had traces of blood along it – Scanlon's, no doubt.

Boxworth took the pipe from his mouth and pointed the stem at the blade. 'What's that?'

'It's an *assegai*, a Zulu disembowelling knife,' I said, queasy at the sight of it. It had a long, narrow blade, like a spear with a short handle. 'The warriors tucked them in their shields for use during close combat.'

The young troopers gasped with amazed horror.

'It has to be Fitzgerald's,' I said. 'Highly prized as souvenirs by soldiers in South Africa. Where did you find it?'

'Up the first creek after Cemetery Hill – I think it's called Insolvency Creek,' the trooper said. 'We walked up through the creek, watching for pigs. The heavy rains dislodged a lot of the creek bank. Found these in a shallow hole, been uncovered by the rush of water.'

Boxworth nodded slowly. 'Trooper Scott, the black tracker, said he

thought that creek should be searched. You noted that, Hawkins, in one of your reports. Should have been followed up. Scott's a smart lad, knows what he's doing.'

'You'd have to ask Northrup about that – he pulled him off the job.'

Boxworth grunted. Northrup was the super now and nobody dared question him. I was struck by a fit of coughing and went back to my seat, glad to have nothing more to do with the investigation. Although this was the evidence we needed. It was a shame Fitzgerald was dead, and you can't kill a bloke twice so that was that.

The sight of that weapon, so feared by the Boer, reinforced my decision to get away from this posting. I did not want to live in this town and ride past the rocky outcrop and remember that day, see the blood, feel the horror. I was not Bucky Barrett. The same post for thirty years? No thank you.

And as to the Light Horse, I'd made up my mind. My father was right: I wasn't frontline material anymore. My stamina and endurance were badly compromised by my injuries. I just didn't like hearing it from him, even though I asked him for advice. I didn't know what to make of that.

And with the excitement of a frontline role ruled out, I could not bear to go back and be some broken-down staff officer in remounts, defending my patch from those fucking upstart militia types.

I'd resign my commission. Once I'd done that, I'd think more about the horse breeding venture my father had suggested, which we'd talked about. Breed walers for the army and the police. Start with two top mares and then expand. I'd be my own boss, have things run the way I liked them to be run. No more rash and reckless decisions for me. I would be a model of prudence, shunning all impulses. My second chance at civilian life and the dawn of my return.

~

The men who delivered the timber planks and bricks for the stable didn't cover the timber and now it was sodden. The station was still a mess of burnt timber and mucky debris and there'd been no response from Bathurst to my request to get it cleaned up, to get the horses in a warm, dry stable, to get me into a warm, dry station. But there had been a reply to my query regarding the disposal of Scanlon's skeletal hand. Burn it, they said. But I didn't.

I fetched a trowel and dug a deep hole beneath the manna gum in the horse paddock. Then I dug up the hand and placed it in the new hole. Mrs Owen had a bay tree by her fence, *Laurus nobilis*, the plant the ancient Greeks used to make wreaths for their heroes. I picked a few sprigs and placed them in the hand, then I buried it and tamped down the earth. After a quick glance to make sure no one was watching, I stood to attention and saluted.

I'd done my duty by Scanlon, and if by chance we passed each other, sauntering along the long, colourless boulevards of the Underworld, asphodels in the buttonholes of our jackets, I could look him in the eye and he would know he'd been avenged.

I went back to my fire in the late afternoon, my goats' wool tam-o'-shanter on, a thick blanket around my shoulders, coughing and watching the flames dance. Alfie pressed up against me. Since his brush with death, he'd become clingy and had to be by my side, if not directly on top of me, to feel safe. He'd grow out of it as he regained his strength. But as we sat there, watching the white moths dance through the long grasses, listening to the noisy corellas in the manna gum, the shadows lengthening and the

scent of woodsmoke and mutton stew filling the air, Alfie suddenly jumped up and barked.

Down by the road was a man in the khaki uniform of the army. He had a stick and what looked like a stiff leg, and was limping up through the long grass towards us. At first, for a terrible moment, I thought it was me, coming from my past to gloat or warn. Then I thought it was some minion from the Light Horse, come to rap me over the knuckles for failing to report for active service. There was nowhere to hide: I couldn't rush into the tent and refuse to come out, as then I'd really be seen as off my chump.

He raised his hand as he hobbled towards me, and I recognised him. Oliver Winterton, a mate from officer training, but unmistakeable even after twelve or more years.

'Hawkins,' he called, panting from the effort of getting across the grass.

'Winterton,' I replied, acutely aware of my goats' wool get-up. We shook hands. I fetched the chair from my tent and placed it close to the fire, and he lowered himself onto it with a wince, one leg obviously unable to bend.

'Africa?' I said, nodding at his leg.

'One of those new motorcycles. Tremendous fun until you crash.'

'Ah.'

'Devil of a time tracking you down.'

'Oh?'

'You have to act, one way or the other. Resign or return.'

'They sent you?'

'No, I wanted to talk to you before you made up your mind.'

'Ah.'

'Have you given it any thought?'

'Been rather busy.'

'Yes, I heard.'

Alfie sniffed around him, then came back and leant against me. I put my arm around him. My tam-o'-shanter, broken furniture and sooky dog raised not an eyebrow with Winterton. He was a gentleman and so was I, and as such he would trust that I had a perfectly good reason for my appearance. It was not for him to question it. That was the code.

'Staff in the Light Horse, during peacetime, wouldn't suit me,' I said.

'I quite agree,' he replied. 'Not a good fit for a man like you. But that's why I'm here. We want you in the new Australian Army Intelligence Corps.'

I stared at him for a long moment. 'But doesn't the War Office ...'

'Times change. There's a new army, a defence force. No more Imperial wars – the defence of Australia is the job now.'

'When did this happen?'

'You were out in the bush a long time, eh?'

'Studiously avoiding the papers.'

'I can understand that you had a hell of a time of it.'

'And you want me to go back?'

'Let me tell you what we do and where we see you fitting in.'

'Not in white tie, drinking cocktails at embassy receptions and going through wastepaper bins, because I won't.'

'It would be foolish to deploy you on such missions,' he said, with too vigorous a laugh, because actually I scrubbed up well, could modestly claim to be a good dancer and drank cocktails with sophisticated restraint. I was not always coated in mud and dog hair and sucking down brandy like mother's milk.

'You'll be very useful on other missions. Besides, that's more Atlee Hunt

in External Affairs sort of thing, when they're not fussing over skin-colour charts and reading people's mail.'

'Nor will I have anything to do with the British.'

He shook his head. 'They don't have Australia's interests at heart, not really. Events in the Pacific are of vital importance to us, not so much to them. The truth is, if push came to shove, they'd cast us adrift, no matter how much we call England home.'

Australian defence. My country. Australian interests and up yours to the English. My ears flicked forward. But my understanding of military intelligence was limited to textbooks and overhearing senior officers cranky with the results. It wasn't straightforward salute and execute, then slope off to the mess for a drink. But what did I know? I'd been ten years in the wilderness, after all.

'I read about the work you did in the Kirkbride case. All of Australia did.'

'That's how you tracked me down?'

'It is, indeed.'

'And you are in Intelligence now?'

'Major,' he said, with a smile. 'After Africa I stuck with the regulars, and when it was decided to put an Intelligence Corps together, I wanted in. We're based in Melbourne but there's a branch at Victoria Barracks in Sydney. It's where I'd envision posting you to start with.'

'How did you go in Africa? I never heard, and after my return ...'

'I went over after you and came back long before you. Bad case of the shits within a week of arriving, hospital in Cape Town and a slow boat home. Never saw a japie, never fired a shot.'

'Bad luck, old man.'

'It was rather, yes,' he said, looking down at his leg.

An awkward moment passed.

'Whereas you—'

'Pushed my luck too far.'

'A distinguished record, though.'

Here we go, I thought. The flattery, the talk of noble sacrifice and glory. I had given my body and mind for my country, for that glory and distinguished record, and now pain every day and night was mine to suffer. My nerves had been shredded by ambushes, sieges, blood, guns and horror. I'd barely slept since the siege, and I knew in my bones that I would never have peace of mind until I turned away from policing and the military. But that was not for him to know.

'No,' I said, shaking my head. 'I'm finished with all that. I want work that will mean something to me.'

'Defending your country? *And how can a man die better / Than facing fearful odds ...'*

'*For the ashes of his father / And the temples of his gods* – yes, I know it,' I said. 'But my father is still alive, and last time I looked the Church of England was doing extremely well, thank you very much.'

'Hear me out,' he said, raising a hand. 'When the corps was formed, we had training at the new place near Canberra: Duntroon. We war-gamed Melbourne being invaded by the Germans – can you believe it? The scenario was that there were German agents in Australia who sabotaged the Ballarat and Bendigo train lines. As a port and cigars conversation, it would have been amusing, but training intelligence officers on this when our real threat comes from closer to home? The field commanders were all saying, "We don't want this rubbish, because if we are to be invaded it

won't be on the three-ten from Bendigo, it will be the Japanese, and they will come in from the north."

'We need men who can work in the north, recruiting and training the locals, the blacks, the pearlers, the ringers, as scouts, train them in reconnaissance. We need officers to do this, men who can work with the blacks, who can live off the land, who can drink with the locals and get their hands dirty, men who put Australia's defence first, not England's, but ours.'

'Send me up to—'

'Based in Darwin, working the coastal areas and bush, getting to know the locals, gaining their trust.'

'Let me think about it. Are you staying in town?'

'Yes, in that ghastly hotel. Stinks of kerosene. I'll get the early coach back to Bathurst tomorrow.'

'Just let me confirm – you'd base me in Darwin?'

'That's the plan. Nine months' training at Duntroon, then up to Darwin.'

Tanidgee Downs via Darwin.

We agreed to meet for a drink before supper and shook hands. He got to his feet and limped back down the paddock.

Military intelligence, eh? Where all the nutters ended up. I'd met a few British intelligence officers in Port Elizabeth and they were some of the most alarming men I'd ever come across. But, on the other hand, scouting in the top end of Australia, miles and miles of unmapped land. What a lark, what an adventure. I knew then that I'd do it.

And what was more, I'd do it because it would be an opportunity to see my dear, dear friend Mrs Flora Baillie-Hamilton.

Maybe I didn't know when I was beaten.

READING GROUP QUESTIONS

1. How did the setting of a dying gold rush town contribute to the plot?

2. In 1912 many Australians called England 'home' even though they'd never been there. Being part of the empire gave them a sense of security. How is this imperial presence depicted in the daily lives of the characters?

3. How does the legacy of imperial wars contribute to the plot?

4. What did you think of the novel's female characters and how they made their lives in a man's world?

5. How do you think women like Mary, whose story would have been common, coped?

6. How authentic do you think the depiction of same-sex love in that era was?

7. Poet Alfred Lord Tennyson said, 'Love is the only gold.' Was he right?

8. Can you see some of the old Australia depicted in Skull River in the ways we now live and think?

ACKNOWLEDGEMENTS

This story takes place on the traditional lands of the Wiradjuri people, and I pay my respects to Elders past and present.

Writing is mostly a solitary pursuit but publishing a book is a collaborative venture and so I'd like to thank Ruby Ashby-Orr, Elizabeth Robinson-Griffith and the team at Affirm Press. Also thank you to Julian Welch for his thoughtful editing, and to Bill Bennell Kooyar Wongi for his reading.

I'd like to acknowledge the dedication and generosity of the volunteer staff of the Bathurst District Historical Society Archives who guided me to the most useful resources and whose conversations, filled with anecdotes and memories, were so interesting and useful, particularly on the topic of the visit of Lord Kitchener to Bathurst in 1910.

Thanks also to Penelope Edwell, Curator, Justice and Police Museum, Museums of History NSW, for her generous help. Also thank you to the librarians at the State Library of NSW and the archivists at the NSW State Archives.

Thanks also to my family and dear friends, both in Adelaide and Sydney, for their support and encouragement.

EarthTrek® EarthTrek® EarthTrek® EarthTrek® EarthTrek®
EarthTrek® EarthTrek® EarthTrek® EarthTrek® EarthTrek®
EarthTrek® EarthTrek® EarthTrek® EarthTrek® EarthTrek®
EarthTrek® EarthTrek® EarthTrek® EarthTrek® EarthTrek®
EarthTrek® EarthTrek® EarthTrek® EarthTrek® EarthTrek®
EarthTrek® EarthTrek® EarthTrek® EarthTrek® EarthTrek®
EarthTrek® EarthTrek® EarthTrek® EarthTrek® EarthTrek®
EarthTrek® EarthTrek® EarthTrek® EarthTrek® EarthTrek®
EarthTrek® EarthTrek® EarthTrek® EarthTrek® EarthTrek®
EarthTrek® EarthTrek® EarthTrek® EarthTrek® EarthTrek®
EarthTrek® EarthTrek® EarthTrek® EarthTrek® EarthTrek®
EarthTrek® EarthTrek® EarthTrek® EarthTrek® EarthTrek®
EarthTrek® EarthTrek® EarthTrek® EarthTrek® EarthTrek®
EarthTrek® EarthTrek® EarthTrek® EarthTrek® EarthTrek®
EarthTrek® EarthTrek® EarthTrek® EarthTrek® EarthTrek®
EarthTrek® EarthTrek® EarthTrek® EarthTrek® EarthTrek®
EarthTrek® EarthTrek® EarthTrek® EarthTrek® EarthTrek®
EarthTrek® EarthTrek® EarthTrek® EarthTrek® EarthTrek®
EarthTrek® EarthTrek® EarthTrek® EarthTrek® EarthTrek®
EarthTrek® EarthTrek® EarthTrek® EarthTrek® EarthTrek®
EarthTrek® EarthTrek® EarthTrek® EarthTrek® EarthTrek®